Despera

"Havoc, go while you can," Ennui said.

Hoard whirled and struck her. She managed to block it partly with one arm, but the force of the blow knocked her to the floor. She fell with a cry. She wasn't being much of a heroine.

Havoc grabbed the bars and strained, meaning to rip them apart. But they bent only slightly, and more fire drove him back. He had become vulnerable.

Hoard nodded. "You're prisoner. You don't have enough magic left to get out." He considered. "But you might be faking some, so I think I'll just leave you in there for a while, and you can watch me with this bitch. I want you to suffer before you die."

She couldn't look, but felt Havoc's mind as he strained at the bars again, exhausting his last strength. His thoughts faded as he lost not only his magic but his physical resources. She realized that he had sent all he had left to her, to help her fight back. Now he was unconscious.

She was on her own—and she lacked the power to fight off Hoard's brutal brawn.

She hung on, determined to die in style. To take him with her. Bright little stars and planets appeared, whirling around her head. The chamber seemed to spin like a whirlpool, curling down into some awful abyss. Void—they were spiraling into the stellar black hole! Utter doom. Still she clung.

KEY to DESTINY

PIERS ANTHONY

KEY to DESTINY

Mundania Press

A Mundania Press Production
Mundania Press LLC
6470A Glenway Avenue, #109
Cincinnati, Ohio 45211-5222

To order additional copies of this book, contact:
books@mundania.com
www.mundania.com

Cover Art © 2004 by Stacey King
Book Design and Layout by Daniel J. Reitz, Sr.
Production and Promotion by Bob Sanders
Edited by Daniel J. Reitz, Sr. and Audra A.F. Brooks

Hardcover ISBN: 1-59426-043-5
Trade Paperback ISBN: 1-59426-044-3
eBook ISBN: 1-59426-045-1

First Trade Paperback Edition • June 2004

Library of Congress Catalog Card Number 2004107189

Production by Mundania Press LLC
Printed in the United States of America

10 9 8 7 6 5 4 3 2 1

CONTENTS

Chapter 1—Loom

Ennui was at her desk, reviewing papers, when it happened. A clip slid off the desk and bounced under it. She pushed back her chair and leaned down, reaching for it, her chin almost colliding with her knees. She got the clip and straightened up again. And paused, amazed.

She felt a sudden surge of energy and desire. She felt wild and wanton, like flinging away her clothing, laying open her body for the gaze of a virile young man. When he hesitated, she went to him, kissed him, took his hands and placed them on her bare breast and buttock. "Take me," she breathed, kissing him again. She felt his huge erection rising against her thigh, seeking its avenue of penetration. Yet there was also a nasty thrill of nervousness, of fear; there was danger here. This was not a safe situation.

She blinked. She remained at her desk, the papers undisturbed. She was fully clothed, and there was no handsome young man. Yet her heart was beating hard, her breasts were tingling, and her cleft was moist. And she still quivered with sexual desire.

What was the matter with her? She was forty-one years old, her seductive days past if they had ever existed, her children grown and gone. She had never been a siren, even when young; she remained moderately homely. And she didn't need a virile young man; she already had a man of her own generation, who loved her, and was quite virile enough. So why this illicit dream?

Yet still the mental image teased her, and her body yearned to it. She wanted sex *now*, and not the routine kind. The desire had touched her, and it wasn't going away. But she had to stifle it, because someone was coming to the office.

Nonce entered. The girl was sixteen and lovely, as was required for her position as First Mistress of the Royal Bath. She was in charge of washing the King and other members of the royal household, as directed. If the King felt an itch for sex, she accommodated that too, on a strictly no-fault basis. The prior two girls to hold her office had soon gone on to far more important roles. In fact, when it came to sex—

"Lady," the girl said.

"Surprise," Ennui said, trying to suppress her rascally imagination. "You are on leave. You don't have to work this week."

"Privacy," Nonce said.

That meant it was important. Nonce had the kind of face and body Ennui could hardly even dream of, but she was a sensible girl, not given to irresponsibility.

Ennui stood and walked away from her desk. She led the way into a nearby private chamber and closed the door behind the girl. "Speak."

"Message: 'Bring two ikons.'"

Ennui stared at her. This was a treacherous surprise. "What do you know of ikons?"

"Only that if anyone knows what this means, you do, Lady. You are Havoc's oath friend."

Bath girls were trained to keep secrets. Often they learned things in the course of their duties that were best kept private. Such as just how rapidly a king could be brought to climax from a limp start. But this thought was that sexual charge possessing her mind again. She had to banish it and get serious. "No other words?"

"None. But the circumstance—"

"Speak."

"I was bathing in a forest pool, when—"

"Don't you get enough of baths here?" Now that rogue desire was taking over her voice.

Nonce smiled. "Bathing alone, Lady, I can pretend I am a person of consequence."

Ennui returned the smile. "You are such a person. The king likes you." It was true, but she shouldn't have said that.

"The queen won't let him bathe alone."

"The real king," Ennui clarified. "My oath friend."

The girl's mouth fell open. She blushed prettily. "Oh!"

And that gave Ennui a certain vicarious satisfaction. Oh to have enough naiveté back to be able to blush like that! "But I distract you from your circumstance. Continue."

"When a—a tree spoke those words. I knew it had to be magic, so I came immediately to you."

Ennui nodded. A tree. That was definitely a message from Havoc. "Prepare to take two anonymous people to that pool. Meet them here an hour hence."

"Yes, Lady."

Ennui left Nonce to her preparation, and went to see her closest female friend. This was the lovely Lady Aspect, widow of the former king, and Havoc's social advisor. "Greeting."

"Acknowledged."

Message from Havoc: 'Bring two ikons.' Nonce will take us there in one hour.

Aspect gave no overt sign that she had received the mental news. She answered with her own thought. *Of course.*

Ennui provided the background mentally while they exchanged routine verbal compliments. *And I felt a weird sexuality just before Nonce arrived.*

Aspect met her gaze. *So did I.*

Astonished, Ennui could only stare. *So it wasn't from inside me.*

It was from elsewhere, Aspect agreed.

This was interesting, quite apart from its emotion. They would have to discuss it further. But not at this moment.

Aspect nodded agreement. Then Ennui left her and sought her man.

Throe was snoozing outside the King's chamber. He woke as she walked by, but pretended to stay asleep. Without speaking aloud she acquainted him with the message and her decision to go, and her urgent state of passion, then went on to their private chamber.

Soon, seemingly coincidentally, he joined her there. They kissed, stripped, and made vigorous love. Their sharing of minds heightened the effect; she felt his passion of fulfillment, and he shared her echo. There was no such thing as an unfulfilled woman, with loving telepathy. Then he helped her become anonymous. She donned a peasant shawl, wooden shoes, and arranged her hair in a messy mop.

"You look beautiful," he said, presenting her with two small wooden trinkets: fake ikons, so that anyone who might have heard the message would think that these were what had been asked for. "Truly."

What made it so nice was that he meant it. Ennui was at best a plain woman, without special talents, but he loved her. She kissed him again, then went to the chamber by the reception desk. At least she had a pretext to leave the dull papers alone for a while.

Unfortunately her sex with Throe, delightful as it was, had not abated her wanton desire. She craved something more than a licit interaction. She hoped he hadn't realized that, for he was a good man and she did love him and did enjoy sex with him. But the vision was something else. It had the thrill of a dangerous liaison that could not be duplicated by a familiar man, even if he could have the staying power of a Glamor.

Soon the Lady Aspect joined her in the chamber. Aspect had undergone a similar transformation, becoming a severely handsome older woman with baggy clothing, netted hair, and a gnarly cane.

Nonce reappeared, also in peasant guise, her allure muted. She glanced at the women, recognizing them but honoring their anonymity. "Are you two visitors ready to return home?"

"Appreciation," Ennui said. "Indirect route." She made a small show of putting the wooden ikons in her pocket.

"It's a long walk," Nonce said. "Is there any chance to get transportation?"

"Would peasant women be able to afford magic floating?" Ennui asked rhetorically.

"Only if they traded for it," Aspect replied, also rhetorically. That meant sex for transport; Nonce could do it, but the older women would have a harder time finding suitable takers.

"We walk," Nonce agreed.

"Negation," Aspect said. "We'll have to use the Traveler's Exchange,"

The girl nodded. She was not telepathic, but she understood the need for secrecy. She was aware that the King Havoc and Queen Gale who resided in the palace were both impostors who had to be treated according to their roles. The girl who played Gale was Spanky, the prior Mistress of the Bath. The Mistress before Spanky had been Bijou, who had also played Gale, to the extent of having an affair with the real Havoc. Nonce longed for a similar affair.

And so do we, Aspect thought, amused.

But with her it's a realistic prospect, Ennui thought enviously.

They followed the girl to the private stairs and down to the lower levels of the city, sharing her innocent thoughts. The difference between the telepaths and the non-telepaths was that the former could read the unguarded thoughts of the latter, while the latter could not read any thoughts. Havoc and Gale were more than telepaths, so knew what was what. Havoc did like Nonce, and would probably oblige her some day. But of course Havoc liked all young women—and all of them liked him.

Delete qualifier 'young' Aspect thought.

And there was a secret the two older women had shared with each other when they became friends. They both loved Havoc in vaguely maternal fashion, but also as women. If the occasion ever came where one of them had to play the part of mistress to him, neither of them would be truly loath. But that was a truth they had confessed only to each other, shielding it diligently from all others. If either Havoc or Gale suspected, they had the wit to let it be.

Could it have been Havoc in her impassioned fancy, his features masked by her shame of the desire? No, because the man was inexperienced, and that hardly described Havoc.

They rode an elevator down to the concourse floor of the city, then walked to the Traveler's Exchange. "How far is the pool?" Ennui asked. She had the answer from the girl's mind, but did not want to reveal that she had done so. Nonce knew that the women were telepathic but never spoke of it.

"Five Chroma zones. I traveled on a King's Pass, but I can't do that anonymously."

"What can we offer?" Ennui asked.

"I prefer to save my body for the King's Bath," Nonce said. She meant that she did not want to exchange sex for a magic ride, though she could readily have found takers. She regarded herself as belonging to her position.

"Sensible," Aspect agreed. "We shall see what else offers."

The Traveler's Exchange was a chamber with a raised stage and a group of people standing around it. As they entered, a man was finishing his statement. "...beyond the Dead Zone."

"I'm going that way," a man said. He was a Cartographer; they had to canvass the planet regularly, to update their maps, because the geography was constantly changing. "Got an assignment."

"Excellent! Brothers, mutual protection, no fault?" No fault was a system used primarily in traveling, whereby people assumed family relationships to each other without any commitment beyond the trip. Men and women often became no fault marriage partners, and this was not considered any violation of their formal marriages elsewhere.

"Done," the Cartographer said. The two shook hands and departed together.

A yellow woman stepped onto the stage. "I am going home to my zone, two Chroma to the east. I have food, need protection."

"I'm going that way," a green Amazon said. "My zone is just beyond yours. What food?"

The yellow woman held up a large basket and tilted it to show an excellent variety of fruits and breads. "Sisters?"

"Agreed." The two joined and left.

Several others followed, without takers. Sometimes it took several days for a person to find the right company with the right assets going the right way. Then a blue man stepped up. "I have transport home five Chroma to the north. It is a bus globe that needs cleaning. My wife and daughters normally do it on the return trips, but this time there were too many passengers and they had to stay home. All conveniences provided, but the thing is filthy."

"That's near the pool," Nonce murmured. "I rode that bus."

Ennui exchanged a thought with Aspect, then spoke. "Two sisters and a daughter, no fault."

"Welcome!" the blue man said.

Another woman spoke. "And a wife, no fault, to the adjacent Red Chroma."

The blue man looked in her direction, and so did Ennui. She was a moderately handsome red woman. She was offering sex for travel, rather than cleaning. Men of one Chroma normally liked the notion of sex with women of other Chromas, so this was clearly appealing. Of course men liked sex anyway, but the novelty was said to enhance the effect.

"Agreed, if my no fault family does not object," the blue man said, smiling.

"No objection," Ennui said, glad that this eliminated any chance that the man would want sex with any of them. Sometimes no fault agreements changed along the way.

They walked up to join the man and meet the red woman. "I am Bus," he said, introducing himself.

"I am Nine," the red woman said.

"We are anonymous peasants," Ennui said. "On, Speck, and No." She indicated herself and the others, using adaptations of their names. Many folk preferred to travel anonymously, so this was not remarkable. "We are not experienced at cleaning buses, but can follow directions."

"Satisfactory," he agreed. He led the way down to the exit ramp at the edge of the city.

They took the ferry across the lake. As they rode it, they gazed back at the city of Triumph. It was a huge wooden pyramid, floating on a lake, anchored to the center. The lower tiers were populated mainly by peasants, the middle tiers by more important folk, and the apex was the king's palace and household.

So now they were cleaning women. It was an irony, because either Ennui or Aspect could readily have commandeered magic service when traveling as themselves; they were two of the king's closest associates. But there would have been no privacy; everyone would have known or suspected the king's business. If Havoc had wanted publicity, he would not have sent his directive in code.

For they carried very special objects: two ikons. Not the wooden trinkets, but metallic statuettes. Few others knew their nature, or even that they existed. Ennui's was in the shape of a tree with eight stubby roots; Aspect's resembled a ball of moss. They were the counterparts to two very special people: the ikons were remnants left behind when people became Glamors. Whoever held a Glamor ikon had considerable power over that Glamor. The Glamors themselves could not touch their own ikons.

The message "Bring two ikons" meant that their bearers should come immediately. This was Glamor business.

They reached the staging area at the edge of the Translucent Chroma zone adjacent to the nonChroma zone surrounding the city of Triumph. There was the bus: a big roughly spherical structure with portholes around its waist. They entered it through a round door that opened from the underside. Inside was a central deck surrounded by comfortable chairs, one by each porthole.

Bus was right: this dome was filthy. His prior passengers must have been slobs. There were fruit peels, bread crusts, and colored smears on floor and seats, and smudges on the glass of the ports. He showed them where brushes and mops and cloths were, and they started in. Nonce took the portholes, and the two older women took the floor.

Two Translucent men came. In a moment the bus was levitated onto a boat, and the boat was moving across the liquid terrain that was the Translucent Chroma zone. They were on their way.

Then Bus went to a closed chamber. Nine didn't say a word; she followed him in. Men usually wanted sex first, and it was best to get it out of the way early. Male capacity was generally less than male ambition, so a woman could thoroughly oblige a man with relatively little actual sex. All women knew that; men should, but constantly deceived themselves.

It was dull scrubbing. *Shall we become better acquainted?* Aspect inquired. *I know you, Ennui, but not as you were before we met.*

I was dull, as my name shows.

Your name evinces lassitude rather than dullness. How were you named?

And there was the request for her early life story. Ennui thought back to her childhood.

꒰꒱

She was the fourth of the required four children, the youngest, and of mixed lineage. Every married couple was expected to have four children, one of which was sired on the wife by a man other than her husband, or adopted from elsewhere, to mix the blood. Fourths, as they were called, were supposed to be treated equally in all respects, but were always aware of their difference. They tended to associate with each other, because they had a common basis, no matter how different they were otherwise.

Ennui's father tried, but his knowledge that she was the product of another man's embrace of his wife generated distance between them. He could not love her equally. That diffidence spread across to her mother. The child was correctly treated, but the emotion was emulated rather than genuine. She felt the lack, but didn't know how to deal with it, so pretended not to care.

Her associations with other children were not much better. Some children were pretty; she was not. Some were smart; she was not. Some were athletic; she was not. She was absolutely ordinary in every apparent way. Boys were not eager to play Tickle & Peek or Touch & Touch with her; girls did not invite her to share confidences. She was dull, and everyone knew it.

She sank slowly into indifference. Her typical answer to any question of preference was "I don't care," or "It doesn't matter." Thus in due course the others named her Ennui, the one who didn't care. But she did care, in her secret heart. She just didn't care to show it.

When she came of age and the other youths paired off for sex and marriage, she was the last girl left single in her village. She had to marry the last single boy, another fourth and a dullard. They did belatedly discover some interest in sexual merging, and did have three babies. Ennui didn't even try to ask another man for the fourth; they adopted a baby no one else wanted. And both lavished unusual affection on that fourth, for a reason they did not care to express. But as a family they remained dull.

She worked, of course. She took the first job that was open, knowing nothing about it: research clerk. She was one of a number of dull women who delved into the voluminous royal files for information when the king required it. Planet Charm was governed by the one group of people who lacked magic: the nonChroma. There were a dozen Chromas, regions colored by their local volcanoes, each completely magical. Each Chroma had many zones, for the volcanoes of any particular color were scattered randomly across the planet. Seen from space, they formed a pretty patchwork of colors. Hence the planet's name: Charm. Residents were the colors of their Chroma zones, as was everything else. Those of the Blue Chroma did blue magic; those of the Red Chroma did red magic, and so on. But blue magic did not work in a red zone or any other, so a blue person who traveled was at a disadvantage. Brigands knew this, and lurked on the trails between Chroma. So few folk traveled; they did not like being magically naked and helpless. Except for the nonChroma folk; they never had magic anyway, so did not miss it when traveling in or out of Chroma zones. They depended on purely physical and mental skills, like swords and wit. They went everywhere that magic wasn't, between and around Chroma zones. This gave them global power. They were also inherently impartial about magic, having no brief for any one Chroma over another. Thus nonChroma became the ruling group, and Triumph City was the capital of the world.

When there was trouble between Chroma, the king settled it. When there was a natural disaster, the king arranged for relief. When something strange occurred, the king investigated. For these services, all Chroma answered to the king, and paid taxes to him. But it was essential that the king be well informed before he took action. He had advisers, and they had assistants, and the assistants gave directives to their clerks and researchers, who did the dull work of finding what was relevant. If there was trouble between a Blue Chroma zone and a Green Chroma zone, Ennui might be one of the ones who dug out the entire thousand-year history of those two zones and filtered out what was relevant. She did not get personal credit for this; it was her job. She was anonymous.

Thus her life proceeded for twenty years. The children grew up and found their own abilities and commitments, and Ennui's marriage was little more than a shell. They had done their job, perpetuating the species in the prescribed manner. And she was bored to oblivion. She knew too much about planetary affairs, and not enough about personal satisfaction.

She had dreamed, once, as an isolated child, of somehow finding her ideal ability and situation, and becoming a person to be envied. But she had always known that she lacked any qualities to make that happen. She had always been dull, and would remain so. She was a creature of the lower levels of the city, and would never be anything else.

Her husband suffered an unsuspected malady, was ill two months, and died. Suddenly Ennui had no marriage. It wasn't that she valued it, but neither had she wished her husband any ill, and it was a shock. The laws of society didn't care: she had one month to find a new husband, or one would be assigned.

Then King Deal died in an accident. She didn't know that at the time; it wasn't publicized immediately. Instead a competition was announced, open to anyone, whose winner would achieve phenomenal notoriety. The losers would not be heard from again; they would disappear. This appealed to her; she had never been visible, so disappearance was no problem. And if by some weird chance she won—maybe it would make her life interesting at last. She knew that something significant was occurring, because the excitement of it filtered down through the echelons. This competition surely related.

Ennui had no life, and it promised to get worse. She didn't want to remarry. Her situation seemed hopeless. She realized that this was the one time in her existence that she could truly afford to gamble. What did she have to lose?

So she entered the contest. She found herself in a chamber with every sort of equipment or pleasure: food, weapons, clothing, amenable young men and women. There were a number of other contestants, who found this delightful. Until the first acid wash coursed through.

They leaped for high pedestals that rose from the floor to get clear of it. Ennui was lucky enough to get one, so she survived the first wash. But now the dark nature of the contest was apparent: there was one fewer of the stools than contestants. It was musical chairs, with the loser apparently being dissolved by the acid.

One of the contestants was a big barbarian man. He approached her, asking her help. But she demurred, and told him why: "I am afraid of you."

"I mean you no harm. How can I convince you?"

"Then make me an oath of friendship." She knew about barbarian oaths from her researches; sometimes the king had to deal with outlying nonChroma villages. This man was deadly, but he would keep his given word. In some ways barbarians seemed more civilized than big city folk.

Finally he did it, and they became oath friends. And that was the act that changed her life, and gave her all that she had dreamed of, and more, though she did not know it then.

The game continued, and barbarian Havoc was true to his oath. He protected her from others, and guaranteed her a pedestal for each wash.

Between washes they talked. She acquainted him with the likely nature of this competition; it could be for some high position or special mission for the king. She had entered it voluntarily, but it seemed that he had been abducted from his distant home village of Trifle to the north and put in unaware. That was why he needed the advice and guidance of someone familiar with the city. He was, it turned out, ignorant but amazingly sharp minded.

There was a lovely young woman in red who had rejected Havoc's first approach. Now, seeing the way of it, that woman came to him, reconsidering, offering sex, but he rejected her. She then fomented an alliance against him. Two men charged him with sword and spear. Ennui screamed, but he dispatched both with a knife—and it was evident he could have done it barehanded, because he didn't stab them, he knocked them out with the hilt. Ennui realized that though he had chosen her for an alliance, she was the one who was profiting most. She had a warrior on her side.

Now they were three: Ennui, Havoc, and the woman in red, named Futility. Futility stripped her cloak and stood naked on her pedestal, offering her dancer's body again to Havoc. She was an ice maiden: desirable but heartless. But the barbarian was on to her, and refused to touch her.

Ennui, knowing that very soon the end would come to two of them, and that the survivor would be Havoc, found her personal restrictions loosening. She told him her secret: that she was depressed, and saw little value in life. He was her oath-friend; he understood.

Then came the wash. Ennui went to her pedestal. Futility ran to push her off. Havoc intercepted Futility, who wrapped her bare legs about him, pressed her torso close, and kissed him avidly. Ennui saw him trying to pry the dancer loose as the acid surged toward them, but she clung desperately. Then he tickled her and she screamed and let go. Ennui would have laughed, had the situation not been so desperate.

Futility drew a knife from her hair, but Havoc disarmed her and threw her down as he got on the second pedestal. The acid swept over her. Futility was gone.

Now they were two. Ennui knew it was over for her; Havoc was the rightful winner. She would not take the pedestal again. She bid him thanks and parting, and asked him to knock her out so that she would not suffer as the acid took her. She had known him only briefly, but he had brought her a marvelous termination, far more interesting than her life.

But as the acid surged again, Havoc swept her off her feet and held her in his arms as he mounted the last pedestal. She had seen him in action, and knew he was fast and strong, but as his easy strength took her she was amazed. She protested, asking him to put her down, because this was surely breaking the rules, but she also loved him for his power and his conscience. "Oh Havoc," she murmured as the awful sea of acid surrounded them. This was a dreamlike way to die, in the arms of a handsome young barbarian.

The acid receded. A door opened, and the king's herald came, presenting Havoc with the fabulous ten-spiked gold crown. "King Deal died yesterday morning. You are the new king. All power to you, King Havoc."

Havoc thought it must be a joke, but Ennui knew it wasn't. She assured him that this was the prize he had won.

And Havoc surprised her again. He didn't want to be king. He just wanted to return to his home village.

But he didn't have a choice. Archers appeared, their bows drawn, orienting on him. It was plain that he would be killed if he did not take the crown. Ennui pleaded with him, and because she was his oath friend, he took her word. One had to trust an oath friend, however recent, and an oath friend had to be trustworthy. It was the barbarian way. He donned the crown, and all present bowed down to him, calling him Sire.

"Stay with me, Ennui," he said. "I need you." And it seemed he did, because she knew the ways of civilization. In this manner she ceased being a lowly peasant woman and became the Lady Ennui, the king's advisor.

He asked her to give the men whatever directives were needed, since he had no idea what to do. But she, overwhelmed by the excitement of recent events and their phenomenal conclusion, fainted. Some help she was! The last thing she felt was his arms around her again, as he caught her and picked her up. She felt marvelously safe.

When she recovered consciousness, they were on an elevator. Havoc didn't know what it was, and didn't trust it. He really was a barbarian. When it moved, he wanted to leap to safety. She had to grab his arm and hold him, reassuring him about the nature of the mechanism. But they wound up climbing a spiral ramp instead. When she got too tired to continue, he picked her up a third time and carried her. Oh, that muscle!

She explained things to him as they went. There was an enormous amount to cover, because he knew almost nothing about the city, let alone about being king. He made her stop calling him Sire; she was his oath friend.

The herald advised Havoc that all the prior king's staff were awaiting word of their dismissal, so he could install his own people. Baffled, as he had no people, he asked Ennui. All she could think of was to suggest that he keep the old ones, until he had more information. He did that, and thereby won the instant devotion and loyalty of the entire establishment. It was the kind of naïve thing no civilized king would have done. But apart from that, there was something about Havoc. Ennui was one of the first of many to realize that.

First they talked to the majordomo, the head of the palace household staff. He introduced them to the assembled staff. There was awkwardness, until Ennui stepped in and gave them sensible guidelines in Havoc's presence, therefore at the king's bidding. She was surprised to find herself reasonably competent at this, and it was clear that he really did need her. He had saved her life; now she was saving his stature before those who had known the old king.

Then she had to persuade him to honor another royal custom: being bathed by three lovely young women. He saw no need of a bath just because he was sweaty and smelly, but he took her word. She persuaded him to think of it as a game of Statue, where he was blind-folded and subjected to being Peeked and Touched by girls, losing only if he moved or protested. She knew he feared getting a masculine reaction, but that was part of the point of such a game; the girls could safely test their power to arouse the victim. In this manner he was thoroughly cleaned and garbed for his next interview.

When he saw the royal outfit he was wearing, he said he felt like a clown. He wanted to leave all this and go home. Ennui managed to persuade him that he couldn't do that. She found his sincere diffidence charming.

"Ennui, I think I am coming to love you," he said, giving her an illicit thrill she struggled to suppress. "Do not leave my side." She promised not to, except when protocol required it. Now she was quite certain that he needed her, and she reveled in being needed. She had made him make the oath of friendship because she feared him; now she was coming into the full significance of the oath. He was the king, but she was like a mother to him, guiding him, being trusted by him. There was no way she would ever betray him or let him suffer any avoidable embarrassment.

She joined him in a meal, being the only one he felt comfortable with, and that was just as well, because he did have the manners of a barbarian. Then they met the Chief of Staff, and Ennui helped smooth over the awkwardnesses. They agreed that she should be designated the king's social secretary, serving as liaison between him and others.

Then they went to met King Deal's widow, the Lady Aspect. She was in the process of packing her things to move out. She had been widowed only a day and a half, and had not expected it. Now she had to vacate, and remarry within a month, as no women were allowed to be single. She was a handsome woman of Ennui's age, and by all accounts a good person, intelligent, accommodating, and decent.

Havoc was blunt in his barbarian way. First he ascertained the limits of his social authority: members of the king's staff were exempt from the marriage requirement, the better to serve the king. Ennui realized that her assignment as his secretary had freed her from the need to remarry, a more than incidental blessing. Now he made the Lady Aspect his household organizer, let her keep her residence at the palace, and asked her to let Ennui board with her. He wasn't aware that such a request by the king had the force of command; he thought he was being polite. Then he lay down on the floor and slept.

And that was my introduction to you, Ennui concluded. *My best friend, next to Havoc.*

≈≈

The Lady Aspect did not pause in her scrubbing, for she did not want to give away the fact that the two of them had been in intimate mental contact. Instead she responded with her own personal history.

I was a creature of the nobility from the first, she thought.

She was the first child, and favored from the outset because she was pretty. She was well cared for and was provided with excellent education and life experiences. She grew up in the upper sections of the city of Triumph, and her parents had responsible positions in the king's hierarchy. On occasion they were invited to royal parties, and once when she was sixteen King Diamond danced with her. She was utterly thrilled, and in that moment dreamed of becoming his mistress. But of course he already had a wife-approved mistress, and was loyal to her, and there were hundreds of lovely maidens eager to get into the king's bed. So there was no realistic chance, but she dreamed for weeks.

When she approached eighteen she was required to marry, as all folk were. She had played Tickle & Peek with a number of boys when she was a child, and explored sex with several when her breasts developed, as was normal. She never lacked for male interest, so could afford to be choosy. She liked one boy especially, and wanted to marry him, but one disadvantage of her class was that social connections were often more important than private preference. Her parents selected a man with excellent prospects, and they married on her eighteenth birthday. He was a thirty-year-old widower. She despaired of her life.

His name was Deal, and he was handsome, smart, and connected. For an older man. There was something magnetic about him that she fought to resist, without perfect success. From the start other married women asked him for their fourths, and he was of course obliged to accommodate them. Aspect could have no legitimate objection, but privately she seethed. She was his wife; she wanted him all to herself, even though he was of another generation. She did not like being alone at night, knowing that he was in the bed of another woman, getting her pregnant. Her pride was taking a beating.

Deal was sensitive, and picked up on her mood. "Statement," he said seriously. "We married not by our own choices. It was political and expedient. But you are the prettiest and finest woman I know, and I love you, and would rather be in your embrace than any of theirs. I do not wish to cause you to suffer. I will tell them no henceforth."

Something tore inside her. She had been determined *not* to love the man she had not chosen for marriage, but his statement burned that away. "I would rather have your love than your penis," she said. "I love you too, and would not have you be known as unsocial. Do not tell them no."

He was taken aback. "You do not want—"

"Misunderstanding," she said quickly. "I do want you in my bed, always." As of that moment, it was true.

They proceeded immediately to sex, and it was wonderful. "Henceforth," he announced, "I will require any other woman who requires a fourth to tryst briefly by day, so I can spend all night with you."

And so it was. They had three daughters at yearly intervals, and then it was time for her fourth. She still loved Deal, and did not want to suffer the embrace of any other man, but it was required.

Deal came to her rescue again. "I have a friend in another zone you do not know. He is your age, reliable, and I trust him absolutely. I would like to have his child in my family."

"I will get you his child," she agreed, relieved.

Deal made arrangements, and his friend visited Triumph City. Deal brought him to their apartment, introduced them, and departed on a business trip of his own.

The eldest girl, three years old, was curious. "Daddy must travel," Aspect explained. "This man will take his place until he returns." The girl nodded, satisfied.

So the man joined her in bed that week, and had sex with her every night. They did not pretend to love each other, but actually the sex was good; they seemed compatible.

When Deal returned, the men shook hands and the other departed. It had been enough; Aspect was pregnant, and in due course birthed a fourth daughter. Ironically, this was the one who most favored Aspect, and Deal had no trouble loving her the same as the others. Meanwhile the deed was done, the fourth had been gotten, and they had no further children. Aspect wore the wire, as it was called, that prevented conception, and they had sex with abandon.

Meanwhile King Diamond resigned as king, and was replaced by King Cheer, a jovial man. Aspect was surprised, because King Diamond had seemed quite competent. But perhaps it was wearing being king, and six years was enough.

It turned out to be an improvement for Deal and Aspect, because Cheer was a more social man, and encouraged parties and celebrations. Deal became a secondary advisor for affairs of state, and Aspect became a supervising hostess for entertainments of state. Both were good at their positions, and were well regarded at court. As Aspect got to know the king better, she was impressed; his smiling countenance masked a very sharp and realistic mind. She had the impression that there were things going on that he did not speak of, but that he was on the right side of whatever issues there might be. The government of the planet slowly improved during his reign. She liked his wife too; she was similar in nature, smiling, but serious beneath.

But in five years King Cheer also resigned, surprisingly, and joined Diamond in comfortable retirement. There must have been a reason, but neither he nor his wife ever spoke of it.

The next king was Enterprise, a decade younger but still mature. He took hold with a will, and things changed rapidly, but he was not foolish. Deal became one of his leading advisors, and the man listened and acted sensibly. It looked good—until, after just two years, he too resigned. What was going on? As before, neither he nor his wife would speak of it; it was time to retire, they agreed. As retirees they had a comfortable existence and no need to take any subsequent position.

There was a veiled selection process, and suddenly a new king was presented—and it was Deal! Her husband! He was almost as surprised as she. But he knew the business, and set out to do the best job he could. The first thing he did was appoint his friend Chief of Staff. Thus the father of their fourth was now an important member of the royal household.

Aspect paid him no direct attention. What was past was past; they had no personal relationship and certainly no romantic one. On the occasions that they interacted, they treated each other with appropriate formality. No one other than Deal knew about their past.

Now the Lady Aspect, as queen, was high profile. Everyone knew her, and many came to her with pleas intended for the king. She considered them carefully and passed along those she deemed worthy of his attention. She was concerned for their children, and did her best to keep them in the background, lest they be spoiled by attention. But they were used to attention, and conscious of the gravity of their father's position, so behaved reasonably well. As they came of age, all were in high demand for marriage, and all four married early and well. All girls had to marry by eighteen, but could do so at fifteen with parental approval. Some had clear understandings with their young men before that age.

There was another, more private aspect to the kingship that she had known about but not fully appreciated before. The king was a very public figure, and was attended by others in every minor respect. There were servants to dress him, a girl to brush his teeth for him, and three girls to bathe him, the Mistresses of the Royal Bath. Mistress was an appropriate term, as they normally performed their office nude, and if the king was intrigued by their shapely young bodies, they cooperated gladly, not only performing sex with him in the bath, but washing off his genitals afterwards. King Deal did not indulge in this manner, remaining true to his wife, but they were more than eager to oblige. One night one of them sneaked into his room and bed just before he retired, hoping to seduce him there.

As it happened, Aspect had already retired, and was lying in the bed in the dark. The girl, finding her there, was appalled, thinking she would be executed. But Aspect found it funny, and realized that this was a rare opportunity to have a small adventure. "Stay," she said. "Don my nightdress, and if you can fool him into thinking you are me, welcome to his attention."

The girl did so, and Aspect quietly left the room. Then she did something she had never done since marriage: she Peeked. She used a special crevice in the wall to watch the bed. The chamber was dark, but not completely so, and her eyes were acclimatized.

Soon Deal came, got in, and was instantly embraced by the eager girl, who flung off the covers in her enthusiasm. There followed a vigorous clasping and engagement, obviously mutually satisfactory. And Aspect, to her surprise and chagrin, discovered that she was turned on by the scene. There was something about seeing that lush young body kissed, stroked, and penetrated that excited her in a way that regular sex did not. She loved her husband, but sex had become dull. She normally did it to oblige him, pretending more pleasure than she felt.

Only when the culmination was complete did Deal take note. "Who are you?" he demanded.

"The bath girl," she answered meekly.

"Return to your station."

She departed, still wearing the nightdress, which had been sadly abused by the action.

Then Deal spoke directly to Aspect. "Did you see enough?"

She entered the room. "I thought it would be a good joke. You really didn't know the difference?"

"Naturally not. I thought there could be only one body as fine as yours."

She almost blushed. She was twenty-seven and had birthed three babies; her body could not compete with that of a sixteen year old girl selected for her beauty. He was teasing her.

"Nor did I know you were watching through the crevice," he continued, smiling.

So the joke had been on her. "Oh, Deal!" Then she fell upon him, kissing him as avidly as the girl had, as eager for sex as the girl had been. And soon enough they achieved it.

But in the morning, having pondered the matter, she gave him the word: "It is time for you to take a formal mistress. I will not have bath girls perpetually displacing me in bed."

He smiled. "I will seek one. But no bath girl will do. I want one that is to at least to some extent an echo of you."

She could not argue with that. And within a year he found one: a young woman of the Invisible Chroma named Symbol who was educated, intelligent, and extremely well formed, though she had to don tight nonChroma clothing to show it.

"What do you see in her?" Aspect asked teasingly.

"When I embrace her, I picture you. She does not interfere with that vision."

Literally true. Though Aspect had demanded it, it took her a while to adjust to the notion that Deal now had a regular mistress who was, it became apparent (as it were) a better sexual partner than Aspect herself. When Deal traveled, as he often did, Symbol traveled with him, for Aspect had four children to care for, ages six to nine. Even when he was home, he often went to the invisible mistress instead of Aspect. Symbol had a room in the royal suite, so was always available.

Yet there were compensations. When Aspect was tired and simply wanted to sleep, she had but to glance at Symbol's veil, and the woman took the hint and drew Deal away, returning him an hour later with no further need for sex. If Aspect preferred, she would hold the king for the full night. No other woman ever got close to him; the mistress saw to that. Symbol also became a reliable caregiver for the children. On occasion she even took the children out for some incidental entertainment so that Aspect could have private sex with her husband. Symbol became a companion for Aspect, for she was an excellent conversationalist, and never imposed in any way. Aspect knew this was because the woman knew that the wife could abolish the mistress with or without cause at any moment; it was part of her profession to cater to the wife as well as the man. But she was so good at it that it was easy to like her, and Aspect did.

"Truth," Aspect said one day as Symbol was helping her dress for an occasion. She did not need to do this, as this was not her job and there were handmaidens for the purpose, but seemed to like being helpful.

"Always," the young woman agreed. That meant that she would answer any question without evasion or distortion, regardless of the consequence. But Aspect would have to answer with similar candor in her turn. Truth was a two-edged game.

"What is your real nature and desire?"

"I am cynical, perceiving and acting to achieve my best situation. The king has much to offer, and I mean never to give him reason to replace me."

That was an honest answer. "Do you love him?"

"Yes, in my fashion."

Qualified, yet surely true. "What do you think of me?"

"I would prefer to evade that answer."

"Why?"

"Because you might not believe it."

"Speak." That was a command.

"You are the most elegant and competent woman of this court, and the king loves you."

This could not be empty flattery, because she was bound to speak truth. "That is all?"

"Negation."

"Speak."

"And I want to be your friend."

Aspect had been prepared to dislike Symbol, but found herself disarmed. There was something about her, just as there was about Deal. This answer surprised her, for it meant that the woman was not merely catering, she truly desired friendship, given and received.

Rather than respond, as she was not certain how she felt, Aspect ended her questioning. "Your turn."

"Needless. I have no need to know what you do not wish me to know."

Which returned the onus to her. Aspect made a decision. "I will be your friend."

"Appreciation." Her veiled (literally) smile was genuine.

Thereafter they were friends as well as business associates. Aspect came to truly appreciate Symbol's qualities, and to value her presence. In time Symbol was given her own apartment, but she spent much time with Aspect, and they remained close.

There were problems with the kingship. Deal was doing a good job, but discovered nebulous resistance to his policies. He labored to pin it down, but it evaded him. Then the council impeached him on spurious grounds. He fought it and won, keeping the crown.

Then, suddenly, he was dead. It was labeled an accident, but Aspect knew better. The anonymous enemy had done it, eliminating the genuine reformer. But she had no proof, really no evidence. This lent a sharper edge to her grief. She was woefully unprepared for this.

She was doomed. The last daughter had married and moved away the year before, and Aspect was now alone. She would have to vacate her suite to make way for the new queen, and within a month she would have to remarry.

Symbol was in a similar situation. The new king would have his own mistress. She tried to console Aspect, but her grief was similar. So she turned it aside. "I will look for an apartment in the city, for this month, for the two of us, if you wish." That would economize on the cost, in their reduced circumstances. Aspect had gemstones to trade, but did not wish to use them up any faster than necessary.

"Thank you." What little comfort to be had was there: Aspect was not alone in her mourning or her situation. "I will pack our things for removal."

The following day the new king was selected. Aspect thought things could hardly be worse, but they were: he was a barbarian youth. Evidently the secret powers that existed had decided that civilized kings were too difficult to control, so they had arranged for an uncivilized one. He would be far easier to handle.

Aspect smiled reflectively. How little any of them had known!

The new king was Havoc from Village Trifle far to the north. News came to her of his barbarian blunders. He belched, he farted, he spoke with embarrassing bluntness. Somehow he had picked up a commoner woman who stayed by his side; it seemed he had made her an oath of friendship. Now she was handling things, buttressed by the power of her oath-friend. What was the planet coming to?

Yet they had done one thing so different and remarkable that all were astonished: they had reappointed all of King Deal's personnel. It seemed that the barbarian knew he was ignorant, so depended on the judgment of his predecessor. The bath girls were already agog, for Havoc was a remarkably handsome and dynamic man just eighteen. But the more sober folk like Majordomo and Chief were also impressed, and found sudden loyalty to the new king.

King Havoc came to see her. Surprised, she paused in her preparations. He was now the king, and she had to call him Sire despite being his mother's age. He questioned her briefly, then did what he had done with the others: he asked her to stay, and to be his household advisor. Thus at a single stroke he relieved her of the inconvenience of moving, of her loss of status, and of the need to remarry. In that amazing moment, she began to love him. Like a son.

All he asked in return was that she allow his oath friend Ennui to share her residence. This was simplicity itself, as there was plenty of room for both her and Symbol since the children moved out.

Then Havoc got barbarian blunt: "Was King Deal murdered?"

"Sire!" she protested, for this was a forbidden thought despite her own suspicion.

He saw through her implied denial immediately. The man was barbarian, ignorant but not stupid. "Do you know anything?"

She confessed that she believed that her husband's sudden demise was not natural.

If that was true, he said bluntly, he wanted to know it, if only, as he put it, to save his own hide from a similar fate.

Then somehow the dialogue was about King Deal's mistress Symbol, and she had to explain about that. The ways of a king were not the ways of a barbarian villager. Havoc asked if Symbol could have done it, and Aspect quickly exonerated her; Symbol had loved Deal as ardently at Aspect had.

Then Havoc dropped lithely to the floor in an amazing display of muscle and coordination, and went to sleep in a similarly amazing display of naiveté.

Startled anew, Aspect looked at Ennui. "He *is* a barbarian," Ennui said. "He has his little ways, some of which are crude, and some endearing."

"Endearing?"

"He keeps his word. He cares about people. He is loyal to his own. He recognizes his areas of ignorance. And he listens when you speak."

Those were sterling recommendations, and she had already seen evidence of them. But Aspect suspected that civilization and the power of the office would soon abate such naïve qualities. Ennui argued that Havoc was ignorant, but neither weak nor stupid; he would remain a good man. But Ennui was of common stock; she would not have had occasion to see or experience the corrupting influence of power.

It bothered Aspect to see the man lying like an animal on the hard floor, so she fetched a blanket and pillow and tucked them around and under him. She had not had a son, but he continued to feel like one.

Ennui helped her move her things back where they belonged, and she helped the commoner woman move in to her rooms. All the while Havoc slept. To her surprise, he didn't snore; he was quite quiet. Perhaps that came of being a hunter in the outlying wilds, learning not to give away one's location. He certainly trusted the two of them, and she was determined to see that that trust was warranted. Perhaps later he would change his mind about letting her remain here, but even so, it had been a kind gesture.

Ennui was tired too, and soon she washed and slept. She refused to go to her room, concerned that Havoc might wake and need her, so she lay down beside him on the floor. That was touching; she seemed to take their oath of friendship as seriously as he did. But also comforting, because Ennui was no innocent girl; she was Aspect's age, and had raised her four children and lost her husband too. They had things in common. Aspect had come to know her somewhat as they moved the belongings, and recognized in her a certain core of commitment and common sense that were worthwhile.

Aspect could not sleep; too much had changed too suddenly to allow her to relax. The grief of her loss loomed like a monster at the window, ready to consume her the moment she eased her defense. Thus she was the one who was awake when Havoc woke. She saw him get up and look around, searching for something. She had a notion what.

"Sire," she murmured, so that he would know she was at hand.

"I need—"

She indicated the bathroom door. He entered, then ran his hands ineffectively over his clothing. Evidently the staff had dressed him, and he didn't know how to get the necessary anatomy clear. "Sire," she said.

"Yes, Lady Aspect."

"If you find your clothing unfamiliar, perhaps I can help you."

She explained the workings of the self-adhesive straps and guided his hand to manipulate them. Then she left him alone to perform his functions in private.

It took him some time, surely because of his struggle with the clothing. When he emerged she had to suppress a smile; he had reassembled himself correctly but clumsily, so that he looked like an oversized boy. She took him back into the bathroom, dropped his pantaloons, adjusted his underwear, and put the pantaloons back neatly. In the process she caught glimpses of his supremely healthy private anatomy, but of course pretended blindness. She explained that she had often assisted her husband when he required it.

"What are my crudities?" he asked bluntly.

She realized that he had not been wholly asleep when she and Ennui had discussed him. Probably any potential attacker would have been rudely surprised had he approached the sleeper. She should have been more careful. She tried to demur, but he insisted on having an answer.

She explained that she did not wish to risk giving offense. But he persisted. "Please."

"The king never says please to an underling," she said, alarmed. And of course that was part of his ignorance. She had to do it. Not only was he the king, he did need to know. "Very well, Sire, I will speak plainly, though it pains me. It is crude to utter expletives in conversation. 'Hell' is an expletive. It is crude to cut directly to the point, such as asking 'Why?' It is crude to scratch or belch or fart in public. It is crude to meet a person's gaze for more than a moment, and may even seem threatening. It is crude to sleep on the floor, or in your clothes."

Havoc wiped his nose. "I guess so."

"As is wiping your nose with your bare hand." She continued to instruct him, and had the impression that he was paying close attention. He was, she was discovering, an extremely intelligent man. He was almost visibly becoming civilized.

He was observant, too. "How long has it been since you slept?"

"Not since my husband died, Sire."

"Then sleep now, and when you are refreshed, come to me. My fiancé Gale will also need instruction, when she arrives here."

Then at last they emerged from the closed bathroom. Ennui was outside. She had the wit not to look askance at discovering the barbarian king closeted in the bathroom with the former king's widow.

Havoc and Ennui departed for his own apartment, and Aspect went to her bedroom to lie down. Somehow the recent interaction with Havoc had reassured her, and she was at last able to sleep.

In due course Symbol returned, and Ennui, this time alone. The two seemed well acquainted by the time Aspect was active again. At any rate, Symbol had doffed her headdress and veil, so that her head was invisible; she never did that in public. They agreed that Symbol would have an early appointment with Havoc, and would continue his education in civilized and royal ways.

"But you know I will try to seduce him," Symbol said to them both. "It's my nature, and my business. Do either of you have a problem with that?"

Aspect and Ennui considered. They exchanged a glance. "No," Aspect answered for them both. For to object would be to imply that they had some sexual interest in the king themselves. Aspect could not object on the grounds of disloyalty to King Deal, because Deal was dead. And Symbol did indeed need to secure her position, lest she be cast out as superfluous. Actually she held another formal position, that of Invisible Chroma Representative, but Chroma Representatives did not normally associate closely with the king. They were a nominal check on his power, and reported to their Chroma.

"Actually I will merely tempt him, at first. I will need to get his fiancée's approval before taking him to bed."

And none of them knew Havoc's fiancée. She was surely a barbarian girl, with abundant ignorance.

Symbol had her interview with Havoc, and returned impressed. "That's the smartest man I have encountered," she reported. "I gave him the full dose of culture and history, and he understood immediately though it was mostly new to him. And there's something about him. He's barbarian, but he reminds me of Deal."

Aspect was surprised to realize it was true. Havoc was as different from Deal as it was possible to be, superficially, but his underlying presence was similar. "That must be why we like him."

"I really would like to seduce him," Symbol said dreamily. "He's a decade my junior, but he has a remarkable body."

"Yes." Aspect had seen that body. Deal might have looked like that, in his youth.

In another day Havoc's fiancée arrived. She was Gale, of peasant stock, but a remarkably healthy and lovely girl of seventeen. She reminded Aspect of Symbol, oddly. Aspect was there when she entered the palace and met Havoc. He swept her into his embrace. "What's this about your being king?" she asked. "Why are you wearing a clown suit?"

He grinned ruefully. "Talk with the Lady Aspect." He pointed her out to the girl. "And the Lady Ennui, my oath friend."

"Oath friend!" Gale exclaimed, shocked. She was barbarian, all right. She knew about oaths.

"Go with Aspect now."

Evidently not pleased, Gale went with Aspect to her apartment. Aspect could hardly blame her; this was even newer to her than to Havoc. "King Havoc is an extremely quick study," she said to the girl. "Are you also?"

"When I have to be. Who are you?"

"I am King Deal's widow."

The girl's face was a study in surprise and sympathy. And as Aspect prepared her for the coming ordeal of attendance at the king's coronation, she found that Gale, too, had endearing qualities. She was lovely, smart, and sensitive, very much the female counterpart of

Havoc. They were obviously well matched. Aspect found herself liking her.

Then she passed Gale along to Ennui, who had ugly news for her. It was obvious that Gale did not like Havoc's having an oath friend, and she really objected to the idea of Deal's mistress being near Havoc. This was understandable, but there were necessary adjustments the girl had to make. Still, when she learned that Deal had been murdered, and that Havoc might face a similar threat, she focused instantly.

Later Aspect learned what Ennui told Gale: that she had to go on a secret mission to investigate the changelings, which were a mysterious class of babies occurring as fourths. King Deal had been investigating that mystery when he was killed. King Havoc was going to investigate it also, which put him in immediate danger. So Gale would have to leave the city anonymously to seek information, while Havoc would go about the king's business with another woman emulating Gale at his side. A woman who would share his bed, and be enchanted to believe she was Gale.

Woman that she was, Gale agreed to this. She attended the coronation speech, as did they all. He made quite a show, telling the huge audience that he didn't give half a wad of stale dragon poop for the job of king. He said he hated King Deal, and wanted to kill him, but the idiot had leaped off a cliff and bashed his brains out, and good riddance.

The audience was stunned, and so was Aspect. But it got worse. "They told me not to be crude in public. Well, all I have to say to that is—" He paused, as the members of the vast audience stared. Then he let fly with a resounding belch.

Then they laughed, and Aspect found herself laughing with them. Havoc had broken the ice in a big way. He went on to more positive things, and his crudity faded. He complimented the prior king's staff, which he had kept on, and complimented Lady Aspect and the Lady Symbol. He summarized the challenges facing the king, and concluded: "I need you. I need all of you. Are you with me?"

And they cheered. He had completely won over the audience, and the others, and Aspect herself. The man was a natural politician.

After that he took the field on the king's business, traveling with the former First Bath Girl, Bijou, made up to resemble Gale. Aspect did not like that business; the girl had agreed to play the role, but would be locked in love with Havoc, and in time would discover that what she thought she was and had were illusion. Indeed, when the two got infected with the mental disease and became mind readers, she did learn the truth, and was appalled. But later Havoc associated with her as herself, privately, though she still played the public role of Gale, and she was more than satisfied.

When Gale returned from her mission, she had much to report, but she insisted on seeing Aspect first, even before Havoc. Surprised, Aspect met with her, and learned that she had been attacked by a succubus. She had defeated the demon, a remarkable accomplishment, but feared that it was merely quiescent, and would steal Havoc's soul if Gale had sex with him. Also, she had learned that the two of them were changelings, as was King Deal, more alike than twins, so they could not afford to marry. So the two had to stay apart, an awful grief for them both. Yet Gale was handling it, doing what she had to. There were queenly qualities in this barbarian girl.

Havoc went on an anonymous mission with Bijou, and a minstrel was coached to emulate Havoc and take his place as king, with the new First Bath Girl, Spanky, now emulating Gale. Spanky turned out to be good at it, as Bijou had been, and it became a regular role for her, for both Havoc and Gale spent a lot of time away from Triumph. Aspect and Ennui, of course, supported them in every possible way, because it was Havoc's wish, and because formidable respect was developing. Aspect had never seen a new king and queen take hold like this.

Chief, the father of Aspect's fourth, took an interest in Ennui, who was at first amazed. Symbol had a fling with Throe, the bodyguard, who had never been a fan of hers; perhaps she regarded it as a challenge. Then Ennui and Throe got together, and found true love. And in time Chief and Aspect decided to see whether they were capable of a genuine association, for the purpose of companionship rather than generating a fourth. Naturally sex was part of it, and she discovered that it was good to get back into this aspect of a relationship. She was into aspects, hence her name.

Meanwhile Havoc turned out to be a truly meritorious king. He went far toward solving the mysteries of King Deal's murder, and of the changelings. Of course he was impeached, but he not only beat back that challenge, he invoked the help of the mysterious Glamors, and eliminated all traitors in high places. He had accomplished what none of the prior four kings had. Most of his associates had been involved in challenging missions for him or with him, and been profoundly affected by them.

If there was one thing Aspect regretted, it was that she had been peripheral to all this. She had never risked her life or status for Havoc, or undertaken a dangerous mission. She had wished to be more of a part of his activities than she was. But that was her secret, shielded from mind reading.

Still, there was one vital way in which both she and Ennui had become extremely close to Havoc and Gale. It had finally turned out that changelings were of different types, and could marry and have children, so that Havoc and Gale could at last formally recognize their love. In the process of this discovery, they had fathomed the riddle of the Glamors, and become Glamors themselves. Each Glamor left behind an ikon, the key to his or her enormous magical power. Havoc had given his to Ennui, his trusted oath friend, and Gale had given hers to Aspect. So they were the holders of the ikons of the two most important people on the planet. It was a unique privilege. They guarded both the ikons and the secret of the ikons from all others. So she could hardly consider herself neglected, even in her secret thoughts.

Now Havoc had summoned the Ladies Aspect and Ennui for a private rendezvous. This had the feel of adventure. She was thrilled.

꧁꧂

Ennui looked up from her scrubbing, as Aspect's extended mental review concluded. They had just about completed the job, but there was something odd. Neither she nor Aspect had spent much time scrubbing in decades; their hands and knees should be raw after this extensive workout. But she felt fine, and saw that Aspect did too. Nonce, in contrast, was tired, despite doing the easier vertical work.

The ikons, Aspect thought. *They lend power.*

And that had to be it. The ikons were the essence of magic, and their full nature was unknown. Gale had fetched an ikon from a volcano just as it erupted, and been blown far through the air, and had survived: that was an indication. Ennui's ikon seemed to have lent her extra sexual appeal, interest, and stamina, and she knew the same was true for Aspect. Both of them looked better than they had in years, being more slender and shaped. They tried to mask it, but a number of court personnel had noticed. Others gave the men credit, thinking that regular attention and sex was responsible, and neither woman demurred. But Ennui had had plenty of sex in her life, and never thought much of it, until she carried the loom ikon. Then she had become a wildly sexual creature, to Throe's amazement. He had had recent experience with several extremely sexy women, so had a basis for comparison, and told her she was a match for any of them. She knew it was true, because their minds were open to each other. She had regretted having to return the loom to its refuge when the need for it was done. The Glamors had seen to that somehow, for all the ikons, though they could not handle any of them themselves. But then she had acquired Havoc's Tree ikon, and the youth and power were back.

It is true, Aspect thought. *I had become portly, and Deal seldom had sex with me any more. I didn't blame him; Symbol was so much better. But now my appetite in that respect matches Chief's. Chief had an affair with Symbol, and said I had come to match her in passion. It wasn't so before I got the ikon; I did sex for the sake of the larger relationship, to have some company. Now—* She made a mental shrug.

Ennui wondered what else there might be about the ikons they had yet to discover. No one had carried ikons before Havoc set out to find them, so as to locate the missing Glamors; indeed, their existence had been unknown. Thus there was no prior information.

We must find out, Aspect thought. *We are the ones most able.*

"Take a break," Bus said. "You ladies have done a fine job—better than I expected. You must have had plenty of experience."

"We have had our four," Ennui said. "It comes with the territory."

"You look so fresh," Nine said. "What is your secret?"

"We're traveling," Ennui said. "Getting away from the routine is uplifting."

He shrugged, not quite believing it. The red woman served supper; that was part of her wifely duty. It was good; the bus was well stocked with foods from a number of Chromas, and Nine clearly knew her business.

When they were done, Nine cleaned up, and then the five of them relaxed. The bus was parked for the night at the edge of the Yellow Chroma zone; in the morning Yellow levitators would take it on across. Bus provided curtains so they could make private cells for sleeping. He and Nine shared one; the other three decided to share one also.

"They're right," Nonce said. "I'm worn out, and both of you worked harder than I did, yet you don't look tired."

There would need to be an explanation, yet they could not tell her the truth. Aspect tackled it. "As you know, we are close to Havoc." The girl smiled; that was a significant understatement. They were his personal secretary and his social guide, and their word was taken without question in the palace, and a fair distance beyond it. "He is now more than he was. He was able to lend us a certain magic power of restoration so that we could better serve his needs. We prefer not to call attention to it."

"Then you'd better work slower tomorrow," Nonce said. "Bus doesn't really care, so long as the work gets done, but that Red Chroma woman is afraid he'll put her to work scrubbing and take one of you to wife instead."

They hadn't read the blue man's mind, but she was surely correct. "No fault has to be mutual," Ennui said, amused. "And why would any man want either of us in his bed, rather than Nine or you?"

"Stamina." She glanced at each of them. "You don't by an chance have any of that spell left over that I could use?"

She thought it was a potion or an amulet. Either ikon would indeed lend her similar properties, but they could not let go of them for any reason other than dire emergency. But there might be a way. "Perhaps we could share with you by proximity," Ennui said.

Ennui took Nonce's right hand, and Aspect took her left hand. Immediately the girl brightened. "Oh, I feel it! Strength and health coursing through me! But you shouldn't deplete yourselves for me."

"No danger of that, I think," Aspect said. "Sleep between us, and we will charge you through the night. That will restore you for the journey ahead."

They arranged themselves, and did hold her hands. But soon there was a complication. "I feel—I want to get hold of a man and—"

"That is a side effect," Ennui said. "The magic enhances health, and sexuality is part of it. We can let go if you prefer."

"No, I'll bear with it. It really is helping me. But I won't speak for the consequence if I encounter a virile man."

Aspect laughed. But thus warned, Ennui and Aspect focused on dulling sexual interest, hoping that this would reduce that portion of the transferal. This seemed to work, and they slept well.

Still, this was interesting. Both of them had assumed that it was their enhanced interest and performance that turned their men on, but perhaps the physical contact lent enhancement directly to the men. They were indeed discovering something about the ikons.

The purpose of the ikons, as they understood it, was to collect and convey magic power to their associated Glamors. Most ikons were in altars in chambers close to volcanoes, reaping the tremendous magic power there. This was transmitted to the Glamors, who could use it to perform amazing feats of magic anywhere. Normally the residents of Chroma zones were limited to their types. Some special gemstones could enable people to take their magic along, a blue stone for blue, and so on, and this made such stones extremely valuable. The king's crown had ten such stones in it, and they protected the king from both magical and physical threats. But when used, they soon became depleted.

Glamors, in contrast, were not limited. The Blue Glamor might seem like an ordinary person in the heart of a blue Chroma zone, but his magic did not fade when he left it. This was because he really didn't leave the source of blue magic behind; his blue ikon remained, and sent him power. If that stone were taken from its refuge and carried out of its Chroma zone, then it could no longer send power, and the Glamor would slowly lose magic ability. It had happened when Havoc arranged to fetch in all the ikons of the other Glamors. Havoc's own ikon, when he became a Glamor, seemed different but wasn't: it did not need to reside near a volcano, because it was nonChroma. It needed to remain in nonChroma zones. The same was true of Gale's ikon that Aspect carried. So though they were traveling across Chroma zones, they would not remain in them any longer than necessary. Were they to spend several days in a Chroma zone, Havoc and Gale would lose their magic powers and become ordinary people.

Obviously there was energy stored in the ikons, because of their effect on their carriers while they crossed Chroma zones. But it was something to keep in mind. Ennui and Aspect would never care to relax in any Chroma zone for long. Not unless someone else took their ikons, or they were hidden in a safe nonChroma place. The power of two Glamors depended on it. This was the real indication of the esteem in which the two women were held.

The ikon! Ennui thought. *That's what did it!*

The passion, Aspect thought, receiving her concept.

When I first felt it, at my desk—I was bent over against my legs, reaching to the floor. The ikon was pinned between my breasts and thighs, near my crotch.

It was squeezed there, Aspect agreed. *The pressure must have activated it, or caused it to radiate more strongly through your flesh.*

My sexual flesh, Ennui agreed.

And when that happened, my mind picked up that passion from yours, for we retain constant contact. I put my hand on my ikon and pressed it to my breasts under my blouse, involuntarily, and felt the desire.

And once I had been aroused, it took time to fade. Sex with Throe did not abate it.

Nor sex with Chief, Aspect agreed. *Both are good men, but not Glamors.*

And they were Glamor ikons. But Glamors could not approach their own ikons or any others, so sex with any of them was not feasible. *Are we stuck with insatiable passion?*

Aspect laughed mentally. *All we have to do is move the ikons.*

She was correct. They didn't have to carry the ikons near their female parts. They could fasten them to their feet, or hide them in their hair. That would solve the problem.

But Ennui didn't hurry to do it. She was becoming used to having sexual interest like that of a man, and wasn't immediately ready to give it up. The passion was frustrating, but also pleasant.

Woe betide the handsome young man who falls into our clutches, Aspect thought with a mental smile.

In the morning the bus resumed flight, now powered by yellow magic. They saw the flames beyond the windows, and at one point the distant cone of the Yellow volcano. Meanwhile they continued the scrubbing, more slowly, and got the bus looking almost like new. Bus was pleased.

They crossed a Gray Chroma zone, and Red, where they left Nine. Then as they crossed the Blue Chroma zone, there came the question they had known was coming. "Would any of you ladies care to shift no fault?" he asked hopefully.

"Appreciation," Aspect said. "Negation."

"Negation," Ennui agreed, though she was tempted. She would have liked to try it, but two things balked her: she was afraid the man would find her older body less than enticing, and she wasn't sure the sex would abate her passion. It hadn't with Throe.

Exactly, Aspect thought.

But Nonce could no longer hold out. She was in excellent spirit, but overcharged. "Agreement," she said, and practically dragged the blue man into his private chamber.

The two older women smiled. At least it would ease the girl's restlessness, for which they were responsible.

He dropped them off at the edge of the White Chroma zone. "If you have a return trip soon, welcome, in any capacity."

"Perhaps," Aspect said. Actually it had been a satisfactory journey, not onerous, thanks mainly to the aid of the ikons.

The White Chroma zone was typical of its type. The landscape was white, including the trees and bushes. Everything was in shades of white, just as everything in other Chroma zones was shades of blue, green, red, or whatever. But it was the White Science magic that made many people uneasy; it did not work in conventional ways. It was hard to explain.

"We have about an hour's walk," Nonce said. "There's a boiling lake ahead, but we don't go that far. I found a warm spring, and that's where it happened."

They walked along the path. Soon they became acclimatized to the whiteness. Texture and shade were all, in a Chroma zone; the full panoply of colors was there, once properly interpreted. It just required an accustomed eye to perceive it.

Ennui tuned out, not particularly interested, and knew that Aspect was doing the same. Both of them were curious what this summons was about. What had Havoc found, that required their attendance? That couldn't be told by messenger? That was what was interesting, and soon they would know.

The path wound between hills, tracing a shallow valley. White trees filled in on either side. Then, suddenly, three men appeared. They were rough-hewn, and carried metallic objects in their hands that Ennui recognized from her social studies text as weapons. They were called "guns," and used magic explosive to propel balls of metal violently forward. The metal could lodge in a victim's body with serious consequences, perhaps even death. It was like getting stabbed by a pole that had no length. These were brigands.

"Intimidation!" a man said. That confirmed it. "NonChroma travelers." That meant they were probably helpless, here in a Chroma zone.

And Ennui, her mind distracted, and not been aware of them lurking. She had been a fool. This was not the king's palace, where life was safe; this was out in the real world.

"We'll take your valuables," the brigand leader said gruffly, tucking his gun into his waistband. "And more. Do you want to submit quietly, or be beaten into submission first?"

Theft and rape: according to formula. What were they to do? Ennui saw Nonce glance their way; she had a knife, of course, but that could take out only one man, at best. The two older women did not even carry knives or other weapons. Surely they should have, but hadn't thought of it. So much for their prowess as adventurers. They had no means to resist.

But they could not give up the ikons. They wore these on chains around their necks; they would readily be spotted by the brigands when they ripped open their shirts to get at their breasts, as brigands traditionally did. Now Ennui realized how absolutely crazy she had been not to hide her most precious possession more carefully.

But she remembered something. When she had carried the loom ikon in her mouth, Throe had not been able to kiss her. Ordinary people could not touch the ikons; they could be passed from person to person only by acts of will. She also remembered how Gale had survived the eruption. The ikons had phenomenal power, and perhaps would safeguard them.

Aspect caught her thought. "Nonce, stay behind us," she murmured. The girl moved to stand where told, realizing that the women had something in mind.

"Satisfaction," the leader said. He meant that he liked dealing with struggling women. He stepped forward, reaching out to grab Ennui.

His hand came near her bosom and shied away. Surprised, he tried again, with no better success. Baffled and angry, he grabbed instead for her shoulder and yanked her forward. Except that she didn't move; he did, jerking himself off balance. He fell against her without quite touching; he slid to the side and stumbled beyond her.

"Magic!" he said, disgruntled. "But what Chroma?"

"No Chroma," Ennui said, heartened by the protection of the ikon. She had been able to get closer to others in the palace, and to Nonce; evidently the ikon distinguished between friend an foe, or maybe it made a difference who was approaching whom.

"Shoot them!" the leader snapped, drawing his gun again.

Ennui didn't like that, but couldn't escape, so she held her ground. The leader's gun made a loud bang and smoke poured from the hole in its front. Something plowed into the ground at the leader's feet. It was the bit of metal, the "bullet" the gun had "fired." It had evidently bounced away from her body and struck the earth instead. The ikon had repelled it.

Then Havoc was standing beside them. He hadn't walked or run in; he had just appeared. He wore peasant clothing, and looked like a hick villager. "So you attack helpless women," he said. "Outrage."

The brigands stared, bemused. Havoc didn't wait. He reached for the leader so rapidly that his arms were a blur. A metal collar appeared around the man's neck, too tight to be removed over his head. On it was printed the word BRIGAND.

Havoc turned to the next man, and in a moment he had a similar collar. Then the third, the same. "If you try to molest any person, the collars will hurt you," he said. "Now be gone."

The leader put his hands to the collar, but it was too strong for him. He was stuck with it until he found a White Chroma metalsmith to remove it—and who would remove such a warning? The man would be arrested the moment he appeared at any village or outpost, and all his crimes would catch up with him.

He leaped for Havoc—and bounced off, as he had with Ennui, except with greater force. He fell to the ground, bruised.

Havoc turned to the women. "Nonce I could transport," he said. "The others, no. Let's walk."

Because he could not approach his own ikon or Gale's. Ennui nodded. They followed him on along the path.

Before long they came to the white pool Nonce had bathed at. Gale was there, with a nice meal set up for them. She too was garbed as an ignorant villager, but nothing could entirely mask the amazing beauty of her person. She had always been lovely, but now that she was a Glamor her perfection fairly radiated from her.

"Gratitude," Havoc said to Nonce. Then he kissed her.

The girl fainted. Havoc caught her before she hit the ground, and set her gently beside the pool.

"You forget your place, Havoc," Aspect reproved him. "A Glamor can't have such contact with a normal person."

"He can," Ennui said. "Provided she does not know his nature— and she doesn't. It was sheer exhilaration that did it. The king kissed her."

"Neither," Gale said. "He put her down deliberately, in a manner that will not dismay her, so that we could talk."

They nodded. They had after all been summoned here for a purpose.

"How did you know we were in trouble?" Ennui asked. "At least, that we thought we were."

"I got your thought," Havoc said.

"But I didn't try to reach you mentally," she protested. "Telepathy is only short range, except in special circumstances such as close friendship."

"We have it, oath friend. But there is another. You carry my ikon. That gives you much stronger association with me, and Lady Aspect with Gale. Distance seems to be no barrier."

"We did not realize this until that point," Gale said. "There is much we don't yet know about the ikons and Glamors."

"So we didn't have to use an intermediary," Ennui said. "You could have signaled me directly."

"We are still new to our roles," Havoc said, nodding. "We have the powers, but are still learning how to use them, and how to relate to our constituencies. I love trees, but there is much I do not yet know about their needs, and it is similar for Gale and the mosses. Those needs must be served; it is the inherent oath we made when they accepted us as their representatives. We need time, yet we believe that the larger quest must still be pursued without delay. So we wish to ask the two of you to handle a spot mission for us, if you are amenable."

"Of course we will," Aspect said.

"There may be danger," Gale said. "The ikons will protect you, but we do not know their limits."

"We understand that," Ennui said. "We like the idea of adventure. It does not come readily to older women."

"And there may be sex," Havoc said. "It can be a tool."

Aspect smiled. "Something you may not know about the ikons. They strengthen us, making us seemingly indefatigable."

"And they make us sexy," Ennui said. "In body and nature."

Havoc was surprised. "We knew they protected, but not that they were sexual. Still—"

Ennui exchanged a glance with Aspect. Then both let down their mind shields and thought of sex.

"Whew!" Gale murmured. "Amazement."

"Point made," Havoc said. "I suspect that the ikons are lending you perfect health, and part of that is sexuality. That may fade as you become accustomed to it, but you will always have the capacity, just as Glamors do. As long as you do not object—"

"We don't object," Ennui said. "But I don't understand why we dreamed of having sex with a healthy young man. We do have men of our own."

"The ikons seem to echo the nature of the Glamors," Gale said. "We do not have precognition, but sometimes we do have hints. There may be such a session in your future."

"But we're old women!"

Havoc shook his head. "You are mature women—and I think the ikons have deleted a decade from your physical age. You could seduce healthy young men if you wished to."

Ennui realized it was true. Aspect had the body she must have had in youth, and Ennui had a better body than she had ever had. "We thought you honored us when you trusted us with your ikons. Now we know that they are rare gifts. We have lives again."

"We are glad of that," Havoc said. "You have been invaluable friends. I think the single best decision I have made in my life was to betroth Gale, and the second was to make the oath of friendship with you, and the third was to befriend the Lady Aspect."

"Oh, surely not!" Aspect said, speaking for them both, impossibly flattered.

"You feel he should not have betrothed me?" Gale asked severely. Then, before they could protest, she laughed, and they joined her. Havoc was not given to empty statements. "But I might argue that making the oath of friendship with the Blue Dragon would rank in there somewhere, and becoming a Glamor."

"We'll accept fourth and fifth places," Ennui said. The glow of the compliment suffused her. She had been the one to demand the oath, and it had changed her life. She had done her best to honor the spirit of the oath, and to help Havoc in any way she could, but had never felt it was that important to him. Like the ikon, the oath had transformed her.

"Oaths do," Gale said. "That's why I resented yours at first, before I came to know the two of you."

"You questioned my judgment?" Havoc asked her, frowning.

"Well, you're a barbarian. And a man. How can you have judgment?"

"You should be spanked."

She lifted her skirt, baring her firm bottom. "Have at it, hero."

"Maybe that should wait until you finish your business with us," Ennui said, though she enjoyed their interplay. They were Glamors, but still quite human and in love. "You were about to assign us a spot mission."

"And your sex play teases us with what we can't have," Aspect said. "You must give over until we have young men to fascinate." She was speaking humorously, yet there was considerable substance.

"Awww," they said together, laughing.

Then Havoc got serious. "Still, we wish this to be an optional mission for you. We can do it ourselves at a later time, if—"

"We want the mission," Aspect said for both of them.

Gale nodded. "Then there is another thing. Havoc and I have dragon seeds. They buzz in our ears when we encounter an untruth, or danger, or a wrong course. They have been invaluable, and perhaps have saved our lives on some occasions. Now, as Glamors, we no longer need them; we have their powers ourselves. We will give them to the two of you, provided you will make oaths never willingly to betray their source, the dragon."

"But dragons—" Ennui said, taken aback.

"Are now our allies. No dragon will attack you while you wear the seeds. You must respect them similarly."

Again Ennui exchanged a glance with Aspect. "We will make that oath."

Havoc nodded. There appeared beside him the Brown Glamor, a dragon. It was long and flat, with sleekly overlapping brown scales, and it fairly glowed. Dragons were of the worm family, having but one leg; that made them second only to the demons in fewness of legs, as the demons had none. Ennui and Aspect had met the Dragon Glamor at the time when Havoc had summoned all the Glamors to the palace, so this was not a total surprise. She knew it was not there to attack, but as an associate of Havoc.

"Brown will take your oaths," Havoc said.

Of course: the dragon seeds owed allegiance to the Dragon Glamor. She faced the dragon. "I say my name: Ennui, human, and make this oath: I will carry Havoc's dragon seed, and never abuse it or play false to any dragon, so long as I carry it."

Then Aspect made a similar statement with respect to Gale's dragon seed. The dragon extended a tentacle and made the signal of acceptance. Simultaneously its mind sounded in theirs: *Accepted.* And it vanished.

Havoc touched his ear and brought forth a tiny blue speck. He gave it to Ennui. She took it and wedged it into a fold of her ear, as that was where he seemed to have worn it. It lodged comfortably, adhering, and she knew it would not come loose accidentally.

Aspect received a similar seed from Gale. "These are old friends," Gale said. "We exchanged them when we betrothed each other. Do not let others know you have them, and learn to receive their warnings without reacting overtly. Some folk do know of dragon seeds, and might try to take them from you."

"Test them," Havoc said. "Approach something dangerous, or try to deceive each other."

Ennui looked around. She saw a white thorn bush. Such plants did not merely have thorns, they snapped their fronds forward to stab any unwary flesh that came within range. Any creature that stumbled into one was in for a painful and perhaps lethal experience.

She walked toward it. Just before she came within range there was a buzzing shock at her ear, not painful, but a clear signal. She stopped, and it abated. She had been warned.

She turned to face Aspect. "This plant is harmless."

Aspect straightened up. "It buzzed!"

"Because you heard a lie," Gale said. "It will also react if there is something wrong with a situation, even if no lie or danger is present. Then you must be cautious. The seeds aren't intelligent, they just know when something is wrong. Sometimes you have to figure out what it is."

"One other thing," Havoc said. "When Gale and I came together, wearing our seeds, they buzzed. We represented no threat to each other, but they seemed to sense a wrongness. We never did discover what it was, and conclude that they might simply have been acknowledging the presence of another seed."

Ennui and Aspect approached each other and linked hands. Their seeds buzzed. "That must be it," Ennui said.

"Now the mission," Havoc said. "There are several unresolved mysteries, and it may be that if we fathom them, we will better come to understand the larger picture. One of these is the loom."

"The loom," Ennui breathed. "I love that loom."

"We want to know its origin. Who made it, where, when, and why. Where did he get the power to make it? There must have been a design. Fathom its genesis."

"I'd love to! But I think I would have to fetch it, and perhaps carry it with me."

"Why?"

"Because I carried it before, and there was no indication where it came from. But ikons relate to their Glamors, and if this is an ikon, it may relate to its maker."

"A Glamor!" Gale exclaimed.

"Or something equivalent."

Havoc nodded thoughtfully. "Do that, as you decide. The mission is yours, to handle as you must."

"It lent me the same sort of power your ikon does. Since ikons can't approach each other, at least not when held by people—"

"Good point. Someone else may have to carry it."

"But who? That loom has a will of its own. It knows me and Aspect, but I'm not sure any man could touch it."

"Perhaps we have a candidate," Gale said. She glanced significantly at the sleeping Nonce.

"She's a good girl," Havoc agreed. "I like her."

Gale shot him a glance. "You can't have her."

"Not even when Symbol is absent?"

"No even when *I'm* absent."

"Awww."

Ennui and Aspect smiled. The two were teasing each other again.

Gale looked back at the ladies. "Acquaint her with the loom. See if she can weave on it. If it accepts her, let her carry it. It will give her ikon protection."

"It will also drive her crazy with desire," Ennui said.

"Then let her make some no fault man very happy."

"She's already good at that," Ennui said.

"Mistresses of the bath are," Gale agreed, with another dark look at Havoc. She was remembering Bijou.

"We are done here," Havoc said. He went to Nonce, slid his arms under her, and picked her up with such easy strength that she looked feather light. He set her on her feet, then kissed her again.

The girl's eyes popped open. "I feel faint," she said.

"Havoc kissed you," Gale said. "And caught you before you fell. You should be all right now."

Nonce found her balance and stepped away from him. "Welcome," she said unsteadily, answering his prior statement of gratitude.

"We have been given our mission," Ennui told her. "We must return to the vicinity of Triumph City. There may be a mission for you too."

"I'd like that." She still seemed bemused, but was evidently not aware of the time that had passed.

They bid parting to Havoc and Gale and set out for the Blue Chroma zone. This time no brigands waylaid them.

As it happened, the bus was still at the campsite. Bus emerged as they approached it. "Going back?" he asked. "I'll have a full load."

"We'll work," Ennui said. "Two old sisters, one young wife, no fault, as we finished before?"

Bus looked at Nonce. "Sisters will have to sleep in the storage chamber."

"Agreed."

So Ennui and Aspect catered to passengers, bringing them food, seeing to their routine needs and cleaning up after them, while Nonce took the man into his chamber every few hours. Whenever she could, she paused to hold hands with one of the older women, getting recharged.

At one point a male passenger beckoned Ennui. She started toward him—and the dragon seed buzzed. She hesitated; was that a warning? Then she went to him, and as she came close, he reached up under her skirt to put a hand on her bottom.

"Negation on no fault," she murmured, and he quickly removed the hand. That was all there was to it, but she knew that the timely warning by the seed had enabled her to handle it without making an awkward scene. No stranger had sought that sort of favor from her for decades, and the surprise feel might have freaked her out. She wasn't sure whether it was the man's act or her likely reaction that caused the seed to buzz; maybe it was just preventing a scene that could have drawn more attention to her than was safe. She certainly appreciated it, and her respect for the seed increased. It was not confined to warnings about prickly plants; it could help her socially too.

They left the bus at the Translucent station near the city. Bus was emphatic in his appreciation. "No was great, of course, but you two ladies were great too. I had compliments on the service, and you left the bus clean. If you ever wish permanent service—"

"We'll keep it in mind," Aspect said with a smile. "But we do not know where we will travel next."

"It's nice to know we have a potential profession," Ennui remarked as they walked away.

Nonce laughed. "The two ranking women of the palace! You certainly are anonymous."

"As we prefer to be," Aspect agreed.

"That must be why you didn't box that man's ear when he goosed you."

"Agreement." The girl was observant. It reminded Ennui of the fact that she had evidently become attractive to strangers, and that pleased her despite its inconvenience. The man had not tried to insult her; he had been genuinely interested. And her bottom had been firm. She liked that, even if she would never care to brag about it.

It was late in the day. "Our next task is nocturnal," Ennui said. "We will stay at a cabin beside the lake, then proceed in darkness."

She led them to the suburbs surrounding the lake on which the pyramid of Triumph City floated, and to the lake itself. But they did not take the ferry; they walked around to the side. There was the cabin she had visited with the Black Glamor, vacant but well stocked. They approached it, and the seeds did not buzz. That confirmation helped; the absence of a buzz could be as significant as the buzz.

"I'm worn out and famished," Nonce said.

"This is for our use," Ennui said. "Rest; Speck and I will prepare a meal."

"But you should not be doing that work!" the girl protested. "I should—"

"You are tired; we are not. Soon you will have our stamina, I think. Rest."

The girl did not question it. She flopped on a bed and lay staring at the ceiling. Ennui delved into the supplies and prepared a modest but filling meal.

"When you and Throe went on a private mission—this was where you came?" Aspect asked. She and Chief had helped by emulating the two of them so that their absence would not be known.

"And Bijou—and The Black Glamor," Ennui said. "For the loom, as it turned out." She paused, considering. "There was an orange female sphinx on the way there. I wonder whether she'll be there again."

"The Sphinx Glamor, surely," Aspect said. "I suspect she is alerted when anyone approaches the loom."

"She liked to have a dialogue with a person of sufficient intellect. I doubt that any of us qualify."

Aspect shrugged. "We are on a mission for Havoc. She'll know that."

"I hope so."

"Perhaps it is time to move our ikons."

"Good notion. We wouldn't want to lose them in the water."

The two of them lifted their loose string necklaces and removed the ikons, which adhered to their fingers. They bound them into their hair, under low mats of hair at the upper backs of their heads so that the bulges hardly showed.

Ennui expected the level of sexual awareness to fade, and it did, but there was another effect. Now that the ikon was in contact with her head, it affected the things of her head. Her sight and hearing became acute, and her thoughts preternaturally clear.

"Confirmation," Aspect murmured. "I think I like this better."

When it was dark out, and Nonce had recovered sufficiently, they went outside to the lake. "We shall have to dive to a cave below," Ennui said. "There is a float with a stone ring. We will take the float out, then use the stone to bear us to the bottom."

"The bottom!" Nonce exclaimed. "I can swim, of course, but I would drown."

"We will hold your hands as you hold your breath. There is a cave there, with air. I will have a lamp. You must trust us."

"I trust you, but I'm terrified."

I barely trust this myself Aspect thought.

The dragon seed did not buzz, Ennui reminded her.

They did it, and held the stone and Nonce's hands, and plunged swiftly to the bottom. Then they swam the short distance to the cave, and emerged into the air. Ennui held the small lamp she had found in the cabin, and it illuminated of its own accord, showing a passage.

Again, the absence of a buzz had helped. Ennui was sure the seeds would not have let them risk their lives without warning. She appreciated the strength the ikons provided, but the seeds were also reassuring.

In due course they came to a chamber with an orange glow. There was the sphinx in all her splendor.

"Glamor," Ennui said. "We—"

Understood. I will converse with the Lady Aspect.

"With me!" Aspect said. "But I have little intellect."

You have the recent history of the doings of the human kings.

"That interests you?"

Everything interests me. Including those ikons and dragon seeds, and the recent clarity of your senses and thoughts.

"You're elected," Ennui said. "No and I will go on."

Aspect nodded, knowing that Nonce would have to carry the loom. "I will rehearse the kings."

Ennui and Nonce went on. They came to the inner cave. There stood the great old loom: a machine formed of wooden planks and pulleys and treadles. It was set up exactly as Ennui had left it, ready to weave. Warp without weft.

"What an instrument!" Nonce breathed.

"Can you use it?"

"I have done some weaving on a loom, but nothing like this. This is the grandfather of looms!"

"Try it."

The girl approached the loom hesitantly. "I'll need some yarn."

Ennui fetched a hank from the collection, and Nonce carefully attached it to a bobbin and flung it back and forth. She was not skilled, but did know how.

"We need to ascertain when and where this was made," Ennui said. "And by whom."

"Maybe there's a maker's plaque."

Ennui hadn't thought of that. They checked around the loom, and found a plaque: PENTER 803.

"What does it mean?" Nonce asked.

"I think this was made by a man name Penter, in the 803rd year following the arrival of mankind at Charm," Ennui said. "I suppose we'll have to return to the city and research in the records for that name and date."

"But we still don't know where."

"I think we had better take this with us while we look. It's a magic object; it may even help us." She did not care to advertise the private dialogue with Havoc and Gale.

"Take it with us! That would take ten men to carry."

"Perhaps not. Touch it."

"I don't understand. I've been touching it all along." But the girl put out one hand to touch the nearest plank.

And the loom shrank into a tiny model of itself, falling into her hand. Ennui breathed a silent sigh of relief; it had accepted Nonce. "You may carry it in your mouth or on your person," Ennui said. "It's an ikon, and will provide you with endurance and abilities similar to ours. You are one of us, for the duration of this mission."

"You have ikons?" Nonce asked, bemused.

"Yes. That was the meaning of Havoc's message. But we prefer not to let it be known."

"Silence," Nonce agreed. She put the miniature loom into her mouth. "I feel stronger already. And—"

"Sexier."

"Suddenly some things are coming clear."

"I thought they might."

"If the loom is an ikon, what is its Glamor? I know other ikons can change into threads, but this one changes into a whole loom."

She had a point. If the ikon was proportional to the Glamor, that would be a super-Glamor! "Perhaps we'll find out. Now let's return to the surface." Ennui led the way out.

Next day they returned to Triumph City, and Ennui did what she knew best, researching in the archives for the name and date on the loom. She found it: Penter was the name of a skilled carpenter two centuries before. There was no record of such a project, but of course the loom would not have been unknown if it had been a matter of record.

What was in the record was the grant of an ideal farmstead to the Penter family in that period. It was a nonChroma region nestled between four closely set small volcanoes, so that the outlying fields overlapped light magic. The family still farmed that land, and prospered. The ancestor must have made an excellent deal with someone. That was the next place to investigate.

Ennui and Aspect had savage romantic sessions with their men, and Nonce took on several eager young men of the palace, reveling in her suddenly extended abilities. Then they headed out again.

෫෧

It took three days and nights to get there, traveling with a convoy, doing the type of work they had found they were good at. On the way Nonce discovered that the loom ikon had a sense of direction. It knew where something was—and they were going that way.

"Maybe your mind affects it," Ennui said. "Decide you want to go back to Triumph City."

Dubiously, the girl did. "The direction faded," she reported.

But when she focused on the place of the loom's manufacture, the awareness returned. The loom did not know, or perhaps did not care, where a human city was, but did know where it had been made. That was just as well, because the records had been somewhat vague about details, and the dragon seeds did not seem to be able to guide them toward the site.

Then they arrived at the Penter farm. This was run by a stout woman of Aspect's age named Gala. It was soon evident that she knew something about the loom, but refused even to think of it. "My ancestor got this farm, and we keep it," she said. "That is all that matters."

"We need to see the workshop where an ancient loom was made," Ennui said.

"Negation. That room is sacred to us; no one has been in it since our ancestor died."

There seemed to be no way they could move her. So they checked her mind. Few non-telepaths had effective mind shields, but it wasn't necessarily easy to pick out relevant information from the welter of incidental thoughts.

There was, however, one thing that brooded. It concerned one of the woman's children.

Aspect led into it, so as not to reveal her ability. "Who helps you farm?"

"My son Bashful."

There was the key. "He is shy around girls?"

"He just hasn't found the right one," the woman said defensively.

They had the boy's age from the woman's mind: seventeen. He would have to marry within the year. That promised to be awkward. Gala wanted him to marry well, so that she would have solid help on the farm, but feared he would have to settle for a leftover or lazy girl.

"If we could cure him," Aspect said. "Give him more confidence, so he could be selective—"

The woman laughed bitterly. "For that, I would let you look anywhere you want. But it's hopeless."

"I could do something," Nonce said.

Both dragon seeds buzzed; Aspect felt hers directly, and Ennui's from her mind. This was a wrong decision.

"I need you with me," Ennui reminded her, picking up on it immediately. Because the connection of the loom ikon to the loom's place of manufacture was evident. Ennui knew the loom best, and Nonce carried it. Certainly that would do for a rationale.

Suddenly it fell to Aspect, to her dismay. But when she started to demur in her mind, the dragon seed buzzed. She was definitely the one. "I will do it," she said. "Allow my friends to inspect the shop, and I will teach your boy what he needs to know." Her words were much bolder than her belief; she had little idea how to address an over-shy youth. She doubted that any mere pep talk would suffice.

Gala stared at her a moment. "This is a stinking deal."

"Agreed," Aspect said. "We must see the shop, and have nothing better to trade."

They waited.

Gala's resistance collapsed. She did want what they offered. "Reluctant agreement."

Soon Aspect found herself in a private chamber with Bashful. He was well named. Universal convention required each person to be named by his associates, in their own time, and the names were usually descriptive and often less than kind. But they could be changed if the person changed enough to warrant it. Again, it was up to the company he kept.

"Do you know why we are here?" she asked him. He was a wild-haired young man of fair complexion and musculature, as farmers generally were.

He wouldn't meet her gaze. "You have to change my nature."

"You have a problem with women."

"I—they—" He shook his head miserably. "Affirmation."

"I suspect your nature is good. You merely don't know how to proceed."

"They laugh at me!" he said, blushing.

"To make you blush," she said. "It gives them power over you."

He nodded, ashamed.

"They do it because they are nervous about sexual relations but don't want to admit it."

"I don't want sex!"

She paused, disgruntled. "Confusion."

He backed off immediately. "Apology. I did not mean to say that."

But there was a powerful burst of something strange in his mind. Something other than shyness was bothering him.

"Truth," she said.

"Negation."

"I have a secret. I think you have one too. I think we must exchange secrets."

"No secrets!" he cried. He lurched at her, putting his hands around her throat. "Get away from me!"

Aspect did not resist, but his hands lacked force. Yet she saw his straining. He really was trying to choke her. The ikon was protecting her, especially about the head. The dragon seed, evidently knowing that, had not buzzed. But those were secrets she couldn't share.

"You don't want to hurt me," she said, drawing his hands gently away. "I don't want to be here any more than you do. I promised your mother."

"I don't want to hurt you," he said, believing it. How else could he account for the seeming powerlessness of his hands? "But I don't want to talk to you."

"I will tell you a secret. Then you may tell me yours—if you choose."

"Negation!"

"I can read minds."

He stared at her. "You're no Translucent!"

"I got a mental disease that made me read minds. At first it was awful—so many thoughts coming at me at once. Then I learned to shield my mind, so I don't hear the thoughts unless I want to. I did not want to deceive you about this."

"Disbelief." But it was hope rather than certainty.

"Perhaps I can demonstrate. As we talk, my friends are visiting the closed workshop."

He was eager to focus on the new subject. "Where my ancestor made the magic loom."

He had let slip more than his mother had. "Yes. We need to know its origin. My mind is linked to that of my friend On. I should be able to learn from her what they are discovering."

"No one has entered that shop in generations."

"Agreement. Certainly I have not; I have been here with you." Aspect focused on her friend, whom she could reach at some moderate distance because they *were* friends and knew each other's minds. "They have entered the shop, and are gazing at the signs of the work of two centuries before, undisturbed. They see where the loom stood as it was crafted."

"You could guess that."

"Now No takes the ikon from her mouth. She restores it—and it fits that spot exactly. And—" She broke off, hearing the warning buzz of the dragon seed.

But it was too late. "You have the loom!" Bashful exclaimed.

"Affirmation. But we don't want it known. Our mission is special, and there may be danger."

"You would have trouble getting out of the village, if they knew. The loom is a legend; no one knows where it went when it disappeared. We keep the shop eternally ready for its return. But you aren't going to return it."

"We aren't." She looked at him. "I ask you not to reveal that we have it."

He hesitated. "Deal: will you return it when you are done with it?"

Aspect shot a thought to Ennui. Ennui considered a moment, then made the compromise, which was reasonable in the circumstance. Both of them knew that Havoc would go along with it, since he had delegated his authority to them in this matter. In fact she could contact him mentally for confirmation; they tended to forget that new long-range ability. "Yes."

"Make an oath."

"Made."

Bashful had gained confidence. "Then I will be silent, in the hope that I have achieved what we desire."

"Appreciation. But we do not know how long we will be using the loom."

"But you are honest folk."

"We honor oaths, at any rate." She smiled. "We serve Havoc, our barbarian king."

"And I believe that you can read minds." He pondered briefly. "You—know my secret?"

"I want you to tell me your secret."

"Negation! This is not part of our prior agreement."

"Acquiescence. Deal: tell me, and I will help you in any way I can."

"How can you help me?"

"I promise to find a way to make it right with your mother, if I can."

"You know my secret anyway?"

"I have told you mine, so you know that I know. But I want it to be fair between us. Tell me, so we are even. Then we can discuss how to proceed."

"You are not revolted?"

She laughed. "I am twice your age. I have seen many things. This is not unusual." And now she realized why the dragon seed had put her in this place: because she did know something about this situation.

He hesitated, not really believing. Then he shrugged. "I want sex with men, not women."

"Now we are even," she said. "I worked in Triumph City. There are many people there. Maybe one in twenty is like you in this respect. Their problem is that they are still required to marry and have four children."

"Yes!"

"But there is a way around it. Sometimes they marry women of similar persuasion."

He was amazed. "There are women like me?"

"Yes. They want sex with other women."

"Then how can they have children?"

"They want sex with women, but they can have it with men. They can pretend, or simply endure it. If they do, they get children. It is desire, not ability, that is changed."

"But I—can't do that."

"Perhaps. But here is your solution: marry one of these women, and adopt. You don't have to have sex with her; no one else need know."

Hope was dawning. "If I could find such a woman, and she kept my secret—"

"She would. It's her secret too."

"But there would be suspicion, if we had no natural child."

Aspect nodded. "You might have to do it once, or enough to have that one. You would both hate it, but it would allay suspicion, and you might like the child."

"But how could I find such a woman?"

"Perhaps I could find her for you."

"Because you can read minds!"

"Agreement. It might take a while, as I would have to meet a number of the local girls, but I believe it can be done. This is how I can help you."

His embarrassment and anger dissipated completely. "Oh, Lady! If you would!"

"This is our deal with your mother: to fix things with you. Does she know?"

"I hope not. She—"

"Would not understand. We'll keep that secret."

"Oh, Lady!" he repeated. "Mortification! I attacked you! Yet you bring me salvation."

She smiled. "Remember, you didn't really try to hurt me." That was not quite true, but it was important that he believe it. "I do it because we made a deal. But had I known before, I would have helped you anyway. You are a decent ordinary young man, apart from one difference."

"Affirmation," he agreed wryly.

Aspect stiffened. She felt a sudden overwhelming urge to do something. "Oh!"

"Lady! Are you well?"

She recovered awareness of him. "I—believe so. I feel a great compulsion to fashion the loom. The girl No has the loom ikon in her mouth, and is standing in the loom site, and my friend On is receiving her feeling, and I through her. It can not be resisted."

"That's how my ancestor Penter made the loom! He received instructions from the spirit of the world."

Aspect smiled. "Perhaps. We understand he was an experienced loom craftsman, but that would not account for its magic nature."

"He was the best loomer of his age," Bashful said proudly. "It took him years. He sought special woods and twines, and magic imbued it, and when he was done he was rewarded with this excellent farmstead, and we keep the faith. But the loom vanished. It's all part of our family and village lore."

"And that power remains there to this day," Aspect said. "That spot must be an access to a channel of strong magic."

"It must be," he agreed. "We didn't know, because we never go in the shop."

"Just as well, I think. Perhaps that is part of the deal: no one must go to make another loom." She nodded, glad to have the matter understood, if not resolved. "Are we done here?"

"Agreement." But then he thought of something else. "Suppose a woman asks me for a fourth?"

That set her back. "I had not thought of that. If you declined, she might wonder why."

"Affirmation."

"And there is the problem of how you can ever be with another man for such purpose, without more suspicion."

"Negation. I know a man. That is how I know my nature. We are circumspect."

"Still, it would be better if you could service a woman, when you had to."

"And I couldn't." But the dragon seed buzzed. He was telling an untruth, though he believed it.

She come to a decision. "Bashful, I think I must teach you sex after all. Not for joy, but for safety. I believe you can learn to do it, if you understand the necessity."

"I don't know. When I played with a girl, and she decided to have sex, I couldn't—do it. That's when the laughter started. Now all the girls know that I was so bashful I was unable."

"Then they must be disabused. If you perform well with one, word will get around. Then you won't have to do it again, or at least not often."

"How can I do what I can't do?"

She considered. "This is not my area of expertise. I may be wrong. But I think you could do it if you pretended."

"Pretended?"

"Do you know the play of the boy and the teacher?" That was academic; everyone knew the plays, because they were put on by educational tours that made sure to cover every village. In this one, a young man asked his favorite female teacher to teach him sex, and she did. In the play, she looked old and sour at first, but became luscious when she threw off her clothing. It was understood that it was just the way he saw her, but the actresses were always indeed luscious. The Lady Gale had once played the role, enhanced by the succubus; that must have truly wowed the villagers!

"Affirmation. But she couldn't teach me like that."

"Think of me as that teacher. I am her age, and you are his age. I hope to teach you how to fool a young woman."

He smiled ruefully. "If only I could!"

"You must compliment her on her body, her face, her intellect—anything, and it doesn't have to be true. She may know it's not true, but she'll like hearing it anyway. Try it on me."

"Lady, that's not hard. You don't look my mother's age. You're beautiful! If I were normal I would be desperately eager for your sexual favor. But—"

"No buts. Remember, this is a play. You must speak the lines."

"And you promise me a way out of my predicament. That makes you the nicest, smartest woman I've met."

"Very good. You have flattered me and made me interested in your wish, which I naturally assume is to have sex with me. Now strip."

"But—"

"Accept my guidance. I have a purpose."

Reluctantly he removed his clothing. He was well constructed, but evinced no sexual reaction.

"Now comes the difficult part. Gaze on me as I strip." She removed her clothing, until she stood naked before him. She knew herself to be formidably feminine, thanks to the ikon. Still he had no reaction. He did not merely *think* he was disinterested in women; it was the case.

"Close your eyes."

He did, standing there awkwardly.

"Pretend I am a man." Was she really doing this? She had barely gotten used to the idea of being an attractive woman again, and never dreamed of being a man.

"I can't!"

She labored to make her voice husky. "Try. Remember, this is a play. I am a handsome man approaching you for sex." She stepped toward him and touched his penis.

He jumped away. "Negation!"

"Try again," she said patiently.

This time when she touched his penis he stood still. She send a mental signal of maleness, not sure how he would receive it.

His member stirred in her hand. He was succeeding in thinking of her as male. But it was only a stir, not a stiffening.

Would the ikon have effect in a case like this? She brought her head down, angling it to bring the ikon close. And the member swelled, becoming rigid.

"Suddenly it lives!" he said in wonder.

"Your imagination is focusing," she said, though she knew it wasn't merely that. "Hold the thought." Because she couldn't keep the ikon constantly close. With Ennui and herself there had been considerable residual effect; she hoped that would be the case here.

"I am holding it," he said, his member throbbing.

"Now I am going to assume a position. Find me, eyes closed, and see what you can do." She got down on her hands and knees.

He stepped forward, almost tripped over her, and found her back with fumbling hands. She sent another male signal. He got down behind her, his member erect.

But then he balked. "I can't do it!"

She turned around, and saw that he had opened his eyes. "Maybe with practice. In this position there is not a great difference between a woman and a man. Work on believing it is always a man. Then when you must be with a woman, do it that way."

"But I *don't* believe!"

"Yet you still have an erection."

He looked down. "I do," he agreed, surprised.

"That is all you need." She thought of another aspect. "If you marry, your wife will understand. She will want you to have this ability too. Practice with her. When you succeed in doing it with her, not only may you get a baby with her, you should be able to do it elsewhere."

"Yes," he breathed, seeing it. "I couldn't do it this time, but I did get part way. If I practiced over and over, I could get there."

She did not confess that she was relieved. She had been ready for the sex, but the notion that she was emulating a man turned her off. So in this case she was like a woman of that persuasion. That helped her appreciate the magnitude of the challenge.

"Now we just need to find you a suitable woman. I need to meet a number, so I can read their minds. Keep my secret about that."

"Yes! There is a dance tonight. I dreaded attending it."

"You dance?"

"Yes, well enough. But I asked no girl to this one, because—"

"I will go with you. We shall pretend I am younger than I am."

He smiled. "Readily done."

"We'll dance together, and I will make sure you know how to hold a woman close. Remember, holding is not sex; it is part of the necessary show. A woman can be pleasant to hold for dancing; you don't need even to pretend there is anything more. Then I will walk around while you dance with others. By the time the evening is done, I should know."

"Oh Lady, I think you have shown me the way. I love you."

"Then kiss me."

He paused, for the moment appalled. "I didn't mean it that way."

"Understood. There are different kinds of love. Two things. If you are to fool a woman, you must at least kiss her. You don't need an erection for that. And you really can love a woman, as perhaps you will your wife. You don't have to have sex with her." She stepped into him, still naked. "Now kiss me."

At first he fumbled, but then something came over him, and he held her close and kissed her. "Thank you, Lady."

"Practice that too, with your wife. Do it in public, so others know your romance is real."

"I will!"

"For it may indeed be real. Just not sexual." She was hammering on that point, to enable him to disassociate love from sex, appearance from reality. "Remember that: you can have friendship with a woman."

"You have shown me that."

Then they dressed and went out. "The problem is he hasn't found the right woman," Aspect told his mother.

Gala's jaw dropped. "That's all?"

"That's enough. Let him choose his own, whoever she may be, and accept her, and all will be well."

"I don't believe this."

Bashful smiled. "Believe it, Mother. This woman has made me a man."

Gala did not look entirely pleased, yet she had to accept what was offered: a normal, marriageable son. Did it matter that it had taken a woman of her own age to accomplish it? Naturally she assumed they had had sex, and Bashful was encouraging that notion.

Ennui and Nonce appeared. Aspect compared thoughts with Ennui, more thoroughly at closer range. They had gotten what they could, but it was complicated to impart at the moment, and Aspect had her own input. So she addressed her own project. *We must locate a secret lesbian girl,* she thought. Ennui nodded, understanding. She took Nonce aside, so as to explain verbally to her.

They attended the dance. Aspect danced with Bashful, and he was competent. She required him to hold her very close, as though they had indeed been lovers, and saw the jealous glances of other young men. Oh, it was nice to seem young and sexy again!

Then Nonce cut in on her, making a stir, because Nonce was truly young and lovely. She too danced him extremely close, and brushed his cheek with her lips. The local girls followed, suddenly finding Bashful interesting, and the boys found Nonce more than interesting.

Aspect and Ennui walked along the sidelines, searching minds. Of course Nonce was popular, for she was a lively girl and knew every dance. But so was Bashful, who belied his name now that he had reason to hope. He was getting into it, enjoying the act, holding girls close. It was the appearance that thrilled him rather than their bodies, but they didn't know that.

Ennui approached. *I found two. One is pretty, the other not.*

But it would depend on other qualities. Aspect walked close to each girl in turn, and learned that the unpretty one was smart and determined, an excellent worker, though she hated the options available to her. Her name was Pear, the unkind description foisted on her. The pretty one was neither smart nor skilled, but was prepared to tolerate the attentions of a man for the sake of social approval. She would get by.

When the unpretty girl stepped outside the dance hall, as she was not kept busy by boys, Aspect trailed her out. "Dialogue," she murmured.

The girl looked at her. "You danced with Bashful and made him confident. Are you his cousin?"

"His friend. He has a secret."

"Don't we all!"

"Which you share."

The girl looked sharply at her. "Who are you?"

"I am called Speck. I have a secret too."

"Curiosity."

"I can read minds. An illness left me this way. Keep my secret and I will keep yours."

"What's my secret?"

"You detest sex with a man. No one has asked you, but you don't want it anyway. You prefer a woman."

Pear was shocked. "You know!"

"I read your mind. You face forced marriage with a man, and forced sex. You dread it, but see no feasible alternative other than death, which doesn't appeal either. I may have a way out of that abyss. Are you amenable to a marriage of convenience?"

"I don't want to marry anyone!"

"With a man of your persuasion."

"A man who doesn't like women? What would he want with me?"

"To keep the secret. To make a good life with a woman who can manage well, pleasing his family and the community. A woman who would not question or expose his private association with another man."

Pear considered, suddenly seeing the relevance. Such a man would not demand sex with her or object to her having a private girlfriend. "We could adopt."

"Affirmation."

"Bashful?"

"Affirmation."

"How can I trust you? This could be a cruel joke."

"Would Bashful play such a joke?"

"Negation."

"I will tell him to dance with you. Take him outside. Talk. Become a couple. Others will try to take him from you, but he will be loyal. He will say you are the smartest and best worker he knows, which is true. But you know the real reason." Aspect buttressed this reasoning with a mental projection of acceptance. Pear was not telepathic, but might receive some of the mood, and decide to do it.

The girl considered again. She was not slow to appreciate a possible answer to her dilemma. "I'll risk it."

Soon they returned to the dance. No one had missed Pear. Aspect cut in on Bashful. "Pear," she murmured. "Dance with her. Others will think she is grateful for your attention. You will say she has a good mind. She does. Become a couple. Others will think you are nervous about pretty girls, so like the one you can get. Let them."

"Affirmation," he replied, amazed.

By the end of the evening, everyone at the dance was sharing the news. Handsome Bashful had taken the ugliest girl to be his own. What was the matter with him? She was smart, but since when did that count with a man? Yet it seemed to be so.

Gala did not seem completely pleased with her son's choice, but realized that social acceptance was more important than prettiness. The girl was certainly competent. Her son would marry and provide heirs to the farm. That was what counted.

When Aspect was alone with Ennui and Nonce, in a cabin for the night, she got the rest of their story. She explained that the dragon seed buzz had been for her, not Ennui, because she had inadvertently told of the loom. But she had learned things from Bashful that related.

"It must be an access to a channel of magic," Aspect concluded. "The ikons are responsive, and its own loom ikon more so."

"But this is way beyond us," Ennui said. "It would take a Glamor to handle it."

Nonce laughed, thinking she was joking, then realized that she was not.

They had accomplished their mission, and in the process found what might be a portal or avenue to greater understanding. Havoc and Gale would have to judge.

Now all they had to do was get home to Triumph City and make their report.

Chapter 2—Family

"Havoc."

He glanced at her, aware that she was excited but was masking the cause. Glamors had superior mind reading abilities, but since both of them were Glamors, they remained even. They could hide things from each other when they chose. "You crave twice as much sex?"

Gale laughed. "Not exactly, incubus. Walk with me."

What was she up to? He set down the tiny fern tree seedling he had been communing with. *I will return,* he thought to it, and felt its acquiescence. Much of his time was spent studying trees in intense new detail, so as to better understand their needs and desires. He intended to make all the trees that had accepted him as their Glamor satisfied that the choice was apt. Gale was similarly studying the mosses. "Acquiescence."

She took his hand. A Glamor's mere touch could transform an ordinary person, and had similar effect on another Glamor, but Glamors were proof against being overwhelmed. They had been married only a month, and it was hard to tell where love left off and magic began. "Love."

"Total," he agreed, kissing her. In public they made little shows of their mutual devotion, enjoying the game, but in private they simply basked in it. They had loved each other since childhood, but fulfillment had been balked until recently, so it seemed new again. They did not need to speak of it at all, as they constantly shared minds, but there was satisfaction in all the nuances of expression.

They walked through their cave-house to the front. The other Glamors had made them a wedding gift of the knowledge of the site and the initial preparations, so that they had been able to move in immediately. It was just about perfect for a Glamor couple, being isolated in the heights of unscalable mountains, actually the unrecognized remnant of an ancient nonChroma volcano cone, so that no intrusions were likely. The base of the cone had become a lake, and the cave was in the inner wall, both heated by the lingering deep fires of a mountain that was not quite as dead as it seemed. The jagged ridge of the cone was covered in snow; the subterranean furnace did not reach that far. They lived at the fringe of heat, so were comfortable rather than hot or cold, and could reach either extreme by moving down or up. If the volcano ever decided to return to full life, they would know; its rumblings were hardly subtle. Meanwhile, it was ideal for a family. Not that they had one yet.

"But we do," Gale said.

"Confusion."

She merely looked at him.

He caught on. "Already! You're sure?"

"I feel the dawning entity within me, apart from me."

Havoc was thrilled. "What—?"

"I can't distinguish gender yet. Does it matter?"

"Uncertainty. I think I want both, to be like me and like you."

"Well, choose one for this time."

"And if I don't?"

"I don't want to birth a neuter."

He capitulated. "Like you."

"Female," she agreed.

"There's no other female like you." Then he paused. He was getting a mental signal. *Ennui.*

Symbol must see you, Ennui thought.

And there was the refutation. Symbol *was* like Gale in key respects. *Relay her message.*

Too complicated.

He sighed. Symbol was not a woman to make a fuss over nothing. She was his official mistress, and had precise awareness of her duties and limits, apart from the fact that she loved him with a commitment verging on desperation. He would have to bring her here, because he didn't want to show himself at the palace and mess up the routine of the pretend king, the "mock." "I must fetch Symbol," he told Gale.

"*I'll* fetch her," Gale said. "She's not getting her fourth of you this day."

It was true he had promised Symbol a forth, and she would hold him to it. Gale had no problem with that; she just liked to remind him that any sex he had with Symbol was now with Gale's acquiescence more than his own. *Hide her in your chamber,* he thought to Ennui. *Gale will fetch her.*

Ennui made a mental nod. *Ten minutes hence.*

Agreement.

The connection faded. The ikon facilitated it, but it required considerable concentration by both parties. "Ten minutes hence in Ennui's chamber."

"That gives us nine minutes for love." She meant it literally; she was not speaking of sex, which could distract from the purity of the emotion.

They took that time, holding hands, gazing across the warm water of the lake, sharing thoughts of their baby to come. "We'll call her Voila," Gale said.

"But her peer group must name her."

"What peer group?"

There it was: this would be the first child of two Glamors, unique until they had another. In time she might mask herself and join village children, if they could arrange it, and then she might gain a name. But until then, she would be theirs. "Voila," he agreed. It was an exclamation of success, quite fitting in the circumstance.

Gale disappeared. They had been practicing virtually instant magic travel, as it was useful when Glamors wanted to get around, and were becoming reasonably proficient at it. Other Glamors had aided them with instructions, because such travel could be dangerous when clumsy.

He sat at the brink of water, gazing into its depths. "Vwa-LA," he murmured, liking the sound of it. Starting his family with Gale—what could be better than that?

Gale reappeared, clasping Symbol, who was swathed in form-fitting clothing throughout. Havoc was struck by how similar they looked in outline. They were not close in age, a decade apart, but both were lovely self-possessed changelings. Symbol was an excellent adviser and sexual companion, though for his taste no one could match Gale in that or any other respect.

"Appreciation," both women said together. He hadn't tried to conceal his thoughts, and one was telepathic while the other was apt at reading faces.

Symbol disengaged and looked around. Her veil was so tight it resembled a facial mask. "Oh, this is beautiful! Your secret house, garden, and lake."

"Location unknown," Havoc agreed. "What brings you?"

"Private message from Mneme she did not want trusted to thought sharing." Symbol was not telepathic, but was able to mask her thoughts; she could keep a secret. "She knew I could find you soon. I knew Ennui could reach you."

Both Havoc and Gale frowned. Mneme was the mistress of the changeling complex, a changeling herself and one tough woman. She would not bother them for nothing. This was not likely to be simple news.

"We are private here," Gale said, meaning that no one else could hear their speech or read their thoughts.

"She says she has a situation that she believes will interest you. She requests your attendance as soon as feasible."

Havoc exchanged a glance with Gale. This had to be important. They would need to attend.

"Appreciation for the message," Havoc said. "We'll attend to it."

"Stay and watch the premises," Gale told Symbol.

"Oh, I don't need to intrude on—"

But Havoc and Gale had already linked hands and traveled, not hearing the end of her protest. The woman would treat the premises with respect, and become familiar with them. They might need a baby-sitter some day.

They arrived in Mneme's office at the changeling complex. It was one of the locations they had zeroed in. The complex was in the process of reconstruction; Havoc had nearly destroyed it before Mneme yielded to his authority. However, the activities were proceeding efficiently. The complex was warded against Glamor intrusion, but that did not seem to apply to Havoc and Gale, perhaps because they were nonChroma Glamors, unknown when the complex was crafted.

In a moment Mneme returned to her office, aware of their arrival. She was about 40, and handsome in severely feminine way. She wasted no time; she was an efficient woman. "Greeting, Sire, Queen."

"Acknowledged."

"We have a problem that you may be able to resolve, in part, if you so choose."

This was curious. They could not read her mind; she was not telepathic, but was another person able to mask her thoughts. "Problems are to be dealt with," Havoc said.

"Some require finesse. We have three super-changelings we may be unable to manage much longer."

What was a super changeling? "Amplify."

"We normally deal in zygotes which are implanted in willing women, who subsequently birth them as their own, as fourths. These are the standard changelings, as you know. On rare occasion we get rejects. These can normally be handled via adoption or disposal, but some are challenging. We gambled on a limited brood, and perhaps made a mistake."

"Your broods are selected from the laboratory mergence of donated sperm and eggs," Gale said. "You select them carefully. How can you make a mistake?"

"This was a small experimental second generation changeling brood."

"Donated by grown changelings!" Havoc exclaimed. "They did not grow true?"

"Most did. But three that we know of may have mutated. We had to take them back."

Gale frowned. "They were implanted in women in the temples, and later birthed—and then returned? I did not know this was ever done."

"We stand ready to recover changelings who are threatened or whose families are unable to maintain them. It is done through the Temple without publicity. These three were simply beyond the capacity of their families."

"How can a baby be beyond any mother's capacity?" Gale demanded. This was obviously a fresh concern of hers, as she would not want any such mischief with her own baby.

"They have what appear to be incipient Glamor powers."

The two of them stared at her. "And they would need Glamor parents," Havoc said.

"Us," Gale said.

"It must of course be by your choice, and not merely because no one can dictate to you. These are healthy feeling living *babies*. You have to want them and be able to love them. If one of them is to your liking."

"What's the alternative, for those not chosen?" Havoc asked.

"Destruction."

"Of *babies*?" Gale demanded sharply.

"Children must be disciplined, or they spoil. All prior human Glamors have been changeling adults, already civilized. There have been no child Glamors. These may not be full Glamors, but rather partial ones. Still, they are beyond the competence of ordinary families. They can not be allowed to run wild."

She was making tough sense. But Havoc was in deep doubt that he wanted any such adoptees in his family. He wanted their own children—three of them, anyway.

"Show them to us," Gale said tersely.

Mneme spoke into a tube. "Bring the three." Then, to Havoc and Gale: "We have given them temporary names for convenience. These need not be honored beyond these premises."

Soon three women arrived, each one carrying a swaddled baby. All three caretakers were nursing their charges as they walked.

"It is the only way we can pacify them," Mneme explained. "They are willful."

Havoc knew that there were amulets that made women freshen instantly. He saw them on the women. Babies did like to feed.

Mneme signaled the first woman, who stepped forward. "This is Warp, male. He can levitate."

The woman lifted the baby clear of her breast and let him go. Havoc stopped himself from diving to catch the infant, knowing that these folk knew what they were doing. Warp hovered in the air, scrambling to return to her breast, his black hair lifting out from his head. In a moment she drew him back in.

"In a Chroma zone this power is not unknown at six months," Mneme said. "But this is a nonChroma Zone."

And only Glamors could do such magic in nonChroma zones. This baby was extraordinary.

The second woman stepped forward. "This is Flame, female," Mneme said, indicating the red haired baby. "She is pyro. When annoyed, she ignites her bedclothes. Do you wish a demonstration?"

"Pass," Havoc said quickly.

The third woman stepped up. "This is Weft, female. She conjures." Mneme held a bright string of baubles before her. The yellow haired baby reached for it, but Mneme drew it back. Suddenly it jumped to the baby's hand. Satisfied, Weft returned to her nursing, clutching the prize.

"They are young yet," Mneme said. "Perhaps they will develop other powers. But these suffice; they can not be governed by normal means."

"We'll take them," Gale said.

"Which ones?"

"All three."

Havoc turned to her, disgruntled. She already had her own baby starting; this would completely disrupt their schedule and their lives. But she sent him a preemptive mental warning, and he stifled his protest. This was her department.

It was Mneme who raised a question. "Can you nurse all three? Even with the amulets this may be a challenge."

"I can do what I have to do, without an amulet," Gale said, her bosom expanding. She had not inhaled; her breasts were growing larger. Havoc had not realized she could do this, and perhaps Gale had not known it either, prior to the need. They were still discovering Glamor powers.

"I must caution you that any one of these would be a challenge," Mneme said. "I had hoped you would take one, possibly two. But three—"

"We'll manage," Gale said. "Havoc, you take Flame. I'll take Warp and Weft."

Mneme nodded to the three women. They cooperated, giving the babies to Havoc and Gale. Then they removed their amulets, so that their swollen breasts could subside.

Flame, not recognizing him, began to fuss. Havoc stood helplessly, not knowing what to do. He knew that women could quiet babies by nursing them, but that was not his province.

"Project assurance of safety, comfort, and sleepiness," Mneme advised him. "That's one thing about your status: you can reach her mind directly."

He tried it, and the baby quieted. He received a mind trace from Gale, who was doing the same.

"Appreciation," Gale said. "We shall take them home."

"Gratitude," Mneme replied. She was the toughest of women, but she truly cared for her charges. She knew that this commitment would be honored.

Havoc touched Gale with his free hand, and they conjured back to the home site. They had to touch each other, because otherwise they would not align perfectly in timing or positioning, and could separate or collide.

They landed just outside the cave-house. Symbol was there. "Babies!" she exclaimed, startled but pleased.

"Adopted," Havoc explained. "Super-changelings."

"Super?" she asked, stepping close to admire the babies,

Then Flame focused on Symbol's blouse. A curl of smoke rose from it, as if a magnifying glass was burning it. The woman jumped back, tearing off the blouse and slapping the incipient flame to stifle it. It was clear that she didn't mind baring her breasts, which were excellent. They were invisible, like the rest of her torso, but she had powdered them so that their fullness showed. The rest of her wasn't powdered, so the breasts seemed to swell from the empty air beneath her head. Actually she had lived in a nonChroma zone long enough to suffer some attrition despite a native magic stone she carried; her heart and lungs showed faintly.

"Pyro," he explained. He glanced at the others. "Levitation, conjuration."

Symbol got over her startle. "Delight! May I hold one?"

Havoc handed her Flame, who was looking around as if seeking more mischief. "She'll want to nurse," he warned her. Gale was already nursing the two she held, having somehow bared her breasts without setting either baby down.

"Maybe I can do that," Symbol said. "I have a bauble." She brought out a little nursing amulet, which she had on a string, so that it dropped down between her ghostly breasts. They swelled. "Yes, it works." She held the baby to one breast, and Flame nursed. The milk might be invisible, but it had the same substance as Gale's.

Trust Symbol to be prepared! Possibly she had guessed the nature of Mneme's problem and sought out the amulet.

"We did not require this of you," Gale said.

Symbol shrugged. "I serve the king and queen in any way I can." She had the grace not to glance at Havoc as she spoke, but her mind carried the trace: she was eager to embrace him again.

"This way is as good as any," Gale agreed, flashing Havoc a mental picture of naked Symbol being hauled away from his bed by the scruff of her neck. It was all teasing; she would send him to Symbol if she wanted to be left alone. Of course her picture wasn't literal, because a truly naked Symbol was almost invisible and there was no scruff to grab.

Havoc left them and walked around the cave-abode, considering how it might be adapted for small children. There was plenty of room, because offshoots of the cave extended in several directions. All they had to do was designate them and prepare them for use. Of course at first the babies would stay close to Gale, whose abrupt motherly capacity was a pleasant surprise. But as they grew—

Havoc. It was Ennui again.

You need Symbol back already? She's busy at the moment.

Chief says we need you back. There's a crisis the mocks can't handle. The mocks were the mock king and queen emulating Havoc and Gale at the palace.

That was bad news. *This is not convenient at the moment. Is it urgent?*

Chief says, quote, "Tell him to get his barbarian ass here in a hurry."

Havoc laughed. *He didn't mean that to be quoted.*

True. But the need is urgent.

Havoc signed. *You said mocks. You need Gale too?*

Ennui sent a mischievous smile. *Unless you care to come alone and night with Spanky.*

I'll ask Gale. But there's a complication.

There always is. We'll handle it. She faded out, her limit expended.

Havoc returned to the others. The babies had finished nursing for the moment, thanks to Symbol's help so that they could do all three at once, and were now entertaining them with demonstrations of spot magic. Symbol's charred blouse was on again, so that her figure was complete.

"We need to practice control," Gale said, seeing him. "So that they can't make mischief."

"Agreement. But there is another problem."

"We have more than enough already."

"Chief wants us back in Triumph City."

"We can't go now! The babies—"

"Ennui said I could go alone and night with Spanky."

Symbol tittered. "Sire, if you want young flesh, Bijou will make the sacrifice. No need to bother Spanky." Bijou had been the first bath girl Havoc had encountered, and of course she loved him; they had had a considerable relationship. Terms like "sacrifice" and "bother" were sheer tease; the girls were more than eager and competent.

Gale's smile was restrained. "Symbol, you have demonstrated your ability to help in a new way. But nursing is more than is expected of a third party. How can we repay you?"

"Gale, I am Havoc's mistress, with your concurrence. I want to be yours too. Let me nurse your babies. The service is its own reward."

Havoc kept his mouth shut. That was about as direct a statement as could be made.

Gale nodded, unsurprised. "We shall have to return to the palace. You will become my personal maid, to help with the children, in addition to the chores with Havoc. We will not be able to conceal their abilities from the palace staff, but we do not want them known beyond. You will assist in that. This is apt to be an enduring commitment, because we shall want the children always in familiar hands."

"I like these children," Symbol said. "They have character."

"As you know, we are now Glamors. This, too, we wish to conceal beyond the palace staff."

"Commitment."

Gale nodded. "Take her back, and prepare the way," she said to Havoc. "Then fetch me. I don't want to try carrying three together."

Symbol glanced at the babies. "I can carry Flame, if—"

"Feasible. Havoc will take you and Flame. You will explain to the staff while Havoc finds out what requires our presence. Tell Berm and Spanky to make way for us."

Havoc put his arms around Symbol and Flame, and transported them to the Ennui's room in the palace.

Ennui was there, expecting an arrival. She was nevertheless surprised. "A baby!" she exclaimed.

"I told you there was a complication," Havoc said sourly.

"What are you doing baby-sitting? Whose is it?"

"Mine. Gale adopted three."

"Three!"

"We underestimated that girl," Symbol said with a smile. "This is Flame. Gale will bring Warp and Weft once we clear the way."

Ennui glanced at Havoc. "Who needs to know about the babies?"

"You, Aspect, Chief, Throe—" Havoc began.

"The bath girls," Symbol said. "Soon the whole palace staff will know, but we'll try to hold the line there, until the formal announcement is made." The baby had finished nursing, and Symbol handed her to Havoc and covered her breast. Some of the powder had been rubbed off by the baby, so that only intermittent portions of the breast showed anyway.

Havoc didn't argue. Symbol knew protocol better than he did. He held Flame, liking the way she cuddled; she had gotten to know him. "However, there's another complication," he said.

Ennui faced him. "This time I had better listen."

"They have magic powers. Here in nonChroma. This one is a pyro. She sets fires with her mind."

"Oh, my." Ennui took a moment to work it out. "That's why you took her? Because it will take a Glamor to handle her?"

"And the others," Symbol said. "They levitate and conjure. So far."

"So we need to move the mocks out, oblivious," Ennui said. "And enlist competent help, so you and Gale can get some sleep."

"That's best," Symbol agreed. "I will be doing what I can, but this promises to be a challenge."

"Understatement." Ennui reoriented. "Moving out the mocks will take an hour."

"An hour!" Havoc said.

"If we rush them, they'll catch on that something's up," Ennui explained patiently. "They have been alerted to be ready to move out at an hour's notice, so that's proper."

She was right, of course. Havoc sat on Ennui's bed, holding the baby. "Go get it done."

Ennui and Symbol nodded and left the room. Havoc would not leave it until the way was clear for him to resume his role as king. Actually he was finding Flame to be good company.

Until she looked at the bed, and the bedspread started to smolder. "Don't do that!" he said, alarmed.

Flame scowled. An open flame appeared on the bed.

Havoc hastily conjured a splash of water. It doused the fire and sank into the bed, soaking it. Ennui wouldn't like that!

However, the water distracted the baby. Flame cooed, touching the wet bedding.

But what would he do when the baby got bored again? Havoc lacked experience with babies. This promised to be a long hour.

There was a knock on the door. *Bijou*, the thought came.

"Get in here!" Obviously Ennui had sent her.

Bijou entered and quickly closed the door behind her. She was seventeen, with brown curly hair, and as comely a figure as was to be found. In fact she strongly resembled Gale, except that she wasn't a changeling. Havoc knew her quite well, having traveled no fault with her after she was done emulating Gale. Naturally she knew all about his accession to Glamor status. He was very glad to see her now.

"Oh, nice!" she exclaimed, stepping up to take Flame from him. "But she wet on Ennui's bed."

"*I* wet on it," he said. "That is—" He sent a mental image of the fire and dousing, to stifle her smile.

"I'll fix it, Sire." She returned the baby to him and rummaged in a closet for sheets. "Or could you project heat to dry it?"

He hadn't thought of that. "I'm still learning my powers. Maybe I can." He concentrated, thinking hot.

The whole bed burst into fire. Hastily he conjured more water and doused it again.

Flame chortled. Bijou smiled. "Maybe better to leave it to me, until you get better control." She got to work, stripping the bed and turning over the mattress.

"Appreciation," Havoc said weakly.

"You know," Bijou said as she worked, "I've hardly seen you since you matriculated." That was her word for his accession to Glamor status. "I danced with the Black Glamor, but couldn't have sex with him. Is the same true of you now?"

"I don't know. I haven't tried it with anyone but Gale."

"Not even Symbol?"

"We've been on our honeymoon without her."

"Then let me be the first to find out." She spread a sheet on the bed and lay down on it, spreading her legs under her skirt so that her inner thighs showed. The view was compelling, as she knew; she had seduced him many times.

Havoc wasn't sure she was serious; she could be playful. "But I'm holding the baby."

"So you are. So maybe I'll just kiss you." She approached him and lifted her face to his—and stopped. "I can't get there."

"It seems that regular folk can't do it knowingly with Glamors."

"That means it's psychological."

"Or magical," he said. "Some magic works better when it is known. Maybe it's like mind reading: both minds become attuned."

"Maybe," she agreed crossly. "How will I ever get my fourth of you, if I can't embrace you?"

He hadn't thought of that. He did owe her a fourth, when the time came; she had certainly earned it. "Maybe if you slept I could come to you."

"Like an incubus," she said, making a moue. "Aggravation! I want it hot and conscious." She took the baby back.

"We'll have to figure out a way." Bijou wasn't the only girl he owed a fourth; there would have to be a way.

Soon Symbol returned. "Things are in motion. I thought Flame might be getting hungry." She took the baby from Bijou and opened her shirt. Flame started nursing. It seemed that babies did that often.

"He's trying to renege on my fourth," Bijou complained.

Symbol smiled. "Negation. There's a way. Remember, I used it with the Green Glamor."

"Fifty times," Bijou said, remembering. "Envy."

"It's a matter of partial distraction. You have to make believe he's someone else, and that you are someone else."

"Like Minstrel and Girl?" For they had played those roles when traveling together.

"Yes. Whatever works. If you can come to believe it enough, you can do it."

"I'll believe it!"

"I will be devising something similar myself, lest I slight my role," Symbol said.

Bijou laughed. "A mistress who couldn't get close to her lover!"

"It would be embarrassing."

Havoc hadn't thought of that problem before either. He had formally taken Symbol as his mistress before turning Glamor. Well, she would surely manage.

Ennui returned. "Things are in motion. Chief has been notified, but we felt it better to wait until you and Gale are in place, so there's no possible confusion. Berm has been meeting with Chief regularly, nominally to give him directives, actually to be advised what the directives are." She glanced around. "What happened to my bed?"

"Havoc wet on it," Bijou said with a momentary straight face.

"I thought that barbarian was house broken." The women loved teasing him.

By the time Gale arrived, they had it straight. Ennui and Bijou were instantly charmed by Warp and Weft, but when Weft conjured Symbol's nursing amulet to her hand, it was clear that proper control had to be exerted.

Soon the hour was done. Havoc and Gale moved into their own royal apartment, but had no occasion to get comfortable. It was time for Havoc to see Chief, who was the cause of their abrupt return to the palace.

"Parting," he said.

"Put on your crown, oaf."

Havoc sighed. The king's ornate crown was sitting on a table where the mock king had left it for him, beside the smaller queen's crown. He had gotten used to being without it. "Observation: you wouldn't dare call me oaf when I'm king." He picked up the crown and set it on his head.

The room spun crazily. Havoc heaved off the crown as he fell on the bed.

"Alarm!" Gale cried as the crown rolled across the floor. Suddenly Symbol was balancing three babies while Gale hauled Havoc's head to her half bare bosom. "Comfort."

"Recovery," he said. Her embrace was indeed supremely comforting. "The crown attacked me."

"Amazement," Symbol said. "Berm would not substitute a magic bomb."

"And Ennui would have known it if he did," Gale agreed. "But there must have been a change."

"*Havoc* changed. He turned Glamor."

Havoc sat up as Gale released him. "The crown has ten magic stones, to protect the king from physical and magic threats. That concentrated magic must interfere with my Glamor powers, or vice versa."

"Both," Gale said. She went to pick up the fallen crown. "I feel its struggle." She glanced at Symbol. "You try it?"

Symbol set down the last baby and took the crown. "Nothing."

"Put it on your head," Havoc said.

"By your leave, Sire." She set the crown on her head. "It is marvelously light."

"It was not made for a Glamor," Gale said. "The currents of magic must conflict."

"Perplexity: how can I be kingly without my crown?"

"Conjure an emulation," Symbol said, removing it. "Then I will hide this one until the mock king needs it again."

Havoc nodded. He concentrated, conjuring metallic substance and shaping it into the semblance of the crown. This was a new exercise of magic, and he was clumsy, but Gale helped, and soon the new crown

seemed indistinguishable from the original. Havoc donned it, satisfied.

"Now I will call you oaf again," Gale said. "Sire." She affected a
look of surprise. "That was supposed to be oaf!"

"So the crown works," Symbol said, sharing the joke. "Now you
must make one for the queen, too."

They verified that the queen's crown had a similar conflict, and
made another emulation. Gale donned it. Havoc made as if to call her
a name, but it came out "Lady." They laughed.

But there was business to handle. Havoc kissed Gale, donned his
formal robe, and went to the private audience chamber, curious what
emergency had come up. Chief would not have summoned him without excellent reason.

≈≈

Gale watched Havoc go. All three babies were sleeping for the
moment, which gave her time to focus on other things. She had a
foreboding that life was about to get more complicated, and they were
already far enough in that direction. "How are we going to manage?"
she asked Symbol. "I was foolishly impulsive, I confess it. I just couldn't
let any of these babies be destroyed. But I fear we're in for a difficult
twenty years."

"I love you," Symbol said. "You are everything I would have chosen to be. How could you be other than you are? Of course you saved
those babies. We'll manage."

"I am also with child."

Symbol paused. "With help, we'll manage. But I think we had
better get professional counseling."

"Question?"

"These three babies have spot Glamor talents. You and Havoc
surely have the means to handle them—if you know how. The folk of
the Chroma routinely handle magic children. I remember my childhood in the Invisible Chroma. Unfortunately I don't remember how
my parents controlled us as babies, and I have been long away from
home. But I believe Ine is about to return home."

"The sorceress," Gale agreed. "She had more of a way with Havoc
than I liked."

"Throe had experience with all four sisters, Ina, Ini, Ine, and Ino.
Ino is the fourth, a changeling, and she remains at home until she mar-
ries the Black Glamor. Their parents should have excellent advice."

Gale nodded. "Affirmation. I surely could use that. But things are
bound to be so hectic with our catching up on the palace routine that
I don't see how we could summon them and keep their visit private."

"Problem," Symbol agreed.

Gale set about rearranging the suite. The mock king and queen
had left so suddenly that much of their private setup remained, and of

course they had not had three babies to accommodate.

Greeting.

Gale nodded. "Greeting, Swale," she said aloud so that Symbol would know. Swale was Berm's sister, rendered into a succubus by a cruel process; Gale had first defeated then befriended her. She could be a great help in some situations.

"The succubus returns," Symbol remarked. "Spanky get too dull for you?"

Swale, now inside Gale, borrowed her mouth with her acquiescence. "I'm desperate for sex, but damned if I'll have it with my brother. Do you want company when you tackle Havoc?" Gale's voice sounded different when Swale used it.

Symbol considered. "You know, he's hard to approach now that he's a Glamor. I know I can do it, but I wonder: would you be able to help me do it as myself?"

"I'm eager to try! I've never tackled a Glamor."

"You can try it with me," Gale said, borrowing her mouth back.

"That's not the same. You're a Glamor too, so don't have the mortal limitation. Anyway, you're pregnant."

"I can still have sex."

"Would my presence affect Voila? You know I share your womb with her."

That set Gale back. Obviously the succubus could visit Gale in her Glamor aspect, and in her pregnant condition, but when she got sexually active it was a transforming state. "Try it with Symbol," she agreed.

There was a gentle knock on the door. "Bijou," Symbol said. "I know her knock."

Gale extended her awareness and verified the mind. The girl had an urgent message. "Enter, Bijou," she called.

Bijou opened the door, slid through, and closed it silently behind her. "Lady Gale," she said. "I have a message from Sire Havoc."

Gale still had not gotten quite used to being addressed as Lady, and she had never felt at ease with Havoc's title, though it was standard; too many attractive women seemed to take it literally, wanting him to sire their fourths. But she knew she would simply have to get used to all of it. She knew that Havoc could have reached her mentally, but was trying to follow protocol. "Speak."

"He must go immediately with Chief to handle a situation. He is not sure you will find it convenient to accompany him—"

"Exclamation! Of course I can't go now!"

"So perhaps the Lady Symbol—"

"Negation," Symbol said. "The babies need me more than Havoc does, for the present."

"But it seems a formal appearance is in order," the girl continued. "The queen or mistress should be with him."

Gale exchanged a glance with Symbol. Both well understood the requirements of formal missions, but this was out of the question.

"Idea," Bijou said.

I wondered how long it would take her to think of getting into Havoc's bed, Swale thought.

And there it was, in her mind. "Emulate me," Gale agreed.

"Problem. I can't touch a Glamor."

"Solution," Symbol said. "I told you how. Practice."

Gale kept silent. She knew Bijou loved Havoc and wanted to embrace him, and now could not. That problem didn't really bother Gale, but it was true that if Bijou emulated her, she would have to be in Havoc's bed. She would have to learn to pretend it wasn't really him. Surely the girl would rise to the challenge.

I'll help her, Swale thought. And of course it hadn't taken the succubus long to think of sex with Havoc, either.

"Challenge," Bijou agreed with evidently mixed feelings.

"Swale will help."

Bijou nodded. "I may need her."

Parting. Swale left Gale to join Bijou.

"You will also need the crown," Gale said. She fetched it.

"Agreement. By your leave, Lady." Bijou accepted the Queen's crown but did not put it on. "I must assume the likeness."

"Affirmation," Gale said. She and Symbol helped put the girl in a queen's robe, and redid her hair to match Gale's. It was surprisingly easy to make the conversion; the clothing fit, and the hair was already close. Soon they stood beside each other facing a large mirror; they looked like twins.

"Appreciation," Bijou said, now emulating Gale's voice.

"Don't do anything I wouldn't do," Gale said.

That broke Bijou up for a moment. "It is doing what you do do that is the challenge." She departed regally.

"Remark," Symbol said. "She is as worthy to embrace him as I am. She has earned her keep."

She certainly had. "Marriage makes me jealous of the designs of other women."

"Sympathy. But also opportunity."

"Question?"

"You are now officially invisible again, as long as Bijou emulates you. You can travel."

"Travel?"

"To see Ine's folks in the Invisible Chroma."

Gale knocked her head with the heel of her hand. "Idiocy! Where has my mind gone?"

Symbol smiled. "The babies took it."

They got to work changing their appearances, becoming anonymous. Meanwhile, Gale summoned Ennui, the one person who had to be cognizant of royal identities.

Ennui appeared just as the babies woke. "Confusion," she remarked, seeing their preparations.

"Havoc's on an official mission," Gale said, picking up Warp. Ennui quickly took Weft, competently checking her diaper for wetness. "Bijou will emulate me. Symbol and I will be anonymous, traveling to see Ine's folks to learn baby care. Cover."

"Covered," Ennui agreed, returning Weft to Gale, as the baby was starting to fuss. She would inform whoever else needed it, and keep the palace operating smoothly. Gale knew that the woman's oath friendship with Havoc had been a sudden, almost random thing, but she had taken hold and become completely competent as well as loyal. She was in certain respects the most important person in the city.

But the woman lingered. "Problem?" Symbol asked as she changed Flame's wet diaper.

"Oddity, perhaps irrelevant. The loom is active."

That made Gale pause in the act of baring her breasts for Warp and Weft. "Clarify."

"Nonce carried the loom ikon, but it brought an urgency on her, and she invoked it as the full loom in a storage chamber. Now she is weaving—and so is Lady Aspect. And me. We all feel the need of the loom, and the dragon seeds do not object."

"What pattern?" Symbol asked.

"Unknown. Intricate. Precise. We are instituting four hour schedules so that it can proceed continuously, but we don't know its ultimate nature."

This was more than interesting. Neither Ennui nor Aspect was given to idle distraction. "Continue," Gale said. "Keep us informed. And the Brown Dragon Glamor."

"Appreciation." Ennui departed.

"So the loom isn't done," Symbol said.

"We have yet to fathom its full nature. We need to. Maybe it's helping us."

Then they returned to the businesses at hand, with another round of nursing and changing. When Flame slept again, Symbol went to see the Sorceress Ineffable, to arrange for their travel with her. Ine's body was invisible, as was Symbol's; she was garbed in inclusive underwear and stockings beneath a conventional opaque long-sleeved blouse and skirt, with gloves and a veil under her hood. She could make herself visible, but that would be a waste of precious magical energy, here in the nonChroma zone. That was why Symbol handled this; it was clear that she understood the concerns of the Invisible folk, being one herself. She had gotten along well with Ine throughout.

Soon they were on their way, providing Ine with a king's coach, her friends Gal and Bol and their babies accompanying her as a courtesy. Ine was delighted to take Warp and nurse him; she had that power as a sorceress with a magic gem to provide some of her home-Chroma power. She had to unwind and stretch her body bands to do it, making it look as if there were a hole through her body, as she had not powdered her breasts. That left one each for Gale and Symbol, which simplified things. The three babies seemed to have worked out shifts, taking turns to fuss, and the breast did not necessarily satisfy them. They did have active little minds and were accustomed to getting their own way. Gale well understood why their original families had been unable to keep them. Glamor or no, Gale herself would have been overwhelmed by now, had she not had the support of Symbol and other women.

As they traveled Ine regaled them with the adventure the three sisters had had with Throe, making him have sex with each of them in order to decide which one was the best mate for their boyfriend Jamais Vu, who was actually the Black Glamor in mortal disguise. But Throe had gotten them back by selecting none of them, choosing their younger sister Inoffensive instead, recognizing her as a changeling. They had gotten him back, in turn, by really working him over on their trip to Triumph City. It seemed that the girls had compared notes, so knew the most intimate details of all the sexual encounters. It was apparent that all of them had high libidos and enjoyed playing with men.

Meanwhile Gale looked out the coach window to see the giant blue animals hauling them along across the blue landscape. It had been scarcely a year since she had first left Village Trifle and come to the center of the planetary kingdom, and the Chroma magic still intrigued her. They had known of it as children, but hardly experienced it; riding in a coach was THE way to enjoy it. Everything was shades of blue, and she could see magic everywhere as people flew by without benefit of wings.

One little blue girl in a blue dress and hair ribbon flew up to the window and offered her a blue fruit; she opened the window and proffered a coin for it, but the girl handed it to her and zoomed away, giggling.

She showed it to the others. "Is this edible?"

"Looks like a blue banana," Symbol said.

Ine was wary. "Let me see it." She took it and held a transparent gem close. It flashed. "Toss it out the window," she said. "It's a stinker."

"Question?"

"Demonstration. I'll set it off, then toss it, so you know without getting stenched." She held the fruit up and scratched it with one nail.

The blue hide of it ripped open along the scratch. Blue powder puffed out. Then Ine tossed it out her window as the thing exploded into a blue cloud. The little bit that was inside the coach smelled awful. Gale realized that had the whole thing been confined inside, they would have been completely soaked in the stink.

"Child's joke," Ine said. "We have an Invisible variant. It seeds itself by emulating fruit and exploding into pollen when bitten. The creature's efforts to rid itself of the smell spreads it widely."

"The babies wouldn't have liked it," Symbol said, sniffing as if to clear it.

Gale realized that she should have been warned. Normally the dragon seed did that, but she no longer had it, since she could perceive spot errors for herself. But she had been so used to the dragon seed, and her Glamor powers were still so new, that she hadn't invoked that awareness. This was her lesson; now she attuned. She would not be caught like that again.

The next Chroma zone was Black. Black made her nervous, because it was the imploding zone, though she knew it really wasn't any more dangerous than any other volcano. Here everything was in shades of black, odd as that seemed; shiny black alternated with dull black to form clear outlines of trees and creatures. Their coach floated right over the vast empty central cone, which made even Symbol nervous; they knew the Black Chroma guides knew what they were doing, and would not have used this direct route had an inruption been imminent, but that fathomless funnel was scary all the same.

The next zone was Translucent, whose natives specialized in mind reading. The three of them used their mind shields to mask their thoughts, though they doubted that anyone was peeking.

Next was an Invisible zone, but not the one where Ine lived. The various Chroma zones were scattered all around Planet Charm, with hundreds of each color in no clear order. The same was true of its sister world Counter-Charm; they could see its patchwork colors. What governed the color of a particular volcano no one seem to know; somehow each remained true to its Chroma, regardless of its neighborhood. Mixing of colors occurred only on the surface, where the border of one zone overlapped another. Symbol and Ine compared notes, as both were of Invisible origin.

Then on to a Green Chroma zone, with exotic plants galore. Their tentacles lifted and swung the coach rapidly across, until at last they reached the fringe of the next Chroma zone. And so on, until they reached Ine's home Air or Invisible zone. Gale was relieved; the babies' almost constant need for attention of one kind or another was wearing.

Now Ine could fly, and so could Symbol. They got out of their clothing and made themselves beautifully visible nymphs. For the first time Gale saw their hair, which was long and silky. Of course they might be enhancing its appearance, but Gale thought they weren't; both were too apt at fascinating men to have such a detail unreal. All Invisible Chroma women were lovely, because they formed their own appearances, but these two were real.

Ine led the way, carrying Warp. Symbol followed, with Flame. Gale carried Weft. This was another new experience for her: flying in company with others. In nonChroma zones she was likely to be the only one who could do any magic, and normally she tried to hide it. But here everyone could do it, so they could be quite open. Others would not be aware that Gale was not an Air Chroma native.

The scenery was varied and quite interesting. The reality was invisible, but both creatures and plants clothed themselves with illusion so that color was everywhere. Air was the Chroma of illusion, of necessity, and everything here was good at it. Gale knew that what she saw was not necessarily what was there, but probably most of it was merely enhanced for better effect. Then she remembered: as a changeling before, and a Glamor now, she could penetrate illusion to see the reality. What she saw conformed her guess: things were close to their appearances, merely less so.

The babies, too, were intrigued. They gazed around, appreciating the riot of colors and forms. That was just as well, because it meant they made no mischief.

They arrived at the house of Ine's parents. Ine's illusion clothing formed around her, so Symbol did the same.

A young woman opened the door as they landed. She was absolutely lovely in a conservative way; she was not trying to flaunt herself, yet could not conceal her beauty. This was Ino. "Ine!" she cried hurrying to hug her sister. But she stopped just before making contact. "You birthed a baby?"

Ine laughed. "Not yet, tyke. This is Gal's baby." She turned to the others. "Introduction: Gal and Bol. My little sister Ino."

"Greetings, visitors," Ino said shyly. She was about sixteen and clearly unspoiled. She might be betrothed to the Black Glamor, but as yet she had not explored the married state. It was evident that she had been raised well and strictly.

"We come to ask a boon of the parents, and perhaps you too, if you have babysitted infants," Ine said. "We need instruction in raising babies."

Ino could not conceal her surprise. "But these are six months old! Surely—"

"Adopted this day," Gale explained.

Ino nodded, understanding. She was a very quick study, as was typical of changelings. Gale suspected that she had caught on that Gale was more than she seemed, but her mind was shielded. "My parents will surely help."

"Appreciation."

The girl ushered them into the house. There stood two older folk, dully garbed and nondescript, obviously by design. "Introduction," Ino said. "Gal of Triumph, Bol of our Chroma and Triumph. My parents, Intrepid and Innate." The parents nodded. "They wish instruction in raising infants. These babies are recently adopted."

"More," Gale said. "They have magic abilities—in nonChroma

zones."

"Disbelief!" Intrepid said, then caught himself, not wishing to be discourteous. "Figurative. There is no magic in nonChroma."

"Privacy," Gale said.

The parents hesitated, then nodded. They would respect secrecy. "Agreed," Ino added.

"Do you know of Glamors?"

They hesitated again. "They know," Ino murmured, this time allowing a thought to escape so Gale could read it: she meant the Black Glamor, whom she was to marry. Her parents were trying to keep that secret.

"Affirmation," Intrepid said, trusting his daughter's insight. "But babies are not that."

"I am a Glamor." Gale rose slightly into the air, and glowed. It was clear that she was no Invisible resident, so she should not have been able to do magic here. "I associate with the Black Glamor, and others." She settled to the floor and faded to normal.

"But you are nonChroma!" Innate protested.

"I am the nonChroma Glamor of mosses. I draw my power from them, and serve their interest." Gale extended her hand. Moss sprouted from it. She smiled. "Recently ascended. I do not wish this to be generally known."

"But you are Queen!" Ino exclaimed. "How can it not be known?" Then she blushed. "Oops."

She had indeed caught on to that aspect, recognizing Gale. The girl had evidently studied politics. She was extremely sharp, but young enough to make slips.

"Affirmation," Gale said. "Queen and Glamor. I am King Havoc's wife. I adopted three babies because they can't be governed by less than a Glamor. But I have no experience with magic babies. I need instruction."

Now Innate smiled. "That we can provide, Lady."

"Demonstration." Gale glanced at Ine, who had learned of the babies' talents during the journey. She held Warp out at arm's length. She let him go. He bobbled and floated.

Gale tucked Weft into the crook of her left arm, and conjured a bright bauble to her right hand. She teased the baby with it, and in a moment it jumped to Weft's little hand. "I did not do that," Gale said.

"And this little mischief is pyro," Symbol said. "she sets fire to things. Surely she does not mean harm, but enormous harm can come in a city made of wood."

"There are several ways," Innate said. "Each has its application and its caution." She glanced at her husband.

"The man's way is to punish the child for infringement, Intrepid said. "Make the child hurt when it transgresses and it will quickly desist. If the child makes fire, burn her on the bottom so she understands it is not a plaything. If the child levitates when told not to, levitate him out of control; he will learn. If the child conjures what is not hers, conjure a prickle to the offending hand."

"But such measures stifle the child," Innate said. "It comes to fear the exercise of its power. This is not good."

"Yet the child must learn of consequences," Intrepid said. "Some magic is dangerous. The fear of that danger must be instilled. Thereafter a mere warning suffices."

"Still, love must be ever be paramount," Innate said. "The child must fear danger, never the parent."

Obviously the two had differences, but they had succeeded in raising four magic children. Everything they said made sense; Gale remembered the loving discipline of her own parents, especially when it came to safeguarding her welfare as a fourth. She just had never before thought of it from the parent's side. She had considerable re-learning to do in a hurry.

"I see this will be a solid task, educating me," she said. "I am barely older than your daughters, and have been a mother for only a day. I must not take your time without exchange; I must trade a service for a service. What can I do for you?"

"Negation," Innate protested. "We are at the service of the king and queen."

"Negation. I am here as a woman needing help. I will exchange."

The parents exchanged a glance, but it was Ino who spoke. "That appeal must be honored."

"But we need nothing," Intrepid said. "We would not ask a pointless service."

"Ini," Ino murmured.

That set both parents back. Yet they were clearly ill at ease about this.

"Our sister Initiative is the smartest of us all," Ine said. "She is much interested in the essence of all things. She has even made a lens to study the surface of Counter-Charm, perceiving detail and creatures there unknown to others. But because of that, she is not a good prospect for marriage; men don't like wives who know more than they do."

"But a smart woman learns to mask that," Gale said. "I did."

"She is also unpretty. Of course every Invisible woman wakes herself pretty, but in close embrace a man can tell."

"Maybe she needs a wider field of men," Gale said. "In Triumph City there are all kinds."

"So I have told her," Ine said. "She was there briefly, when we delivered Throe home. And you know, we had fun with him, but his love was only for an older and unremarkable woman, Ennui. A man of that nature might love Ini. But she saw only the crowded business of the city, and the tight enclosure of it, and fled it. She does not want to go there."

"Yet she faces an uncertain marriage here, in two years," Innate said. "She deserves so much better."

Gale saw the problem. No girl wanted a leftover man; there were reasons why those men were rejected by other women. "I do not know what I can do, but I will make the effort. Perhaps I can persuade her to give Triumph another chance."

Innate smile gratefully. "While you make that effort, we will start training your babies to mind, so that simple signals will maintain their discipline in a kindly manner."

"Done!" Gale looked around. "Where is Ini?"

"I can take you to her," Ine said. She passed Warp to Ino, whose young breasts immediately expanded, ready for use. The girl was only fifteen, but knew what was what. Perhaps her contact with the Black Glamor was already stretching her horizons.

"I will remain here, learning," Symbol said. She was still holding Flame, who seemed to like her; there had been no further outbreaks of fire.

Gale nodded. While she had no reason to doubt the motives or competence of the parents, she trusted Symbol in a special manner. Also, the woman would quickly relay what she learned, so that Gale would not miss anything important.

She gave Weft to Innate. The baby girl started to fuss, but a miniature display of circling colored stars appeared, distracting her. Gale made a mental note: she could use illusion to divert the babies.

"Take my hand," Ine said.

"You can transport?" Glamors could do it, and some Chroma folk, but Gale understood that it was difficult magic that most left alone.

"I am a sorceress; I try to master all magics."

Which made sense. "Lead me." Gale took her hand.

Ine transported herself to another part of the Chroma zone, guiding Gale there. This was another new experience; Gale had done it with Havoc and other Glamors, learning how, but never with a regular Chroma person. The magic seemed identical; what was unusual was Gale's ability to invoke it anywhere.

They landed at a simple home site with a workshop, and the surrounding landscape was invisible; obviously the proprietor was not much for appearances. "Iniquitous!" Ine called.

Ini appeared, forming as a plain young woman. Vanity was evidently not her forte. "Yes, Inefficient?"

Gale burst out laughing. "Apology," she said after a moment. "The way you tease each other."

"Surprise," Ini said. "Queen Gale."

"Heed her, sister," Ine said. "She needs you." She vanished.

Ini gazed at Gale. "You do not command?"

"I have not been queen long enough to learn how. I am exchanging a service with your parents."

"Situation."

Gale explained it: Glamor, babies, deal. "So I must persuade you to come to Triumph City, if I can."

"I would not do that voluntarily."

"They wish you to marry well, and fear that will not happen here. There are many men in Triumph, some of whom appreciate intelligence in a woman."

"How many appreciate plainness?"

Gale shrugged. "I lack experience there. But since you can make yourself appear as you wish—"

"Disinterest."

This was not working. Ini wanted to be valued as she was, and that was indeed a challenge. "What do you most desire?"

"Knowledge."

It figured. This woman was dedicated to learning. That was not Gale's strong suit. Uncertain how to proceed, she stalled. "Example?"

"Counter-Charm. Everyone knows it is our sister planet, very like our own world, with Chroma volcanoes. Many folk stare at it in fascination, wondering whether there are people like us there. But I don't want to wonder, I want to *know*. And I am trying to find out."

"But all we can do is look at it," Gale said. Actually she understood that Glamors could go there; there was supposed to be a Glamor retreat there. But she hadn't had time to follow up on that since becoming a Glamor. Marriage, the study of Glamor powers, research into her constituency of moss and lichen, and now the babies had kept her thoroughly occupied.

"I fashioned a magic lens to peer at it more closely. Throe helped me make a breakthrough; we were supposed to have sex—you know about how he had to check all of us for Jamais Vu?—but the lens was more interesting. We saw strange animals! Since then I have watched further, and catalogued the creatures I see. But as you say, just looking from afar is limited; how I wish I could go there and survey it from up close!"

"But would it be safe?" Gale was getting interested.

"I tried to analyze the quality of light reflected from it, and believe it matches our own, close enough; that suggests that the air is similar. The two planets are so close in size and composition that gravity must be similar. Some of the life forms resemble our own, so I think they managed to cross between worlds, or were colonized from the same source. But most are different. Since the known plants and creatures interact with the strange ones, I think they must have similar biology. And of course the magic is similar; the volcanoes and Chroma zones are just like ours, with certain intriguing exceptions. So yes, I think it would be safe for us, in the sense that we could survive there, if we protected ourselves from predators." She sighed. "But such speculation is foolish; I will never walk that phenomenal surface."

"I am not sure that is impossible," Gale said.

Ini paused. "Glamors may be able to go there. But why should they take any of us?"

"Compromise: join our mission for a year or less, and help us fathom the riddle of ourselves: who set up the things of the Glamors, the ikons, the altars, the loom. What opposes our quest for this knowledge? There is a power we do not understand. Thereafter, solved or unsolved, return here as you were, if you wish. If it is possible in that time, I will get you to Counter-Charm, at least briefly."

Ini's eyes glowed, literally. "Deal."

Thus readily she had found the key: the woman wanted to *know*, and this was worthy knowledge. She would surely be a great help in the quest. And Gale was curious about the sister world herself. In her home village it was called Mystery. By whatever name it was fascinating.

҉ ҉

Havoc left the chamber—and there was Throe. *Good to have you back, Sire,* the bodyguard thought. He could not say it aloud because theoretically the king had never left the palace, apart from a brief honeymoon after his marriage. Throe served the mock king in the same manner, maintaining the pretense, but his heart was not in it.

"Question: have you any idea what's up?"

"Trouble between Chroma, Sire."

"I'm sure you'll keep me safe."

"I will do my utmost, Sire." They both knew that Havoc needed no guardian as a Glamor, but maintained the pretense that he was a still a normal man.

Havoc reported to the counseling chamber, Throe fading into the background as was his wont. *Where are you, Chief?* he thought.

Close by, Havoc. I must not enter until officially summoned. It is a matter of protocol.

Oh. Havoc raised a hand and snapped his fingers. "Chief!"

Chief entered in a moment, half smiling. "You summoned me, Sire?"

"I understand there is a problem."

"There is, Sire." Even in a private meeting, Chief maintained the formal address. Protocol counted for a lot.

"Speak."

"There is mischief between a Green Chroma and Yellow Chroma zone. Their areas overlap, and unusual plants grow there. Both Chroma want control of the region, so as to exploit the produce of those plants."

"They can't split it down the middle?"

"They are unwilling. They are threatening to go to war."

"Question?"

"It is possible where zones overlap. Fireballs versus huge green tentacles."

"Interest."

Chief shook his head. "It behooves the king to make peace, not applaud war."

Havoc sighed. "Even a barbarian king?"

"Especially a barbarian king. He must demonstrate control over his nature."

"I could issue a directive."

"Sire, I think not."

"Question?"

"It may be that this product is too important to leave to either Chroma. I believe the crown should expropriate it for universal use."

"Clarification."

"The plants produce a potent magic aphrodisiac. I understand that the fruits and the juice of the fruits cause many creatures, including humans, male and female, to suffer virtually insatiable sexual desire."

"Exclamation! Everyone will want it."

Chief smiled. "Agreement, Sire."

"And in this case the king's decision will have to be enforced."

"Agreement."

"Do it."

Chief shook his head. "Protocol, Sire."

"Damn protocol! What do I have to do?"

"Sire, you should make a formal visit of state, with the queen, survey the situation, consult with the sides, confer with other Chroma, and come to a conclusion as to the appropriate course for the betterment of all parties."

"Gale can't handle that right now." He shot Chief a mental picture of the three babies.

Chief suppressed his astonishment at this family news. "Yet a decision of this magnitude, at least in the popular image, requires due formality. Appearance is as important as substance. The people must believe that their king has given this matter his best attention."

"Problem."

"Perhaps the queen will after all see fit to accompany you." Chief knew she wouldn't, but was leading up to something.

Havoc shrugged. "We can ask her."

"Bijou," Chief said, not loudly. The girl appeared almost immediately, as palace personnel were trained to. "Ask Queen Gale if she would be amenable to accompanying the king on a royal mission. If not, perhaps the Lady Symbol."

The girl nodded and departed. She knew as well as Havoc did that Symbol was tied up with the same commitment as Gale. They couldn't leave the babies.

"There is another matter," Chief said. "It seems the loom is active. Nonce brought it to the palace, and invoked it, and she and the Ladies Ennui and Aspect are taking turns weaving an ambitious tapestry. This may not be completely voluntary on their part."

"Surprise! I thought that turned out to be a dead end."

"I suspect the end is alive; it is merely our comprehension that is inadequate. Perhaps this is the loom's way of acquainting us with the next stage. I believe we should let the weaving proceed, and try to fathom the nature of the tapestry as it progresses."

"How long does it take?"

"A small simple effort may be accomplished in a day. This one looks more like a year."

Havoc looked at him. That was bound to be a phenomenal creation. "It must be relevant."

"Agreement. But this aspect, it seems, can not be hurried."

Gale appeared, formally attired in robe and crown. "Havoc, you know I can't travel right now! Neither can Symbol. You'll have to settle for something less."

Havoc touched her mind—and burst out laughing. It was Bijou, playing Gale. She was so good at it that she had fooled him for an instant. "I'll settle," he said.

"Then I think we are ready," Chief said.

"Complication," Havoc said. "If that is the real crown, I can't touch her."

"It is real," Bijou said. "Question?"

"My new nature conflicts with the crown's magic."

"I can remove it in private."

"Experiment," Chief said. "Ascertain the limits."

Havoc approached the girl and took her hand. There was a tingle. He moved into a slow embrace. The tingle intensified. He made as if to kiss her—and was repulsed. "It's like an ikon," he said. "Resistance increases as I get close."

"Sufficient leeway for public display," Chief said. "Can you carry her?"

They tried. It turned out to be possible if Bijou removed the crown and held it out from their bodies. That would have to do.

Bijou took Havoc's arm, walking a bit apart from him, and they made a regal exit, followed by Chief and Throe. The news was proclaimed that the king was making an official journey to handle an affair of state. A retinue of servants of several types appeared; the king never went out alone. They descended to the water floor, marched to the ferry, and crossed to the outer city. People had assembled as if by magic—impossible in this nonChroma zone—to line the road on either side.

Havoc hated it. He remained a village man, accustomed to knowing everyone in the community, and being the object of cynosure only when he was conducting a class in martial arts. Being stared at simply because he wore a crown was ridiculous. He didn't recognize any of the faces, and they surely knew little about him that was not crafted for their attention. He felt like a circus freak.

Havoc, smile at that little girl, Bijou thought, indicating the direction in her mind.

He dutifully turned to smile at the child. She reacted as if blown back by a gust of wind, awed.

You have to be king, Bijou thought. *They have to be in awe of you. It's the system.*

Havoc made a mental picture of a sausage labeled SYSTEM being rammed into an enormous and rather messy rectum.

Bijou tried to maintain a straight face, but lost it, and had to cough into her hand. Chief and Throe, walking behind them, picked up the image and had similar problems. "Sometimes it's fun serving a barbarian," Chief murmured to Throe, just loud enough for Havoc and Bijou to hear.

There was a royal coach waiting, drawn by six legged horses. Throe stepped up to assist the king and queen's entry, then joined them inside. The coach moved out at a brisk pace, leaving the gawkers behind. The formalities had been completed.

They reached the southeast campsite at the edge of the Brown Chroma zone. Huge brown golems came to pick up the royal coach. Airborne, it moved swiftly on into the Brown zone.

"We have a dull trip of two days and nights," Chief announced. "I can acquaint Havoc with the details of the mission."

"Which will put him to sleep," Bijou said. "If you two men were not here, I could entertain Havoc in better style." She removed her crown, signaling her intention.

"Doubt," Chief said. "But I would like to see you try."

"Challenge." She turned to Havoc, oriented on his face, and slowly approached for a kiss. Havoc did not move, satisfied to have her explore the limits. Her lips stopped just short of his. She struggled to complete the contact, and finally did touch him.

And fell back, swooning.

"Confirmation," Chief said. "She'll be needing practice."

Throe, seated opposite the girl, learned forward and took her gently by the shoulders. "Lady," he said, as if concerned about the fainting spell. "Lady Gale."

She stirred, woozy. "Where?"

He gave her a miniature shake. *You are Lady Gale.* "Are you well, Lady?"

She remembered. "Yes, thank you, bodyguard. Is the king well?"

"Unscathed," Havoc said.

Bijou glanced around. "We are private?"

"Agreement," Chief said. "But unsafe to assume we will always be."

"I kissed him and was stunned?"

"Affirmation."

"We can't have that happen in public—or in private when others may be spying on us."

"Affirmation," Chief repeated.

"So now is the time to figure it out, with only those who know the secrets present." She meant that she was not really the queen, and that Havoc was a Glamor.

"We won't tell," Throe said with a smile.

"I need to imagine that you're someone else," she said to Havoc. "I'm already someone else. May I try again?"

"How can the king deny the queen?" There was reason behind this game, but Havoc liked the game.

"I am the queen," she said firmly. "You are a sexy barbarian. You—" She broke off. "Plea: remove the crown."

Havoc obliged, so that she could better pretend he was not the king. It was its symbolism rather than its magic that interfered with her pretense, in contrast to the effect her crown had on him.

"The queen would not cheat on the king," Throe said.

"They are traveling," Chief said. "No fault."

"Still, she's the queen."

Chief nodded. "Put your crown out of sight, Lady. You are traveling incognito."

Bijou smiled. "You boys are really getting into it, aren't you. Are you trying to be helpful, or merely voyeurs?"

"Helpful voyeurs," Throe said.

She frowned, but did hide her crown. She faced Havoc again. "Well, Hayseed, you have not traveled with a woman as lovely as I. You are too country boy shy to make the first move, so I will help you. We shall start with a kiss."

"Delight," Havoc murmured.

She approached him slowly. "Of course I wouldn't touch a barbarian ordinarily, but folk might suspect my identity as the queen if I acted too regal. So I will act like a barbarian girl, and smack you one."

Then, suddenly, she lunged. She caught him hard on the mouth with a compressed kiss. There was an electric jolt and she bounced away, reeling. Havoc realized that the jolt was hers; he had picked it up from her mind.

But this time she managed to hang on to awareness. "How did you like that, Hayseed?" she demanded.

"That was some smack," he agreed, remembering how his kiss had put Nonce out for the duration.

"You kissed Nonce?" Bijou demanded. He hadn't shielded his thought.

Chief chuckled. "Hayseed's in trouble now. He kissed a bath girl."

"And they weren't even traveling," Throe said.

Bijou recovered and donned her crown, delivering a queenly glare. "There will be another encounter," she said grimly.

Havoc hoped so. Bijou was fun and deserving.

They looked out the coach windows. Everything was brown: trees, vines, grass, even the birds flying near. The shadings made it possible to distinguish details, but it seemed dull to Havoc. Soon he nodded off.

He woke to a kiss. Bijou was practicing again, her crown off, and this time she managed to hold lip contact for several seconds before the resistive tingle became too strong. It was good progress, but still a long way from full sex.

"But I will get there, Hayseed," she murmured. "Just wait until night."

The coach came to the far edge of the Chroma zone. The giant golems set it gently down at the staging area and hitched a new set of horses to it. They rolled some distance out of the zone, seeing the brown fade. They entered a zone of nonChroma colors, then came to intensifying yellow. This was a Fire Chroma, but not the zone with the problem. Chroma folk could travel to their own colors and have no difficulty, but because the zones were isolated from each other, they tended to be autonomous. That meant that whatever happened at the farther Yellow zone would be unlikely to affect the near zone's attitude toward the king. In fact it was the disunity of zones of any particular Chroma that made centralized government by nonChroma folk feasible. The king lacked magic power in any one zone, but all other zones would support his decisions.

The horses were released, and yellow Fire folk came to see to the coach's next leg of the journey. Of course Ennui had set up the itinerary and sent messages out to coordinate the route. Ordinary folk had to pay their way with caravans or walk, but the king had priority throughout. The yellow men worked yellow magic to lift the coach into the sky and float it on the wind. Here everything was in shades of yellow, monochrome of the current color. They were high enough to see the distant central volcano, intense yellow clouds clustering around its cone. It occurred to Havoc that volcanoes could be dangerous apart from their magic, because of the force with which they spewed out gas and rock; he had a healthy respect for them.

But again it got dull. Bijou tested her mettle, managing to hold a long kiss without fainting, but it remained a challenge. Havoc did not try to conceal his enjoyment of her effort; it was fun having a lovely young woman play ardently up to him. Of course Bijou had gone much farther with him in the past, and he liked her a lot, and not just because she resembled Gale. She was worthy in her own right.

"Thanks, Havoc," she murmured breathlessly. Her effort was straining her physically as well as mentally.

"Caution: I don't want you to hurt yourself."

"It hurts me to have such a chance at you, and not be able to consummate. Maybe if you approached me—"

Havoc tried it. He moved slowly to hold her and kiss her. Her body went taut as if experiencing pain. Frustrated, he stifled that reaction, and she relaxed so that he could complete the kiss.

"Oh, Havoc, you numbed me," she breathed. "I didn't know you could do that."

He hadn't known it either. It was another Glamor power, there for the asking—if he but knew to ask it. Maybe the Green Glamor had used that to help Symbol have sex with him, fifty times in succession.

"I was with the Green Glamor," Bijou said. "He called himself Thumb. We were captured by White Chroma men, who were going to rape me, but I was rescued just in time."

"And Symbol got him," Havoc agreed.

"I saved myself for you."

He laughed. "You'll get there."

They snoozed until the coach landed at the far verge of the zone. New horses were hitched, and they moved across the nonChroma zone to the fringe of a Green Chroma zone. Here tall trees reached down stout tentacles to haul the coach up, and swung it along across the green landscape.

Bijou continued her effort to get close to him, and with his numbing help was able to do it with less consequence. "Just wait until tonight," she murmured in his ear. "Swale will be with me."

The succubus! Havoc had had sex with her once, in Gale's body, and it had been phenomenal. The succubus was a creature of sex, and she was expert.

After the Green zone they crossed a Black zone. This made Bijou nervous. It wasn't the unremitting darkness of the terrain so much as the fear that there could be an inruption that sucked them all into its funnel and destroyed them. "I know it's no more dangerous than any other volcano," she said. "But it gets to me in a special way."

"It's a female volcano," Chief said. "In instead of out."

That made them all pause for thought. It seemed like a valid analogy. Maybe the magic matter that was hurled out by the other volcanoes was drawn back in by the Black Chroma funnels, restoring the source. They discussed it, wondering whether they had come upon a significant understanding.

Night was closing as they reached the far side of the zone. They were glad to move out of it to the surrounding nonChroma zone, where there was a staging area and campsite. A modest royal banquet was ready for them, which Havoc and Bijou consumed in royal style, while Chief and Throe ate with less flair, not being royal. They could not be sure who might be spying on them. It would not be magical, but any of the local servants could report to other masters. So the four of them were obliged to act as if on show, though it probably was not the case.

King and queen shared a nice chamber for the night. They undressed, washed, and lay together on the bed. "Sire, do you desire me this night?" Bijou inquired.

What kind of question is that? he demanded mentally.

It's the style the mock king and queen employ, she thought. *They don't know how you are in private, so err on the formal side.*

So now he had to emulate the fake king, lest others think Havoc was the fake. "Disgust."

"My lord! How have I offended you?"

He realized he shouldn't have spoken that word, as it would seem to be in response to her offer of sex. She knew it, but was playing the role. "Disgust that you should ever suppose I did not desire you, this night or any night."

"Apology. I am yours."

Actually she wasn't. She had progressed to clasping and kissing, but sexual penetration remained beyond her threshold of pain. She struggled valiantly to accommodate him, and was mortified that she could not. Aware of that, he changed his mind, with sincere regret. "I am more tired than I realized. Tonight we shall merely sleep."

"Acquiescence, my lord."

And we'll have to educate the mocks. Damned if I want stilted sex! Then something else occurred to him. *What of the succubus? Couldn't she help?*

I asked her to let me try it alone this time. Tomorrow she'll step in if needed.

They concluded that an aspect of the failure was that for this he had to play the role of king, not the hayseed barbarian, so she could not complete the diversionary image. She did not want to be numbed for this; she wanted full awareness. They would have to work out a new ploy.

Havoc spread out his Glamor awareness in a routine check of the local environment—and made a discovery. *Our crowns have been stolen!*

Astonishment! She did not doubt his perception. The two crowns on the table were fakes.

A servant must have exchanged them while we were distracted. I would have been aware of magic.

"Agreement," she murmured aloud. *Servants can be sneaky. I know; I was one.*

Havoc laughed. *An excellent one.*

We must get them back. Do you know where they are?

I can locate them. But I prefer to let it be, until we know the rest of this mischief.

The two crowns protected the king and queen from hostile magic. Havoc's was now his own fake, but Bijou's was real. So now the fake had been replaced by a fake. He sent his awareness back—another ability he had not known of before—and spied hands appearing from behind the desk, taking the two crowns, and seemingly putting them back immediately. It had happened so quickly and quietly that they had not noticed.

He followed the crowns along the floor just out of sight of eyes on the bed, and out of the chamber. Then the servant stopped crawling and stood, carrying the crowns to an unoccupied chamber and hiding them in a closet there. That was all; the servant returned to the servants' quarters. Havoc followed her a bit farther, but she seemed to be entirely ordinary. Returning to the present, he reached out and touched her mind, but found no memory of the event. She had evidently acted under some other compulsion, and did not know what she was doing.

This had the aspect of a sophisticated plot. He did not know where it would lead, but now he had been warned. The plotters did not know he was a Glamor who did not need the protection of his crown. That was his means to foil it, once he discovered its nature.

Pretend you don't know about the crowns, he thought. *I will fathom this in due course.*

Acquiescence, Havoc she thought nervously.

He took her hand, and they slept.

In the morning the routine continued. They breakfasted and returned to the coach. Havoc acquainted Chief and Throe with the matter of the crowns. *Be alert.*

They nodded. Their telepathy was a secret from those beyond the palace, and like Havoc's ascension to Glamor, was at times a significant benefit. Now they knew there was dirty work afoot, and would be alert for it, physically and mentally.

Havoc also sent a long distance thought to Ennui. *Our crowns were swapped with fakes. We pretend not to notice. Advise the Glamors.*

Havoc, don't risk it! she thought with motherly concern. *Return swiftly and let Throe handle it.*

Negation. They don't know my nature.

She grudgingly accepted that. *But if other Glamors care to intercede, I won't stop them.*

Havoc smiled. It was her way of telling him that she would urge the other Glamors to get on his case. Especially Gale. But he knew that Gale was going out on her own mission with the babies. He could not commune telepathically as readily with Gale as with Ennui, but they did have a certain awareness of each other's location and state of mind. By the time Ennui reached her, Havoc might well have solved the case of the missing crowns.

By the time they landed for the second night, Bijou had succeeded in putting Havoc's hand on her breast without flinching. It was an interesting experience; her breast was throbbing with her racing pulse, but it was effort rather than passion that caused it. She was pushing her limits. Chief and Throe pretended not to notice, knowing that this was exactly the progress she had to make.

But when they arrived at the campsite closest to the quarreling Chroma zones, Havoc made a seemingly arbitrary decision. Actually they had discussed it mentally and agreed it was the prudent course, considering the theft of the crowns. They wanted to surprise both the Chroma zones and the unknown enemy.

"Pack the meal; we are moving on immediately," Havoc said. "Keep the horses."

"But my lord, I'm tired," Bijou said, forming a queenly frown. "I don't want to have to camp in the field."

"Woman, when I desire your opinion, I will require you to speak," he said gruffly. She made a moue and was silent. This was very much in the manner the mocks had adopted, so was in character for their public image.

The local servants hastened to pack the meal. The other coaches of the royal retinue turned about, rehitching their steeds, and made ready to travel again. They stashed the meal in the coach and moved on.

There was just one coach-navigable trail leading to the zones. It passed close to the overlapping territory. "I prefer to examine the situation myself, before hearing the arguments of the quarreling factions," Havoc announced for the benefit of any eavesdroppers. "We shall camp at the edge tonight, and hold audience on the morrow."

"In a Chroma zone?" Bijou protested.

"A little magic will do you good, woman."

Bijou made a show of biting back a caustic reply. *I'm going to get a bit of that magic inside me tonight, or freak out in the attempt.*

They unpacked the meal and ate while traveling. In due course they reached the green/yellow overlap, which was a pale green hue. The king's coach halted at its verge, and the other coaches drew themselves into a roughly circular formation around it. The king never traveled alone or unguarded. In fact the king couldn't even crap in the pot without attendants close by.

Throe went to supervise the defensive preparations, and Chief met with his traveling staffers who would liaison with the Yellow and Green Chroma staffers, hastily revising the arrangements for the coming royal audience. Of course no one would complain openly of the inconvenience the king's arbitrary change of course made, but there was surely grumbling at a safe distance.

A considerable party was forming, as was usually the case when the king made an appearance. Attractive young green and yellow women showed up, bringing food for the supplementary staffers and servants. Tents were pitched, and it was apparent that the girls were available on a no fault basis for male hands who were interested.

Havoc walked out into the zone. Throe immediately appeared to accompany him, and guards deployed inconspicuously in the vicinity. This was of course why Havoc detested being king; he couldn't go anywhere alone. He much preferred traveling as Hayseed the Minstrel, with a good woman by his side. As soon as this mess of a mystery enemy was finished, and the riddle of the origin of the Glamors solved, he would see about an early royal retirement. Then he and Gale could raise their children in peace.

"It is a worthy ambition," Throe murmured. Havoc hadn't bothered to mask his thoughts. "When you do, I hope to do similar with Ennui, albeit without children."

"Understanding. You have had yours."

On one side the zone verged into green; on the other, yellow. In the center it almost glowed with the intensity of the juxtaposition of Chroma, and the plants growing there seemed to have a special vigor. Most were familiar to Havoc, as the same plants grew everywhere on the planet. A few were new to him, and he studied them with interest.

What are you? he inquired of one, touching it gently with one finger.

Fire Fern, it replied in its manner, not in words but in identification.

I love you, fire fern, he thought, caressing it. He was the Glamor of trees and plants, and cared about all of them. If any were mistreated, he would be aware, and would respond if he could. He had not yet learned enough to fully implement his protection, but he was working on it.

Danger, the fern thought. But it lacked the mind to be specific.

Other plants had a similar warning. They knew his nature, and valued his company. From them he drew a special strength, because he was the Glamor of *all* plants, not just nonChroma plants.

Throe stood by, receiving the silent communion because Havoc shared it with him. "Amazement," he murmured.

"I am not what I was," Havoc said. "This is better, and not merely because of the power it brings me. I am part of a special global community. I can live apart from the human kind, but I couldn't not endure apart from these." He gestured, taking in the whole region.

They returned to the camp. A beautiful green girl approached them, lifting a hand in a request to speak.

"Speak," Throe said. Normally a common person did not address the king directly unless she was part of his personal staff, and then she was cautious.

"I am here for your comfort, warrior, no fault."

Throe smiled. "Needless. But thanks."

She shrugged. "I will remain within beck."

"It seems you don't have to sleep alone tonight," Havoc murmured as the girl faded back.

"I remain amazed that when offered delights like that, I still would prefer to be with Ennui. She was neither young nor pretty, until recently, and makes no pretense to special intelligence, but she has something."

"Commitment."

"Maybe that's it. When you exchanged oaths of friendship, she took it as seriously as you did. I like that in a woman."

"So do I. It was that way with Gale."

Throe did not seem to look about, but he picked up something Havoc had missed. "There are many local Chroma zone girls—more than necessary for servant duty."

"And all are young and pretty," Havoc agreed.

"Their minds are innocent of any bad intention. But I do not understand why so many are here. The king's party does not usually attract such a number."

Havoc nodded. "Something is afoot, surely related to the theft of the crowns. But I can't fathom it either. We shall have to wait for the trap to spring."

"Agreement. But if I alert my men, that may betray our awareness."

"They are good men. Normal discipline should suffice."

"It should," Throe agreed. "For a normal circumstance."

"We do have two advantages."

"I hope they remain unknown."

"The queen and I will retire," Havoc said loudly. "Dismissed, bodyguard."

Throe bowed his head, and departed. Havoc went to join Bijou in the royal tent.

We are on show? her thought inquired.

Assume so. Throe and I note too many maidens present for the occasion, so we suspect the trap is closing. Act normal.

She smiled, appreciating the irony. They were playing parts; real normal would give them away. "My lord, you must be tired. Let me assuage your fatigue."

Of course Havoc wasn't tired; the Glamor power made him indefatigable. "Appreciation, my love." He disrobed and lay prone on the mat.

"How I treasure those words, my love," she murmured. She knew he did not love her, but she did love him, and the words sent a thrill through her that touched his mind. She set about massaging him, her hands strong and competent, the legacy of her time as a bath girl. It felt good.

I do not love you as I love Gale, he thought, *but I do care for you and value your presence and your touch. Were I free to love another, I would love Symbol, then you.*

"Third on the totem," she murmured. But she was thrilled again;

it was a high ranking.

A faint, funny, appealing smell developed. Night blooms?

Havoc, may I beg a favor? Can we interrupt this massage for a fast bout of raw sex?

That suggested that the succubus was on duty. *Can you handle it?*

Her hands on his back trembled with feeling. *Yes.*

He was amenable. He turned over as she tore off her negligee. "Answer to my desire, my love," he said for the benefit of any listeners.

Bijou flung herself down on him full length, kissing him avidly. It was true; she was handling the proximity better than before. *Don't wait!* she thought urgently.

He was ready. He positioned himself and came at her slowly, giving her the chance to demur, but she didn't. As his member touched her cleft and found the hot wet place she stiffened, clenched her teeth, and sucked in a shuddering breath, but then forced herself to relax. *Don't stop; I want it more than it hurts me. Don't numb me; I want it fully real.*

He nudged cautiously into her, feeling her body and her mind react as though she were being raped, but she held on, enduring it. She did want it, desperately, and to withdraw would be to make her suffer worse. So he continued, sliding deeper in the hot channel, finding the margin between discomfort and desire as her tolerance slowly increased. *Think different identities,* he reminded her.

She did, and her body relaxed somewhat, enabling him to complete the entry without hurting her as much. Then she kissed him and tightened rhythmically inside, massaging his member, triggering his climax. She screamed through clenched teeth as he jetted into her, then fainted.

Consternation, Swale thought. *I pushed her too hard.*

He had forgotten the presence of the succubus, though he should have recognized her touch that brought him off. *She wanted it. You made it possible.*

But it was difficult for me too. Now I know: Glamors are proof against my kind.

He smiled. *That's good to know.*

Havoc waited a bit, then withdrew. In a moment Bijou woke. "Apology," she murmured. "I couldn't stay with you for the finish."

"You did well, my love, as always." *Another woman couldn't have tolerated it at all.*

I had to. I'll clean up and finish the massage.

No need. I'll give you one.

"My love!" she murmured as his hands kneaded her small muscles. The queen would not expect such reciprocation from the king—at least, not as played by the mock king and queen. Havoc intended to change that.

Bijou melted, physically and mentally, loving his touch. But he had not been at it long before she touched his mind again. *Havoc— can you—more sex?*

She was ready for another siege already? He could certainly oblige, as Glamors were capable of continuous sex when they chose. "Attend my renewed desire," he said.

She rolled over, welcoming him. He approached her again, on guard against her reaction to the Glamor diffidence, but it was less than before. *Swiftly,* she thought.

This is not my doing, Swale thought.

This was unusual. Bijou loved him, but this repeated eagerness for sex was not like her. She liked sex with him because she liked pleasing him; if she could please him without sex, she was glad to do that. Now it was the sex she craved; the raw desire suffused her mind.

Responding to her urgency, he entered fully and climaxed again. This time she managed to retain consciousness. "Glorious!" she gasped.

They broke again, and she resumed massaging him. But soon she wanted sex again.

Something was wrong. *What brings this passion?* he thought. *It is not your normal way.*

She paused, considering. *Agreement. I feel insatiable. I have never been like this before; it has always been for you rather than for me. Swale says she mistrusts this.*

So did he. The odd smell was stronger. Suddenly Havoc caught on. "The aphrodisiac pollen!" he exclaimed. "It must be from night-blooming flowers. We assumed it was merely the fruit that brought on the urge."

"That's it!" she agreed. "But that means that everyone is breathing it."

"And no one is on guard," he agreed. "It's a neater trap than we figured." He laid his hands on her and focused. *This will abate it for a time.*

She nodded. *My passion is gone. I didn't know you could do that. I mean, not that way.*

He hadn't known either. It was another Glamor power, discovered when invoked. "Stay safe. I must roust Throe, and discover what's happening next." He was already getting dressed.

"I'll help." She dived for her own robe.

Havoc doubted that she could do much, but let it be. He left the tent and went to the next one. *Throe,* he thought strongly.

Awkwardness.

Havoc sent a blast of passion abatement. Freed of the erotic compulsion, Throe disengaged. "Don't leave me!" a woman's voice came. "I'm not nearly satisfied." Havoc recognized the voice: it was the green girl who had broached Throe before. She had been ready when the urge came, and Throe had not been able to resist her. But Havoc saw from her mind that she had not known this would occur. She had simply been inclined to be in the vicinity.

Throe emerged. "I suddenly had an overwhelming urge. Apology for my neglect."

"Aphrodisiac pollen," Havoc said tersely. "The thing we came to investigate."

"Trap?"

"Suspicion. Yet how can sex hurt us?" He knew the answer, but wanted verification.

"Distraction. The girls were sent to be sure all men were busy. But what is the threat? I detect no hostile minds near."

"But there is magic," Havoc said, sensing it. "Fire."

"From the Fire Chroma!"

Havoc extended his awareness. "Perhaps. It is forming a circle around our camp and burning inward."

"Alarm!"

"Fetch Bijou. Cover for me." Havoc conjured himself to the palace at Triumph City. He knew that Bijou would act queenly, pretending that Havoc was close by, and Throe would rouse the camp to the extent possible.

Ennui jumped as he appeared before her. "Havoc!"

"We are in the trap. Fire—too much for me to douse. Tell the Glamors." He returned to the camp.

It was already in near chaos. The erotic aroma remained, but now the fire was evident, and that was a marvelous aid for concentration. The Chroma girls, appreciating the danger, were vanishing, literally; this was a Chroma zone, and they could do their magic. The men of the king's retinue were lurching into their clothing and forming a ragged formation for Throe to direct.

The Black Glamor appeared beside Havoc. "Preference?"

"That my accession remain anonymous. This is Glamor business. Douse the fire."

"Granted." The Black Glamor vanished.

Satisfied that the matter would be handled, Havoc used the distraction of the crisis to make his own investigation. He conjured himself to the outer edge of the fire, making himself invisible and inaudible. He extended his awareness, searching for hostile minds.

There was nothing. Magic had started and shaped the circular fire, but the source of that magic was gone without trace.

So they had sprung the trap, but hadn't identified the source of it. It was clear that neither the Yellow nor the Green zones had devised this plot; they were only now becoming aware of the fire, and were hurrying to help douse it.

There was nothing to do except conjure himself to their prior campsite and exchange the crowns for the real ones, so that their enemy would think the plot had fouled up and their crowns had protected them long enough for the Glamors to come.

He conjured himself to his tent. "Give me your crown." He shared his plan with Bijou mentally.

Can you put tracers on them? she thought. *So you'll know who collects them.*

He looked at her. "Brace yourself." Then he kissed her. *Great idea.*

Braced, she withstood the impact of the kiss, thrilled. But she had another thought: *You can't handle my real crown.*

She was right. "It's good one of us has common sense," he muttered.

But you can take me there, and I'll take it and hide it for me to recover on our return trip.

He kissed her again. Then he embraced her and conjured them both to the other campsite.

No one was in the room, and the two crowns remained where they had been left. He impressed the two they were wearing with a finder signal—another abruptly discovered Glamor ability—and exchanged his crown while Bijou exchanged hers. Then she took hers outside and hid it in the thick foliage of a nearby tree. He conjured them back to the fire, where they hadn't been missed.

"Tomorrow I will declare the pollen too dangerous to be left to the Chroma," he said. "It will be reserved for disposition by the crown."

Bijou smiled. "You had decided to do that anyway."

"I needed a pretext. After what happened here, both zones will not peep protest."

"My Lord, I love you."

She was speaking as the queen, but she meant it for herself too.

"We may travel again soon." Because with both Gale and Symbol occupied with the babies, Bijou would have to emulate the queen again for any formal excursion.

"I love traveling with you."

So do I Swale thought.

He kissed them both with one kiss. Then they had to get to work sorting out the chaos of the camp.

⚶

Gale was glad to return to the palace, for once. The session with the invisible Chroma family had really helped, and the babies were already better behaved. Innate had drilled them in certain simple words that they recognized and responded to, and schooled Gale and Symbol in others they could learn. Mostly it was a matter of anticipating likely mischief and avoiding it.

Ennui, she thought. *We're back. Initiative—Ini of the Invisible Chroma—is with us.*

Apology, Ennui replied immediately. *I was weaving and didn't realize. I will be with you shortly.*

"I don't wish to be any trouble," Ini said. She was now invisible, because her body was in its natural state while she had lost her magic ability to make herself visible. She was familiar with the problem, having visited here before, but it remained an awkward adjustment.

Gale smiled. "We can use the help with the babies." She saw that Ini was dubious; her mind showed it. "You don't have to nurse them. Can you change a diaper?"

"Acquiescence," Ini said, relieved. Two of her sisters had been happy to nurse babies, but Ini was different, and of course lacked both her Chroma magic and a nursing amulet.

Swale popped in. *That girl is really trying* she reported. *She has learned to kiss him, and got his hand on her throbbing left breast.*

"I'm so glad to know that," Gale said wryly.

I let her try it alone last night, but she couldn't do it. Tonight I'll help her score. The succubus thought came through with a certain hearty zest. Sex was most of her life.

"What about the mission?" Symbol asked.

"They're walking into a trap," the succubus said with Gale's mouth. "Havoc wants to spring it."

"He would," Gale muttered. Actually Ennui had already advised her of this.

I must return to duty. Parting.

"Parting," Gale and Symbol said together.

"Is there something I don't understand?" Ini asked.

"Gale tamed a succubus," Symbol explained. "She acts as a liaison, entering one of our bodies and communicating."

"A succubus! Concern."

"This one can be trusted," Gale said. "You'll surely meet her, in due course. Her name is Swale. Her brother sometimes emulates Havoc, pretending to be king, when Havoc is away anonymously."

"Understanding."

The babies woke and began fussing. Gale and Symbol hastened to pick them up. They were wet, so there was immediate use for Ini. She tackled the third baby, Flame, who was not alarmed by being invisibly handled; it was touch she reacted to. But it was evident that Ini wasn't good at this. Her invisible hands were clumsy, and the diaper was far from tight. Flame fussed, and made as if to start a fire.

"No," Gale said. That was one of the words: don't do what you're about to. Innate had emphasized it with projected disorientation that the baby found unpleasant, so the lesson had quickly taken. Gale had learned how to do the disorientation, but hoped she wouldn't need to. She was in luck. This time.

Ennui knocked, then entered. "Success?"

"We now have a much better notion," Gale said, nursing Warp. He was floating, but that took his weight off her, so she let it be. "We should be able to manage." She glanced at Ini. "Ini will be staying with us for a time. Can you establish her in her own room?"

"Affirmation." Ennui led Ini from the room. Gale knew she would get the Invisible Chroma woman established and oriented. Ini would have to don nonChroma clothing, because her own was invisible.

"You know, we'll have to tell the populace some time," Symbol said. "Three babies can't be concealed forever."

"I prefer to get comfortable with them first. For one thing, I'd rather have their magic powers not be known. Most folk think magic is impossible in a nonChroma zone without a magic gemstone."

"Maybe we should give them little stones," Symbol suggested. "They don't have to be magic; they just have to look as if they could account for the magic the babies do."

"I like it! I'll make them up as soon as the babies are asleep again."

Symbol continued to ponder. "I wonder about the babies being little Glamors. Shouldn't they have ikons?"

Gale's mouth fell open. "Astonishment! You're right! Only Glamors can do magic on their own in nonChroma zones, and they all have ikons. The ikons collect the magic and transmit it to the Glamors so they can go anywhere, as long as the ikons remain in their home Chroma. We can't do magic without the ikons—and the babies must be the same."

"Which means their ikons are lying around somewhere, unrecognized. Hadn't we better find them?"

"Yes!" Gale was almost bewildered by the realization. "Bafflement. How to proceed?"

"That invisible sister you picked up, Ini—I understand she's quite intelligent."

"And we need a smart mind to figure this out," Gale agreed. She send a mental thought: *Ennui! Send Ini here.*

Acquiescence.

Gale set Warp in his crib and picked up Weft, who had been content to wait her turn. The babies' manners had improved significantly since their stay with Innate. It was evident that the babies had not before encountered parents with complete magic, and had learned limits in a hurry. Weft started nursing on the other breast.

Symbol was still nursing Flame, who took more time about it. She was accustomed to Symbol's invisible breast, and seemed to be the most sociable of the babies. "We shall have to nurse different babies on occasion," Symbol said. "So that all are used to either of us."

"Agreement." But for the present, it was convenient to leave Flame with the Invisible Chroma woman.

Soon Ini returned. She was now completely swathed by visible clothing, and wore a veil to clarify the outlines of her face. "Problem?"

Gale explained their revelation about the babies' ikons. "You're the smartest woman we know; how do you see it?"

"Challenge." Ini considered briefly. "If they are Glamors, and have ikons, they must have constituencies. What ones are available?"

That set both Gale and Symbol back. "I thought all were accounted for," Symbol said.

"No, the pattern of the threads suggested that there should be eighteen Glamors" Gale said. "We have accounted for fourteen."

"Then these babies could be three of them," Ini said.

"But how can a baby be a Glamor?" Gale asked. "These ones merely have spot talents, not full Glamor powers."

"They have limited powers *because* they are babies. As they grow they may develop other powers. Is there any age limit for ascension to Glamor status?"

Gale exchanged a glance with Symbol, their minds similarly daunted. Ini was surely correct; it explained much.

"So they have constituencies," Gale said. "We shall have to figure out what's left. Their ikons will surely reflect them."

"So if we find the ikons, we'll know their constituencies," Symbol said. "And if we knew their constituencies, we would know what ikons to look for." She rolled her eyes. The effect was not visible, but her mind reflected it.

"I think we must first identify the constituencies," Ini said. "If we list all the ones we know of, we should be able to identify the others by elimination."

They reviewed the list, in order of the number of legs, beginning with the demons, who had no legs, and following with the worms or dragons, with one leg. Then on through fish with two fins, birds with three wings, humans with four limbs, insects with five, vertebrates with six, spiders with seven, plants and trees with eight roots, the sphinx with nine limbs, the mollusks with ten tentacles, the millipedes with a hundred, Gale's own mosses with a thousand, and the saprophytes with ten thousand.

"So the logical continuation would be a hundred thousand," Ini said. "A million, ten million, and a hundred million."

"That's a lot of legs," Gale said weakly.

"It may be a convention of convenience, rather than literal," Ini said. "Consider an amoeba: it extends pseudopodia as it chooses, and shuts them down again. So it could be considered to have any number."

"Like a hundred thousand," Symbol said. "There's a category."

Ini nodded. "And it may be that one of these babies expressed an interest, and the community of amoeba accepted. Similarly the other babies reached out, and two other communities accepted. Let's assume that Amoeba is one. I think the large creatures are covered, but what about the other small ones, like bacteria or viruses?"

"Are they living?" Symbol asked.

"I believe so, and they are very common. Babies soon encounter them, without the aversion adults have. They could desire representation. And what about the fungi?"

"Aren't they the same as the saprophytes? Gale asked.

"Some are, some aren't. Some are like plants, some like tiny animals, and some are yeasts. They are a class by themselves, as much as vertebrates or mosses are."

"I suppose then a baby could represent them," Gale agreed dubiously. "What sort of ikons would such constituencies make?"

"My guess would be a mushroom or toadstool for fungus, and an amorphous blob for amoebae. Bacteria have several shapes, some like tiny spirals. Virii hardly have their own forms, being infectious agents; their name means slime."

"A slime ikon!" Symbol exclaimed, laughing.

There was a gentle knock. Gale recognized the mind of a trusted servant, arriving with a meal for all of them. Ennui had informed the royal kitchen who was where and what each preferred. "Bring it in!" she called.

The door opened, and the woman drew in a wheeled cart laden with fruits, cakes, drinks, and covered platters. She carefully unloaded it onto the central table, then quietly departed, drawing the cart after her.

Gale put Weft down to nap. They got to their meal, which was delicious.

Then Symbol looked around. "Where's Warp?"

Gale looked. The baby was gone. "He must have floated out of his crib while we were distracted." She looked around, but didn't see him. She sought his mind, but didn't find it. "The little twerp has learned mind shielding!" she exclaimed.

"And the door is open," Ini said, appalled. "The servant was pulling the cart and forgot to turn back to close it. He must have floated out."

"He picked his time," Symbol said. "I have to admire his cute little cunning. We underestimated him. He must have been paying better attention in the Air Chroma than we knew, and picked up on mind masking when the adults did it."

"Very smart baby," Ini agreed. "Dangerously smart—for his own safety."

"We have to find him!" Gale cried, alarmed. She lurched for the door.

"Caution," Ini said. "The other two should not be left unattended, especially considering the powers."

"You watch them," Gale said, plowing on.

"Go with Gale—she's dangerous too," Symbol told Ini. Gale heard, but was heedless. Where was Warp? How could she have let him get away?

Ini followed her. "Caution," she repeated. "Not everyone knows about the babies."

She was right. "I'll try to present a calm demeanor. Help me search."

"He hasn't been gone long, and we don't know how much control he has. Probably he's moving slowly, and along open halls."

"Agreement." But her alarm scarcely abated.

The palace was a many-chambered section, occupying the whole of the top several floors of the wood pyramid that was Triumph City. Passages interconnected and ran parallel to each other, so that servants could do their business without ever blocking the way of the king, queen, or leading staff members or visitors. Gale bore right, and Ini bore left, following different passages.

Gale, running, turned a corner and almost collided with a servant. "Apology, Lady," the servant said, though it had been Gale's fault.

"Did you see a baby?"

"Yes, Lady. It—it—" The woman balked at saying it.

"It floated?"

"Affirmation, Lady. I hardly believed—"

"Where?"

"This way, Lady." The woman hastily led the way to an alcove. "I sought to tell Lady Ennui, but she's not at her desk."

"She's weaving," Gale said tersely as she looked desperately around.

Ini appeared. "No sighting," she reported.

Belatedly Gale recognized the place. "This is the private ramp!"

"Yes, Lady," the servant said.

"A ramp?" Ini asked. "Where does it lead?"

"To several floors of the main city. If he got in that—"

"He is out in the city, somewhere," Ini finished.

Gale entered the ramp and ran down it. Ini followed, somewhat clumsily. There was nothing like this in her home zone, and she would have flown down it if there had been. She wasn't used to running down a winding ramp on her feet.

Neither was Gale. In a moment she thought to fly down it. But she didn't want to leave Ini behind. "I'll carry you," she said.

Ini did not protest. She suffered being picked up and carried. Gale floated them rapidly down the spiral, watching for an open portal. If there was none, the baby should still be in the ramp, and the secret was salvageable.

Unfortunately, one was open. Had the baby exited there, or continued on down the ramp?

"If he remains within the ramp, he should be safe for a while," Ini said. "If he exited, he will quickly cause a commotion. Can you track that?"

"Affirmation. Ordinary folk don't mask their minds." Gale extended her awareness—and immediately located the commotion. People were amazed at the appearance of a floating baby, and word was spreading rapidly. It was too late to stifle it; the secret was out.

She set Ini down and ran to the site of the most recent excitement. There was Warp, hovering before a woman standing with her mouth open. Gale quickly captured him and bore him away.

"Appreciation," Ini said to the woman, though all she had done was distract the baby for a moment with her odd expression. Then she followed Gale.

Back in the palace nursery, all babies safe, they discussed the situation. "Did you do any magic in anyone's presence?" Symbol asked.

"Negation. I just took Warp and carried him."

"Then one secret remains. They don't know you're a Glamor."

"But they do know there's a magic baby," Ini said. "I think you will have to make a public announcement before wild rumors start. Just about the babies."

"Agreement," Gale said. "I'll have Ennui set it up." She went for Ennui, still carrying Warp.

"Stay with her," Symbol said, and Ini obeyed. Gale knew that Symbol remained concerned that she, Gale, would do something foolish in her distraction, so was putting a guard on her. It was probably a sensible caution.

Gale entered the loom chamber, and paused at sight of the tapestry. It was only a tenth finished, but that bottom segment was magnificent. "Awe!"

Ennui glanced their way. She was sitting at the loom, while Aspect and Nonce were sleeping on bunks across the room. That was surprising: the former queen and bath girl sharing quarters. It showed their mutual commitment to this project. "Lady."

"Chore," Gale said, reverting to her spot mission. "Warp floated loose, and people saw him. I must make a formal announcement about the adoptions. Not about Glamors. Can you set it up soon?"

"Affirmation. I will wake Nonce to take my place here—"

"Negation. It can wait its turn." Gale approached the loom, and Warp cooed, fascinated by the complicated device. "I have been distracted, and have not before seen the tapestry. This is a wonder."

"Agreement," Ennui said, resuming her work. "We are curious as to its nature, and there is a mystery about it."

Gale studied the fragment. "Complex colorful scene."

"And it changes even as we weave."

"Well, of course, as more of it is revealed."

"Negation. What we have woven changes."

"Confusion. This does not seem possible."

"Magic," Ennui said. "Both loom and yarn are magic. We weave the picture as directed—yes, something tells us—and the scene is magic. We three are agreed that the picture is shifting, not greatly, but slowly and subtly, as though what we have done is not quite perfect and requires revision. Yet since we are working under direction, why shouldn't we do it correctly? We are mystified."

"Familiarity," Ini said, gazing at the tapestry. "I believe this is not a scene, but a map."

"Revelation!" Ennui exclaimed. "Maps must constantly change, because of the weather's effect on the Chroma zones."

"Speculation," Gale said, excited. "Could the tapestry be showing us where the answer to the mysteries of the origin of the loom and altars is?"

Ennui nodded. "Possibility." She focused on the placement of a thread. "Problem. We are running out of yarn."

"And ordinary yarn will not do," Gale said. "You'll need more magic yarn."

"Affirmation. We can't come close to completing the tapestry without it."

"Is there more in the cave where you found the loom?"

"Negation. We have it all."

"Frustration. Any notion where more might be found?"

"One chance," Ennui said. "When Nonce carried the loom ikon, it guided her toward its physical origin. When that was found, it generated the urgency to weave. Perhaps it will lead us to the yarn."

"But you are in the middle of a tapestry," Gale protested. "You don't want to destroy that to travel."

Ennui smiled. "The loom knows better than that. The tapestry becomes part of the ikon when the loom is carried. We can take it with us."

"Travel," Gale said. "We can provide you with an entourage, guards, transport—"

"Negation. That would spoil the secret. We must travel alone."

"Concern. Three women, unknown destination. Mischief."

"The ikons protect us," Ennui reminded her. "We are like minor Glamors. And my mind contact with Havoc enables me to summon help if it is needed."

"Acquiescence," Gale said, not entirely satisfied. "Travel masked."

"Of course. If the palace can spare us."

Gale smiled. "We'll make mocks of the three of you. It will do."

Ini had been staring at the tapestry. "Observation: this is not necessarily Charm. Perhaps a Cartographer can confirm."

Gale glanced at her. "Why do you suspect it isn't?"

"There is too little as yet to be sure. I have studied Counter Charm, and this fragment could match a segment."

"Counter Charm!" Gale said. "Astonishment."

"My supposition may be misplaced."

"And it may be correct. We shall have a Cartographer view the tapestry."

"Preference," Ennui said. "Get the yarn, complete more of it first, so that identification can be more certain."

That did make sense. "Agreement."

"Question," Ini said. "If the map identifies a place on Counter Charm, where perhaps something is, what use is that to us? We can't go there."

"You forget that Glamors can go there," Gale said, though she suspected that Ini hadn't forgotten. She simply didn't know whether the others were party to Gale's promise to take Ini there if possible. "And I think if we do, we should take you, since you will be more familiar with its nature than we are." That abated that concern.

"Disbelief!" Ini said. "Dream."

"It may be realized. But first we must complete and verify the map."

"Acquiescence," Ini breathed. Had she been in her home zone, she would have floated. Apparently she hadn't allowed herself to believe that the promise wasn't empty.

Gale and Ini returned to the nursery room. "We may have more use of you than we anticipated," Gale said. "And you may like it better than you expected."

"Affirmation," Ini breathed. "Is it possible we are being guided? I mean, that the loom wants you to get the answers you seek, and is helping not only with a map but by summoning others who can help?"

Gale considered. "Possible. But more likely chance. If the loom could spread such influence, why wouldn't it simply summon someone with the answer?"

"The answer may be masked for reason," Ini said. "So that the wrong folk don't get it."

That made sense. They entered the nursery, where Symbol was holding Weft and Flame, who were beginning to fuss. "Relief," she said. "Flame will abide with me, but Weft wants you."

"Adoption is a two way process," Gale agreed, taking Weft with her free arm. She was able to nurse both Warp and Weft, but the two were becoming competitive about her attention at other times. She would have to see whether Havoc could distract Weft on occasion, to keep the peace. "We have made progress in understanding." She and Ini explained.

Next day Havoc returned, having braved the problems of attempted assassination and sex with a non-Glamor, and stood with Gale as she made her formal announcement. It was actually her first, and made her nervous, but she felt this was her province and she shouldn't make Havoc do it. He stood beside her and let her carry it. Offstage Symbol, Bijou, and Ini held the three babies, who were miraculously quiet. For the moment. They were dressed in fancy little outfits, the boy in blue, the girls in red with red ribbons in their hair.

She stood on the dais overlooking the great assembly room of the city, with massed faces looking up at her, and she felt nervous in a way that singing and playing her hammer dulcimer never had caused. She was not performing this time as a minstrel, but as queen, and the expectations were different.

She froze.

The sea of faces gaped at her, making it worse. She couldn't speak.

Havoc, reading her locked mind, sent a thought to Ennui, who hurried away. Then he spoke to the audience. "Queen Gale and I have an announcement to make, but it is of such nature that we decided that a special presentation was warranted. I'm not supposed to belch."

There was a roar of laughter. Havoc's deliberate loud belch at his first public address as king had become a social landmark; he was the *barbarian* king. The mock king did it frequently at appearances; it was expected. Bless Havoc; he was covering for her, making her silence part of the act until she could recover. *If* she recovered; she had never before messed up like this.

"We have done something that not even experienced barbarian watchers anticipated," Havoc continued after a pause. "We hope you will approve and support us. There have been some wild rumors; rest assured that the truth is much worse." He paused for another appreciative laugh. The people loved to see Havoc live up to his name. He was such a showman, bless him.

Ennui returned with two musical instruments: Havoc's dragon scale and Gale's hammer dulcimer. Now she understood his ploy: he was making this into a musical presentation, something she had done many times before. She might be tongue tied in speech, but she knew she could still play and sing. She accepted her dulcimer, and put the little hammers on her fingers, feeling much better.

Havoc strummed his scale, evoking its peculiar resonance. He sang: one of the oldest of the folk songs dating from their ancestors of Planet Earth, a thousand years before. He had a fine voice and barbarian enthusiasm. This was new to the citizens of Triumph City; Havoc had never sung in public before—not as king. He was surprising them, and that was good.

> I gave my love a cherry that had no stone
> I gave my love a chicken that had no bone
> I gave my love a ring that had no end
> I gave my love a baby with no crying

The last line roused the audience, for the wild rumors concerned a baby who indeed had not been crying. That was the least remarkable thing about it.

Now it was Gale's turn. Havoc faced her, silencing his instrument, assuming a pose of listening. She lifted her dulcimer, hammered the refrain, addressed him, and sang:

How can there be a cherry that has no stone?
How can there be a chicken that has no bone?
How can there be a ring that has no end?
How can there be a baby with no crying?

Havoc nodded knowingly, and so did many heads in the audience; they were of course thoroughly familiar with the song. He made the revelations as if they were the first ever heard, his dragon scale lending authority.

A cherry when it's blooming it has no stone

He produced a flower and presented it to her with a flourish. The audience didn't know he had conjured it; it seemed like prestidigitation.

A chicken when it's pippin' it has no bone

An egg appeared in his hand. He held it to his ear as if to hear the chick knocking on the inside of the shell, ready to break out: pipping. And in a moment the shell did break and the chick started to emerge. He quickly returned it to the mother hen, who appeared at the side of the stage.

A ring when it's rolling it has no end

He produced a ring, rolled it across his dragon scale, then put it on her finger, kissing her hand. There was an oooh of appreciation from the women in the audience.

He paused, setting aside his instrument, and took Warp from Ini. He held him aloft with a flourish and sang:

A baby when it's sleeping has no crying.

At that moment Warp, not comfortable with the exposure, began to fuss. Havoc's personal magic had finally messed up. The audience laughed, loving the irony. Gale hastily put aside her dulcimer and took him, the hammers still attached to her fingers. He was quiet, intrigued by the hammers. The audience applauded.

Havoc fetched Flame from Symbol and presented her to the audience and to Gale. "But I think two is better than one," he said. Now there was a wave of surprise; one baby explained much of the rumors, but two went beyond them.

Gale accepted the second baby, affecting surprise. She faced the audience, showing them off.

Havoc fetched Weft from Bijou. "And three is better yet," he said with mock barbarian naiveté. "Might as well do it right."

Gale, her arms full, merely looked at him. The audience roared its delight; this was exactly the kind of mistake a barbarian would make, overdoing it.

Havoc looked at the audience as he cuddled Weft, who clearly liked the attention. "Maybe I better stop there," he confided. The audience agreed. Then he changed his mind. "But we need a fourth." He pondered a moment, then lifted a finger. "I know: I put the fourth inside her." He glanced significantly at Gale.

Gale couldn't help herself: she blushed. The audience saw this confirmation, and cheered. They did indeed have the required four, albeit in reverse order.

After that it was easy. Gale explained how she had learned of the magic babies, and felt that no ordinary family could handle them, so it was her obligation as queen to adopt them. That went over well; the king and queen were expected to be larger than life. They had the babies demonstrate their magic, using key words learned in the invisible Chroma. Warp floated, confirming the rumors; Weft snatched a bright bauble by conjuration; and Flame ignited a torch. They were definitely magic babies, and the audience was highly impressed; most of them had never seen nonChroma people of any age do magic.

Havoc had the last word: "After all, how could a barbarian king give his love an ordinary baby?" The applause lasted long after they departed the stage.

They returned to the nursery. Gale was overflowing with delight and gratitude for the way Havoc had rescued her from embarrassment and made such a great show of it. "Take over for a little while," she told Symbol. "I've got to make fantastic love to Havoc."

Symbol, Bijou, and Ini took the babies, and Gale took Havoc into the royal bedroom and flung herself at him. She was flushed from the on-stage experience, and her desire was overwhelming. They were out of their robes in a moment and on the bed. She made Havoc climax three times in five minutes, in one continuing Glamor act of love. "I think I just figured out why I married you," she gasped as she climaxed herself.

"Three times as much sex?" he asked.

She clamped her cleft on him, hard, as mock punishment. "That, too."

Then they got up, cleaned and dressed quickly, and rejoined the others in the nursery.

Symbol, Bijou, and Ennui were sprawled suggestively in chairs, while the three babies were in their cribs with stares of wonder. None of them got up when king and queen entered. Only Ini was alert. "Confusion," she said. "They all just collapsed in bliss."

"Oops," Havoc murmured. "We forgot to shield our minds."

And the women had gotten a stiff mental dose of phenomenal sex at very close range. Only Ini, who was not telepathic, had escaped. "Apology," Gale said. But she wasn't unduly chagrined, knowing that the three other women could have closed their minds to the incoming emotion if they had wanted to. Then she realized that the babies might have received it too; Warp had demonstrated mind shielding, which implied telepathy, and the others might not be far behind. She hoped they hadn't understood the feeling.

That afternoon Gale left Symbol in charge again, and took Ini with her for a Glamor conjuration to the changeling complex. Mneme saw them immediately, of course. "Problem?"

"Mixed," Gale said. "We like the babies, but we judge they are young Glamors, therefore left ikons behind. We need to recover those ikons. Give us the addresses from which they were recovered."

Mneme nodded. "You understand, Lady, that such information must not be imparted to the families?"

"Affirmation. We hope to recover the ikons without notice. My associate is of the Invisible Chroma, so can search inconspicuously."

"That seems best," Mneme agreed. She gave them the information. Warp and Weft had been implanted in sisters at one village, and Flame at another village.

Gale clasped Ini and conjured them to the region of the first village. Then she extended her awareness—and found a small region of blankness. "I think I have located one," she said. "Glamors can't handle ikons directly, so it makes sense that there would be a bit of mind blanking too. But I can take us closer to it."

She did so. The fuzzy patch was in a village, which meant that they would have to fetch it from a yard or house. "I can change my appearance," Gale said. "But I'm not very good at that yet."

"Let me investigate," Ini said. She stripped away all her clothing and disappeared. "Give me as precise a direction and range as you can; I lack your ability to track it."

"This direction," Gale said, pointing. "About a hundred paces."

"On my way."

Gale followed her by her mind as she entered the village and walked to the indicated spot. It was behind a house, and Ini circled the house, but didn't spot any ikons. *Idea*, she thought. *Can you emulate my Chroma? Make yourself invisible?*

Chagrin! I never thought of that. Because emulating invisibility was much easier than designing alternate clothing. Then she realized that Ini was not telepathic, and could not pick up her thought; she had merely made her thoughts distinct for Gale to read. Gale focused on her hand, causing it to fade, and when she had the technique she extended it to the rest of her body. She was invisible. Then she focused on sound, making herself inaudible too. And on smell, to fool the village dogs.

She walked into the village to join Ini. There were a few children playing, watched by an older woman; they were unaware of her. She joined Ini. "I am beside you," she murmured.

Make a more precise location of the ikon.

Gale did. It was between the raised roots of a tree behind the house. She whispered it to Ini, who got down and peered into the region. *Success,* she thought. *Two ikons.* She picked them up with two hands and held them aloft for Gale to see.

A little mushroom and a little spiral. Warp and Weft, surely. A double victory.

These must represent the fungi and the bacteria, Ini thought. She couldn't receive Gale's thoughts, but knew Gale could receive hers, so formed them clearly. *The third one may be a blob for amoeba, or slime for viri.*

"They won't give you diseases," Gale murmured. "Put them in your mouth, and I'll carry you clear of here."

Ini obliged, putting them in her two cheeks. The ikons seemed to float in the air at head height, as her invisibility did not affect them. *I can't put them together; they repel each other.*

That was interesting; ikons were cautious about their own contacts. Gale did not remember such an effect when they had gathered the ikons of the existing Glamors, but it might not have been noticed in the rush of other events. Gale sought to clasp her for the conjuration, but couldn't.

The ikons. Glamors can't touch them.

"But we can carry those who hold them, if we're careful. It must be that one is the limit."

I will set one down. We'll have to make two trips. The mushroom separated from the spiral and floated to the ground.

Gale tried again, and this time was able to clasp the woman. She conjured them to the place they had been outside the village. Ini set the ikon in the crook of a tree, and they returned to the village for the spiral.

"This is apt to become cumbersome," Gale said.

"Especially with three."

"Also, who will keep them? I hadn't thought of that."

"Does anyone need to carry them?" Ini asked. "Why not simply store them in a safe place?"

"Ideal! Where no stranger will find them. I know a place near my home village, Trifle. It's an island in a stream, just below fierce rapids, accessible only via the fringe of a Red Chroma zone into which the river flows. So neither Chroma nor nonChroma folk go there."

"Let's fetch the third ikon, then ferry them there." Ini put the second ikon with the first, in the tree, not touching.

Gale clasped her, and conjured them to the vicinity of the second village, where Flame had come from. She spread awareness, and located the ikon. It did turn out to be a realistic bit of slime, made of impervious metallic material. No one had noticed it, lying near a small spring where the baby must have been set while her mother dipped water. No one would have wanted it.

Now they ferried them to the island. Gale carried Ini there three times. Then they considered how to stash the ikons.

The island was hardly larger in diameter than Gale's spread arms, with the water coursing past on its way into the red Chroma zone. Thick brush grew on it, surely holding it in place. "I think I'd better make a tight container the shape of a mossy rock," Gale said. "With a magic warner so that I will know if anyone molests it."

"Suitably anchored," Ini agreed. "But I will know where it is. Suppose someone reads my thoughts?"

"It is time you learned mind shielding," Gale said. "I will teach you. You deserve some mental privacy." Meanwhile she formed the rock, not yet putting the moss on it. Ini set the three ikons into it, in three corners. Then Gale used her mind to excavate a hole to set it in—and paused. "Something is here."

It turned out to be a buried metal chest containing a collection of Chroma gems. "Brigands must have stored their loot here," Ini said. "They may return. Can you tell how long it has been?"

Gale discovered another Glamor ability. She touched the chest with her mind and found that it had been undisturbed for more than fifty years. "They must have gotten killed, and their secret died with them. You can have their treasure."

"I can't use any but an Invisible gem."

"Take the others anyway; they will be excellent for trading to Chroma folk who are traveling." Gale smiled. "You are now rich."

"Would they buy me a good man?"

"The kind you want can't be bought."

"Agreement," Ini said sadly. "I wish I could find one interested in everything except beauty."

"Such men exist." Gale liked Ini, who was so unlike her sexy older sisters Ina and Ine. She made a private resolve to find a suitable man for her before the year was out.

"It won't work," Ini said. Then, as Gale glanced at her, startled: "No, I'm not telepathic. But I have had this dialogue with others, so know their next thought. I shall have to find my own man."

"Idea. Maybe I can increase your opportunity. We have that other quest I mentioned, the search for the altars. That is bound to take a party to far places around the planet. Havoc thought to send Bijou to enlist two Chroma changelings for that, since Glamors can't approach the place. But Bijou now needs to emulate me when I travel. That leaves an opening, and I think you would be ideal."

"How do you know Glamors can't approach?"

"My friend Swale the succubus discovered another vague region that could be it. The Red Glamor tried to explore it, and could not. If you are willing to host Swale for a time, she will lead you to it."

Ini laughed. "It will take more than a succubus to make me sexy!"

"I am not sure of that. Swale is very good at what she does. Anyway, if you are amenable—"

"Amenable," Ini agreed.

They abolished the chest and set the stone in its place, tied firmly into the ground. Then Gale grew a special type of moss on it, that was poisonous to most creatures. Only a person who knew exactly what he was doing would find it safe to meddle here. While they worked, Gale explained the nature of a mind shield, that not only concealed private thoughts, but made it seem that they did not exist. She told Ini when she started to get it right.

The job was done. Gale clasped Ini, and they returned to the palace. It had been a challenging but good day, all told.

Chapter 3—Altar

Augur was surprised to see the invisible woman. She was completely swathed in clothing, including hat, veil, and gloves, so that no part of her flesh was exposed. That was the way it had to be for travelers from the Invisible Chroma.

"Salutation," he said.

"Acknowledged," she responded. "I seek Augur and Aura."

"I am Augur, and my fiancée is Aura. We live here in the Purple Chroma zone, where our respective Red and Blue Chroma overlap."

"I am Ini, of the Air Chroma, now on duty for King Havoc. The king requires your participation in a quest for the source of certain objects. Read my mind." She assumed a pose that suggested she was laying her mind open.

"I am not telepathic, but I can judge sincerity. State your thoughts."

"It is true; I am on the king's business, and you and Aura are summoned. You are to assume charge of the mission."

He nodded, believing her. "Acquiescence. The day is late; retire with us this night, and we will proceed in the morning."

Ini nodded. "Appreciation."

Augur exchanged a glance with Aura. The king had surely sent a worthy emissary. This would also get them safely away from their home Chroma zones, which was good.

They provided the woman with suitable lodging and conjured dinner. She removed her veil, making her head seem empty, so that she could eat. The food remained visible as it passed through her face and descended into her torso. Neither Augur nor Aura had had much experience with otherChroma folk, so this was interesting, but courtesy prevented comment. While they ate, they explained their situation, as Ini was not conversant with it.

"I am of the Red Chroma, obviously," the red man said. "My friend Aura is of the Blue Chroma. We met in this overlap zone in the course of our work. I am a specialist in plants, and she in animals; we were studying and cataloguing them, and worked together for a time."

"But we were also spies for our Chroma zones," Aura continued. "I deceived him, seduced him, and prevailed on him to betray his zone, then joined him and was condemned with him. An outside jury consisting of two travelers was selected to decide which one of us should die, and which would suffer that loss."

"Cruelty!" Ini exclaimed.

"We did not know then that the travelers were Throe, the king's bodyguard, and the Lady Gale, the king's fiancée," Augur said. "They arranged to provide an answer that prevented any execution and caused the authorities of both our zones to reconsider. Now we are free to depart at such time as the king requires it."

"As he is now doing," Aura concluded. "Our zones do not want us back; we are exiled. So this mission, whatever it may be, is to our liking. It will enable us to be together, and useful to the king."

The Air Chroma woman had listened with attention, her face invisible but her swathed head turning alertly to face the speakers. "I will clarify the mission when we are in a nonChroma zone, secure from Chroma magic."

"We shall be traveling far?" Augur asked.

"I believe so."

"No fault?" Aura asked.

The woman's head looked at her, and for an instant there was something eerie in her veiled expression. "I do not seek to preempt your man. Even if I wished to, I am of homely aspect and would not appeal to him. So in that sense, no."

Augur was relieved. He could of course indulge in sex with any woman, and on occasion did, but his overwhelming preference was for Aura. He knew she felt the same about him.

But he had another caution. "You are aware that we are Chroma folk, but we are unable to do magic in other Chroma or in nonChroma. Unless we travel in Red or Blue Chroma zones, we will be in effect nonChroma folk."

"My own experience," Ini said. "I am not comfortable outside my Chroma, and not merely because of the way I must dress. But there is a reason the mission must be this way."

They nodded. After dinner they showed Ini around the Purple Chroma zone with its unusual plants and animals. Then they retired for the night.

In the morning they packed staples and set off walking. They had hardly started out before Augur suffered a miscue. He tried to conjure a walking cane to his hand, and it didn't come: no magic here in the nonChroma zone.

Aura noticed. "I just tried to fly up to treetop height to verify the trail ahead," she murmured.

"We know better, but we have automatic habits."

"I had similar problems," Ini said. "Magic is so convenient, it is hard to give up. We depend on it in so many ways."

When they were well into nonChroma territory, Aura had a question. "Though we are not telepathic, there are those in our Chroma zones who are, and there are other ways to eavesdrop in a Chroma zone, so we did not question you closely about a private mission. But I am curious: how did you find us? Did you have specific directions?"

"Negation. I was guided by a spirit. Perhaps it is time I introduced her. She is Swale, a succubus."

"Horror! You are possessed?"

"Negation. The woman you met, Queen Gale, tamed her, and now she serves as convenient liaison and protection."

"Disbelief! Sexual spirits are notorious; we are warned against them as children."

"Agreement. But Queen Gale is an unusual woman. When the succubus tried to take over her body, she fought, and such was her strength and determination, she prevailed and made the spirit captive. Thereafter she treated Swale with courtesy, and helped rescue her mortal brother from captivity, and won her loyalty and friendship. She has become a vital member of the king's team of supporters."

"I agree that Gale is a remarkable woman. But a succubus! How can she ever be trusted?"

"I was doubtful myself, but I have had experience with Queen Gale and with the man you met, the king's bodyguard Throe. They both swear by Swale, and I believe their judgment. At any rate, Swale guided me here, and will guide us to the region we suspect is the source of the ikon altars."

Augur found this dialogue interesting and alarming. A succubus had a special appeal and threat to men. "Plea: keep her away from me."

Ini smiled. "You have but to avoid indulging in sex with me. That should not be difficult."

"You say you are of homely aspect, but your face and body are invisible. I am not sure you would not be sexually compelling if possessed by a succubus."

"And a succubus could draw out your soul at the moment of climax," Ini said. "You are right to be cautious. But if you care to feel my face and form, you will verify that I am no seductive maiden."

Augur glanced at Aura. She nodded. She was of course just as concerned as he was about such a threat, and if they shared company continuously for an extended period, it was better to ascertain the situation at the outset.

"I will touch you, no fault," he said.

"No fault," she agreed, stripping away her upper clothing and becoming invisible from the waist up.

He put his hands slowly to the region of her head, found it, and ran them across her hair and face. The hair was lank rather than bouncy, and her facial features were rough-hewn for a woman. He moved on down to her neck, shoulders, and breasts, which were respectively scrawny, bony, and small. She was definitely no beauty.

"Do you wish to check the rest?" her voice came from air.

He glanced down into the oval of her skirt's waistband, and saw the insides of her leggings and shoes. The form of the leggings made it plain that her legs were muscular rather than shapely. "Negation."

"So even if I came to you at night, naked, I would not be very seductive," the invisible voice said as the upper clothing reformed around her body. "And I have no intention of doing so."

"But if you were governed by the succubus, it would be a different matter," Aura said.

"Do you wish to see her use my body?"

"Presuming that this would be for demonstration only, not for real seduction," Aura said. Augur heard the nervousness in her voice; she had a healthy wariness of the power of a sexual spirit.

"No need," Augur said, not easy about this.

"I want to know the limit of the threat," Aura said. "Now, in full daylight, to be sure I need not fear it at night."

"I will give Swale control for a limited time," Ini said. "I would not do so, were I not assured she means no mischief. I have come to know her during my travel here."

Then the swathed figure changed. She put her hands to her head, setting the hat at a jaunty angle. She converted the veil to a loose scarf. She adjusted the blouse to make it fit more closely about her bosom. She lifted the hem of her skirt, pinning it shorter. One swathed leg angled in to touch the other at the knee, and her opposite hip became more prominent. Then she addressed Augur. "Introduction: I am Swale." Even her voice was different; it had become sultry.

"Augur," he said, surprised by the extent of the change. She had become several degrees sexier despite being entirely covered.

"I am not going to seduce you, red man," she said. "This is merely to demonstrate that I could." She shifted her hips, and even masked by the unattractive skirt they became intensely appealing to him. There was something about their motion and angle that inspired his sexual interest.

"Acquiescence," he said, not wanting to challenge her to further effort.

"And if I did seduce you, I wouldn't take your soul," she continued, subtly adjusting her pose for greater effect. "I could, but would not. Gale first defeated me by power, then tamed me by kindness; I love her and serve her will." She shook her upper section in a small but significant way, making her breasts quiver under the cloth. That, too, was remarkably effective.

"No contest," he said. She was attracting him far more than he cared to reveal. It was amazing that such an ordinary body could transform to such allure without even showing itself. Had she been naked and visible, he would have had to fight to stop from clasping her.

"And even if I took your soul, I would return it. I took King Havoc, by his request, so that he could travel with me and spy out his situation expediently."

"King Havoc!" Augur exclaimed.

"He had sex with Gale, while I possessed her, and I took his soul. Once his mission was done, I returned him to his body, via his penis. It was quite an encounter."

"*I* had sex with Gale!" Augur said, appalled in retrospect.

"I could have taken you then, had I been with her, had she wished me to. But I don't ask you to trust me, just to be aware of my presence and power." The figure stepped forward, whipped off her veil, and kissed him with her invisible face. There was a musky woman smell about her that made him think of glistening naked anatomy.

Augur would have stepped back to avoid it, had he not been caught by surprise. He would have broken it immediately, had her lips not been marvelously compelling. Instead he found himself holding her evocative body, his groin yearning toward hers, his chest aware of her feminine breasts against it. Her expressive mouth sent radiations of longing through him. Oh yes, she could seduce him, even in this body, if she chose.

She broke and stepped back, leaving him half stunned. "Now you know. If you ever truly desire me, let me know and I will borrow the Lady Ini's body again for the occasion, and neither she nor you will regret it. I love sex, and always want more of it. But you will have to ask, so that I know I am not going beyond social limits."

Augur desired her right now, but did not want to say it. She had instilled in him a phenomenal sexual urgency. "Acknowledged," he said, hoping his racing pulses were not evident.

"Do it," Aura said. "Now."

Such was the compulsion of the succubus he had forgotten his beloved's presence. "Aura, this is not wise."

"I want to know the limit of the threat," she repeated. "If she means to take your soul, she can do it at any time. Give her opportunity now, and if she does not, we can believe that she does not mean to."

Ini spoke; her voice was unmistakable. "She does not mean to take your soul. But she does not have to demonstrate this with my body; she can instill herself in Aura's body for the demonstration, if you prefer."

"Negation!" Aura snapped.

"But that way she could demonstrate, without slighting you," Augur said, still trying to mask how desperately he now wanted sex.

"I will not have that demon spirit in my body!"

Swale returned. "I do not take women's souls, I merely occupy their bodies so as to seduce men. But it would not be an effective demonstration with you, because you are a beautiful blue woman. You could seduce him on your own."

"Point," Aura agreed. "I have done so. Use the Invisible body, if Ini is willing."

Ini returned. "I said not no fault because I did not wish to cause discomfort, either to you for seeing your man borrowed, or to him for being required to do it with a homely woman. But I am sixteen, and must soon enough marry; I have little experience with sex, for obvious reason. I would like to have such experience, and I would love to be embraced by a man as handsome and intelligent as Augur, even if I am not the one who stirs his passion. Swale's presence and nature arouse me. I am more than willing."

That was uncomfortable candor. "I wish to watch," Aura said.

"Naturally," Swale said. "But there will not be much to see. Let's find a bower, unless you prefer it standing in the open."

Augur was so charged up that he hardly cared. In a moment they were under a spreading tree, forming a bed of soft needles. Swale threw off her clothing, becoming completely invisible, and he stripped also. Then she stepped into him, kissing him again, and her body felt lush and eager. His soul might be in danger; at this moment he didn't care. They sank to the ground, embraced, and almost immediately he was thrusting into her, climaxing powerfully.

As he ebbed, he became more aware of the situation. He was lying on invisibility; only his own jet of semen showed just below him, a little red puddle in the air. Aura stood beside them, her face expressionless; he hesitated to judge what she was thinking.

"That—that was amazing," he gasped.

"I did not take your soul," Swale reminded him.

"Acknowledgment. I can't remember having such urgency or fulfillment before." He glanced up at Aura. "No offense, beloved."

"None," she agreed. "She is certainly a succubus."

"Now it is done," he said, ready to disengage. He was still in her, but flaccid.

"I can make him do it again," Swale said to Aura, not releasing him.

Aura cocked her head. "Interest."

"Doubt," Augur said. He knew his limits; twice in rapid succession was not likely.

For answer, the succubus resumed activity. She kissed him, this time using her tongue, and her breasts slid against him, swelling. Her buttocks tightened and her cleft closed around his member, massaging it peristaltically. He had no choice but to respond. His softened member hardened again, and soon, carried along by what felt almost like suction, jetted a second time. This time the succubus rolled him over while it was happening, so that Aura could see every detail. His penis was spewing over his own belly, the viscous red liquid hovering at its tip.

"Satisfaction," Aura said, sounding not entirely pleased. She had indeed been shown up as sexually amateur, though neither of them had thought that before.

"Technique is everything. Almost any body will do." Swale gave Augur another internal squeeze, and he realized that he was not through with her until she was through with him. "I can instruct you," she said, still speaking to Aura.

"Agreement!"

Augur, surprised by her vehemence, had to laugh.

"I enjoyed it too," Ini said.

That embarrassed him, obscurely; he had been aware only of the succubus. Now the anatomy had lost its intensity; Ini did not have command of such technique.

She let him go, and they stood. A coating of needles showed the invisible woman's backside before she brushed them off. Ini went around the tree to clean up, and he realized that she did not want to embarrass them both by cleaning out his red essence before them.

"Maybe next time I will let her use my body," Aura said. "That was a considerable demonstration, and she did not take your soul."

"Considerable," he agreed.

Ini donned her clothing, becoming visible again. They resumed their walk. "Question."

"Yes, it is permissible to talk about the recent experience," Aura said.

"Swale has gone elsewhere at the moment. She comes and goes, staying in touch with the folk at the palace. I came to know her during my journey here, but there was no sex. My only prior experience was with Throe, when he was required to have sex with me and my sisters to decide which of us was best for our boyfriend." She chuckled ruefully. "Throe fooled us all; he selected our little sister Ino, whom he had not even met, and she was indeed the best choice. Anyway, it wasn't perfect with Throe; neither of us really wanted it, but we were obliged. But this time, with the succubus—it was wondrous."

"Agreement," Augur said. "You—your body—became awesomely conducive. I could not help myself."

"Evident," Aura said wryly.

"Swale is a spirit, and I think her essence extends beyond the body," Ini said. "So she was intersecting you before she touched you with my body. She probably heightened your desire with her magic. There may also be some illusion; for example, I felt as though my breasts were larger."

"My impression too," Augur said. "Remember, I felt them before we started, so I had a basis for comparison."

"And my—my interior—"

"Took hold of me, kneaded me, sucked me," Augur said. "I'm sure that was not your doing."

"Agreement! Yet overall, it was an outstanding experience, even though I don't believe I climaxed."

"Apology. Normally I regard sex as a mutual endeavor. But my urgency was such that I was unable to wait."

"Accepted. I believe I had a better experience with her control than would have been the case had I climaxed on my own. But if we ever—that is—"

Augur exchanged a glance with Aura, who nodded. "Perhaps no fault is in order after all."

"Negation!" Ini said. "I don't want to interfere with your relationship. I should not have spoken."

But it was clear that she had had a good but partial experience with sex, and deserved completion. "No fault *means* it does not affect other relationships. I admit to curiosity about the difference between sex with your body and sex with you. I will be with you this night."

Obviously feeling guilty but gratified, Ini was able only to nod.

They followed the winding trail between Chroma zones, because they could do magic only in their own Chroma and it was better to remain where no one else could do magic. This was a private mission, so they could not say they were on the king's business so as to commandeer cooperation.

They came to one of the camping areas that were judiciously spaced along the trail. There was a fireplace with wood and tinder. Augur set it up, then snapped his fingers to make fire—and paused, reminded again that even this simple magic did not work here. They found suitable stones and struck sparks somewhat clumsily until the fire caught.

"There is something else," Ini said as they ate. Augur couldn't help noticing how the food seemed to masticate itself in her facial region, then flow in gobs below it. He knew it would disappear as she digested it, but the effect was interesting. "There are dangers along these trails, because brigands know that Chroma travelers are without their magic here. So we shall have protection. But it has to be inconspicuous."

"We are armed," Augur said. "We both know knife fighting."

"Brigands try not to give travelers an even chance. They may come with swords."

"Now I am interested in protection," he said, trying to make light of it though he was concerned.

"Glamor protection. You know of Glamors?"

"Only by rumor," Aura said. "Are they real?"

"It turns out they are, and they support the king. This is a king's errand, so Swale is keeping watch, and if there is a threat, she will notify a Glamor. The Glamor will investigate, and take appropriate action. But the Glamor will try to make it seem that our salvation is coincidence, masking the action. So things could become strange on occasion."

"Understanding," Augur said. "Appreciation."

As it happened, their first day was uneventful. Tired from the unusual amount of walking, they settled into a campsite at dusk. They used the facilities, which included a supply of food, washed, and settled for the night.

"I will take a separate room," Aura said. She was honoring their agreement to let Ini try it alone with Augur.

"I do not demand this of you," Ini said awkwardly as they stripped for the bed.

"I demand it of myself," he said diplomatically. "I used your body, rather than having a relation with you. That was unfair."

"You are a decent man. Still, I feel guilty. You should be with your beloved." She had disappeared, but her voice made her location plain.

"Aura understands. Soon we will marry. We would have married a year ago, when we turned eighteen, but first our spy missions and then our trial put us in limbo and we could not. Now the king's mission has freed us from that stasis, and when it is done, we shall at last have full joy of each other."

"I am glad to be the agent of that freeing. Yet—"

"And even were we married now, no fault remains. Now I will touch you."

"Acquiescence," she murmured.

But this time he found her invisible body stiff and barely responsive. "I understood you wanted this," he said, taken aback.

"I do. But I know myself to be inept in this respect, and am ashamed to put you through this ordeal."

Unfortunately, the way she was now, it *would* be an ordeal, for both of them. He could perform the sexual act, but her body was not evocative the way it had been with the succubus, and his entry would surely pain her. Yet he was reluctant to give up on it, because he knew she truly wanted it. He needed to make her relax, to warm to him, to forget her stage fright. But he couldn't ply her with praise for her beauty; they would both know he was lying.

So he stalled, hoping that something feasible would occur to him soon. "May we talk for a while instead?"

"Relief!"

He had to smile at her candor. "Let me tell you about our studies in the Purple Chroma zone, where we were when you came to us."

"Interest."

They had given her a token tour, showing off the purple poisonous snake Aura had tamed and the land squid they called Grandfather Tree, but there was much more. "I am a specialist in plant life, and Aura in animal life, as you know," he said. "We discovered that our disciplines overlapped; there is no perfect distinction between some plants and animals. Odd forms developed in the overlap zone, as if stimulated by the influence of two colors of magic. We were both fascinated, quite apart from our missions as spies. This surely contributed to our interest in each other; we respected each other's minds and expertise."

"Enthusiasm. I love to learn all I can about all I encounter."

She was clearly serious; he felt her body relaxing. So he continued, telling of their discoveries in detail. Ini reacted with questions that showed her quick understanding. It became evident that she was an intelligent woman, dedicated to acquiring knowledge. It was a pleasure sharing it with her, and he was glad he had thought of this. She was coming alive.

"But I am talking too much," he said at last. "Tell me of your interests."

She was glad to. "The Chroma—the colors of magic—I believe they are not so much magic in themselves, but catalysts for the larger magic that is everywhere, even in nonChroma zones. So your purple Chroma has a double catalyst."

This was unexpected. "But the volcanoes blow out all that colored magic matter! The effect abates where the color does, and there is no magic in the nonChroma zones."

"You know better than that. Consider Swale: she is magic, and she functions readily in nonChroma. Consider us: if there were no magic here, how could you be red, Aura blue, or I invisible? Lingering stain might account for the two of you, but not for me. And the Glamors do magic anywhere."

"Revelation," he agreed. "There *is* magic in nonChroma. But it is because we retain our natures. The succubus is a demon spirit with no body of her own; she borrows from those she inhabits. And the Glamors—I suspect you know more of them than I do. How can they do magic anywhere?"

She was glad to answer. "When they become Glamors, they fission into two aspects: the Glamor and an ikon. The ikon is like a little stone, a pebble, in a relevant shape, like a fish, dragon, or bit of moss, depending on the Glamor's constituency."

"Constituency?"

"Each Glamor represents a category of life, such as the fish, birds, insects, or trees. That life form sustains the Glamor, and the Glamor supports that life form."

"I had heard that each Chroma had a Glamor, and that all are human."

"Half true. Each Chroma has a Glamor, and nonChroma has several."

"Several! But nonChroma—"

"Does after all have magic. A number are human, but others are animal."

"Shock! Animal Glamors!"

"Who are as smart as the humans, and telepathic, for the most part. They work through their Chroma, but represent their constituencies. And they can't be detected when they do not wish to be known, even by other Glamors. It is believed that their ikons remain in their home Chroma and transmit magic power to them, enabling them to function anywhere. But I believe that it is not magic that is transmitted, but a—a catalyst, a mechanism to translate the local magic into usable power. It is similar with ordinary Chroma folk: your Chroma enables you to draw on the universal magic of the planet. It is a—a language, a way to enable you to relate. I think this is a better explanation."

"Amazement! You know more of this matter than I do, and have thought it through more carefully. I am impressed."

"Appreciation," she said, melting.

Then, wordlessly, he embraced her, kissed her, stroked her, and entered her, and she responded avidly. Now there was no tightness; her body was animated and eager to cooperate. There was no hurry; in fact he preferred to prolong it, which was easy enough to do after the two times he had performed earlier in the day. Only when she climaxed did he do so himself, and it was a very satisfying experience, though it was neither as intense nor as polished as before.

"Oh Augur," she gasped. "Eternal appreciation! Now I know what sex can be."

"Now you know," he agreed.

"Favor."

"Ask."

"May I continue to hold you for a while? I know it is over, yet I have such longing to extend the pretense while I can."

"Granted." He held her and turned them both so that she was lying on top of him. "But it is not pretense. When you offered your body, it was not appealing, but when you offered your mind it was conducive, and I responded. Your intelligence, your animation, your initiative, your commitment to knowledge—these are beautiful in their own fashion, transforming my perception of you. I simply had to have you, and believe you had similar emotion."

"Affirmation!" she exclaimed, clasping and kissing him. "I forgot to be afraid of my ugliness or incompetence. It became natural to follow through with my body."

He nodded in the darkness. "I did it because it was natural, and I did not think you would object."

"Object!" She giggled, running her hands across his body, stroking his sides and thighs. "Did you mean to say 'initiative'? That's the long form of my name."

He smiled. "Affirmation. Initiative was in order at that point. I knew you wanted it, but would not demand it. You are not the succubus. Even to speak of it, before the act, would make it negative. So I obliged you—and myself. And it was as wonderful in its way as it was with the succubus, albeit it less intense."

She shuddered with pleasure. "Tell, me, Augur—is this what love feels like? Because in this moment I think I love you."

"Affirmation. In this moment I love you also, with no detraction from my love for Aura. It is passion-inspired, and will not last, but it is nice for a time."

She kissed him again. Her body remained lively, and evocative because of it. "I do not wish to presume, to become troublesome."

"Speak."

"May I touch you and kiss you when I wake in the night? Not for more sex, just for the feeling."

"Delight."

"As you say, the feeling will surely pass. But I think there will always be a little love for you in me. You have opened a door and shown me what is possible. Perhaps I will never experience it again, but I am so glad to have done so this once."

"And I am glad to have discovered you, apart from the succubus." He put his arms around her, stroking her back and bottom. "You are invisible, so my imagination must picture you. You have become lovely." He squeezed a buttock.

"Gratitude."

They lapsed into silence, then into sleep. She slid off him and slept apart, but in the night he woke to feel her hands stroking him, not sexually, just appreciatively. Then she kissed him, and slept again. Indeed it was not sex she craved, but acceptance of herself a worthy of such attention.

In the morning he woke before she did. He felt for her body, carefully, located her face, and kissed her awake. Again she responded, returning the kiss with passion. Then she broke. "If you were mine, I would try to seduce you, just for the feeling of power. But it is a new day and my time with you is done. I love you, and will have the courtesy not to say that again." She rolled off the bed and soon was washing and dressing. He tracked her by the sounds; she remained completely invisible.

"Yet should we have occasion to night together again," he said, "I would not be loath. You are a good woman, Ini."

"I love hearing it, the more because I believe you mean it." Now her visible clothing took shape about her. She was returning to normal.

In due course he performed his own morning ritual. Then, clean, dressed, and in order, they emerged to face the day.

≈≈

Aura saw the two emerge, and knew immediately that they had been successful in sex. Both had been somewhat awkward the night before; now both were relaxed and satisfied. Sex tended to do that, even when no fault.

"Permissible to inquire?" she asked.

"I was all wrong," Ini said immediately. "So we talked instead, and when we forgot about sex, we did it and it was wonderful. I envy you your man, but I need no more of him. He has made a woman of me, and I will always remember."

"You talked of sex, and made it work?"

"Negation," Augur said. "We talked of plants and animals, then of Glamors and ikons. Ini is a remarkably intelligent and knowledgeable woman."

Now it came clear. "And you were always turned on by that."

"Affirmation."

"I have prepared us a breakfast. You must tell me all about Glamors and ikons, and if that makes me hot, you know how to abate it."

Augur smiled. "Agreement."

They ate, and shared information. Aura was glad that Ini had gotten it on with Augur, but also satisfied to have it ended. She preferred having him to herself. However, the information Ini shared about Glamors and ikons was fascinating; before this she had not even known of ikons, but they did make sense. The business about animal Glamors and Chroma as magic catalysts was astonishing. And the fact that there were even nonChroma Glamors—Aura had thought she had a fair understanding of magic, but these were phenomenal revelations.

"Swale has returned," Ini announced as they started their day's trek. "She says we have a long way to go, so may prefer to seek magic transport."

"We lack suitable trading goods," Aura said. "They don't give rides for nothing."

"She says the two of you are handsome folk, as all changelings are. You can sell your favors for transport, and she can enable me to do similar."

"And be the plaything of ugly men?" Aura demanded. "And watch my love seduce middle aged Chroma women? I prefer to walk."

"She says she could make you desire ugly men, and that he could make it with those middle aged women's delicate daughters, who would be glad for the experience with a man like him. She says there is a special appeal about no fault sex with those of alien Chroma."

"We know," Augur said, smiling. "I love my blue alien."

Aura realized that she was being teased. "I prefer to walk," she repeated firmly.

The trail continued between Chroma zones, the colors faint at close range but intensifying in the distance. Aura had not taken such a walk before, and was intrigued. The animals here were of different colors rather than shades of monochrome, and were more furtive than those that had magic defenses. She saw Augur gazing around at the vegetation and knew he was similarly interested.

Then a big animal appeared, barring their way. It was a giant yellow serpent, evidently a stray from the adjacent Yellow Chroma, hunting in this interim territory. It lifted its head, eying them.

"That creature is dangerous," Aura murmured as they halted. "It can digest only one person at a time, but we don't care to lose one third of our party."

"I can use my red gem to repel it," Augur said. As travelers they carried gems that were concentrated aspects of their home Chromas, so that they could do emergency magic. But each use of such a gem depleted it, and their reserves were limited.

"Save your gems," Ini said. "Swale is on it."

"How can a succubus stop a serpent?" Aura asked. "Make it desire sex with us?" She winced at her own facetious remark. What would it be like to be raped by a snake?

"Actually, she could," Ini said. "But it would not be mutually satisfying to the participants. No, she is notifying the Brown Glamor, whose constituency is the one legged creatures."

"Worms!" Aura exclaimed.

"And serpents—and dragons."

Oh. Theoretically the Glamor of Worms could order the serpent off. Aura was dubious, but such an act would confirm part of what Ini had said about the Glamors.

"It is done," Ini said.

"But the serpent is still there."

"It will not attack. In fact—" Ini paused, surprised. "It will now guard us."

"Disbelief!"

"Shared," Augur agreed.

"Understanding," Ini said. "Swale says the Brown Glamor has agreed to make a demonstration."

"The Glamor will show himself?" Augur asked.

"Negation. The direct appearance of a Glamor would prejudice the privacy of this mission. But the serpent will do things you ask, to prove it is now tame."

"I know that species," Aura said. "It is sheer predator; it can not be tamed, only repelled or discouraged."

"All worms are tame for the Glamor. Ask."

"Tell it to roll itself into a loop," Aura said, calling the bluff. She still had her hand on her blue gem. She had no aversion to serpents as such, but this was the most vicious breed, and she was extremely wary.

After a pause, the huge serpent twisted around, caught its tail in its mouth, and formed a circle with its body.

"Coincidence?" Augur asked, obviously impressed.

"Tell it to wrap itself around a tree and lay its head on the ground upside down," Aura said.

Another pause. Then the serpent slithered to a nearby tree, coiled around it, extended its head, and laid it down inverted. That could not be coincidence.

"Surrender," Aura said. "It obeys."

They resumed their walk, and the serpent slithered along parallel to them for a while, then disappeared.

"It is not gone," Ini said. "Swale says it prefers to be out of sight, but it remains on guard."

They had the proof of that an hour later. They encountered three nonChroma men walking the other way. They did not wear brigand outfits, but looked tough and carried obvious weapons: sword, spear, club. "A greeting to each," the sword man called as they approached.

"Acknowledged," Augur said.

They sought to pass and move on, but the men spread out across the trail. "A red man, a blue woman, and a swathed woman—invisible?"

"Confirmation," Ini agreed.

The man took a good look at Aura. "Lovely."

"Appreciation," Aura said tersely.

"No fault?"

"Negation."

The man looked at his companions. "Colored folk don't have magic outside their colors, right?"

The other two nodded. The spearman brought his weapon about in a nominally non-threatening manner, but it oriented on Augur. The third man was hefting his club, as if pondering whether to use it. If these were not brigands, they were nevertheless more than willing to grasp opportunity. Aura grasped her red gem.

"So I ask you again, red girl: no fault?"

"Negation, again."

"Unfortunate." All three strode forward, two brandishing their weapons, the sword man reaching for Aura.

And the big serpent slithered in from the side, so rapidly that its body knocked down the two henchmen as its jaws opened to take the sword man. It never paused; it carried the man screaming into the brush. Then it flipped its head, tossing the man into the air, and caught him with a new grip. The second scream stopped halfway.

The other two men scrambled up and fled.

"I developed an appreciation for serpents," Augur remarked as they resumed their walk.

"It will store the body for later, and return to guard us," Ini said. "It seems we brought it good hunting."

"Welcome," Aura said. But she was shuddering with reaction. She had had no intention of letting herself be raped, but neither would she have killed the man. The denouement had been far more surprising and violent than she cared for.

They walked through the day without further ill event, and camped outside, as there was no prepared site here. Now the huge serpent stretched out and formed a half circle around them, protecting them in sleep. Aura was by now reconciled to that; the serpent had proved itself, and it was true that it represented about as good protection as could be had in the field. She was looking forward to a close evening with Augur; she needed to sleep in his arms, after the horror of the day.

And another woman appeared, walking from the other direction. She was gray, a color Aura hadn't seen before, and slightly heavyset, no beauty. "Greeting, three."

"Acknowledged," the three said almost together.

"Introduction: I am Stevia, of the Gray Chroma, said to be unbearably sweet."

"Aura and Augur, of the Blue and Red Chroma," Aura said. "And Ini, of the Air Chroma."

"Request: I have come far, am fatigued, and have found no campsite. May I share yours, no fault?"

What was there to say? Travelers never denied legitimate no fault. "Welcome," Aura said. "Share my man." With luck, the woman would decline.

The woman turned her gaze on Augur appraisingly. "Appreciation."

Augur had the grace to make the best of it, though Aura knew he was as annoyed as she was. This gray woman was not his type. "It is the traveler's way," he said.

"I have food," Stevia said, removing her backpack. She produced a surprising variety of fruits, vegetables, breads, wine, and smoked meat, all gray. "Enjoy."

"We have protection," Aura said. The serpent had disappeared the moment Stevia hove into view, but of course was close. "Warning: its nature may be alarming."

"That big snake? Acceptance."

Aura was surprised. "You saw the serpent!"

"A lone traveler must be alert." But she did not explain why she had not been alarmed by the serpent's presence.

Aura realized that this was no ordinary lone traveler, but saw no issue to make. Stevia would tell more about herself in due course, if she chose.

They pooled their food supplies, and had an excellent dinner. The gray food tasted exactly like red or blue food, and was surely as nutritious. In this respect color didn't matter; the food wasn't magic. Augur and Aura gave their capsule histories without clarifying their mission, and Ini called herself a fellow traveler. Then it was Stevia's turn.

"Confession," she said. "I did not come upon you three by chance. I happen to know that you are on the king's business. I was sent to help protect you."

"Astonishment!" Aura said.

"Verify it with your succubus," Stevia said, glancing at Ini.

"Already accomplished," Ini said. "This woman has special resources. She can help us."

"Interest," Augur said, understating the case. How could she have known about Swale?

"You may not before have encountered a person of my Chroma," she said. "It is rare. Gray nullifies other magic. This can be helpful on occasion. My hair can also function in particular ways."

"Curiosity," Aura said. She wanted to know a lot more than just about the woman's hair.

"Observe." Stevia did not move, but her hair did. It lengthened, rippling, extending down around her body like a cape. It reached the ground, then flowed across to the others. When it reached Aura's foot, it moistened it. It was wet!

"Suffocation of a hostile creature is possible," Stevia said as her hair drew back into itself, becoming relatively normal. "Or warm enclosure for a friend." She glanced at Augur.

"Surprise," Augur said faintly.

They finished their meal, handled natural functions, and retired for the night. Augur took Stevia at her word, depending on her hair for warmth and protection from bugs, and lent his cloak to Ini. Then Augur lay with Stevia, while Aura lay down beside Ini. But not before she glanced over at the other two, seeing the woman's gray hair rippling out and around both their bodies until it enclosed them in a gray cocoon. That cut off both the sight and sound of them. Aura wasn't sure whether to be annoyed or relieved. She hadn't minded Augur having sex with Ini, who deserved the reassurance, but this Stevia was something else.

Ini reached out to touch her hand. *Swale here*, a thought came. *I have information to impart privately. It will be better if you clasp Ini so we three can commune mentally.*

Surprised, Aura acceded. By this time she had accepted the succubus' legitimacy; like the huge serpent, she had been tamed. The king had strange allies.

We may be observed, Ini's thought came. Aura recognized its identity without knowing how she did; Swale was different. *This news must not be shared outside ourselves.*

And Augur, Aura thought.

Some not with him.

Dismay! I have no secrets from my love.

But it turned out that this one was necessary, for a time. *Stevia is the mortal identity of the Red Glamor*, Swale thought. *Her constituency is human: she represents us. She is lusty, as are all Glamors, but normal humans cannot have sex with Glamors, or if they do, only with extreme discomfort. So she cannot seduce Augur if he knows.*

The Red Glamor! But she's of the Gray Chroma.

That is her masquerade, deliberately different from her real identity. She is of the Red Chroma.

Aura's feelings were mixed. Why did a Glamor need to bother her beloved at all? Couldn't they get their sex elsewhere?

Consternation, she thought. *I mislike my man being seduced by a creature likely to be as sexy as you are, Swale.*

We do need her protection, Ini thought. *There are brigands ahead who possess serpent repellent. Stevia will persuade them to let us be, but she will not reveal her nature. Traveling no fault with a handsome man like Augur justifies her attendance, so that she can work her magic unrevealed.*

Aura reluctantly agreed that this did make sense.

Then she remembered something else. *What was that Swale said about Augur and me being handsome folk, as all changelings are? What is a changeling?* Actually Queen Gale had discussed this matter with them, but neither of them wanted to believe it, because it suggested that they could not marry.

Swale answered directly. *You both are fourths, are you not?*

Not exactly, Aura thought. *My parents had their three, but neither wanted my mother to have to embrace another man for the fourth. So she went to the temple, and after a long pregnancy I was birthed. I counted as a fourth, because I was not sired by my father, but no other man touched her. I believe it was the same with Augur.*

Ini made a mental nod. *That was the way of it with my parents too. My little sister Ino was a temple baby. Those are the changelings. They are not sired, they are implanted. They derive from specially crafted genes, and are superior human beings. The two of you resemble my sister, as you resemble King Havoc and Queen Gale, who are also changelings. You differ in color and in detail, but you could be in the same family. You are all handsome, intelligent, thoughtful, and socially aware. That was surely why King Havoc selected you for this mission: he trusts changelings to be competent and honest.*

This was not a kind revelation. Aura had been attracted to Augur because he was a superior man with qualities she liked, and he felt the same about her. Cross-Chroma relationships were rare, but she had encountered no Blue Chroma man to rival him. Now she had to confirm the worst. *But if we are like siblings—*

Baseless, Swale thought. *Havoc and Gale feared the same, and postponed their marriage, until they learned that there are different broods, and distribution is scattered so that two of the same brood are unlikely to encounter each other. They would not send two to adjacent Chroma zones.*

Aura relaxed, immensely relieved. So they were all right after all! Just the thought of Augur stirred a longing in her loin. It would be devastating to lose him because of something that predated their births.

There is something else about changelings, Swale continued. *They have the potential to become Glamors, though all those posts are filled now and there may not be any more. They heal faster and better than ordinary folk, they have or can develop eidetic memory, they can mask their private thoughts so well that telepaths don't realize they are hiding anything, and they can penetrate illusion.*

I can't do these things, Aura thought. But she realized that maybe she could. As a child she had had less trouble with injury than others, and had seemed to heal faster and better. She was not telepathic, but had learned to mask her thoughts to fool telepaths. Her memory for the animals she studied was very good; she never forgot one, and Augur never forgot a plant. She fought off another surge of passion as she thought of Augur. What was he doing inside the cocoon of Stevia's hair? But illusion shows fooled her just as they did others.

Such talents have to be learned, Swale thought. *You should practice seeing through illusion, because you never can tell when that ability will be useful.*

Aura considered, and realized that was true. Illusion could be dangerous, if it covered a threat or made something seem like what it wasn't, such as poison looking like food. *How do I do that?*

I can make spot illusions, Ini thought. *I'm native to the Chroma of illusion, and they require very little magical energy. I can use my gemstone without depleting it.*

That would be good, when morning came. Aura found Ini's invisible face and kissed it. The woman kissed back. Then they were hugging each other and stroking each other's bodies.

Oops, Swale thought.

They paused. *What is happening?* Aura demanded.

My spirit links you, so we can communicate mentally, and avoid betraying out secrets, the succubus explained. *But I am a sexual entity. I have inadvertently turned you on to each other.*

Ghastly, Ini thought.

Appalling, Aura agreed.

Then they resumed kissing and fondling.

I can depart, Swale offered. *That will allow you to settle back to normal.*

Aura thought about Augur and Stevia, realizing that her washes of eroticism had been sponsored by contact with the succubus. But she couldn't have Augur this night, and was only frustrating herself thinking about it. She had sex in mind, and no other way to implement it. *We're in this far,* she concluded. *Let's finish it—and never speak of it hereafter.*

Agreement! Ini thought.

Neither of them was experienced in this kind of lovemaking, but the presence of the succubus made it work out. Overall, Aura concluded, it was equivalent to male-female sex, just different. She made a mental note: some of these female strokes might be adaptable to a male partner. She would find out, in due course.

At last, satisfied, they slept, embraced.

In the morning they got up, separated, cleaned up, and waited for Stevia's cocoon to dissipate. Soon it did, revealing the gray woman as quite full breasted and full thighed, rather than heavyset as she had first appeared. She was solid in a shapely way. Some men liked that.

Augur glanced up, saw Aura, and glanced away. He must have had a considerable workout.

"Your man is virile," Stevia remarked as she took cloth and water and washed herself.

"Agreement." Was this really the Red Glamor? Aura had no reason to doubt Swale, but it was hard to believe while watching the gray woman clean herself in quite ordinary manner. There was a touch of red at her genital region, confirming her action with Augur. Why was it supposed to be impossible for normal people to have sex with Glamors, only if they knew the Glamors' identities?

We don't really understand that aspect ourselves, the woman's thought came. *But we have learned to be circumspect.*

Startled, Aura stood frozen. That was telepathy! She had received Stevia's thought. This was quiet proof of the Glamor's power, for even a Chroma telepath would not be able to do it in a nonChroma zone.

Correction, blue woman: there are different types of telepathy. Normal Chroma is limited, unless a person carries a magic stone. But another type of telepathy is an illness that breaks down the mind's natural barriers. A number of palace officials have that kind. It is not proof of a Glamor. So beware.

There it was again. Obviously telepathy *was* possible in nonChroma. *Warning taken,* she thought faintly.

Stevia smiled and continued her washing.

The big serpent appeared. Ini approached it and spoke with Swale's voice. "We thank you for your protection, but know that you can't make the next leg of our journey. Return to your natural range."

The serpent slithered back the way they had come. "He would just get himself killed," Swale said. "There is no point."

Soon they traveled again. Ini, guided by Swale, led the way, followed by Aura and Augur, with Stevia at the rear. "Apology," Augur murmured.

"Needless. No fault."

"For—for the intensity. She's like the succubus."

And she had seen what Swale could do with him. "How many times?"

"Four—five—I lost track. When I thought myself depleted, I found myself recovered. I think she has a gemstone she used to restore my potency. I never before felt such continuing desire or urgency. I had to have her, over and over. It made me feel unfaithful to you. Regret."

And she couldn't tell him he had been with a supernatural creature. "Understanding. Our love is based on more than sex."

"Agreement!"

At midmorning Ini halted. "Swale says the brigands have spied us and are coming. They are numerous and vicious."

"Best to hide, or veer into a Chroma zone?" Augur asked, concerned.

"The local zones leave them alone. It seems there is some trade between brigands and zones."

"Outrage!" Aura said.

"Agreement," Stevia said, catching up to them. "But it is best to be circumspect. I will remonstrate with them."

Aura stifled her response. If this was truly a Glamor, she could do what she said, and it was best to avoid trouble.

They resumed walking. Soon a group of rough-looking men appeared before them, barring the way in much the manner of the three on the prior day. But these ones wore brigand emblems: shoulder patches with raised clubs. No, Aura realized after a moment; those were depictions of erect phalluses, unrealistically big and hard. Below them was the motto SCREW YOU. That made this band's nature quite clear.

"A man and three maids," the leader said. "Good takings for hardons."

Stevia spoke. "We seek no mischief or complication. I am sure you are reasonable folk. I shall give you a kiss for our safe passage through your terrain."

The brute stared at her. Then he burst out laughing.

She leaned forward and kissed him on the cheek.

His demeanor changed. "I guess you're right. Maybe some other time, eh?"

"Some other time," Stevia agreed.

The leader gestured his henchmen to stand aside. Surprised, they did so. The travelers walked on by them, unmolested.

The henchmen weren't the only ones who were amazed. How could a simple kiss, not even on the lips, have wrought such a change?

I could have changed his mind without contact, but that would have betrayed my nature. This will give us time to get clear.

Oh—Glamor magic. She was supposed to be the Glamor of Humans, so could control human minds. She had probably done some of that during the night with Augur.

Correct. Your man loves you. I had to override some formidable resistance to repeated sex with me, because he had not done it repeatedly with you.

That irritated Aura. She didn't like anyone messing with Augur's love for her.

Then a seeming ripple passed through her mind, and she realized that she had no cause to be upset; no fault followed its own rules. She also realized that the Red Glamor had just changed her mind, much as she had changed Augur's mind, but the idea no longer bothered her.

Ini joined her. "I was forgetting," she murmured.

"Confusion."

The woman lifted her gloved hand. Her fingers held—nothing. Then Aura realized that she was holding an invisible gem. Her magic, to enable her to project illusion. She nodded.

A green goat appeared standing in the trail ahead of them. Stevia, in the lead, ignored it. In fact she forged right through it. It was illusion.

Augur's jaw dropped. "Astonishment!"

"Illusion," Aura told him. "We should be able to penetrate it before we know what it is. Practice with me."

He was quick to catch on. Of course that was a changeling trait. When she had the chance, she would tell him the good news about changelings.

A big tri-beaked bird appeared ahead. Again Stevia ignored it. She had to have seen it, but she knew it for what it was. Aura knew it couldn't have appeared so suddenly; a real bird would have flown or run in. So it had to be illusion. She focused, trying to see through it in a way that would not be possible with a real bird.

The outline fuzzed slightly. She was beginning to get it! Augur seemed to be having a similar experience. "Amazement," he murmured.

Soon they were able to see through the illusions as if they were translucent. They were still there, just permeable. So it was true: changelings could discern illusion, and know it for what it was. This was a rare discovery, for all that it seemed she could have done it all along, had she but known to try.

The illusions became less obvious, and finally ceased. But Aura didn't quite trust this. She looked around, using her penetrating gaze, and spied a tree by the side that wasn't really there. She nudged Augur, and he followed her gaze. "No tree," he agreed.

"Sufficient," Aura said to Ini. "Appreciation."

The Air Chroma woman nodded.

There was no more illusion to see along the path, but where a Chroma zone squeezed close there was some monochrome illusion. Some of it surprised her; aspects of plants she had thought physical turned out to be illusion. Some had wicked spines for defense, but only one thorn in three was real. Some had small flowers that illusion magnified to big flowers. Augur had surely known it, because his specialty was plants, but she hadn't. In fact it had not occurred to her that plants used illusion at all. The real world was not as formidable or pretty as the one enhanced by illusion.

Stevia fell back. "Brigand scout ahead. Strip and scare him off."

Ini did so, handing her pack and clothing to Stevia, whose hair grew to cover and conceal them. Now Ini was invisible.

The scout appeared ahead, wearing the penis patch with the SCREW YOU motto. "Hey, where you going, girls?" he called, putting his hand on his bow. He could fire arrows into all of them before they could close the distance, if he chose. Evidently the gang leader had changed his mind about letting them go.

A stone heaved itself up from the trail and whirled around, suddenly flying toward the scout. It missed him, but he was startled. "What the—?"

Another stone lifted and flew at him. He dodged it, but was plainly shaken. "Magic!" he said. He retreated as a third stone lifted, then fled into the brush.

Invisible Ini had done the job. Soon she returned to reclaim her clothing.

But half an hour later the gang was there again, having somehow managed to get before them—and behind them. They were surrounded.

"I see this will require a stronger measure," Stevia said. "Trust me."

Aura was not easy with this, but they seemed to have little choice. They stood still as the Hardons closed in on them. "Well now," the brigand leader said. "You're a pretty slippery bunch, know that? But now we've had our little games and it's time for the action." He glanced to the side. "Strip them."

Rough hands took hold of them and ripped away their clothing. In moments the four of them stood naked, with Ini invisible again. Hardons sorted through their belongings, separating out items of interest.

"That gray gemstone accounts for the mind changing kiss," the leader said with satisfaction. "And the invisible bitch accounts for the flying stones."

He paused as if pondering. "Now ordinarily we'd just rape all of you, take your stuff, and be done with it. But you made trouble, so we'll have to make an example of you. We could rob you, rape you, and kill you, but we want the word to spread. So we won't kill you, just rough you up a little and set you loose. Your four Chroma should get the word, and the others too, soon enough. Nobody screws the Hardons; it's the other way around." He laughed, and of course the whole band laughed with him.

The four did not answer. Aura was increasingly alarmed; Stevia had said to trust her, but then had done nothing to defend them.

"Set four posts in line," the leader said. "No—in a circle, so they can see each other, and what happens to each of them."

Men got to work, bringing up heavy posts, digging holes in the ground, and setting in the posts. Then they bound the four victims to the posts, facing inward. Ini was visible only by the ropes circling her neck, arms, waist, and feet, anchoring her to the post so that she could move a bit but not escape. All of them were similarly tied.

Aura quietly tested her bonds. They were snug about her wrists, not painful, but impossible to loosen. Trust brigands to know how to immobilize captives! The brigands wanted them to be able to struggle, but not to escape. The struggling of a victim might emulate passion, to a man who would not otherwise receive it. Her feet were tied somewhat apart, so that it was not possible to clamp her legs together to resist penetration. She couldn't even bite if one kissed her; they had set a bit in her mouth that prevented it.

"Now we'll draw lots for first dibs on the girls," the leader said. "And on the boy." Several brigand women were clustering around Augur's post. "Those who want seconds have to wait until all have had firsts. We have a fine variety this time: blue, gray, invisible, and red for the women."

The greatest male demand was for Aura, so the lots took longer. She schooled herself to be calm; there was nothing to gain by freaking out, and if she screamed and cried it would only show how badly they were humiliating her. Better to remain passive and contemptuous of their efforts. Ini and Stevia seemed to have the same attitude.

Stevia had told them to trust her, and she was the Red Glamor, so presumably they would not actually get raped. Still, this was no pleasant experience. The brigands had to be stopped soon, or it would be too late.

There were only a few brigand women, so they were sorted out first, and the first one addressed Augur before any of the three bound women were attacked. She kneeled before him and felt his penis, then took it into her mouth, teasing it erect despite his obvious aversion. The second woman in that line held what Aura recognized with horror was a dildo: a sex toy used to serve in lieu of a penis. Such instruments could be used on men as well as women, and some women did have a taste for such reverse sexual penetration.

Now the others were ready. The leader approached Aura, evidently having a preemptive right to the best. Other rough men approached Ini and Stevia. All of them were naked below the waist and had prominent erections. Raping was no bluff; this was the trademark of the Hardons. They lined up before their choices, but did not start yet. Even the lead woman paused, holding Augur's erect red member in her hand. They were waiting on the leader's performance before indulging their own appetites. This was surely a matter of gang discipline.

It seemed they were doomed. The Red Glamor had done nothing. She had not even saved herself.

Patience, woman, the Glamor's thought came. *The situation is under control.*

Some control! The man was feeling her breasts with his dirty hands. "Kiss me, blue honey," he said, his scraggly face looming near hers. "If you squeeze when I get inside, I'll see that nobody punches you in the gut."

The brute was bargaining for her enhancement of his pleasure. The awful thing was that it was surely no bluff; any of these rough men could beat her while she was tied, to soften any possible resistance. They would probably kill and burn or bury all the victims after they were done with them, so that there would be no hard evidence of their fate. No—the leader had said he wanted them to survive, to warn others. Did it really matter?

I can make you enjoy it. It was Swale, visiting with Aura's acquiescence.

Negation! I don't want to enjoy it.

Then I will visit Ini. The spirit was gone.

The man oriented his member. It touched her groin. He bent his knees, bringing it down for more effective entry. Maybe she should have accepted the succubus's offer, if it was going to happen anyway. Maybe Swale could have caused the man to wear himself out with repeated efforts, and collapse before his brigand band. Serve him right.

A breeze sprang up, catching Stevia's gray hair and tossing it about. Aura felt her own hair stirred.

Then there was a cry to the side. "Smoke!"

The leader paused, his member still nudging her cleft. "Who cares?"

There was coughing. "Bad smoke. I can't see; I can't—" The man was choking.

"Poison smoke!" another man cried. "Must be a blaze upwind."

That got the leader's full attention. His member lost position as he turned to view the smoke. "The damn wind's bringing it right down on us. What a break! Get clear!"

The men ran, avoiding the smoke that was bearing down on them. In a less serious situation the sight would have been comical: their erections preceded them, swinging from side to side as they lost elevation. The women too, their bared breasts bouncing. But of course the four bound captives could not escape it. Worse yet!

Then Aura saw that the smoke was illusory. This was a trick, a device to scare away the brigands. But why had those exposed to it been choked and blinded?

That would have been the mental suggestion of the Red Glamor. Stevia had been on the job after all.

Confirmation.

The smoke swept through, enclosing them. And suddenly Stevia was free, coming to Aura, touching her bonds, which dropped. "Do

Augur," she murmured.

So that Augur would not realize what the Glamor had done, thus preserving her secret. So she could have more sex with him. Had the situation not been so desperate, Aura would have resented that. But now she knew that they had never been in serious danger; the Glamor had planted suggestions in the mind of the brigand leader, that he thought were his own ideas, to make this a history making display. That had delayed the rapes while the illusory poison fog formed, and the wind to carry it to them.

Affirmation, the Glamor's thought came. *Now they will curse the ill chance that denied them their sport, never suspecting that they never had a chance for it. But this grows tedious; I will see about getting us transport.*

That would certainly help. Aura approached Augur as the fog dissipated.

～

Augur was relieved to see the women loose. Aura came to kiss him and untie him. Then she paused "Maybe I should leave you bound until I have had my will of you," she said teasingly.

"Quick, before the gray woman comes."

She laughed and loosened the ropes. "She got free first, and loosed me."

"How could she do that? Those brigands are good at bonds; I could make no headway."

"I think her hair can be prehensile."

"Confirmation." Stevia's remarkable hair had not only enclosed the two of them in its comfortable cocoon, strands had tickled him in sensitive places. She was a truly accomplished lover, really the rival of the succubus. "But we were fortunate the fog came, though it turned out to be illusion."

"The fog was no coincidence."

Surely not; it had been too provident. "Swale must have notified a Glamor."

Aura did not answer, concentrating on the ropes. Soon he was free. Then he embraced her. "Oh, beloved! I could not bear to see you raped!"

"I wasn't too keen on what those brigand women were doing with you, either."

Neither was he. It had not been a matter of appearance; the woman ranged from ugly to sexy. But he did not like being compelled to perform, and it had become clear that they knew how to do this. A man could indeed be raped by a knowledgeable woman, in more than one way; he had seen the dildo the second woman held.

Now the other two joined them, donning their clothing. "I thought I had more control of the situation than I did," Stevia said. "Their numbers were too great. Fortunately the succubus was here to summon help. I do not care to risk further mischief. We should obtain transport."

"Our mission is private," Augur said. "We lack goods to trade for passage across Chroma zones."

"I have gray gems reserved for this purpose."

If she had gems, why hadn't she used them before? Augur suspected he knew: she had wanted to travel no fault with him. She was an extremely lusty woman, and he knew himself to be a handsome man. Men and women were known to scheme to travel with those who appealed to them; it was an open secret. Aura was subject to similar schemes by men.

They went through the baggage left by the fleeing brigands, recovering their own things and adding to them. Then they made a pile of the remaining brigand things and set fire to it. It seemed only fair to repay the brigands in kind for their hospitality.

They made their way to a staging area at the fringe of a White Chroma zone. Here everything was in shades of white, distinguishable in the usual monochrome manner. A white man approached them. "Greeting."

"Acknowledged," Stevia said. "We are travelers of four Chroma, banding for convenience. We wish to obtain faster transport than walking around the zones."

The man gazed at her with open assessment. "What do you offer in trade?"

"Gray gems. They will nullify magic in their vicinity if invoked. That can be useful for travelers."

"Demonstration?"

"Acceded." She held up a gray gem. "What do you wish nullified? The effect is temporary."

The man produced a metallic tube with a projecting handle. "This is a gun, operating by magic explosions that propel small balls rapidly toward some target. Observe." He held the tube by its handle and pointed it at a small block of white wood sitting on a stump about twenty paces distant. There was a loud noise, a puff of smoke, and the block jumped off the stump.

Augur realized that this was more than a demonstration; it was a warning. Such a weapon could strike a person well beyond the range of sword or club. They needed to treat this man with respect.

"Impressive," Stevia said as the white man stuffed white powder and another white ball into the tube. "Now take the gem and hold it next to your gun." She proffered it.

The man pointed the gun at the empty stump, holding the gem beside it. He moved his finger below the tube. Nothing happened. Then he held the gem away from the gun and tried again. This time it banged. Obviously it remained functional when its magic wasn't being damped out.

"One gem per traveler," he said, satisfied.

"This gem for one car," Stevia said.

"Two for the rental of the car one day."

"And sustenance for that day."

"Done."

Stevia produced a second gem. The man pocketed them both, then led them to a coach that seemed to have no hitching for a horse. "Who is to drive?"

"The red man," Stevia said.

"Humor, Gray. We use our own drivers, so as not to trust our science to the ineptitude of otherChroma efforts."

"And the two gems cover that," Stevia said.

"Negation. They cover the car and sustenance for a day. The driver is extra—"

The white man paused, for Stevia was kissing him.

"Extra careful to see to the welfare of the passengers," he resumed after a puzzled pause. "Yes, covered by the gems. Now I shall summon her."

A white woman appeared. She was young and pretty, in a white blouse and short white skirt, and of course her hair and skin were white also.

"These four have rented a car for a day, sustenance and driver included," the man said.

The woman's white eyes narrowed momentarily; evidently she had expected additional payment. Then she surveyed the four travelers and made a trace private nod. She addressed Augur. "Sit beside me as I drive. You three ladies ride in back."

She opened the car door and climbed into the vehicle. Augur walked to the other side, opened its door, and came to sit beside the driver. Aura, Ini, and Stevia climbed into the back seat, which was just wide enough to hold them. This device was odd, but he had learned of it in school, understood the general principle, and was a quick study. He intended to learn how to operate it, in case the woman tried to hold them up for further compensation. She might take them to hostile terrain and threaten to desert them; such ploys were known.

"Introduction," the woman said. "I may be called Driver." That suggested that it was not her normal name; she was preserving her anonymity from people she expected never to see again.

"Augur," he replied. He did not volunteer the names of the others, as yet uncertain what kind of a relationship the white woman intended.

She moved her hands and her feet. There was a hiss and a puff of vapor from a vent, and the car moved forward, gaining speed. "Direction?"

"Far side of zone," he said. "Inquiry: what is the operative magic of this vehicle? What propels it?"

She glanced sidelong at him. He had seen such looks before; she was considering a no fault liaison. This might be her only chance for the novelty of embracing a Red Chroma man. The appeal of otherChroma sex was strong. "I can teach you to drive it, if you wish."

"Acquiescence."

"No fault?"

It really wasn't a difficult decision; he wanted to learn, and she was pretty. The three woman behind them were listening, and understood. No fault during travel was sometimes mandatory rather than optional. Such exchanges were more often broached by men to women, but it could go either way, and this might prevent her from trying to extract a gem from them. "Agreement."

That was it; she would choose the occasion at her convenience somewhere along the way.

"We have a small furnace," the woman said, commencing the instruction before he had a chance to change his mind. "We burn coal, and the fire heats a boiler to make steam. The steam is piped to cylinders that drive the two rear wheels. I control it with this foot pedal." She paused, giving him opportunity to gaze at her foot and bare white leg. He had to lean down to see the pedal clearly in the shadow of the region. "I steer the car with this wheel, and use the brake pedal with my other foot to halt the car's motion." She demonstrated by pressing the other pedal, and the car slowed dramatically, causing him to slide forward. He put out a hand to catch himself, and his fingers came up against her white knee. As she had intended. "Soon," she murmured, as if it was passion that motivated him. Actually her body was quite nice, apart from its color, being shapely and firm. Passion would be easy to achieve.

She continued the instruction, and he observed carefully, recording it permanently in memory. The girl probably did not appreciate his capacity in this respect. She thought he was admiring her body, when actually he was cataloging her every motion directing the car, and its response.

Ini put an invisible hand on his shoulder, having removed a glove and rolled back her sleeve for the purpose. *Swale here*, the thought came.

He was surprised; he hadn't realized that she could communicate directly with him. *Question?*

The White Chroma woman means to seduce you.

He smiled. *So I discovered. No fault, in exchange for instruction controlling the magic of this vehicle.*

You knew? Embarrassment. I was traveling, and just returned, and did not verify details.

Warning appreciated, nevertheless, he thought. *I prefer to see it coming.*

Appreciation. Parting. She was gone.

They moved rapidly along the white road, through the white terrain. Augur knew he should be used to seeing monochrome of other zones, but this endless white fascinated him. Every plant was white, from leaves to bark to flowers. Every flying bird, every fleeting animal, and of course every human person: white. In the distance he saw hills, and beyond them the great conic mountain that was this zone's volcano, the source of all its magic. Or, if Ini was right, and he rather thought she was, its catalytic agent. At the moment it was quiet; innocuous white clouds floated above it. Then Driver pulled up at a rest stop where there were sanitary facilities, food, and places to rest. A man approached to put more white coal in the car's hopper.

The three traveling women went to the facilities without comment. Driver led Augur to a separate chamber, intended for men but unoccupied at the moment, and shut them in. Then she hoisted her skirt, drew down her underpants, and bent over, presenting her plush bare white bottom. "Give me my fourth, red man," she said.

So that was it! If her timing was right, she would have her fourth by him. Fourths were by definition no fault, and required no art of lovemaking unless the participants wanted it. Neither could they reasonably be declined. He bared his member, which was quite ready despite the cynicism of her ploy, and set it carefully to her spreading white cleft. The channel was hot and slick; she was ready too, and needed no further lubrication. She might be pretending it was a mere business transaction, but in tempting him she had tempted herself as well, and was truly hot for it. She squeezed as he slid the tip to the inviting depression and lodged, his red denting into her white; then she rocked back to take him rapidly and firmly in. The effect was formidable; he climaxed explosively as she achieved his full depth.

"Give it a moment," she murmured, keeping her bottom tight against his groin. She wanted to be sure she got all the ejaculate, which was still pulsing forth. Her vagina was kneading his softening member, milking it of the last drops. Then she drew herself off him, placed a small clamp on her external cleft so that nothing would escape, drew up her pants and dropped her skirt. It was done.

Bemused by the efficiency of it, Augur went to the urinal and used it. He used water at a sink to clean himself while she waited, indifferent to this process. Then they went back outside.

Driver paid him no further notice. She had gotten what she wanted, and was making it clear that she had no interest in any romantic notions he might entertain. She had evidently sized him up as a suitable donor for her fourth, a man she would probably never encounter again after this day, and taken appropriate action. She had obviously been well prepared, so must have been looking, ready to seize the opportunity when it presented itself. She had been just seductive enough to obtain his agreement for the liaison; now she was not at all enticing in manner. He realized belatedly that he had never seen her breasts, just her bare legs. And of course her bottom, her business end. No fondling, no words of endearment, just a hot hole to plug, rapidly. She had not let him waste time, but had jammed down on him and squeezed. He had never even kissed her. She had wanted no more of him than his seed for her baby. That, in recent retrospect, was a letdown.

They resumed the drive. There was no delay or holdup; Driver wanted to complete this job and go home. It was probably hard for her to urinate while wearing the clamp, so she needed to get to a secure environment.

The scenery remained just as varied in all respects except color, and there some fine examples of plants he ordinarily would have liked to pause to study. There was also much illusion, as there surely was in every Chroma zone, only now he perceived it as such. But he was in a mild depression because of the comedown the sex had proved to be; he had been used, and though he had no legitimate complaint, it annoyed him. So he knew he was missing much he should have appreciated.

As evening closed, they arrived at the far side of the zone. Driver dropped them off at the station, took on more white coal, and drove back the way they had come. She did not even bid them parting.

"Augur's glum, and Driver couldn't wait to get away," Ini remarked. "What happened, a quarrel? I saw nothing."

"She must have had him at the lunch stop," Stevia said.

"Agreement," Augur said.

"That fast?" Aura inquired. "There was hardly time."

"Her fourth."

She nodded, understanding; that explained everything.

"She looked hardly older than I am, and not worn," Ini said. "She's borne three children?" Then she caught herself. "But of course the fourth is a status, not a number; she could be leading off with it."

"Getting the chore out of the way first," Aura agreed.

"Chore?" Augur asked.

All three women laughed. "Who would ever have sex with you for the fun of it?" Stevia asked.

And of course they had all done just that. He had had a lot of sex recently: twice with Swale in Ini's body, once with Ini herself, at least five times with Stevia, and once with Driver, technically. With every one of them except Aura, his beloved. Each one of them was different, and it was more than body or technique. They were qualitatively distinct. In fact Stevia had been different each time, as if her personality and anatomy changed with each performance, regardless how rapidly one followed another. She seemed superhuman. Did the Gray Chroma folk have special powers? But she was away from her Chroma zone, so should be ordinary except for her hair, which seemed to be inherently magic. It still seemed doubtful that the hair could have untied the brigands' bonds. Unless she chose to use one of her gray gems, or—

Like a light, it flashed on him. "Glamor!" he exclaimed. "You're a Glamor!"

"Defecation!" Stevia swore. "You caught on."

"He's not stupid," Aura said with a certain muted pride.

"Changelings aren't," Ini agreed.

"That's why you weren't concerned about the brigands," he said. "You knew you could handle them at any time, if you revealed your nature. But why did you even bother with me?"

"We crave variety, and the joy of innocence," the woman said. "Yes, I am the Red Glamor. A mortal person can't do it knowingly with a Glamor."

"Why not? How are you different, if you keep your present form?"

"Watch," Stevia said, speaking to the other two. She approached Augur. "Kiss me."

He tried, but his face would not touch hers. "Something opposes me."

"Moreso for penetration," she said. "There's something about knowing that balks the mortal, male or female. So I could have my fun with you only so long as you did not know. But you were too smart."

Augur's feelings were mixed. Stevia had worked him over thoroughly, but it had been an almost insane pleasure doing it, and educational. He wanted to be rid of her and back with Aura, but he suspected Stevia had more to teach him, and he wanted to learn it. He did not want to be denied her because of his own inability. "Could Swale enable it?"

"Negation. She might help a mortal woman embrace a male Glamor, but would be helpless in this situation."

"Affirmation," Swale said, from Ini's body. "Glamors already have all the powers of sex I do. If I could operate a man's body it could get interesting, but you need an incubus for that."

"The white woman simply exposed her bottom and bent over," he said. "It was an act of minimal contact and very brief duration. Is that kind of sex possible?"

"Experiment," Stevia said. She bared her gray bottom and bent forward. They were outdoors, in the open; evidently she didn't care.

The sight and novelty stimulated him. Public sex? He glanced at Aura. "Objection?"

"None," she said tightly.

He bared his member, which was erect and eager for this new experience. He approached the proffered target. He almost touched it, but halted. Somehow he could not close the last fraction of the distance.

"Push?" Aura asked.

He laughed, then reconsidered. "Affirmation."

She got behind him and shoved him forward. His member collided with the bottom—and he received a jolt of current that nearly paralyzed him. He twisted away, falling.

"Apology!" Aura cried, dropping to her knees to tend to him. "I did not realize!"

"Needless," he gasped. "I must be reacting wrongly."

"Negation," Stevia said. "The knowledge prevents you. You could do it with one of the others."

"Doubt," he said. "At least, not at this moment."

"Try."

He looked at Aura. "Acquiescence?"

Evidently half nervous, half curious, Aura stood, inviting his embrace. He enfolded her, and there was no resistance, personal or magical. It was sheer bliss, because he was able to do it, and he was doing it at last with Aura. But this was demonstration, not romance. "Continue?" he asked doubtfully. He feared he was embarrassing her. They normally were not demonstrative in public.

"Affirmation."

He kissed her, and it was as nice as ever. "Gratitude!" he murmured. The feeling had not been as intense as sex with the white woman, but it was far more meaningful.

"Welcome," Aura said, melting against him. She had been as concerned as he, and as relieved.

"Confirmation," Stevia said. "No fault in you. The fault is in me, for being discovered as a Glamor." For a moment she shimmered and appeared as a beautiful red lady, outshining blue Aura. Then she reverted to dull gray.

Augur disengaged from Aura. "Apology for experimenting on you," he said.

She smiled, embracing him again. "Needless. I'll take you any way I can get you." It was almost as if they had had sex; both their emotions were overflowing.

"Still—"

"Understanding." She kissed him once more, deeply.

"Gratitude," he repeated.

Then Swale spoke from Aura's body. "Had it been up to me, you would have duplicated your performance with the White Chroma woman with the Blue Chroma one, right here and now."

"Aura let you in?" he asked, startled.

"She trusts me now. But she doesn't need me." Aura's expression changed, and it was evident the succubus was gone.

They went about the evening routine, and that night Augur slept with Aura. They did not need to have sex; it was enough just to be together again. But they had it anyway, and not because of any succubus.

"Now you are spent," Aura murmured mischievously. "If only I had a dildo to use on you!"

Swale must have put that notion in her mind. "Anything you do with me is nice."

"You did know I was teasing?"

He affected disappointment. "You were?"

She spanked his buttock smartly, then kissed him. "This time."

Next day they crossed an Air Chroma zone. Stevia's gem purchased a trip on an invisible floating coach. Ini removed her clothing and became visible in a colored dress.

"Surprise!" Augur said.

"This is Air Chroma," she said. "We are not invisible to ourselves. We clothe ourselves with bright illusion."

He saw it was true. Now he saw through the illusion, penetrating the dress and seeing not her body, but nothing.

"Comprehension. You have disappeared.

Then her body appeared, lean but female. "I made the dress, not needing to make my body," she said. "But if you are seeing through the dress, then my body should show."

He laughed. "Apology for peeking."

"Needless."

He could see the dress again; his power of penetrating illusion did not mean it disappeared, merely that he could cause it to fade somewhat, revealing whatever it covered.

They looked out of the invisible coach, and saw a land of phenomenal color.

It was true: the folk of the Air Chroma not only clothed themselves with illusion, they covered everything else, making this a far more interesting zone than others. Or was it all by the people? In the Purple Chroma zone plants used illusion to enhance their flowers and apparent defenses; did they do the same here?

"Question," he said to Ini.

"Yes, it is true that almost all Air Chroma women are beautiful," she said. "Because all want to be, and with illusion each person crafts herself."

That had not been his question, but it was surely the one visitors most often asked. He followed it up. "But what of you?"

"I believe in being exactly what I am: a woman too smart and plain for her own good. So my illusion emulates my actual form as closely as is feasible."

"Argument," he said. "Were you and I isolated together for some time, perhaps on a small island in a nonChroma zone, I would find both your mind and your body desirable, now that I know you, without help from Swale."

"You are too smart a man for your own good," she retorted, blushing.

"Your illusion replica recreates even your embarrassment!" Aura said.

"Compulsive honesty," Ini said, blushing worse.

Augur glanced at Aura and saw her trace nod. "Favor." Then without waiting he put his hands on Ini's shoulders, carefully turned her upper body to face him, and kissed her firmly on the mouth, which was accurately marked by the illusion.

She gazed at him a moment after he let her go. "Favor? For whom?"

"For me. You have become appealing to me. I believe that with similar association you will become appealing to some other good man who is available."

"Doubt." But her blush continued.

"And if—*when*—it happens, be prepared to accept it. You are worthy."

Ini looked half desperately at Aura. Aura nodded. She looked at Stevia, who also nodded. Her gaze dropped, and her flush faded. "Hope."

Their coach landed at the far side of the zone, and they got out and crossed to the next zone, which was Black Chroma. All the landscape was black, including the trees. Even the clouds floating above were black. Augur found himself admiring it; he still had not gotten accustomed to the colors of other zones than Red, Blue, or Purple.

Stevia approached the black attendant, a middle aged woman, and made a deal for a rapid crossing.

"That will be directly past the cone," the woman said. "It is quiescent now, but there is always risk. You may prefer to take the longer route around the fringe."

Augur hoped she was agree to the longer route, but she didn't. "The direct route will get us there by dusk. That seems best."

The black woman shrugged. "Agreement." She led them to a great round door set in the side of the adjacent black hill. She drew on a large lever, and the door swing grandly open. Inside was a black chamber whose far side was convex. This turned out to be the wall of a huge black bubble with a smaller round portal set into it. They entered that and took black seats. It was like a coach, but without windows.

"Question: have you traversed a Black Chroma zone before?"

"Negation," Stevia answered for the group. She herself surely had, but the others had not.

"Explanation: Black Chroma cones implode rather than explode. They suck all matter into themselves, where it disappears. Nevertheless, enough magic ambiance remains to empower the zone." The woman floated near the floor, demonstrating. "We protect ourselves by developing our establishments largely underground, hollowing out the rock. This is secure from most inruptions. We use vacuum to suck our transport bubbles through the tunnels from station to station. You are advised to hold on; acceleration can be sudden."

Augur discovered handholds on his seat. He grasped them, and the women did likewise. He did not care to display his nervousness about being in a Black Chroma zone.

"This globe is routed close by the central cone, per your request," the woman continued. "Suction is greatest at the cone, so it will accelerate toward it, and decelerate as it proceeds away from it. You will be aware of it, but will not experience discomfort, and your landing will be soft. The risk is not from the travel, but from the small chance of an inruption occurring during your trip. If a significant inruption occurs, you are lost. But the chance of that is very small at the moment." She glanced at them. "Satisfaction?"

"Agreement," Stevia said.

"Do not attempt to open the capsule while it is in motion. That would be foolhardy; the vacuum would probably kill you. Merely wait. The door will open of itself when the pressure equalizes at the far station. Parting." She closed the door on them.

Almost immediately Augur heard a peculiar whine, as of a wind blowing through a crevice. Then their globe moved, accelerating as if flung from a slingshot. The vacuum had taken hold, sucking it in toward the center of the zone.

"Emotional discomfort," Aura said.

"Comfort," Augur said. "Reassurance. Love."

"Appreciation."

The sharp acceleration continued, pressing them back into their seats. The whine intensified. Augur felt as if he were in the grip of a violent storm that was blowing him wherever it wished. Its power was awesome; he could not affect its course. He hardly blamed Aura for her fear.

The whine increased in loudness and rose in pitch. Then there was a kind of ping and it changed, beginning its descent. "We are past the cone," Stevia said. "It remains quiescent."

"Relief," Aura breathed.

The slowing continued, feeling like falling. Finally they came to a halt, and the portal opened. They were there.

A black man was there. "Greeting, travelers. All is in order?"

"Agreement," Stevia said.

"Your trade for the travel includes lodging and sustenance for the night, if you wish to accept it."

Augur wanted to say no; he wanted to get well clear of this scary black Chroma zone. But Stevia spoke first. "Acceptance."

The man showed them to a suite of chambers and shut them in. "Portals are kept closed between uses," Stevia explained. "For protection against a surprise inruption."

"Concern," Aura said. "Wouldn't it be safer in the next Chroma zone?"

"Negation. The next has no facilities, while this one is well equipped. Observe." She went to the lavatory chamber and stepped into the shower sphere, her clothing dissolving as she did. She was not bothering to conceal her nature from them, now that it had been exposed. Warm water cascaded down on her body. "Few stations have this kind of shower."

Augur saw her point; this was nice. They took turns in the shower, and it was refreshing. They did not bother to dress after it; instead they put their clothing into a laundry hamper, and it disappeared for cleaning. Then Stevia demonstrated their dinner service: she spoke into a tube, and soon a small globe arrived with four complete meals. They were completely black, from potatoes to wine, but were excellent; the taste was normal.

"I think I am not used to this," Ini said from her chair. She was invisible except for the food she was taking in; it outlined the upper portion of her alimentary tract before slowly dissolving into fuzziness and fading out. Her body seemed to be weaving slightly.

"The wine!" Augur said. "It is intoxicating."

"So I discover. I liked the taste, but it seems stronger than I thought. I may become ill."

"Swale," Stevia snapped.

"Present," the succubus said in Ini's body. "I will handle this." The body straightened and ceased wavering. Evidently Swale was accustomed to wine, and had no problem with intoxication. "Of course I would like some sex in exchange for this service."

"Since I can't have him, you might as well," Stevia said.

"Objection," Aura said.

"Suggestion," Stevia said. "Let Swale put Ini down for the night, and transfer to you."

That notion intrigued Augur. He glanced at Aura.

"Acquiescence," she said. Evidently she was intrigued too.

In due course Ini was safely asleep on her bed, beyond the danger of illness. Swale, in Aura's body, joined Augur on his. "Favor," she murmured.

"We already agreed," he reminded her.

"Request: let me remain in control, but treat me as you would a real woman."

He paused, considering. The succubus wanted to act like a real woman? She was like Ini in that respect, wanting simple recognition for herself as a person, rather than as a performer. "Agreement."

He made love to her, in leisurely fashion, and she responded cautiously, as though not quite sure how to do this. There was no compulsion, just a slow accommodation. When at last they climaxed, she kissed him with a muted intensity that was unlike Aura. "Gratitude," she breathed. Then she left; he felt the change.

"She was like an innocent maiden," Aura said. "She really has little experience with making love rather than sex. It was wonderful feeling with her."

"Agreement," he said. Then they slept.

In the morning they considered it again. "As we get to know those of other Chroma," Aura said, "we find they are like us in basic respects. They have hopes and fears and desires despite their magic."

"Ini is under her intelligence an innocent teen girl," he agreed. "Searching for true love, and fearful she won't find it. But she will."

"And even Swale longs for similar fulfillment. Her obsession with sex is in her nature, but she longs for true love too. Is there any hope for her?"

"With an incubus?"

"She's a tamed succubus; there may be no other like her. I think she'd rather have the love of a normal man. Last night, with you, she just floated, pretending she was like me. I felt sorry for her."

"You have a tender nature."

"It came upon me when I met you."

They kissed, used the facilities, and emerged from their chamber to join the others. "You're right," Augur told Stevia, as they breakfasted on tasty black fruits and porridge. "This lodging is better than sleeping outside where bandits lurk."

Stevia nodded. "I have had experience."

"Curiosity," Aura said.

"I am approximately two hundred and sixty five years of age. I achieved Glamor status at age fifteen, and have not aged since. I have enormous Glamor powers, yet at heart I remain a lonely girl in search of love."

"You too!" Augur exclaimed.

"I, and all women." Stevia's gray form faded, and the bright red form of the Glamor emerged. This was the first time Augur had fully seen it, and he was awed. Her face and form were perfect; she was scintillatingly lovely. Beside her even Aura looked comparatively plain. "That is why I seek solace anonymously in the arms of mortal men."

"But there are male Glamors," Aura said.

"And I have had intermittent affairs with them all, over the centuries," the Glamor agreed. "We know and understand each other, and have no trouble relating, emotionally or physically. But it does get monotonous. There are only so many times you can have sex with the same man without exhausting the variations."

Augur nodded. He had begun to see a pattern, even in the variety of sex Stevia had provided five times. Suppose it continued five hundred times? It would indeed get dull. "Regret," he said. "Had I known, I would not have fathomed your identity. That is—"

"Had you known that Stevia's secret needed to be maintained, you would have left it," the Glamor said. "But I will find other innocent men. This merely clarifies my nature. I must separate from you soon anyway."

"We're almost there!" Aura said.

"Agreement. I will take you as far as I can, and point the way, and leave you." She faced Augur. "But if you encounter a willing maiden hereafter, and suspect she is me in another guise, do not seek to confirm your suspicion. I would dearly like to embrace you again, and I will not take you from Aura."

"Deal," he agreed.

The red beauty faded, and the plump gray Chroma woman formed. "Actually there are ways," Stevia said. "But they require more time and effort than we have to spare at present. I explored them with Havoc, and it was fun."

"King Havoc?" Aura asked, surprised.

"She and my sexy sister Ine took on King Havoc together," Ini said. "I received a stroke by stroke description." She shook her invisible head; the ribbon in her hair moved. "For days I dreamed of being seduced by a Glamor. But that's impossible, even were one interested in me."

"Only if you know his nature," Augur reminded her.

"And if I don't know, what is the point?"

The dialogue lapsed. They completed the meal, then left the suite. "Appreciation," Stevia told the black attendant. "Your hospitality is excellent."

"Welcome."

They walked the short distance to the edge of the Chroma. "I shall no longer be so wary of Black Chroma zones," Aura said. "I was superstitious."

"All Chroma are ultimately similar," Stevia said. "All volcanoes are similarly dangerous, whether they blow in or out. And all people are similar under their colors."

"Understanding."

The adjacent nonChroma zone was thicker than usual. Volcanoes were irregularly scattered across the planet, so some were crowded close together while others were widely spaced, and the nonChroma zones represented the regions where no magic color extended. They could be vanishingly thin, or quite extensive.

They came to a formidable mountain range that extended to either side beyond the horizon. "This is the region," Stevia said. "It is a patch of land that would be a solid day's walk across, were it a flat plain. As it is, it cannot be walked; the peaks become sheer, and the cartographers record sheer cliffs. It obviously hides a secret, since it is proof against Glamors, and we suspect it is the secret of the origin of the altars. Perhaps this is where the material was mined to make them. We doubt there are dangerous animals or plants here, but we don't know."

"We are specialists in plants and animals," Augur said. "We should be able to recognize their natures."

"One reason Havoc selected you for this mission. Find your way over or through these mountains to the interior valley, and I will meet you when you return this way. Parting."

She faded out before they could acknowledge. The Red Glamor was gone.

ᗡ᭙

Aura shook her head. "Confession: I was coming to depend on her protection and guidance. Now I feel nervous."

"Agreement," Ini said.

"And I wanted to learn more from her about sex," Augur said.

Aura considered a sharp retort, but had learned enough recently to understand that he was serious. Such knowledge did have its place. "Maybe if she comes to you in another guise, you can learn it."

"Meanwhile, I suppose I'll have to settle for you."

"Much more of that attitude, and you'll be settling for Ini." She caught herself too late. "Apology," she said to the Air Chroma woman. "Affront not intended."

"Needless. Your implication was that he must not disparage you lest he be denied you."

"Accuracy."

They set off for the mountains, following what trace paths offered. It was obvious that this was sparsely settled terrain. The way became rugged, and progress was slow.

"Assistance?" Swale inquired from Ini.

"Can you spy out a good path ahead of us?" Aura asked.

"Simplicity. Provide a moment while I check." After a moment she was back. "This way." Ini moved out.

It was indeed improved. They wound around and over rocky outcrops, avoided aggressive vegetation, and found a ledge leading upward. "This leads to a cave that may go through the mountain," Swale said. "I was unable to explore it as a spirit; I think there are barriers. When you enter, I shall have to stay body-bound, or leave you. Preference?"

"Use my body," Aura said promptly. At first she had been diffident about the succubus, but familiarity had reassured her, and the session of gentle sex with Augur had abolished any remaining doubt. Swale was a highly sexual person, but a person nevertheless.

"Or mine," Ini said. "Will you be fixed in one for the duration, or can you transfer?"

"I can transfer, but only with your cooperation. You must make physical contact with each other."

"Then remain with Ini, and tell me when you wish to be with me."

Even with the way clarified, it was no easy trek. It was midday, and they were hot and tired by the time they achieved the cave. It did seem to be their destination; it looked unnatural, its sides being smooth and with a faint phosphorescence. They could see its interior, which curved on the level into the mountain.

"Crafted," Augur said. "This is meant to be entered."

"Crafted," Aura agreed. "But as an aid to travel, or as a trap for the unwary?"

"It would seem pointless to set up a trap where no folk go," Ini said. "Or to make an opening that is not supposed to be used. Easier simply to let the mountain balk intruders, if passage is to be denied."

Aura wasn't sure of that, but had no better case to make. Of course there was danger; they were entering a region forbidden to Glamors. It was bound to be a challenge, of what nature they could not know.

The cave opened into a chamber with five passages leading directly into the mountain. "Definitely crafted," Aura murmured. "But which one are we to take?"

"Try them all," Augur suggested.

"Caution," Ini said. "We need to judge: crafted for what? This could be a sieve."

"Question?" Aura asked.

"A sieve sorts thing by size or type. These seem to be passages intended for human beings or creatures of similar size, but we can't be sure what their selection is. I think we need to find additional information."

"There are marks above the passages," Augur said. "Each one different."

"Those may be the key," Ini agreed. "It could be a test for sapience."

Aura studied the marks. They were simple lines. The first passage on the left had a single vertical line. The second had two lines crossing, forming an X. The third had three lines crossing imperfectly, forming a small triangle in the center. The fourth one had no mark. The fifth had five lines crossing imperfectly, forming a five-pointed star.

"Why is one missing?" Aura asked.

"Erased?" Augur asked.

Ini peered closely at the place. "Negation. This surface is untouched. There was never a figure here."

"There must be reason—or meaning," Aura said. "This must offer the hint. It should be a set of lines crossing with a small square in the center."

"Agreement," Ini said. "As a riddle, it is elementary. But by itself it seems meaningless."

"So we explore," Augur said. "I see no indication that there are traps like falling ceilings; presumably we are intended to scout the region and draw a conclusion."

They checked each of the passages. Four were dead ends, going nowhere. Only the unmarked one led to the next chamber.

"I wonder if this is a game?" Aura said. "A puzzle we need to figure out, to win."

"Only intellects of a certain level are partial to games," Augur said. "Even competitive games, like chess or anagrams, can be phrased as puzzles. We will prove our fitness by solving it."

"And if we are not fit?" Aura asked.

He shrugged. "We won't get through."

She hoped it was that simple. Some mysteries had deadly answers. But they seemed to have little choice. They took the passage to the next chamber.

That chamber had five more exits, also marked with small symbols. They were formed of marks of equal length, again: two lines parallel, three forming a triangle, four forming a square, and five forming a pentacle. As before, one was unmarked. But the symbols were not in progressive order; they were random.

"Now we have a riddle," Ini said. "All these passages seem to go somewhere. Surely four are wrong. How do we know which one is right?"

"Maybe the unmarked one, as before," Augur suggested.

"Perhaps the fourth one from the left, as before," Aura said.

"Or the one marked with the four lined symbol—the square," Ini said. "As implied before."

They nodded. "The random order of the symbols this time suggests that a straight left right progression is not valid," Augur said.

"And the unmarked one is not the same one as before," Aura said. "That suggests that that rule is also invalid."

"Which leaves the square," Ini said. "We had to establish its nature, then search it out, applying intelligent selection. Does this make sense?"

"A sieve," Aura agreed. "A selection for intelligence. Mere animals would be unlikely to grasp it, if they even noticed the symbols."

"We can explore all of them, again," Augur said. "Just to be sure."

"I wonder." Ini peered down the passage without a symbol. Just before it curved out of sight, there was a barred gate on a vertical hinge at one side. "That appears to be a rotary mechanism. Does it move both ways?"

Augur walked to the gate and pushed it without following. It swung forward, and a second gate swung out behind it. "A rotary gate," he said. He caught the second and pulled it backwards. It balked. "One way."

"So we don't explore all passages, this time," Aura said. "We have to guess right the first time."

"Surprise," Ini said dryly. "But I prefer not to guess. We don't know where the wrong ones lead. It could be to the outside, or to a boiling fissure."

"The fissure would stop a person from going outside, returning to the entrance, and trying another passage, negating the selective process," Augur said. "So danger seems likely."

"In any event, we want to go together," Aura said.

"Agreement!" Augur said, touching her hand.

"What does Swale think?" Aura asked Ini.

"I'm not sure what would happen to me if my host died while I was locked in," Swale's voice answered. "I want to survive, and I think that is more likely as a group."

"Together," Aura repeated, satisfied.

They reviewed their theories, and concluded that the most likely correct answer was the square. With a certain trepidation, they walked down the passage as a group. They passed the rotary gate and followed the curving passage to a new chamber.

This one was different. It had just two passages going on, and one of those showed daylight beyond another turnstile. They could leave if they chose, and perhaps could return at another time. The other was blocked by—an altar.

"This is what we came for," Ini said. "Or a confirmation that it is here: the secret of the origin of the altars."

They studied the altar. It was roughly cubic in shape, with 18 small pockets at the top. All were empty. They could see that there was a squared off passage beyond it, just large enough for the altar to fit in.

They tried to move the altar out of the way, but could get no grasp on it; it could not be pulled, and they could not get behind it to push it out. It seemed that the only way to move it was into the passage.

They considered. "It seems we can leave, or push," Augur said. "So we had better push." He put his hands on the side of the altar opposite the passage and pushed. The altar didn't budge.

Aura joined him. When they braced and pushed together, suddenly the cube moved into the passage and stopped.

"Now it's truly blocked," Aura said.

"We don't know how far the passage is," Augur said. "Presumably it goes somewhere. We merely have to push the altar into the next chamber and get around it."

"As a test of strength, this may be apt," Ini said. "As a riddle it seems less so."

"We must have faith that there is a way through," Aura said. "Even if we have to do some hard labor."

"Perhaps I should take a turn at pushing," Ini said.

"Welcome," Augur said, standing aside.

Aura and Ini put their shoulders to the cube and shoved. To Aura's surprise, it moved forward another square, though she was sure that Ini did not have Augur's strength. Apparently any two pushers sufficed; it might be a matter of position and balance as much as power.

"Maybe this represents a selection for number," Augur said. "Two people rather than one."

Now a space opened to the right. The floor here was dark and polished, in contrast to that of the prior chamber and passage. There was another polished space beside the cube, and a short passage extended from it, to the right.

"It seems we have found the way through," Aura said.

The passage to the right led them to a second altar in its own chamber. There was another passage to the left, then left again, bringing them to a third altar sitting in the middle of a chamber. There was a passage leading back toward the chamber with the polished floor, and it was clear that the second altar could be pushed in that direction. Beyond it was another square passage, which turned left, bringing them to a fourth altar in its own chamber.

That was all. There was no other exit from the linked chambers, except the way they had entered.

They considered. "There seems to be no point in going back," Augur said. "So there must be something we have yet to understand."

"And that would be the next riddle in the sieve," Aura said. "Four altars, a central polished section, connected chambers. What can we make of this?"

"The polished squares are the same size as the bases of the altars," Ini said. "Perhaps they are supposed to rest on those squares."

"We could push them there," Augur said. "There is no apparent reason, but maybe the selection is for those who are able to think beyond the obvious."

"Agreement," Ini said. "The three polished squares form a pattern that can be completed by the square our first cube is on. We have but to push the other three into their places."

"But the altar we first placed blocks the access of the one opposite," Aura said. "We need to push it back a square."

"Where it will block the altar to the left," Augur said.

"So it seems that we have another riddle," Ini said. "How to push the cubes in place. Perhaps we should make a map."

They sketched a crude map on the polished floor. It showed the four polished squares, and four passages leading out to the four altars as originally placed. Now it was clear that all could be pushed in from the outside, but that the manner of the placements mattered. If they did it wrong, the figure could not be completed.

They numbered the altars 1 to 4, clockwise from the first one they had pushed in. The pattern would have been simple to complete if they had not pushed #1 in prematurely—but they had had to do that to get into the chamber. Now they were stuck with it interfering with the other placements.

"I fathom it," Ini said. "Place #2 first, in the southwest spot. Then push #1 back to the spot it crossed to let us in."

"But that will block our exit," Aura protested.

"We don't want to go that way anyway," Augur reminded her. "Then we can place the other two, and it is done."

They got to work. Augur and Aura got behind altar #2 and pushed it across the southwest square and to the southeast one. This blocked their prior route, so they backtracked around the outside to pass altar #3 and go down the passage to reach altar #1. Ini remained behind. "Are you there?" Augur called.

"Affirmation," she called back.

They pushed, and the block slid into place. This reopened the way through the center. They walked back to altar #3 as Ini walked around to join them. They pushed it into place, right where #1 had been before.

Then they went around to push altar #4 into place, completing the pattern.

There was a melodic sound, and the four blocks faded out. In their place was a circular stairway winding down.

"It seems we passed the test," Ini said, pleased.

So indeed it seemed. Aura was relieved; she had not been sure of their course, but this confirmed it. They had realized that they needed to move the blocks, and figured out how, and done it. But why did this elaborate setup exist, and who had made it? The makers of the altars?

The stairs led to a new and larger chamber. Four altars were in it, more or less along the far wall. Two were blocking the exit passages.

"We have learned how to play this game," Ini said. "Now, I suspect, comes the serious challenge."

They took time to check the situation before doing anything. The problem was that they could not see down the passages as long as the altars were there, and if they pushed them into the passages they would be committed, right or wrong.

Ini made another map. They pored over it. "Look," Augur said. "Move this one south, and that makes a place to move that one south without blocking. That opens one passage, and we can go down it and see where it leads, before committing."

They did so. It led to a passage parallel to the wall of the chamber, connecting with the other blocked passage. It went on to another chamber where there was a placement square. That was where the altars were supposed to go.

It was still tricky to figure out the exact movements necessary to move the cubes without blocking up, but they worked carefully and got them to the receiving section, one by one. Aura took a break after the third while Augur and Ini went back for the last one. This was wearing work!

She gazed around the second chamber. There was another exit to the outside, perhaps for those who were unable to solve the puzzle. They had no need of that; the problem wasn't that hard. Then, idly, she practiced her illusion penetration. The chamber, passages, and alters were real, of course; they had been working directly with these. So there was no illusion here.

Then her gaze fell on the remaining square for the last altar. The floor was not polished there. How could that be? They had just been moving the altars there because the squares *were* polished.

She blinked and looked again, and the polish reappeared. It was illusion!

The last altar came sliding down the passage toward her, Augur and Ini hidden behind it. "Halt!" she cried. "We're making a mistake."

They peered around the cube on either side. "Question?" Augur asked.

"Come look at the fourth spot. It's illusion."

He came and looked. "Confirmation. I never thought to question it."

They pushed the other blocks off their spots. None of them were polished.

"You're sure?" Ini asked. "They look polished to me."

Aura laughed. "You can make illusion, but can't see through it."

"Accuracy. Only Glamors and changelings can penetrate it, like my sister Ino." She paused. "This is a sieve for changelings! An illusion trick that normal humans would be deceived by."

"The nature of the selection is coming clear," Augur said.

"With distressing specificity," Aura agreed. "This passage is allowing only a very special contingent to pass."

They checked around, and found an alcove with four real placements. To Ini they were ordinary floor; now the illusion was of floor, covering the polish. That made quite certain that no non-changeling would be successful, even if suspecting the trick.

They moved the altars to the correct site. They merged and faded, and another stair appeared, this one winding up. They followed it, and in due course emerged to the light of declining day—on the other side of the mountains.

Now they saw across a vast caldera to the far side of the ring of mountains. Colored plumes hovered in parts of the depression. Plants grew there in abundance, and many birds were in evidence. That made sense, Aura realized: birds could fly over the mountains and get inside, while most animals could not. So this was a private paradise of birds of many types.

"Where do we go now?" Augur asked.

"Probably to the center," Ini said. "That's the obvious place."

Aura saw a small round peak in the center. That disturbed her, though she wasn't sure why. "Caution."

Augur glanced at her. "Question?"

"There's something I don't like about this. I want to understand my concern before we proceed."

"Acquiescence," Ini said dubiously.

That doubt nettled Aura. "Ask Swale."

I am here, Swale thought. *I am able to travel again, at least within this valley. May I join you?*

Aura thought an affirmation, and was aware of the succubus entering her body. She did this via the vagina and the womb, where her main portion stayed; from there she could reach out to take control of the host body if invited to do so. The womb made sense; it was close to the site of sexual activity that the succubus related to so ardently.

So what's your answer? Aura inquired.

This valley is strange. I have never seen one quite like it. I agree that we should understand it before proceeding into it; it could be dangerous.

"Swale agrees with me," Aura announced.

Augur shrugged. "We can camp here, perhaps within the tunnel; I think no creature will bother us there."

"Appreciation."

They made camp, and ate from their knapsack supplies. They sat gazing out at the darkening central valley. It was like a great pool, a lake, a sea, filling in from below. It was deepest in the center, except from the lone round hill there. That dark sea rose as the night thickened, until it lapped at the steep cliffs of the ring of mountains.

"Volcano!" Ini exclaimed. "This is a giant caldera!"

And that was it, Aura realized. The ring of mountains—the remnant of the cone of a giant volcano. But what a monster! It would take a person a day to walk across it. She had never seen a cone that big, never imagined one. This was awesome.

"The point in the center," Ini said. "That could be the result of new eruptions, starting over after the main blast. In time it could build up to the size of the original."

"What Chroma?" Augur asked.

That stumped them. There was no color near the center point. In fact, the center appeared to be nonChroma. It floated like an island above the pool of shadow.

Swale borrowed Aura's mouth. "I never heard of a nonChroma volcano."

"NonChroma!" Ini exclaimed. "Oxymoron."

"Is it?" Augur asked. "Now that we know magic exists also in nonChroma zones, why not volcanoes to feed it?"

"The Cartographers have never recorded a nonChroma volcano," Ini said. "I have observed Counter Charm though my lens, and seen none there either. NonChroma is what exists when there is no Chroma, by definition."

"What about the past?" he argued. "This caldera is ancient, dating from long before the time of man's arrival at Charm. Maybe in the early days of the planet, there were nonChroma eruptions, just as on our origin world of Earth."

"Earth's volcanoes are Science Chroma," Ini said.

"But not white," he said. "So at least one kind of magic is possible without Chroma. Maybe it was similar here."

Now that her concern had been supported, Aura found herself questioning it. "I saw color around the edges of the valley—the caldera. That suggests that there are Chroma here. How could they be venting within the cone of a nonChroma volcano?"

And now that her skepticism was being supported, Ini also argued the other side. "As Augur says, this crater is ancient. Volcanoes change all the time; every day there is some starting, somewhere on the two planets, and old ones going quiescent. That's why the Cartographers have to constantly revise their maps. So the huge nonChroma vent could have disappeared, and now otherChroma are invading. There has certainly been time to do it."

"Doubt," Swale said. "This was the biggest cone ever imagined on the planet. It must have had an immense reservoir of magma. How could that dissipate so completely?"

"In time," Augur said. "In sufficient time, the universe can change."

"Yet there is a new cone forming in the center. That suggests that the magma remains."

"And no Chroma in the center," he said. "The nonChroma could have been blasted out across the planet, exhausting itself, and now only a tiny fraction remains. So the Chroma invades the perimeter."

That seemed viable. The discussion lapsed, and they settled for the night. "Depart?" Swale asked.

"Can you inhabit a body without governing it sexually?" Augur asked.

"To a degree. My very presence enhances a body's sexuality, even if I do not govern."

Aura remembered the effect, when she had been with Ini. "Stay," she said.

"But do not govern," Augur said.

Then they made love, as they had to, for the succubus's nature did make it urgent. It was Aura doing it, albeit with greater intensity than normal. It was as though she was walking, but somehow taking running steps; she was buoyed, so that her slight reactions became significant ones. She could tell that Augur was reacting similarly, whether because of her enhanced responses, or direct overlapping by Swale's spirit. Overall, it was very nice.

For me also. I feel almost as though I am feminine rather than sexual. I could acquire the taste.

Aura smiled in the darkness, acknowledging.

Then they slept, and it continued nice.

In the morning they watched the great shadow sea diminish to a lake as the light spilled over the perimeter and brightened. The lake shrank, until it was merely a pool around the center point, and finally evaporated entirely.

It was time to hike. "I want to reach it well before night," Aura said.

They set off across the caldera, which was fairly even apart from its gradual slope down to the center. Flocks of tri-beaked birds were foraging and nesting, hardly spooked by the intruders; it was evident that they had never been hunted. They were of different colors, reflecting the small Chroma vents of their spot regions; this was a mini-world, with Chroma zones ranging from several hundred paces in diameter to barely an arm-spread across. Aura had never seen such small ones, and was considerably intrigued.

"Plants of many Chroma," Augur remarked. He of course was noticing the things of his specialty, as she was noticing those of hers.

"And a few rats," Ini said as a six legged one ran across their path. "They must have made their way through the caves, too small to be balked by the blocks."

"I can range this region," Swale said with Aura's voice. "I find no larger animals. This is a paradise for birds."

They came up against a larger Chroma patch, this one black. "Let's go around it," Aura said.

They skirted it, and that was just as well, because it had a small inruption while they watched. Black dirt and stones sucked down into the hole, and a cloud of dust formed and funneled down too. Then it was over as fast as it had begun, and the air sweeping in to the vacuum swirled chaotically, stirring up more dust.

"If I have to be this close to an inruption," Augur said, "that's the kind I prefer."

But the experience started Aura thinking again. Eruptions brought magic out from the depths of the planet; inruptions sucked material back below. How could there be such a cycle, where there had been a monstrous nonChroma zone? Other Chroma might have leaked in from outside, but how could a vacuum leak in?

She gazed ahead at the small mountain they were headed for. It did not look like a volcano, either current or extinct. It looked like a fused pile of rocks. Where could they have come from?

It is inert, Swale thought. *No volcanic activity, and I think there never was.*

Then Aura suffered a revelation. "This is not a caldera—it's an impact crater!"

"Confirmation!" Ini exclaimed. "I knew there was something wrong with it, but not what. The center is the debris thrown up in the heat of the aftershock."

"So there were no giant nonChroma volcanoes," Augur said. "That explains much."

"There must have been many impacts of many sizes," Ini said. "All over the planet. Then as time passed, these became fewer, and the volcanoes took over, obliterating most of the prior traces. But there was no major Chroma pocket in this region, so the remnant of the crater remains."

"And whoever set up the altars used it as a base," Aura said. "It is safe from molestation by the wrong people."

"Or they made it safe," Augur said. "Using Glamor-proof wards, and perhaps sealing off any other routes over or through the mountains."

"Question," Aura said. "This is ancient. How could it have been made Glamor-proof before Glamors existed?"

The others paused to stare at her. "Bafflement," Augur said. "There must be more here than we suspect."

But Ini was on it. "This must have been fashioned in connection with the Glamors someone knew were coming. So the way was prepared, but the Glamors themselves were barred. Whoever set this up knew the nature of what was to come."

"That would be precognition," Augur said. "Has there ever been evidence of such magic?"

"Not that we know of. But maybe they merely put in place instruments that would cause Glamors to develop, without actually seeing the future."

"And now we come to fathom their secret," Aura said.

"Nervousness," Ini said.

"Agreement," Augur said.

They forged on, avoiding most mini Chroma zones, passing through the Red, Blue, or Invisible ones, and watching out for bird colonies or dangerous plants. They reached the center mound by noon.

It was certainly no volcano. Fused glassy rock rose up in a pointed peak rather higher than it had looked from a distance. A closed round portal was set in the base. They had merely to slide off a panel and pull a small lever to release it. The lock swung open, admitting them to the interior.

Inside was a chamber containing a single altar. That was all.

They considered it. "Confusion," Augur said. "I expected more."

"Disappointment," Ini said.

"There has to be more," Aura said. "We have but to fathom it."

They walked around the altar. It seemed exactly like the ones they had pushed through the chambers. It had eighteen small pockets on top, all of them empty.

"Conjecture," Ini said. "Other altars contained single Glamor ikons. They were in chambers very near active volcano cones, to be near the sources of their power. Perhaps this was intended to contain a nonChroma Glamor ikon, but there were no nonChroma Glamors at the time, so it remained unused."

"Belief?" Augur asked.

Ini sighed. "Negation. There were no Chroma Glamors either, at the time. This surely has some other purpose."

"You mentioned a loom," Aura said. "That acted like an ikon, but with no Glamor attached."

"The magic loom," Ini agreed. "The Ladies Ennui and Aspect, and the girl Nonce who carries it—they are weaving a magic tapestry map on it. It is what may be a map of a section of Planet Counter-Charm, where perhaps something important lies."

"Amazement!" Augur said.

"Awe, for me," Ini said. "I have studied Counter-Charm, and long to learn more about it. The Glamors may go there in quest of their origin, and may take me with them. Absolute longing! But the relevance to this altar is uncertain."

"Point," Aura said. "Could this alter be like the loom? With some particular purpose it will take time to understand?"

"We must understand it now," Augur said. "Once we leave it, it will be too late to use it."

"Unless it is another ikon," Aura said.

The others stared at her.

"Surmise," Ini said. "If it is, it will convert to portable form." She touched the altar with her gloved hand. Nothing happened. She removed the glove and tried again.

The altar disappeared. In her invisible hand was a tiny replica of it, the same in detail.

"So we can take it with us," Augur said.

"And understand it later," Aura agreed.

"Confirmation," Ini said. Then after a pause. "Complication."

"Question?" Aura asked.

"The ikons affect their bearers. They give them protection, a suggestion of Glamor powers, and may become attached to particular persons so that others can't handle them. Who should carry this one?"

"You don't wish to?" Augur asked.

"Privilege. But I understand they also arouse sexual appetite."

Then Swale spoke with Ini's voice. "Confirmation. She's getting hot already. Problem?" Of course the succubus saw it as an asset rather than a liability.

Aura laughed. "Borrow Augur!"

Augur averted his gaze. Aura knew he was not averse, but did not wish to suggest that he wanted any woman other than Aura herself. She could handle that; she liked Ini. So Augur would be having a lot of sex on the return journey; he would survive.

"Perhaps you or he should carry it," Ini said.

"Doubt," Aura said. "Augur and I are evenly matched, both being changelings and of an age. Powers added by an ikon would distort our relationship. But you it would help."

"Acquiescence," Ini said. Her hand holding the ikon became visible. "It is acting like a Chroma gem, restoring my home Chroma magic."

"Deserved reward," Aura said. "Now let's return to the rim before nightfall. I think our mission has been accomplished."

Chapter 4—Tapestry

Ennui paused, gazing at the expanding tapestry. "We are almost out of yarn," she said.

The Lady Aspect nodded. "Havoc says that Ini is on her way back, with Red Chroma Augur and Blue Chroma Aura, and another ikon. He wants us to delay our quest for yarn until they arrive, in case there is interaction between the ikons."

"Understanding. But I confess I hate to delay on this even a day."

"Commiseration. The tapestry wants to be made."

They endured the delay, and in a few days the altar party arrived. Ini carried the ikon, which was in the form of a small altar, and it showed: she was visible and had a certain hungry sex appeal despite her plain face and body. Ennui understood exactly how that was.

They met with King Havoc and Queen Gale: the three of them working on the Tapestry, the three who had fetched the Altar, Symbol, and Swale. Nine people and a succubus spirit intent on fathoming the mystery of the origin of the Glamors. The three royal babies were present also, alternately nursing on Gale or Symbol, gazing at the folk in the room, or napping. When they were active, Havoc entertained Weft, so that each baby had one adult to be with. Symbol wasn't a Glamor, but Flame liked her well enough and gave her no trouble.

Ini introduced Augur of the Red Chroma and Aura of the Blue Chroma, both of whom Gale had helped save from execution. They were both handsome changelings. She reported on their trek to find the altar ikon, which had turned out to be in a huge ancient impact crater, an isolated region largely isolated from the rest of the planet.

"Mini-Chroma zones?" Gale asked, intrigued.

"With mini-Chroma plant and bird communities," Ini agreed. "Too small to have much effect on their neighbors."

"Let's see this altar," Havoc said.

Ini brought the ikon from her mouth, and set it on the floor. It expanded to full altar size. "It is clearly a magic ikon," she said. "But we have not fathomed what its purpose is."

The group clustered around it. Neither Havoc nor Gale were able to touch it; it was proof against Glamors. But it did not seem to do anything.

"When I carry the loom ikon," Nonce said, "It guides me where it wants me to go. We expect to be guided to find more magic yarn, to complete the tapestry. Does the altar ikon have any similar effect?"

"None," Ini said. "It protects me and animates me, but leads me nowhere."

"Let's see if it relates to the loom," Havoc said. "Fetch the loom."

"I have it here," Nonce said. "We ran out of yarn, so had no need for the full size loom." She stepped back, removing the ikon from her mouth. She set it down next to the altar, and stepped back.

The full loom appeared, larger than the altar but less solid. The partial tapestry was on it.

Side by side, the two magic items glowed. There was the sound of faint music. It was as if they were recognizing each other. Then the effect faded and both were quiescent.

Havoc nodded. "We have more to learn. Altar crew, remain at the palace and study it. Loom crew, go where it leads. These mysteries will allow us to unravel them when they are ready." He grimaced. "Meanwhile, the rest of us will get on with running the kingdom."

Weft squirmed, and he amended his statement. "And raising fine children." The baby relaxed, satisfied. The little Glamors did not yet speak, but seemed to pick up on thoughts. They were eerily precocious.

Symbol smiled. "He's got three remarkable babies, two sexy women, all the power of the planet, and he feels confined."

"Understanding," Augur said. He was the only other man in the room. "Adventure is better."

"Typical men," Aura said. "Augur had endless sex with two women, a succubus, and a Glamor, and he's bored too."

"Let's leave these dull creatures and get drunk," Havoc said to Augur.

"Enthusiasm," the red man agreed.

The two left the chamber.

"Fake," Gale said. "A Glamor can't get drunk, and Havoc didn't do it when he was mortal."

"Augur neither," Aura agreed. They all laughed.

Soon Ennui and Aspect went to see Havoc. She had access to him at any time, both as his secretary and his oath friend. "We have to go find more yarn," she said. "This may take some time away from the palace. Can you spare us?"

"Not readily," Havoc said. "I depend on both of you to steer me right, in decision and protocol. I have little competence for kingship."

"You have competence," Aspect said. "What you lack is taste for it."

He nodded. "I need both of you as I need Gale and Symbol, only in different ways. Suggestion: I'll go find the yarn; you remain here to run the kingdom."

Both smiled. "Understanding," Ennui said. "But negation. We have the loom ikon to lead us, and we know how to use it. You can't touch it."

"Agreement." He sighed. "Go, ladies. Return soon."

"Love," Aspect said. "Parting."

"Parting," Ennui echoed.

He reached out and caught them both around their waists, drawing them into him. The ikons resisted, but allowed this. He kissed each on the cheek, with evident effort; it was not easy for him to touch them. "Love," he said. "Parting."

They found themselves in the hall. Ennui was reeling. "He said 'Love,'" she breathed.

"And 'Parting,'" Aspect agreed. "But I know what you mean. We're his mother's age."

"It must be the ikon. It not only makes me feel sexy, it links me to him. I feel so guilty."

"For what?"

"As if you didn't know!"

"As if I didn't know," Aspect echoed. "But we must bear in mind two things: we can never touch him that way as long as we bear the ikons, and it is the ikons that turn us on, not our natural inclinations. So we should feel neither threat nor guilt. He is surely oblivious; let's leave him that way."

"Agreement!" Ennui found herself flushing. "He meant friendship love, not passion." But still she felt like a teen girl after her first serious kiss.

"We must bid parting to Gale and Symbol."

They went to the baby chamber and knocked. "Welcome, Ladies!" Gale called.

At the moment the babies were quiet. "We must seek yarn," Ennui explained. "For the tapestry. We may be gone some time. We came to bid parting."

"It is a worthy mission," Gale said. "Do you need guards?"

"Negation; that would end privacy. We'll travel as On and Speck. The ikons protect us."

"Advice," Symbol said. "The ikons do more than protect. Use them to advantage."

"Question?" Aspect asked.

"They turn you on sexually, and make you sexually appealing. You could seduce a random man almost as readily as I could."

"Doubt," Ennui protested. But she suspected it was true.

"Anonymous travel means you must pay your way," Symbol continued. "Not every Chroma man will be satisfied with cooking or housecleaning. Use the universal offering: no fault. It is expected of nubile travelers."

"I am beyond nubility," Ennui said, feeling the flush rising again.

"Not any more. With proper expertise you will have no trouble."

"I'm forty one years old!"

"Not any more," Symbol repeated. "Your body is thirty, pushing twenty nine, and rarely formed. You have but to show it, and the terms of travel are yours to set."

"Disbelief."

"Demonstration. You know how I am formed, but I can't show you nudity." She glanced at Gale. "Show?"

Gale stood and removed her robe, quickly nude. Her pregnancy did not yet show. She was as shapely a young woman as any in the city.

"Now the two of you," Symbol said. "Before the mirror."

"Protest," Ennui said.

But Aspect understood the demonstration. "Withdrawn," she said, removing her own clothing.

Overruled, Ennui did the same. Soon the three of them stood before the large wall mirror.

Ennui gasped. They were three beauties, a young one and two mature ones. All had slender bodies and outstanding breasts. The main differences were in the faces and hair. She had thought she would be ashamed to stand nude beside a beauty like Gale, but she had become remarkably comely. That was of course why Symbol had set this up: to show the two older women just how far the ikons had taken them. Certainly it was magic.

"Some adjustments," Symbol said. She put her fingers to Ennui's hair and removed the combs that bound it into a bun. Her dark tresses dropped loosely to her waist, half masking her breasts. Aspect did the same with her hair. Ennui's hair had been somewhat lusterless; now it was lustrous, falling in silken hanks. Aspect's hair had been good; now it was perfect.

The figures in the mirror looked even more similar. They were three sirens.

"And makeup," Symbol continued, applying it to Ennui's face. In a moment her eyes were darker and larger, her lips prominent. She could be a king's dancer. Aspect, doing the same, was similar.

"Amazement." Yet her appearance merely reflected the way she felt. "I was never like this."

"The ikons are potent," Aspect said. "They have been working on us both, restoring me, enhancing you. Yours has indeed made of you the woman you never were."

"Now move it," Symbol said, demonstrating with a flourish of her swathed hips. Aspect readily emulated her, remembering her youthful beauty, but Ennui couldn't.

"The knees," Gale said. "They power the hips."

Ennui bent her knees in turn, and saw her hips flaunt in the mirror. It was astonishingly sexy. Could that really be *her*?

"Try the rear," Symbol said, giving her a hand mirror and turning her to face away from the wall mirror. "Do the knees again, and watch."

Ennui held the mirror so that she could see the reflection of her backside as she moved. Her back was narrow, her hips remarkably wider, and her legs were impossibly shapely. Suddenly her bottom flexed, radiating sex appeal. "That can't be me!" But it was. It was like a dream of transformation, and she half expected to wake at any moment.

"Buttressed by the right clothing, you will be a killer," Symbol said approvingly. She got to work on it.

"But we need to be anonymous," Ennui said. "This—this will make of us a tour of courtesans."

"Masked by dingy outer robes," Symbol said. "Now when you approach the proprietor of a Chroma transport, bear in mind that he will be intrigued by your nonChroma appearance. Chroma men love to have sex with otherChroma and nonChroma women, just for the novelty. So you should show very little, and that briefly, until the deal is made. A little goes a very long way, when you have such a body."

"But to—to solicit strange men for sex—I could never do that," Ennui said.

"One does it subtly," Symbol said. "Pretend you are a man for a moment. Gale?"

Gale, now fully dressed, came to stand before Ennui. "I need to cross this Chroma zone. I have little to offer in trade." But her robe had fallen partly open, revealing the shadowed contour of one full breast.

"And the man will say he has a better idea," Symbol said as Gale inconspicuously drew her robe closed. "You will demur at first, but not strongly, and soon allow him to persuade you to acquiesce to his suggestion. You never openly solicited him. You don't need to."

"But still—to sell sex—"

"It is expected," Symbol repeated. "No fault can be a great tool. Women with your forms can do quite well, and there will be no complaints."

"But sex!"

"Which is what the ikon is making us desire," Aspect reminded her. "We want to be wanton."

It was true. They wanted to travel anonymously, and this was the way it was done. And it would allow them to indulge passions that were becoming overwhelming. Already Throe, a good man, was surfeit, being unable to satisfy her completely, and she knew it was similar with Aspect and Chief. Nonce had less trouble, because while the loom was full size it wasn't enhancing her, but when she carried it as an ikon, it would. To travel without men would be asking for trouble, unless they had a plan to handle it. And they had to get more yarn. This would get the job done.

Considerably educated, they postponed their journey until morning. That gave them one last night's fling with their men, and a few more hours to adjust to the notion of serious no fault traveling.

Yet they were restless. Their men, thoroughly satisfied, were sleeping, but the women were still up. "I feel nostalgia for the palace, and we haven't even left it yet," Ennui said.

"Agreement. I find myself pondering who will perform our functions while we are absent."

"And I find myself pondering whether we really should keep our secret from Havoc."

Aspect smiled. "Let's choose our successors, and tell Havoc."

"Let's be naughty, and tell Havoc about our secret passion for him."

Aspect agreed. Perhaps, with luck, they would succeed in shocking him. They departed for the royal chamber, mentally signaling their intention to meet him so that he could see them privately if he wished.

Later, satisfied that they had surprised Havoc and nudged him in two new directions, they returned to their beds and slept. It had been naughty fun.

In the morning the three of them set out, wearing rather dingy robes over rather tight outfits. Their hair was caught up in dull efficient hanks that could readily be loosed to let it flow at need. They crossed the moat, as some called it, and walked to a staging area. Nonce guided them; the loom knew where to find what it needed.

When they were clear of other company, Nonce raised a question. "The loom ikon makes me feel sexy as anything. When I carry it in my mouth, I want kissing or oral sex. When I wear it between my breasts, I want to smother a man with them. When I have it near my crotch, I want straight raw penetration."

"Familiarity," Ennui said.

"Here's the thing: if we're going to have sex with men to pay our passage, where do we carry our ikons? I mean, if I know there'll be sex coming, I should have it near my cleft—but then I won't be able to let him in. If I have it in my mouth I'll want to kiss him—and won't be able to."

She had a point. The issue hadn't come up when they weren't considering sex, but now they were. "We may just have to move them around. But it does suggest that we are doomed to be frustrated, because we can't explain our limitations to strange men." Ennui had moved her ikon around when having sex with Throe, sometimes holding it next to her cleft until the moment of his approach, then putting it behind her. He was patient, knowing her reason: the closer the ikon, the more intense her pleasure.

"The ikons offer a lot," Aspect said. "But they have their price."

Ennui concurred. Part of that price was a guilty desire for a man they knew they shouldn't try to seduce.

They started at the fringe of a Brown Chroma zone, where huge golems waited to carry coach-loads of passengers. There were several

coaches waiting, as there was a good deal of travel to and from Triumph City.

They started toward the closest. Ennui's dragon seed buzzed,
and she knew Aspect's had buzzed also. "Wrong one,"

They turned toward a second, and got buzzed again. It seemed
that there was a difference between transports.

Finally the seeds allowed them to approach the most distant of
the coaches. It was far from the most impressive; it was small, and its
golem looked battered. The man himself was of middle age and un-
handsome. But they had learned to trust the seeds.

"Question: who tries first?" Aspect inquired.

"Answer: I will," Ennui said. "I'm the one who is most nervous
about it. If I can do it, you certainly can."

"Impeccable logic."

Ennui approached the brown man. "We are three traveling women
who need transport across your zone and others." She twitched her
shoulder so that her robe opened just enough. She was half surprised
that it worked correctly the first time. "We have little to offer but the
skills of householding, such as cooking, cleaning, or minding children.
We don't need any fancy accommodations, and are good workers."

"I have a better idea," the man said. For a moment Ennui thought
she was imagining it, because it was exactly what they had said in
rehearsal. But a man was a man, regardless of the Chroma; they were
all much alike in certain situations. She could read it in his unguarded
mind: the sight of just a portion of her firm breast had set his pulses
racing. Sex, it was turning out, was amazingly easy—now that she had
the body for it.

She looked up at him with eyes that had been subtly shadowed to
look larger and brighter. "Question?" It was the maidenly pretense of
ignorance.

"No fault."

She smiled carefully. "But I am beyond youth, surely not of such
interest." Her misbehaving robe fell farther open; she drew it mod-
estly closed after providing the man with a sufficient additional glimpse.
His desire had been thoroughly stirred; the lust in his mind was feeding back to her, making her similarly eager.

"You'll do. I am not young either. Deal?"

"Agreed." And she had done it, to her passing surprise. "But we
are three. What of my companions?"

"Let me look at them."

Aspect stepped forward, her robe drawn tight at the waist but
hardly concealing the underlying figure. Nonce paced her, requiring
no clothing wiles at all, because of her youth. "Introduction," Aspect
said, providing what Ennui had forgotten to do. "I am the woman Speck,
and this is my companion the girl No."

"And I am the woman On," Ennui said.

"I am the man Nocount." He grimaced. "The one my peers concluded would never amount to much, no account. They were correct."

"We are anonymous," Ennui said. "At present we are of no more account than you, and satisfied to be so." This was a sensible qualification, because once he saw any of them nude he would know they were not washwomen drudges. The dragon seed had not buzzed to stop her, as it could have done. She was subtly enlisting his cooperation in maintaining their anonymity.

"I have a notion," the brown man said, thus encouraged. "It may not appeal to you."

"We need very much to get where we are going," Aspect said with a hesitant but appealing smile. "We are open to anything within reason."

"I have dreamed of having a bed of lovely women. Several together, all amenable."

"Several?" Aspect asked as if not understanding. Of course she understood quite well; Symbol had mentioned this variant. To a man, the only thing better than a single lovely amenable woman was several of them, at once.

"In my bed at the same time. For the duration of the trip." Caught up by the vision, he added to the offer. "Food provided. No housework. Just that."

Aspect looked at Ennui, then at Nonce. The other two hesitated, then reluctantly nodded. "It is a bit unusual," Nonce said, "but we should be able to manage if there is no unkind stuff." That could have been what the dragon seeds had warned them away from: unkind stuff, which could include sadism or truly ugly sexual tastes.

"No unkind stuff," the man said quickly. "No pain, no discomfort, just loving."

"And no telling," Nonce said. For three attractive women in the bed of a homely man would be considerable news.

Nocount hesitated. It was a man's nature to talk about his conquests. "Tell as long ago?"

That was a decent compromise that would keep them anonymous. "Agreed," the two said together.

"Deal," Nocount said, and the three of them nodded affirmation.

They entered his coach, and the brown man directed the huge brown golem to carry it carefully across the zone. Of course that was for show; the golem would do it as it always did. By this time it had probably worn a track along its familiar route.

As the coach was lifted and carried, the brown man closed the window shutters and cleared the seats to the side so that the interior became one big bed. Then he put a hand to his brown clothing, and paused. "You first."

He still wasn't quite sure they would do it, despite their agreement. Ennui smiled and undressed in leisurely fashion, knowing that

the man wanted to savor every part of his dream. She was pleased to
see that he got a masculine reaction, barely masked by his brown
trousers; she was being a success as a siren. When she was naked,
she lay down on the bed, her legs slightly apart. She was discovering
that not only was she able to do this seduction, she was enjoying it.
She was flaunting the body she had never had before.

Aspect then did her languorous strip, more artistically than Ennui had managed, causing Nocount's breathing to accelerate. Finally
Nonce did hers, at which point the man almost ripped off his own
clothing and stood erect in more than one sense. His body was middle
aged but clean, fortunately.

The three smiled warmly at Nocount. This was his fantasy, and
they were obliging it to the best of their understanding and ability.
Ennui realized that it was really a play, with the cast catering to the
lead character.

Some choreography, Aspect thought to Ennui. *I'll take the head,
you take the groin. We'll have to keep our ikons clear of our action
areas. When he's done with you, we can change positions.*

Action areas: their mouths, breasts, and clefts. An unromantic
description, but realistic. *Agreement.*

Still bemused that they were actually doing it, Ennui found herself quite ready. This was a man's fantasy, but she was reveling in her
newfound capacity to *be* a stranger man's dream. They kept their ikons
always on their bodies, never in their clothes, because they couldn't
afford to be separated from them. It wasn't just a matter of the protection the ikons provided them; it was that each ikon was incalculably
valuable in itself and could not be risked. They owed it to Havoc, Gale,
and the loom. *What of Nonce?*

She can start with his legs.

Ennui put it into motion. "Don't tease us, virile man; come find
your lodging." She spread her legs farther, invitingly. Oh what a naughty
show!

Nocount was drawn to her as by a magnet. He came down on
hands and knees, and she caught him about the waist and drew her
groin into his. She avoided his face, as she had her ikon in her mouth;
he would not be able to kiss her, and she didn't want him to realize
that.

Meanwhile Aspect, kneeling, caught his head and drew it in to the
pillows of her breasts. She had her ikon in a little pouch tied to her
ankle. Nonce, guided by a glance from Aspect, sat by his legs and
massaged them. Her ikon was in her mouth.

The coordinated effect was overwhelming for the man. He thrust
into Ennui and jetted instantly. She held him close, making little sighs
of pleasure, as she had so recently learned to do from Symbol. Men
wanted to think that their pleasure translated automatically to the
women, even when it was far too fast for that to be possible. But the

fact was, she was so ikon-hot that mere penetration was enough to bring her to climax, and of course she was receiving his climax from his mind, triggering hers anyway. Telepathy transformed sex, making the woman share the man's urgency. So she really didn't have to pretend pleasure; she was having it.

Spent, the brown man rolled off Ennui and let his head loll between Aspects generous breasts. Nonce continued massaging his legs, slowly working her way up. "Oh, that was great," he gasped.

"It has just begin," Aspect murmured. "You must do me next." She stroked his brown hair.

Ennui faced away and used a tissue to do a spot cleanup while the others occupied Nocount's attention. Men were not much on the necessary supplementary details of sex; they preferred to focus only on the act itself.

Constantly stimulated, it wasn't long before the man was ready for the next bout. Chroma men could recharge rapidly with the help of magic when they needed to. Aspect slid down and stroked his penis, while Nonce moved up to become his breasts pillow. Ennui took over the leg massage. They helped him get into position for Aspect, and she facilitated his penetration. But it was after all too soon; he was erect but not quite ready to climax again.

Spank him, Aspect thought to Ennui.

Surprised, Ennui hesitated. But Aspect sent her a mental picture: both men and women liked being sexually spanked. This was not something Ennui had ever had experience with, but she could not doubt Aspect's experience. Aspect had been a beautiful woman long before Ennui, despite their being the same age. So she tried it, lightly smacking Nocount's bottom as he lay on Aspect. His brown buttocks tautened, and his mind reacted; it was indeed stimulating him sexually.

She spanked him harder, making it sting a little, and that sting translated into further desire. So there really was a connection between pain and pleasure; she had never believed it, but now was experiencing it through him. Soon he was pumping into Aspect, long and slow. Amazing how well such small signals worked.

After another interlude of pillows and massage, during which Aspect quietly cleaned up, it was Nonce's turn. She was so eager she didn't wait for Nocount to initiate it; she got on him as he lay supine, set him into her, and clenched and bounced on him until he had no choice but to climax a third time. Ennui and Aspect felt it telepathically, and shared her urgency. His conclusion was slow, but almost painfully intense when it finally got there; the two of them gasped with him.

Sexually exhausted, he lay among them, still appreciating their incidental catering, not noticing Nonce's quick cleanup. "You are the hottest three women I've met," he said in wonder.

"We intend to satisfy you," Ennui said. "Let it never be said that nonChroma women are inadequate."

"Never!" he agreed fervently. Then, perhaps fearing that they would want another round, embarrassing him by his lack of further ability, he remembered his promise to feed them. "There's good food in the locker."

Ennui got up and located it. She did not dress; the man's dream wasn't yet over, and three naked women were part of it. There was an ample supply of brown bread, wine, potato salad, meat, and pudding. She portioned it out, and they sat cross-legged in a circle and ate. It was good food, and welcome.

"Comment," the brown man said. Now was the time to get to know each other, when there was no urgency.

"Welcome," Ennui said for the three of them.

"I know it's no fault, and you're just keeping your end of the deal. I figured you'd honor it technically, but it wouldn't really be all there. It can make a big difference, how a woman is, even when she's doing it, if you know what I mean."

All three smiled. "We know," Ennui said.

"But you three gave me more than I ever expected. It's as though you're really into it, liking it the way I did. And you're all beautiful; I figured you'd be less so when your clothes were off. Even now, you're letting me see your breasts and cracks, when you don't have to. If that's an act, it's a damn good one."

It was phrased as a comment, but it was really a question, and required an answer. "We are traveling, and will be returning in due course. It will be easier if we can cross the Chroma zones with the same people as the first time, so we wish to make a good impression."

"No offense." This meant he had a negative remark.

"None," Ennui agreed.

"I think this is horse manure. You could have made a good impression on me with a lot less enthusiasm. You could impress *anyone* without half trying. In fact, why did you choose my coach? It's the least of the ones available. I usually get the riffraff." He frowned. "I took the job I could get, apprentice to a coachman, and when he retired twenty years later I took over the business. Strictly no account. Some women do pay with sex, but none of them have been anywhere near the class of any of you three. I'll bet you are part of a troupe doing pro entertaining. You had no need to ride with me, let alone make my dream."

"We have ways of judging," Ennui said. "We felt we would be more comfortable with you."

"Even with my dream?"

"Especially with your dream. It's one we are equipped to accommodate."

"You sure are!"

More explanation was needed. "And as it happens, we are lusty women. We don't like pain or degradation, but straight passion is nice.

Some men are too cynical, some too brutal, and some insist on telling too much. So you were the one for us. We can oblige you, and you will keep our secret." She allowed him to believe that he had guessed correctly about their employment; that was far safer than the truth.

Nocount pondered a moment, thinking of the obscure tastes of some of the other coachmen; just the bits of it Ennui picked up telepathically were enough to make her glad the dragon seeds had guided them. "Well, you've done it," he said at last. "And I'll be glad to take you back when you return, if I'm there. I just wish I had more time and vigor."

"Yours are sufficient," Aspect said.

"Negation. I wish I could do at all again with you, but we're getting near the other side of the zone, and I'm not ready."

"And the moment we're gone, you'll regret it," Aspect said. "That you couldn't take it while it was there."

Nocount laughed ruefully. "I regret it already."

"Let's see what we can do," Ennui said, loving the unfamiliar role of seductress.

They cleared away the remnants of the food and closed in on him. They kissed him, fondled him, rubbed him, and soon had him sexually excited again. They knew that the nearness of the three ikons affected him, restoring him more rapidly than would otherwise be possible even with his Brown magic. Then Ennui did the honors, taking him into her and bringing him to a slow climax while the others stroked his body.

"You see, you were ready after all," Ennui said, kissing him as she held her ikon in her hand, behind her back. Then Aspect kissed him as Ennui quietly returned her ikon to her mouth. Finally Nonce kissed him similarly. He was still inside Ennui, softening; she felt twitches as the others kissed him, but that was all. He was truly done.

The coach was lowered to the ground. The four of them hastily separated and dressed. "Maybe on the way back, you'll tell me more," the man said. "There's got to be more."

"Maybe we will," Ennui said. "If you keep the faith."

"Oath!"

That set Ennui back for irrelevant reason: it reminded her of her oath with Havoc, that had transformed her life. Suppose she hadn't thought to demand it of him? It was possible that both of them would be dead, and someone else would be king. The thought appalled her.

Fortunately Aspect covered for her. "Fond Parting," she said, kissing Nocount again. Nonce followed, and then Ennui, reminded. They walked away, leaving the nice brown man bemused.

⁂

Aspect smiled as they left the Brown Chroma zone. That had been more of an adventure than anticipated, but a pleasant one. Nonce, by far the youngest, was nevertheless most experienced in the art of man-pleasing, being a bath girl. Aspect herself knew it, but had not practiced it in decades; it was good to verify that she could still do it, albeit with the considerable aid of the ikon. Ennui was least experienced, because there had not before been general male interest in her body, but she had come through well. They had demonstrated that they had what it took to travel with sexual no fault.

Then next Chroma was Air, or Invisible. Of course it wasn't invisible; it was a riot of colors, as every person, animal, and plant projected its own image, the way it wanted to be seen. It was only when folk left their Air Chroma zone that they lost their magic of illusion, and became invisible. Symbol suffered that, and the three Air sisters who had visited Triumph City. One might have thought that they would become dully visible when they lost their magic, but that wasn't the way Chroma worked; people retained their colors, until they slowly faded in new territory. Few regarded this fading as desirable; their colors were much of their identities, beyond their Chroma.

They had no trouble making a deal with a handsome (naturally) pair of Air men, who took one look at their figures and had better ideas. They made a competitive game of it: one had sex with Ennui, the other with Aspect, simultaneously, and the first one who recovered enough to achieve a full second erection got Nonce for the follow-up. As it turned out, the second got her too, in the interest of maintaining male harmony. Thereafter the men concluded that they had had enough, their sexual ambition being slightly larger than their capacity. Symbol had covered that too: give men all the sex they wanted, because it was self limiting, despite their expectations. Meanwhile they floated magically across the zone in a large open basket, supported by piled pillows. Evidently these men had entertained traveling women before.

By the time they reached the other side of the zone, night was closing, and they camped for the night. "It has been interesting," Aspect said as they ate their supper, "But I think I have had enough sex for the day."

"Agreement," Ennui said. "But it certainly is easier to travel this way."

"I always travel this way," Nonce said.

"You have always been young," Aspect informed her. "The two of us have only recently gotten young again." Actually she had understood that Nonce preferred to save her sex for the king, in case he should ever want it, but it was her business.

The next zone was Green. Fabulous plants were everywhere, but the green men were just like the men of other colors in what counted. The three ikon-enhanced bodies lured them uncontrollably, and a deal was easy.

In due course they came to a Gray Chroma zone. "I think this is the last one," Nonce said. "I feel it getting close."

"It will be a pleasure to let no fault be for a while," Aspect said.

They approached the Gray Chroma fringe station. This one had a nondescript gray-haired woman. That meant they would have to make some other kind of deal.

"Confusion," the gray woman said. "You wish to cross the zone?"

"We believe so," Aspect said patiently. "We are not sure of our destination, but believe it is close beyond."

"That would be Death Valley. No one goes there."

"Question?"

"It is part of a thick ribbon of barren terrain that extends throughout this region. It is nonChroma and deadly; few things live there, and only knowledgeable folk even approach it. Your mission is surely elsewhere."

The three of them did not need to exchange a glance or thoughts. This sounded like the kind of place where something essential would be hidden, like magic yarn. "Perhaps. But we feel the need to check."

"Introduction: I am Malkin."

Sometimes peer-naming could be unkind. The word Malkin meant a rag mop or an untidy woman. Evidently she had reason for more comprehensive dialogue, so was taking a necessary step toward it.

"We are the women Speck and On, and the girl No."

"If you are determined to visit Death Valley, you will need a guide from Village Edge, adjacent to it. Otherwise you will be in peril. But even their experienced guides are not keen on penetrating that wilderness. They will make a demand."

Here it came: the price. "Continue."

"They have a situation in Village Edge. They are looking for a person or persons to represent an unpopular side in a decision on exile."

"And this will be their price for a competent guide into Death Valley," Aspect said. She wondered whether this could resemble the situation Throe and Gale had faced when they had been required to judge Augur and Aura, the cross-Chroma lovers. Travelers were liable for what local folk avoided.

"Affirmation."

"What is the side?"

"That is something they decline to divulge, but it must be extremely awkward. I am unable to make a recommendation, other than caution."

This time Aspect did exchange the glances. "We seem to be without choice. We will go there and negotiate with them. But first we need to obtain passage to that village."

"I will provide it without other requirement. The villagers have agreed to recompense me for any effort I make on their behalf."

"Agreement," Aspect said. Her dragon seed had not buzzed. Of course the seeds had limits, and did not seem to be concerned about things like awkwardness or embarrassment, only safely and truth. Malkin had not lied.

The gray woman ushered them into her coach. Actually it was more like a boat, having no wheels and being open above. There were three seat-benches across it with room for two people on each. Aspect sat with Malkin in the front seat, and Ennui and Nonce sat in the real seat, leaving the middle one empty for balance.

"Fasten belts." Malkin demonstrated by drawing up straps that were tied into the seat, and knotting them across her lap. She waited while the others did the same. "The ride can veer."

Aspect tried to peek into the gray woman's mind, but it was thoroughly opaque. The gray Chroma really did stifle other magic, it seemed, to a degree.

The craft moved. It slid forward along a shallow indented track, self propelled. Its progress was smooth, as if the track were a slippery chute, as perhaps it was. She saw that the track curved sinuously ahead, and the boat followed it, gaining speed. When it came to a curve, it swung around it, throwing the passengers outward with surprising force. But the seat belt held, and no one toppled off the seat or out of the boat.

"Comment: Each Chroma zone has a different type of transport," Aspect remarked.

"We prefer our own." Evidently the woman wasn't much for conversation.

They zoomed across the gray monochrome landscape at considerable velocity. Aspect saw gray trees, houses, lakes, and people, all looking much like those elsewhere, except for the color. She saw other sliding tracks, some with boats moving. Sometimes tracks diverged into two, or merged; they interconnected in much the manner of roads, except that there were no right angles. Some tracks formed bow-like loops. Aspect didn't understand that until she saw a boat zoom from one track, around a loop, and onto a new track going a different direction, without ever stopping or even slowing much. That was it: no stopping, therefore greater efficiency.

After a time they came to a gray village. The boat smoothly slowed, and finally glided to a stop at an outlying house. An old man emerged as they untied their seat belts and got out of the boat.

"Greeting," the man said.

"Acknowledged," they chorused.

"Welcome to Village Edge."

"Appreciation."

"Introduction: I am Elder Reaper."

They named themselves.

Then Malkin got to business: "These travelers need to visit Death Valley. They may be willing to serve your need."

Reaper didn't hesitate. "Hospitality of the village for the duration, and a competent guide to Death Valley when the matter is concluded."

Aspect paused momentarily, listening for a buzz from her dragon seed. There was none. "Agreement."

"Parting," Malkin said, returning to her boat. She seemed relieved. Perhaps other attempts had not worked out.

"Parting," they echoed as the boat slid away.

"You did not inquire as to the matter we contemplate," the elder said.

"Our need is urgent," Aspect answered. "Your terms seem fair."

"Nevertheless, we shall give you the option of declining, after you understand its nature, provided you will agree to keep it private."

"We agree not to bruit it about elsewhere," Aspect said.

Reaper glanced at the others; they nodded acceptance.

"We have in our village two women whom some wish to exile; others wish to let them be. There will be a hearing and a decision. The women need a person or persons to argue their case effectively, as they are not apt at public presentations." He paused, awaiting their response.

Aspect had appeared in public many times, as queen, and was fair spoken. Now, with Gale's ikon enhancing her body and mind, she knew she could be quite effective. "I am apt, if there is a reasonable case to be made."

"That depends on your view." He paused again.

Something was up, but the dragon seed did not buzz. The man was not lying, merely being unusually cautious. His mind was opaque to telepathy, as the gray woman's had been, so she was dependent on the guidance of the seeds.

"My view is much as that of any other mature woman." Seeing his brow wrinkle, she explained: "I am forty one years old, and past my four children. Magic has improved me somewhat."

"Understatement!"

"Appreciation. Similar is true for my companions. We have become more attractive than we were, but we remain normal in other respects. We should react to issues as other women would, but perhaps with greater tolerance than some, for our experience has educated us." It wasn't necessary to clarify that that experience had been at the king's court, where acquaintance with and tolerance for many divergent types and attitudes was necessary.

The gray elder nodded. "The women are lesbians."

So that was it. By sheer coincidence, Aspect had recent experience handling such a case. "There are those who do prefer their own gender. If this does not interfere with their households, it should not be occasion for concern among others."

"They have had their families, and are considered to be good mothers. Now that their four are done, they wish to leave their husbands and live together as a couple. The village is divided whether to allow this. If it is not allowed, they will be sent into exile. They say they would prefer to die."

Aspect had managed to deal with the young nonChroma man's situation by arranging his marriage to a lesbian woman, masking their natures. But this was open. "And you wish us to try to persuade the villagers to accept them."

"I wish you to make their case, so that no unfairness may be attributed to the village for ejecting them."

So he was one of the naysayers. This was a job likely doomed to failure. But it was the price of their guidance to Death Valley. "We will make their case," Aspect said, and Ennui and Nonce nodded.

"This way." He led them to an empty gray house that turned out to be fully functional and provisioned. They would have no trouble staying here for the duration of their business here.

"The lesbians are in the adjacent house," Reaper said. "The hearing will be held tomorrow at noon. Parting."

"Parting," Aspect said somewhat faintly to the man's back. They had barely a day and night to prepare their case. It occurred to her that a day and night of wild sex with all the village men would probably have been easier than what they faced.

"But they will guide us to Death Valley, win or lose this case," Nonce said.

"Nevertheless, I want to win this case," Ennui said grimly. "I know discrimination when I see it."

"You two get settled," Aspect said. "I will make contact with our clients, and set up a dialogue for this afternoon. We shall need to marshal our thoughts."

She went next door and knocked. There was no answer, but she knew people were there. "I am your representative," she called.

The door opened, reluctantly. A gray woman of middle age was there. "Greeting," she said unenthusiastically.

"Explanation: I am one of three nonChroma travelers who need to see Death Valley. We are informed that we must make your case to the village tomorrow at noon, in return for a guide. We have sympathy for your situation, and want to do our best. But we have little notion how. Perhaps if we can talk with you for a while, we can work something out. We mean well, and are competent in our fashions. Perhaps we can help."

"Enter," the woman said, seeming relieved.

"I do not mean to visit, just to exchange introductions and agree to meet later today," Aspect said, entering the house.

In the main room stood another gray woman, much like the first. To Aspect, one middle aged Gray Chroma woman looked much like another.

"Introduction," the first woman said. "I am Mender, and my companion is Sympathy."

"I am Speck, and my companions are—"

"The Lady Aspect!" Sympathy said. "King Deal's queen. I saw you on a tour a decade ago, and you look even better now."

This was awkward. "Favor. You have recognized me, but I am traveling anonymously. I ask that you keep my secret."

"Agreed," Sympathy said.

"We are good at keeping secrets," Mender said. "We kept ours for twenty years." She glanced at Sympathy. "This woman is really the queen?"

"Not any more," Aspect said. "My husband died, and now Havoc the Barbarian is king, and his wife is queen. I am on a mission for them. We fear it would be compromised if known."

"We understand compromise," Sympathy said. "Surely you can make our case well, if anyone can."

"I will do my best. But I need to know you better. Can my associates and I converse with you this evening? We have little time."

"We will come to your house at dusk," Mender said. "Apology for mistrusting you at the door. We have been shunned or condemned by some."

"Needless. Understanding." Aspect stepped back, in a half unconscious mannerism signifying the letting go of something unwanted— and her dragon seed buzzed.

Alarmed, she turned. The floor she had been about to step on consisted of gray boards like the rest, but these seemed less solid. In fact, she recognized the contours of a removable panel, perhaps covering access to a cellar. It was not quite tight; her foot might have dislodged it and sent her tumbling.

She turned back to the two women, and caught mutual expressions of alarm. "Problem?" she asked.

"None," Mender said quickly. "Here is the door."

But the seed buzzed. The woman was lying or at least concealing something.

"There must be candor between us, if we are to help," Aspect said. "I have no intention of exposing any secret of yours, just as you are keeping mine. Is there something I should know?"

Sympathy sighed. "Confirmation." She indicated the stove, where a pot was boiling. "We are making poison."

"Horror!"

"Not for you or anyone else," Mender said quickly. "For us. It is a herb that puts a person to sleep so deeply that soon death follows, painlessly."

"You expect to be banished," Aspect said.

Both nodded. "Exiled," Sympathy said. "We can't face that. All our lives have been here. So we mean to remain, the only way we can."

"But we do not want our bodies to be despoiled or removed,"

Mender said. "So we have made another brew, a lot of it, that will dissolve our bodies and enable them to sink into the ground where they can never be recovered. That brew is in the cellar."

"Which I might have fallen into, had not some fluke stayed me," Aspect said. She was really getting to appreciate the dragon seed!

"We did not mean to burden you with this information," Sympathy said.

"It is better that I know. It impresses on me the importance of my assignment. I shall try to save you from the necessity, but will not interfere if that is your only choice."

"Appreciation," Mender said. "The villagers would prevent it, if they knew."

Aspect stepped to the door. "Parting, until dusk."

"Parting," the two women echoed.

Back at the other house, she found Ennui and Nonce comfortable. "This gray food is excellent," Nonce said.

"As is their lavatory," Ennui said. She was in a gray bathrobe, having just washed.

"I have met our clients," Aspect said as she disrobed and went to the lavatory herself. "They are nice women in a cruel dilemma. They mean to die if they are exiled. We must prevail."

"How can we persuade reluctant villagers to be tolerant?" Nonce asked. "Triumph City has many visitors and many variants, and leads to tolerance, but isolated villages tend to be bigoted."

"I don't know how, only that we must," Aspect said. She discovered a shower chamber that magically pumped warm water. That was a luxury almost unknown in nonChroma, but common in Chroma zones. Her voice resonated in this confined space.

"Sing," Ennui suggested. "I did. I was surprised how good I sounded."

Aspect had sung in youth. She had been fair, not great. "Black, black, black is the color of my true love's hair," she sang, and indeed it sounded good. "Her lips are something rosy fair."

"You need to be a man to sing that," Ennui said.

"Or—" Nonce started, but broke off, embarrassed.

"Or a woman who loves a woman," Aspect finished. "Suddenly I have a weird notion."

"We shouldn't tease them about being lesbian," Ennui cautioned her.

"That's not precisely it. But before I finish my thought, let's find out whether we really can sing. The ikons may have enhanced us in this manner too."

They tried it. Soon they were singing in three part chorus, and it seemed quite melodious. The ikons *had* enhanced their voices, and now they were near minstrel level.

"I believe we can do it," Aspect said. "Song—music—has evocative qualities. It can move the heart and spirit. That's why young men sing to young women."

"I know," Nonce said dreamily. "Two years ago, when I was fourteen, a boy sang to me. Of course he just wanted to Poke & Tell, and I knew it, but he succeeded."

"Full sex?" Ennui asked. "At fourteen?"

"I had breasts," Nonce said defensively. "And he had such a voice. It would have been a shame to let his effort be wasted."

"This time I want to move some villagers," Aspect said. "I know Havoc and Gale could do it, both being minstrels; they could make the rafters weep. If we can do it too, we can save those poor women. It's a wild idea, but I think it's possible."

"Not much else is," I suspect," Ennui said.

They selected songs and practiced harmonies. There was little doubt about it: they were better singers than they had ever been before, and their voices related nicely. Nonce was soprano, Ennui alto, and Aspect could manage countertenor. The ikons might be responsible for the interaction too, relating magically to each other.

At dusk the two lesbian women came. After introductions, they all sat and talked. "How were you named?" Aspect asked them. That was always the signal for an interesting little story that also clarified a person's nature.

"I was from a needy home," Mender said. "Instead of new, we patched the old. As third daughter, I was last in line, and all my clothing was well worn before I got it. So I learned to patch it well, sometimes so that no sign of repair was evident. Realizing this, other children came to me with their repairs, and I become Mender."

"From the start, I was sympathetic to others," Sympathy said. "I was always interested in their stories. I don't know when I was named; it just seemed to be my identity. We met when I had a tear in my skirt and she had a scratch on her leg. She fixed my tear and I commiserated about her scratch."

"We were friends from then on," Mender agreed. "But we didn't know our natures."

"Confusion," Aspect said.

"Then came the dread eighteenth birthday," Mender said, proceeding to what she knew the visitors wanted to know. "Neither of us were really pretty, so we lacked choices in men. But after the pretty girls were taken, there was less choice, and our turn came. We were lucky; our men were decent. We knew our duty to the village and humanity, and they knew how to get us with child. We did love our children, and all other children; they congregated at our houses."

"And when the time for our fourths came, our men simply exchanged partners and did it," Sympathy said. "They said it was intriguing, and perhaps it was. We did not find it any more interesting than it had been with our husbands. It was effective, and we each had our fourths, and we loved them too, as they tied our families together. Then one day when she was mending for my family, I remarked on how little I felt the need for sex; were it not for my husband's desire, I would be satisfied to live without it. Mender agreed; it was no better for her. We know that it was not because of the men, because we had clasped each other's men and found them no better. Most women find the seeding of their fourths to be exciting or revolting; we found neither. We knew that other women had some genuine interest, at least when that man was handsome or especially attentive. So the lack seemed to be in us."

"Then, somehow, it happened," Mender said. "The children were all out elsewhere, and so were the men; we were alone in the house, her house. I was holding a mended blouse up to her chest to verify the fit, and she put her arms around me to maintain her balance, and then we came together and kissed."

"And it was magic," Sympathy said. "We got a thrill we had never had from the men. We kissed and kissed, and it just got better. Then we stripped away our clothing and lay on the bed and fondled each other's breasts. I had never done that before; I had only been fondled by a man, and while I was glad to give him what pleasure I could, there was little in it for me. I had learned to be stimulating to him so that he would grow more quickly urgent, and do it, and sleep, letting me be. Now I discovered what he felt: the touch of a woman's breasts can be marvelously exciting. And her bottom. And her kisses. And when she kissed my breasts, I became eager for more. It was all so novel and exhilarating and wonderful."

"So we made love," Mender said. "We adapted the techniques we had used on our men, and that they had used on us, and now they worked phenomenally well. We knew that this was what true sex could be, and true love."

"And kept it secret from all others," Sympathy said. "No one thought it remarkable that we were together so much, for we had always been close friends, and cared for each other's children. But when we were alone, it wasn't talking or mending we did, but sex. We had discovered its meaning at last."

"Once our children were grown," Mender said, "we realized that if we were ever going to know complete happiness, this was the time. We told our husbands."

"That was our first mistake," Sympathy said. "We thought they would understand. They did not."

"They told others," Mender said. "And others condemned us. Our marriages were over in all but name. There was nothing to do but be open about it, and move in together. That freed our husbands to take other wives, which actually helped the village, because there are more women here than men. So our husbands became reconciled."

"In fact, having younger wives, they became enthusiastic," Sympathy said. "It seems that passively cooperating women had left them somewhat unsatisfied. Once they discovered how active women could be, they were ready to make up for lost time. So it seemed to be a good solution for everyone."

"Except to a good many other villagers," Mender said. "They felt there was something obscene about it, and petitioned to have us forced to return to clasping men or to be exiled. So the elders arranged a hearing, but there was a problem."

"No one wanted to plead your case," Aspect said.

"Accuracy."

"So it was in limbo for some time," Sympathy said. "Until now."

"Suspicion," Aspect said. "It might have been better for you had we not come."

"Negation," Mender said. "It has to be settled. We can not endure indefinitely in limbo."

"One way or the other," Sympathy agreed.

They talked further, and got to know each other reasonably well. There would be others to interview in the morning. If they were able to put it together well enough, they had a case they had a chance to win.

The two women returned to their house, and the three travelers settled down to sleep. Aspect had no certainty that they could prevail, but they did have a chance. It depended on how well her idea for the songs worked out.

In the morning they practiced their singing, making sure they had not lost their voices. They worked out a medley of adaptable songs. This would be an unusual hearing.

Then they went out to interview the two husbands and some of the supportive friends. The village was closely divided; no one could be sure the way the vote would go.

By noon they had a pretty good idea of who favored the women and who wanted to be rid of them. The children generally favored the women, who for twenty years had been highly supportive of all children, not just their own. But children would not vote; that was a privilege of adult status. Many of the younger adults who had recently been children felt the same; their votes would count. The two ex-husbands had changed their minds. "If I had known it would come to this, I would have kept my mouth shut," one said candidly. "Sympathy was always a good woman, always there for me, and great with the children. The village needs her."

But there was a hard core of older women and their husbands who absolutely rejected the notion of women loving women. A number of their supporters might change if the prime movers did, but would not be weaned away from them. There were as many of them as there were young adults, making the issue too close to call. Those were the ones to be addressed.

The hearing started on time, as Vivid was at zenith. Mender and

Sympathy took seats in the center of the village square, the cynosure. They looked awkward and afraid. It was obvious that they would not be able to speak effectively in their defense. They never tried; they just sat there, eyes downcast. Aspect would have felt sorry for them even if she hadn't had the job of defending them.

Two children came to the women, a boy and a girl. Aspect knew these were the youngest of those they had raised, now ten years old: the fourths. They understood what it was like to be set apart, even if there was no official discrimination. Each of them hugged each of the women, tears flowing. They did not want their mothers to be lost.

Aspect glanced with assumed casualness at the villagers, and saw the effect. These two had been good mothers, and the whole village knew it. Sexual preference was one thing, parenting another.

A severe-faced older woman stood first, a female elder, addressing the assembled villagers in the circle around the stage. There was no introduction; all that mattered was the statements. "The question is whether we wish to have among us women openly practicing perversion," she said. "After the presentations, there will be a division of the village by all adults, and a clear majority will carry the issue." She looked around. "First the case for exile."

Another sour woman rose and stepped into the center. "Outrage. It was bad enough their doing it in secret, but doing it openly is worse. If we countenance this, we become supporters of corruption. They must either return to their men and do their duty by them, or depart far from our sight."

Several more spoke, most of them mature women. Aspect found it interesting that the women seemed to have stronger feelings on the subject than the men. Perhaps it was that to a man, any woman was looking for a man, and only if she could not find a man did she turn to a woman. That wasn't true, but men's sexual notions were crafted largely on illusion anyway.

Then it was time for the defense. Aspect spoke first. "You have known these two women throughout. You know they have already done their duty by their husbands and the village, raising eight fine children. If the vote were put to the children, there would be no question of their fitness."

"Falsity," one of the prosecution women said angrily.

Aspect pounced on it; she had long experience managing the reactions of large audiences and knew the advantage of flair. She also knew the nature of children, whatever their Chroma. "You believe I speak falsely? Then let's have a showing of the children." She looked around, her eye catching those of many of the children who lurked around the outside of the group. Usually children were seated up front, but this was no entertainment play, and they were excluded from participation. "Children!" she called. "This doesn't count, but you can still show how you feel. Come here to the center, all of you!"

"Irregular," the elder woman protested.

"You challenged my statement," Aspect said firmly. "I must defend my credibility."

Other villagers nodded. Aspect's statement had been rhetorical, but now needed to be defended. The elder had unwittingly opened the door.

The children were glad to have the attention. They flocked in, about thirty of them, ranging from just below marriage age to toddler. They were tittering excitedly at this unexpected recognition.

"Now we'll have a division of the group," Aspect said. "All who want to banish these two mothers stand here." She indicated a spot near the prosecution elder. "All who want these women to stay in Edge Village stand here." She gestured to a spot near Mender and Sympathy.

Perhaps five gray children walked toward the exile place. The rest ran to the seated women. They didn't just stand, they clustered around them, chorusing their Greetings, taking their hands, hugging them. Some were crying. It seemed that most of the children of the village had close relations with these two mothers. The five saw that, hesitated, and then went to join the others. It was hard for a child to be part of a clear minority.

Aspect made a grand gesture with her hands: Observe. She had made her point. One thing was sure: the other side would not challenge her again. They had discovered the hard way that she was an experienced handler of groups. That was important, because this was going to be an unusual presentation.

It took a while for the children to clear the stage. Several of the older ones lingered, looking seriously out into the adult audience. They were silently challenging their own parents, making them feel guilty about the proceedings.

"What is more important than motherhood?" Aspect asked rhetorically. "The children know. What business is it of anyone else whom a woman embraces at night, as long as she's an asset to the village by day, and there for the children? You know these are fine people—whom you now propose to punish for their honesty. You think no woman ever loved a woman before, in secret? As if forcing them to embrace men again would do the village any favor, when there are more women here than men. Which other women will have to be exiled, because there are no men for them to marry here? You should be thankful you have an alternative." But she saw that wasn't going over; the specter of unnatural sex did not allow for convenient alternatives.

"But argument is useless," Aspect continued. "Instead we propose to show you the essence of what you contemplate."

Now Ennui and Nonce came to the stage, swathed in encompassing cloaks. Nonce carried a staff, though it was evident she did not need support. Ennui took center stage, an obscure figure facing away from Aspect.

Without preamble, Aspect sang, drawing on all the power of her restored voice. She was aware of the surprise of the villagers; there had been no prior hint that she was a singer. Indeed, she had not been, since her youth. Nonce joined in, providing a supportive chorus; this was a standard device in minstrel presentations, and understood as such. The song was of course well familiar; all the ancient songs of Origin Earth Planet were constantly circulated throughout the human community, and the monoChroma zones did not affect the wording. It was its sudden rendition at the serious hearing that was startling.

> Black black black is the color of my true love's hair
> Her lips are like some rosy fair
> The prettiest face and the neatest hands
> I love the ground whereon she stands.

As Aspect sang, Ennui slowly turned, letting her cloak fall to the ground. She shook out her dark hair, which was surprisingly luxuriant. Here in this gray Chroma zone, the effect was considerable; no woman here had hair like that.

> I love my love and well she knows
> I love the ground on where she goes
> If she no more on earth I see
> My life will quickly fade away.

Ennui smiled and removed her shirt, showing her fine breasts. There was a murmur through the audience. After the first shock of the emergence of the song, they were realizing that this serenade was by a woman to a woman, and not merely spiritually. The woman was a sex object.

The fact was that while any man could relate to a well formed woman, so could many women. Ennui now had the kind of form most women longed to have. The kind that was a magnet for male attention.

Then Nonce advanced. She gestured with her staff in a Go Away signal. Ennui, obedient, picked up her shirt and cloak and walked off the stage.

Aspect, seeing that, bowed her head in projected sorrow. The village authority had denied the right of a woman to love a woman. She sang, drawing on the ikon to project feeling.

> I go to troublesome to mourn and weep
> But satisfied I ne'er could sleep
> I'll write you in a few little lines
> I'll suffer death ten thousand times.

> So fare you well, my own true love
> The time has come and I wish you well
> But still I hope the time will come
> When you and I will be as one.

There it was: love and exile. Changing it to female-female made all the difference. The villagers were uneasy; they well understood the joys of love, but didn't want to understand this type of love. It was a popular song, generating powerful emotion—which was uncomfortable in this circumstance. Especially since Ennui had become a truly lovely woman, so that anyone could understand loving her.

Aspect brought out a little pad, and quickly wrote on it. These were the "few little lines" to her lover. Nonce glided up, took the note, and carried it offstage. Then Aspect departed to the other side.

Ennui returned, reading the note; she had received the letter. She hurried after Aspect, but was too late; Aspect was gone, facing away from the stage.

Then Ennui broke into song, and Nonce supported her vocally too. Ennui was not as apt as Aspect, but her ikon gave her a better than average voice, and it, too, projected well. This time it was "Greensleeves," with the color understood despite the Chroma monochrome.

> Alas, my love, you do me wrong
> To cast me off discourteously
> When I have loved you so long
> Delighting in your company.

Now it was Aspect who faced away, dropping her cloak to reveal her own figure. She joined with the other two for the chorus; this too was standard, and did not mean she was really participating. Everyone had to sing, in dramatized songs.

> Greensleeves was my delight
> Greensleeves was all my joy
> Greensleeves was my heart of gold
> And who but my Lady Greensleeves?

The song continued, as the lover poured out her grief at being denied. It concluded:

> Greensleeves, now farewell, adieu
> God I pray to prosper thee
> For I am still thy lover true
> Come once again and love me.

Ennui gave up and walked away. Only then, in the measured timing of such drama, did Aspect turn back and address her again in song. By this time the fact that this was woman to woman love was established, and the audience was accepting it, at least for the assimilation of the show. This time the song was less familiar but nonetheless beautiful and feeling:

> In the gloaming, oh my darling,
> When the lights are dim and low
> And the quiet shadows stealing
> Softly come and softly go.
> When the winds are sobbing faintly
> With a gentle unknown woe
> Will you think of me and love me
> As you did once long ago?

For this was the voice of the one who had left, despite loving. It was painful, and the pain came through as the ikon lent Aspect even more evocative power. She could feel it affecting the audience.

> In the gloaming, oh my darling
> Think not bitterly of me
> Though I passed away in silence
> Left you lonely, left you free
> For my heart was crushed with longing
> What had been could never be.
> It was best to leave you thus, dear
> Best for you and best for me.

But Ennui had not yet departed the stage. As Aspect sang, she paused, and turned, and slowly oriented on her. When Aspect finished, she stepped toward her, and sang, with Nonce providing support and Aspect joining the refrain.

> Tell me the tales that to me were so dear
> Long long ago, long long ago.
> Sing me the songs I delighted to hear
> Long long ago, long ago.
> Now you are come all my grief is removed
> Let me forget that so long you have roved
> Let me believe that you love as you loved
> Long long ago, long ago.

As Ennui completed the song, they came together, reunited. Aspect was aware of the audience feeling for them, relieved that reconciliation had been achieved.

They embraced and kissed, woman to woman. Aspect knew it was an evocative moment.

"Outrage!" Nonce cried. "Obscenity!" She charged in from the edge of the stage and thwacked her staff hard against Ennui's back. The sound was loud in the quiet of the kiss.

Ennui dropped to the floor and lay still. She was stage dead. The blow had not hurt her, because of the ikon; in fact it had required special technique to cause it to land at all. But it was impressive in this context.

Nonce faced away, careless of the deed she had done.

Aspect seemed not to know what had happened. This too was a conventional stage device, dramatic irony: the leading character did not know what the audience knew. She walked away, lay down as on a bed, closed her eyes, and sang:

> I dreamed a dream the other night
> Lowlands, lowlands, away my John
> I saw my love dressed all in white
> My Lowlands away.

As she sang, Ennui quietly got up and stood, in white.

> She came to me by my bedside
> Dressed all in white like some fair bride

Ennui walked to the "bed" and stood beside it.

> And proudly in her bosom there
> A red red rose my love did wear.

And Ennui did have a red patch of cloth there, suggesting the flower.

> She made no sound, no word she said
> And then I knew my love was dead.

In shock, Aspect sat up. Simultaneously Ennui dropped, lying sprawled as she had before. This was reality returning. Ennui in the gown had been a vision, a ghost.

Aspect kneeled by the body, horrified. She looked beseechingly at Nonce, but she remained adamantly facing away. No help there.

Aspect sang once more, a fragment from "Barbary Allen," one of the most familiar ballads. Just one word was modified.

> O mother, mother, make my bed

> O make it long and narrow
> Sweet Willa died for me today
> I'll die for her tomorrow.

Then she collapsed over the body of her lost love. She was dead too. Nonce remained standing, facing away, unrepentant. The message was plain: bigotry had slain the lovers. A needless tragedy.

The tableau held, none of them moving. Then one of the children started crying. In a moment several more joined in, and then some of the adults.

"Division of the village," the female elder snapped. She was calling the vote before there was any more erosion of her case.

The villagers got up and moved. Some went to join the elder; more went to stand beside the seated defendants. The children went there too.

Still the tableau on stage held. Nonce did not move. She was facing the elder woman. Aspect and Ennui lay as they were; Aspect's head was to the side so she could see Nonce and the elder and part of the audience. They were forcing the issue.

Nonplused by the disparity, the elder looked around, but found only her closest supporters. She had lost the vote.

She made the best of it. "The village must be united," she said, and walked across to join the other side. Her companions went with her. Now it was unanimous.

And now at last the stage tableau ended. Nonce turned back to face the others, and Aspect and Ennui got up. As a group they walked to Mender and Sympathy. "Live as you choose," Aspect told them. "Your village supports you."

They embraced each other and dissolved in tears.

≈≈

Next morning the guide reported to their house. "Introduction: I am Crow. I will take you safely to Death Valley." He was a young gray man, burly and rough-hewn.

"I am On," Ennui said. "My companions are Speck and No. Appreciation."

They were packed and ready to resume travel. They left the house clean, not knowing when or whether they would be back. They followed Crow out of the village. The path was wide enough for two, so Ennui paced the man, and Aspect and Nonce followed.

When they were clear, Crow spoke again. "Comment: you are some women!"

"Response," Ennui said cautiously. "We are not lesbian, despite the play. We had a case to make."

"Understanding. And what a case you made! Admiration."

"Appreciation."

Crow was now talkative, as the ice was broken. "I thought the case was lost, and I was amazed when you started singing. I never thought you were a minstrel troupe."

"Recent formation."

"Those songs—you changed them to fit. I thought it was crazy at first, but then I got into it and it seemed sensible. I never realized women could love women, but it began to make sense. I'm glad they're staying. When I was a child I cut my finger once and Sympathy comforted me and Mender mended it. I never forgot."

"They are good women," Ennui agreed. Then, curious, she asked a standard question. "How were you named?"

"I practiced with my sling," he said, showing the small weapon he carried. "I wanted to hunt with the men, but I was only twelve and they thought I'd be a drag. But they gave me a chance. 'Try that crow,' one told me as a crow flew by. I hurled my stone and brought it down. After that they let me hunt, and I had my name. How were you named?"

Ennui smiled. "I am not going by my real name, because our mission is private. I can't tell you. None of us can."

"Understanding," he said, disappointed.

Ennui's dragon seed buzzed. That surprised her; how was she going wrong? Crow had wanted to get to know her better, and she had denied him. But surely she couldn't tell him her real identity. The buzz had come as he spoke, but she was sure he wasn't lying. So where was the wrongness?

Then it came to her: they had been warming to each other, and she was now a beautiful woman. She kept forgetting. Men always thought of one thing when they encountered such women. She had denied him that by declining further personal knowledge. He thought it was all or nothing.

"I will make it up to you," she said impulsively.

"You don't owe me anything. I'm honoring the village's deal."

"You assume I was offering no fault sex?"

Crow blushed. "Apology."

She liked that. She had never before been pretty, but neither had she ever been naïve in the village manner. "I was."

The blush was worse. "Confusion."

"Travel is customarily no fault. I have no objection. I can't tell you my real identity, but we can relate in other ways. That's the nature of no fault."

Now he understood. But it seemed he wasn't used to no fault, as he had never traveled to other Chroma. "You—Lady, you—when you stripped halfway down yesterday on stage—I thought you were older, but then—"

"I *am* older. Over thirty."

"Doubt."

"But I encountered magic that enhanced me. Perhaps there will be something I want of you. Then we can trade." That gave him a chance to earn it, and should make him more comfortable. The seed hadn't buzzed again, so it seemed that this was what it had in mind. Actually the dragon seeds didn't have minds, but it was easier to assign rationales to their warnings.

"Excitement!"

What delight to encounter youthful directness. "You are married, of course?"

"I love my wife. But she—a month ago she got stung by a poisonous nettle when foraging, and came close to dying. The healer saved her, but her recovery is slow, and she can't work. That's why I agreed to return to guiding to Death Valley; no one else will. It's dangerous. But I have to make our way."

He was in a tough situation. And if his wife could not work, she probably couldn't have sex either. She felt sorry for him.

Do it, Aspect's thought came. *It's smart to befriend him.*

That was also Ennui's thought, especially considering the seed's warning. "Is there a place we can safely pause?"

"Affirmation. But if you want to get there and return by nightfall, it is better not to delay." Then he made a connection. "Oh—you mean for private business?"

He thought she needed to urinate. "Not precisely. Take me there. It won't be long."

"There's a place to the side, here," he said. "Behind that rock. Let me check it to be sure no predator is close, then I will leave you."

They started to the side. Nonce started to follow, but Aspect held her back. Nonce was not telepathic, so missed some things. But she quickly caught on.

They came to the rock and went behind it. Crow lifted his nose and sniffed. "It is safe, for now." He started to go back around the rock.

She caught his arm. "No fault," she murmured.

Crow licked his lips, though evidently not quite daring to believe it. "Serious?"

"Affirmation." She removed her shirt, then her skirt, conscious of his eager gaze. She liked being a compelling woman; she hadn't been one long enough for it to become stale. She spread her clothing on the ground and lay down on it. She spread her legs, just enough to be enticing. "As you said, best not to delay unduly."

"Agreement!" He hastily dumped his own clothing.

He was on her in a moment, and in her, erupting instantly. "Oh Lady!" he gasped. "Gratitude!"

Oh, the ardor of virile youth! "Welcome." She held him close until he had drained, then released him. Once again she had succeeded in climaxing at a man's pace, despite not being able to get into his mind telepathically. The ikon made it possible. She hadn't thought to remove it from her mouth, but he hadn't thought to kiss her, so it was all right.

They did spot cleanup and quickly dressed. "But Lady—why? We made no trade."

She wished she knew, apart from feeling sorry for him, and the warning buzz of the dragon seed. Naturally she couldn't say that. Now she had to come up with a rationale. "It is a taste of what I—and my friends—offer. If we make a deal with you, you will know that we are worthwhile."

"Known!" he agreed. The wonder of it remained in his expression.

They returned to the others. Aspect and Nonce saw them and resumed travel. Evidently Aspect had updated Nonce, who was now ready to do her part when necessary.

"Negation!" Crow shouted, diving forward.

Things happened rapidly. Aspect, slightly ahead, paused, startled by the shout. Something erupted from the ground just ahead of her. Crow landed on his shoulder, and did a forward roll between Aspect and the eruption. He righted himself and kicked with his boot, knocking aside a strange point that projected from the ground.

"Question?" Aspect asked in confusion.

"Thorn tree root," Crow gasped. "Poison."

Now it came clear. The root, foiled, disappeared into the ground. Ennui saw that there was a tree nearby that had large thorns. Evidently its roots were thorny too, and it used them to stab unwary prey. Crow had saved Aspect from an ugly encounter.

Actually the ikon probably would have made her invulnerable to the stabbing, but the man did not know that. He had done what he thought he had to do.

And it had happened because he had been approaching from the side, and recognized the tree and its access to the path. He might have missed it, had they not had their brief diversion. That explained the dragon seed's buzz. It wasn't pro sex, but anti-danger. Ennui would have been walking where Aspect was.

But it wasn't over. Crow was baring his teeth in pain.

Ennui kneeled beside him. "Question."

"Grazed," he gritted, showing his leg. Gray blood was flowing from a scrape on the calf. There would be poison in that wound.

Your ikon, Aspect thought. *Havoc's the Glamor of Trees.*

That was right. That meant that he drew his power from trees, and had power over them. Maybe his ikon did too.

Ennui spit the ikon into her hand and held it concealed in her fist. "I have some healing ability," she said. "Allow." She reached for his leg.

"Can't heal," Crow said, wincing. "Gray Poison—gray magic can't stop. Same as my wife."

"Negation." Ennui put her fist right up against the wound. She could do this because she was wielding it; it would have stopped him from touching her on his own initiative.

The bleeding stopped. "The pain is fading!" Crow said in wonder. "Your touch is healing me!"

"Travelers have some magic," Ennui said. "So as not to be vulnerable." That explanation would have to suffice. She continued pressing her fist against his calf, impressed by the speed of the effect. Aspect was right: this was Tree magic, effective against tree poison. It could prevail in a situation other magic would not; trees responded to their own.

Crow gazed at her with continuing amazement. "First you give me fantastic sex. Then you heal me. What are you—a Glamor?"

He was closer than he could be allowed to know. Ennui forced a laugh. "Considerably less than that. I have an amulet." She paused, but the seed did not buzz. She opened her fist, showing the little tree ikon. "Just a healing stone, effective for such an injury." That was a lie, or at best a quarter truth, but her seed did not buzz. She was allowed to be untruthful; the seed reacted only to others she encountered. He did not recognize the ikon's true nature, and that was best.

"Love."

"No fault," she reminded him.

"Of course." He was embarrassed again. "I meant—"

That he was passionately grateful for what she had done for him. "Understood."

Soon Crow's injury was gone as if it had never been. He got to his feet, testing the leg, shaking his head in amazement to find it sound.

They resumed travel. Now Crow was ebullient, perhaps affected in another way by the healing contact of the ikon. He sang, with a fair voice and considerable enthusiasm. It was "The Crow," a song that associated with his name.

> There once was a farmer a-traveling to town
> Hey boom fa-le-la, sing fa-le-la, boom fa-le-la lay!
> Saw a crow in a fir tree, way up in the crown
> Hey boom fa-le-la, sing fa-le-la, boom fa-le-la lay!

They joined him in the refrain, augmenting the luster of the melody. He smiled, loving their support, for they had been recognized in the village as minstrels. Ordinary villagers normally loved to join in with minstrels; it lent brief excitement to their routine lives. Ennui had known that was true for nonChroma folk; it seemed to be true for Chroma folk too. There really wasn't much difference between the two, other than the magic.

The sling from his shoulder he quickly brought down

He hit that black crow and it fell to the ground.

He had changed two of the words to fit his situation; that was common, as many of the ancient Earth terms did not relate well to Charm society.

That black crow was useful in numerous ways
The keel-bone was sailed over oceans and bays.

The feathers were made into featherbeds neat
And pitchforks were made from the legs and the feet.

More things were made from this wondrous crow
You may all doubt this story but it really is so!

They applauded themselves at the conclusion, laughing, their fingers crossed in open denial of the claims of the song. Children loved such games. They were bonding, and it was a pleasure. Ennui made a mental note: it was easy to relate to a man sexually, but better overall to relate to him in friendship. Perhaps she had known that once, but her dreary life (before Havoc) had erased it.

Meanwhile she had learned more about the ikons. They were turning out to be anything but inert tokens. They had powers akin to those of the Glamors themselves, albeit smaller and more subtle, because they were filtered through the people who held them.

The gray countryside gave way gradually to nonChroma. "But Death Valley is weird," Crow said. "It's mostly nonChroma, but I have seen Chroma vents here and there. That's part of what makes it dangerous."

This was interesting. "NonChroma vents?"

"Like tiny volcanoes. Little patches of color, and magic. I know of no other region like it."

But they did. Augur and Aura had described a huge impact crater with exactly such vents. That suggested that this was the right place.

"We shall have to observe those," Aspect said, as if dubious."

"Agreement," Crow said. "But it will help if you tell me what you are looking for. Death Valley is not a place to wander aimlessly."

"We hope we know it when we see it," Ennui said.

"I do not mean to pry into what is not my business, merely to get you where you are going," he said, a trace defensively.

"Pause," Ennui said. Then she took him by the face and kissed him, her ikon safely away from her mouth. "We are not being secretive at the moment. We merely are ignorant of what we seek. Fortunately No has a sense of direction that may enable us to find it."

"Persuaded," he said, somewhat faintly. As Ennui had suspected, the kiss had impact. Oh, what fun to be beautiful!

Crow led the way up the slope of a hill. There was no discernible trail, which was one reason they needed a guide. He looked constantly about, alert for danger. Once a six-legged panther crouched beside a stream. Crow waited for it to drink, then lifted his sling so that the animal could see it. The panther considered, then loped away. Ennui knew it might not have done so had the women been alone. It evidently recognized the weapon, and respected it. The man was competent in the wilderness.

Which made her wonder why he preferred to avoid Death Valley. He had to have good reason. Should she inquire?

"I see you wondering," Crow said. "There are only so many times a man can go into danger and emerge unscathed. That thorn tree—I could have been caught, but it's a calculated risk. But there are things in Death Valley I don't understand, and that makes the odds worse. I can't afford to die or be incapacitated while my wife is ill."

"Persuasion," Ennui said. "When we finish here, we will visit your wife. Perhaps my amulet will help her."

"Hope!"

"Intention."

He looked at the stream. "This is the last water before the Valley. All the creatures here share it. You must take what you need now, lest you be thirsty."

Good advice. They drank, then filled their water bags. They had not discovered whether their ikons protected them from hunger and thirst. They had remained mostly in the city, in the palace, where all physical needs were served. Now they were learning much more about their ikons.

They continued up the slope. "Observation," Crow said. "You ladies walk well."

"Sexily?" Ennui inquired.

"That, too," he agreed, embarrassed.

He had expected them to tire. The ikons made them virtually tireless. "We have had to walk before," Ennui said.

"Yet you look so—" He faltered. "Delicate."

"We have good legs."

"Agreement!" Then he blushed again.

The man is a delight, Aspect thought. *Today he is yours. Tomorrow mine.*

That seemed fair.

At length they crested the hill and saw a circular valley ahead. Surely an impact crater. There were small patches of color scattered across it.

"Necessary to go into it?" Crow inquired warily.

Ennui looked at Nonce. She nodded.

"Affirmation. What we seek is there."

He led the way down. "There are few predator animals in the

Valley itself," he said. "But those vents are tricky. Winds can shift erratically and sweep Chroma vapor across new sections without warning. They can contain Chroma pollen and insects. Their magic can be awkward."

"Awkward?"

"There are stories, and some are true. Insects can paralyze animals, so as to make living food for them. Or cause a person to become ravenous so as to become fat for the larva. Pollen seeks not only flowers, but places for new plants. It can rot the flesh to make rich soil. Or cause a person to sneeze violently and continuously, so as to better spread it. And since Death Valley is extremely dry, everything seeks water. They can rapidly suck it out of a body. So it is best not to get caught by the magic."

His reasons for avoiding this region were becoming sensible. "We have some magic defense," Ennui said carefully.

"Unsurprised. Still, best to remain no longer than necessary."

"Agreement."

They wended their way down into the valley. Crow selected a route that took them well wide of any Chroma vents, but it was not possible to avoid them all, because some were tiny. Ennui looked down to see a dish sized cloud of blue around a small crack in the ground. A tiny Chroma zone.

As they reached the roughly level floor of the valley, a breeze sprang up. "Annoyance," Crow said. "Retreat is best."

Ennui was about to agree, but her dragon seed buzzed. "Negation. We must press on." She looked at Nonce.

"This way," Nonce said. She forged on into the valley.

"Alarm," Crow protested. "Dangerous."

"Still, we must proceed," Ennui said. Still, she wondered; the dragon seed had never been wrong, but this did indeed seem dangerous.

The Chroma zones smeared out in the wind, becoming elongated streamers. Some were low enough to jump over; others high enough to duck under. They jumped and ducked, following Nonce.

She led them toward a low mound. "Nothing here but Chroma," Crow called. "I have been all around this region. We must get out of the valley."

But Nonce continued. And suddenly came to a hole in the ground, just beyond a yellow Chroma vent. It was big enough to allow standing entry. "Caution!" Crow warned, but Nonce dodged by the vent and forged on into it. Ennui followed, and Aspect and Crow had no choice but to do the same.

"Amazement," Crow said. "I never saw this hole."

It was dark below, but Nonce seemed to know where she was going, and the dragon seed did not buzz. In a moment the passage opened into a fair sized cave with another small Yellow Chroma vent.

They hurdled this and landed within it, then looked around by the light of the Chroma fire.

"This is man-made," Crow said in wonder. "But empty, with no other exit."

Ennui wasn't sure how he knew, because it looked natural to her, but trusted his judgment in this respect; he must have explored many caves. "This must be the place."

"This is the place," Nonce agreed.

They explored it. There was an opening in the far side of the chamber, with another glowing Yellow Chroma vent, and beyond it was another chamber. Crow was amazed. "Illusion," he said. "All I saw was wall."

This one had a hole in the center, and in the hole was dark liquid.

"And now we don't have to go back over the rim," Ennui said, dipping her hand in it and tasting. It was good water.

"I couldn't see that either," Crow said. "Just floor." How is it that your ladies can see through illusion?"

Ennui exchanged glances with Aspect and Nonce. This had to be another attribute of the ikons: penetration of illusion. "We have had some experience with special places," she said. "Things are not always what they seem, so we verify. Once we know what is there by touch, we are able to see it."

On the far wall of this chamber was an outcropping of crystalline rock, reflecting different colors. Aspect stroked it with her fingers, found a loose fragment, and took it down. She brought it to the light of the Chroma fire.

It was a bright blue crystal. "Do you suppose?" she asked.

"It does look like it," Nonce said.

"And if it is—" Aspect said.

They left that thought unfinished, and explored farther. They found another passage and another chamber. In it was an altar. They immediately turned back, not speaking of this to the guide, who remained fascinated by the water he could feel but not see. Ennui knew they had to get him clear. She took the blue crystal and addressed him.

"Crow, we are not expert in crystals," Ennui said. "Is there someone in Edge Village who can tell whether this is innocent colored stone—or a Chroma gem?"

"A Chroma gem!" he exclaimed. "That would be incomparably valuable."

"Yes, this could be a gem mine. You need to return soon; we shall not. We must remain here for an indefinite time while we figure out exactly what we are doing here. We have enough for a while, but soon we shall need supplies—mainly food. Take this stone with you, find one who knows, and verify its nature. If it is Chroma, it is yours to keep or trade. If it is not, we shall try to find some other way to make another trip here worth your while." She smiled at him. "In addition to our no fault acquaintance."

He was in doubt. "To leave you here, in this dangerous valley—"

She embraced him, pressing her bosom against him. "We must do what we must do. Perhaps we will find that there is nothing here for us, and will return to the village with you. We should know by the time you return with supplies. Shall we say three days?"

"But villagers will question—"

"It must be secret. Please, Crow." She kissed him, and felt him giving way. It was almost impossible for a man to resist a beautiful woman's plea. She had seen it in her past life; now she was practicing it.

"If that's what you need. But—"

"This way." She led him to the entrance passage, and they returned to the first cave. Aspect and Nonce remained behind.

Ennui removed her clothing, as before, and lay on it. The tacit nature of the deal was clear: if he had sex with her again, he was committed.

He couldn't help himself. In a moment he was with her. This time she held the ikon in her hand, away from her body, so that she could do everything with him. As before, he was on her and in her in a moment, eagerly jetting. This time she held him longer, kissing him and stroking his back with her free hand. "Oh, Lady, oh Lady!" he said.

She knew it was more than sex she was giving him. Sex was to an extent a pretext for him to clasp her and allow his emotion to show. Comfort his wife could not provide at the moment. "And first opportunity I will return with you and see if I can help heal your wife."

"For that alone I would do your bidding forever!"

"When you come in three days, it will be Speck's turn with you. You will find her as accommodating as I am. After that, No, who is closer to your age. We will take turns, as long as we are here. All we require is your silence, and supplies."

"This is not no fault, then."

"For the supplies, the gems," she agreed. "For your silence, this."

"Agreement," he said.

They got up, and he dressed and departed. Ennui rejoined the others. "Deal made."

"We know," Aspect said. Ennui had not closed her mind during the sex or dialogue. The dragon seeds had not buzzed. This had to be the correct course.

Meanwhile, Aspect and Nonce had examined the altar. "The eighteen pockets are filled with seeds!" Aspect said.

"Seeds!"

"Flax seeds, by their look."

"Flax—the source of linen yarn."

"So it seems."

They looked at each other, temporarily baffled. "We can't weave the seeds," Ennui said. "We need the yarn. Are we expected to grow it ourselves?"

"Seeds do grow, if planted and watered," Aspect said.

"But we need magic yarn," Nonce protested.

"There are multiple small Chroma zones outside," Ennui reminded her. "Plants will grow to match whatever Chroma they are in."

And there it was. "I think we are about to become farmers," Aspect said.

⚘⚘

They surveyed the land beyond the cave. There turned out to be vents with all the different Chroma. So they had seeds, Chroma, and water. It would be work and take time, but they could do it.

Aspect nodded. "I never anticipated this, but in retrospect it makes sense. No animal or ignorant person would go to such trouble. Only one who knows what she is doing."

They reconsidered the caves as a temporary home. They would need bedding and better lighting.

"We can forage outside," Ennui said. "We may be immune to Chroma threats as well as nonChroma ones."

"We are not helpless women," Aspect agreed. She looked at the crystal wall. "I wonder if there is any moss here?"

"Glamor of Moss!" Nonce said.

"The Tree ikon did heal tree damage," Ennui said. "But we aren't threatened by moss."

"Some moss glows," Aspect said. She focused her attention on moss, willing it to glow. Would this work?

Slowly dim light appeared on the cave walls. The moss was responding. She walked closer to a wall, and the brightening intensified until the light was significant. The whole wall was covered with moss that had been invisible before, but now made its presence known.

"I think we have learned more than how to make light," Ennui said.

"And I think I will do whatever I can for any moss I encounter," Aspect said, amazed and gratified.

"And I for trees," Ennui said. "We have become committed, and they have accepted us."

"I don't think my ikon has a constituency," Nonce said.

"Unless it is those seeds," Aspect said. "Certainly the loom."

"Maybe this cave," Nonce said. "I wonder—could my ikon affect local Chroma?"

"Question?" Ennui asked.

Nonce walked to the passage between caves, where the Yellow Chroma vent was. She squatted beside it. Suddenly the seeming fire brightened, becoming fierce. Then it faded, and the passage behind it disappeared. There was only the blank cave wall.

"Alarm!" Aspect said.

"Illusion," Nonce replied. The passage reappeared. "The Chroma responded to my will."

"Explanation," Aspect said. "You found these caves, when Crow had never seen the entrance. Your ikon showed you reality."

"You saw it too," Nonce said.

"Once you did," Ennui said. "We can penetrate illusion when we know it is there, but you were the one who saw it first. The loom ikon gives you that power over its demesnes."

"Agreement," the girl said, gratified.

"Illusion is a good protection," Aspect said. "But fear is better. Can you make the main entrance seem threatening?"

"Discovery," Nonce said. They went out of the caves and stood by the entrance. She addressed the vent.

First the passage disappeared, showing merely the slope of the mound. That was what Crow and any others had seen. Then the fire became intense, and they felt its heat. Aspect put her hand toward it, and the heat became pain. It might be illusion, but it was burning hot. "This will be effective."

They explored the region around the mound. Now that they were cataloguing spot Chroma zones instead of avoiding them, they realized that this section of the valley was quite well endowed. All the Chroma were represented.

Then they gathered dry brush. Very little grew in Death Valley, but there must have been more water at some time in the past, so that shrubs and low-lying plants could grow. This brush could be centuries old. Even the dry grass might be ancient, preserved by desiccation.

They carried armfuls into the cave and made three beds in the first section. By this time it was evening. They broke out their food packages and ate conservatively, knowing the supply had to last three days.

"We have our home for the duration," Aspect said. "It does not seem quite up to the standard of the palace, but neither is it out in the dangerous wilderness. Surely we shall make do."

"Tomorrow we must start planting," Nonce said. "The seeds all look the same. Will they differentiate as necessary?"

"Surely they will," Aspect said. "Each Chroma zone will make its plants magical in its own manner, and those will make magical threads equivalent to the ones we have already used. The magic of the loom is to integrate all the different Chroma into a single magical tapestry. We have but to enable it."

"And when we finally have the complete tapestry," Ennui said, "we will try to integrate that into a single important quest for the ultimate riddle of Planet Charm. Who made the loom? Who hid the altars? How did the system of Glamors and ikons come about? There is so much to know!"

Indeed there was. Not least, the effect the ikons were having on the people who carried them. Nonce was young and pretty, and hadn't changed, but she was now invulnerable to attack and smarter than she had been. Aspect herself had returned to her physical and mental prime. And Ennui had gained most, becoming a strikingly lovely woman. They all had developed an ability and passion for sex, and had become excellent singers. They could penetrate illusion, and heal, and were indefatigable. The ikons were remaking them, and so far that was delightful. But where was it leading? At what point would they cease to be themselves and become something else?

Should she share that concern with the others? What good would it do? They were locked into their mission, and had to complete it, regardless of personal cost. They had to keep the ikons, to safeguard the Glamors they related to. And perhaps the icons were merely enabling them to be all that they could be.

She decided to let it be. She put it from her mind—and it was gone.

In the morning they got to work. The first problem was water: they had the spring, but little way to carry water to their Chroma garden patches. They had their water bags for drinking, but were loath to expend that water.

"Consideration," Ennui said. "We have water here. If it is sufficient for our flax gardens, it should be sufficient for us. We can use the water bags and refill them."

Aspect had to agree. "If we believe in this mission, and in this site, agreement. But those bags will be tedious to fill here. Buckets would be better."

"We will have a number of patches, some distant," Nonce said. "We will spend a lot of time carrying water regardless. This is a desert; they will need a lot."

Then Aspect had a wicked idea. "We could carry more, if we care to."

"Not without more containers," Ennui said.

"We have containers. We merely don't think of them as such."

Both looked at her blankly.

"Our bladders," Aspect said. "We can drink hugely, and urinate. The plants will not object; they might even prefer it."

"Pee on them!" Nonce said, laughing.

"Havoc makes offerings to plants," Ennui said. "Not just piss. When he and I needed the good graces of a plant, he made me do it. I was not pleased at the time, but soon I understood the necessity."

Aspect nodded. "We'll have to defecate somewhere. This settles that."

"If we drink now, we'll have some ready when we plant the first ones," Ennui said.

They took turns drinking copiously from the spring, then fetched seeds from the altar and headed out. They approached the nearest Chroma zonelet, a green one. "Should one person service the same zones?" Aspect asked.

"Negation," Ennui answered. "I will have to visit the village, and will not be able to tend my zones then. They should get used to all three of us, assuming they care."

That made sense. Aspect kneeled at the edge of the green zone and reached into it. There was no problem; it was like a regular zone, magic but not hostile. Crow could be correct about pollen and insects, but she rather thought not, because these isolated little zones would need to interact with others if any life were to survive in them. In fact they would want animals to visit, and leave offerings of urine and manure.

"We could use trowels," Aspect said as she dug her fingers into the hot green sand.

"We can ask Crow," Ennui said.

Aspect made several small holes in the ground, then carefully pressed the seeds into them, one to a hole, and covered them over. She did not know the proper procedure for flax, and hoped this would do. Then she tilted her water bag over the region and let some water dribble onto it.

"What, no piss?" Nonce asked.

Thus challenged, Aspect responded. She stepped into the zone, hoisted her skirt, squatted, pulled aside her panty, and let go with a small amount of urine. She didn't want to waste it, but it was an effort to cut it off in mid flow. She let go rather more than she had intended.

They went to the next, which was blue. Ennui tried this one, carefully placing her seeds, then squatting and letting a limited flow out. She was better at it than Aspect had been.

Nonce took the third zone, a brown one. When she squatted, she let go too freely, and squirted with too much power, overshooting the garden area. "Obscenity!" she swore.

"Piss on it," Ennui said, smiling.

They continued to other patches. Long before their supply of seeds or zones was gone, they ran out of water, both internal and external. They had to return for more. But they had watered perhaps twice as much as they might have done with just the water bags. It was a good start.

By day's end they had processed a lot of water, two ways, and managed to plant seeds in all their designated Chroma zones. They were not physically fatigued, thanks to the ikons, but were emotionally tired. They ate and slept quickly.

The following day they checked their gardens and watered again. All the patches were dry, which suggested that they needed more water. But even with voluminous imbibing and full use of the water bags, it was hard to give enough. They were spending all their time going back and forth, and as yet had nothing to show for it. No shoot had shown, and they couldn't even be sure the seeds were fertile. They might have remained in the altar in the cave for centuries, and died. But probably, they reassured each other, the seeds were just taking their time.

On the third day Crow returned. As it happened, Aspect was just then squatting over a brown Chroma patch, squeezing out her last available drops of urine, and didn't see him until she was done.

He was standing there, blushing furiously; his gray face was almost black. He must have seen her squat, and not realized what she was doing until too late. He obviously did not know what to say or do.

Poise was best. Aspect stood, turned to him, and smiled. "We have planted seeds. We have no water buckets, so we use what we have. Apology for embarrassing you."

His mouth worked. "I would have—have turned away, had I known. Abject apology."

"Needless. You have not seen anything I was not about to show you anyway. This day you are mine. Come to the cave with me."

She led him to the cave. Ennui was returning from her own watering mission to another patch, saw her, and halted. *Do him first*, she thought. I *will tell Nonce*.

Aspect nodded, and led Crow on into the cave. They had turned down the Yellow Chroma pain fire for the day, knowing the man was scheduled. Inside she gave him time to remove his heavy pack, then led him to her bed and stripped.

There followed a very fast clasping and penetration. Ennui had warned her, but still it was surprising. The man was practically jetting before he made it into her. He must have been eager for this event, and unable to hold back. She was not able to climax herself, so swiftly, and that annoyed her, but she said nothing to him about it.

Instead she engaged him in dialogue. "What did you bring us?"

"Everything I could think of," he said happily. "That gem stone— It was Chroma! Valuable. It paid for all of it and more. They wanted to know where I got it, but I just told them I found it in Death Valley. They wanted to know where you three women were, and I told you had found a cave to rest in, and that I would go back for you. Only to my wife, I told the truth, I mean about that, no fault, you know."

"We know," Aspect agreed amicably.

"And she—she cried. I did not know why. She wasn't jealous, she knows about no fault, she expected that, but she cried. I didn't know what to do."

"She cried for what she could no longer give you," Aspect said. "But soon she will be able, again."

"Hope!" He got up, went to his pack, and started unpacking it. He was right: there was everything. It was a large pack, and well filled. They would eat better than they had, because now there was enough. "My wife told me what you would need. She was very helpful. I told her how the Lady On had healed me, and she cried again."

Sure enough, there was more than food there. There was fresh gray underwear, and washcloths, and a small mirror. There were little candles, and inflatable pillows. These would be a blessing.

"Your wife is thoughtful," Aspect said. "Appreciation. We will thank her more properly when we are able, soon."

"It has been awful, half without her," he said soberly. "Not just because of—you know. I hate having her in pain." He paused, turning his face away.

Aspect put her arms around him, and he cried into her shoulder. Then she drew him back down onto the mat and slowly stroked him. This time there was no urgency; she led him in leisurely manner into sex, lying on top of him, kissing him, setting his hands on her body where she chose, building him up to a culmination she could share. The climax was long and slow, but nonetheless potent. His gray Chroma mind was closed, but she had come to know him enough to pick up some of the surge of feeling, and so she shared it.

"Oh Lady, I never had it like that before!"

"This is how it will be with your wife, when she can do it again. It must be slow, so as not to strain her."

"Agreement!"

She held him for a time, schooling him in gentle sex, and he marveled at it. He had not realized there was any other way but instant. Now he knew.

They finished, and dressed. The others returned, seemingly by coincidence. There had never been any secret what he had been doing with Aspect, but they pretended innocence.

"We need buckets," Ennui said briskly. "We shall be staying here after all, and we have water to haul."

"Buckets," Crow agreed.

"We are gardening," Nonce said. They had agreed that they would have to explain this much to him. "We have found that the little Chroma zones are just right for our flax."

"Flax?"

"Special flax, for weaving," Ennui said. "Pretty colors, hard to get in nonChroma zones. We will grow it, then depart."

His face lit with comprehension. That was why the "Lady Speck was in the Chroma!" But the recollection of the scene embarrassed him again, despite their recent intimacy.

"Why we need buckets," Aspect said. "So we have a better way to carry water."

He nodded. "You shall have them." He glanced around the cave. "I feared you would be in bad straits here, but you seem to have done well."

"We are tougher women than we look," Aspect said, smiling.

"You look beautiful."

"Appreciation."

Aspect gave him another gem, this one red. "Do not spend it all on our supplies," she said. "These are worth far more, and you should have things for your wife."

"For her," he breathed. "Agreement. Appreciation."

It was time for him to go. Aspect saw him out, and walked with him to the edge of the valley. "We will see you in three days," she said.

"Agreement." He was ready to go, but lingered. There was something he wasn't quite able to say.

Men were so easy! "Pause," she murmured.

She embraced him, kissed him, then led him to the vertical face of a boulder and leaned back against it. She opened his trousers and brought out his member. It was throbbing. Youth was so resilient! She guided it up under her skirt and into her cleft, then closed her legs about it and pushed forward as her hands drew his groin in to hers. This tight penetration set him off, and he pumped and jetted into her. This time she matched his climax despite its speed. It was partly the naughty novelty of doing it vertically, outside, in daylight. She had never done that before, and it was a private thrill. He didn't realize that she had controlled this liaison throughout; that, too, stimulated her.

"Oh Lady!" he exclaimed. It seemed to be his only way to acknowledge such interaction.

"Welcome," she said. "Next time, it will be On."

"You are so—so understanding."

"We are women." She disengaged as his member slackened. She put it back into his trousers and closed them. Then she kissed him. "Take good care of yourself, Crow. We depend on you."

"Death Valley no longer repels me."

She laughed, and patted his behind as he started off. "Fortunate."

He climbed the slope, and she waited, reaching under her skirt and wiping her crotch with a tissue. He hadn't even thought to question why she had not worn underwear when leaving the cave. As he crested the ridge, he turned back to look at her, and she waved, smiling. Only when he was out of sight did she turn and make her way back to the cave.

They continued their labors, largely on faith that the seeds had to be alive, perhaps magically preserved in the altar, and next morning as Aspect squatted at the green patch—the first one—she spied a tiny shoot. She was so excited she splashed urine on her foot. "It's growing!" she called.

In a moment the others were there. "Better clean it off before it forms a sixth toe," Nonce said, observing her wet foot.

"The plant," Aspect said, though she knew it was teasing. "There!" She pointed to it.

Indeed, it was true. Soon Ennui found one in a red patch, and Nonce a yellow one. They were breaking ground all over.

"We should celebrate with wine," Aspect said. "If we had wine."

That dampened the mood for a moment, reminding them how isolated they were. They missed the comforts of the palace and Triumph City.

"But now we are on our way," Ennui said. "We are accomplishing our mission."

"We'll celebrate with water," Aspect decided.

"I'm so full of water I squish when I walk," Nonce protested. But she joined them in the pretense that water was wine.

The following day all the patches had shoots growing, and the first ones were thicker and taller. Aspect was no farmer, but she was sure this was very fast growth. They were in Chroma zonelets, to be sure, but even so, they were fast. So the seeds must be special. It made the chore of constant watering seem worthwhile.

On the third day Crow returned. This time he brought six gray leather buckets and three yokes, and showed them how these were worn over the shoulders so as to suspend a bucket on either side. They would be able to carry twice as much water with half the effort. They were thrilled, and Nonce flung her arms around him and kissed him all over his face. Then she led him into the cave. It was her turn.

"I'm getting to like that man," Ennui remarked as they returned to their watering with what they had. They would not be able to use the yokes and buckets until Nonce was through with him, but they practiced with the empty ones, getting the feel of the yokes. This was a much better solution than they had anticipated.

Then Nonce poked her head out of the cave. "Come in!" she called. "There's more."

There was indeed. Crow had brought them some wine. Not a lot, because of the weight, but enough to let them have one merry celebration. They had it immediately, insisting that he sip with them.

Nonce nudged Aspect. "He asked me a question one of you can better answer. Talk to him." She made a cute forbidding frown. "But no sex; he's mine today."

Ennui was busy filling buckets from the spring, so Aspect took Crow outside. "Question?"

"My wife—she can't do it, but she wants to know how."

"But surely she knows sex," Aspect said, surprised.

"Affirmation," he agreed, turning a darker gray. "But if—when— she's better—she knows the three of you have—you're so good at it! She knows she was never like that. I love her, and never said—but she took one look at me and knew."

"Women do," Aspect said, smiling.

"I don't know what to tell her."

"Crow, On and I are older than we look. We have had experience. No has had experience too; she had a special position where beauty and ability count. And we—we have had magic enhancement, sexually as well as physically. So we have advantages over normal women. We do not mean to spoil you for your wife." Yet they might inadvertently have done so. It had not occurred to any of them that their newfound sexuality could have a negative side.

"I can tell her that," he said dubiously.

Was there a way to fix it? "It's not just physical," she said. "It's an expression of love. It starts with you; you must show her that you love her."

"I do!"

"Not once a month," she said. "Not once a day. Not just during sex. Constantly. Build your relationship."

"Confusion."

He was a typical man. He meant well, but he wasn't given to romantic expression. This might require considerable instruction. "First things first," she said. "We should be able to keep up with our gardening better, thanks to the equipment you brought. Next time On will return with you to try to heal your wife. Thereafter, if necessary, I will go with you to talk with her. Perhaps we can accomplish something."

"Gratitude!"

Ennui emerged with her filled buckets. She hooked them to the yoke and walked toward the farther patches. Aspect and Crow went inside, and they filled her buckets. Then she gave him a Chroma crystal and left with Ennui, leaving him with Nonce for another session.

The yoke worked well. It was shaped to conform to her shoulders, so that when she walked erect the filled buckets seemed much lighter than they were. She walked to other patches, and carefully poured water.

By the time she and Ennui finished, Nonce and Crow emerged. She would see him off while Aspect and Ennui refilled their buckets from the spring.

"Wife problem?" Ennui inquired.

"We may have been too good to him; his wife is concerned."

"Dismay! I never thought of that."

"I told him that after you healed his wife, I would go talk to her. Perhaps that will be enough."

"Hope."

They took time filling the buckets, so that Nonce would have whatever time she needed. Aspect could see the shape of their future routine. But the wife would have to be reassured. What could she say to her?

Nonce returned. "Answer," she said, though they hadn't asked. She knew they were curious. "It was only a kiss. I think he feels guilty doing so much with us, while his wife is ill."

Guilt. That could be it. "We may have been too free with him," Aspect said. "We are sexually charged. We can't blame his wife for her concern."

"But how else can we reward him?" Nonce asked. "We need those supplies."

"I will talk with her."

The plants grew vigorously. All the seeds they had planted had sprouted, and each plant was the color of its Chroma zone. Because they were close to the vents, the changeable winds did not deprive them. They were definitely successful little gardens.

A six legged desert panther cruised by, one of the deadly predators. Aspect saw it first, when her dragon seed buzzed, and was alarmed. She was alone in the vicinity at the moment, and had no weapon. But when the creature sniffed too close to a garden patch, she advanced on it, hefting a stone. It faced her and crouched, snarling.

She hurled the stone. It flew straight and fast, striking the big cat on the shoulder. Surprised, it shied away. She was surprised too; she had never had any kind of throwing arm. Credit one more to the ikon.

She picked up another stone. The panther oriented on her, not quite sure enough of itself to attack. She threw, and the stone smacked into its nose.

That decided the issue. The panther bounded away. Only then did Aspect relax, shaking. How could she have done such a thing? She was a soft royal woman, a city girl, completely untrained in combat. She should have fled screaming helplessly. Yet that had never occurred to her; instead she had braved the panther like an Amazon and driven it off.

True, she suspected it could not hurt her, because of the ikon. Still, she hadn't thought of that aspect either. She had simply done what she had to do. No single woman ever stood up to such a predator, yet she had not only done so, she had been the aggressor. She had attacked it, and driven it off.

Now the others arrived. "Amazement!" Nonce said. "You tackled a panther!"

"Barehanded," Ennui said.

"Negation. I threw stones at it."

"Spooked it?" Nonce asked.

"No, actually I hit it. I didn't know I could throw that hard or accurately."

"The ikon," Ennui said.

"They make us immune from attack," Nonce said. "They must also make us able to attack." She picked up a stone and threw it at the standing tower of a long-dead tree. She hit it.

Ennui tried it, and also hit the tree. "There seems to be no end to their powers."

"That concerns me," Aspect said. "They are changing us, remaking us. Where will it end? Are we truly ourselves?" She had been silent about this before, but now it came out.

"Similar concern," Ennui said. "I didn't want to cause alarm."

"Ditto," Nonce said.

So they had all thought of it, and been silent. "We must assume that the ikons are beneficial, or at least neutral," Aspect said, now arguing the other case. "Otherwise we must fear the Glamors are bad."

The others nodded. They couldn't afford to believe that this was the case.

Next time Crow came, with regular supplies and more wine, Ennui returned with him. They were efficient enough to handle the watering with two, thanks to the yokes and buckets. Other plants were sprouting along with the flax, and these seemed to have a protective effect, holding the water close. They had decided not to weed them out; Ennui's ikon related to plants, and they were plants. Mosses also formed, making small colored carpets on the ground; those too were left, for the sake of Aspect's ikon. Increasingly they were thinking like Glamors.

"This is not the adventure I anticipated," Nonce confided. "But I think I like it."

"Agreement."

They had to work harder, with Ennui absent, but were capable. Worse than the work was a gap in the fabric of their association. The three of them had come together almost randomly, but now they were a team, and it felt like a three legged stool with one leg missing.

On the third day Crow and Ennui returned. "She did it!" he exclaimed exuberantly. "She healed my wife! She's well now."

Aspect realized that he had never referred to his wife by name. That might be part of the problem.

In due course Crow returned to the village, and this time Aspect went with him. She discovered to her surprise that she remembered the route perfectly, in every detail. Her memory had never been that good before; it had to be another gift of the ikon. When they passed the place where Ennui had taken him for a spot liaison, thus saving them from the attack of thorn tree, she saw him glance that way.

"Show me," she said.

They went behind the rock, and she kissed him and drew him close. Things proceeded according to the script, and soon he was spurting into her. "Oh, Lady!"

Now all she had to do was discover what she had that his wife lacked. If the wife were not pretty, it would be a problem. Character, competence, and dependability were important, but generally went for nothing without appearance. When a man chose a women for her pleasant nature, it was actually the pleasant nature of a pretty person, not of a plain one. Ennui's life had been transformed not by the intelligence, endurance, and other ikon-sponsored gifts, but by the wonder it had made of her face and body. Aspect herself had become supremely appealing to men not because of her qualities of character, but because she had recovered the physical splendor of her youth. She was without illusions on this score. Crow's wife would have no ikon to transform her.

"It's so good to have her healthy again," Crow said as they resumed travel. "But she feels it isn't enough. She thinks you can help her."

"I hope I can," Aspect said sincerely.

The trip back was faster than the trip out had been, because he had become well familiar with the trail and its dangers, and because he had discovered that he did not need to slow his pace for these women. Nevertheless, it was late afternoon when they reached the village.

The wife met them at her door. She was hardly plain; her body was well assembled, bordering on generous, and her face was cute. "Introduction," she said. "I am Blackbird, Crow's wife."

"I am Speck, traveler."

"You saved Sympathy and Mender!"

"We did what we could."

Crow gave Blackbird the Red Chroma crystal he had received this time. She filed it in a drawer, knowing its nature and value. The house was neat and well kept; no problem there.

Blackbird served a nice evening meal. Here too she was plainly competent. Their incidental dialogue was pleasant; Blackbird was neither smart nor stupid, but pleasant in the middle range. Her manners matched those of her husband: adequate for village life, crude by city standards. Why did this woman feel she was inadequate?

"I'll go check with the men," Crow said as they finished. "Parting." He was gone.

Blackbird wasted no time. "Crow says the girl is good, but the women are wonderful. He can't get enough of you. What is your secret?"

There had to be something. "He likes sex, as all men do. Surely he likes it with you."

"Not as much as he likes it with you. Oh, he loves me; it's not that. But somehow you compel him. He says he can do it several times a day with you."

"And not with you?"

"Well, for a time, not at all with me. But your friend On—she put her hands on me, and I felt the poison leaving. She made me well, and I'll always be grateful. Then I could do it with Crow again. But he really wanted it with On; I could tell. And with you. So it was just once with me. On wouldn't do it with him in my house, but would when traveling. No fault. But he wanted her throughout."

Aspect considered telling part of the truth, and the dragon seed did not buzz. "The three of us are on a special mission, and we carry amulets that aid us in this. On's amulet helped heal you. But they also make us healthy and sexy; it's a pleasant side effect. When one of us gets close to a man, it makes us eager for sex with him—and of course he wants it with us. It's magic."

Blackbird considered that. "I wish I could find such an amulet. But it's not just that. He thinks about you when you are not close. He speaks your names in his sleep."

Ouch! "My dear, I am sorry! We never intended to interfere with your marriage. To us it's just no fault, and payment for his silence about our mission."

"Negation. You're not interfering. Sex was never that much, even before my illness. You three are good at it, and he loves it. I just wish it could be like that with me."

She had to find an answer. "If there is any way I can help you, I'll do it. But this is not something to be healed by a laying on of hands."

"I wonder. Maybe we should try it."

Aspect couldn't say that the ikon of mosses could heal a problem not caused by mosses. She would simply have to demonstrate that it didn't work. She reached out and put her two hands on Blackbird's arms, willing whatever healing was there.

The woman's eyes widened. Her breathing quickened. Her mouth opened. "Ooooh!"

Aspect felt it returning. It was sexual passion the woman was feeling, the other legacy of the ikon. She removed her hands.

"What was that?" Blackbird asked breathlessly. "I never felt the like."

"It was the effect of the amulet: desire." But this was curious: how could the woman not recognize it?

"If Crow were here right now, I'd—I don't know what, but I'd try. No wonder he longs for you."

"I can't give you the amulet." Indeed, staying too long in the Chroma zone could cause Gale a problem, since the ikon needed to be in a nonChroma zone for full effect. She hadn't thought of that before. But if Gale did not draw on her Glamor powers too much, it should be all right. Meanwhile, there was something to clarify. "You haven't felt such desire before?"

"Never. It's weird and wonderful."

"Then perhaps we have an avenue. All men and most women feel sexual passion, when the circumstances are right. It is unusual if you have not."

"Confusion."

"Tolerance, if you will. I have rather personal information I wish to know."

Blackbird shrugged. "Tolerance," she agreed.

"Show me how you have sex with Crow."

"Simple. He says he wants it, we get on the bed, he does it. Then if it is night, he goes to sleep."

"Show me," Aspect repeated. "Pretend I am him."

Blackbird led the way to their bed. She removed her dress and lay down on it, spreading her legs. Her face assumed a passive expression.

"This may be the problem," Aspect said. "You are not participating."

"He plumbs me in an instant!"

"I know. But this is only a fraction of what sex can be."

"What more is there?"

"Seduction. Passion. Mutuality."

"Confusion."

"Pretend you are Crow—or any man. I will be the woman."

"I am not like Mender or Sympathy."

"Neither am I. Pretend."

Blackbird got up and dressed. Then Aspect sat on the bed. "You are looking handsome today," she said, leaning forward so that her blouse hung loose, showing her breasts. She smiled and crossed her legs so that her thighs showed.

"If Crow saw that, he'd want it right away."

"Precisely. You have the equipment; you have but to show it in the right manner. And when he asks you, you must kiss him and act as if this is what you have wanted all along. When you are on the bed, hug him close, wrap your legs around him, and keep kissing him. Tell him how much you like his manliness. Encourage him to do it again, as soon as he can."

"Again!"

"He will be slower the second time. Give him your breasts to stroke. Massage his back. Act as if your desire is greater than his. And perhaps by the time he can do it again, you will climax with him."

"Climax?"

"Women can do it too, just not as readily as men. Make it a drama, a play, with your bed the stage. With practice it can become real. Then he will speak your name in his sleep."

"Far fetched."

"Men are easy to fool in this manner. They want to believe that you share their passion, and you can share it if you want to."

"I can get that feeling?"

"You may. No guarantee it will work. But it might. Then you will be like us."

Blackbird nodded. "I will make the effort."

Ennui had used a bunk in the corner of the main room. Aspect was happy to have it. They sat and chatted.

Crow returned. Blackbird remained seated. She faced him, leaned forward, and smiled. She crossed her legs. "You look handsome," she said.

This was a bit too sudden and obvious, but Aspect couldn't caution the woman without giving away the ploy. But it worked. Crow took one glance down inside her blouse and glanced toward the bedroom. Then he glanced at Aspect, who was sitting absolutely decorously, showing nothing, unsmiling. Obviously he did not want to broach the subject in public.

Blackbird got up and approached him. She hugged him and kissed him. "Desire," she said.

That did it. They went to the bedroom and closed the door. They did not emerge.

Aspect lay down and slept.

They were late rising in the morning. Could a single lesson have been that effective?

It seemed it was. When they finally emerged, Crow looked surprised and gratified. "You made her be like you!" he exclaimed.

"She was always like me," Aspect said. "You just hadn't realized."

Blackbird didn't comment, but she was clearly pleased. She might not have learned how to climax, yet, but she had succeeded in evoking far more attention from her man.

After breakfast, Crow went to see about the next pack of supplies, Blackbird settled down to sew clothing, and Aspect went to visit Sympathy and Mender. They were doing well; there were children constantly in and out.

Before she left, Crow came to find her. "I know I'm clumsy about shopping for supplies, Lady. But if you would come with me, we can get it right this time."

"Negation: you have done well. Acceptance: I will do what I can." She bid parting to the two women and went with him to assorted houses where they obtained particular supplies. Crow had put the first Chroma crystal up as collateral with the village elders, and they were keeping accounts; there was no difficulty about requisitions.

That evening Blackbird monopolized Crow again, managing to tempt him away from the middle of the meal. She was getting better at playing the game, and Aspect was pleased to see it.

After a time, Blackbird rushed out, naked. "It happened!" she exclaimed. "I—I climaxed! Now I know why he wants it so much!"

"Now you know," Aspect agreed. "Congratulations."

Blackbird dashed back into the bedroom.

Next morning the two were late getting up again. Aspect found her own breakfast, well satisfied. Ennui had healed Blackbird's body; Aspect had managed to heal her sexuality. It had been surprisingly easy, with no magic required.

Then her dragon seed buzzed.

Something was wrong. Not with Crow and Blackbird; they were in a private paradise of discovery. Something else. But what? She was sure she couldn't ignore it, but the buzz have her no hint of its nature.

She got up and went to look outside. There were villagers surrounding the house.

She hurried to the bedroom and rapped on its door. "Trouble!" she called.

They joined her, both pleasantly disheveled. She explained about the villagers, and they verified it. "Confusion," Crow said.

"I can inquire," Aspect said. She knew what they did not: that she was invulnerable to attack.

"Negation." He forged on out to confront them, while Aspect and Blackbird watched from inside.

"That's Scheme," Blackbird said. "Always up to no good. He should have been banished long ago. What mischief is he up to now?"

They surrounded Crow immediately, far too many for him to defend against. Meanwhile several men thrust their way into the house. "You are captive, witch woman," Scheme said to Aspect. "And you are hostage, Blackbird, to Crow's performance."

"Outrage!" Blackbird exclaimed. "Home is sacrosanct!"

He ignored that. "Where are the Chroma gems?"

So that was it. The village had been overwhelmed by greed. The Chroma crystals were simply too valuable to let be.

"They are for Crow and Blackbird, for trade," Aspect said. "Not for taking."

"That is for us to say," Scheme said. "Crow will lead a party of us to Death Valley, to where the stones are, so we can harvest them all."

"Negation!" Blackbird said.

"If he wants to see you again," Scheme said grimly. He turned to Aspect. "And the other witch women won't try anything magic as long as we have you."

Aspect wasn't sure how to handle this. They were not going to let the greedy villages raid the cave, but Crow and Blackbird were vulnerable to their plot; they had to live here. Aspect could probably fight her way clear and go to warn the others, but that would reveal more of her nature than was expedient. How could she defuse this politely? She saw no way. The seed had warned her too late—and she might not have been able to do anything if it had buzzed sooner.

So she called for help. Ennui could reach Havoc long distance when she tried; maybe Aspect could reach Gale similarly. The Glamors would know what to do. *Gale!*

The answer came, faintly. *Aspect.*

Trouble in Edge Village, Gray Chroma zone. We need your help.

Acquiescence. The mental presence faded.

Had it been enough? She hadn't had time to explain what kind of trouble, or that it was immediate. Had Gale picked it up from her mental background?

Meanwhile the men were searching the house. They quickly found the Red Chroma crystal. Then they hustled the two of them outside, and to the village square.

Crow was there. "Lady!" he cried. "I don't know what to do."

"Help will come," Aspect said. She hoped it came soon.

"Attention," Scheme said. "Crow will lead me and my party to the source of the Chroma stones. His wife and the witch woman will be held here until nightfall. If we aren't back with the stones then, start raping them. If anything happens to us, kill them."

"How can you do this?" Blackbird cried. "We're a civilized village." A number of villagers looked ashamed, but did not speak. Scheme had control of the situation.

Then a dot appeared in the sky. It expanded swiftly. It was a big gray bird. A huge one. It came to land in the square beside the captives. It stood the height of a man, on three legs, and it glowed.

Aspect recognized it. "The Gray Glamor!" she exclaimed, amazed. Gale must have notified him.

The bird's head turned toward her, nodding.

The villagers stared in awe. Surely they had never seen a Glamor before; few people anywhere had.

Then the Glamor's head turned to orient on Scheme. Obviously it was his cue.

"I don't care if it *is* a Glamor," the man blustered. "Those gems are ours."

The bird did not react. He merely stood gazing at the man. But now the sky filled with specks that became gray birds. They were small, but in a moment the villagers recognized the species: they were called piranha birds.

The villagers scattered. But Scheme, held by the Glamor's gaze, did not move. The birds flocked around him, and on him, pecking viciously with their tri-part beaks. Blood flowed.

The man screamed, once. Then he fell, his body entirely covered by birds. Soon there was nothing left but bones.

The birds, gorged, departed. The Glamor glanced once more at Aspect, then flew away.

Aspect kept a tight rein on her emotion and went to Blackbird, who stood in shock. "It is done," she said, taking the woman's arm. "No one will interfere with us again. Come to the house." She glanced at Crow. "No change in our schedule."

"You *are* a witch woman," he said, stunned.

"Negation. Merely a woman on an important mission, protected by Glamors. They take exception to interference."

They returned to the house. It took Crow and Blackbird some time to recover emotional equilibrium, and it was not easy for Aspect. But the point had been made, savagely, as seemed usually to be the case when Glamors took open action. Aspect remembered when they had intervened on Havoc's behalf, the first time, and his enemies had dissolved into dust. No one ever forgot a Glamor point. Gale had done what needed to be done.

Aspect realized that, shocking as the event had been, she was much better equipped to handle it than she would have expected. This was surely another gift of the ikon: it shored up her ability to handle emotional shock.

A villager came to their door and prostrated himself. "Apology," he said. "Abject. For all of us."

"Just go about your normal routine," Aspect said. "We seek no quarrel with you, merely cooperation. But do bury the bones." She knew there were more guilty villagers than just Scheme, but there was no need to punish them. They would never interfere again.

"Acquiescence," he said relieved. He departed.

Next morning Crow and Aspect set off for Death Valley, both carrying substantial packs. Blackbird remained at the village. They knew she would be safe. Absolutely safe.

"In three days I have seen joy and horror," Crow remarked.

"The good and bad of human beings."

"Blackbird—you transformed her. I can hardly keep up with her. I love it. Gratitude."

"Appreciation."

When they came to the spot near the thorn tree, he hesitated.

"Desire?" Aspect asked.

"Curiosity."

She was curious too. They went to the rock, and had sex. This time he took time to kiss her and stroke her breasts before entering. She responded, enjoying the progress he had made; it was a private credit to her time with Blackbird. It was a marvelous mutual climax. "Oh, Lady!"

"Oh, Crow!" She was teasing him, but he liked it. "Comparison?"

"She's not as good as you, technically, but is much closer now, and I love her, and that makes it more."

"Gladness."

"In time you ladies will finish and go, but Blackbird will always be with me."

"Agreement."

"But I will never forget you."

"We will remember you, too, Crow."

They completed the trek without further event. "Something happened," Ennui said. "What?"

They told the story of Blackbird's conversion, and Scheme's plot and punishment. "I think there will be no more complications at the village," Aspect concluded.

It was Nonce's turn with Crow, which she took while they were unpacking supplies. Then he was gone, eager to return to Blackbird. "He's changed," Nonce reported.

"Another woman is working on him now," Aspect said.

Things settled down to routine. Time passed. The flax plants grew to chest height, and it was time to harvest them. They pulled them up by the roots and laid them on the ground in their Chroma zonelets, watering them to encourage decomposition. This was the retting process, to separate the long strong fibers from the woody sheaves. There was no way to hurry it; it took the time it took. When they cleared the plots they planted more seeds, because they weren't sure they had enough fibers yet.

Finally they had the fibers they needed, and were able to resume weaving on the loom. Nonce set the loom up in the second chamber, and they took turns at it, as before. The picture took further shape, growing, and they knew it was a true one because they could see it change after appearing; it was tracking the section of Counter Charm it depicted.

They planted more seeds as plots cleared, and in due course had enough to complete the tapestry. It was a truly marvelous thing, fascinating them with its constant shifts of color and detail.

Crow appeared regularly every three days with more supplies. He reported that Blackbird was pregnant with her first. The three of them gave him extra attention as his wife's condition progressed, making sure he suffered no sexual deprivation, and in due course he was a father.

By the time they were done, a year had passed. They had been long away from Triumph City, and were eager to return. They bid fond parting to Crow and Blackbird, and set off for home.

Chapter 5—Counter Charm

Havoc was antsy. With Ennui and Aspect away, he and Gale had had to remain mostly at Triumph City truly being king and queen instead of leaving it to the mocks. He hated it, but knew they couldn't risk having no truly committed and knowledgeable people in the palace. Symbol served as social reminder, and Ennui had left her top lieutenant, a competent and discreet woman, but she was not his oath friend. Bijou filled in where she could, as secretary and bed-mate when necessary, but both were a strain on her in different manners.

Chief and Throe were similarly out of sorts, with their women gone. They had shifted suddenly from too much sex to too little, as other women did not compare. But Ennui had made a sly suggestion before she departed. Havoc smiled, remembering it. She and Aspect had come to him in the night, oddly, looking strangely sexy in their nightrobes. "Apology for disturbing you at this hour."

"Needless." She always had reason.

"I was restless, and I thought of something."

"Your thoughts are always welcome."

She smiled appreciatively. "I don't know how long we'll be gone, Havoc. I believe Ini can handle my job, with the assistance of my assistant; she's twice as smart as I am, and has an organized mind. But you need a substitute for the Lady Aspect, to organize social functions. Neither Aspect nor I care to have substitutes that might replace us in your esteem—"

"Negation! You are my oath friend."

She smiled. "I'm teasing, Havoc. Still, there's something to it. Ini I'm sure can be trusted, but anyone in Aspect's place is at risk of getting ideas of permanence. So how about Futility?"

"Question?"

"Remember when you contested for the kingship, and oathed me in the process? That beautiful deceitful woman in red?"

He remembered. "Ire!"

"Precisely. You will never be inclined to keep her. Excavate her from her banishment, and assign her. I suspect she will be competent, and there will be no danger of permanence."

She was right. Havoc would never trust that particular woman.

"But how could I trust her in a position of responsibility? She has little conscience."

"She is in Limbo now. She surely hates it. Offer her freedom if she performs well—and a return to Limbo otherwise. She will conform."

He glanced sidelong at her. "This is a tougher stance than I have seen in you. You are not a hard woman."

Ennui smiled. "Havoc, I'm not hard to *you*, and not just because of the oath. If you needed a bed mate and no young woman was convenient, I would serve. But experience as your personal secretary, confronting the myriad folk who seek to gain advantage by contact with the king, has made me cynical. I have learned how to make people conform to royal convenience. Anyone will bend if correct and sufficient force is applied."

This surprised him on several counts. The thought of her in his bed had never occurred to him; she was his mother's age. But as he gazed at her now, he saw that she was not the woman he had first oathed. She looked no more than thirty, and a remarkably robust and lovely thirty at that, almost akin to Symbol. What had happened?

"Your ikon happened, Havoc," she said, picking up his thought. "It has transformed me to a health and shape I never was in youth. And it has made me sexy, perhaps in the Glamor manner. Getting to know the succubus Swale has done nothing to abate that. I remain your oath friend, with all that implies, but all else has changed."

Symbol was ten years his senior, and a fine mistress. Ennui was more than ten years her senior, yet looked quite capable of similar performance. Indeed, all else had changed. But he could not approach her, because of the ikon.

"I could set the ikon aside for long enough, Havoc, and would, if the occasion warranted. But my point is that I have changed. I am a mentally harder and a physically softer woman than I was. I think you can trust my judgment with respect to making Futility behave. You could even take her for a no fault mistress if you choose, if she believes that is a requirement for the position you offer. Swale could help, if your knowledge of Futility's nature turned out to be too much of a turnoff. In fact that might be best, because she will think that is *why* you offer it. Her appearance is her main power."

Ennui was cynical indeed! And surely correct. "What is Limbo?"

"It's where they hide the folk who officially no longer exist. Where you and I would have gone, had we not survived the kingship contest. They are not mistreated, but they can never return to normal human society."

"I doubt I like this. They are not criminals?"

"Correct. You can disband it if you prefer; as king you have that power. But it may do better to keep it as a threat for now."

Havoc looked at Aspect, who had let Ennui do the talking so far.

"Concurrence?"

"Concurrence," Aspect agreed. "Fetch her, control her, bed her. As for Ini—I have an additional use in mind for her."

"Beyond replacing Ennui as my personal secretary?"

"Agreement. If you are going to bed my surrogate, bed Ennui's also. And more."

"Confusion!"

Aspect smiled. "We thus bed you in surrogate, Havoc, perhaps a fitting compromise. We know the thought of sexuality in us embarrasses you, as it would have embarrassed us before we got the ikons. But there is reason. You plan to travel far—to planet Counter Charm— and you will be taking some nonGlamors along, including Ini. She carries an ikon. That will make her sexually charged, and in time more physically appealing than she has been. But most vital, you need to discover how to transport an ikon-bearing person so far a distance. So do it; practice traveling with her, no fault, and do not tease her with your close manly presence. She is young and impressionable despite her intellect; she will soon be smitten with you. Let her slowly learn how to clasp you, as Bijou did."

"Consideration," Havoc said, taken aback.

"You have trusted our judgment before, Havoc," Ennui said. "Trust it now."

"Agreement," he said, half dazed by their boldness.

"Favor," Aspect said. "We wish to kiss you."

"Amenable, if possible." He doubted it was.

Ennui removed her tree ikon from her mouth and gave it to Aspect, who held it at arm's length from her body. Then Ennui approached Havoc, embraced him, and kissed him passionately on the mouth. Her sexuality was like the splash of a warm wave against his body. Indeed, she had changed!

While he stood bemused, she disengaged, returned to Aspect, recovered her ikon, then took Aspect's ikon. Aspect came to him, took him in her arms, and kissed him similarly. She too smote him with her ardor.

These women were signaling their interest in changing the nature of their relationships with him. He would have to consider it, though there was considerable emotional resistance. He and Gale were after all responsible for their change, having given them the ikons.

Thereafter Ennui and Aspect went on their mission, relieving him of that particular quandary, and Havoc followed up on their suggestions, after checking with Gale and Symbol. Neither objected, knowing that such things were expected of kings, that Ini would appreciate it, and that it meant he would not reveal his Glamor nature to the other woman. "But take Swale along to Limbo," Symbol said wisely.

"You trust the succubus more than me?"

The two exchanged a glance. "Of course we do," Gale said, laughing.

"She's female," Symbol agreed. "She doesn't think with her gonads."

Havoc wasn't sure about that, after the demonstrations the other two women had just made.

The succubus hovered near, touching his mind. *I can turn sex off, too, you know.*

He hadn't known. That could be useful. "Agreement: Swale accompanies me to Limbo."

Chief knew of Limbo, and guided him there. It was on an island in a boiling lake some distance from Triumph City. It was reached by specially insulated boats whose boatsmen had strict orders to transport no one *away* from it, on penalty of being confined there themselves. Havoc entered it alone, as Hayseed the Minstrel.

You could have a ball here, Sire, and no one would know, Swale thought teasingly. She could not occupy his body, but she hovered beside him, and he could intersect her spirit by moving slightly, maintaining contact. She was actually good company, in part because her interest in sex was as keen as his and she never disparaged it. There were no sexual fantasies he could have that were beyond her compass.

Agreement.

And having a ball, anonymously, was one such. "Especially if you occupied any balky maiden," he agreed.

Affirmation.

Limbo was actually a pleasant enough place. The boiling lake warmed it so that it was never cold, and many exotic trees and plants grew there; he had to stop himself from examining them, lest his interest be suspicious. It was supervised by a former official of Triumph who had inadvertently caused King Deal embarrassment and had to be banished for political reason. He had become a minor monarch in his own right, and governed fairly. It was really a village economy, quite peaceful. There was no requirement for marriage or four children here; in fact most of the younger women wore the wire, not wishing to bring children into perpetual isolation from the main human society.

Swale floated ahead, scouting, returning to guide him to the single tavern on the island, where his quarry was to be found. He entered, finding a few men and women there. They glanced his way, recognizing him as a new resident, but made no issue; minding one's own business was evidently the custom here. Surely everyone knew everyone; it was not a large community. Probably the process of getting to know a new resident was savored as ongoing entertainment, stretched out.

Futility remained beautiful, with her trim figure and lustrous red hair, and was employed as a dancer and serving wench at the tavern.

That was probably all that offered that wasn't farming drudgery or boring labor. He entered the establishment and sat at a table.

She came to it, as she was bound to; he was a patron. She flashed an artificial smile. "Welcome to Limbo, stranger. What'll you have?"

"A loaf of bread, a jug of wine, and thou."

She has no interest.

"Bread and wine are on the house, this first time. Me you'll have to earn." She moved away gracefully, returning soon with the goods.

"Join me," he said.

"Unlikely."

Shall I touch her?

Just enough, he replied mentally.

"Until another patron comes." Futility sat down opposite him.

"Introduction: I am Hayseed the Minstrel. I am hot blooded."

"They call me the Ice Maiden. I am cold blooded."

"You look more like Futility to me."

She glanced at him sharply. "I have not used that name here. Where do you know me from?"

"The acid contest."

Now she surveyed him carefully. "The barbarian! Wreckage. No that's not quite it. Destruction."

"Havoc."

"That's it. You and that motley older woman. So she must've won, if you're here. Funny about the delay, though."

"I won, and took her with me."

"Interest. What was the prize?"

"The crown."

She laughed, not pleasantly. "And here you are, rendered forever anonymous. Try again, barbarian."

Havoc shrugged. He still didn't like this woman, but that was why he sought her. "Do you still carry the stiletto?"

"Are you still fast enough to intercept it?"

Havoc merely gazed at her. She made a tiny feint with her right hand, but he did not react. Then her hand flashed for her hair—and his hand shot out and caught her wrist before it got there. He held it just a moment, then let it go. "Perhaps."

She dropped her hand, nodding. "You're him, all right. But if you want to clasp me, you'll have to tell me the truth. What did the woman win, and why did you let her?"

"She is now the personal secretary to the king, and my oath friend."

"And you're the king," she said derisively.

"Agreement."

"So why'd you come here?"

"I remembered you."

She sighed. "Well, I gave you your chance." She stood.

"I offered you a liaison once. You declined. I made it instead with

Ennui."

She paused. "That was my mistake."

"Agreement."

"That was humor. Parting." She turned to leave.

Touch her.

A harder nudge this time, Sire. In fact I'll assume temporary occupancy. Swale was enjoying this. It had been long since she had infiltrated a hostile woman.

But do not let her know.

Awww.

Futility grimaced. "Oh, hell, there's nothing to gain, nothing to lose. We're all stuck here for eternity, and you're a handsome hunk of a man. Very well, barbarian, this way."

She led him to a small chamber in back that was evidently hers. She stepped lithely out of her clothing and stood before him, strikingly nude. Swale had truly turned her on, an unusual state for such a cold woman.

"The stiletto too," Havoc said as he stripped.

"Negation. That never leaves me."

"I could take it from you."

"You'll have to."

He caught her by one arm, twisted, and forced her face-down on the bed. He poked his fingers into her hair just above the neck and lifted out the little dagger. He set it aside. He released her arm.

She turned in place, serpent-like. "That's the one thing I like about you: you're man enough to take me if you want me."

But without the succubus, she would have been coldly furious. Her fury had been translated to passion.

Then they were in furious sex. Her legs wrapped around him as she hooked her hands behind his head and hauled him in for a savage kiss. Her internal muscles clasped him as he penetrated her, urging him to a convulsive climax.

Havoc still didn't like her, but that was one fine sex experience. She would do for a mistress, at least when assisted by the sexual spirit.

"You have done your part," he said as they broke. "Now I will do mine. Collect your things and come with me."

"I have no things worth collecting." She returned to her clothing, dressing as he did. "Not that we're going anywhere. To Limbo is a one way trip. Didn't you know?"

"Except for the king."

"Yeah, sure." But she accompanied him, perhaps playing out the game. Swale was also guiding her, keeping her interested in the possibility of another sexual encounter.

He led her out of the tavern and to the arrival wharf. There was Throe. He inclined his head. "Sire."

"This is Futility. She will take the Lady Aspect's place for the interim."

"Lady Futility," Throe agreed. He turned and signaled the boatman.

"Yeah, sure," Futility repeated. "Joke's about played out."

The boat came in. "Sire," the boatman said.

Havoc conducted the woman onto the boat. He and Throe took their seats. The boat moved out.

Futility faced Havoc. "Disbelief."

They crossed the boiling lake and tied up at the outside wharf. Beyond it a carriage waited, drawn by two horses. Havoc escorted her to it. Throe got up on front with the coachman. They started moving.

"Dream," Futility said.

Havoc shrugged.

The coach took them to the edge of a blue Chroma zone. They got out and walked to a huge basket. "Sire," the blue man said. They got in. Huge blue birds came, and the blue man slipped big loops over their feet. They took off together, carrying the basket into the sky.

Now Havoc doffed his minstrel hat, fetched the crown from under the seat and put it on his head.

Futility stared. Swale nudged her with belief. Then she faced Havoc and bowed her head. "Apology, Sire."

"Needless. When we reach Triumph City, you will be confined to the palace. You will not contact anyone you knew before, or betray my interests in any way, on pain of being returned to Limbo."

"Understood," she breathed.

"You will answer to the Lady Symbol, who is my mistress, and the Lady Gale, who is my wife. When I come to you, you will never deny me in body or manner."

"Of course, Sire."

"You will arrange my formal social schedule. There will be helpers to advise you. You will be the ice maiden to all outsiders, barring my caution otherwise."

"Sire," she agreed.

And so it was. Futility actually turned out to be competent, because her self-interested mind was like a metal trap, and she knew she owed everything and more to the king. He did take her sexually every so often, so that she remained persuaded that this private letch was his reason for rescuing her from Limbo. Swale did not need to touch her again; she was quite capable of the pretense of interest, and the pretense was all Havoc wanted. Later she asked, and was granted, the right to entertain palace guests by dancing as the anonymous Ice Maiden. She was good at it, and on occasion became the no fault bed partner of some Chroma male dignitary who was taken with her appearance. She did this as a service to the king, normally having no interest in sex for its own sake, and was rewarded with significantly greater freedom. She and Havoc were honest with each other: they were not friends, but he was the king and she was competent in her position, beautiful, and talented in the dance, and so they had use for each other.

Ini was another matter. Gale had made a deal with her family to bring her to Triumph City in the hope of improved marriage prospects, and she was proving to be useful and reliable. She was the smartest person he knew, but rather plain physically, to the extent her invisibility allowed it to be known. That was a double liability for advantageous marriage, but worthwhile for Havoc's purpose. Aspect was right: close association with him would cause the girl to be smitten, and it would be unkind not to oblige her. But he really wished she were more shapely.

"As you know, we anticipate travel to Counter Charm," he said. "Your knowledge of the surface of that planet makes you a likely member of the party. I, or another Glamor, will carry you there. But first I must be sure it is possible."

"I could give the altar ikon to someone else, so as to be more transportable," she said.

"Negation. We may have to transport the loom, or at least the tapestry, and they are ikonic. I need to learn how to do it. I propose to practice with you."

"I am at your service, of course, Sire."

"We will travel extensively across Charm. No fault."

"As you wish, Sire."

"Call me Havoc. Reconsideration: call me Hayseed. I prefer to be anonymous."

"Then I will be Ni. Candor?"

"Granted."

"I suspect you proffer no fault in the belief that I would like to clasp the king. I would, as any girl would. But I am aware of my limitations of body, and do not wish to cause you discomfort. The delight of discovery of new things is my passion, and I have already been well rewarded there. So there is no need to clasp me."

Ennui and Aspect had addressed this point. "The ikon charges you sexually."

"Agreed, Sire. I was not sexually hungry before, but my interest in men is now akin to men's interest in attractive women. However—"

"You are surely more physically attractive than you were. I have seen the change in the Ladies Ennui and Aspect."

"They are rare women."

"It is difficult for a mortal person to knowingly clasp a Glamor, and difficult for a Glamor to clasp a mortal with an ikon. This may relate to the problem of transporting such a person. Therefore it may behoove us to tackle these problems also."

The shrouded woman considered. "It is a challenge I would delight in tackling, Sire. Still—"

Havoc remembered something. "Swale was with you when you sought the altar."

The figure nodded. "Swale can make me compelling. If you wish—"

"Do *you* wish?"

"Negation, Sire. What the succubus offers is effective but artificial. I wish I were lovely, but I orient on reality, and accommodate to it."

She was determined not to require him to clasp her if he didn't want to. He did not argue the case further. He had other business to attend to, so set a future date for their first attempt at distance traveling. He might indeed call on Swale for assistance, if sex turned out to be warranted.

When that time came, Ini was ready, and had a suggestion. "Such an effort is bound to be observed sometimes, as there may be people where we arrive. If I remove my clothing I will be invisible, concealing the fact that I am with you. This could simplify the mission."

He liked the notion, but saw a problem. "It may be cold in some regions."

"The ikon keeps me warm. I will not suffer."

"Does the ikon show?"

"Negation. It has adapted to the host, and is invisible."

"Agreement. Travel invisible."

The clothing fell away, and only her mental presence was evident before him. He stepped to her and put his arms around her—and stopped. The ikon was resisting. "Problem."

"I will hold it away from us." He felt her slight motion; then it became possible to hold her closely to his body. But he felt the continuing resistance of the ikon, diminished with the distance.

"I will try to move you across this room," he said.

"Acquiescence."

He jumped magically across the room. It worked, but he felt the drag. It was as though she weighed much more, because of the ikon. He concentrated, and jumped again, doing better. Then he jumped to his own chamber.

There was Gale, nursing Weft. The baby girl was seven months old, and quite aware of herself and her surroundings. She stopped nursing immediately. Her eyes focused on something in front of Havoc.

"She sees the altar ikon," Ini said, surprised.

"Hold on to it," Gale said. She perceived Ini the same way Havoc did, by her mental presence. "She conjures."

"I feel the tug."

"Ini has to hold it out so I can hold her close enough to move," Havoc explained.

"And that's why she's naked?"

"To be invisible."

Gale laughed. "Obvious, so to speak. Now get out of here so Weft will finish her meal. You're too much of a distraction for her."

Because he took the baby's attention whenever he could, so that Gale could tend to Warp effectively. Weft had a possessive nature, yet was cute, and she behaved well when with him. But she did need to nurse.

Havoc moved them back to the original chamber. "Not every man's wife would be so tolerant of his bringing a naked women to their bedroom."

"Gale is perfect."

"Envy. But what if you had brought Futility?"

"Gale knows that Futility is only business."

"Apology for teasing, Sire."

"Needless. Are you ready for greater distance?"

"Ready."

He traveled to Limbo, landing near the wharf, and let her go. No one was there, because it was used only when new exiles were brought in. That was the way he preferred it. He wondered how the denizens had reacted when the stranger had vanished with the Ice Maiden. Not that it mattered.

"Where?" Ini asked, looking around as he turned her loose.

"Limbo."

"Ignorance."

He explained about the island.

"Interest. I never knew of it."

"Neither did I, until very recently. It's where I fetched Futility."

"You should have set up this practice with her."

"Negation. I don't like her. I like you."

"Joke?" she asked as he took hold of her again, preparing for the return jump.

"Serious. She's lithe and beautiful, but cold, calculating, and dishonest. She won't betray me because there is nothing to be gained by alienating the king, but our association is mutual convenience, no more. You are not pretty, but you are smart, reliable, and you mean well. You could be my friend."

He felt her invisible jaw drop. She had no rejoinder.

He jumped them back to the chamber in the palace. He was gaining confidence with practice. "Enough?"

"Question?"

"We have traveled to a distant place and back. Is this enough for the day? I do not wish to strain you."

"Apology. I was distracted by what you said before. Negation; I am enjoying this, and the ikon provides me stamina. I would relish more."

"Then I am minded to try a jump to an unfamiliar spot. That may be chancy. My Glamor power prevents me from hurting myself by overlapping a tree or rock, but we could land in a public place. I might

have to put you down, to use my hands. There could be embarrassment."

"That's an advantage of invisibility: no embarrassment."

"Then on." He took hold of her again, and jumped as far as he
could, eastward across the planet.

They landed knee-deep in a red lake. A six-legged croc spied them
by sight and smell, and nosed smoothly in. Havoc waded out of the
water, urging Ini with him. The croc couldn't hurt him, and probably
couldn't hurt Ini either, but he preferred that that not be apparent.

"Interest," Ini said, looking around as he released her. Again, he
'saw' her via her mind, not her body. "I have not before had occasion
to catalogue Red Chroma fauna and flora."

"Nor this time," he said. "But after this practice is done, I will
bring you back here, if you wish."

"Deal."

"Do you know how far we have come?"

She glanced at Counter Charm in the sky. "Judging by the changed
position of our sister planet, about one twentieth of the circumference
of Charm."

"Amazement. I can't figure distance like that."

"It's just a matter of perspective. I can detail the process if you
wish."

"Negation. Just keep tracking us."

He took hold of her again, and jumped east again, to his limit.
This time they were near a Black Chroma volcano. He made an immediate short jump to get to nonChroma terrain.

"Appreciation," Ini said. "Black makes me nervous."

"Distance?"

"Another fifteenth of the way around the planet. You are getting
stronger."

They jumped again, this time a tenth of the circumference, and
landed in a White Chroma zone. Again Havoc made a smaller jump to
get them to a nonChroma zone.

Now they were in late afternoon. "I didn't realize it was so late,"
Havoc said.

"Explanation: you have traveled between a fifth and a quarter of
the way around the planet. Night falls here five to six hours sooner
than at Triumph City."

"Appreciation! I hadn't thought of that."

"One reason you have me along."

He looked at her position. "I am minded to night in this vicinity,
and continue east in the morning."

"Amenable."

Havoc drew on a Glamor power to scout the vicinity and locate a
friendly tree with a trunk diverging into several large spreading
branches. This formed a safe basket for them, as the tree would not

tolerate any intrusion by a hostile creature. He harvested succulent fruits that provided liquid with their substance. They ate, contributed offerings of fertilizer at the tree's base, and settled down for the night. Havoc, stronger and invulnerable, lay in the basket and held Ini on top of him, making her secure.

In the process, one hand came up against her small breast. He considered, and left it.

"Appreciation," she murmured. "For pretending my anatomy is worth touching."

That was exactly why he had left his hand, after the accidental contact. Her lack of confidence in her appearance was showing. She was sixteen, an age when appearance was vital. "You have helped me gain proficiency. Maybe you can return the ikon to your mouth now."

She did so, cautiously. He felt her body became more resistive to his proximity, but it was tolerable.

"I find myself awake," Ini said after a bit. "This is night, but hours before my normal sleep cycle."

"Similar."

"Dialogue?"

"Amenable."

"I have been thinking about the Glamor and ikon effects. I see them as physical and psychological. When a person tries to strike an ikon bearer, the blow sheers away. That is physical; the heavier the weapon, the faster and closer it moves, the greater the magical repulsion. So were you a normal person, you could not strike me."

"Agreement."

"But perhaps you could hold me as you are doing, by approaching slowly and without malice. In fact I'm sure you could, because Augur clasped me after I possessed the ikon. I had to move it from my genital area to enable him to penetrate me, and from my mouth so he could kiss me, but he was able to touch me closely."

"But I as a Glamor have more trouble."

"True. The ikon wards you off more effectively than it does a mortal person. You would not be able to have sex with me unless I held it well away from my body. I am speaking analytically, not invitingly."

"Understanding."

"Comparison: if I lacked the ikon, and did not know you were a Glamor, I could have sex with you. But once I knew your nature, I could not. Since that barrier obviously is not physical, it must be psychological."

"Agreement," Havoc said, surprised. "I can have sex with Futility because she doesn't know. But Bijou, who knew, had a real struggle to get to it."

"Could your inability to have sex with an ikon holder be similarly psychological?"

"Possible," Havoc said, surprised.

"I am minded to experiment, for the sake of knowledge. Amenable?"

"Amenable."

"We contemplate likely failure, so it probably will not happen. But if you care to attempt it with me, perhaps we can ascertain the limit." She turned over so that she was straddling him.

Havoc, normally the lustiest of men, especially since becoming a Glamor, found that he was not ready for this. "Embarrassment: I lack hardness." Actually he realized he was partly hard, but unable to touch that area.

"Needless. I am holding the ikon near my groin. See if you can bring your groin to contact. Completion is unnecessary. Remain clothed."

Havoc tried, but though there had been reasonable proximity before, now with the ikon in that region he found he could not achieve contact. He pushed hard, but her invisible groin eluded him.

"Observation," she said. "I am floating."

"Astonishment!"

"Feel with your hands."

He did so, and discovered a space between their bodies. She was floating above him, pushed away by his effort to bring their groins into contact. "It's physical!"

"Physical," she agreed. "You can not have sex with me because you are unable to approach close enough for penetration near the ikon. So it is not after all psychological. This requires rethinking." She turned over so that her back was toward him, moved the ikon away, and settled comfortably against him. Her backside was more interesting than expected; the ikon was reshaping her. "I am minded to experiment further."

"Amenable!"

"Again, I do not wish to cause you awkwardness. But now I wonder whether a mortal's inability to have sex with a Glamor is after all not psychological. I would like to remove the ikon and attempt a genital contact. There is no need to complete it, or to remove your clothing."

"Proceed." They were discovering things that even the older Glamors didn't know. This woman's approach was a marvel for discovery.

She held the ikon well out from her body, to the side, and faced him, first straddling him, then trying to lie wholly against him. She did not succeed. In fact she was floating again. "Physical," she concluded as she gave up the effort.

"Mystery: if it is physical, why does ignorance enable sex?"

"This is the problem. Psychological seemed to explain it, but now we are lost. How could a mortal's mere knowledge evoke a physical repulsion?" Then she jumped, startling him. "Revelation: we are looking the wrong way! It is psychological not for the mortal, but for the

Glamor."

"Confusion."

"The magic lies with the Glamor. He can invoke it by mere act of will. You can transport me around the planet; you could as readily make me float. The power is yours."

"Agreement. But why would that prevent me from approaching you when I wished to?"

"Psychology can be subtle and devious. It can make it seem that the other person is doing something instead of you. If you believe a mortal woman is unable to clasp you, then your magic can make it true. If you believe that her ignorance makes it possible, then that is true also. Similar could be true for the ikons: you believe you can't approach them, so you can't. Your psychology becomes physical, because of your great magic."

This was approaching sense. "That means I should be able to clasp you, if I truly believe I could."

"If my conjecture is valid."

Something changed in him. "Ini, your rationale appeals to me, perhaps because it offers me greater understanding and control of my own actions. Now I want to clasp you sexually."

"No need. It can wait. In time the ikon may make me more physically desirable, as has been the case with the Ladies Ennui and Aspect."

"Negation. I want to do it now, before you reach that state. Your mind turns me on."

"Willing," she said breathlessly, getting out of his way.

He almost ripped off his clothes. Then, fully erect, he caught her body and drew her into him. He kissed her mouth, and felt a tingle as of a departing stasis. He kissed her breasts, and felt them expand. He clasped her, and penetrated her, and erupted into her with a phenomenal climax. He felt her reacting against him, her body tightening as she achieved her own climax. Then they lay plastered together, breathing hard.

"You are right," he said.

"Appreciation." Then: "Curiosity: is it true that a Glamor can do it many times in succession?"

"True. You wish it?"

"At this moment, yes. To see if I can too."

He had not yet slid out of her. Now his member hardened again. "Tell me when to stop." He thrust, and jetted again, and she flung her arms around him and pushed her groin as close as possible, for maximum reception. After a moment he hardened a third time, thrust, and jetted. He felt her convulsing against him, matching his climax.

After six times, she relented. "Now stop, if you care to, Sire. I fear we are depleting ourselves, delightful as this is."

He relaxed, and they lay again with entry complete but not driving. "You stayed with me. Yet you are not a Glamor."

"I gained it from you. When I felt your body around me and in me, I responded. There is phenomenal joy in your essence. I think my ikon helped."

"Instead of hindering. You enabled the breakthrough. Now we know that Symbol did it fifty times with the Green Glamor because he believed she could; they did not need to play a game of charades."

"Affirmation. And appreciation."

"Question?"

"For demanding it before I become desirable. That makes it much better."

"Welcome." Actually she had become desirable, but there was no need to point that out. Something else occurred to him. "Glamors can have sex freely with other Glamors. If there were true repulsion, surely it would be worse with Glamors than with ikons."

"Concurrence."

"So the answer was there all the time, opaque until you found it."

"Answers always seem more obvious in retrospect than in anticipation."

"Opinion."

She laughed against him. "Whose?"

"Yours." He was requesting her perspective on another matter.

"Welcome."

"As we know, Ennui and Aspect have become far more sexually appealing with the ikons than they were before them. The ikons also make them lusty."

"Agreement."

"They have suggested that they would like a change in our relationship."

That surprised her; he felt it in her body. "They desire you!"

"Affirmation. I respect, trust, and value both them enormously. But they are the age of my mother. I find this awkward."

"How old is the Red Glamor?"

That stopped him. "Over 250 years. And I have no problem with sex with her."

She wriggled against him. "I'm 16. Red's 250 plus. That makes Ennui and Aspect middle range."

"And I have been answered."

"Suggestion: let's do it once more, then sleep."

For answer he clasped her again, stiffening, and they went into a final bout of sex. And slept.

In the morning they resumed jumping, and by day's end had circled the planet. On later occasions they did it again, until Havoc was satisfied that he could take her any distance, with or without the ikon. That problem had been abolished.

So had whatever problem of appearance she thought she had.

Invisibility could not hide the fact that the slow transition inspired by the ikon she carried was making her the match of any of her sisters. They had sex often when they traveled, but it was for the fun of it, not for any reassurance she might need. She was coming to accept that. Sometimes she teased him about having a second Air mistress. He did not argue; it was close to being true. With his wife increasingly pregnant, and his mistress fully occupied helping her cope with the children, sex tended to get left behind. Ini understood, and was obliging, and discreet.

But still he longed for the return of the Ladies Aspect and Ennui. He felt clumsy running the kingdom without their guidance, and worse when Gale birthed Voila; true fatherhood was its own challenge. And finally the Ladies came.

⸙⸙

Gale knew it well before the three arrived; she sensed the approach of her ikon. "They're back!" she exclaimed.

"Relief," Symbol said. "I know they have ikons, but such a long distant mission had to be chancy."

"The Gray Glamor kept an eye on them. When there was trouble, he took care of it."

"I remember your comment. It's hard to believe we lived all our lives before without Glamor contact"

Gale smiled. "Things change."

"And now we'll go with the Glamors to Counter Charm."

"Now that we'll have the complete tapestry and the altar," Gale agreed.

The three children were playing while the baby slept. Symbol went to prepare nutritive puddings for them. Warp liked dark chocolate, Weft Vanilla, and Flame strawberry; their tastes matched the colors of their hair, approximately. Voila's hair was light brown, matching that of her parents; she was too young to have developed a taste for light chocolate, but it would surely happen soon.

Gale watched them while Symbol was busy; they had learned that one of them always had to be alert, because mischief erupted the moment the three were left to their own devices. Sure enough, as Symbol put the puddings out to cool, the strawberry one lifted into the air and floated slowly toward Warp. Then a little ball of flame appeared over the chocolate one, threatening to burn it to ashes. The strawberry pudding reversed course and returned to its place.

Gale stifled a smile. She had observed with extended peripheral awareness, giving no sign. Warp had tried to steal Flame's pudding; Flame had warned him off. So that was ploy and counter-ploy, self correcting. That was best.

Then a brown ball of Warp's—their toys were color coded too— appeared in Weft's hand while Warp was distracted by the puddings incident. That needed to be dealt with, lest it trigger retribution. The children were normal, but also Glamors, and a serious quarrel could lay waste the area.

Gale focused, and a little black cloud complete with projecting lightning jags appeared before Weft. It was illusion, and Weft knew it, but abruptly the brown ball returned to its place behind Warp. They all knew that an illusion warning could readily be replaced by an unpleasant reality. Discipline was constant, but mainly in cautions rather than punishments. Gale had heeded the sage advice of Intrepid and Innate, Ini's Invisible Chroma parents. It did require magic to handle magic children, but it was working out, and Gale had never regretted adopting them.

Symbol passed out the puddings. Voila woke and demanded feeding too. Gale picked her up and nursed her.

"I lose track," Symbol said. "How many Glamors are there now?"

"Fourteen adult, three child."

"And eighteen pockets in the altars. One more Glamor to go."

Gale paused. "I wonder what constituency?"

"Ini would know."

The children took their attention then, with a threatening food fight, and the subject lapsed, but Gale didn't forget it.

The three Loom travelers were warmly welcomed home. They had been looking younger and fitter when they left; they were more so now. Ennui and Aspect looked hardly older than Nonce, while Nonce looked more mature. It seemed that the ikons were taking them toward a common ideal.

Gale hugged Aspect and Havoc hugged Ennui. Both women were amazed. "How can you touch us so close?" Ennui asked.

"Ini figured it out," Gale said. "The key is in the Glamors. We can touch when we want to."

"Not the ikons themselves," Havoc said. "But we can come close."

Ennui and Aspect exchanged a glance. Then they went with Nonce to set the loom up in its former chamber.

"Jealousy," Symbol muttered.

"Question?"

"Never in my life did I see either Aspect or Ennui as sexual competition. Oh, Aspect was King Deal's wife, and could have him any time she made an issue, but I was the one he came to for pleasure. As for Ennui, she was Havoc's oath friend, and that made her supreme in court, by definition, but sex had nothing to do with it. But now the ikons have wrought such a phenomenal change that they both look younger than I do, and sexier, and I know they can and will perform. If they want Havoc, they'll take him."

"Doubt."

"As mistresses, I mean. You're his wife and his love; not even an ikon can change that. But I am merely his mistress; I can be replaced.

Ini could readily do it; he truly likes her. Her ikon has transformed her similarly. I really haven't been giving him enough attention recently."

"Because your time has been monopolized by the children."

"And I don't regret it. But it has shifted the nature of our relationship."

"Symbol, I need you. I can tell Havoc to—"

"Negation. Such things have to be natural. I am merely suffering the pangs of seeing others as others have seen me."

That was true, but it bothered Gale. Every woman desired Havoc, and he rewarded a select number with sex when it was appropriate, but Gale and Symbol were his home ports. The notion of the Ladies Aspect and Ennui entering the sexual arena was disturbing, in part because they were not mere passing doxies. They were vital, formidable women, essential to the operation of the kingdom. Symbol was right: they had become disturbingly sexual creatures.

"Was it a mistake to give them the ikons?" Gale asked.

"Negation. They are to be trusted beyond all others. It merely requires some realignment of perspective."

"I will ponder the matter." She intended to consult Swale, who remained the sexual expert.

They collected the children and went to the loom chamber. Nonce had reverted the loom, and there was the tapestry, complete. It was an amazing picture, seeming alive. "We had some adventure along the way," Aspect said.

"We want the whole story," Gale said. Then, realizing that the women had been without their men for a year, she added "Tomorrow."

It turned out to be a considerable story of travel, sex, gardening, and village conspiracy. It seemed that the once-staid older women had made excellent use of their flashy new bodies. But they had gotten the job done.

Later, Symbol remarked on that. "Those ikons really made a difference."

"We thought they would merely keep them safe," Gale said. "But the ikons almost seem to have wills of their own."

"Agreement. They're not just leftovers from Glamors."

That reminded Gale. This time she followed up, bringing Ini in to discuss it. Ini, too, had changed; she carried the altar ikon, and though she remained invisible, her swathing showed a shapely outline. Havoc had confirmed that she had become an apt sexual partner. Swale was also present.

"There are seventeen Glamors we know of," Gale said. "But eighteen pockets in the altars. What would be the constituency of the last one?"

"Amoeba," Ini said promptly. "That's the only significant class that's missing."

Gale remembered. "You thought it would be for one of the babies, but it wasn't."

"So it remains to be assigned a Glamor."

"I wonder," Symbol said. "Are these things invariably random?"

"Negation. Havoc and Gale chose their constituencies, and were accepted by them."

"So someone could choose the amoeba, and perhaps become a Glamor."

Both Gale and Ini were surprised. "Possibility," Ini agreed.

"Do we want that?" Symbol asked. "How do we know who would turn up as a new Glamor?"

Now that the question had been asked, it required an answer. *Don't risk it*, Swale thought. *Ikons are bad enough; Glamors are potentially dangerous.*

"We need to choose that Glamor," Gale said.

"Suggestion."

Suddenly Gale realized that Symbol had an idea. Was she thinking of going after it herself? "Speak."

"You have three Glamor children. What of Voila?"

"She's three months old!"

"With Glamor parents and siblings."

Suddenly it was making sense. "But Voila is too young to make such a choice."

"So her parents should make it for her."

Gale looked at Ini. "Sense?"

Ini nodded. "Sense. That would eliminate the chance of an ugly surprise, and she would grow up properly prepared. It would be a perfect completion of the roster."

Sense Swale agreed.

Gale sent a mental signal to Havoc, and in moments he was with them. "Agreement," he said. "But the other Glamors should be advised."

In a moment he advised them, telepathically. They thought it was a good idea.

Gale nodded. "Maybe when she's a little older," she said, uncertain how or whether to proceed. "I would want her to understand, before commitment."

"Agreement," Ini said, and departed.

Then Gale braced Symbol. "You thought of it. You don't want it for yourself?"

"Temptation," Symbol admitted. "It could make me more than competitive with the others. But I think better for Voila. She can grow up knowing, instead of being spoiled by mortal distractions."

"I thought you were cynical, looking out for yourself."

"I was. Then I fell in love with Havoc. And with you. And with your children."

Gale was touched. "You deserve your own life."

"Cynical, looking out for myself? I am better off, and surely happier, patterning myself after you." She smiled. "Anyway, Futility is better at those old qualities than I could be."

"Agreement!" Gale said, laughing.

The children were becoming restive. It was time for entertainment. This was one way in which Symbol was supreme: she could distract the children for hours at a time by showing them illusion stories from her comprehensive collection. She used an Air Chroma stone to power it, and though the stories had been crafted for older children and adults, they appealed to these three too. The fact was, the little Glamors were precocious; it came with their genes and health. They might not understand all the ramifications of the shows, but they followed enough to be distracted, and that was what counted.

Early in the adoption, the babies had fixed on particular stories and insisted on the same ones repeatedly. But now they preferred variety. They were making progress through Symbol's repertoire, and some were borderline appropriate, but the children demanded them. "Next one in line features Death," Symbol said. "I'm not sure—"

"Let's try it," Gale said. "If it spooks them, cut it off. They know it's just a story."

I'm interested too, Swale thought. *I know about death.* She did; her body had died, and she lived now because Gale provided a regular host.

The show started. The three children immediately oriented on it, sitting around its edges, facing inward. They liked to see themselves disappeared by the illusion; it made them feel like part of the story. Gale and Symbol watched from farther back. Voila slept in the crib beside Gale.

"Once upon a time there was a boy," the narrator said.

Warp clapped his hands. He liked boy stories.

"He was caught late away from home, and had to hurry before it got too dark to see the way." The boy appeared, a tow-headed lad of about six, running along a path through a forest. The path wound between colors on the left and right; everyone knew that it could be dangerous to go into Chroma zones, so the paths meandered as necessary to avoid them.

"But the way was blocked by something dark and scary." The boy came to a sudden halt, for a formless blob blocked the path. It shimmered darkly and seemed menacing. In fact it was darkly terrifying.

But the boy had to get home, and had no other route. So he did what he had to: he addressed the blob. "Please, Blob, let me by."

The blob became aware of him. Two or three big eyes appeared and focused on him. "Who?" it asked with eerie windiness, as of the exhalation from an uncovered crypt.

"Introduction," the boy said bravely. "I am Todd of Village Minor."

"I am Death."

Todd stepped back. "Death! I fear you."

"All mortals fear me, and rightly so."

But this wasn't getting him on his way. "Please, Death, let me by. I need to get home before dark."

"I would if I could. But I am bound."

"How can Death be bound?"

"I was chasing an errant soul, and blundered into an old spirit trap. It's an embarrassing nuisance. I can't depart until the confinement enchantment is nullified."

Todd was beginning to be curious rather than afraid. After all, if Death was trapped, then he couldn't grab Todd. "If you get it nullified, then will you go away and leave the path clear so I can go home?"

"Agreement."

The boy nerved himself. "How is the spell nullified?"

"That requires a drop of fresh warm blood and a spoken spell."

"Can I do that?"

"You can—if you have the courage."

"I'm just a small boy. I don't have much courage."

"So it seems."

"But if I did have the courage, I could do it?"

The blob had a somewhat resigned patience. "So I said."

"If I did, would you promise to go away and not kill me?"

"I can not promise that. All mortals come to me in time."

"I mean, not right now."

"That I can promise."

The boy screwed his courage to the sticking point. "Okay. What's the spell?"

"The blood must be dripped onto the enchantment, and these words spoken: 'Ill mode, with this fresh blood I banish thee.'"

"How do I get the blood?"

"Scratch your finger with a razor fern."

Todd found a razor fern growing beside the path. He held his hand out near the blob and stroked the fern across it. The serrated edge opened a cut, and blood welled out. "Sick zone, get out of here before I bleed on you."

"Irregular, but it will do," Death said. The blob dissolved, and a tall black vaguely human form loomed up before the boy. "You have done me a favor. How may I return it?"

"I just want to go home!"

Death considered. "Another time, perhaps." Then it disappeared.

The path was clear. Todd ran quickly along it, and soon was safely home, except for the cut on his hand. He bandaged that himself, not trusting his mother to understand about his encounter with Death, even if she believed it.

There was a slow fadeout, and fade-in to a new scene, signifying the passage of time. Todd was now a young man, handsome and confident, proceeding along the same path. He came to the same place where he had encountered Death as a child. There, coincidentally, was a strung net. He charged right into it before he realized it was there, and was abruptly wrapped and suspended just above the path.

Before he could free himself, three ugly brigands appeared. "Well, look what we caught!" one exclaimed.

"A healthy young man," the second said.

"We'll cut him up and roast him for our supper," the third said.

They were serious. They gave Todd no chance to plead for his life. They came at him with knives drawn, about to cut him up where he hung. He was entangled, and could not defend himself.

"Assistance!" he called desperately. But it was obvious that the chance was small that anyone was close enough to hear, or would be able to stop the brigands if he came.

Then a tall dark shape formed behind them. "Greetings, brigands," it said.

They whirled at the sound. "Death!" one cried. "Flee!"

They tried to run, but Death made a small gesture with one hand, and the three fell to the ground. Their bodies puffed into smoke. Only their clothing, knives, and booty pouches remained.

Death turned to Todd. "I owed you a favor. Parting." The figure vanished.

Todd worked his way free of the net and dropped to the ground. He checked the brigands' things. He had no use for the clothing, but the knives were good, and the pouches contained a small treasure. He knew it was now his, by right of survival; anyone who killed a brigand was entitled to the brigand's things. He was suddenly well off.

"Thank you, Death," he said. "I appreciate the return favor." He picked up the things and went on his way.

That's nice, Swale thought. *That's the way Death should be.*

Gale had to agree. She was glad that it had turned out to be a wholesome story for children.

The illusion faded, and the playroom came back into sight. Gale looked around. Symbol was slumped in her chair, having fallen asleep. She had of course seen this show many times, and was bored with it. The babies were gone.

What happened?

Alarmed, Gale spread her Glamor awareness, seeking them. There was nothing. "Wake!" Gale snapped.

Symbol's swathed form came alert. "Question?"

"The babies are gone."

"Alarm! Who would have taken them?"

"Who *could* take them?" Gale was rapidly building up extreme nervousness.

I would have known if a demon spirit came.

"Only someone they trusted," Symbol said. "Ini. Nonce. Bijou."

"Or a Glamor."

"Who would?" Symbol asked.

"Without our knowledge? None."

"And why did I sleep? I don't sleep while watching the children."

They stared at each other. "An attack?" Gale asked, horrified.

"Who *could*?" Symbol asked, echoing Gale's prior question.

"Unknown," Gale said grimly. *Havoc!* she thought desperately.

He was there beside her, catching on immediately. "Mischief."

They quickly organized a thorough search of the palace, knowing it was futile, because the mental traces of the babies weren't there. Then they spread out beyond. And found nothing.

Use your past-seeing, Swale suggested.

Gale exerted a power she had developed after Havoc demonstrated it, to see the recent past connected to whatever object she focused on. In this case, the youngest of the babies: Voila. She was sleeping in the crib beside Gale. Then she faded out. The crib was empty.

"It's magic, all right," Gale said. "She was conjured away."

They notified the other Glamors. None of them knew what had happened. There was no question of complicity; they laid their minds open.

"Who could have taken them from a Glamor's side?" Symbol asked.

"Only a Glamor she trusted," Havoc said.

"I trust them all—but none are guilty."

"Unless—" Symbol hesitated, then continued. "Unless there is that eighteenth Glamor, that we don't know about. Isn't it true that not even a Glamor can detect a Glamor who wants to hide?"

"It is true," Gale agreed. "But if there is such a Glamor, why would he take my children?"

"To stop you from making Voila a Glamor?" But Symbol immediately corrected herself. "If he's already a Glamor, he can have no such fear; there's no other Glamor to be made. And if he isn't, he would lack the power to steal the children from a Glamor's side. This doesn't make sense."

Gale controlled her burgeoning horror by organizing for action. "We must search everywhere! Again! Until we find them." But she feared it was hopeless.

Then Ini had an idea. "If they are anywhere near, and hidden so you can't find them, there should be a patch of obscurity, as there was at the altar crater. Use your extended awareness to locate that patch."

"Yes!" Gale did so—and found a patch outside Triumph City, in an unsettled region of the nonChroma zone surrounding the city. She grabbed Symbol and transported them there.

It was a glade with a small pond, a fairly pretty place. The patch was beside the pond. They walked toward it.

Symbol paused, glancing down. "What is that?"

"A shiny blob," Gale said impatiently.

The hell it is, Swale thought.

Symbol stooped to pick it up. "This is ikon substance."

They stared at each other in wild surmise. "The Amoeba Glamor!" Gale said.

"I have a marvelous suspicion," Symbol said. "The children—they helped Voila do it. They heard us talking about it, and took action themselves."

"The children!" Gale said. "They are Glamors! They could have done it. Except that they haven't yet developed more than single Glamor skills."

"Haven't they?" Symbol turned and faced the far side of the pond. "Game's over, kids! Get your little rumps over here, now!"

"Awww!" Four small forms appeared the other side of the pond.

The little devils!

Gale opened her mouth.

"Caution," Symbol warned. "They meant well, and seem to have accomplished well." She lifted the amoeba ikon.

Gale stifled her threatening outburst. Symbol was right—and the children were Glamors. Including, now, it seemed, Voila. Somehow they had done it.

"Impressive array of skills," Symbol said as the children made their way around the lake. Voila was floating, surely not by her own initiative. "They blanked themselves and Voila out, Glamor style, so that we were not aware. They made their way unobserved out of the palace and out of the city. They found a private spot where amoeba were likely to congregate. They addressed the amoeba, made an offer, and obtained their acceptance. They made their little sister a Glamor, like themselves. Now the whole family is Glamor."

"But the risk!" Gale protested. "They could have been destroyed out here!"

"Doubt. They knew what they were doing. We underestimated them, though we have been with them throughout. We should cease doing that."

They showed great nerve, too. They'll be real terrors when they get older. Makes me sorry I'll never have children. The succubus had a taste for mischief.

Gale realized that it was true. The children had demonstrated abilities of planning and performance well beyond what any adult had suspected. They had also saved Gale the trouble of tackling the Amoeba Glamor matter herself. Now all she had to do was find a placement for the ikon.

I have a notion. The succubus gave it. Gale nodded.

The children arrived. Voila floated up, and Gale took her from the air. There was a subtle difference about her, a quality change. She was indeed a baby Glamor.

"Impressive," Symbol told the three. "But we worried. You must let us know before you go out next time, so we won't cry."

They tittered. "'Greement," Warp said.

Havoc appeared. "Found," he said.

"They made Voila a Glamor," Symbol told him.

"They wanted her to be like them," he said.

Gale's knees felt weak, though they could never really *be* weak. "Havoc, take them back. We'll follow."

He nodded. "Let's float," he said brightly to the children, and lifted into the air himself. He wasn't much help in taking care of them, except with Weft, who let him know what she wanted, but he was good when playing with them. He always picked up swiftly on Gale's wishes, too.

They did the same, smiling as they floated. Obviously all three of them knew how to do it, now.

"Question?" Symbol asked when they were alone.

"The ikon."

"It should join the others, safely hidden."

"Negation."

"Gale, those things have too much power to be left lying around! We've seen their effect on several people. You've got to put it away, for the sake of your baby."

"I want you to keep it."

Symbol stared at her, assimilating the meaning of that request. Then, slowly, she dissolved into tears. Gale embraced her, reassuring her that this was indeed what she wanted. Symbol would have not only the responsibility of protecting the vital magic connection of Gale's daughter, but the impressive benefits of ikon possession. She would become younger, stronger, tougher, prettier, and sexier. She would be able to hold her own with the other ikon bearers. Most importantly, perhaps, she would be able to hold her own with Havoc. She was no longer in any remote danger of being replaced.

Oh come on now. She was never in that danger.

But she thought she might be, Gale replied. *Ini is younger, smarter, and has an ikon. Now Symbol is sure she won't be.*

The succubus had something else on her mind. *Will you take me to Counter Charm?*

Certainly, if you want to come.

I am not sure I can travel between planets.

Gale smiled. *What a fate! To be stuck with us on an alien world.*

I have served as courier of information. If I can cross between worlds, I can still do that.

Gale considered. *We can take you there with me, then you can try to return to a familiar host on Charm, like Spanky. You won't get lost if you can't make it?*

No, I would simply return to you.

Then we can safely experiment.
Appreciation.

⁓

Havoc liked the change. "There's something about the ikons," he said as he lay with Symbol in the royal bed. Gale was tending the children; she had sent Symbol here.

"I feel it already," Symbol said. "I know the effect is slow, but my breasts feel firmer, my torso more limber."

"Agreement," he said, running his hands over those parts. Her form had always been excellent, but did seem improved.

"And if you want to do it fifty times, I believe I can keep the pace."

He laughed. "There is no mark to be made. Just whatever pleases us."

"It is enough just being here with you. I love you."

He knew it. "Let's just talk, and sleep."

"I love Gale too."

"And you love the children."

"Affirmation."

"You will need to make your own family before too long, but I don't think we can spare you."

"Who would I marry? I'll never love another man."

He shook his head. "Your self of two years ago would be appalled to see you now." He squeezed her, appreciating her nature. He remained amazed, when he thought about it, how Symbol had adapted. She had become so much more than a sexual partner.

She changed the subject. "Are you going to bed Aspect and Ennui?"

"I don't know," he said seriously. "They have changed remarkably, and they indicate they want it, but I don't think of them in that manner. Opinion?"

"Do it once with each, ceremonially. Then decide how you feel about it."

He nodded. "Solution." Then he kissed her, and proceeded to sex with her. She felt slightly firmer inside, too. Part of his mind found it odd that she carried the ikon of his daughter, and that it was making her sexier than ever. But he insisted to himself that this was no more surrogate sex with his daughter than it would be with his mother, with the two older women. The ikons were entities in themselves, owing nothing to human relationships. But he was glad Gale had given Symbol one. She had become part of their family, and this meant she would be ageless also.

Next day he consulted with Ini. "The Tapestry is complete. You confirm that it shows a section of Counter Charm?"

"Indubitably, and in fine detail."

"There must be something there we want. Is it marked on the

map?"

"Nothing we can see. It is just a current map."

"Then how can we find what we need?"

"I suspect that is what the alter ikon is for: to point the direction."

"You have reason for this suspicion?"

"Yes, Sire. When I go near the Tapestry, the altar ikon reacts. It points me at the Tapestry."

"But not at any specific part of it."

"Correct, Sire. I take that to mean that we must get the altar ikon to the actual scene depicted in the Tapestry. Then it will point the way."

That made sense. "Can you carry the Tapestry as well as the altar ikon?"

She shook her head. "I doubt it, Sire. I can try, but ikons seem naturally to repel each other."

That was surely the case. "I'll find another carrier."

"That may be best, Sire."

Havoc went to Chief. "Get together with Ennui. Organize the expedition to Counter Charm."

"For whom, Sire?"

"The Glamors. Symbol. Ini. Augur and Aura."

"Not the Ladies Ennui and Aspect?"

"I need them here to help you run the kingdom during our absence."

Chief smiled. "Relief."

Havoc nodded. "You and Throe suffered a year without them. No need for more."

"Question. Symbol and Ini I can see. Why Augur and Aura?"

"They represent two more Chroma, enabling them to function magically where Symbol and Ini can't. We don't know what we'll encounter, and that could be important. They really have no home zone, being inter-Chroma lovers who are tacitly banned from their home zones. They are changelings who have rendered me significant service. They are specialists in flora and fauna, which should help as we encounter new ones. They volunteered, and Gale and I like them."

"Augur is like a red version of you, and Aura a blue version of Gale, pre-Glamor."

Havoc fixed Chief with a royal glare. "Are you implying that we want to get them into our beds?"

"Yes, Sire. Who wouldn't?"

Havoc shrugged, smiling. "But the other reasons are valid, aren't they?"

"Agreement, Sire. Detail: the Ladies Ennui and Aspect have resumed their normal roles, displacing their substitutes Ini and Futility. Ini will travel with you, so that's no problem, but what of the dancer?"

Havoc hadn't thought of that. "Futility isn't easy to get along with."

"Not personally. But she does have talents."

She did: dancing, sex, and organization. Little else. "You are suggesting that for the sake of smooth relations here at the palace, we should take Futility to Counter Charm?"

"That would be a pat fix, Sire. She believes you desire her as an alternate mistress."

"Correctly. There's something about possessing a woman I know I would never want to marry or even keep as a formal mistress."

"I felt that way with Symbol, before she went to you. In addition, Futility has an ability you can use: she was once a clerk, and can take rapid and accurate notes."

"How do you know this?"

"It is my job to know such things."

Havoc nodded, thinking of something else: someone to carry the Tapestry. "Add her to the roster. I'll inform her." He had to do it himself, because the woman knew nothing about the Counter Charm project.

"Appreciation, Sire."

Havoc told Futility. "You have served well, this past year, but you are no longer needed here now that the Lady Aspect has returned."

Her face froze. "Limbo, Sire?"

"Negation. I am not punishing you. I want you with me on a special mission."

For an instant she showed honest emotion. "Gladly, Sire!"

"It requires far travel. There may be danger. There will certainly be inconvenience. You may be the object of more male attention than mine."

"Anything, Sire."

"We can arrange for the succubus to join you, if necessary, to facilitate such encounters. She'll be with us. Your choice."

"That would make it easier, Sire" she agreed. "But I am quite capable of faking it, as I do with you."

He nodded. She was not being humorous. She did fake it, and he had made it clear throughout that he wanted nothing but absolute candor from her about it. "Report to the Lady Ennui. Speak these words: 'I am to join the mission, by order of the king.' Then follow her directions."

She frowned. "I am to work for the Lady Ennui?"

"Negation. She will not be on this mission. She merely sets it up."

"Of course, Sire." Again, her relief was evident. She knew she could not compete with Ennui for his attention, though he had never had sex with Ennui.

Now it was in the hands of Chief and Ennui. Havoc went with Gale, Symbol, and four children to their mountain hideaway for a break. Of course he didn't get it; the children took up all their attention. If this was the way it was likely to be on Counter Charm, he might be glad to have Futility along.

Still, the children were fun. They were learning more abilities, day by day. Even little Voila was learning to hold her own: she would start fussing just before one of the others did something unkind to her, summoning Gale or Symbol to the rescue. It took the adults some time to catch on, for at first the fussing seemed to be without cause. But gradually it became apparent: she could see briefly into her own future. This was an ability unknown before on the planet; no divinatory magic could truly foretell the future, because such foretelling, unless too obscurely couched to be useful, invariably changed that future. Thus the ability nullified itself. But Voila used it to eliminate the bad things in her near future. Such as having a blanket conjured away, or a burr set under her little bottom.

They realized that she had had this ability since she turned Glamor. It was her sole expression of her new status. At first she fussed just an instant before something untoward happened, but her range was slowly extending, and the end was not evident. Would she grow up to see hours, days, or seasons into the future? The three older siblings were already becoming wary. They were mischievous children, and Glamors, but Voila could get them restricted before they managed to do their mischief. If she could do this as a baby, what would she be able to do as a child?

"I'm nervous too," Symbol confided during a two-minute tryst they were able to squeeze in while all children were temporarily distracted. Squeeze was definitely the proper term; she hiked up her skirt behind, used two fingers to draw aside her panties, and sat sideways on his lap as he bared his ready member. It wasn't elegant, but it was efficient.

"It's a necessary defense against three predatory Glamors," he said as his rod wedged into her cleft, seeking the well at its base. It had to be there, but the position seemed to set it at an awkward angle. Most of her weight was on her bottom, her buttocks flattened against his thighs, so there was little free play.

"But what about when she concludes that parental supervision is a threat? That a necessary nap is something to be avoided?" She squirmed, and then member and aperture aligned and he slid firmly into her.

"She will discover that a nap can be avoided only so long, and that parental authority is better than anarchy." The tight fit set him off, and he erupted into her.

"If she doesn't get herself into trouble we can't fix, because her foreseeing is too brief to understand the later consequences." Her channel clenched around him as her own climax came. Since she had the ikon, she was much faster in this respect. He liked it, but it could also be disconcerting, because now her pleasure was genuine instead of feigned for his benefit. He was as aware of her finale as she was of his.

"All parenting is a challenge," he said as he subsided comfortably, knowing that once was the most they had time for. "Ours more than most. We'll do the best we can."

"We certainly will," she agreed. She regarded herself as the third parent, and neither he nor Gale was inclined to disagree; Symbol's help was invaluable. She gave his member one final squeeze as it diminished, though the compressed closure also prevented its exit.

At that point a big questing, floating, blue eyeball found them. Its painted eyelids widened with discovery as it focused. Then all three older children appeared as the eyeball puffed into smoke, so it was hard to tell which one of them had made it. They plumped into Symbol's lap, which was covered by her skirt; this was one reason for such a position. There was no evidence of the nether connection they had; she merely seemed to be sitting on Havoc's lap. Her flesh would not have shown regardless, but his would have been visible through hers.

Symbol hugged the three together while sliding off his lap, keeping them facing inward and occupied as Havoc used a bit of magic control to get his exposed anatomy back in his pants and covered. The children already knew about sex; it was impossible to conceal something that significant from them. They thought it hilarious. That was one reason to mask any such performance. But they suspected that something was happening, and were already squirming out of her embrace.

Havoc, now separate, offered his own distraction. "Who can do this?" he asked. He curled into a ball, his wrists at his ankles, and floated just off the floor.

Immediately all three emulated him, curled and floating. The time was long since past when only Warp could levitate.

Havoc turned in place, doing a slow somersault. That was more of a challenge; Warp managed it, but Weft spun out of control, giggling, and Flame floated almost to the ceiling before correcting herself. They were learning a new trick.

Then Havoc righted himself and made looping progress forward, as if riding a difficult horse. They followed with further giggles. Havoc rotated to face backwards, continuing his motion toward the door.

He collided with something soft. All three children burst out laughing. So did Symbol. It was a bosom.

"Well, now," Gale said, reaching around him as if he needed support. "What a big baby." She kissed the top of his head. There were titters.

Havoc tilted forward in air, reached between his legs, under her skirt, and caught her with a four fingered goose from below.

"Yeeek!" she screeched, sailing up to the ceiling.

After that all six of them were strewn across the air and floor, laughing helplessly. Parenting did have its fun moments. The children enjoyed the naughty ones the most.

But the reprieve at the hideaway was temporary. Details required Havoc's return to the palace for a day and night at a time when neither Gale nor Symbol could make it. It would be a formal appearance, meaning that he would have to displace the mock king, Swale's brother Berm, for that time.

"Summon Bijou," he told Ennui. "Privately; I need her to emulate Gale again."

"She is not available. I sent her to another city on a routine mission, not knowing you would need her. She can't be extricated today without generating suspicion."

"But I need to be seen with the queen."

"You will have to use Spanky. She can certainly do the job."

Spanky was the bath girl who had assumed the role of mock queen. She was certainly competent. "But she's with Berm."

Ennui eyed him. "You have a point, Havoc?"

"Aren't they—?"

"In love? Indeed, and once their duty here is done, they will marry, with Swale's blessing."

"I don't want to use his woman."

She laughed. "By your assignment. The fact that they like each other has little relevance. She will serve your need. You're the king."

Havoc realized it was true. "I don't think of them as subjects. They're people."

"You think of everyone as a person. That's one of the lovable things about you. But if it makes you feel better, remember that you have promised her a fourth, for this service, when the time comes."

"Agreement. Still—"

"And like every maiden here—every woman here—she would like to be clasped by the real king, if only for a night. This does not impinge on her feeling for Berm. It's just the abiding dream of every bath girl. You would find her a most willing partner for the night."

"But Berm—"

"Will understand. He would like to clasp the real queen or mistress similarly. Just to know he had done it."

Havoc considered. "Would Gale—?"

"She can't spare a night, but she would spare a clasp. Take him to the hideaway as a spot visitor, and she'll fit it in."

It seemed like a fair exchange. Soon Havoc met with Berm and explained, and took the man to the hideaway, where Symbol promised him a guest lodging for the night. He seemed awed. He knew the children, because the mock king had to be familiar with all Havoc's public functions, so in a sense this was homework for the next appearance. But whether it was Gale or Symbol who took him on, or both, he would have an occasion to remember.

Spanky performed perfectly in the public appearance, only slightly shaken by the substitution of the real king for the mock one. Then it was night, and they were alone together.

"Sire, I am not clear what role you have in mind for me overnight. I will do my best, regardless."

She was offering to leave him alone, during the hours when others assumed they shared a bed. "You have served well, and I like you," he said with perfect honesty. "I will spare you if you have a reservation about sharing my bed. Otherwise I hope to enjoy you."

She seemed to glow. "Sire! I am yours."

And she was. Her name derived from her exceptionally well formed bottom, and it turned out that she could make it count sexually. It was a fine experience.

After the first session, she broached a corollary matter. "May I say the word, Sire, this one night, as myself?"

"Acquiescence."

"I love you, Havoc." She kissed him. "I love Berm, of course, but you are something else."

Havoc couldn't say the same to her, so he just kissed her and stroked her and held her hand as they settled down to sleep, and she was in rapture. In the night, when she woke and stirred, he brought her in to him again for another encounter, knowing that the idea of being desired by the king was the ultimate compliment. It helped that it was true; she was a fully worthy girl.

In the morning he wrapped up his business, then fetched back Berm, who looked dazed. Havoc did not need to read his mind to know that someone had given him a night never to forget.

It had been nice with Spanky. They would have to do it again sometime. Meanwhile, Havoc was quite satisfied to leave the mocks in place during his coming absence.

Soon enough they were ready to travel. For this they needed a private open space so that they could see Counter Charm plainly. Short hops were easy, but teleporting to another world was serious business. Chief had arranged coaches to the same glade the children had taken Voila to, scheduled separately so that there was no obvious indication of a rendezvous from the palace. Throe had set guards to keep stray intruders out of the area. Now they stood there: Havoc, Gale, Symbol, four children, Ini, Augur, Aura, and Futility. Waiting.

"There will be another coach?" Futility asked Ini. They had worked together for a year, and Ini got along with the woman better than others did. Futility had not been told where or how they were going, so there was no chance of her betraying the secret.

"Of a sort," the Air Chroma woman agreed.

"Certain private information is about to be revealed," Havoc told her. "I expect your discretion."

"Complete," the woman agreed, mystified.

"We shall be traveling with Glamors. You will know them by the colors."

"Glamors! Aren't they mere stories?"

"Many think so, and so did I, until I encountered them, and became one."

She laughed nervously. "Humor."

"I told you I was king."

She stared at him, unwilling to credit the implication. She had not believed he was king at first.

"Believe him," Symbol murmured.

"But a Glamor—I couldn't have had—" She glanced at Gale, and cut off, embarrassed. She knew that a king could take any mistress he wanted, at any time, but the presence of the king's wife made the matter awkward.

"Those who don't know, can," Gale said. "And those who do know—if the Glamor wishes it."

"Understood." But Futility plainly doubted.

"We are going to Counter Charm," Havoc said.

Futility looked desperately at swathed Ini, who nodded.

A figure appeared, shrouded in an encompassing black cloak. "Greeting," the Black Glamor said.

Then the others appeared: Red, Air, Blue, Green, Yellow, and Translucent. Followed by the animal Glamors: the White Goat, Brown Dragon, Gray Avian, Silver Spider, and Orange Sphinx. Futility looked as if about to faint.

"We have fourteen adult Glamors," Havoc said. "And four child Glamors who will have to be carried. Plus five normal humans who will also be carried. We will complete assignments before departing. The same assignments will hold for the return." He smiled. "We wouldn't want to forget anyone."

The assorted Glamors nodded.

Havoc lifted the little boy. "Here is my son Warp. Who will transport him to Counter Charm?"

The Blue Glamor stepped forward to take the boy. "I will. I have a way with young men."

Warp looked nervous, but the moment she touched him, he relaxed. She was the Glamor of Insects, and conjured a fascinating big bug for him.

Havoc lifted Weft. "Here is my daughter Weft. Who will take her?"

The Yellow Glamor came forward. "I am a girl; I can handle her." She took the child. Her clientele was the Demons, and a yellow wraith appeared to intrigue Weft.

"Here is my daughter Flame."

The Translucent Glamor, male, came to take her. A small fish appeared, swimming in air; his domain was fish. Flame was interested.

"I will take Voila," Gale said.

Futility stared. "You?"

"She's a Glamor too," Symbol said.

Havoc turned to the adults. "Here is Ini of Air."

The Black Glamor stepped forward. "I will take you," he said to her. "Your sister is my fiancée." Ini nodded.

"Here is Augur of the Red Chroma."

"Mine," the Red Glamor said.

"Here is Aura of the Blue Chroma."

"Mine," the Blue Glamor said. She was a remarkably pretty woman, resembling Aura.

"Here is Symbol, my mistress of the Air Chroma."

The Glamor of Air, visible only because he shimmered, stepped forward. "I will convey her."

"And Futility, nonChroma," Havoc concluded.

There was a pause. Then the Green Glamor took a stop forward—and changed his mind. The Silver Glamor, in the form of a giant spider, moved forward. Futility stiffened. But the spider moved back.

"I suppose I had better transport her," Havoc said. He stepped forward to join her.

"You were teasing me," she murmured, relaxing. "I do not tease well."

"True. But neither Green nor Silver would have betrayed you. You must accept all of them as superior beings, because they are what make this excursion possible. We do not know what we will encounter; any of them will protect you there."

"Understood."

Havoc looked around. "Make sure the count is complete before leaving the staging area. If any do not arrive—"

"I will check," the Green Glamor of Mollusks said.

"Then it is time." Havoc clasped Futility to him and jumped to Counter Charm. He felt her stiffen with nervousness, but it didn't matter.

They arrived safely at the Glamor's retreat on the other planet. Havoc released the woman. "Keep the count," he told her tersely. "This journey is not as easy as it looks."

She stared at Charm. It looked quite similar to Counter Charm from this distance. "We really are there? On the other planet?"

"Correct."

Gale arrived, holding Voila. "What, you didn't take advantage of the moment?" she asked him with mock surprise, glancing at Futility. The woman's neck reddened, whether from embarrassment or anger; indeed, she was not good at being teased.

Havoc scuffed the ground with his toe. "I forgot."

Futility looked elsewhere, her face set.

Then the others arrived, in rapid order. "All present," Futility said as the last appeared.

"Appreciation." He gazed at the others. "I think it best to establish ourselves at this base before tackling our mission. Have any of you explored the region between here and what is covered by the tapestry map?"

The Red Glamor turned Augur loose to join Aura. He was disheveled; she had evidently had some fun with him on the way. "Negation. We came here only to relax, and have not probed beyond a reasonable safety perimeter. This will be our opportunity to take it farther."

"There have not before been mortals or children here," Havoc said. "We need to be more careful on their account. I believe we should extend the safety perimeter."

"Agreement," Gale said.

"Those who transported children or mortals can continue to watch their welfare," Red said. "The others can extend the perimeter."

"Question," Ini said. "May the mortals explore too? In the company of their Glamors, for safety?"

"Agreement," Red said, beckoning Augur back. Now that it was possible for mortals to have knowing sex with Glamors, she had further business with the handsome man.

"Agreement," the Blue Glamor said. She was with Aura.

"Affirmation," the Black Glamor said.

"I need to stay with the children," Symbol said. The Air Glamor nodded; he was free to go alone, as were the Animal Glamors and Green.

"Preference?" Havoc asked Futility.

She had no hesitation. "To remain with you, Sire."

Havoc repressed a smile. It wasn't just association with the king she wanted, but to avoid associating with Gale and Symbol or being saddled with child care chores. Or teased.

"Let's divide the region into sectors," Havoc suggested. "Each of us can explore outward from where he stands around a circle here, so we don't overlap or miss a section."

They formed the rough circle: five human Glamors and five animal Glamors: white goat, brown dragon, silver spider, gray bird, and orange sphinx. Then they started disappearing, taking along whatever companions they had. Havoc was the last. He embraced Futility and jumped outward an hour's walk.

They landed in a green thicket of tentacular saplings. The tentacles writhed, orienting. Havoc was invulnerable, but Futility wasn't, so he jumped a short farther distance out. Now they were in a yellow field. It would do.

He turned her loose. "Stay close to me. I can protect you, but local creatures can do magic, and I don't have any more power than they do, in their Chroma. We want to spy any likely threat to the enclave. Since it is nonChroma, probably no Chroma plant or creature will bother it, but we need to be sure."

She looked at him. "You didn't bring me here for sex."

She was catching on. Well, it was time for truth. "The Ladies En- nui and Aspect preferred to have you absent from the palace during my absence."

"It was never for sex."

"Actually I did like it."

"Because it was a contrast to the loving sex you got from the La- dies Gale and Symbol. And Ini."

"And Bijou," he agreed. He did not like to admit it, even to him- self, but sex with Futility was as close as he could get to the feel of raping a woman without actually doing it. She did everything perfectly, but he knew she didn't like it. On occasion he asked her to express open revulsion, and she did so, without in any physical way resisting. Once he had asked her to resist, but not seriously. She did that too, stopping just short of what would have been effective. She never went for the stiletto in her hair. Her craftsmanship had to be admired. Thus he could have a type of sex with her he could never have with the women he liked. Only Swale understood about that sort of difference, and she kept the secret. She had assured him that such aberrant desires were not uncommon in men, though only brigands openly practiced them. Futility, too, kept the secret.

"You know I am calculating and emotionally uncommitted," she said.

"Agreement."

"Then why did you rescue me from Limbo?"

"The truth is unkind."

"I prefer to know it."

"We needed a competent substitute for the Lady Aspect who would never replace her or the Lady Ennui in my esteem."

"My respect for those ladies grows. Ennui recommended me?"

"Affirmation. She rescued you from Limbo."

"Creditable cynicism. I owe her."

"You do."

She pondered briefly. "I remain sexually available to you, of course, Sire, and to whomever else you require. But if your interest in this aspect of our relationship is no greater than mine, shall we dispense with it?"

This realism on her part was making her ironically appealing. "Perhaps."

She opened her blouse without removing her backpack, expos- ing her perfect breasts. "As you wish, Sire. I will emulate whatever emotions you prefer. Rape sequence? Screaming? Crying?" A tear welled from her eye; even that she could evoke on command.

That particular candor turned him off, as she had calculated. "Some other time."

She had a tacit victory, but pretended to be unaware. "What other way can I serve?"

"First by keeping the secret after this is done. We do not care to advertise our mission here to others."

"Naturally."

"Second by helping organize the mission we are on. What the Lady Ennui does for me on Charm."

"Deskwork without the desk."

"Agreement. It is a necessary chore."

"Better than the chore of sex."

"Third, by entertaining us with your art."

"Gladly! I will dance while the others relax."

"Do these things well, and on our return to Charm I will free you to live your own life in whatever manner you choose, anonymously, marriage and children optional."

She paused a moment, her expression indefinable. "May I kiss you, Sire?"

She was clearly pleased; he had reached her true desire. She was asking leave to step out of character and express honest emotion. "Permission."

She flung her arms around him and kissed him avidly. It was the most passion he had seen in her. It was genuine; he felt it in her mind. All her life she had acted to please others she despised, hating the necessity except for the joy of the dance itself. Now she would have the chance to truly please herself.

"Sire," she breathed. "Now, if you wish—it is the only time in my life I have desired it."

A rare event; never before had she honestly asked for sex. It did turn him on. He clasped her clothed, standing. She opened his clothing and hers and made the connection for them, lifting her legs athletically to wrap around him. It was a position known from ancient times as "The Tree," which was coincidentally fitting for the Glamor of Trees. She managed to kiss him constantly. Her dancer's body was capable of whatever contortions required to hold the position and maintain the connection. Her firm channel rhythmically massaged his member. He slowed his response just enough to be sure she had hers, then pumped into her with a strong climax. She was there with him, contracting in time with his thrusts, making the most of them. She certainly knew how to do it, and now was using all her expertise for the outright joy of it.

Then, panting, she had to break the kiss. "This one is real!" she gasped. "Thank you, Sire."

"Thank you," he echoed. They both knew that this was likely to be the only time they did it with true mutual passion. It was an experience to remember.

It seemed warranted, Swale thought.

Havoc realized that the succubus had been in Futility, probably facilitating her desire. That explained much. *Don't tell her.*

Agreement.

It ended. Futility lowered her feet and disengaged, maintaining balance throughout. A moment's cleaning up, then she returned to business. "If you will explain the nature of the mission, Sire, I will do my best to facilitate it."

"We seek something unknown, in a region displayed by a map on an animated magic tapestry. Ini carries an ikon that should point the way. You carry the map."

"Sire?"

"It is time to tell you. Check your pack; now you will find it."

She checked, and found what seemed like a folded handkerchief. "This is not mine."

"Open it."

The material unfolded several times, finally forming a large animated map. It was the tapestry, put in her pack and spelled to resist discovery. "It's beautiful!"

"It is a tapestry, woven on a magic loom. It is ikonic in nature. That is to say, magic, operating independently of its environment, just as Glamors do. It shows the area we shall be exploring. It can't be marked, but you will make notes of what we find. You will be working with Ini, whose ikon we hope will point the direction. If the route is devious, you will note it so we can retrace it. We do not know how difficult the traverse will be, or what barriers there may be, but you will have Glamor protection and support."

"You set this up before I knew of any of it."

"Agreement."

"You used me in more than one manner."

"Agreement."

"Obviously I am appropriate for this mission, being suitably cynical."

"Agreement."

"Appreciation."

"Welcome." They understood each other.

They explored the sector, discovering a number of interestingly different plants and animals and one odd green cloud floating very low. That seemed harmless, but might warrant further study.

In due course Havoc returned to the base with Futility. "We found nothing unduly threatening," he reported to Gale. Then he settled down to divert the children, giving Gale and Symbol a break.

"And he did take advantage of the moment," Futility said.

"There may be something else," Gale said.

"The Tapestry map."

Gale nodded. "What did he promise you?"

"The rest of my freedom."

"That is a promise only he can make. It will be kept."

"I am to work with Ini. I have worked with her before. I would not go so far as to say I like her, but I find her compatible."

"She has a similar promise from me."

"Your promises are persuasive."

Havoc conjured a pack of playing cards. "Who wants to play War?" he inquired. Warp was eager, Flame amenable. Weft just settled down beside him, snuggling.

The Black Glamor returned with Ini. She was almost glowing through her shrouding. "There is so much here! I must note it all."

"This is my job," Futility said, bringing out a pad and pen. "I will record what you tell me."

"Unfeasible. I have so much, no one could keep up."

"Try me."

"The Chroma zones are similar, but the plants and animals differ in slight or major degree. In addition there are forms unknown on Charm, such as Chroma clouds. I am not sure those last are inanimate; they seem to show volition." She paused. "How much of that did you record?"

Futility's pen had been moving throughout. Now she read it back, perfectly.

Ini was surprised. "How can you do that?"

"Shorthand. Before I danced, I clerked. It can be a useful skill."

"Agreement! How is it I worked with you a year and did not know of this?"

"It did not seem relevant to our relationship."

Havoc smiled to himself. Futility was indeed good at keeping secrets. But Chief must have taken the information from her mind, knowing what to look for. Or perhaps Ennui, an efficient clerk herself, had researched it from the files.

Ini resumed dictating. Havoc was glad to see it working out. Probably most of it was owed to Chief and Ennui's management; they had steered him right in detail as well as general direction. Still, this was only the beginning; none of them really knew what they were here for, or how to get it.

✑ ✐

Gale was too busy at first keeping the children under control to truly appreciate the magnitude of what they were attempting: a mysterious mission on the sister world of Counter Charm. But as the Glamors returned with their reports, there was a cumulative effect. This was truly a new world.

However, there were immediate practical matters. Symbol watched the children while Gale conjured the raw substance for their first big meal of the mission. She formed a mound of it in the center of the glade, then shaped it magically into familiar foods: potatoes, carrots, lettuce, eggs, milk, meat, wine. Conjuring was really summoning from elsewhere, in this case fresh moss, her constituency, pulped into an organic mass. It was not necessarily appealing in such form, which was why she was changing the form. The nourishment was the same, but what counted was the appearance and taste. She had been learning how to do this, for the time when she would need to: now.

She made a big metal pot and filled it with conjured water. The Yellow Glamor, who had carried Weft, made a magic fire under the pot. Gale could have done it, but courtesy required her to leave it to the Glamor of Fire. She piled vegetables into the pot so that they would cook, and started in on making bread by a similar process.

Actually little of this was truly necessary, because Glamors could feed themselves, and perhaps did not even need to eat. As king and queen, they had had to eat regularly and often publicly, concealing their Glamor natures, and hadn't had occasion to experiment with fasting. They didn't dare experiment on the children. But probably they could last a long time, perhaps indefinitely, without food. Still, it seemed best to maintain the forms, and foster a communal attitude. Certainly the mortals needed food.

As evening came, all the Glamors and their companions returned. The women came to help with the preparations for the meal, and the men set about making a shelter suitable for a group of this size and diversity. Soon they had what resembled a wayside inn, with several rooms and a central plaza. There was a big round table and chairs for all who wanted them. Regardless, there were places for all twenty three physical members of the party, human, animal, and child.

Dinner was served. Gale and Symbol tended to three of the children while Voila slept contentedly in a sling Gale wore. The Red and Blue Glamors assumed rather sexy serving girl outfits and brought plates to the others, leaning far forward when serving the men. The Yellow Glamor assumed the form of whatever animal Glamor she was serving, bringing appropriate dishes: a huge twitching fly for the silver spider, a bucket of grain for the white goat, a salad of berries and buzzing insects for the gray bird, a pile of scorched rabbits for the brown dragon, and what looked like writhing sand for the orange sphinx. All of them had flagons of multi-colored wine and free access to assorted forms of bread.

The Glamors ate and drank, and as the meal progressed became tipsily convivial, though of course wine had no such effect on them. Several showed off for the children, who were fascinated. The Black Glamor, always the most formal entity, opened his mouth impossibly wide and issued a resounding burp that floated up and away as a small black cloud. The white goat grew several extra horns, extended his tongue until it wrapped around the largest one, and pulled it off, to be drawn into the mouth and chewed up. A big translucent fish swam over the head of the Translucent Glamor, darted down to snap at Warp's nose, missed, and swelled so much in disgust it finally exploded and disappeared. The children were thrilled.

Then the center of the table was cleared, and Futility got up on it, garbed in a dress with a low décolletage and high cut skirt. Gale brought out her hammer dulcimer and played a merry melody. Havoc produced his dragon scale to accompany her. Futility danced, at first sedately, then with increasing abandon, kicking her legs high. Glamors they might be, long experienced in sexual relations, but every man watched with full attention.

"She goes for the night to the one she's closest to when the music stops," Havoc announced, waving his wine so that it almost slopped. Privately he signaled Gale when to stop, holding it for the right moment.

When the entertainment was beginning to pall, Havoc gave the signal, and both of them stopped the music. Futility flung herself right off the table at the closest human male, landing in the Translucent Glamor's lap. He stood, holding her, and carried her into his assigned chamber.

"Pawning her off on another Glamor?" Gale inquired as they cleaned up the remnants of the meal.

"With Translucent's agreement," he said. "He lacks a woman at present, and she's shapely."

"That means you'll be after Symbol and me again."

"Affirmation."

She sighed. "It's a cross we'll just have to bear."

"Well, there's Ini."

"She's nighting with the Air Glamor, being of his Chroma."

"Then Aura."

"She's with the Green Glamor."

"Not with Augur?"

"He's with the Red Glamor, of course."

"Maybe I can catch Symbol briefly."

"As you did last time? She's occupied."

"Oh? With whom?"

"With the children, while we relate." She took his hand, and guided him to a private spot she had located in the day while seeking a suitable site for human wastes. She had made a bower and lined it with fresh straw, shielded from general view.

"Oh, Gale," he said, dropping the banter as they made love. "I would give up the crown and Glamor status, just to spend forever with you."

"I know it. I feel the same."

"Maybe once all this is done."

"It will never all be done."

Now he sighed. "But it becomes bearable, with you."

She clasped him closely, sharing his emotion. "When we were children, we wondered whether we understood love. In retrospect, I think we did."

"Agreement. I never loved you more than then, and want never to love you less."

They lay for a while, clasped. "Have we climaxed yet?" she asked rhetorically.

"Do we have to?"

"It's customary, when we're as close as this." For he was throbbing inside her, and she was stroking him externally and internally. As Glamors they had control, and could climax many times in rapid succession, or go through the motions without climaxing at all. Normally they took turns: one would climax, while the other shared the sensation telepathically. That enabled them to get the most from it.

"But then we'll have to separate and resume normal life."

"We'll have to do so soon regardless. Voila is getting restive." She was in constant mental touch with their daughter.

"Then so it must be. Your turn."

She moved immediately into her climax, milking his hard member, kissing his mouth and face, caressing his flanks, her mind and passion completely open to him so that he could follow her appreciation of him. Her culmination was normally longer and less intense than his, more of a superlative loving than a release, and she knew he enjoyed it as much as his own. By similar token she enjoyed his urgent jetting; telepathy enabled her to truly appreciate the male response. But this time she slowly drew his essence from him, cherishing it, and then they sank into the declining rapture of the aftermath. It didn't matter, ultimately, how they did it, as long as they were together.

"Now we have the physical capacity to extend it indefinitely," he said. "But not the situation."

She knew it. Their dreams of endless rapture were futile, but she wouldn't have it otherwise.

Then Voila's summoning became more urgent, and they had to end it. But it had been wonderful taking this brief time together.

"Agreement," he said as they separated and prepared to return.

"Do try to give Symbol more time," she said. "She loves you."

"Sex I can share. You preempted my love."

"Apology," she said, kissing him with as much passion as others might have before the climax.

Then they returned to the camp and resumed family duties.

Next day Havoc and the male human Glamors took Ini and Futility to the region marked on the tapestry. They joked that it was to be one big sexual liaison, and perhaps there would be some of that, but their underlying purpose was serious. The truth was that Ini's passion was knowledge, and Futility's was dancing, but both could handle sex, and sex with a Glamor was something special. So they would not be loath, but there was plenty else to do.

Augur and Aura, watched by the Red and Blue Glamors, went out to explore the nearest Red and Blue Chroma zones, to ascertain whether they were the same as those on Charm. If they were, then the two of them would have their magic power back, in those zones.

Gale and Symbol explored the camp area in detail with the children, while the Yellow Glamor faded out of sight, watching. The children were Glamors, but this was an alien planet, and the young ones were likely to be the most vulnerable to mischief. In general, the guardian Glamors stayed invisible, so that possible predators would not know of their presence until committed. It was deemed best not only to avoid trouble, but to discover danger that might lurk for the unwary.

The animal Glamors continued the wider exploration of the planet. None of them knew exactly what they might find, so they were checking everything.

Gale paid special attention to the mosses and lichen, her constituency. They were of different varieties than those of Charm, but essentially similar; she related to them well. She was sure Havoc was relating similarly to the trees.

The children, too, were relating. Warp was fascinated by fungus, Weft was eager to wade in a stagnant pool surely thick with bacteria, and Flame was sniffing for viruses. Gale wasn't worried about any of them getting ill; they were proof against that, both because they were Glamors, and because of their specialties. So it didn't hurt to let them explore in the manner they preferred.

But Glamors or not, they were young children. At mid morning Gale called a temporary halt. "Time for snack and rest," she announced. "Get out of all that dirt, clean off, and gather around me."

"Awww," the three chorused. Voila was too young to make a similar protest, but she looked as if she wanted to.

They snacked on puddings and milk, then settled on the straw that Symbol gathered and spread. But they were rebellious; they didn't want to nap, though they needed it.

"I'll show an illusion," Symbol said.

That got their attention; they loved the illusion shows. In a moment it formed in the center of their circle, a three dimensional animation of a children's story.

The inevitable announcer came on. "This is the story of the little ifrit," he said. "An ifrit is one of the demonic beings, related to the afreets, the djinni, and the jann. They can dissolve into smoke, jump instantly to a far place, and reform as a solid human being, animal or object. Some become thunderstorms, others sexy maidens." As he spoke a storm appeared in the background, rumbling ominously, followed by a shapely young woman in harem clothing.

The children were now hidden, covered by the illusion, but Gale knew they were smiling. Even at a year and a half, they liked violence and sex, because these always led quickly to dramatic complications in stories.

The Little Ifrit, it turned out, was lonely. His name was Ifor, and he appeared as a towheaded little boy in shorts. The bigger ifrits refused to play with him, because he could not jump as far as they could, or form as big a man shape, and he didn't like doing evil mischief. They became animated scimitars and menaced passing mortal folk; Ifor was sorry for the threatened folk. They became giant squishy pies and hurled themselves into the faces of housewives carrying laundry; Ifor wanted to help the poor women clean it off. The larger female ifrits liked to assume the forms of lovely nude young human women and lead mortal men into attempted liaisons. Then they would dissipate in smoke, laughing. Ifor hated that kind of teasing. So he was walking by himself.

Then he heard something. It was someone crying, a mortal child by the sound of it. He fuzzed into a cloud and scudded rapidly toward the sound. Yes, it was a little human mortal girl, about six years old. She was sitting under a spreading umbrella tree and bawling.

Ifor floated near, checking the situation. The cause of the girl's misery was soon apparent: she held a decapitated doll. Some cruel boy, or maybe an ifrit, had torn the head off it. Obviously it was her only possession, and she was heartbroken.

Soon Ifor was crying too, which was a very un-ifrit thing to do. He couldn't help it; he felt the girl's sorrow. He wanted to help, but wasn't sure how. He looked for the missing head, but all he found was a thin trail of sawdust stuffing. The neck of the doll had leaked as she carried it. The head must have been destroyed.

Then Ifor had an idea. It wasn't a great idea, because he wasn't big enough for that, but it was credible considering his size. He formed himself into a doll just like the one the girl carried. But he didn't know what the head was supposed to look like. So after a moment's consideration, he copied the head of the girl herself, with her pert nose, blue eyes, and flouncing yellow curls. It was a cute head, and would do for the doll. Then he laid himself down before the girl and waited.

After a time she ran low on tears and looked about. She saw the doll. Her mouth dropped open. Then she dropped the corpse of the old doll and picked up the new one. "You are lovely!" she exclaimed. "I love you." Forthwith she took the new doll home with her, much cheered.

It turned out she was a fourth, with three big brothers. "What's this Blondie's got?" one demanded. He snatched the doll away from her. "She must have stolen it."

Blondie resumed crying. The boys smiled, satisfied. Now it was apparent what had happened to the old doll. The mean brothers had ruined it, just to make Blondie cry.

Ifor acted before he thought. Had he been bigger he might have had more restraint. He twisted in the boy's grasp, put his face to the boy's thumb, and bit.

"Ow!" the boy cried, dropping the doll.

Now the other boys were interested. "What kind of doll is that?" one asked.

"Who *cares?* Step on it."

A boy raised his foot to do that, but Ifor quickly scrambled out of the way.

"It's alive!" another brother exclaimed, amazed.

"A living doll!" The oldest brother turned on Blondie. "Where'd you get this, you little girl dog?"

Gale had to smile. They had rendered the term into a child-appropriate form.

"I just found her," Blondie said. "She was lying in the dirt in front of me."

"A likely story! Now tell the truth, or I'll twist your head off like I twisted the doll's."

There was confirmation. As the brute boy reached for the girl, Ifor knew he had to stop this immediately, whatever it took. So he marshaled his magic and swelled into a big crude shape.

"I am the ghost of the doll you killed!" he roared in the boy's face. "And if you ever make Blondie cry again, I'll twist *your* head off and dump it in the soup. Then I'll turn the rest of you into another doll for your brothers to rip apart. A *girl* doll!"

That did it. The boys fled, thoroughly cowed.

Ifor shrank back into doll form. "I'm sorry you had to see that," he said. "But those boys are just too mean."

Blondie picked him up. "That's okay. I love to see them scared. But I guess you're not really a doll."

"Agreement."

"So I can't keep you."

"Apology." He felt very bad about it.

"What are you, really?"

"I'm an ifrit."

"An ifrit! But they're big bad scary evil demons!"

"Most are," he agreed, ashamed. "I'm too little to qualify."

"I'm little too!" she said. "Maybe we can be friends."

He had never thought of that. "Let's try it and see what happens."

So they introduced each other. "I'm Blondie Baby Girl."

"I'm Ifor Ifrit."

"Could you really twist off Big Brother's head?"

"Negation," he confessed. "I'm not solid enough in the big scary form."

"But he doesn't know that." She tittered. "Let's not tell him."

So they were friends, and it worked. Blondie had a companion instead of a doll, and Ifor had a companion too. Every so often he made an appearance in the boys' bedroom to terrorize them again, so they would not get cocky. He discovered that he could indeed be a big bad scary evil demon when there was good reason for it.

The years passed, and both Ifor and Blondie grew older apace. In time he became a full-grown ifrit, and she became a beautiful woman, so of course they fell in love.

The announcer reappeared. "But that's another story. Tune in for that when you are grown." He faded out and the illusion ended.

"Yuck!" Warp cried. "With a *girl*?"

"What's wrong with a girl?" Weft demanded dangerously. She was verbally precocious, and could talk circles around her brother when she chose to, which was usually.

Symbol glanced at Gale. "Maybe it's time to resume exploration?"

Gale agreed. Usually the children fell asleep during the illusion shows, but this one had caught their attention, though surely for the wrong reasons. They weren't going to nap now. That was bound to result in early crankiness, but it couldn't be helped.

They got moving again. They were following a nonChroma corridor between a Brown Chroma zone and a Silver Chroma zone. On Charm, Brown was the magic of golems and silver the magic of electricity, but there was no certainty that the same held true here on Counter Charm. Theoretically any Chroma could enable any kind of magic, and the alignments might differ here. That was one reason to stay out of Chroma until they had a better notion of the potentials.

"Pause," Symbol murmured.

Gale and the children stopped. They looked where Symbol was looking. Something was moving on the Brown side. It looked like a low-lying cloud, one of the kind they had seen scattered around. This one came to the edge of the Chroma zone and shrank. It drew into itself, getting much smaller, and a brown blob formed. This was a new phenomenon, and it interested the children as much as it did the adults.

Soon the cloud had disappeared into the blob. Then the blob rolled into the nonChroma zone, right ahead of the human party. It went down a slight incline—then rolled up a slight incline to the other side. It reached the Silver Chroma side and entered it.

Gale exchanged a glance with Symbol. This was curious indeed.

But it wasn't over. The brown blob paused at the edge of the Silver zone. It fuzzed, and vapor rose from it. The vapor expanded while the blob shrank. It was turning back into a cloud!

They watched, fascinated, as a brown cloud the size it had started spread into the Silver zone. But it did not float away. It remained in place, slowly fading. The brown lightened, and then turned silver. The thing had changed Chroma affiliations!

"Ifrit!" Weft cried.

And that was as good a term as any. A smoky thing that could coalesce to a smaller solid when it needed to, and return to the diffuse form later.

The cloud, now fully silver, floated away, disappearing into the silver Chroma zone.

They went to the place the ifrit had passed. There was a worn path there. This was evidently a regular crossing site.

They continued exploring, but that single observation weighed on Gale's mind. Nothing like that existed on Charm. This would bear further investigation.

Swale rejoined her during another rest. "Oh, I forgot about our experiment," Gale said.

That's all right. I was with Futility and Havoc. They really got it on, upright in a field.

"I'll bet."

He pretends to desire her sexually, and she pretends to desire to be desired. So they have passionless sex, maintaining the forms. But this time it got away from them, and they indulged in phenomenal ardor. They like each other better than either admits.

"That happens. Are you ready to try for Charm?"

Affirmation. I'll orient on Spanky, as she's the one I have most been with. Parting.

Gale felt the succubus depart. But in a moment she returned. *Couldn't make it,* she reported with regret.

Gale had an idea. "Try for the Lady Aspect."

But I hardly ever go near her.

"She has my ikon. That gives us a closer connection. I can't reach her telepathically from here, but maybe you can follow the ikon channel to her."

On my way.

This time she did not return. Gale was getting concerned, but then Swale reappeared. *I made it! I explained to her, and she is willing to help. Once I was there, I had no difficulty reaching Spanky.*

"Satisfaction." They had established a viable contact with the home world that did not require a physical Glamor trip, which was a more complicated matter.

Now all she had to ponder was the matter of the ifrits.

The whats?

Gale explained what they had seen.

I wonder if they are related to spirits.

"I doubt it. These seem to be physical entities, normally diffuse enough to float."

She discussed it with Havoc that evening. The quest for whatever was on the map was not going well; they were encountering things that balked even Glamors. He seemed glad enough for this distraction. "We have seen more of those clouds, but thought they were confined to their Chroma. You actually saw one change Chroma?"

"An ifrit," she agreed. "Weft named it. Those things are more than clouds. That was what looked like a conscious decision. It couldn't float across the nonChroma zone, so it coalesced into a form that could cross, did so, then returned to normal—taking on the new color. This is something we need to know more about."

"Agreement."

"Do you need Augur and Aura for the main mission? It occurred to me that they might go into a Red or Blue Chroma zone and study those clouds."

"We can spare them. They are good people, but they can't move the way Glamors can, and Glamors have to be assigned to watch them in case of danger. If they got into their own Chroma zones, they could protect themselves. In fact, Ini and Futility could join them; they could protect those two as well as we could, in Chroma."

"Ini can protect herself, in an Air Chroma zone. But yes, let's do that, because this could be important."

"Agreement."

Then things got complicated with the children, and further dialogue was impossible.

Chapter 6—Ifrits

Augur kissed Aura good morning, and went out to help organize breakfast. The beauty of this Glamor bower struck him again: it was nonChroma, except for particular trees, which must have been planted and specially maintained. They were all the colors of the Chroma, each tree one color: Blue, Red, Silver, Black, and so on. Spot monochrome, surely tended in each case by the relevant Glamor. He had never imagined such an effect before coming here. They must have adapted miniChroma zones of the kind he had seen in the impact crater where they found the altar. The Ladies Ennui, Aspect, and Nonce had also done some farming in such zones, to make the tapestry. So obviously it was possible, but still a novelty.

Gale was already out, generating foodstuff to shape into assorted types. She reminded him strongly of Aura, and he realized that this was to be expected; both were changelings of similar age.

"Surely you should not have to be doing all this in addition to caring for your children, Lady," he said. "Aura and I can—"

"You can't conjure food in a nonChroma zone," she said. "Symbol is handling the children at the moment. And you deserve your rest."

That was another remarkable thing: the king's mistress spending more time with the king's wife and children than with the king. "But—"

"I'm a Glamor, remember. I don't tire physically. But I'm glad you're here. We have a special assignment for you and Aura."

"We are happy to do whatever we can."

"We want you to go into one of your Chroma zones and study the ifrits."

"Question?"

"The children named them. They are traveling clouds that can condense into balls to roll across nonChroma sections. Then they seem to return to cloud status, and assume the new Chroma zone's color."

"This is more than interesting."

"Agreement. Take Ini and Futility and make an extended observation. We want to know all about the ifrits."

"Lady, this could take some time."

She stepped close and kissed him, exactly as Aura was apt to do to stifle his protests about something. "Take the time. I suspect this could be important."

"As you wish, Lady." Already he liked the notion; this was a chance to be genuinely useful to the mission.

"How is Red?"

He hesitated. "In what sense?"

"In the sexual sense. I understand she was with you when you fetched the altar ikon, but then you caught on to her nature. That would have stifled things. But now that Havoc and Ini have figured out how Glamors can have sex with knowing mortals, Red can be with you again. How is she?"

"Candor?"

"Naturally."

"The sex is great, and I am learning things. But there's no human feeling; I might as well be with Futility. And of course I'd always rather be with Aura."

She nodded. "And I with Havoc. But with Glamors, sex is a prime pastime and variety is spice. The other Glamors have known each other in every sense for decades or centuries, so the new Glamors—Havoc and I—are in demand for novelty, and the mortals along on this mission also. We just have to put up with it until this mission is done."

"Understanding." He pondered a moment. "You and I met in sex, before we knew each other."

"Before I turned Glamor," she agreed.

"You reminded me of Aura."

"And you reminded me of Havoc."

"So it was good."

"Agreement."

"I liked the kiss."

She smiled. "We changelings are attracted to each other. It's the combination of the similarity of form and mind, and understanding of being the fourth, the odd one out."

He nodded. "It's what I found in Aura, though she was of a different Chroma."

"Chroma means less than it seems. As the ifrits may demonstrate. They may have mechanisms we can use."

"Agreement. Rapid exchange of Chromas is unknown on Charm." He hesitated. "Question."

"Ask."

"This diversion of resources to study the ifrits—won't it delay the primary mission?"

"Negation. That is already delayed."

"Surprise."

She made a gesture of "no concern." "Reason: we are well aware that this is an alien world to us, and there are surely dangers we don't anticipate. Perhaps not for Glamors, but for you mortals. We value you and don't want to risk you."

"Appreciation," Augur said, smiling.

"So we are exploring the boundaries of the region covered by the map, defining them and seeking news of anything hostile or dangerous. There are no humans here, but there could be something else. While we make this check, you are free for other pursuits."

That did clarify it. "Understanding."

Aura emerged. "How can I help?"

Gale considered. "I'm not sure dancing on the table is appropriate for breakfast."

"Then I'd better scrub pots."

"The Lady Gale wants us to go into a Chroma zone and study the ifrits."

"Question?"

Now the children burst forth from their chamber, followed by Symbol, who carried the baby. "Ifrits!" Weft cried. "Clouds who turn into balls and change colors."

"Appreciation for that clarification," Aura said.

"We saw," Warp said.

"It started Brown and went Silver," Flame explained.

"Rapidly," Weft said. "Within half an hour."

The children had better vocabularies than Augur had realized; they were precocious, perhaps unsurprisingly. "And we will be observing how they do it," he said. "We'll go with Ini and Futility."

The Red Glamor appeared. "And I will guard you."

Augur saw Aura considering: him with four women, one a Glamor, two with ikons. But she shrugged, accepting it. "That should be interesting." He wasn't sure exactly how she meant it.

Now others were appearing. They proceeded to breakfast, and discussed the mission.

"I wonder," Augur said. "Could we locate a region where Red and Blue Chroma overlap?"

"Delight!" Aura said. For this would mean that both of them would have magic, as well as a zone whose essential properties would be familiar to them. Delight indeed!

"There is such a region," Ini said. "At the edge of the Tapestry map. I remember it from my study of it before we came here."

Futility brought out the map, and they checked. She was correct. There seemed to be a small area of overlap. "There is our study site," Augur said.

Then little Weft asked a question. "Will the ifrit go there?"

And there was the problem. Why should an ifrit go there? It would be sheer chance to have one of the clouds pass through that limited spot, and since there was no nonChroma zone there, no condensation to solid form would be necessary.

"But there are other borders," Aura said. "We can use the Purple zone as a base, and work outward until we find an ifrit crossing path. Then we can wait for one to cross."

"Meanwhile there will be plenty else to study," Ini said, satisfied.

When the meal was done, they organized for the trip. The region was too far for them to walk in less than several days, so Glamors transported them. The Red and Blue Glamors took Augur and Aura, as before, while the Green and Translucent Glamors took Ini and Futility. Augur was aware that Futility had spent the night with Translucent, and he might seek further liaisons with her, just as Red would with Augur. Blue matched Aura's Chroma. Green seemed just to be helpful.

Each Glamor embraced his or her mortal companion. Then they jumped, as they called it, to the site. They landed in the middle of the Purple Chroma zone. It was larger than it had seemed on the map. It felt like home.

"Joy," Aura said.

"We will return in the evening," Red said to Augur. "But we are attuned; if you have trouble, scream mentally for help."

"In this zone, we should be able to take care of ourselves," Augur said. "That is part of its appeal. But we appreciate your alertness."

"Parting." Red disappeared. But in a moment he felt her near presence. She was embracing him and kissing him, invisible. "I am not through with you, Red man," she murmured. "Any more than Green is through with the Air girl." Then she was truly gone.

The Green Glamor had an interest in Ini? That would explain his helpfulness. Maybe he was simply ensuring that she would be amenable for sex. Ini with the ikon was a different creature from the socially shy girl whose family despaired of placing well, as Augur knew. But with or without the ikon she was a worthwhile person. He hoped the Glamor was making it plain that sex was all he wanted. It would be a shame to see Ini hurt.

"Clarification," Ini said for Futility's benefit, half startling him. He was glad for the moment that they weren't telepathic. "The two of you can do magic in this zone?"

"Accuracy," Aura said. "We have had experience, and are comfortable in Purple."

"And of course in your own colors. So Futility and I should not depart these colors without making sure you know it. So you can protect us."

"Agreement," Augur said. "Unless you find an Air Chroma zone to step into."

"That would be nice, but there is none here. So we will stay with the two of you, unless some other arrangement is expedient."

"That's fine."

"We should catalogue what we find here, so as not to waste time while waiting for the ifrits. With luck an ifrit will pass this region. Then we can focus on it."

"Affirmation."

They got to work. First they delimited the Purple Chroma zone. Its boundaries were fuzzy, fading into red on one side and blue on the other, with nonChroma corridors at either end as the two Chroma zones curved away from each other. This was exactly as it had been on Charm. The plants here were purple, and surely the animals too.

He checked the plants avidly. There were some he recognized, and more he didn't. The theory was that all the living inhabitants of both worlds had come from elsewhere in the universe, so it made sense that some would be the same. Presumably they were carried on planetoids and dust that flew through space and crashed on the planets. Possibly some had been seeded by colonizing ships from other worlds, as was the case with human beings and a few of the plants they brought with them. So some would land on one world, some on the other, and some on both.

He wasn't sure whether he was more interested in the ones that were the same, or the ones that were different. Both were important. So he asked. "Ini."

The Air Chroma woman was there immediately. "Here."

"Ultimately I want to catalogue all the plants here, and Aura will do the animals. But which should I tackle first: familiar or unfamiliar?"

"Familiar," she said. "Rationale: you can do them more efficiently, and establish classifications. Then you will have a notion what Charm flora are missing here, and what Counter Charm ones are new."

That did make sense. "You have thought about this."

"I live for knowledge," she said sincerely. "This is paradise."

"We'll start at one end, where the Red and Blue Chroma zones converge, and work our way across the center, noting the familiar plants. On the return trip we'll note the novelties. I'm assuming that the great majority of plants will have global distribution, and that the Purple Chroma ones will be a representative sample. This is not necessarily the case, but will do for this present purpose."

"Agreement."

He smiled. "I like working with you already."

"It's the ikon. It makes me sexy."

"That must be it."

"But let's omit the seduction for now."

It was not entirely banter; he did know her and like her, and she really was sexy now. She was also competent. "I believe you are familiar with the broad classifications."

"And the narrow ones," she agreed. "However, I am not a specialist."

"I am. Here is a slime brier, virtually identical to those of Charm."

"Agreement. Futility."

"Present."

Ini spoke the technical term for the slime brier, and Futility noted it rapidly on her pad.

They moved on, and it worked remarkably well. Augur could have made the notes himself, but that would have slowed him. He judged that Ini's cooperation doubled his speed, and Futility's doubled hers. He called out the familiar plants at a faster rate, and they kept pace.

He glanced across at Aura. She was stalking animal life. When she saw his glance, she gave him a hand signal, then disappeared. She could do magic now, as could he, and could spy on timid creatures far better if she became undetectable. He felt her mind trace; neither of them was telepathic, but they had the connection of love, and in-Chroma were aware of each other's nearness.

Augur strode forward—and the ground gave way beneath him. Startled, he reacted instinctively: he floated in place, refusing to fall. It was good to be back in Chroma!

"That's a feeder trap," Ini said. "Don't enter it."

"Agreement," he said, using telekinesis to move the loose material below him aside. This exposed a deep pit with a smooth rounded dirt bottom. He concentrated to penetrate illusion, and saw the reality: a nest of writing tentacles, some with stout pincer claws. Had he fallen to the bottom, those tentacles would have wrapped around his legs and the pincers would have started chopping him up. "Confirmation. This is a feeder. It will go on Aura's list."

He used his magic again, this time to restore the artful cover over the pit. But he made one change: he conjured a red stick to set on top of it, so that the site was plainly marked amidst the universal purple. That would prevent Ini or Futility from falling in. Not that they were likely to.

They worked their way across the zone. In the center, where the overlap of red and blue magic was thickest, was a clearing with bare ground. They approached it carefully, but there was no masked pit. It was just packed dirt.

"This would make a good campsite," Ini said. "We could conjure material for a tent and sleep in comfort."

The notion appealed. "And resume work that much sooner in the morning," Augur agreed.

"Without having to service Glamors all night," Futility said. "Or be alert for rambunctious children."

Aura appeared. "That would be nice."

"Actually, my ikon makes me lusty," Ini said. "I don't mind Glamor attention; it can really satisfy me."

"You could signal for the Green Glamor," Augur said.

She was suddenly embarrassed. "Oh, I wouldn't do that. He surely has other business."

"Take Augur," Aura said with a certain resignation.

"Apology. I don't wish to—"

"If we return to the main camp tonight, we'll all be taken by Glamors," Aura said. "If we stay here, two of us can rest, and the benefit of an early start remains."

The others nodded. "We can pretend I want a night with three women," Augur said.

"Pretense is fine," Futility said. She made no secret of her preference to be left alone, though Augur understood that she could perform phenomenally when she chose to.

"How is it going?" Augur asked Aura.

"Not many animals here," she said. "Tree squirrels. Moles. Distant birds."

"Counter Charm has phenomenal creatures," Ini said. "I saw them with my telescope." That was an optical device she had crafted that could greatly enhance vision; she had explained it during their sojourn for the altar ikon.

"I'm sure. Perhaps our presence here makes them stay clear. There will be more as we explore beyond the Purple Chroma."

"Few would make such a limited zone their permanent home," Augur said.

Aura kissed him and disappeared again, resuming her own survey.

They moved on. The cataloguing got faster as they encountered repeat species. Both women continued apt. They reached the far end in the early afternoon. "We should be able to reach the center glade again by dusk," Augur said. "Then we can make camp."

"Agreement," Ini said.

Now they catalogued the unfamiliar plants. Augur and Ini were similarly fascinated, but it was obviously just a job to Futility. Most varieties were variations of types on Charm; they had evidently evolved from similar stock, responding to a slightly different environment. So all were essentially familiar, just different in detail. The colonization by the plants had surely been by one event that caught both planets.

In late afternoon they reached the center glade. Augur and Aura had magic to sustain them, and Ini had the ikon, so they were not tired, but Futility was plainly worn. She did not complain, but it was best to make allowances. "Rest," he told her. "You have done well. We'll make the camp."

She flashed him a smile of appreciation. "I'll dance tonight."

Augur conjured Red Chroma plant fibers from the neighboring zone, and Aura used Blue Chroma magic to meld them into tough, waterproof fabric. Aura conjured dead blue wood saplings, and he used Red magic to shape them into suitable supports. They had done this sort of thing before, and liked the interaction of their magics. Then, as Ini tackled the making of the tent, he gathered purple stones for a fireplace and Aura summoned dry purple wood for the fire. Finally they conjured organic substance, shaped it into familiar foods as Gale had done in the nonChroma zone, and Ini cooked it.

The work was warm, and Aura doffed her clothing and worked naked. Ini stripped to white bra, panties, shoes, and a purple flower in her hair so as to be approximately visible. Augur was struck again by the contrast with her original body; the underwear shaped a strikingly sexy creature. Augur, also naked, had to exert some control to prevent a masculine reaction; there was something about the way panties and bra moved, with nothing else in sight, that was highly conducive. It would not be any chore to oblige her this night.

"Swale is here," Ini said. "I'll lend her my mouth."

"What are you folk up to?" a different voice asked from Ini's body. "This looks like a regular camp."

"Affirmation," Augur said. "Greeting, Swale."

"Acknowledged. Are you changing the subject?"

"We have concluded that we can work more efficiently if we remain here overnight. So we will not need transport back to the main base. That should relieve the Glamors."

"That should drive the Glamors wild," Swale said. "You four are prime mortal diversion."

"However, this is supposed to be a serious mission."

Swale looked around, the action indicated by the motion of the flower. Futility had now stripped and stood beside Aura, two beautiful women smiling expectantly, while Ini was an invisible wonder. "Serious, my burning vulva! You're planning on private group sex!"

"I did not say that," Augur said, doing his best to sound insincere. "We have excellent reason to remain here."

"Oh, yes. I'll tell them. But I'll be dropping by to get my piece of the action."

"Appreciation."

"Parting."

"Parting," they chorused.

"She's gone," Ini said. "That was fun."

"It was," Aura agreed.

They had supper at dusk, and Futility danced. It was amazing how much sexual passion she conveyed, considering that she had no interest in sexual performance. They had conjured and ignited torches for light, and the flickering shadows enhanced the effect.

"Observation," Augur said. "Were you attempting to seduce me by such a dance, you could readily succeed."

"The object is to entertain by the dance alone," she replied coldly.

"He knows," Aura said. "He was attempting to compliment your performance."

"In that case, appreciation."

A thick purple fog closed in around the camp as they retired. It muted the sounds of the night creatures, and had a pleasantly odd, musky smell. This was a nice place to stay, apart from its convenience.

The tent was no larger that it needed to be for the four of them to lie beside each other on a common pad: Ini, Augur, Aura, Futility. That way he could oblige the Air Chroma woman without separating from Aura, while Futility was shielded from any direct contact with him.

Ini was passionate. She straddled him, naked, lying on top, kissing him avidly. He was satisfied to be in darkness, not because of the concealment, but because it relieved the awkwardness of embracing a woman he couldn't see. "Just get the edge off, and I'll try to leave you alone thereafter," she whispered.

"I will try," he whispered back. "But I'm no Glamor."

"You will do."

They got the edge off, and she rolled back to her place on the mat. "Personal question," he murmured.

"I do care for the Green Glamor," she answered, knowing his concern. "As I do for Havoc. But I know that any relations I have with either are of a temporary nature, as is the case with you."

"I regard you as a friend. That need not be temporary."

"Appreciation. I need a friend."

"Friendship between Chroma is hard to maintain."

"Yet you and Aura show it is possible. Perhaps somewhere there is a man for me."

"Surely somewhere," he agreed.

"Meanwhile there is sex."

Half a loaf. "Parting," he said.

"Acknowledgment."

Augur took Aura's hand, and they slept.

He woke in darkness. Something was wrong. The fog seemed gone, but he was having trouble moving.

"Problem," Ini gasped beside him.

It was an effort to speak, but he made it. "You too?"

"Paralysis," she breathed. "Limbs don't work."

He struggled, and managed to move a hand enough to touch Aura. "Wake," he said, not sharply.

She woke. "Tired."

"Problem. Check Futility." He let his face go slack, having expended most of his energy.

She made her own effort, and touched the other woman. He heard a squeak of protest, then of alarm.

He summoned what remained of his strength and spoke loudly enough for them all to hear. "We. Are. Bound."

They lay there, assimilating that.

Then there was a sound. Something was approaching from outside. It sounded like a rat. Several rats.

"Trap," Aura gasped.

"Use," Futility said. "Magic."

Augur tried, but discovered that his power of magic was similarly depleted. Somehow it had drained away.

"Ikon," Ini said. "Helps." She made a heroic struggle and sat up. "Must. Get. Out." But then she fell back to the mat exhausted.

Meanwhile the sounds grew louder. Something—probably a horde—was coming in, and Augur doubted these were innocent rodents. They would be after paralyzed flesh.

"Swale," Ini said. The succubus had arrived. Then "Go. Tell. Glamors."

But after a moment the news was bad. "Sw—Swale. Trapped. Too."

Even the succubus! There was no doubt now that hostile magic was involved. They were caught in a different kind of feeder trap. Augur realized, far too belatedly, that there was a reason the central spot was bare. It was where a serious predator lurked.

But if magic deprived them of magical and physical mobility, what of the rats? Was this selective? Probably they had developed resistance to it, living in this area. But Augur and Aura had long experience with Purple Chroma, so might be able to resist it also. Or were the rats zeroed in, tolerated by the magic? Why, when they came to steal its prey?

Slowly he worked it out: something here, perhaps buried in the ground beneath this spot, wanted the magic and perhaps also the life force of other creatures. Their bodies didn't matter, just their lives and magic. So the rats did it the service of cleaning out the flesh, of killing them faster and taking away the refuse. It was at least partially symbiotic.

But it was purple. As it happened, he and Aura had long experience with the Purple Chroma. What the rats could do, they should be able to do also.

The flap of their tent moved. A six legged rat appeared, its whiskers wiggling. He could see it mainly with peripheral vision. It was the same general type as on Charm. Normally harmless to human beings, but not when they were helpless. One rat could inflict a painful bite. A swarm of them could kill.

Aura spoke. "Ill," she said. "Usion."

Illusion! That might help. Ini had an Air Chroma stone. Illusion was an Air specialty, and was just about the least challenging magic in terms of energy. In fact only telepathy was said to require less energy—but none of them were telepathic. A lot could be done with a little. Illusion was obviously known here on Counter Charm, but perhaps not as intricate as the Charm Air Chroma folk could make it.

"Ini," he said, fighting for strength. "Illusion."

"Um." Then a snake appeared, one of the category of worms and dragons, single legged. It was slithering through the air, its eyes glowing, its tongue forking. It looked absolutely real, except for its location. Were there similar snakes here? He didn't know. But perhaps it would manifest as a suitable predator to the rats.

The rat spied the serpent. It skittered back, alarmed. So it did recognize a rat predator. So the illusion was effective. As long as the rats didn't catch on.

Augur returned to his focus on the larger problem: how to get out of this trap. If rats were immune, could thinking like rats bring them immunity? Or if this were a special function of Purple Chroma magic, could he and Aura draw on their experience to nullify the paralysis?

They had better try both approaches. "Aura," he breathed. "Think. Like. Rat."

Meanwhile, he would think purple. What qualities did Purple Chroma have that they could draw on? The Red Chroma related to demons, to blood, healing, and ectoplasm. The Blue Chroma related to animals. They had found combinations of qualities in the Charm Purple Chroma zone: demonic animals, and creatures adept with ectoplasm. As a Red Chroma man he was adept with ectoplasm. It was sometimes used to form illusions, though it was relatively slow and clumsy; its advantage was that it had some substance. Used to buttress illusion, it could be effective. And it did not require much physical or magical energy.

He opened his mouth and concentrated. The ectoplasm stirred in his stomach, separating itself from its lining. It became a sinuous column and wended its way through his throat and out his open mouth. It formed a faint red cloud above his face. Then it stretched down toward the illusion snake on the floor.

The rat reappeared, perhaps suspecting the illusion. The snake made a feint at it, warning it back, but this time the rat held its ground. If it bluffed out the snake, there would be no stopping it or its more timid companions.

The ectoplasm curled down to touch the rat's tail. It coalesced around the tail, grabbing on by adherence. Then it twitched, tugging. Of course it could hardly move the tail, but the rat felt it. It scrambled back, thinking the snake had touched it.

But soon the rat came again. It was hungry, and here was live meat. Others crowded behind it. It would not be possible to hold them off much longer.

Then there was a new sound outside. The ground shuddered; larger creatures were striding toward the tent. The rats scattered. What was coming now? They were unlikely to have any chance against it.

The tent flap whipped open. Light shined in. "We're in time," a human voice said.

It was the Lady Gale. And the Red Glamor. And the other Glamors. They had come to the rescue.

But how had they known?

"Swale," Gale said, reading his question. "She was supposed to check on you, participate in only one episode, and return to me. When she didn't return I knew that either it was one remarkable party, or something was wrong. I tuned in on the ikon, and felt Ini's desperation. Then I knew."

Glamors could tune in on different ikons? He hadn't realized. But it was fortunate they had done so.

The Green Glamor bent down and lifted Ini. Augur saw the bra and panties Ini had put back on rise. Then the Red Glamor bent to take hold of Augur. She looked like a small, slight, weak woman, but her strength was phenomenal. She lifted him up effortlessly and carried him out of the tent and away from the deadly ground, following Gale. Behind them came the Blue Glamor, carrying Aura, and the Translucent Glamor, carrying Futility.

"You thought you would escape us," Red said to him, reprovingly. "We'll make you pay."

At this point he was glad to pay.

⁓⁓

Aura was never so relieved to see the Blue Glamor, and not just because she was of her own Chroma. She had almost given up hope of escape, despite making some progress thinking like a rat. That had returned some strength to her body, but not enough to enable her to fight back. She had never before felt so helpless, and she hated it.

Once the whole party was well clear of the glade, they jumped back to the base camp in nonChroma. There, while the four mortals slowly recovered, they talked, one on one.

"So it is some kind of demon," Blue said. She was no longer bothering with her mortal camouflage identity of Lucent the Amazon. "But not the kind we know on Charm."

"Agreement," Aura said. "This one seems to suck out the magic and life from its victims. Probably it starts with desire: we wanted to camp there. We thought it was our own idea. Now I think it wasn't; we merely found reason to do what we wanted to do, which was to submit to the life-eater. We were such fools."

"Not fools, merely ignorant of the ways of this world, as all of us are. We Glamors have visited here for years, but never bothered to learn much of anything about the larger planet. We just planted our trees and relaxed. That was, in retrospect, foolish."

"How were you able to rescue us without being caught yourselves?"

"Excellent question. I think we may have overwhelmed it with numbers and speed; it took time to subdue the four of you. But it may also be that it doesn't know how to handle Glamors. This world is as ignorant of us as we are of it. We may bring a concentration of magic it is not equipped to handle."

"Ini will surely develop a theory."

"Affirmation. Meanwhile the presence of mortals here is helping us to discover liabilities we hadn't noticed before. We shall try to be more careful. Now I think it is time for you to rest in comfort."

"For that I need Augur," she said wanly.

"You will be with him, alone, this night. Futility, too, will be let be. We are not entirely ignorant of your needs."

So it was. Augur joined her, and the Glamors let them be. She held his hand throughout the night, comforted by his presence. Ini remained with the Green Glamor, who seemed genuinely concerned for her.

Next day they returned to the Purple Chroma zone and completed the survey of plants. Then they ranged outward and tackled the animals, her specialty. But this time they had the more active support of the Glamors, both for safety and effectiveness. The Glamors fashioned a magic bubble that floated invisibly across the landscape, regardless of Chroma, masking them from the awareness of the wildlife below. This turned out to be a much better way to spot and study animals.

At first Aura was distracted by the wonder of it. She had known magic like this in her home Chroma zone, but had never seen much purpose in it, other than to transport travelers across the zone. But this was beyond Chroma, indifferent to the changes in colors, and it worked just as well when they crossed nonChroma zones. The ability of the Glamors to use magic anywhere was now revealed as far more than mere duplication of Chroma ways.

Then she settled down to business. The animals had been rare in the Purple Chroma zone, and now they understood why: those that hadn't been killed were wary of the life eater. They were common in the other zones. At first she spied the birds, because they were readily visible in the air. No—not birds, but giant flying insects. Insects were not her specialty, but she quickly saw that these were different: they had six legs, not five. There were none like that on Charm. So they had come from a different colonization.

Then she spied true birds, but again they were different: one wing whirling overhead, rather than three. Another separate colonization. So would the legs classification of Charm hold here? Every essential type of living thing belonged to one of the major groups, identified by their number of legs. None for the Demons, one for the Worms, two for the Fish, three for the Birds, and so on. Humans were four legs, using two to walk on, two as appendages. There were no humans native to this world; did some other creature have four legs? She was eager to find out.

"There!" Ini said, pointing.

Aura looked. It was a large creature with five legs moving rapidly along below. But there was something odd about its progress. She couldn't see the legs moving.

"I saw one of those with my telescope," Ini said. "They have wheels."

"Wheels!" Aura had never imagined that. This was certainly no insect!

The bubble moved close, and the wheels became apparent. This was a Yellow Chroma animal, moving along an almost level channel through the forest, surely a path made by its own kind. With such a clear path, wheels were clearly superior for motion; the animal was moving faster and with less apparent energy expenditure than any footed creature could. But what would it do when it needed to go off the path? Suppose an obstruction fell across the path?

Then the creature came to just such a case. Its path crossed another path, but the two were not joined smoothly. The second passed over the first, so that there was no intersection. But the creature slowed, orienting on the other path. Then it lifted two front legs, balancing neatly on the remaining three, and set their wheels on the new path. It now straddled both paths. A third leg lifted, joining the two on the other path. Then the last two legs lifted, coming to join the front three. The animal rolled away on the new path.

"I call it a wheeler," Ini said.

"Agreement," Aura said faintly, and Futility made a note. This was so far different from anything on Charm that it was difficult to assimilate.

"Interesting," Augur said.

"I suspect I could spend a month just studying this one creature," Aura said.

"And there's another I saw," Ini said, pointing again. "I call it an animate sponge."

They moved across to it. It did indeed resemble a huge moving sponge, with no visible feet. Its substance showed no eyes, ears, antenna, or other perceptory organs; it was just a blob. "A sponge," Aura agreed, and Futility made another note.

They moved on to another Chroma zone. There they spied a normal animal: a six legged bear-dog. It wasn't identical to either, but obviously derived from similar stock. It had to be the result of the same colonization that Charm received.

"Problem," Ini said.

Aura nodded. "Six legged insects. Six legged vertebrates. We have a duplication of classes."

"So it does not follow the Charm pattern," Ini said.

"Which could be sheer coincidence," Augur said. "We classify by legs because there is only one major group for each number of legs. But elsewhere in the universe that may not matter at all. Counter Charm could have a number of duplications."

"Agreement," Aura said weakly. "We may have to rethink basic classifications."

They continued, discovering many half-familiar and many quite different types of creature. Then they spied an ifrit from above. It was vague against the similar color of the Chroma, but could be made out as it obscured trees and ridges. It was orange, moving slowly toward a Blue Chroma zone.

"If it crosses—" Aura said.

"It will be in your Chroma," Ini said.

"I want to meet it."

"Caution."

"Agreement. We must notify the Glamors."

"We should be able to contact them mentally. We aren't telepathic, but if we open our minds, they can attune."

The Blue Glamor appeared. "Needless. We are attuned. Proceed with your encounter."

"Appreciation," Aura said.

The bubble floated down into the Blue Chroma zone. "But remain within," Blue said. "We are averse to ugly surprises."

"Such as life eaters!" Aura agreed, laughing. "So are we. We have no idea of the real nature of the ifrits, but I doubt that they seek to befriend human children." The story of the naming of the ifrits had of course circulated through the mission.

"Concurrence." The Blue Glamor departed.

They waited in the bubble, hovering opposite the path across the nonChroma band between the Orange and Blue Chroma zones. Slowly the ifrit approached the path. "Boredom," Futility said.

Aura laughed. "Ask Augur to service you."

Even the cold woman had to smile. "I will sleep instead." She curled up in her place in the bubble.

"However," Ini said.

There was the urgency of the ikon again. "Take him," Aura said. The woman had nighted again with the Green Glamor, and surely been done as many times as she desired, but it seemed the ikon urge soon built up when any time passed without sex. Ini would definitely need a man of her own soon, as long as she had the ikon.

So while Futility slept and Aura watched the slow progress of the orange cloud, the red man and the invisible woman came together. There was no hurry; they were mainly passing time. Aura glanced every so often, intrigued by the way Augur seemed to be playing alone. He kissed an invisible face, stroked invisible breasts, and finally entered an invisible groin. Of course Augur and Ini had done it before, many times, but not in Aura's presence in daylight. Well, they had when the succubus Swale had governed her, making a demonstration, but that was a year ago. She found it a turn-on, and when she saw him jet into seeming air she suffered a surge of desire herself. But it would be unmannerly to show it, so she focused mainly on the ifrit.

Did ifrits reproduce? Did they have males and females? Did they mate? Did they have sex? How? Probably they were asexual beings, but at the moment Aura preferred to ponder the sexual alternative.

How could two clouds have sex? Did one form a gaseous member, the other a nebulous cleft, and did they put the one in the other? More likely they simply exchanged puffs of vapor, in slow motion.

Unless they did it in the solid form, meeting in a nonChroma zone for the purpose. Could two balls mate? That did not seem feasible. Suppose they assumed solid form without leaving their Chroma? Then they would have magic to facilitate the process.

Augur and Ini were done for the moment; they dressed again and resumed watching the approaching ifrit. Aura considered sharing her thoughts with them, but decided to let that wait, lest it betray her jealousy of their recent pleasure. Had a male Glamor happened by, she would have been glad to clasp him. It would have been a nice contrast if the Green Glamor had come for Ini, found her occupied with Augur, and been clasped by Aura instead. She found herself pondering the fifty times he had done it with Symbol; what must that have been like? Fifty climaxes in an hour? It was hard to imagine, but Aura was making the effort.

The cloud reached the fringe of Orange Chroma and squeezed down into a ball. The ball rolled across the nonChroma zone, following the path. It was apparent that it rolled uphill toward the Blue Chroma zone.

"How?" Futility asked, amazed.

"Partly inertia," Ini explained. "A ball will roll almost as far up a slope as it has rolled down. Partly internal balance: it evidently shifts its weight to the front to facilitate motion in that direction. Partly it must be magic, as it intercepts the fringe of the opposite Chroma zone. A fairly sophisticated adaptation."

"The demons of Charm are not intelligent of themselves," Augur said. "Neither do they assume solid form. If this is demonic, it's a different type."

"Just as the animals are different," Aura agreed. "Maybe a different colonization."

"Fascination," Ini said. "Fundamentally distinct varieties of demons."

"Which means we can afford to assume very little," Augur said. "The ifrits may be dangerous, harmless, or indifferent."

"How does it feed?" Aura asked rhetorically. "Does it hunt, kill, absorb?"

"Assuming it needs to feed," Ini said. "If it is a creature of the air, it may simply gather floating dust."

Now the ifrit was in the Blue Chroma zone, expanding back into cloud form. It remained orange, but the outer edge was turning blue. It was changing Chroma.

"Amazement," Ini breathed. "It truly is converting. Slow for animal motion, but rapid for Chroma assimilation. It takes years to accomplish such a change on Charm."

"And never occurs, if a person uses a Chroma gem stone to retain Chroma identity," Augur said, glancing at Ini's filled clothing. "Curiosity: if you took no precautions in a Blue Chroma zone, how long would it be before you became fully visible?"

"The same time it would take you to become invisible, unprotected in an Air Chroma zone," Ini said. "Perhaps a decade for the process to be complete, because the bones are slow. The intermediate stages would be visually messy."

"You would look like a skeleton!" he said, smiling.

"Negation. My skin, lungs, and digestive tract would become visible blue first, as they have the most contact with the other Chroma. That is to say, with the air and water and food of that Chroma. So you would see me seemingly full formed, but the internal process would not be complete for some further time. You would be able to look into my ear and see my head seemingly empty." She was surely smiling.

"Acknowledgment," he agreed.

"You, in contrast, would indeed become skeletal," Ini continued. "Your skin and lungs would become invisible first, but only the skin would show it. Underneath, your muscles and bones would remain red for some time."

"Interest," Aura said, still watching the ifrit. "A skinless red man."

"Conclusion," he said. "I will not reside long in the Air Chroma. I would prefer to remain red, or change slowly to blue."

The ifrit was now almost the size of cloud it had been before, and well on the way to being blue. Only a small portion remained solid; the rest funneled broadly upward.

"I want to go out to meet it," Aura said.

"Negation," Ini said. "We agreed to remain protected."

"Then let's summon the Blue Glamor back. I can't study this entity well from afar."

The Blue Glamor appeared, accompanied by the Red Glamor. "We are curious too," Blue said. "We will guard you outside." They disappeared.

"Joy!" Aura jumped through the wall of the bubble, which became porous to her passage. Augur followed. Ini stripped off her clothing, becoming invisible again, and joined them. Only Futility, more vulnerable, remained behind.

They strode toward the cloud as the last of it turned vapor. Aura lifted her arms and waved her hands. "Hey, Ifrit!" she called. "We want to talk with you." She felt giddy with the audacity of this approach. But how else could they ascertain whether the thing was aware? She had to do something out of the ordinary, that would attract the attention of a sentient entity. If that was what this was.

For a moment nothing happened. Then the cloud changed. It had been floating at about small treetop height; now it slowly descended to the ground, angling toward them. It was responding!

"Hello!" Aura cried. "Introduction: I am Aura, a human being of the Blue Chroma. This is Augur, a human being of a Red Chroma." Was she making any sense at all to this thing? Even if it could see and hear her, how would it know her language? More likely she was coming across as a tasty morsel to consume, if it ate morsels.

The cloud gathered on the ground before them. It extended a smoky tendril of vapor toward her.

Aura nerved herself and stood her ground. She didn't think vapor could hurt her; even if it was poisonous, she could use her blue magic to withstand it. Certainly it couldn't harm her mechanically. "I am Aura," she repeated. "I am from Charm—the other planet."

The tendril touched her face. There was a tingle of magic. It spread out to encompass her head, slightly cool. She stood firm, with measured breathing. There was a musky odor that was somehow familiar. Then she placed it: the fog that had been in the Purple Chroma zone at night—it must have been an ifrit! But not an enemy, for it had been gone by the time they got caught by the life-sucking demon. It must have been passing through, on its way to wherever ifrits went. It hadn't recognized them as significant, any more than they had recognized it.

The mist spread downward around her body, permeating her clothing, coming up against her skin. It touched every part of her, like water in a bath, but much lighter. It was shaping her outline in complete detail.

Some of the vapor entered her mouth and nose. She controlled her aversive reaction and breathed it in. She wanted to know the nature of this entity; it was fair to let it knew her nature too. She was not suffocating; the air remained breathable.

The vapor thickened about her head. It covered her ears and eyes. She kept her eyes open, staring straight ahead. She was looking through thick blue fog—and did she see a vague core of orange? The ifrit had made the same change a human being would have made, from the outside inward; its core would be the last to conform.

The tingle of magic intensified. The thing was trying to get inside her head, literally. *I am Aura—human being,* she thought as clearly and forcefully as she could. *From the other world.*

For what seemed like a long time, the mist enclosed her head. The magic played around and through her, not hostile, not friendly just—curious.

She had little doubt now that the ifrit was sentient. It was aware of its surroundings, and of her as a special creature. There was no thought message, no meaning in the magic; it was just exploring. Possibly it took her for an interesting artifact, something to be catalogued and identified for future reference. Perhaps there were things on Counter Charm that attacked ifrits, so they needed to know about what they encountered. Needed to classify friends and enemies and neutrals. Which category was she being placed in?

Aura, she thought carefully. *Friend.*

At last the vapor around her thinned. It separated from her body and head; it withdrew from her lungs. The tendril retracted into the cloud. She had not been harmed.

Then the cloud lifted. The action was slow, as vapor in an open space normally was, but she was acclimatized, and saw it as a conscious, determined action. Soon (it seemed) the ifrit floated away.

She looked around. Augur still stood beside her. "Did it enter you too?" she asked him.

"Affirmation."

"Did you recognize the smell?"

"The fog last night!" he exclaimed. "An ifrit!"

"Surmise: it was just passing by, and had no connection to the evil demon."

"Likelihood," he agreed.

The Blue and Red Glamors appeared. "Impressive," Blue said. "You two have nerve."

"Augur has nerve," Aura said. "I'm in my home Chroma; I can protect myself if I have to. He can't."

"When I saw you do it, I realized the ifrit was exploring, not attacking," Augur said. "So I added to its information."

"Swale wants to know whether there was sexual contact," Ini said. She remained invisible; Aura had forgotten her presence for the moment. "She did not dare go through its vapor, after the way she was trapped last night."

"No sex," Aura said. "I felt the vapor touching my most private parts, but was aware of no sexual aspect."

"Similarity," Augur said. "It was concerned with shape rather than function."

"Sapient?" Red asked.

"I was not aware of intelligence, just sentience," Aura said. She was speaking surprisingly objectively, considering the confused exhilaration she felt. Contact with an alien thing! "It was—curious. I think it saw us as odd animals, so it checked to see whether we were friendly, hostile, or neutral. I tried to think 'FRIEND' but have no certainty that it either received or understood. Now it surely knows we are animals and not threatening it, so it has moved on."

"Classification?" Blue asked.

"Not animal or vegetable, I think," Aura said. "But aware, so it must be alive. I'd say demon. Augur would know better than I about that."

"Definitely demon," Augur agreed. "Not the hungry type we encountered in the Purple Chroma zone. An ifrit seems to have passed through when we were there, but moved on. I take this as confirmation that there are fundamentally different classes of demons here, probably separate colonizations. The ifrit was not attempting to suck out our life force. It was merely checking. My estimate is that it is harmless."

"Incautious assumption," Red said. Aura noticed with a certain bemusement that there was now no trace of seduction toward Augur. They were seeing her in business mode. "We must discuss this with the Glamors."

"Agreement," Blue said. Both vanished.

Aura went with Augur and Ini back to the bubble. They caught Futility up on what had happened, and she made rapid notes as they floated back to the main base.

The Glamors were ready for them. "Request," Havoc said. "Open your minds so we can read the direct experience."

They did so. There was no sensation, but Aura knew the Glamors were getting the full story of the ifrit contact.

"Confirmation," Gale said. "Sentience, not sapience. Demons of animal level. Probably innocuous."

Now the Yellow Glamor spoke. "Demons are my constituency," she said. "Therefore this is my domain. Today I was investigating the demon in the Purple Chroma zone, and impressing on it the need to ignore human beings as potential prey. I believe it understands." She smiled. She was a pretty woman, as all human female Glamors were, but for a moment her even yellow teeth showed glintingly pointed. "Thus I was not on hand for the ifrit contact. I agree that it answers the description of a new species of demon, but this must be verified directly. I will be with you for the next contact."

"Desire," Ini said.

"You and Futility too," Yellow agreed. "To observe and make notes." She glanced briefly at the children. "Others should remain clear, until we have better information."

That was it. The other Glamors yielded to the specialist. On Charm Red was the Chroma specializing in Demons, but Chroma was coincidental with Glamors. The Yellow Glamor lived and breathed demons, drawing her power from them and representing them; she understood them better than any other person of human form. Gale, Symbol, and the children had discovered the ifrits and named them, but they would not be part of this investigation.

They moved on into the activities of the evening, including supper and Futility's dance. Aura had to admit that the woman was good at it; she had an excellent body, and made the most of it. At the end she retired again with the Translucent Glamor, who seemed taken with her. Aura had the impression that the woman's indifference to sex was secondary to her satisfaction at being desired by a Glamor.

Aura was allowed to sleep with Augur again. "I'm still charged up from that experience," she told him. "Maybe they are mere animals in effect, but so different from any I have encountered before that I am fascinated. I hope there can be other contacts."

"There surely will be. At least until the Yellow Glamor is satisfied."

She embraced him, more than ready for sex, but fell asleep before it got anywhere, as far as she knew. That annoyed her; she had been more tired than she realized, but she had promised herself sex with him, then thrown away the chance.

⁂

"Wake." It was the Yellow Glamor standing beside them.

"Question?" Aura asked, surprised. It was barely dawn.

"Two ifrits approach this camp."

Suddenly Aura was totally alert. She and Augur scrambled up, not bothering to dress, and followed the Glamor outside. There was nothing in sight.

"They are near the edge of the nearest Red Chroma zone," Yellow said. "It is beyond coincidence that they approach this base at this time, and that two are together. I believe it best that we meet them."

"Agreement!" Aura and Augur said almost together.

The base was in a nonChroma zone, apart from its special Chroma trees, of fair extent. Several Chroma zones bordered it, irregularly, Red among them. They made their way toward the Red one.

There was an ifrit cloud, condensing to globular form. "The second is beyond, awaiting its turn," Yellow said. "There is no established path here, so this can't be a routine crossing."

"Agreement," Aura breathed. "They must be coming to see us."

"This time in solid form," Augur said.

"We do not know whether either is the same as the one you contacted yesterday," Yellow said. "Considering their slowness of motion, it seems unlikely. This suggests that there is communication between them, and that these are the closest ones to this enclave. There has never before been such an intrusion, that we know of."

"How should we proceed?" Aura asked. Her heart was thudding. The thought that they might be about to make more meaningful contact with the ifrits was exhilarating.

"The two of you should approach them; you are the ones they know, if that is relevant. I will observe, unobserved. Try to ascertain the nature of their interest."

"Agreement." Aura walked toward the coalescing ifrit. Augur followed, deliberately a bit behind, giving her the first chance to make contact.

The red blob was within the Red Chroma zone; evidently Chroma magic was required to make the transition from cloud to solid. Aura stepped into the zone, meeting it there.

Some cloud remained, in a streamer attaching to the ball. It shifted toward her, evidently aware of her. Part of it extended toward her. She extended a hand toward it. Hand touched vapor tendril.

"Aura. Human. Friend," she said, focusing her thoughts. Would that help?

Then the tendril withdrew. It joined the solid body.

Aura waited. What came next?

The solid glob quivered. It was a sphere, but now it became ir-regular. Bulges appeared. These extended into five projections, two below, two to the sides, and one at the top. The two below thickened into stout columns, while the two to the sides lengthened and bent in the middles. The top one became a smaller sphere. All of their sub-stance was at the expense of the main mass, which diminished some-what. What was the ifrit doing? This was no shape for rolling; it was awkward and ungainly.

The columns below broadened at their bases, projecting slightly forward. The side extensions formed small nests of tentacles at their ends. The top ball sprouted fibers above, that lengthened until they bent of their own weight and flopped crazily to the sides. Two blisters appeared, one on either side. The front formed two slight indents, a single projecting ridge below them, and a sideways crack below that. The thing looked like a comical cartoon face.

Aura felt her jaw dropping. "The ifrit is trying to emulate a human being!" she exclaimed.

"It is trying to make contact by adopting our form," Augur agreed. "So we can relate to it."

That suggested more than animal curiosity. "It must be sapient after all," she said. "Or approaching sapience."

"Then let us help it relate," Augur said, as the second ifrit began its slow condensation. "This could be much more of a breakthrough than we anticipated."

"Agreement," she said, awed.

⁂

Augur was excited. Aura's initiative had brought them to the verge of something unprecedented: possible contact with an alien sapience. The ifrits were meeting them more than halfway, which suggested that they had not only understood Aura's effort, but had recognized the two of them as creatures worth understanding better. Oh, it could be that the ifrits were curious, so were mimicking the unknown species, thinking them potential playmates; since ifrits could change shape, that might be a standard device. But it also could be that they had recognized sapience, and wanted an exchange of minds.

The ifrit before Aura was shaping itself into a crude human being. How far could that go? Would it be able to walk and talk? Would its eyes see, its ears hear, its fingers feel? If not, the ifrit would have trouble truly relating. Yet the ifrits must have done this before with animals, so had a notion of animal senses and abilities.

He heard something, and looked around. Ini, this time swathed, and Futility were coming to join them. That made sense, if the ifrits tolerated the extra company.

The ifrit before him was reducing to the solid stage. It had had to wait until Aura's ifrit was done, because the clouds took up too much room to come together in such a restricted area. Aura's ifrit was becoming female, with long hair and breasts. Would his ifrit become male? That seemed likely. They were copying what they saw. Did they have any idea of the significance of the genders? Maybe, because at least some of the animals they had seen here had two sexes. Did the ifrits have male and female forms? That depended on how they reproduced. If they reproduced.

Aura's ifrit opened her mouth. She sucked in air, then blew it out again. "Oooo!"

Aura smiled. "Greeting."

The ifrit tried again. "Hzree-sting."

"Aura. Human."

"Aaaw-rah. Hoo-min."

Was this intellect, or mere mimicry? It might take some time to find out. Ini was murmuring to Futility, who was noting it down.

Augur's ifrit did gradually shape into a man. At least it lacked breasts and had a penis. But imitation was a far distance from understanding.

"This is a creditable beginning," Augur said. "However, this smacks of parody. It needs to be more precise." He was sure the ifrits could not understand his remarks, but they were partly to keep Aura abreast of his thinking.

"Attention," Aura said. "Mine is closer."

He looked. She was right: her ifrit, ahead of his ifrit in the adaptation, was forming into a lovely figure of a red woman. She had outstanding breasts, a small waist, and lustrous hair. In fact she looked very much like Aura, only in red.

He watched his own ifrit more closely. It was improving its emulation. Its head was too big, but now some of it fuzzed off into vapor, which settled around the shoulders and condensed on them. Both head and shoulders were improved. The facial features were crude, but they too fuzzed partly into vapor, leaving a smaller nose and lips, a firmer chin.

"Better," Augur said encouragingly.

"Bet-terr." The voice and enunciation were improving too.

Augur watched as, part by part, the ifrit reshaped its body. It was evident that it could not do so directly; the seeming flesh had to vaporize, then condense again. So the process was slow, but effective. Soon enough a virtually perfect red human man stood before him.

"Caution," Ini said.

"Question?"

"He looks exactly like you. The other looks exactly like Aura, except for the color."

"Actually, mirror image," Futility said. "The human body is seldom perfectly symmetrical. The male ifrit's left arm is slightly more muscular than its right one."

Augur realized that as a dancer, she was highly conscious of body balance. This was an excellent point. The ifrits were copying them as they saw them, mirror-like. Still, the fidelity was remarkable.

"Perhaps it should be left that way," Ini said. "We do want to be able to tell you apart." She was not joking.

"They copy us," Augur said. "We are their models. This makes sense. But there is more to being human than appearance."

"Understatement," Aura agreed, laughing.

Both ifrits stumbled. They caught themselves, a bit clumsily, as they were evidently not accustomed to standing on two legs when in solid form.

"Interest," Ini said. "Your laughter surprised them, distracting them from their concentration on the form. They must never have heard it before."

"Only human beings laugh," Augur said. "Because only humans have a developed sense of humor."

"Only humans have the wit to appreciate the ridiculous," Aura said.

"Wit," he agreed. "Intelligence."

"Hypothesis," Ini said. "No creature on Planet Counter Charm is sapient."

"Rationale?" Aura asked.

"The ifrits evidently travel the planet, and can go anywhere. They will have encountered all landbound creatures, and probably airborne ones too. If they never encountered laughter, there are no creatures who practice it. Therefore none have sufficient wit."

"Correction," Augur said. "They may have humor, but express it some other way."

"Or they may be smart, but not humorous," Aura said.

"Hypothesis unproven," Ini agreed.

"But likely," Aura said.

"So we need to find out just how smart they are," Augur said. "Animal intellect seems probable."

Meanwhile the two ifrits were shaping up. The one before Aura was looking around, her eyes fixing on Futility with seeming interest. Futility glanced at Ini, then walked to stand beside Aura. The ifrit touched her hair, which was red. The ifrit's hair was red too, but not the same shade; it matched the monochrome of the zone.

"Some of us are Chroma," Aura said. "Some are nonChroma. This is Futility, who is nonChroma."

"Futility," Futility repeated.

"Foo-dill-idy."

"All our talking must be confusing to them," Augur said. "The repertoire of animals is limited."

"But we are not animals," Ini said. "Our dialogue helps make that plain. We should not pretend to be animals."

"Agreement," Augur said. "Animals hear us constantly talking, and ignore it, just as we ignore their scratching."

"Question," Futility said. "Shouldn't we name them?"

"Agreement," Aura said. "If they are going to look this much like us, and want to relate, we need to get on a name basis."

"The concept may be tricky," Ini said. "Animals don't have names, except when humans give them names."

"Let's try it and see how it works," Augur said. "What is a suitable name for this one?"

"Ifor Ifrit," Ini said naming the one in the children's story that had brought the term ifrit.

They all laughed, causing the ifrits to pause again, their faces going blank. Would it ever be possible to explain to the ifrits what humor was?

"Maybe Ivor, to differentiate," Ini suggested. "And Iva for the female."

"Agreement," Augur said, and the others assented.

The male ifrit was now complete, looking just like Augur, only left sided. It was time for introductions.

Augur touched his own chest. "Augur," he said.

"Aw-grr."

Close enough. Now he tapped the ifrit on the chest. "Ivor."

"I-vorr."

"Agreement. I am Augur, you are Ivor." Then he walked slowly to Ini. "Ini," he said, touching her swathed shoulder.

"In-ee."

"Ini," Ini repeated, touching her own shoulder. Then she touched Augur. "Augur." And the ifrit. "Ivor."

"I-vor." Already the pronunciation was closer.

But had the lesson taken? "Augur," Augur said, tapping himself. He glanced at Ini.

"Ini," she said, touching herself again.

Then both of them looked at the ifrit.

"Inee." And the ifrit touched himself.

"Negation," Augur said. Then, reconsidering, went for a simpler term. "No." He touched Ini. "Ini." He touched himself. "Augur. He touched the ifrit. "Ivor."

It took some time, but finally the ifrit got the idea. Then they repeated the process with the female ifrit She, having observed the process before, was quicker to catch on. "Ivaa."

When both ifrits had the name of all the party straight, it was time for the next step. What should that be?

"You two must be hungry," Ini said. "You skipped breakfast. Now it is nearing noon."

So it was; time had passed rapidly. "Then let's eat," Aura said. "And see if they do."

They hesitated to leave the Chroma zone, so Ini and Futility returned to the camp and brought food out for them. Augur conjured a crude table and chairs for the six of them.

This confused the ifrits. They had surely seen conjuring before, because it was common magic with in Chroma zones, and animals often used it to fashion temporary refuges. It was the special forms that were strange. "We need to make a demonstration," Augur murmured. "I'll be a courtly man; you be ladies."

"We'll fake that state," Aura agreed wryly.

He approached her. "Aura," he said clearly. "Seat." He pulled out a chair for her. She sat on it. He went on to Ini. "Ini. Seat." She sat. "Futility—seat." She sat. Then he came to Iva. "Iva. Seat." And she, again benefiting from observation, sat. He came finally to Ivor. "Ivor. Seat." And Ivor sat. It wasn't courtly protocol for a man to help a man, other than the king, but this had done the job.

Aura served food similarly. "Augur. Food." He accepted a chunk of bread and a cup of milky liquid, Gale's concoction. Ini and Futility accepted theirs. Then Iva and Ivor. Did ifrits eat? Not in solid form, he suspected. But since humans did, this was appropriate.

When all were served, Augur made a show of biting into his bread. He chewed, slowly and obviously, and swallowed. Then he took a careful sip of his drink. After that, Aura did the same, and the others. But the two ifrits had a problem: their teeth were not hard, and probably they didn't have solid digestive systems.

But they adapted. They opened their mouths, and their teeth vaporized. Soon they reformed as much harder units, so they could chew. But they still couldn't swallow. So vapor issued from their mouths in larger quantity, then funneled back down into them. Now they swallowed; they had reformed their innards to make the equivalent of stomachs.

"And what of elimination?" Ini murmured.

"They'll probably have to eject it undigested," Aura said. "But at least we have succeeded in making a social occasion."

After the meal and a brief discussion, Augur took Ivor to the screening of some bushes and demonstrated urination and defecation. The ifrits surely understood these animal processes; now they knew that humans did them too, and perhaps understood that they normally did them alone. Ivor went through the motions, but was able to produce only a little mist, which was then retracted. "Understanding," Augur said. "You don't eat and eliminate the way we do."

They rejoined the women, who evidently had had similar experience. "What's next?" Augur asked.

The answer surprised him. Iva Ifrit came to him. She placed her arms around him and squeezed, gently. They were both naked, and she was well formed—just about like Aura in red—so this was a pleasant surprise. "Fren," she said.

"Friend," he agreed, pronouncing the word carefully.

"Frend," she agreed. "Ege of."

Augur did not understand the second statement, but hesitated to show his ignorance. He stood embracing Iva, silent. It was Ini who figured it out. "Edge off!" she exclaimed. "That's what I said when we had sex the other night!"

"Amazement!" Aura said. "That suggests two things. First, that the purple fog was the same ifrit, or that they have communication. Second—"

"That Iva wants sex," Ini concluded.

Augur still did not feel free to comment. This development astonished him, and he did not know how to handle it. He remained as he was, holding the ifrit, not moving.

"Conjecture," Ini said. "The ifrit passed that night, noted our presence, heard our dialogue, and recognized a typical animal interaction: sex. This is used in many species as a social lubricant: a male does not generally harass a female who is new to the group if he has had sex with her. The ifrits wish to interact amicably with us, so proffer sex in this spirit. Question: would we be wise to decline?"

"Acceptance," Aura said after a pause. "I will take on Ivor."

"Question," Ini said. "Notes?"

"In this instance, yes," Aura said. "There are bound to be complications. It is a learning process, and we must be ready to clarify things. Let's start with Augur and Iva. Demonstrate sex."

Augur's feelings were mixed. He knew this was not a human woman, not even an animal one, but a form of demon. But she was perfectly shaped, and wished to relate in this way. "Agreement," he said.

He drew away from Iva, and concentrated on conjuration. He summoned substance to make a red bed of straw, then covered it with a red sheet. Then he demonstrated lying down. She understood immediately, perhaps because he and Ini had been lying down in the night. He lay beside her, and kissed her.

That needed a lesson. Her mouth was mushy. "Aura," he said.

Aura came and lay down beside them. The likeness remained eerie: the red woman form and blue woman form. He moved over to her and kissed her. Then Aura addressed Iva, bringing Iva's finger to her pursed lips, demonstrating a kiss. After that Aura kissed Augur again, with exaggeratedly firm mouth. Then she withdrew.

It sufficed. When he kissed Iva again, her mouth was firm. It was far from perfect, but a vast improvement. Ini was murmuring, and Futility was making rapid notes. This was certainly a public demonstration.

He continued, fondling and kissing Iva's breasts. Iva remained quite still. He summoned Aura again, and she demonstrated motion with the touching, adding small moans of pleasure as she clasped him to her.

Again Iva understood. She came alive as he stroked her, and moaned. She kissed him with increasing competence.

It was time for the finale. This time he did not try to do it with the ifrit first; he demonstrated on Aura, making sure Iva saw the exact nature of the penetration. He wasn't quite sure she had made a place. She had the external form, but probably not the internal one. He withdrew, refraining from the climax.

Iva went to Aura. She felt Aura's anatomy, finding the essential aperture. Her own cleft fuzzed into red vapor, then reformed. She returned to Augur.

Now he entered her, but it still was not right. She had made too large a hole, so that it was like poking into an open bag. He returned to Aura, this time demonstrating her tightness with a finger. Iva rechecked, using her own finger, and Aura tolerated this with style. Then the ifrit fuzzed again, and reformed.

This time Augur found the entry pleasantly tight. Well worked up by this time, he kissed her, hugged her close, and thrust to full depth, climaxing immediately. It was a relief rather than a joyful experience, but he knew the worst was over. Hereafter the ifrit would know how to do it.

He lay with Iva for a short while longer, making the point that these things did not have to be rushed. He knew that she had had no actual pleasure from it, but was satisfied to have done it correctly. Then he withdrew. "Your turn," he told Aura, a trifle maliciously.

"My turn," she agreed. "But I'm not sure I can make him climax."

That could indeed be a problem. A woman could take or leave a climax during sex, but a man was expected to have it. "Idea," Augur said. Then, mentally: *Yellow.*

Here, the Glamor's thought came immediately. She had been watching invisibly all along, their protection in case there should be danger. Augur was not telepathic, but the Glamor could read his mind.

Can you read the minds of ifrits?

Not these ones Yellow replied. *They are foreign to my experience. I'm not sure they have minds as we know them.*

He wasn't either. *Can you project feeling to them?*

That I may do. Feeling is less specific than dialogue.

Project her orgasm to his mind, so he experiences it, at the time, he thought.

Agreed.

Aura approached Ivor.

"Preemption," Ini said. "I'm too hot to stand it any more. Let me."

"Agreement," Aura said, looking somewhat relieved.

Ini ran to stand before the ifrit. "Ini," she said.

"Ivor," he replied.

"I will have sex with you." Not expecting him to understand the words, she took him by the hand and led him to the mattress Augur and Iva had just vacated. "But I am invisible, so it will have to be by feel." She removed her swathing and stood in bra, panties, and hair ribbon. Then she doffed the underwear, so that only the ribbon showed.

Augur had seen her invisible before, but at the time he had been the one having sex with her. Now he was a spectator, and that was interesting in another way. Especially since his recent partner Iva stood beside him, also watching, as well as Aura and Futility.

The ribbon moved close to Ivor's head. His lips pursed, as they had taught Iva; Ini was kissing him. Then his hands moved, stroking air; she was guiding them to her breasts and bottom. Her shape was pretty well defined by the motions of his hands. Then he lay on the bed; she had led him down. His member lifted; she was handling it. It didn't stiffen; it lacked the mechanism. Then it fuzzed into vapor, and reformed fully erect; his observation of Augur surely guided him.

Ivor started to insert the stiff member into her invisible cleft, but at that point the action slowed. "Augur," Ini called. "I want him to know about thrusting."

But sex had been too recent, for him. He was not ready. *Yellow,* he thought. *Can you send me a fresh erection?*

It came, forging into his member: such intense sexual appetite that in a moment he was fully erect. "Aura," he said.

Aura joined him on the bed beside Ivor. She lay on her back and spread her legs. He came down above her. "Note," he said. He placed his member appropriately, then made exaggerated thrusting motions, plunging into her full depth, withdrawing almost all the way, then thrusting again. "Like this."

Then Aura wrapped her arms and legs around him and hauled him in close. That, and the fierce thrusting, and the Glamor's sending, set him off, and he went to it in earnest. After several more he climaxed, felt her doing the same, then collapsed beside her. He had made a fuller demonstration than anticipated.

Ivor tried again. This time he penetrated the invisible body and thrust repeatedly, copying Augur exactly.

Ini moaned, achieving her climax. Then Ivor's face showed a blankness that indicated ifrit surprise, and his body quivered. He was feeling Ini's orgasm, relayed by the Glamor. His whole body stiffened, then relaxed as he dropped to the side, still holding the invisible woman. He had just discovered the point of sexual activity.

For a time the four of them lay there. Augur looked up to see Iva's face blank; she didn't know why Ivor had reacted like that.

Yellow? Augur thought.

Agreement.

Augur stood up. "Now it is your turn with each other," he said. "So Iva can feel it too. I let her down in that respect."

They got the two ifrits together. Ivor's member was rigid; he would have to vaporize it to soften it. That was fine. He set it in Iva and started thrusting. She wrapped arms and legs around him, emulating Aura. They kissed.

Then both ifrits changed. They clasped each other tightly, quivered, and relaxed together.

"I asked the Yellow Glamor to send them our climaxes," he told Aura. "Last time, he got Ini's climax, telepathically transferred. Now they both know what it's all about."

The ifrits let go of each other, sat up, then stood. "Sex," Ivor said.

"Sex is great," Augur agreed. "That's why we do it." But of course the ifrit looked blank.

"We need better communication," Aura said. "But we may be at the limit. Animals can learn spot words and actions, but they lack the brains for full language."

"I wonder," Augur said. "I agree that they are at the animal level now. But their versatility in changing form and Chroma makes me think they have more potential. We still don't know why they came to us, and I think we ought to find out."

"Agreement," Ini said. She was now in bra and panties again, leaving her swathing off, and that was adequate. "But how can we learn, if they can't talk well enough to tell us?"

"Maybe they came to observe us," Futility said. "They don't need to tell us anything, just to find out about us."

"To whom do they report, in that case?" Aura asked.

"We had better find out," Ini said.

They tried to question the two ifrits, but made no headway. The ifrits were present, and cooperative to the best of their ability, but were at the limit of their intelligence.

Then Augur got a wild idea. "The ifrits are limited in their solid form, because their natural form is the clouds. Whatever they can do intellectually must be in that form."

"But we can't talk with them in that form," Aura said.

"Which is why they made the sacrifice of assuming our form. But it may be that they are in effect bound, muzzled, and blindfolded when solid. Normally they use it only to cross between Chroma. So we need to find a way to talk to them in cloud form—and I think I know how." He paused, suddenly concerned that his idea was impractical.

"Speak," Ini said.

He plunged in. "There are two of them. Surely they can communicate with each other when in cloud form, and maybe if one is in solid form. So suppose one stays with us, and the other becomes a cloud? We can project our thoughts as well as non-telepaths can, perhaps assisted by the Yellow Glamor, and the cloud can read that and relay it to the solid one. We know they can see and hear us in that form, because they picked up on the words and sex Ini and I had last night. They may be far more intelligent in cloud form—or at least able to understand far more complicated thoughts."

"Possibility!" Ini said. "That form could be like that stories of ancient computers, mechanical intellects, that used special circuits to store and manipulate huge amount of information. The clouds could be three dimensional computers, with phenomenal capacity—if it can just be directed."

"Directed?" Aura asked.

"The ancient machines were not intelligent of themselves, as I understand it. They were merely very good at handling information. They had to be programmed to do it; without a program, a computer was useless. So we may need to provide a program—and hope the clouds will be able to assimilate it. It may not be sapience as we know it, but it might come close."

"Interest," Aura said.

"And if we can achieve this," he concluded, "We may learn why they came to us. There has to be a reason; they have gone to a lot of trouble—more than mere observation should be worth. They could observe us from their cloud perspective; they must want more."

"Let's try it," Ini said. "How?"

There was a silence. Augur was baffled; how could they get the ifrits to be smart enough to understand, before they tried the device that might make them smart?

"Pet training," Futility said. "Teach them to Go or Stay. Then tell one to Go and one to Stay."

Augur exchanged a glance with Aura. Could something that simple work? "Lets demonstrate."

They left the table. "Aura—Go," Augur said. Aura walked away. "Ini—Stay." Ini remained standing. "Futility—Go." Futility went. Now would the ifrits understand? "Iva—Go."

And Iva went.

"Ivor—Stay." Ivor stayed.

But one trial wasn't certain. They tried it again, with a different patterning. Ini went, the others stayed. Ivor went, Iva stayed. They tried several more times, and the ifrits were always correct.

Now it was time to try the key separation. "Iva—go cloud," Augur said. "Ivor—stay."

Iva started to walk away. But that wasn't it. "Cloud," Augur said. He lifted his arms, trying to emulate a cloud. "Puff. Vapor. Smoke. Your natural form. Cloud." But she didn't understand.

I will try, the Yellow Glamor's thought came.

Then Iva started to dissolve into vapor.

I sent a thought: turn cloud, but stay here.

Appreciation. That was the aspect Auger had forgotten: to tell the cloud to stay. Without the presence of the cloud, they would not be able to try the new communication.

The body lost cohesion, steaming into red vapor. The cloud formed and expanded. As the body dissolved, it became a lump, then a mound on the ground. The food it had eaten was exposed, with a smear of a different shade of red: Augur's seed. It was like watching someone dying.

At last it was complete: a small pile of refuse, and a full red cloud perhaps thirty paces in diameter. It remained, surrounding them; the musky odor was there.

But would this device work? Augur was nervous.

≈≈

Aura considered. She wasn't sure this cloud/solid connection would work, but it was certainly worth trying.

"We'll be talking with Ivor," Augur said. "But the understanding will be Iva's. Assuming that they are in close communication."

"That's the big gamble," Ini said. "How do we find out?"

Again, they were baffled. Ivor was standing there, waiting for them to do something. But what?

"Why not ask him?" Futility asked.

And again, it was her direct question that showed the way. Futility made no pretense of intellectualism or caring; this was just a job, and she wanted to get it done. Sometimes that was what was needed.

"Ivor," Aura said. "Can you talk to Iva?"

"Iva. Go," he said.

"Iva. Here." Aura spread her arms through the cloud.

He didn't understand. "Iva. Go," he repeated.

"He thinks we want to be sure she's gone," Augur said.

"Assuming he thinks at all," Ini said. "Animals don't reason things out. They deal with the immediate situation. Iva was here; we sent her away. So she is no longer relevant."

"Maybe the Yellow Glamor can help again," Augur said.

"By sending Iva a thought," Ini said. "Tell her to contact Ivor."

Attempt. It was the Glamor's thought.

Ivor's face went blank a moment. Then he spoke. "Iva."

"Iva!" Aura repeated. "Stay in touch with Ivor. Help him understand." But again she was way beyond the ifrit's capacity.

"I think we need to proceed with a course of education," Ini said. "As with a child. Start with the basics, work up. If Iva stays in touch, Ivor could be a bright student."

They tackled it. They started with simple words for things: tree, stone, the names of the people present, go, stay, walk, lie down, jump, and so on. Then they did position words: here, there, near, far, up, down. Ivor repeated them with increasing fluency. But did he retain them? Did he truly understand them? His physical form surely had very little brain; the real storage would be with Iva, if their understanding of ifrit nature was correct.

They tested him. "Where is Futility?" Aura asked.

"Futility." But he did nothing.

"Here is Futility," Aura said, walking to the woman and touching her shoulder. "Where is Ini?"

Ivor paused. Then he walked to Ini. "Here is Ini."

It had worked! But Aura restrained her glee, in case it was a false indication. "Yes, there is Ini. Where is Augur?"

Ivor strode to Augur. "Here is Augur."

It was looking good. "Where is a tree?"

Ivor walked to a tree and touched its bark. "Here is tree."

"I think he's got it," Augur murmured.

But this remained at the level of an eighteen month old human child. The Ifrit might have gotten there on his own. They needed to verify the higher capacity they presumed Iva in cloud form was capable of.

"Take Augur to the tree," Aura said carefully.

Ivor considered. "Take Augur," he said, going to Augur. "Tree." He caught Augur's hand and tugged him toward the tree.

"We're getting there," Ini said with the same suppressed attitude Aura had.

"Take a stone to Futility," Aura said. "Then to Augur."

The ifrit went to a stone, picked it up, carried it to Futility, and held it out for her to take. But when she reached for it, he withdrew it and carried it on to Augur.

He was definitely getting there.

When they got Ivor to kiss the woman standing closest to the tree, when Aura, Ini, and Futility were at different distances from it, they knew they were getting beyond the range of animal understanding. Either Ivor had greater brain capacity than seemed likely, or Iva was understanding it and assisting him.

As they progressed, remaining doubt faded. Ivor was learning faster and retaining better than any human child could. It had to be the rapid assimilation of information Ini had described in the mythical ancient computers of planet Earth. The cloud was doing it.

But the day was passing. They needed to be sure they could renew process next day. That meant being sure the ifrits understood what was happening.

Aura sat across the table from Ivor. They had agreed that she would make this explanation, as she seemed to relate best to the ifrit. "Ivor, we are teaching you about human beings. But there is more to cover. Can we do this again tomorrow?"

"We can do it again, Aura," he agreed.

"Do you understand the process?"

"Process?"

"We asked Iva to become a cloud again so she could help you understand. We talk to your solid form, but it is your cloud form that understands."

He was surprised. "Iva?"

Aura smiled. "Ask her. You are in touch with her."

"Iva, is this true?" Then he answered himself. "Yes, it is true. She is around us, understanding. But why is it this way?"

"Because you made your solid forms without enough detail to function fully on their own. You had no legs, so couldn't stand until you formed them. You copied our forms exactly, externally, but not internally." She paused, seeing his confusion. "External means outside. Internal means inside. You looked like us outside, but inside you were just—matter. You had no stomach, so had to make one to eat. You had no functional sexual anatomy—" Again she paused to explain. "Anatomy: the structure of a thing, like a human body. Sexual anatomy is the shape of the sex organs, outside and inside. You had an outside penis, but Iva had no inside vagina. So you had to remake yours, and she had to make hers, before you could have sex." It was easiest, now, to define words as she went along, because a single definition was sufficient, and it placed the words in context. However, sometimes this led to cumbersome chains of explanations. "Then we did have sex, which consisted of the male putting his stiffened penis into the vagina of the female, followed by great pleasure."

Ivor smiled—another thing he had learned—reminiscently. Possibly that experience had helped motivate him to learn more. There was nothing like sex to motivate a man! That might also be why she related best to him: a man was more attentive to a woman who could provide him such pleasure. Ini could have done it, but Ini was observing and recording. "I did not know of the pleasure of sex, before," he said. "We know animals do it to—"

"Procreate," Aura filled in. "To start the process of making young creatures like themselves. Every living thing procreates in some manner."

"To procreate," he agreed. "But we thought it was simply because they wanted new animals of their kind. Now we understand that they do it for the pleasure."

"They do it for the pleasure," Aura agreed. "Nature takes care of the rest." Another pause. "Nature: our word for the natural processes of living things. We think of nature as good, but she is merely efficient. Efficient: to do things in the best way, with little waste. So she gives immediate rewards—makes animals feel pleasure—for long term objectives. Objective: something that needs to be done, a goal. Long term: it takes time to happen, perhaps years. Perhaps means maybe—something that happens or doesn't happen. Year: a unit of time. How long it takes the planet to circle the suns and return to its starting place."

She didn't try to clarify that they actually used the year of ancient Planet Earth rather than their own. "Planet: this whole ball of substance we are on."

She stopped. She could hardly blame him for confusion; she was getting into astronomy, something the ifrits would have no idea of. It was also drifting from the point she was trying to make. "I must save that for next day; it is too much now."

"Next day," he agreed amicably.

"One of the things you did not make was a superior brain. Superior: very good. We have superior brains in our heads; you have animal brains. But in your cloud form you have superior brains. So we asked Iva to return to cloud form so she could understand, and enable you to understand. Because we don't know how to talk to ifrits in cloud form, and ifrits don't know how to talk to us in solid form." She was explaining this for Iva's benefit too. The ifrits needed to comprehend the full mechanism, so they could duplicate it. "This is collaboration: more than one person working together to do something better. You and Iva, talking with us and understanding. This is the process."

"The process," he agreed. "I talk, Iva understands. We can do this again tomorrow."

"Excellent. That means very good, favorable. We will come here again tomorrow to meet you and Iva."

"Question."

She had not taught him that; he must have picked it up from hearing their other dialogue. He was getting smart indeed! "Ask."

"May Iva be solid and talk too, tomorrow?"

Oh, no! Did this mean that they did not after all understand? "We need Iva to be in cloud form, so that—"

He held up a hand in a stop signal. That was another mannerism he had picked up on his own, or the pair of them had. "I understand. But Iva likes Augur. He showed her how to have sex, and later she discovered the pleasure in it."

Iva liked Augur. They had explained the concept of "like," but this was more relevant than the ifrit's understanding should have been. Iva wanted to have more experience with Augur, surely including sexual. They had not yet covered the concepts of no fault sex or of permanent relationships. "But—"

Again the hand. "Iva helps me understand. You are correct; we can not have superior brains in the solid state. But does it have to be Iva who makes the understanding?"

This remained difficult. "You wish to be the cloud, so Iva can be the solid one?"

"Negation." Yet another untaught term. His increasing savvy was becoming eerie. "I wish to be solid too. A third ifrit can be the cloud."

There it was. They did indeed understand, and had come up with an improvement in the system. So that both could participate. Aura had been a bit slow to get it. "Understanding. That should work. If the third ifrit knows what Iva knows."

"He will know it all."

There was confirmation that they had high grade communication between themselves. They could transfer information and a program in the manner Ini had described. This was progressing far better than anticipated. "Then welcome. We will be glad to talk to both of you." Aura glanced at Augur, who stood silent at a moderate distance. "Iva can relate to Augur."

"Appreciation. She will like that."

"Then it's a date. We will meet here tomorrow morning."

Ivor reached across the table and took her hand. "A date," he agreed. Then: "Question."

Something else? Aura's head was already spinning. "Ask."

"Must we take the same forms?"

"The human form is best, for this purpose."

"Agreement. But we look exactly like you and Augur, except for your color. May we be more individualistic?"

"Welcome," she said, relieved. It had been mildly unnerving to be talking to a man so much like Augur in appearance. "Assume the human forms you wish. Introduce yourselves to us so we know you."

"Agreement." He lifted her hand and kissed it. Augur had never done that! "Perhaps we can have sex again, tomorrow."

"Perhaps," she agreed weakly.

"It's a date. Parting."

"Parting." She realized that the surrounding cloud was moving off.

He began to vaporize. First his head dissipated into red vapor, then his neck, arms, chest, and stomach. The held contents of his stomach rode the dissolving torso down to the chair, leaving a sloppy little pile. The legs fuzzed out. He had become the cloud.

"Intriguing," Ini said. "The moment you exchanged partings, the Iva cloud started moving. It left at the same rate the Ivor cloud formed, so they didn't overlap. They coordinate well."

"That's not all," Aura said. "Did you hear? He asked me for a date tomorrow. A sexual date."

"Agreement. I will take your place, if you wish."

"How did he learn about kissing a woman's hand? We never told him or showed him that."

"Several things we never demonstrated," Augur agreed. "They evidently know more about us than we thought. Someone must have done it, or spoken of it."

"This experimental contact has become successful beyond our wildest dreams," Ini said. "My guess is that the cloud form is fully as effective as the legendary ancient computers, once given direction.

Have we started something we'll regret?"

"Such as generating a sapience superior to our own," Augur said.

"That's frightening!" Aura said.

"But I think not likely," Ini said. "The ancient computers could assimilate an enormous amount of information, and manipulate it rapidly, but they could not actually think. A human being had to direct them. I suspect we can't create a sapience greater than our own. Or even equal to our own; there will be conceptual liabilities. But it should certainly be interesting."

"Agreement," Aura breathed.

They set off for the base camp.

The others were quite interested in their report. The Yellow Glamor could have given it, but left it to the mortals. "And at the end, he kissed my hand and asked me for a sexual date tomorrow. I don't know how he learned to do that."

"You were naked," Symbol said. "Of course he was interested."

"I mean the hand."

Gale turned to Havoc. "Yesterday when you were mocking the courtly manner, you kissed my hand."

"Was there an ifrit near?" Ini asked, and Futility made a note.

"I didn't think so. But I wasn't alert for vapor."

"Vapor can be invisible," Ini said. "Especially when it matches its Chroma. The ifrits may not have to stay in obvious globular cloud form."

"Which means we had better take warning," Havoc said. "We have no quarrel with the ifrits, but if one should develop, they may know more about us than we think."

"Nevertheless," the Red Glamor said, "we must maintain engagement. They show potential to match or emulate human sapience. This is something we need to watch."

The others nodded agreement. Then Futility danced, and the entertainment of the children began. Symbol showed a family style illusion story for them all.

At night, with Augur, Aura had a different concern. "We showed them sex, on a no fault basis. Now they want more."

"Actually, Iva isn't hard to take."

"And what of Ivor with me? They seem to be learning human emotion too. Suppose they decide to be jealous of our other relations?"

He got serious. "They are utterly nonhuman. They may have discovered the pleasure sex can provide, but we can't know what a relationship means to them."

"We should find out."

"Agreement."

"Meanwhile, it may be improvident to balk sexually."

"Concurrence," he said. "I suspect they will soon be better lovers."

She thought so too. The notion of sex with cloud creatures remained weird, yet it was a direct way to relate.

In the morning they were ready at the Red Chroma zone before dawn. This time they had brought supplies, and were clothed.

The clouds moved in. One hovered on either side, and they condensed simultaneously. One was male, the other female. This time they were not clones of Augur and Aura.

When the formulation was complete, the male approached Aura. He was naked, well formed, and unfamiliar. His features were on the handsome side of ordinary. His body was similar; he could readily have lost himself among a throng of Red Chroma humans.

Aura glanced across at the female. She was similarly different. The ifrits seemed to have taken an average of human types, improved on it slightly, and diverged a few features. The woman was pretty without being outstanding. This showed fair finesse; the ifrits were emulating regular people.

Meanwhile a third cloud was moving in, surrounding the two solid ifrits and the rest of the people. The mind configuration was in place.

"Introduction," the male said to Aura. "I am Ivor. We spoke together yesterday."

"Agreement," she said, smiling. "Compliment: you have rendered your form well. So has Iva."

"Request: I wish to kiss you."

"Acquiescence."

He took her in his arms and kissed her, competently, and let her go. Iva was similarly polished, with Augur. It was hard to find any deviation from the human norm, apart from the lack of clothing.

So she tackled that first, as they sat across from each other at the table. Augur and Iva took the other end, talking quietly with each other. "Explanation: Yesterday we were surprised by your approach, and hurried to join you without dressing. Normally human beings are clothed, as we are now."

"Question: why?"

"Question: do you wish a brief explanation, or a full one?"

"Both. Then I will know what is better next time."

"Brief: for warmth and for modesty and decoration. Full: animals go without clothing, as most of them have fur, scales, feathers, blubber, or some other mechanism to maintain the warmth of their bodies. Humans evolved—evolve: to develop more complicated bodies and habits from simple ones, in the course of much time—on a distant planet which it seems had only science magic volcanoes, so they could not directly warm themselves by other Chroma magic. They had to use fire, which they made from burning wood. But their main challenge was heat: they learned to forage in the hottest part of the day, when furry predators were resting, so that they would not get eaten themselves. They lost most of their fur so that their skin could radiate heat more effectively. But then at night when it was cold, they had to make a substitute—substitute: a thing that serves instead of something that is not available—for the lost fur, to hold in body warmth. They learned to adapt the skins and feathers of dead animals and birds, and to weave plant fibers into cloth for clothing. This is cloth." She removed her shirt and passed it across the table for inspection. "Thus came to be clothing. It was used so often that it became customary—customary: the usual course of action—and was worn even when external conditions did not require it. In fact it was removed only on special occasions, such as for sex."

"Interest."

"Precisely. A woman's removal of part or all of her clothing in the presence of a man is often considered an invitation for sex. A naked woman is often considered a sexual object—that is, one that is available for sexual action."

"Understanding," he said, looking at her haltered breasts. "Is it the same for a man?"

"Less so, because women are less interested in men's bodies than men are in women's bodies." She took back her shirt.

"Aura," Augur said. "Request."

She smiled and handed him the shirt. He gave it to Iva, who put it on with a certain awkwardness. Then he gave Aura his shirt. She relayed it to Ivor, and helped him don it. That meant that both ifrits were clothed only above, but it would have to serve.

Ini murmured to Futility, who departed.

Now Augur and Iva moved closer, making it a four way dialogue. "We inadvertently—by chance, unintended—misled you yesterday," Aura said to both ifrits. "Apology."

"Question?" Iva asked. It was apparent that though their forms differed, the minds of both ifrits were very similar. What was said to one was understood by the other, because the understanding came from the cloud ifrit surrounding them.

"Apology: the expression of regret for a mistake. The other person may accept it, reject it, or dismiss it as needless. The most positive course is dismissal, as it suggests that there was not a mistake."

"Confusion."

"There are assorted human manners that coincide only approximately to reality. Reality: the true state of things. Generally an effort is made to enable the other person to feel good, even if that is not wholly deserved. Such effort is not considered lying."

"Difficulty."

That got them into the ethics of socially correct deception. "Concern," Aura said. "This is a confusing nuance of human behavior whose clarification should wait on more essential things."

"Agreement." But it was obvious that the ifrits would be returning to this.

Futility returned with more clothing. Now the ifrits were able to don full outfits: shirt and trousers for Ivor, dress for Iva. They looked completely human.

They went into Math, Logic, Puzzles, and Humor. The ifrits proved apt at the first three, unsurprisingly, but the fourth was another problematic one. "One of the characteristics of intelligence, of sapience, is humor," Aura said. But she knew it would be difficult to get the nature of human across to beings that lacked an innate sense of it.

"Question," Ivor said. "What is the advantage of sapience?"

That was bound to be another tough one. This time Augur tackled it. "Aura mentioned how heat dissipation and clothing become survival mechanisms for human beings. There are other mechanisms, and perhaps the most important is intelligence. Animals live mainly in the present; they may remember past events but don't dwell on them, and have no concern for the future. Future: what will happen hereafter. Humans are concerned with the past and the future, and it gives them a great competitive advantage. Humans are dominant on Planet Charm because of their sapience. They remember past mistakes, and work to correct them in the future."

The ifrits exchanged a glance, another human mannerism they had picked up on their own. "Confusion," Iva said.

"I think we need a practical demonstration," Aura said. "Question: what do ifrits fear?"

"Question?"

"Fear," Augur said. "A negative emotion caused by danger or the threat of pain or death."

"Question?"

The ifrits had no pain, death, or fear? Because they weren't really alive? Did they have any true emotions?

"What preys on ifrits?" Aura asked. "What attacks ifrits, and hurts or kills them?"

"The sucker," Ivor said.

"Detail."

"It is a creature of meshes that sucks in air and cloud, feeding on ifrit substance. Ifrits try to avoid it."

"Understanding," Aura said. "Sapience should enable ifrits to nullify the sucker. Nullify: render it ineffective, not dangerous."

"Demonstration."

Aura was cautious. "First, discussion. Sapience enables us to prepare ahead, so that we can handle the situation when it comes. We must understand the sucker, then we can figure out how to nullify it."

They discussed it. The sucker used illusion to camouflage itself, and turned up unexpectedly, catching an ifrit unaware. Once the suction started, the ifrit had to fight to escape, and usually lost a portion of its substance. If it was sleeping, it could be too far gone before it woke, and was doomed.

"Sapient discussion," Augur said. "Suggestions for dealing with this problem."

"Learn to penetrate illusion," Aura said.

"Unfeasible," Ivor said. "The sucker has—evolved—with ifrits, and knows how to make illusion that deceives us. It strikes at a weakness in our makeup."

"Then strike a weakness in its makeup," Ini said. "It evidently filters your molecules from the air with its meshes. Meshes are subject to clogging and tearing. The moment you feel the suction, start turning solid, but not as one piece. Form yourself into grains of sand-like substance too big to pass the filter, with points and sharp edges that will lodge and cut. When the sucker's meshes are stifled, it will have to quit or suffocate. Then you will be freed."

Ivor looked at Iva. "This is why it doesn't prey in dust storms," he said. "The dust and sand interfere."

"Agreement," Iva said. "How is it we never realized?"

"Because you lacked the reasoning power of full sapience," Aura said. "With sapience, many things become clear. Now you should arrange to try it, to verify whether this is effective. Can you notify other ifrits of this ploy?"

"Affirmation. We know it will work."

Augur shook his head. "Theory shows the way, but practice confirms. It must be cautiously tested before you can be sure."

"We understand," Ivor said. "With the sapience you have lent us, we appreciate the reservation. We will relay both method and caution."

"Then this is one example of the advantage of sapience," Aura said. "We can make another."

"Needless," Ivor said. "We are satisfied that sapience is worthwhile."

"You have done us a favor," Iva said. "We wish to do you a return favor."

Where had they discovered that concept? "We are merely trying to understand you, and enable you to understand us," Aura said. "It is true that humans normally exchange favors, but we feel this is not the occasion for it."

The two ifrits exchanged another glance. "We will think of something," Ivor said. "It will be an exercise of our sapience."

"Now we would like to indulge in sex," Iva said. "There is more we wish to learn about it."

"We have shown you the mechanism," Augur said. "We assume that it is not natural to you, so is not something you truly wish to do."

"It is true that we do not practice it as you do," Ivor said. "But we do reproduce. It is the pleasure that comes with it that surprised us. We do not understand how the mere temporary insertion of a part of the male into the female can bring such pleasure to either party."

Augur tackled this one. "Humans have evolved to obtain pleasure in this manner, like other animals. Ifrits have not. So further such activity is pointless for you."

"Negation," Iva said. "It is a way of relating positively, and we wish to be positive with you. We believe you will like us better if we are good partners in sex."

"And we wish to know how you enabled us to receive such pleasure," Ivor said. "We recognize that it did not come from ourselves."

Tell them, the Yellow Glamor's thought came. *It is time for the next level of revelation.*

Aura saw Augur nod. He had received the thought too. "There is a brief explanation, and a full one," he said.

"Request," Iva said. "Augur tell me the brief one, as we do it."

"And Aura tell me the full one, as we do it," Ivor said.

All four humans smiled. "That means that you and I will take longer," Aura said to Ivor.

"Agreement. But Iva will know it too."

Because what one learned, the other learned—and all ifrits, in due course. "Then we will tell as we demonstrate," Aura said.

Aura went with Ivor to a secluded glade. "Sex is, as you understand, a social lubricant," she said as they prepared a suitable bed. "Normally one man and one woman form a relationship and confine their sexual activity to each other. But when humans travel, they need additional support, and sex, especially for a young woman, is a standard way to get it. Men generally desire sex more than women do, so a man will provide protection or resources in exchange for sex. This is the usual exchange of favors. My relationship is with Augur; I love him and will marry him."

"Question?"

"Love is a strong permanent attraction. Marriage is a public recognition and commitment, so that all others are aware of it. But travel is generally no fault: no permanent commitment is made, just a temporary one. The sex Augur and I have with you and Iva we consider to be no fault."

"Statement: there is no love between us."

"No love," Aura agreed. "But sex does not require love."

"Conclusion: you therefore lack desire for sex with me."

"Candor?"

"Question?"

"Candor is when the truth is told, when it may not be pleasant for the other party."

"Candor," he agreed.

"I do lack desire for sex with you. The only man I wish to have sex with is Augur, though I wouldn't mind it with King Havoc. But I have done it with a number of men, as no fault traveling or to oblige. I am considered an attractive woman, so men desire sex with me. I will do it with you."

"Conjecture: you will do me a favor, and Iva will do Augur a favor."

Aura laughed. "Perhaps."

"There is humor. I do not understand."

"Sometimes we react to an odd or different perspective. Augur is a man, and he does appreciate women. He probably enjoys sex with Iva. So you are correct, in a way I had not before considered. That is what I found funny."

"I do not wish to require you to do what you prefer not to do."

"Question: why not?"

"I wish you to like me."

"Do you understand like or love?"

"Negation. I wish to learn."

Aura was touched. "I am not sure that such things can be taught. Liking and loving develop from amicable association, in people with the capacity for them."

"Regret."

"I can not give you love, Ivor, but I can give you sex."

"Negation," he said sadly.

"But I think I am coming to like you," she said, kissing him.

His return kiss was hungry. "Appreciation." But he made no attempt to engage in sex.

"There is one more thing," she said. "We needed help to show you the pleasure of sex. Just as you have an ifrit in cloud form helping you to understand, we have what we call a Glamor helping us."

"Question."

"Of course. Glamors are superior humans, able to do more magic in more places. They are telepathic, among other things."

"Question."

"Telepathy: direct communication between minds, usually at a small distance. No vocalization necessary."

"Relevance?"

"A Glamor sent you and Iva the pleasure of sex. It was the only way we could find to enable you to experience it."

"Demonstration?"

The Yellow Glamor appeared. "Here is that pleasure."

Both Ivor and Aura went rigid. Aura felt a phenomenal sexual climax, and knew the ifrit was sharing it, though they were standing apart from each other.

The Glamor disappeared, and the pleasure faded. "Wonder," Ivor said.

"Welcome," Aura replied. That had been a more direct and unsubtle demonstration than she would have chosen, but it was surely effective.

"Wish: I could feel that while kissing you."

She laughed again, and this time he laughed with her. He was either learning humor, or getting expert at emulation. "That is I think beyond my power. But I will kiss you again." She did so.

There was something quite gentle and warm in his reaction. "Impression: I felt some of it."

Was he learning love? That could be emotionally dangerous. "We have what is called a business or perhaps a social relationship. There is no permanence; it is no fault. Soon we humans will complete our mission on this planet and return to our own world."

"Regret."

They returned to the table. Augur and Iva were already there, of course, having finished in the brief explanation time. "Pleasure from a Glamor," Iva said.

"We wish to know more about Glamors," Ivor said.

"Tomorrow they will be here," Augur said. He had evidently cleared this with them.

Aura nodded. "I suspect it is time." Her head was spinning again; they had made almost unbelievable progress, and it seemed likely to continue. She hoped they would not regret it.

Chapter 7—Cloud Formation

Havoc nodded. "Yes, it is time," he agreed. "We have taken two days to check out the region surrounding the section the tapestry map covers, and know there are no ugly surprises there. Now we can sample the key zone."

Avian nodded his gray head. Then he and Havoc moved together toward the zone. The other Glamors stayed back. They had agreed to risk no more than two in the first exploration. That was why the mortals were not here; neither Ini, with the altar icon, nor Futility, with the tapestry map, would be risked until the way was certified safe.

The terrain looked ordinary. They had selected a Gray Chroma zone to sample first, which was why the Gray Glamor was participating. They planned to have human/animal teams, to maximize the senses and reactions. All this care seemed unnecessary, but they trusted the nature of the challenge: extreme caution was best. There could be things here that none of them had encountered before. They needed to be prepared for the unexpected.

Still, the gray terrain ahead seemed exactly typical of Gray Chroma zones elsewhere on this planet. The trees were the same as those Havoc had noted elsewhere, and the odd birds were too, as Avian had noted. It hardly seemed to require a special map from another planet; they could have flown over the zone and quickly sketched their own map. Yet nothing about this quest had been straightforward, and there seemed to be reason for the other aspects; there was surely reason here too.

They stopped just beyond the limit defined by the map, having established that without passing it. "Your sample, Gray," he said.

Avian stepped across the unmarked line. One stride, two, three. Then he paused, squawked, and stepped back. *See for yourself.*

Havoc shrugged and strode forward himself. On the third step, the zone changed. He was standing at the edge of a turbulent sea that had not been there before. Gray waves slapped against gray rocks at the shore, throwing up spume. The sound was consistent, and the smell of the water's edge was pleasant. Drops of water struck him like cool rain.

This had to be illusion. Nothing like this was on the map, and it wasn't visible from outside. It had appeared only when he entered the defined zone. Yet it was different from prior illusions he had encountered, both on Charm and Counter Charm, in that it was apparent only when he was actually in it. Most illusions were visible from inside or outside; they were fixed, overlaying reality at their sites. Symbol's illusion story shows were an example.

Like Symbol's illusions, this one was full-fledged. In fact it went beyond, because hers did not have smell or touch, just sight and sound. This was the most effective illusion he had encountered.

Or *was* it illusion? This was so realistic that it could be reality, and the illusion might be the placid scene seen from outside. That would mean that this entire region was quite other than anticipated. Yet why would they need a map of the illusion, in that case? It would be useless.

Havoc squatted and picked up a wet pebble from the fragmented beach. It had been smoothed by millennia of washing, but the faint lines of its layered formation remained. He stepped back across the tacit line.

There was the ordinary landscape, with Avian standing where he had been. The surging sea was gone. So was the pebble Havoc had held.

"Interesting," he remarked. "You saw the same?" He projected a mental picture of the sea.

Agreement.

"I think that is illusion."

The bird nodded.

They consulted with the other Glamors. Yellow was absent, safeguarding the mortals in their investigation of clouds, but they could update her when they understood more. Gale was with the children at the base. The others crossed the line one by one, experiencing the scene for themselves. All were impressed.

They moved around the perimeter to an Orange Chroma zone. This faced a moderate mountain overgrown with orange trees and shrubs, with a path winding up the side that might have been made by one of the giant snails they had seen elsewhere. The Orange Sphinx Glamor approached it, with the Green Glamor, whose constituency was mollusks; he would be able to relate to a snail if they encountered it.

The sphinx stepped across the assumed line, paused, and returned. The Green Glamor did the same.

The others took their turns. When Havoc tried it, he discovered a scintillating desert, across which glittering things raced, keening melodically. It was hard to get a clear view of them; their courses were too erratic to anticipate well, and they seemed never to pause in place. They didn't leave tracks; instead their motion stirred up dust and sand, which soon settled behind them, leaving no clear prints. The heat was horrendous; as a Glamor he could handle it, but it would be bad for any mortals. This might be illusion, but it was nevertheless uncomfortable.

This time Havoc turned around, facing back the way he had come. There was more desert—and one of the glitter things was angling toward him. It surely couldn't touch him, being illusion, but he had seen enough. He walked forward, crossing the line that had to be there.

Back outside the zone, he turned and looked. There was the overgrown mountain again, quite peaceful. The illusion was completely gone.

"Impressed," he murmured.

"Concurrence," Green said. "I thought to check a snail; I found none there. I tried to penetrate the illusion to find the snail trail we can see from here, but could not find it."

They moved on to another section. This was an Air Chroma zone, showing only vague fog, which was the Illusions Chroma's way of being undefined. The Invisible Glamor checked it, with the Silver Chroma Spider. Again, they withdrew after brief inspection, and let the others try.

Havoc entered with Avian, this time together. And this time it was the base of a deep valley, with birds and small clouds overhead, and a creature reminiscent of a legendary Earth dinosaur roaming through it, questing perhaps for prey.

Havoc looked around. He did not see or hear Avian. *Gray?* He thought.

He got an answer, but it was hopelessly garbled. He knew a mind was near him, but not what it was trying to convey, or even whether it was the bird. It seemed that the illusion covered even telepathy.

Behind him was the near slope of the valley, too steep to support more than crevice-dwelling plants and moss. It rose to a ridge far above. That would be a very long climb.

There was agitation in the nearby thoughts. Something was bothering Avian. Havoc turned back to face the center of the valley—and saw that the dinosaur had winded them and was now striding purposefully toward them. It might be illusion—or it might be something real, like a dragon, modified by illusion. "Retreating," he said, buttressing the thought with the word. He stepped into the steep slope, and was out.

Avian was beside him, his tri-part beak looking disgruntled. The other Glamors nodded with understanding.

"Impressed again," Havoc said. "That is not passive illusion; it is aware of our intrusion."

Those birds sent bird-mind signals, Avian thought. *I received them clearly, but not yours, Havoc.*

"You were fogged," Havoc agreed. "Body and mind."

"Illusion is my Chroma specialty," the Air Glamor said. "But I have not before encountered this type or competence. It covers everything."

"Illusion can be penetrated," the Red Glamor said.

"Agreement. But did you penetrate this one?"

"Negation," she said, frowning. "That surprises me."

"And me," Air said. "I had to focus my entire effort on penetrating just one aspect at a time: sight, or sound, or smell, or mind. So I could make the dinosaur fade, but still heard the beat of its footfalls. This is a surprising challenge."

"Question," Havoc said. "Should we proceed regardless, or delay our investigation until we are better able to handle this special illusion?"

"Delay," Air said. "I need time to study this. I should be able to find a way in due course."

"And we don't want to risk the success of our mission on fouled up perceptions," the Red Glamor said. "We don't even know what we are searching for." She glanced around. "There could be danger, even for us."

"And there is more to study in the normal regions," the Blue Glamor said. "I have found insects of strange types, and want to fathom their natures." Her constituency was the insects.

"True for many of us," the Black Glamor said. "I am discovering different types of saprophytes."

"There may even be a new type of human being, for all we know," the Red Glamor said with a smile. "Let's reconvene when Air has solved his riddle."

There was general agreement. They went to their several pursuits. Havoc returned to the main base, where Gale and Symbol tried to stay even with the children.

"Visit or stay?" Gale inquired when she saw him appear. She was nursing Voila.

"We have encountered intractable illusion. Air is working on it, so we have spare time for now."

She gestured toward Symbol, who was watching Warp and Weft explore dirt while holding Flame. "Deal: Pick one of us for two minutes hot sex in exchange for an hour's baby-sitting with the terrors."

"Both of you together for four minutes, for half an hour with the terrors."

"Done." Gale set Voila down in the crib, went to Symbol, and spoke briefly with her. Symbol smiled and quickly set up a self-playing illusion showing figures made of candy, dancing. The children were immediately distracted by it. She left them and walked toward Havoc.

Gale fashioned an illusion sphere whose surface was reflective. She stepped into it with Symbol. "Four minutes, starting—now."

Havoc joined them in the sphere. From inside it was transparent, so they could see the children clearly. There was a bed in it, and both women were lying on it, nude, Symbol thoroughly powdered. Their breasts tended to lose definition in that position, but remained evocative. Their lifted knees were toward him, showing their shapely thighs to their furred clefts. He could concentrate and see through Symbol's illusion powder, but there was no point in rendering her invisible.

Havoc vanished his own clothing and joined them. Gale grabbed his upper section, kissing him as she bore him down on the bed by the force of her breasts. Symbol grabbed his lower section, and straddled him, lifting his stiffening member to fit into her. Then she plumped down on him, taking him all the way in. In a moment he was jetting into her center.

Then they changed places. Symbol took over the kissing, at the same time catching his hands in hers and pressing them against her ample hot breasts. The powder smeared as his fingers slid across her flesh, leaving streaks of translucence through which he could see the bit of liquid in her center that was his ejaculate; her illusion was thorough. Gale addressed his member, massaging it back to full strength, sliding it in, and clenching rhythmically on it. Soon he was jetting again. As a Glamor he could do it, as both women well knew.

Then the two of them hauled him off the bed and lay back on it themselves. "Time's up," Gale said. "Wake us when the half hour is done." Still naked, they closed their eyes, emulating blissful sleep. Symbol's illusion powder was now streaked across Gale as well.

Havoc got back into his clothes, admiring the two forms. Both were beautiful women, and both loved him. What more could he ask? They had delivered exactly what had been offered: very fast, intense sex. But he could see that the constant effort of keeping up with the children had tired them, physically or emotionally. They had been more than ready for just such a break. *Love,* he thought, projecting it so Symbol could receive it too.

Gale smiled and Symbol blushed. That was interesting; Symbol was far more experienced and cynical, but she was the mistress, not the wife, and a sincere expression of love profoundly affected her. As far as he knew, he was the only man who could cause her to do it. Love had unbalanced her equilibrium, perhaps to her embarrassment. Or *had* it? Her flush had to be illusion too, for it would not show in its natural state. So she was probably having an extra bit of fun with him.

He stepped out of the sphere. There were Warp, Weft, and Flame staring in. The little monsters had set up an illusion scene of themselves watching the illusion show, and scrambled to watch the real show by reversing the sphere's reflectivity so that they could see in without being seen from inside. The adults, preoccupied, had not noticed.

"Our secret," he murmured. The three nodded enthusiastically. They knew they'd never get to see another like it if either woman caught on.

Actually the women probably had caught on, but would pretend they hadn't. There were few real secrets kept from Glamors of any age. There was a lot of necessary pretense in this family, as both young and old understood. Rather than keeping secrets, they were letting the children know that real love abounded here, and how it could be expressed.

"So what's your interest," Havoc inquired once they were safely away from the sphere. "A game of checkers?" He conjured a board.

"Ifrits," Flame said immediately.

"The clouds," he agreed, banishing the board. "What's going on with them?"

"Augur and Aura talk with them," Weft said. Her vocabulary and syntax were strengthening day by day. "They're called Ivor and Iva."

"And they have sex with them," Warp said.

That was a surprise. "How do you know that?"

"Minds not shielded," Flame said.

Another surprise. "You can read their minds from a distance?"

"Just the sex," she clarified. "The raw feeling."

So the strength of an orgasm broadcast far enough to be read at a distance, if a telepath was there.

"Negation, dummy," Warp said witheringly to Flame. "Yellow Glamor did it."

A ball of fire formed and hovered menacingly near to him. "I knew that," Flame said.

Time to break this up. "*I* didn't," Havoc said. "What did the Yellow Glamor do?"

"She sent a—feeling to the ifrits," Weft said. "So they could feel the feeling for sex."

"It's a sort of surging, very strong," Warp explained helpfully. "A nice bursting."

"He knows that, dummy," Flame informed him. "He just did it into Symbol."

"And into Mommy," Weft added.

Warp scowled, floating off the ground, magic coalescing.

"Orgasm, that's the feeling," Havoc said quickly. "Yellow's the Glamor of Demons, and the ifrits seem to be demons. But why did she send it?"

"They want to know," Weft said. "Why humans have sex."

"And ifrits don't know," Warp said. "So they did it with Augur and Aura."

"And the Glamor sent them an orgasm," Weft said. She already had the word down.

"So they could understand," Havoc said, getting it straight. "Because ifrits don't reproduce the way humans or animals do, so don't have orgasms."

"But they do have babies," Weft said.

"Little clouds," Warp agreed.

This was interesting indeed. "I think I need to know more about this."

"Tomorrow," Flame said. "Mom's going to make you help."

"We want to play with them," Weft said.

"Play with clouds?"

"When they turn solid," she said.

"I think I'd *better* be there."

"Affirmation," she agreed, laughing as she floated up and kissed his cheek.

After that he was able to get them interested in a ball game. He conjured a spherical balloon, and they batted it about mentally; the one who made it get within another's circle got to pop it in his or her face. It was no-fair to fill it with water just before popping.

Time passed. Symbol appeared. "The ifrits know an eerie amount," she murmured, picking Flame up.

"Aw, they just read Mom's mind," Flame informed her.

Gale soon enough confirmed it, after the children were down and asleep. "The ifrits are making extraordinary progress. Augur and Aura feel they have taken it about as far as they can. Now it's time for the Glamors to educate the ifrits about Glamors. The ifrits have caught on that Glamors can do more than mortals. Since you are now available, you should be there."

"Is it wise to tell them everything?"

"Yellow says they mean no harm. We're learning much about them; they want to learn about us. It's a two way path."

"And the children want to participate."

"Question?"

"To play with the little ifrit clouds, tomorrow, when they turn solid."

Now she hesitated. "We don't know *that* much about the ifrits. They are alien to all our prior experience. Even Yellow is wary."

Havoc realized he had been had. "I gave them a tacit agreement. I didn't realize you had reservations."

She smiled. "Weft played you like a dulcimer. You can't say no to her."

"Or to any female of this family," he agreed.

She kissed him. "Naturally not. Resignation. We'll just have to watch them carefully."

"As if that's possible."

She nodded agreement. Then she took his hand, placed it on her bare bottom, and went to sleep. It was flirtatious teasing, suggesting that he could do what he wanted, but that she had other business. So he gave it a squeeze, left his hand there, and slept himself.

Next morning Havoc and the family went out to the nearby Red Chroma zone with the ifrit party: Augur, Aura, Ini, and Futility. Sure enough, two ifrit clouds coalesced into a very human man and woman, followed by four little clouds that formed into small human forms. The ifrits had come prepared.

Warp, Weft, and Flame ran out to meet the ifrit children. Gale held Symbol back, masking her own nervousness; she wanted the children to feel free. Symbol went to sit at the table someone had conjured and left there, watching the children as if relaxing. Gale set Voila in her bassinet on the table, then took Havoc's arm, evidently determined to participate in the adult business. He felt her tension; she was definitely not easy about the children.

The two adult ifrits came to meet them. The male was handsome, reminiscent of Augur in color and frame; the female was a fetching red Chroma woman.

Augur performed the modest ceremony: "Ifrits, this is the Glamor Havoc, and this is the Glamor Gale. Humans, this is Ivor Ifrit, and this is Iva Ifrit. They accept the names we gave them, having no naming conventions themselves."

Ivor put forth his hand. "Greeting, Havoc." The handshake, like the rest of him, seemed completely human. Meanwhile Iva exchanged a token hug with Gale. Then Ivor nodded to Gale, and Iva came to give Havoc a warm kiss.

"We have explained and shown what we can," Augur said. "But some questions only Glamors can answer."

"Ask," Havoc said. He had been told the ifrits had learned to make completely human forms, but the reality was striking. Iva seemed as if she would make an excellent sexual partner. He would not have known she was not human, had that kiss been all he knew of her.

"One of our number passed by when four humans were caught in the trap of the life eater," Ivor said. "We thought that would be the end of the matter. Then you rescued them. How did you accomplish that?"

"Question," Havoc said. "Was it to learn this that you made contact with us?"

"Affirmation. We realized that you could not be ordinary animals."

"Concurrence. When we learned of the difficulty our companions were in, we went to rescue them. Glamors can not be overcome the way mortal humans can, so the life eater could not hold us."

"Interest. The life eater can not hold ifrits either. But we are demonic rather than living creatures."

Now Iva spoke. "We discovered far more than we might have expected. We did not know of sapience; our normal level is equivalent to that of animals. You have taught us a remarkable thing."

"Sapience is convenient," Havoc said.

Gale nudged him. "Less so in women."

Ivor looked at her. "Confusion."

She laughed. "I was teasing Havoc. Men prefer stupid women; they are easier to seduce."

"Teasing is a form of humor? We do not understand humor."

"Havoc will explain it," Gale said, as she diverted her attention to Symbol. "Problem?"

Havoc paused to see what the problem might be. He was concerned for the welfare of their children too, and intended to be alert. Weft had privately petitioned Symbol.

"The littlest ifrit wants to play with Voila," Symbol said. "But can't reach her."

Havoc saw Gale hesitate only a trace. Then she lifted the bassinet and set it on the ground at the end of the table, where a tiny red ifrit stood. "Introduction," she said. "This is Voila."

"This is Iolo," Weft said. "He's the littlest ifrit."

"Voila can't walk yet," Gale told Iolo. "But you may join her in the bassinet. May I lift you?"

The little ifrit nodded. Gale reached down, put her hands carefully about him, and lifted him into the bassinet. She set him at the end, facing Voila, who was tilted so she could see him. "She can't talk yet either," Weft said. "But she knows what's up." She dashed off to rejoin her own ifrit companion.

Voila sat up farther, by using magic to float her upper section. Magic was easier for her than physical processes. She smiled at the ifrit, who smiled back.

Now Havoc addressed the question. "Humor: something funny. Example: Gale is as smart as I am, but pretends I prefer her stupid so that I can trick her into having sex with me. I don't need to trick her, and we both know it, so it is humorous."

"It is a game," Gale said. "Men generally are more interested in sex than women, but we exaggerate the difference."

Iva spoke to Havoc. "You would find me more sexually appealing if I were stupid?"

"Only in pretense. Your form is already appealing."

"But you should pretend not to know that," Gale said.

Havoc let her carry it while he quietly oriented his attention on the children beyond the table. They seemed to be playing a game of tag, running madly in complicated patterns. They were not confined to the ground; at times they floated. It was apparent that the ifrits could not do that in solid form, so they reverted to cloud form. Now the little Glamors were flying around the small clouds, zooming close, until tagged by an extended vapor extension. It seemed to be working out.

He glanced at the bassinet, and saw Iolo doing the same. As a cloud he surrounded Voila, who seemed unconcerned. Evidently they were communication in their fashions.

Ivor saw the direction of Havoc's glance. "Your children have named ours," he said. "We do not use names in our native state. They are Ilona, Igor, and Imre."

This was interesting. "You are in mental touch with your children?"

"It is not your telepathy," Iva said. "We do not practice that. One of our adult number surrounds us, as you know, to facilitate contact. She keeps us current."

Havoc remembered that a thin veil of ifrit substance surrounded them, extending to the end of the table but not beyond. That left the bassinet and the open area clear for the children. "I think we are not properly conveying the nature of humor. Perhaps we will come across a clearer example in the course of further dialogue. Meanwhile, I am interested in the nature of your mental state. I gather that you are sapient in your cloud form, but not in your solid form."

"Agreement," Ivor said. "Normally we are not sapient in either form, but as clouds we have the capacity to develop it, and have done so with human guidance."

Ini and Futility were standing behind Havoc, making notes. Now Ini spoke. "I use the analogy of the fabled ancient computers of Earth, which were machines capable of great storage and manipulation of information, but which were not conscious or intelligent in themselves. The ifrits in their cloud state may be considered as computers with the added quality of awareness. Their solid forms are normally used only for crossing between Chroma zones, or as defense against certain threats, so lack capacity for sapience in themselves."

"Appreciation," Havoc said. "So the clouds are the minds, and the solid forms are mere bodies."

"Accuracy," Iva said. "All of us, including the children, have access to the common store of information and awareness. However, the children lack the substance to utilize all of it."

"So we could not be having this dialogue, were the cloud ifrit not surrounding us," Havoc said.

"Correct," Ivor said. Indeed, it did not seem to make much difference which one of them spoke. "Our solid bodies are merely enabling us to relate to you who are normally solid. We regret the clumsiness of this interchange."

"But we are trying to relate to you as effectively as is feasible," Iva said. "We are distinct entities. I approached Augur for sex, to facilitate his positive impression, and will do the same with you if you wish."

"Gale will surely veto that," Havoc said, smiling. "She's a jealous female."

Symbol, at the end of the table, laughed.

Iva picked right up on it. "Humor? This relates to your interactions with each other?"

"Agreement," Gale said. "I am Havoc's wife. He and I and the four children are a family. We love each other. Symbol is his mistress. She provides him with extra sex. I am not jealous."

Havoc nodded. "And, ironically, my mistress spends more time with the children than with me. So I remain sexually starved."

Iva gave him a direct look. "Is this an invitation?"

Gale nudged him. "Oh, go and do it with her, Havoc. You know you want to. She's an entirely new crafted woman, like a golem."

And he did want to, and not merely because golems could be

remarkable sexual partners. The fact that Iva was completely inhuman in essence made her doubly intriguing. "Agreement."

"There is a private place," Iva said, standing.

Why not? Havoc stood. "Brief parting."

"We'll come after you if it is not brief," Gale said with mock severity.

They went to the glade that clearly had been prepared for this activity. "You travel with Symbol?" she inquired as she removed her clothing.

"Sometimes." He did the same.

"No fault."

He caught on. "Negation. My relationship with Symbol is not no fault. She is my permanent mistress, and she loves me. With you it will be no fault."

"Love," she said. "This is another difficult concept."

"More difficult than humor, perhaps," he agreed. "To truly understand love, you must experience it."

"Paradox: we must experience it to understand it, but do not know how to experience it until we understand it."

He laughed. "I think some of our intellectual emotional concepts are as awkward for you as becoming clouds would be for us."

"If you became clouds, we could show you how to become clouds. Is this paradox parallel?"

"Likely." He paused. "Question: is your interest sexual or intellectual?"

"Intellectual. Sex is a means to relate, to induce you to share more intellectual insights. However, one thing we have been shown is the pleasure of sex. I would like to experience that pleasure again."

"Can you receive telepathy?"

"We can receive the raw feeling. We are unable to send such feeling in the manner you can."

"Then I will send my pleasure to you, as I experience it. This will be male pleasure rather than female pleasure, however."

"Acceptance."

Greeting. It was Swale.

"Pause," Havoc said. "I have a visitor."

"I do not perceive this person."

"It is Swale, the succubus. A sexual spirit. I am not sure the equivalent exists on this planet."

"Not that we know of," Iva agreed. "Not among ifrits."

I could show her.

That intrigued him. "Swale could enter your body and perhaps provide you with sexual feeling. Would that be of interest to you?"

"Agreement, if it brings the pleasure."

It will.

"Then accept Swale's infusion of your body. She will enter the female channel you have made to enable sexual participation, and spread out from there. If you wish her to depart, think that thought to her, and she will go. Amenable?"

"Amenable."

Havoc waited a moment. Nothing happened. Then Swale returned. *She has no womb.*

Oh. "You must craft a new place, for the succubus to occupy," Havoc said.

There was further dialogue, and it seemed that the ifrit did a partial vaporization and reformation, internally. In due course Swale entered it.

Iva looked curious, then surprised. "It is like sex, but there is no man."

"There is Swale."

Iva's expression changed. "Suddenly I desire sex in a way I did not before. Request: perform it immediately."

They were both standing naked. He took her in his arms and kissed her. She returned the kiss with surprising competence. He stroked her bare bottom. She pressed her breasts against him. He recognized schooled emulation of passion, having experienced it often enough with Futility, but this was not that. Swale was imbuing her with the reality.

They lay on the mat. She was quiveringly eager, but at the same time looking surprised. He penetrated her and thrust, and she met it with her own thrust, squeezing his member inside. She was certainly good at this. He suspected it was mostly the information stored in the surrounding cloud ifrit, played back for his benefit, but now there was an added urgency. Swale had that effect on a woman. He climaxed, and sent the feeling to her.

"No need!" she gasped. "I am feeling it from myself."

Her schooled cooperation had became genuine, thanks to the succubus. She writhed and groaned, transported by the intensity of the orgasm. Her internal pulses became raggedly powerful. That heightened his own feeling. They writhed together, and slowly subsided, falling apart.

"Forget intellectual," she said. "I like this."

But he felt that once was enough. He held her and moved on to the intellectual. "Human beings find pleasure with each other in this manner. But love is much more." He had an idea. "How do you feel about your children?"

"They are of our substance. We guide them and protect them and would regret their loss."

That wasn't sufficient. Evidently ifrits did not experience family love either. "It may be that intense emotion is not natural to you."

"Idea: can you project love similarly? Swale is with me, but this she lacks."

That might be worthwhile. "Here is my feeling for Gale." He projected the encompassing love he had for his beloved.

"Oh, I wish I were she!" He wasn't sure whether it was ifrit or succubus speaking.

Had he gone too far? He shut off the projection. "Regret if I tease you."

"Negation!" She turned to him. "Plea: to kiss you before it fades."

How could he refuse? "Granted."

She lay against him and kissed him. This time it was not emulation; she was truly passionate. She loved him with the echo of his own love for Gale. Then he felt her tears. She knew she could not keep this feeling.

"I never cried before," Iva said as the tears evaporated and returned to her face as tiny clouds.

"Love is joy and pain."

"Agreement." Then she added: "Swale has departed, but still I feel it."

"You learned that pattern from her."

"Of sex, yes. Of love, from you. Swale departed then, with regret. I do not understand why."

Because she did not want to love him as he loved Gale. That was a likely emotional conflict of interest. But Havoc decided not to explain that.

They got up and dressed. Havoc was about to say something supportive about love and its universality among the human kind.

Then Symbol screamed.

Havoc conjured himself to her side. She was peering down into the bassinet where Voila lay. "She's evaporating!" Symbol exclaimed.

Indeed, the top of the baby's head had dissipated into mist. Horrified, Havoc was for the moment helpless.

⁓⁓

Gale leaped up in alarm as Symbol screamed. The woman was normally unshakable; this had to be disaster. Symbol was staring into the bassinet. Even as Gale looked there, Havoc appeared beside them.

Their baby was dissolving into vapor.

"She's turning ifrit!" Weft exclaimed as she appeared.

But the process was already reversing. The vapor coalesced, and soon Voila's head was complete. She smiled at them. Iolo, the ifrit baby boy, hovered as a little cloud at the foot of the girl's bed.

"Observation," Ivor said. "Humans *can* assume cloud form."

Gale looked at Havoc, then at Symbol. That was it: the baby had been in the process of joining her ifrit companion. She had hastily reversed the process when the commotion started. In fact, she had probably reversed it just before the commotion, having sensed it coming, but the process was slow.

"I was discussing it with Iva," Havoc said. "I compared the feeling of love to the ability to become a cloud: you need to experience it to understand it."

"Conjecture," Ini said. "The cloud ifrit relayed that comparison to the others, including little Iolo, who shared it with Voila. She decided to try it."

"And didn't know it was impossible," Symbol said. "Apology for overreacting."

"Needless," Gale and Havoc said together.

"Suggestion," Ivor said as Iva walked toward them from the forest. "Allow her to proceed with the transformation. We can guide her through Iolo, once she starts."

Gale felt a surge of alarm and hope. "But is it safe?"

"She did reverse it just now," Havoc reminded her.

Gale made a sudden decision. "Permission," she told Voila. "Brief." She augmented the words with strong clear thoughts. Telepathy made sonic communication unnecessary; the baby understood her perfectly.

I hope that's wise, Swale thought. She had rejoined Gale before Havoc finished with Iva, avoiding the love emotion.

Voila immediately resumed conversion. Her head dissolved into vapor, followed by the rest of her little body. Soon her nightie and diaper lay empty in the bassinet. She was all cloud.

The Iolo cloud lifted and floated toward the Voila cloud. He extended a tiny pseudopod of vapor and touched her. Then both clouds rose higher, floating out of the bassinet.

"She is intrigued," Iva said. "We are in touch."

"You can communicate directly with Voila?" Gale asked, restraining her extreme nervousness.

"Indirectly," Iva said. "She is touching Iolo, and we are touching Iolo. Clouds lack your telepathy, unfortunately." She met Gale's gaze with a peculiar intensity.

I sent her love of you, Havoc thought.

Oh. "Keep her safe."

"May we do it too?" Weft asked. The other children were here as well, having been distracted by the more interesting phenomenon.

The other children could do it? "Not yet," Gale said. "We must be sure of Voila first."

"Aww." But she accepted it, knowing that it was a reasonable stipulation.

"Now return," Gale said. This was the key: could Voila resume her natural form, after entirely dissolving and floating away?

The two small clouds floated slowly back to the bassinet. There was no wind; they had their own propulsion. They settled at either end of the bassinet and coalesced. In time they became Voila and Iolo, seemingly the same as before.

Gale reached in and picked Voila up, checking her mentally. She was the same! The baby nudged Gale's bosom, hungry. Gale bared a breast and nursed her.

Iolo, deprived of his companion, looked out of sorts. Symbol reached in and picked him up. He nuzzled her bosom, copying Voila. Symbol glanced at Gale, who made a trace nod. Symbol opened her shirt and let Iolo nurse. Probably he would not be able to assimilate human milk, or any physical substance, but the point was the parallel.

Voila sank into sleep after nursing, and Gale put her back in the bassinet. Iolo, seeing that, emulated it, and Symbol set him down beside Voila. Did ifrits sleep? Did it matter? The children were certainly getting along.

Gale turned to the children, who had been waiting with remarkable patience for them. The other three ifrits, Ilona, Igor, and Imre, were standing with them in solid form. "One hour. Then you're through with clouds for today. Be back here, solid." She remained keenly uncertain about this weird transformation, but knew they would be trying it on their own if she did not let them do it while supervised.

They ran to the center of the field and started in. She knew they were telepathically linking to their ifrit opposites, able to read their technique, following their slow conversions. Voila had demonstrated that it was possible, surprising them all; now the others were determined to do it.

"Amazement," Havoc murmured.

"Our children keep surprising us," she said. That was a fair understatement, this time. They were becoming conscious clouds!

"We are pleased that the children are relating well," Iva said. "We have not before encountered an animal species capable of cloud formation."

"We assume this is because you are Glamors," Ivor said. "We understand most animals, but not Glamors."

Gale glanced at Havoc, who tackled it. "On our native world of Charm, all creatures and plants can do many kinds of magic within their Chroma zones, as is the case here. A few become Glamors, who can do magic anywhere, regardless of Chroma. Because we are not limited to our Chroma zones, our power is far more comprehensive, and we are able to take it farther. Telepathy and teleportation are parts of it. We are also largely invulnerable to physical damage, and have special powers of perception and sex." He glanced across the field toward the children. "And, it seems, cloud formation."

However, the children seemed to be having trouble. The ifrits were changing, but the humans were not. They were eager, but the transformation was not occurring. What Voila had accomplished so readily seemed to be more of a challenge for the older ones.

"They are too accustomed to solid form," Ivor said. "They are unable to release it."

Gale was relieved. It would be far easier to keep track on one child with such an ability to change, than four. She knew the children would be disappointed, but they hardly appreciated the enormity of such a thing.

But she had to let them have their hour, so she tried to distract herself. "The analogy of a fabled ancient computer has been used," she said. "Is this really the way it is in cloud form?"

"Imperfect," Ivor said. "But not irrelevant. Our substance functions best when properly spaced. In natural cloud form we can sense, assimilate, and understand. We are unable to do very much of this in solid form, and marvel that you do."

Havoc nodded. "Our physical forms have evolved for a long time. They are complete in themselves. Just as we can't change into clouds and function, you can't suddenly make solid forms with the infinitely fine detail necessary to live fully, let alone achieve sapience."

"Conjecture," Iva said. "We are able to emulate sapience by utilizing liaison with our cloud form. Could you achieve sapient cloud form if you maintained telepathic connection with one of your number in solid form?"

"Doubt," Havoc said. "If our children are already too set in solidity to change, surely it is well beyond adult capacity."

Gale was glad to agree. "We do well enough in our present forms; we do not need to borrow yours."

"Unfortunate," Ivor said. "In cloud form you could truly discover our full nature."

Gale shrugged. "That may be a necessary sacrifice."

"Observe Warp," Symbol murmured.

They looked. Warp was floating, as he had always done. Now he was fuzzing a bit, as if developing a coating of mist. Was he discovering how to make the change? Gale wasn't sure whether to hope for his success or failure.

But after a time Warp settled back to the ground wholly solid, defeated. He was in tears.

Gale got up, sending a thought. *Here, Warp.*

He appeared in her lifted arms. She stepped back to recover her balance; his arrival had been with a thunk, as he was not yet perfect on teleportation. That was why she had stood. He buried his face in her shoulder while she held him comfortingly close and patted his back.

Weft appeared. "No fair," she said. "He's getting cuddled."

Havoc beckoned her, and she jumped to his arms without passing through the intervening space.

"Hey!" Flame protested.

Symbol took her. Theoretically there were no favorites, but there did seem to be associations.

The three ifrit children considered that, finding themselves abruptly left out. "Take them," Gale murmured to Iva. "They are learning human ways."

Iva glanced at Igor, and he walked to her, and she picked him up. Ilona went to Ivor. That left Imre.

"Here," Aura said. He went to her, and she held him. Their colors did not match, as she was blue and he was red, but the correspondence was that she was a woman. Apart from Symbol with Flame, the women held male children and the men held female children.

"Not everything works the first time," Gale said. "Voila showed that a human being can become a cloud, and resume normal form. I suspect the other children can do it too, if they can just figure out how."

"Ours are trying to show them," Ivor said. "But it seems that what works for ifrits does not necessarily work for humans."

"Voila found the key, whatever it is," Gale agreed.

Warp lifted his head. "Make her show us!"

Gale smiled. "Dear, I can't *make* her do anything. She's a Glamor."

"We shouldn'ta made her one!"

"Then no one would know how to become a cloud."

He considered that. "Make her want to."

Havoc laughed. "He's got you, Gale. You can do that."

"Not necessarily. Voila has a cute little mind of her own, and she anticipates me."

"'Cause she sees what's next," Weft said. "Maybe that's why she knew how to turn cloud."

"Precognition is not the same as ability," Havoc reminded her.

Flame chimed in, from Symbol's embrace. "She sees what's next, and does it. If we could see, we could do."

Havoc nodded. "That may be it. How is it that you three can't precog too?"

All three children frowned with concentration, and the three little ifrits did the same. "We don't know," Weft said. "We just can't."

"Specialization is one thing," Havoc said. "Adults do it too. But all Glamors can do what other Glamors can, when they try."

"Can *you* precog?" Weft demanded.

Havoc paused. "Got me there," he admitted.

Pleased with her spot victory, Weft kissed him on the neck. She wasn't yet big enough to reach for more effective territory without floating, but she would surely achieve it soon enough.

Got all of you, Swale thought.

Gale had not thought about it this way before, but this could be significant. How could Voila have a talent no other Glamor shared? That was not the Glamor way.

"If she can do one unique thing," Ini said, "she may be able to do another."

"Nonsense," Futility said, surprising them all. "The rest of you could precog if you just got the trick of it. You're probably doing it already, without knowing it."

From out of the mouths of babes... The succubus had never had a lot of use for that woman.

Gale thought of the way she and Havoc emulated the warnings of the dragon seeds. How could they—or the seeds—know a mistake, without possessing an element of precognition? Clairvoyance might account for it, but the seeds had seemed to know the future to a degree. They couldn't define it, but knew it. Voila's talent could be similar.

"Let's ponder today, and try again tomorrow," Havoc said.

"Okay," Weft agreed, as if he had been speaking to her alone.

"We'll meet again tomorrow," Gale said to Ivor as she set Warp in the table. Warp, recovered, promptly floated down to rejoin the other children.

The ifrit children disengaged and dissolved into clouds, including tiny Iolo, who really hadn't been sleeping. Then Ivor and Iva followed and floated away. Gale felt they had had quite enough experience for a single day.

Evidently the children agreed, because they ate supper, cleaned up, and went to sleep with minimal fussing. Gale got several uninterrupted hours with Havoc. After satisfying his normal passion, with Swale's help, because of her distraction, she lay beside him and talked.

"Question: can the children become clouds, and is it wise if they do?"

"Privacy."

His mind was closed. He surely had a serious concern, as did she. "Where?"

"Home."

A really serious concern. "Briefly," she agreed.

They held hands and transported themselves between worlds, to their crater mountain retreat, used only intermittently the past year.

They landed on their bed, still naked from their lovemaking. Now she was aware of his tension, evoked by her question. "Speak."

"The children must not become clouds. We must find a way to divert any such effort."

I will check with Ennui and Aspect, Swale thought, politely getting out of the way.

Gale hardly noticed. "But I already told them they could try it tomorrow, and you agreed."

"We were with the ifrits. I had to conceal my disquiet. They are alien creatures; we do not know their real motives."

"And so you let me go ahead and set it up—and now I have to renege?" she asked sharply.

"You should have known not to set it up."

"How—with you encouraging it?"

"Common sense."

She was irked. "You started it. You were making out with Iva, discussing how humans could become clouds."

"I had to, to mask my concern."

"You didn't have to have sex with her!"

"You told me to."

"And you were all too willing. She's got a shape; that's all that counts, isn't it, for a man?"

"What one ifrit knows, they all know. I couldn't hold back without betraying my real thought."

"So you sent her your great orgasm."

"And my love for you."

Gale was hurt. "That's not supposed to be for others!"

That made him pause. "Apology."

"Apology, hell! You shouldn't have done it!"

Symbol appeared. She was in tears. "Please. I can't stand it when you fight. I love you both."

That made them both pause. Symbol was a tough, experienced woman; Gale had never seen her cry.

"Apology," Gale said, feeling her own tears. "I withdraw my jealousy."

"I withdraw my accusation," Havoc said, similarly chastened. "It was unreasonable to expect you to doubt me."

"Gratitude," Symbol said.

But now, with their quarrel abated, other questions occurred. "How came you here?" Havoc demanded of Symbol.

"And who is watching the children?" Gale added.

"The Red Glamor brought me, and returned to watch the children. She will keep them asleep for the duration."

"So our private dialogue is Glamor business?" Havoc asked sharply.

"The ifrits are Glamor business," Symbol replied. "It is too important to risk by internal strife."

So they had acted to break it up. Perhaps that was just as well. "Have the Glamors thought about the risk of allowing our children to become clouds?" Gale asked her.

"Answer: you know we can't stop them from trying, so we'd better encourage them to do it while we watch. Then if they fail, we won't be to blame."

"And if they do it, and something goes wrong?"

"We have to see that it doesn't."

"How?"

"By developing better precog," Havoc said.

That was so obvious in sudden retrospect that she kissed him. "Can we?"

"Conjecture: by studying Voila?"

The children would study her to learn cloud formation. The adults could study her to learn precognition. It made perfect madcap sense. Thrilled with the idea, she decided to share her pleasure with Havoc.

"I must reluctantly satisfy your burgeoning male passion again."

"Don't forget me when you return to Counter Charm," Symbol said, discreetly leaving the chamber.

He was always pleased when she expressed interest in sex with him, however obscurely. "Your turn," he murmured as he embraced her.

"My turn," she agreed, and proceeded to address him and work herself into a fine climax, which she broadcast to him.

Weft appeared beside their bed. "Will you two cut out the mushy stuff?" she demanded. "We're trying to sleep."

They laughed as the child disappeared. "The little mischief tracks our minds for unwonted pleasure," Havoc said.

"We'd better let her sleep."

Then they stared at each other. "This is Charm," Havoc said.

"She made the jump between planets alone!"

"We'd better get back to Counter Charm." He looked as shaken as she felt.

They did, not forgetting Symbol, who went off to be with the children. They settled back in their bed. "I am sorry we quarreled," Gale said.

"And glad we made up."

"Agreement!"

"In future, let's make up without quarreling."

"Agreement!" she repeated.

As she faded out, Gale reflected on how much their lives had changed in the past three years. They had gone from innocent rustic villagers to king and queen, become Glamors, assembled a full four child family, and now were on another planet, interacting with alien sapience. How much wilder could it get?

Havoc squeezed her hand. "All is meaningless, without you."

"Stop trying to seduce me again!" She was overflowing with love for him.

"Never." And they slept, bathed in love.

Somewhere along the way, Gale realized that she had forgotten Swale. Well, the succubus could make her own way back when she was ready.

In the morning the children were eager to return to the Red Chroma zone. So was Gale. The riddle of cloud formation had possessed her imagination; it was a challenge to be overcome.

"How do you do it, Voila?" she asked rhetorically as she nursed the baby.

To her surprise, Voila responded with a thought, showing how she used a process like the recent-past review to review the recent future. Normally what was about to happen didn't matter, as it was routine, but sometimes it made a difference. She lacked the mind to reason it out, but recognized coming pain, discomfort, or frustration when it loomed, and fussed in response. That usually abated it.

Gale emulated the process, and suddenly she was aware of the recent future. It was there, just ahead, like a path through a forest, clear close up, but curving out of sight in the near distance. It was dull, containing only activity she already knew about, but she knew with the magic sensing that it was a true vision rather than conjecture. Should anything untoward occur, she would probably know it in time to avoid it. She was unable to see far ahead when she tried; the path curved in multiple directions simultaneously, losing definition. She could focus on any one aspect, and it clarified somewhat, but remained devious. The forks did not remain separate; they spread, crossed, merged, fudged, and disappeared with seeming randomness. This was definitely a limited vision.

Gale fixed the process in her mind, so that she would never lose it. The clear vision ahead was brief, only a few seconds, but that could make an enormous difference in some cases. She wanted not only to have it, but to share it with Havoc and the other Glamors.

"Thank you, Voila," she said. "I love you."

The baby knew it. She continued to nurse contentedly.

Distracted by the half hectic morning routine of conjuring breakfast and seeing to the children, even with Symbol's considerable and invaluable help, Gale almost missed the first useful manifestation of the new talent. Her left middle toe gave a twinge. She eased the forward power of her leg and set her foot down slightly short, distorting her balance. Why had she done that?

Then she saw the wooden block on the ground. It was one of the ones the children played with, somehow strayed from its companions. Her foot landed just short of it. Had she continued that step normally, her middle toe would have struck the block with some force. Probably not enough to injure it, but enough to make it hurt for a moment. Stubbed toes were never fun, even for Glamors.

The awareness of the recent future had made the toe twinge before it was hurt, and she had reacted just enough to spare it that pain. Just as Voila reacted to bad things before they hurt her. The talent had worked.

"Thank you, Voila," she repeated, though the baby was sleeping in her bassinet at the moment.

At breakfast she shared the news with the other Glamors, explaining how she had received it from her baby and had the early proof of it. She opened her mind to them, so that they could read the process directly.

They were interested; none of them had known of this Glamor ability, but soon verified it. Green conjured a green metallic token, emulating one of the coins of ancient Earth, with a picture of a head on one side and a tail on the other. He flipped it, and others called out the side that was about to be upright when it came to rest on the table.

Soon they were completely accurate. They could fathom the recent future.

They also verified its limitation. More than a few seconds ahead, the overlaying and fudging paths became too tangled to discern accurately and were useless. But close up the process was very nice.

"Appreciation," Red said for them all. "Amazement that a baby discovered what we did not."

She is a Glamor, the Brown Glamor thought.

"Our thinking may have become stultified," Green said. "We have not been stretching our boundaries sufficiently."

"And we should," Yellow said.

"And shall," Black said.

"Another potential interest," Gale said. "Today the children discover whether they can become clouds like those of the ifrits. It will be preceded by a negotiation."

"Question," Translucent said.

"Situation: Voila knows how to do it, having demonstrated it yesterday. The other children do not. They will bargain with her to obtain the information. Then they will try it themselves."

"Voila," Red said. "Who showed us the recent future."

"Agreement." The point had been made: this was more than child's play.

We are aware of your trepidation, the Brown Glamor thought. *But this exploration seems necessary. We will participate.*

That comforted Gale. The other Glamors had evidently discussed the matter more temperately than she and Havoc had.

They went out to the Red Chroma zone. The ifrits were there, already condensed to human forms. The human children ran to join their ifrit counterparts. Gale wondered whether it was coincidence that each human/ifrit pair consisted of one male and one female. Did the ifrits really have genders, or had they assumed them to relate to the humans? Were they truly as friendly as they seemed? There was an enormous amount they still didn't really know about the ifrits. That prevented her from being entirely easy.

Gale sat at the table, setting Voila's bassinet on top. The children clustered around. "Situation," she announced. "Voila knows how to assume cloud form and return. The other children wish to learn how. Voila will surely share her information, but will need to be persuaded. She will want something in return."

The human children nodded. *They know about bargaining.*

"However, Voila is only three months old. She lacks the experience and information to bargain effectively on her own. Therefore she will need an adult assistant, a second, a representative, or advisor. A person who will bargain effectively on her behalf."

"No fair," Warp protested. "We can't argue against grownups."

"Then perhaps you should have representation too," Gale said evenly. "Whom do you want?"

"Daddy," Weft said.

"Mommy," Warp said.

Gale was taken aback. "I'm not sure we are appropriate. We are your parents, and dare not favor one over another."

All three children burst out laughing. But they did make new choices. "Black Glamor," Warp said.

The Black Glamor appeared. "Humor?"

"Serious," Warp said, laughing.

He shrugged. "Acceptance."

"Yellow," Weft said.

Now the Yellow Glamor appeared, similarly surprised. "Acceptance."

"Red," Flame said.

The Red Glamor appeared. "Comprehension: we match your colors of hair."

The children burst into another round of laughter. "Agreement," Weft said. "But you must really do it."

"Acceptance."

"Now who for Voila?" Gale asked.

"Brown!" the three said together.

The Brown Dragon Glamor appeared. *Acceptance.*

Gale looked at Voila. "Is this your wish?"

The baby smiled.

"So be it," Gale said. "I leave the matter to you."

"Request," Ivor said. "We are not apt at your mind communication. May we have a verbal translation?"

"Affirmation," the Blue Glamor said. "I will speak Brown's thoughts." She paused. "Herewith: Voila requires full interaction with her three older siblings, and the young ifrits. Also training in all the Glamor abilities the others have mastered."

"Outrage!" Red exclaimed. "She is too young to participate in many of their activities at this time, and would merely hinder them without benefit to herself."

"Also," Black said, "Voila proffers only one ability. That warrants a return of only one ability."

"Compromise," Yellow suggested. "One per child."

The Brown Glamor hesitated, telepathically consulting with his client. "Agreement," the Blue Glamor said.

"Compromise," Yellow said again. "Full participation in all interplay involving the young ifrits. Partial participation in straight sibling play, as approved by their parents."

Again a pause. "Agreement."

Gale looked around. "Do we have a deal?"

"Agreement," the three said together.

"Then so be it." Gale looked at Voila. "Now you may show them how to form clouds."

"Here is the secret," Blue said. "You must go to your constituencies. That is, the forms of life you represent as Glamors. They give you Glamor power, and can give you this. You have but to request it from them."

"Surprise," Gale said. "Voila did that?"

"She wished to become a cloud. The amoeba supported her. They understand individualism on the cellular level."

"Individual cells!" Havoc exclaimed. "That's what forms the clouds."

"Agreement," Iva said. "We are conglomerations of many. We link to form larger entities for convenience."

Gale realized that this had been obvious, had they but looked at it that way. Fog was a collection of water particles; the ifrits were collections of demon particles. To become sentient clouds, humans needed to fragment into their component cells.

"Still," Havoc said, "There needs to be guidance, to maintain connection between the cells. We must study Voila to find that way."

Voila, satisfied with the deal, was already starting to sublimate. Her body dissolved into mist, forming a cloud above the bassinet.

The three other children protested. "Hey, wait for us!" Warp cried.

"Do it slowly," Weft agreed.

Slow. It was the Brown Glamor's thought, guiding Voila. The Dragon could think in words to communicate with humans, but was using concepts now, and that was registering better with the baby.

Voila's body coalesced, then dissolved again, more slowly.

"Like fungus spores!" Warp exclaimed.

"Like floating bacteria," Weft said.

"Separate viruses," Flame said.

They were going to their constituencies, and getting it. Gale glanced at Havoc. She knew he distrusted this, but he showed no sign of it. He loved the children, as she did, and was concerned for their safely. Yet if this conversion were possible, it was best that it be done here and now, with everyone watching, as Symbol had said.

Warp began to fuzz. A twisting streamer of vapor rose from the top of his head. Then his hair dissolved. He was doing it.

Gale kept her voice even. "Good, Warp."

"Good, Weft," Havoc said. Weft's hands were misting.

"Don't hurry it, Flame," Symbol said. "Do it slow and right."

The pace of conversion increased as they got the hang of it. Their extremities vaporized, then their torsos. Soon Warp was fully cloud, floating clear, with Weft not far behind. Flame was last, but definitely doing it.

The three small clouds were joined by the true ifrit clouds. The six of them floated after the two smaller clouds that were Voila and Iolo. They had done it.

Havoc took her hand. This was nominally his reassurance for her, but she felt his tension. He was worried that they would not be able to return. She squeezed his fingers. Voila had returned, and they were following her.

The clouds played for some time, while all the Glamors watched. Then the clouds drifted back, following the smallest. Voila and Iolo condensed, slowly, and so did the others. Gale fought to prevent herself from snatching Voila, picking her up carefully. The baby nursed, satisfied.

"That was great!" Warp exclaimed. "We talked with Ilka."

"Question?" Gale asked carefully.

"She's the co—co—"

"Coordinator," Ivo said. "The one of us who remains in natural form, enabling us to relate in solid form."

"She's nice," Flame said. "She knows everything."

Havoc picked up Weft, and Symbol took Flame. Gale knew they were quietly checking to be sure the children were as they had been before. Warp seemed to be his normal boisterous self.

The transformation seemed to have been a success. Gale relaxed at last.

Her gaze fell on her own left hand. She froze.

The hand was dissolving into mist.

She clamped down on her threatening scream. She had been following the children too closely. She didn't want to make a scene. *Havoc!*

He responded immediately, understanding. *Reverse the process.*

That was of course the answer. She focused on her hand, willing it to be solid again. The mist swirled down around it, condensing. In a moment the hand was whole again.

She hoped no one else had noticed.

☙❧

Havoc had seen Gale's hand, and been uncertain how to alert her without making a scene neither of them wanted. Then she saw it herself, and took care of it.

Now they knew: adults could do it too.

Havoc set Weft down, and she ran to join the others for one of Symbol's pudding snacks. He did love her, as he loved them all. He suspected that she had actually picked him as favorite, rather than the other way around, because there were limits to the influence the adults could wield. The children had somehow parceled out the choices among themselves, perhaps in a compromise to avoid quarreling. They were children, but they were also Glamors, and that made them formidable. The way Weft had visited them at the Charm hideout—if she had intended to astonish them, she had succeeded. At this point they could not be restrained; only their returning love and respect for the adults in their lives kept them in line.

Gale and Symbol had done most of that, loving and disciplining the children with unceasing vigilance and competence. He had expected it of Gale, who was a loving person; hard-nosed Symbol had been a surprise. But her commitment could not be questioned; he trusted the lives of his children in her hands. She had become a mother, and was indispensable. He suspected that this development had surprised her as much as him; she had never craved conventional motherhood and family. Of course it made her as sexually scarce as Gale, because of the constant demands of the children; the two together did not amount to what either one alone had been before. They had to make an effort to be with him, scheduling trysts. But how could he begrudge that? They were doing a job no other women could do.

And now they knew that Gale could turn cloud, if she chose to. She associated so closely with the children that she had picked up the technique and started to do it unconsciously. Was that another breakthrough—or a danger?

"The venture seems to have been successful," Iva said.

That reminded him of the ifrit female. He did not fully trust the ifrits, not because of any apparent fault in them or their motives, but because they *were* alien entities whose nature and motives were bound to be substantially different from human ones. He would have much preferred to mix children at a later time, once the ifrits were better understood. Sex with Iva had been fine, but that had required far less trust than needed for children to become clouds. "Agreement."

"I was concerned that there could be a problem."

She was concerned? "Such transformation is normal for ifrits."

"We wish to relate well with you. A problem with a child would spoil that."

"Concurrence." He had to recognize that the children had succeeded; the ifrits had not done them any harm. Still, he distrusted this. He wished he could get truly into the mind of an ifrit, to comprehend its ultimate nature. Then perhaps he could really trust them.

"You remain tense. Have I offended you?"

The ifrits were surprisingly swift to pick up on human nuances. Havoc suspected that they had no concept of offense in their natural state. "Negation."

"There is other reason?"

What should he tell her? That Gale had started to become a cloud herself? No, that was best kept private until they had a better notion of the potential. That she had been jealous of his sharing his feeling of love with the ifrit? Admitting that probably would not be wise; were the ifrit a human female, she could be angling for Havoc's further favor, and that would be reason for Gale's concern. Ini and Futility knew their places, in this respect, and would never cause him embarrassment. But Iva—what better way to weaken human unity than to alienate his affection for Gale? That would be impossible to accomplish, but Iva would not know that. That whole subject was best avoided.

He decided on the straight truth. "We do not know you ifrits well. I am wary of exposing my children to the power of beings we do not fully understand."

"Affirmation!" she said with surprising vehemence. "Ivor did not want us to bring ours, but I felt it was the most effective way to relate."

"You distrust humans," he said, wondering whether she was serious, or merely trying to emulate a human concern.

"We do not know humans," she said, qualifying it exactly as he had. "Your ways differ from ours, and you are frighteningly intelligent. If your private motives are hostile, we could be in peril."

"Concurrence. We are necessarily cautious."

"We are trying to understand you in every way possible. We are handicapped by having to use these clumsy solid forms. We wish you could understand us completely, too."

"I would have to turn cloud to do that," he said, smiling.

"Agreement."

He had not been serious. Now he wondered. "Could it be possible?"

"Can you do what your children can?"

Decision came in a flash. No need to hide Gale's ability if he tackled it himself. *Gale—I want to turn cloud.*

Gale was with the children. She did not look at him, so as not to reveal that they were in telepathic communication. *Iva stays solid.* But she was relieved that he was trying it first; her feeling imbued her thought. They both knew that one of them had to do it, now that they knew it was possible.

She was not completely serious, but it seemed like a good idea. "I will make the attempt," he said. "I ask you to remain here, to relay news of me if I succeed."

"Agreement. Ilka is in touch; otherwise I would not be at sapient level. She will guide you."

Havoc communed with his constituency, the trees and plants. *Help me.*

They helped. They understood pollen, which could float in its myriads on the currents of the air, each unit capable of making a full new plant of its kind. Clouds of many types of pollen mixed, yet each remained true to its own nature.

Havoc concentrated on his individual cells, willing them to separate, to become isolated entities. But they clung to their positions in his body, refusing to let go. It wasn't working.

Then Gale brought Voila in the bassinet. "She wants to help."

The baby started to vaporize. Havoc attuned to her telepathically, tracing how she did it. She was in touch with the amoeba, and with the ifrits; both melded into a translation.

Havoc emulated her connections—and saw the fuzz of vapor before his face. He was doing it!

He watched as the vapor thickened. Then he couldn't see it any more; his eyes were going. He was blind. He suppressed his momentary panic and continued; there had to be a way to see in cloud form.

Feel. It was Voila's feeling, telling him to feel.

He tried to feel, and became aware of the touch of her vapor. He could tell its nature and identity by its feel. He was also aware of the temperature of the air. And yes, there were spores in it, and pollen, and he knew its humidity and pressure. There were smells too, of animals and plants. He could neither see nor hear, but he knew much about the air he floated in.

Another vapor tendril touched him. *Ilka.* It wasn't telepathy, just awareness of her identity: the cloud ifrit.

Voila? He thought, concerned.

Coalesced, Ilka thought. *I will guide you now.*

That was probably just as well. *I know things about the air, but my normal senses are gone.*

Ours are better for this form. Then she showed him how to use the vapor senses he had. Pressure gradients of the air allowed him to know and choose his level of floating. Humidity and temperature varied near different types of vegetation, because trees gave off cooling moisture. That helped a lot; he understood trees, and found he could relate to them about as well this way as by sight. He could tell their shapes by it without even touching their surfaces, though the touching confirmed it. In fact by surrounding them he could define their complete configurations.

They traveled, moving by magical propulsion: each suspended cell pulled and pushed against its environment, moving the way he willed. It wasn't fast, but it was sure. There was a slight cross wind; they let it flow through their clouds, maintaining their direction. The cells held their positions in a magic lattice that was largely immune to wind.

Who are you? he asked as they slid across the terrain.

Ilka understood, for the question was not verbal. *I am the parent of Iva.*

That explained much. *How are we communicating?*

It turned out that when vapor tendrils touched, they overlapped slightly, and each cell read the adjacent cell of the other entity. They exchanged complete information, which then spread through the rest of the clouds. A greater overlap enabled faster exchange.

But too much overlap was not in order: that could lead to the generation of a new ifrit. It happened on its own when the overlap was sufficient. The mixed cells of the two entities exchanged such complete information that they became their own entity, with the fused outlook of the parents. They separated, and became a small cloud, which in time would grow.

How did they grow? By feeding on the magical energy available in the air. It was diffuse, so growth was slow, but in time it amounted to enough to form an adult.

The farther they went, the more competent Havoc became. He now had a perfect picture of the landscape he covered. Not its color, for that was a function of light, or its sound, but its real nature. It was a model extending across the lower portion of his being. It was a more detailed awareness than he had had as a man, and he was comfortable with it.

Meanwhile, his dialogue with Ilka clarified the mental nature of the ifrits. Their floating cells related to each other directly, with no interfering flesh: every cell connected by magical lines to every other cell. This enabled rapid and powerful thought. If he wanted information, it was there; if he wanted understanding, it was there. Ilka was organized for sapience, a quality she had developed to accommodate the aspects of human nature being fed in through the solidified ifrits. She enabled them to converse verbally, drawing on the bank of vocabulary developed for this purpose. But now, with direct contact with Havoc, communication was far more comprehensive. There were no limits of substance; information was transferred whole.

Everything was there, including all the dialogues Iva and Ivor had had with several humans. Iva's sexual experience with Augur and Havoc were there, including the orgasms and the love. Both of those were new experiences to the ifrits, the one being intense local pleasure, the other emotional pleasure. Ilka—and all ifrits—wanted to know more about them. And especially about sapience. That last required restructuring of the levels of understanding; it could not simply be copied whole. But now, with Havoc in cloud form, it was feasible to emulate its pattern.

Havoc discovered that there was no deceit in the ifrits. They had no hidden motive. They simply wanted to know. They were the guardians of planet Counter Charm, and needed to understand whatever occurred on it, defining any possible threats.

How did they deal with threats? By understanding and neutralizing them. What was the last threat so handled? A hostile object had struck their world some time ago; they had been unable to remove or nullify it, so had sequestered it.

Havoc's excitement coursed through his being. That was the area defined by the tapestry map!

Ilka's excitement echoed his own. The planet wanted to be rid of that object; did the humans want it? Then they should take it.

They came to the edge of the Chroma zone. To ifrits, color was irrelevant; they simply condensed, rolled across the intervening nonChroma zones, and returned to full form in the next Chroma zone.

That is unnecessary for me, Havoc thought. *I can retain cloud form and cross.*

She was amazed. This was impossible for ifrits. She protested that it was not safe to cross; they had to turn back.

Havoc, flush with the joy of cloud competence, preferred to make a demonstration of his Glamor competence: he floated on into the nonChroma zone, across it, and into the next. He could feel the magic; it was qualitatively different here. He knew from his prior human survey that it was a Green Chroma zone; he zeroed in its equivalent feel, so he would know it in future.

Ilka was no longer with him, being unable to cross without supportive magic. He did not mean to tease her; he would return, having made his demonstration.

Then he became aware of something else: the ground was shaking. His cells nearest it felt the vibration, and now the area was taking on a special charge of magic. The ifrit experience he had acquired from Ilka identified those signs: the local volcano was making ready to erupt. He had to get out of there before it did. It might not happen immediately, but at the cloud's velocity, he'd have to hurry.

But as he moved back, he discovered that something had changed. Ringing the edge of the zone were several funnels lifting from holes in the ground. His thinning fringe defined their shapes. The ifrit information identified them: fog suckers. Creatures that sucked in air and vapor at high power, filtering out the ifrit cells, consuming them. A deadly predator. There was information how to escape: get out of suction range. An ifrit might lose some substance, but could regenerate the lost cells in time.

But Havoc had been caught by surprise, and was too close. The suckers had let him pass over them, and lifted behind him. Had he continued on into the zone he would have been all right, but the building eruption prevented that. As the suckers evidently knew.

Now he realized that he should have paid more attention to Ilka's caution. The information was there: *Bad zone.* He had assumed she meant the nonChroma strip. She hadn't. Now his arrogance had gotten him in trouble.

The air was moving faster as the suckers developed power. One sucker he might have held off, by letting its suction pass between his cells while he slid to the side and out of its range. That was the way ifrits avoided being blown by adverse wind. But there were four there, increasing the effect and broadening the coverage. He could not get away from them.

There was another strategy of defense, an untried one suggested by the solid air Chroma human Ini: do a partial condensation, forming larger cells with hard edges that would abrade and clog the filter meshes. It should be effective—against a single sucker. But not against four; he lacked the mass to stop them all, and would be consumed.

What could he do? The rising airflow was already drawing him in toward their funnels. To late to condense to full solid form; he'd be gone long before he made it. His Glamor invulnerability would not avail him here; he was too diffuse. He had to think of something in a hurry.

His leading edge was approaching the nearest sucker; he felt the increasing air shear.

What would frighten a fog sucker? A sand storm?

His outer wisps were at the funnel, getting drawn in.

Maybe so. But there was no such storm here.

Unless he could make one. By illusion.

He concentrated. His diffuse cells performed marvelously. He formed a vision, using his memory of his human sight. A haze of flying sand appeared. He surrounded himself with it, making every cell seem like a grain of sand. He generated noise, using memory of sound. True ifrits surely couldn't do this, because they lacked eyes and ears, but he was a false ifrit. He made a raging sand storm.

The suckers were animals. They had small eyes on stalks and ears in the ground. They saw and heard the sand storm.

Their funnels dropped back into the ground. The last thing they wanted was to suck in sand.

But Havoc knew the illusion wouldn't fool them from long. He took his chance to condense; he would be much better off in his natural form. Condensation was not a rapid process, but it was faster than the time it would take to float his full cloud over the suckers and across the nonChroma zone. Once he was a man, he could simply conjure himself back to the Red Chroma zone.

He solidified, but awkwardly. He had had guidance when evaporating; he needed it when condensing. His body was forming wrong. He had to reverse, turn full cloud, and try again.

There was another shaking of the ground, but this was not the eruption. It was closer and more localized, and it occurred in beats. What was it?

He focused on forming his eyes before his limbs were complete. He looked, and saw a bounding six legged tiger, reasonably similar to those of Charm. A large predator, coming in for a kill. As if he didn't have problems enough!

Now the suckers, discovering that there was no storm, were lifting their horns again. They were too late; he would be completely solid before they got up sufficient suction. But the tiger was faster; it would get to him before he completed his condensation.

However, now his head was complete, and with it his command of general magic. He conjured a metallic staff, swung it about, and rammed it at the tiger's nose.

The tiger snapped at it—and bit off the end.

Havoc paused briefly to stare. This creature was less similar to those of Charm than he had thought; none of them could chomp metal like that.

Well, there were other ways. He conjured a fireball and lofted it at the tiger. That should set it back.

The animal snapped at the fireball, took it into its mouth, and swallowed it with no apparent discomfort.

Havoc whistled. "You are more formidable than I judged," he told it. But now he had almost completed his condensation; there was a bit of fog around his feet, dissipating.

He conjured a big wad of spruce gum. This was a tree specialty; it was light but solid, and extraordinarily sticky.

The tiger snapped it up—and its teeth stuck in the taffy-like ball. It tried to open its mouth, but the gum clung, distending rather than yielding. In time the beast might work its way clear, but Havoc would be long gone.

One tiger nullified. But two more were on the way. No wonder the ifrits were wary of this region; volcano, fog suckers, and big predators abounded.

He conjured two more wads of gum, but the tigers were not stupid; they had seen the fate of the first, and refused to snap at them. They prowled around him, studying him, aware that he was not defenseless.

The last of the vapor disappeared into his feet. He was wholly solid; now he could jump away from here. But he was ornery; he wanted not merely to escape the tigers, but to beat them back, establishing his dominance. He also wanted to make his mark on the fog suckers. So he dallied.

What would teach both tigers and fog suckers a lesson without actually killing them? Illusion worked only briefly. After the first experience, they would recognize it.

Then he had it. He cast a spell of illusion over the fog suckers, which were starting their suction. He made them look like six legged rabbits. Then he teleported himself out of the way, behind the tigers.

They spied the rabbits and pounced, crashing into the fog suckers. The suction hauled on the feet and tails and the tigers' weight flattened the funnels. There was a horrible growling as the tigers scrambled to extricate themselves from what turned out to be inedible and entangling.

The Green Glamor appeared. "You seem to have the situation in hand," he remarked.

"Affirmation. What is your interest?"

"Ilka Ifrit reported you were in trouble. Unfortunately it took her a while to float back to the rendezvous area."

"I foolishly ignored her caution."

"So the ifrits had no ill will?"

"None. I am satisfied they are innocent."

Then the green volcano roared and shook. "We seem to be having an eruption," Green remarked.

"Affirmation. Shall we depart?"

"Sensible," Green agreed, though he had little to fear from such activity in his natural Chroma.

They jumped back to the Red Chroma zone staging area. "Havoc!" Gale cried, spotting him. "What happened?"

"Own fault," he said. "Ilka told me not to cross zones, but I ignored her caution and encountered some problems."

She ran to embrace him, followed by the three children. "You were always wild," she said, not wholly reprovingly. Then, mentally: *Real story?*

Ifrits are innocent. Now I trust them. Ilka warned me, and summoned help when she knew I was in trouble. But I knew her nature before that.

Gale kissed him. "Next time I'd better come along to keep you sensible."

"Agreement. We can be a family of clouds."

"A family of clouds!" Warp agreed as the children arrived.

Now they were committed.

ᗡᖇ

Gale was more excited than she cared to show. She had seen the children become clouds, and Havoc, so the technique had been proven, as it were. But she would not be able to accept it fully until she did it herself—and she intended to do that today. But what a risk—allowing herself to disintegrate, float away like vapor on the breeze, and return to her natural form. Suppose something went wrong? Who could care for the children?

Symbol, Havoc thought in answer to her concern. *We might have to co-opt Spanky too, to emulate you.*

The bath girl? she thought, appalled.

She's a nice girl, he thought, teasing her. *Phenomenal bottom.*

Berm's not bad either, she thought, teasing him back. But the exchange did ease her concern somewhat.

They came to the Red Chroma zone. Ivor, Iva, and their children were already there, in condensed form. "I want to go first," Gale said. "So that I can track the children before they have a chance to float away."

Iva smiled. "It is the nature of children. But this zone is safe for them."

"They won't stay in this zone."

"Agreement. Ivor will guide you."

Gale didn't question why it was Ivor and not Iva. Iva wanted to be with Havoc, and surely Ivor had a hankering for Gale. They had not had sex in solid human form, while Havoc and Iva had. Gale understood and accepted it. In fact she was curious herself: how was it done in cloud form, and what was it like? Perhaps there would be a chance to find out.

"We shall have to separate as we change," Ivor said. "So as not to overlap at the outset. I will expand in this direction, and you may expand in that direction." He indicated left and right. "I will extend a vapor contact to touch you, and will guide you throughout. Then we will move off enough to give the children room to change."

"Agreement." She remained tight. She really was concerned about suffering some mishap and orphaning the children. Havoc meant well, but he was not a mother. Symbol meant well, but she was not a Glamor. Gale had to be there to do it, and even the slightest chance she would not be was unnerving. But she couldn't track the children unless she could turn cloud when they did.

And, she realized belatedly, she was still holding Voila. She looked around for Symbol, but she was busy with the other children.

Then Voila began to change, anticipating Gale. They would do it together. Gale set her down, giving her room, and focused on herself. What was the first step? She had started doing it unconsciously before, but now had no idea how she had done it.

"Focus on your constituency," Havoc reminded her. "It has to be with their support."

She remembered. She oriented on the mosses and lichen that gave her their support, and they responded strongly, suffusing her with special magic. But how did this translate to vaporizing her substance?

There came a mental signal from Voila, wordless, for she did not yet know how to speak, but it carried the essence of the conversion. *Feel.* Her baby was showing her how, just as she had shown Havoc how before. Voila was the expert. She knew how to become a cloud, and how to return to solid form. Gale found that immensely reassuring.

Gale followed Voila's lead—and saw vapor rising from her hands. She was doing it, this time deliberately. She focused, and the process intensified. Her vision fogged, and she knew it was because her eyes themselves were fogging, literally. She was sublimating, dissolving into vapor. Becoming a cloud.

How did a person see or hear without eyes or ears? She understood that the ifrits didn't need such organs, but she did not like the idea of being blind and deaf. Alarm formed and intensified.

Feel, Voila thought again, and demonstrated. Gale followed her lead again, and became aware of the air around her, its flavor, temperature, pressure, and a myriad other factors. Suddenly she didn't need sight or sound; she had a more direct contact with her environment. Her alarm faded.

Now she was mostly cloud, with only part of her remaining inconveniently solid. Why would anyone want to be solid instead of vaporous? This state was so much more versatile and comfortable. She was glad to be aware of the last of the solidity departing. Now she was all cloud.

Welcome, a thought came. *I am Ivor.*

Going, Voila thought without the word.

Wait! But the baby was already floating clear.

She is joining the other children, Ivor explained. *She is secure. I will guide you now.* His thoughts were competent and comforting.

How was he in such direct touch with her, since the ifrits lacked telepathy? Oh—a vapor tendril. Now she was aware of it. Its mere touch of her vapor communicated his thought and nature with perfect clarity. Now she understood what the ifrits had tried to explain: there could be no deception among ifrits, for touch-understanding was complete. She had had to experience it before she could truly believe it. Now she believed.

Time passed differently. She was aware of it, yet it was less important compared to the rest of the environment. There was so much to explore in this marvelous new form! Her mind seemed somehow improved; she could perform thoughts with pleasant speed and power, and overall she seemed so much more aware. But she was supposed to be tracking the children, finding that she could send vapor tendrils out to touch them reassuringly. As it turned out, she was the one being reassured; they had adapted to cloud formation with the joy and acceptance of childhood, not needing to analyze it.

This is why an adult guide is better, Ivor thought. *We have the patience of age.*

He was right. She let the children be, knowing that they were more competent in this form than she was, and that Havoc and Iva were tracking them, and the ifrit children. They would be all right. Her best course was to focus on her new existence, learning all she could about it.

The child clouds floated exuberantly off to explore the terrain. Havoc and Iva tracked them from the far side; Gale and Ivor from the near side. Soon the others were well ahead, as Gale was still finding out how to travel. Ivor guided her in that, patiently, and she was learning.

But the contact of tendrils enabled such comprehensive dialogue that it wasn't talk so much as the sharing of minds. She had to render it as dialogue in order to fix parts of it in memory that would survive her return to solid form; Ivor advised her on that, and it was impossible not to trust his judgment and experience. So what was covered in much larger, broader, and satisfying exchanges was squeezed into the limited dialogue form so that it would not be lost.

"This is amazing," she thought. "I thought communication would be limited without sound and sight, but its scope is enormously greater."

"We find it so," he agreed. "This is why we never made much effort to enhance our solid forms, until we encountered you human beings and realized what was possible."

"Agreement. How did you stand being squeezed solid for days at a time, to converse with us?"

"We are interested, and the sex helped make it worthwhile."

"Sex makes much association interesting. But I understood you don't normally practice it."

"Not in our natural form."

"How is it that you reproduce, then?"

"We extend significant pseudopods, merge them, and separate them from our main substances. They become the small ifrits you have seen. We nurture them until they are grown, then let them go."

"This is essentially similar to what we do. But this merging of pseudopods—isn't that sexual?"

"It is reproductive, not sexual."

"There is a distinction," she agreed. "But among our kind they normally associate. Nature does not depend on human commitment to regenerate the species; she makes it intensely pleasurable."

"Nature?"

She clarified the concept as well as she could, then continued: "So as it happens, we don't need to be concerned about reproduction; it will take care of itself. We focus on the pleasure."

"We did find pleasure when we did the act with your kind in the solid forms," he agreed. "But it was projected by your other Glamor being."

"Yes, so you would know what it feels like. You feel nothing like that when you make baby ifrits?"

"We do not," he agreed.

"I find that curious. Do you have some other incentive to reproduce your kind?"

"It is our normal course. Our existence is not complete until we pass our essence along to others."

Gale had some doubt about this; altruism seemed seldom to operate among living things. Of course these were demons, not living creatures. But they seemed equivalent. "So you procreate without pleasure. But wouldn't it be better with pleasure?"

"We do not know."

"There is another reason for the pleasure: to facilitate a relationship without necessarily procreating. Families need to stay together even when not seeking to have more children."

"We stay together because it facilitates the welfare of our children."

She changed the subject. "This form has marvelous senses. But we are oriented on sight, hearing, and touch. I miss those."

"We have them."

She was dubious. "Without eyes, ears, and fingers?"

"Those appendages merely collect raw data which is then translated for the mind. They are not necessary in cloud form."

Hope flared. "Interest! You mean I can learn to perceive these ways as a cloud?"

"Confirmation. Here is how." Another pseudopod of vapor touched her, loaded with information.

Gale assimilated it rapidly. This form was good for such ready transfer of information; her floating cells simply copied that data and reorganized to assimilate it. She discovered that she did not need eyes to see; light-sensitive cells accomplished it. She did not need ears to hear; rapid interpretation of the compressions and rarefactions of sound was sufficient. And the vapor was touching all of the ground the cloud passed over; all she needed to do was relay the awareness of the cells to her consciousness and interpret them as larger patterns.

She floated in place, reorganizing. Gradually she saw the red landscape below her, and heard the sounds of animals and wind and moving water, and felt their outlines. All of these impressions were far richer than those of normal human senses; she was in danger of being overwhelmed by information.

"Filter it," Ivor suggested. "All of it is not required on a constant basis."

Which was exactly what the normal human senses did, she realized. She applied the programmed filters, and the flood of sensation diminished until it was comfortable. That was a relief.

Then she became aware of something else. "The children! Where are they?"

"They moved on ahead while we paused. We can seek them."

They applied propulsion, which Gale realized now was not magical in itself, but a magical control of one of the properties of the bright light coming from above: heat. That heat was taken in by the cells, transferred to cells at the rear, and fed into the air. The air expanded explosively, pushing the rear of the cloud forward. Because the network was flexibly fixed, this drove the full cloud. The process was sophisticated in detail in ways she had not appreciated until she considered it. Information was filtered here too, again as it was in her human body; in physical form she did not maintain an awareness of the spot physical and chemical processes that enabled her to move in the ways her brain directed. The cloud was a body, spread out in relatively diffuse manner, but similar in the larger essence.

They came near the edge of the Red Chroma zone. An ifrit was coalescing. "That is Iva," Ivor thought. He sent her a query tendril, and in a moment had the news: "The children crossed to the adjacent zone. The Glamors floated without coalescing. Ours followed, crossing in solid form. Havoc was alarmed and crossed immediately, but Iva can't do that."

Because she was an ifrit, not a Glamor in ifrit form; she had to coalesce, then vaporize again in the new zone, picking up its magic.

"Why was Havoc alarmed?" Because Havoc was not one to worry without reason.

"The adjacent Chroma zone is Black."

Ouch! "I am crossing now."

"Caution. No inruption is imminent, and there are no predators in this region. The children are not in danger."

"Black Chroma makes me nervous regardless. I want them out of there." Gale knew she was being emotional rather than rational, but had to follow her nature. "I must help Havoc fetch them back."

"Recommendation: observe without summoning them. They are interested in exploring, and are surely safe. Children do not like being restricted."

There spoke a permissive father. Gale was a worried mother. "They will know the moment my tendril touches one."

"Negation. Use an anonymous tendril." He sent her the information.

She realized this had possibilities. "Appreciation." She floated on across the nonChroma strip, leaving Ivor behind.

It was indeed a Black Chroma zone. A cloud was there, and she verified that it was Havoc's trailing edge. They touched tendrils, rapidly exchanging information. He acquainted her with the location of the children, which was within a linked network of caves, and she acquainted him with the mechanisms for seeing, hearing, feeling, and anonymous tendriling. Vapor communication was as competent as telepathy, so the exchange was immediate.

"They are right," he thought in speech form. "There is no inruption, and no predators in this vicinity. I was concerned, so came across, but we can afford to watch them for a while."

They floated close to the caves. The children were entirely inside them, shaping themselves to the subterranean configuration and not requiring much space. The adults extended tendrils and sent them into the nearest cave entrance, utilizing the new technique. They repulsed each other magnetically so did not overlap. Havoc and Gale maintained regular tendril contact outside the cave, so knew what each was doing inside. The newly realized senses enabled them to see inside the cave by wavelengths of light normally drowned out by the full light of day, and to feel the qualities of the confined air. It was actually superior to what the human senses could have provided. The human body wouldn't have fitted comfortably in the narrower portions, and its senses would not have been adequate in the darker recesses.

"This is worthwhile experience," Havoc said. It was actual sound that he sent to her and she received, now that they know how to do it. They were enjoying the exploration of their increasing abilities.

"Agreement. I was wary of the cloud form, but now I hope it works as well back home."

"It should. The two planets are similar; only the life forms differ."

"And the demon forms."

"We are now demons," he said, surprised. She did not have to read his mind; surprise was a quality of the communication he sent. In fact they could not read minds; telepathy was foreign to the ifrit nature, or at least had not been developed in cloud form. But other modes of information transferal were so apt that telepathy would have been little if any advantage.

Their two tendrils lengthened endlessly, snaking through the winding corridor of the cave. Now they caught up to the children, who had assumed similarly elongated forms so as to share the caves without overlapping. All eight of them were there, exploring the crevices and playing impromptu tag with each other, in the process becoming hopelessly tangled. Yet they maintained their separate forms, the humans evidently having learned the technique from the ifrits.

"They seem safe," Havoc said. "We can let them play for a while."

Gale agreed. The children were gaining similarly valuable experience, mastering abilities that might be useful later in life; it was best to leave them to it, as long as there was no danger. For one thing, with the adults outside, no threat could come without being known before it got near the children.

"The ifrits procreate, but don't have sex," Gale said, transferring the information about overlapping and forming new entities.

"What a shame. Sex is not for procreation alone."

"So I tried to explain to Ivor. But he does not understand."

"Neither does Iva." Then he got the idea she had known he would. "We should find out whether non-reproductive sex is feasible in cloud form."

"We lack a program for it"

"Because they lack it. We shall need to develop our own."

"But if we do it wrong, we shall make an ifrit baby. That would not be wise, and we couldn't keep it."

"Agreement." He pondered. "I am exploring my information. I know how to procreate, but I find no sexuality in it. It's not a matter of obtaining the pleasure without the baby; there's no pleasure to have."

That was Gale's impression. It seemed to be an insuperable barrier.

Then Iva arrived, having completed her crossing and transformation. She extended a tendril. "The children are well?"

"They are well," Gale agreed. "We spied on them in the cave, and let them be."

"They will tire of it soon," Iva said.

They did. Gale and Havoc quickly withdrew their tendrils as the children floated out and resumed more compact cloud shapes. They were ready for the next adventure.

"They should rest soon," Iva said.

"Agreement," Gale said.

The children were for once amenable. All of the little clouds settled in place for a nap. It seemed the ifrits were similar in this respect to humans. In fact they were similar in most respects, other than underlying nature.

There was a flash from across the nonChroma zone. "Ivor says there is a problem with your mortal humans," Iva said.

In a moment they learned not only what that problem was, but that the ifrits could signal each other at a distance if conditions were right. They formed reflector patches and angled modified beams of sunlight across the terrain, to be received and interpreted. Iva shared the technique, and Gale and Havoc understood it. There was a section of the nonChroma zone that lacked vegetation, and Ivor had beamed across it.

The problem was that Augur had attempted to assume cloud form, and had succeeded. But then the wind had shifted, diluting the Red Chroma zone, and he seemed to be unable to return to solid form. Ilka Ifrit was uncertain what to do, so had signaled Ivor to contact Havoc and Gale.

"Return with Ivor," Havoc suggested. "He's already across the nonChroma zone."

"Acquiescence." She floated in that direction. Havoc was competent to watch the children take their nap.

Ivor was already moving, trailing a tendril for contact with her. Ilka's information was that Augur and Aura had wondered whether this was something ordinary Chroma folk could do, so had tried. Aura had gotten nowhere, being a Blue Chroma person in a Red Chroma zone. But Augur, to his surprise, had succeeded. Ilka had helped him achieve full cloud form and acquainted him with the basics of organization. Distracted, they had not been aware of the slow shift of wind. It was all Ilka could do to hustle him on toward the center of the zone so that he could recover full control. He was not yet apt at traveling, and remained perilously close to the edge of the zone.

"What happens to an ifrit caught out of Chroma?" Gale asked tightly as they traveled.

"Normally we condense to solid form to get past nonChroma. We are unable to maintain vapor cohesion in the absence of sufficient magic. Our substance dissipates."

"Death?"

"We are not a living class of creature, but an individual caught in this manner suffers dissipation and is lost as an aware entity."

"That sounds like the equivalent of death to me. Since Augur is a living entity, it would mean death for him."

"Agreement. We normally take care not to be caught in this manner. This was an unusual coincidence of elements."

"We call it bad luck."

"Luck?"

Gale explained the concept. Like humor, it was alien to ifrit understanding; they had no circuitry relating to it. Ivor accepted her package of thoughts, and would share it with other ifrits.

Augur was in serious trouble. What could they do to save him? The ifrits were willing to help, but didn't know how. That meant that it was up to the humans. Up to Gale. And she had no idea.

Mother.

Gale felt a shock. That was Voila's voiceless, wordless thought. The baby was following her. How could that have happened? She was supposed to be napping.

Gale sent back a tendril. Voila was there, her cloud approaching, one tendril ahead. *How?* Gale demanded, for the moment unable to focus on anything else.

But the baby didn't know how. She had simply followed her mother. Somehow she had eluded the attention of Havoc and the others. Maybe she had used her awareness of the future to thread a course that avoided detection. The developing powers of all the children were eerie at times, and Voila's especially.

That was something to be sorted out at another time. Gale welcomed her daughter to her company. She couldn't pick her up and hold her, but she could touch her with a tendril and reassure her. *Welcome.*

But it wasn't comfort the baby sought. *Others,* she thought, forming the concept with difficulty in the absence of language. *All.* Gale was translating somewhat vague feelings, orienting on their closest meanings. Voila was trying to tell her something important.

Could it wait? With any other child, perhaps. With this one, less likely. What future did the baby see, that urged her after her mother and required her to communicate? For it had to be that talent driving her, focused by her ability to see the alternate futures, the immediate consequences of any action. She was doing what she had to do.

Gale trusted the instinct of her daughter. Voila was too young to speak or even to understand much of what went on around her, but her ability to see the recent future was a potent tool. Gale extended a tendril and joined her mind to that of the baby as well as she could. The clouds did not have telepathy, but this was close.

And now she saw it. Voila knew that Augur was about to die in most of the future paths, but there were some where he didn't. Voila knew there would be pain if he died, and no pain if he didn't. So she was searching out the path of least pain. That meant enlisting Gale's help, as she was doing.

Voila was better at futures than Gale was, having practiced it longer. She could orient on one and ferret it out from the complex interlocking tangle of all the rest. She did not know the meanings or larger significance of any of the paths, but she could locate the ones that

brought most comfort. Gale added her adult perspective to the seeking ability of her daughter, and suddenly saw the answer.

"Ilka!" she thought/shouted.

"Responding," the ifrit replied.

"Tell the Glamors!" Gale sent a plan/strategy that the ifrits would
not understand, but that Glamors would.

The ifrit relayed it to a coalesced ifrit, and in a moment the Glamors had the word. They acted immediately, gathering where Augur
was stranded and projecting magic into the region, sending it somewhat the way the ikons sent magic to Glamors. That strengthened the
Red Chroma ambiance and enabled him, with Ilka's guidance, to coalesce to human form.

Gale and Voila arrived at the site and did the same. Aura was
especially grateful; she picked up the baby and cuddled and kissed
her repeatedly. That, Gale realized, was part of the positive future
Voila had sought; she liked being cuddled.

In due course Havoc, Iva, and the children returned. They discussed the crisis, and concluded that the Chroma mortals should
venture to cloud state only at particular Chroma sites, and with a
Glamor watching. The Glamors were in no danger, because they were
independent of zones, despite associating with particular Chroma,
but the mortals were more limited. Still, it was worthwhile for them to
learn the art of cloud formation too.

Aura tried it in a Blue Chroma zone, successfully clouding and
returning to solid human form. Ini tried it in an Air Chroma zone,
becoming an invisible cloud. Then she expanded on the form, using
illusion to make herself a complete painted scene: lovely trees, mountains, a river, and assorted animal life, quite realistic. What gave it
away was the fact that several of the animals were not native to this
planet; they were the ones she knew on Charm.

That impressed Gale. Ini was an Air Chroma native; naturally
she was conversant with illusion. She had utilized it readily in cloud
form, entirely concealing herself by it. That was another potentially
useful technique. In fact, it might be the key they needed to fathom the
riddle of the formidable illusion hiding the thing they had come to
Counter Charm to fetch.

It was another day before they were satisfied that they understood the process of cloud formation well enough for now, and that it
was safe for supervised children to do it. It was past time to return to
the problem of the illusion masking the object for which they had
come to this planet.

The Air Glamor made a private report. Gale had known him as
Dour, a Cartographer, completely fooled by his disguise. His constituency was the hundred leg millipedes, but at the moment it was his
expertise in illusion that concerned them.

"Failure," he said.

"Amazement!" Havoc said. "How can any question of illusion be beyond your powers?"

"Frustration. I have tried repeatedly to penetrate it, but can null only one sense illusion at a time, as before, so am limited. This is a higher class illusion than any we know on Charm."

Gale, too, was amazed. "You can't plow through, ignoring it, to reach the center?"

"This, too, I tried. Each time I got beyond the boundary of a setting such as the ones we sampled before, I found myself not farther into the illusion fields, but at the fringe, exiting. It affects my sense of direction, not merely by image and sound, but directly, so that my certainty of maintaining progress in a straight line is deluded. If I null that illusion, the others such as balance and body position overwhelm me and I am unable to function. This complex illusion has defeated me."

"This explains why we need the altar to point direction," Havoc said. "And a map to mark progress."

"But these are held by mortals," Gale said. "We don't want to put them at risk."

"We may have to," Havoc said.

"I will keep trying," Air said. "Perhaps there is something I have overlooked." He departed.

"I doubt it," Havoc said. "He knows illusion better than any of us."

"There has to be a way," Gale said. "The mere existence of the tapestry and altar suggest that there is."

"We'll see." He disappeared.

Iva joined Gale in solid form as the children played. "Observation and request," she said.

"Interest and acquiescence," Gale replied. Her experience in cloud form had satisfied her that the ifrits were honest and friendly; indeed they lacked the ability to deceive. Whatever Iva wanted was surely justified.

"We have tried to understand you humans, by assuming your forms and practicing your ways. We have discovered much. But we have need to understand more. We know that you come from our sister planet which you call Charm."

"Accuracy." That was the observation; what was the request?

"Why?"

There it was. Gale had consulted with Havoc and the other Glamors when they realized that the ifrits were achieving sapience of the human style, and they had agreed that when this question came, it should be answered. It was time.

"Complicated," Gale said. "Suggestion: link with Ilka for better understanding as I explain."

The red mist in their vicinity thickened: Ilka, summoned, was establishing a more direct connection with her daughter ifrit. That would enable them to assimilate a situation they might not otherwise have been capable of grasping. "Done," Iva said.

Gale spoke for some time, summarizing the Glamor quest for answers to the riddles of their own existence. She told of the change-lings like Aura and Augur, who came as incipient babies from an unknown source and grew to be superior human adults. Of the transitions of some humans and animals to Glamor status, with ikons that transmitted magic power to them so that they could do magic anywhere, even here on Counter Charm. Of the altars where most ikons were kept. Of the loom and the tapestry that showed a scene on Counter Charm.

"And so we at last came here," she concluded. "Because there is evidently something here that we need, in the region that turns out to be thoroughly masked by layered illusion. Once we locate it we will take it back to Charm and use it to gain the answers we seek. We did not know of you ifrits, but are glad to have made your acquaintance. We believe that humans and ifrits can do each other much good, because each has abilities the other can learn and use. When our mission here is done, and we return to our home world, I hope we can maintain contact."

"Amazement," Iva said. "We have our own history and mystery, which it seems relates to yours."

This was something new. The ifrits had history? And their own mystery? "Curiosity."

"Suggestion: use your telepathy to link with your other Glamors, who may be interested in this."

The ifrit was not fooling, any more than Gale had been. This had the scent of something important. *Havoc!* Linking to his mind, she relayed the context of Iva/Ilka's request.

I hear and obey. And in a moment she felt the presence of the other Glamors. They were all listening.

"Done," Gale said.

"Our planet was colonized in similar manner to yours. Some of our forms are parallel, while some differ, as you know. We had no human arrival, and you had no ifrit arrival, but the general nature of the two planets is the same. Only the details differ. We generally lack sapience, but can achieve it at need. We have achieved it in order to relate to you humans. There was another time when we achieved it or something similar, then lost it."

"You were sapient before—and let it go?" Gale said, surprised.

"Agreement. We do not need it for ordinary existence, as you have seen. But some time ago we did. We retained only a summary, so that we would know what needed to be undisturbed. Now you have come to disturb it."

"The object!" Gale said, prompted by one of the other Glamors.

"The object," Iva agreed. "I did not know of this until you spoke of it, and the information prompted Ilka to consult with other ifrit memory. We do not understand all of it, but believe the information will be useful to you."

"Speak," Gale murmured, fascinated.

"Long ago the object came from space. It resembled a metallic meteor, but it did not crash; it slowed and landed on your world. Our worlds have accepted what came from space, but in this case they did not. The object was dangerous and needed to be eliminated, but it was not capable of being touched. It seems to have repelled magic; only purely physical forces could act on it. We do not know how this could be, only that it was so."

"A spaceship," Gale said. "With means to repulse magic. It landed on Charm." She paused, assimilating the input of the Glamors. "Maybe it was a bomb—a thing set to explode with horrible force, to destroy the planet. But why would such a thing be sent?"

"We do not know. Only that it had to be stopped. Somehow something on your planet shaped physical things around it, using magic beyond the object's range, and rolled it into a volcano. Then the volcano erupted with such force as to hurl the object free of the planet. It seems the object could not prevent this; it had been physically sealed and rendered helpless for a time, and was ejected before that time expired."

"What a story!" Gale said. "How did anything on Planet Charm know why or how to do that, before there were sapient creatures on it?"

"We do not know. Perhaps it resembled your child's ability to see the futures, so that what needed to be done was done. The object was sent away. But in space it recovered its mobility, and returned to land again—this time on our planet. We ifrits recognized it as too dangerous to touch or ignore. But we lacked the ability to shape physical things around it to nullify it, so we used nonphysical means."

"Illusion!" Gale exclaimed. "You made the illusion!"

"We made it," Iva agreed. "We bound the object with confusion so that it could not move or act, and covered it with illusion so that no animals or demons could approach it. We left it there, for no magic can touch it directly, buried and hidden. We want to be further rid of it, but lack the means."

"And this is what we have come for," Gale said. "This supremely dangerous thing from space."

"Agreement. If you wish to remove it from our planet, we will help you accomplish that. But there is a complication."

Gale smiled grimly. "There often is. Explain."

"We no longer have the ability to remove the illusion we crafted. That ability was deliberately sacrificed so that no entity, including ifrits, could ever approach the object casually. Our forebears did not anticipate the appearance of humans or Glamors. So we are unable to help you in this respect."

Gale nodded. "That is a complication, agreed. But we Glamors bring other means to accomplish things. Maybe we can do what you can't."

"That is possible."

"You said no one can approach the object casually. That suggests that there *is* a way."

"Agreement." Iva was surprised. "I have just learned of this, too."

Gale suppressed impatience. "What is the way?"

"The illusion is not random. It is structured in rings and layers, drawing on the nature of those who seek to pass it. It is dynamic, using their own qualities to confuse them. But because it was recognized that at some point there might be reason to reach the object, an avenue exists."

"An avenue!"

"It is a challenge, a—game. You must fathom its rules and follow them. If you do, you can proceed safely through. If you do not, you will be led into treachery. Even if you are immune from physical damage, you will not discover the object unless you prevail in the game. This is intended to ensure that whoever reaches the object has sufficient understanding to handle it. The object is deadly."

"So we gather," Gale said dryly. "But it seems that this is a risk we are obliged to take. Havoc will love it." Because Havoc was a creature of crisis, bored with routine.

"We will assist to the extent we are able."

She knew they would. This was a phenomenal breakthrough. Now they knew a great deal more about the object they sought. Could this be a reason the way had been prepared for the existence of Glamors? To finally deal with this lurking threat? But that implied that there was some intelligent design behind this effort of theirs. In that case, what was the need of Glamors? Why hadn't the originator of that design simply handled the threat itself?

There was still more here than they had fathomed.

A presence come. *Swale!* she thought. *You took your time returning.*

The succubus made a mental nod. *I got involved in something back on Charm. There's a problem.*

There was always another problem. *We are busy here at the moment.*

With the ikons.

Oops.

Chapter 8—Ikons

Chief had been away on business for several days. It drove Aspect crazy. "Eagerness!" she exclaimed as she embraced him, pressing her body to his.

He laughed, as she had known he would, but without the normal force. His trip must have been wearing. She couldn't tell, because his mind was locked closed. Well, she would take his mind off that soon enough.

It seemed forever before she got him alone in the evening. She wore her slinkiest gown, determined to make the most of the occasion. He liked it, of course; he had no choice. But she didn't dally long on admiration; she virtually hauled him to the bed and had at him, kissing and stroking where it counted. All too soon she had him inside her with a mutual climax.

But still his mind was shut. That bothered her. "Question."

He gazed at her. "Reluctance."

"I am here for you, lover. I want to share and ameliorate."

"Postponement?"

This was serious. "Preference: tackle it now, then more sex. We have catching up to do."

He sighed. "As you wish. You have changed. That is my concern."

"I have become more passionate." She took his hand and playfully stroked herself with it.

"You were away for a year. That provided perspective. You are not the woman I came to love."

She was taken aback. "I am a better woman now. My health, my form, my desire. I owe it to the ikon."

"I have known you for some time. Loved you that time."

"You sired my fourth," she agreed. The she glanced askance at him. "Love—then?"

"You were such a remarkable woman, my ideal. I could not help it."

"I didn't know."

He smiled. "You were my friend's wife. I had my own wife and family. No one could know. Especially when you became queen, and I the king's chief of staff."

This was perplexing news. "But when you were free, and I was free, it was Ennui you approached."

"I did not know your sentiment, and feared rejection."

She shook her head. "I never suspected. I thought you wouldn't mind getting me into bed again, but of course I had lost the figure of youth, so believed that was past."

"Negation. But the memory of my friend remained; I did not wish to dishonor it. Yet when it didn't work out with Ennui, I tried cautiously to approach you."

"And I welcomed it," Aspect agreed. "I had of course been aware of you, but assumed there was nothing there. I found I was mistaken."

"Agreement. Then you took Queen Gale's ikon."

"And it transformed me."

"Agreement," he repeated. "At first I liked this, because it changed you to be more like the vibrant young woman I first loved."

"I was pleased to be so, for you."

"But the change has progressed to the point where you no longer seem like that woman. You are beautiful, as you were before, and healthy in the manner of youth. But I am no longer youthful."

"Disregard! I love you as you are."

"And I love you as you were. My age."

She was taken aback again. "You do not wish me young?"

He frowned. "Difficulty. You are man's desire. But it is like embracing a bath girl of my daughter's generation. How long will you be patient with me?"

Aspect had not thought of this. She had assumed that men of all ages liked young women. "I remain my real age, in outlook and experience. I want my body to please you."

"It does. But I can not keep up with you. Your sex drive is now like that of a young man."

She nodded. "Acquiescence. I thought you liked that."

"I do. But you need more sex that I can provide."

He was right. She was already hot for more of it. "I don't know what to say."

"I believe I should free you to find your own level."

She was appalled. "Shock! I love you."

"And I love you. I do not wish to stifle you."

"I will give up the ikon!" she said. "I don't want to be free of you."

"You can't give it up. It is a sacred trust. The Lady Gale depends on you to maintain it safely."

"Agreement. But another person could do that. I would consult with Gale, of course, but I'm sure she will agree."

"Even if she does, you would be giving up more than my association is worth. You may be immortal, forever healthy and youthful. You deserve it."

Aspect felt tears on her face. "If you prefer to go elsewhere, I will not hinder you," she said carefully. "But I love you and do not wish to give you up for any other reason. Especially not for youth, health, and passion you do not desire. I want to be what you want me to be, even if that means middle aged."

He shook his head. "This is what I did not want to ask of you. It is not fair to ask it."

"And you did not ask it. I want it. For you."

"Appeal: Do not be hasty. Consider the cost. Consult with Ennui. Be sure, before taking such a step."

She kissed him. "You're so sweet."

"I am rational. This is no simple decision."

She kissed him again. "I will not be hasty. I will consider. I will consult. I will be sure." She continued kissing him, and he, evidently relieved by her acceptance of the situation, responded. Before long she got him into sex again. And felt guilty, knowing that it was this very urgency of hers that made him wary.

Next day she talked with Ennui. Both of them kept their minds closed. "Chief would like me to be as I was before the ikon."

"But you were middle aged."

"I thought he preferred me this way, but I was mistaken. I want to oblige him. How is it with you and Throe?"

The woman frowned. "The same."

So Ennui had already discussed it with her lover. "He would prefer you as you were?"

"As a homely middle aged woman," Ennui agreed. "I find it hard to believe."

"Perhaps it is that they are middle aged men, and fear we will tire of them."

Ennui nodded. "That might be. At any rate, they are serious. I am ready to give up my ikon, but I don't want to put Havoc at any possible risk. Is there any truly secure place we can put them?"

Aspect hadn't thought of that. "We'll need to find a suitable hiding place, that no one will suspect. Secure, yet readily accessible at need. I have no idea where."

"Similarity."

"Let's think about it. One day's delay won't matter."

"Agreement."

They were wrong; one day did matter, as they discovered when Nonce returned from her leave of absence.

Aspect! Ennui's sudden thought came. *Outrage here.*

Aspect dropped whatever she had been doing and hurried to Ennui's office. Nonce stood there, distraught.

"Nonce was raped," Ennui said. "In a manner."

"The mock king can handle that," Aspect said, putting her arms around the girl. "Who did it? He'll be castrated."

"A golem," Nonce said.

"Confusion."

In time they got the story straight. Nonce, seeking diversion, had gone to a Brown Chroma zone role playing game. This was a physical setting where the players animated golems, so that civilized limits could be dispensed with. Rape and murder were common, with the victims being diminished or ejected from the game. Animated golems seemed just like real people, to both the ones they encountered and the ones who animated them, but what happened to them did not happen to those who controlled them. So when a golem died, the person in it did not die; he or she merely had to start over. There were supposed to be constraints: players could form protective alliances, so that they could avoid or repel aggression while competing for points. One man could overpower one woman, but two women could overpower one man, and women had the option of deception. The men were required to tell the truth at all times; the women could lie when they found it advantageous. Points were awarded for many actions and discoveries: for finding hidden treasure, for killing monsters, for raping, castrating, or killing other players.

Nonce had been wary of entering the game alone, so had made an alliance with a young woman she met at the gathering area: they would be a team for the first day, until they became familiar with the layout and other players and could handle it alone. They picked pretty golem forms, wasp waisted and full breasted, and entered adjacent animation chambers. They would appear together in an isolated spot within the game, then set out looking for adventure and points. Nonce understood that the game provided a rare thrill for those who never in real life faced such threats and opportunities. They could live lives of promise and danger, without truly risking their bodies.

But when Nonce stepped into the game, she found no female companion beside her. Instead there were two brutish men. She tried to flee, but they boxed her in and caught her. Then one held her, screaming in protest, while the other ripped off her clothing. He raped her, still screaming. Then the other man throttled her, and she was dead before she had ever started.

She had found herself back in the booth, out of the game. The bauble she had traded for her day's play had been horribly wasted. She checked the adjacent booth, and found it empty. Her companion had never animated her golem.

"A shill!" Aspect exclaimed. "She set you up for the men."

"They got ten points each," Ennui said. "Ten for raping her, ten for killing her. Accumulated points can be traded for tangible prizes after a player emerges from the game. They must have shared with their female accomplice."

"I can't protest," Nonce said. "Women don't have to tell the truth in the game, and I think there are no rules for anyone outside the game. I was a lamb, and they slaughtered me." She was halfway blaming herself. That was common in such cases, but hardly made it right.

"I still call it rape," Ennui said grimly. "I think we should do something about it."

"It did feel like rape," Nonce said. "And like death." Her eyes were rimmed; she had been crying.

"Agreement," Aspect said. "We shall act."

They acted. They planned carefully, had Throe hire a coach and driver anonymously, and went to the Brown Chroma zone game site. Things were quiet at the palace, which was why Nonce had been given leave; Chief was advising the mock king and would alert them if there were any problem. This was planned as a one day event, handled without wider notice.

"You are gutsy ladies," Throe remarked as they traveled. Theoretically he was a man with two sisters to convey to another region; that was all the coachman needed to know, in case he gossiped elsewhere. They were not speaking loudly enough to be overheard by the coachman anyway.

"We have protection," Aspect said.

"By that you don't mean merely me." He had been the king's bodyguard for many years, and had guarded Aspect too. Now he guarded Havoc and Gale, but they no longer needed it, and were offplanet. He guarded the mocks when they went anywhere, but they too were relaxing at the palace today. That left him free to do them a favor.

"We'll settle for merely you, once we figure out where to put something," Ennui told him fondly. Even in privacy, they did not refer directly to the ikons.

"Suggestion."

"Ear open," Aspect said, cupping one of hers as if to listen closely.

"Crowns."

The two women stared at each other. Put the ikons in the appropriate crowns! Havoc's in Havoc's crown, Gale's in Gale's crown. That would not conflict with the Glamors, because they no longer used the real crowns; they used the fake ones, leaving the real ones to the mocks. Thus the ikons would be securely hidden, and would normally remain in the nonChroma zone.

Ennui kissed him. "And I thought you were hired for your muscle," she said.

"Was," he agreed, pleased.

"Tonight, when Berm sleeps, fasten this in the king's crown," Ennui said, bringing out Havoc's tree ikon. "You can do it, because it is your job to poke around looking for threats to the king."

"Agreement." He reached to take the ikon she proffered. "Observation: you will need to let it go if I am to take it."

"I am trying," Ennui said. "It sticks to my hand."

That seemed to be the case. Throe let go, and she held her hand out, the ikon remaining though she was not holding it. "Confusion."

Aspect had a chill notion. She brought out Gale's moss ikon and tried to set it on the seat beside her. She could not; it clung to her fingers. "Fear: they have become attached, and we can not relinquish them."

"But Throe carried them before," Ennui said.

"Until we became their permanent guardians," Aspect said. "We have not tried to set them aside since we kissed Havoc a year ago. We merely assumed that we could do so."

"It seems we were mistaken," Ennui said. She looked uncomfortable.

"Perhaps in a Chroma zone," Aspect said. "To cut off their source of magic just long enough to allow separation."

"We are going to one now," Throe reminded them.

They nodded. "If we succeed, take them, and keep them clear of us."

"Agreement." He was obviously glad to help, because he wanted Ennui free of her ikon.

In due course they arrived at the Brown Chroma zone. This was set up for tourists, with golem guides directing them to the game complex. The grounds were nicely laid out, with brown trees and bushes lining the wide driveway, and pleasantly designed brown buildings. Intriguing statuary decorated the entrance to the main building: truly handsome nude men and women.

The coach parked at the coach lot, and a brown attendant came out with a bag of feed for the horse. They took care of everything here.

"It will cost you to enter," Aspect reminded Ennui.

"I happen to have a blue stone," Ennui said. "That should more than pay my way for a day." They were speaking now for any possible listeners, acting like tourists, keeping their minds closed.

"Mind you pick the right golem."

Ennui smiled knowingly. "A truly lovely one, outside and in." She eyed Aspect appraisingly. *I must say, you look fetching in brown.*

Appreciation. For while Ennui was garbed in nonChroma colors, Aspect was all in brown: a tight blouse, very short skirt, and dainty brown slippers. Her skin had been tinted brown also for the occasion. Throe was similarly brown. They had prepared carefully.

Ennui climbed out of the coach and walked into the building, immediately escorted by a helpful golem. Then Throe got out, turned, reached in, and draped Aspect over his shoulder in an undignified manner, her bottom and legs in front, her head and arms dangling behind. She was quite limp. He walked directly to the maintenance door to the side, and entered it with his burden. They had researched the complex layout, so knew exactly where things were. They were ignored; service personnel were not tourists.

They made their undignified way to the inner game area, and to the row of booths containing unused golems. One was a brown woman much like Aspect's present form. Throe set Aspect down carefully, she remaining quite limp, opened the booth, removed the golem, set her down, then stood Aspect up in her place. He picked up the golem and carried her away. Wooden golems were stiff when not activated, but these game-golems were more like rag dolls.

Now she was on her own, physically. *In place,* she thought to Ennui.

Good. There are predator males here, but not the ones who did Nonce. It's a pattern, with a female shill; a number use it on new innocents. Be ready.

Oh, yes! Aspect remained standing still in her box, but she was looking around with her mind. She couldn't read the golems, which had no minds, but could see that there were several male golems in booths near her own.

I am concerned about playing this game my very first time alone, Ennui thought. *My virgin voyage. I am making an alliance with a friendly woman who will go with me.*

And alert her henchmen to my location, Aspect agreed grimly.

There was a pause. Then Ennui contacted her again. I have chosen you. My friend is choosing the golem beside you. Oh, say!"

This smelled of something else. *What?*

She really is going with me—but she will animate a male golem.

That was a novel touch. Women debauching women, or perhaps just killing them after setting them up for their male cohorts. Nothing like twisted sexual fun.

Coming now.

Aspect came to life. She stepped out of her booth and looked around as if seeking her female companion.

Two men burst from nearby booths. They charged her from either side. She tried to flee in ineffective alarm, but one caught her, spun her about, and held her with her arms pinned back.

Aspect screamed, as any helpless terrified woman would.

The second man put his hands to her bosom and ripped off her blouse. He hooked his fingers into her skirt and yanked it down, dropping it around her ankles. She wore nothing beneath either, in the golem manner. She tried to kick her feet, but they were entangled. She tried to push him away, but was ineffective. She was helpless. It seemed.

The man in front brought out his stiff member and wedged it in her crotch. She screamed as piercingly as she could manage and twisted her body, trying to avoid the entry, but the man behind her yanked her back harder, keeping her helpless. That would be the woman in male body.

The man in front got his rod angled correctly and thrust upward and inward, completing the rape. And Aspect acted.

First she clamped on his member. The ikon had given her remarkable strength and control there; she grasped it in the manner of a closing fist. Then she caught his ears in her two hands and brought his head down toward hers. Then she bucked her hips with a violent twisting motion.

The golem member, designed for ready amputation, was wrenched off. At the same time Ennui sent a telepathic bolt at the human operator's mind, stunning him. The golem slumped against her.

"What?" the woman-man demanded, confused.

"He fainted," Aspect said. "Something's wrong."

The pseudo man let her go and bent to see to his fallen companion. And Aspect drew her knife and stabbed him in the back. He dropped to the ground, as the golem body was designed to do when killed.

She had castrated one man and killed another. She had just gained twenty points. There was no reason to kill the rapist; ten points was the maximum one person could get from harming another. That was why one man had raped Nonce and the other had killed her; that way each made the maximum. Now Aspect had done the same, to two others.

She pulled the separated member out, and twisted off the ears of the golem she had killed. These were the proofs of her conquest. She had to admit it: she was exhilarated. It was very satisfying to do it back to the bad guys.

She put her clothing back together as well as she could and walked away. There were other men in the area, but they avoided her, having caught on that she was not the patsy she looked. Well, she didn't need them; there were monsters to slay and treasures to find.

Found them, Ennui thought. *All three. Get out of there.*

And leave my winnings behind? Aspect thought with mock petulance. But she walked to her starting booth, entered it, and became quite still. She had been decommissioned.

Throe came to service the battered golems. He carried the original female over his shoulder. He hauled Aspect out, put the other in, and carried Aspect ingloriously away. She suffered herself to dangle, rather more of her anatomy showing than was decent. But of course golems had no decency; they were mere anatomically correct dummies when not animated by human minds.

Throe carried her all the way out to the coach, and no one even glanced his way, let alone challenged him. He set her on the seat and got in himself.

"Were we ordinary folk, I might be tempted to forget my place," he murmured, smiling.

"I have ripped off one member; I'm game to do another."

"Sometimes Ennui traps me that way, teasingly. She's actually stronger than I am, now. I know she would never deliberately hurt me, but it does make me uncomfortable."

"We somehow thought that form and sexual appetite was what

would please you men most."

"We men might have thought so too. Now we know better. There is after all more to a woman than sex."

"After all," she agreed, laughing.

Ennui emerged, having finished her game session. More important, she had located the trio that had savaged Nonce. Those were the ones they were really after; the others were incidental. They had needed to play the game in order to have a pretext to remain there long enough to survey minds and locate their quarry. Ennui entered the coach, and the driver started it moving.

"Now for stage two," Ennui said.

"You have the data?"

"You know I do. We'll intercept them tonight."

They rode to a trail inn for a good meal, acting the part of tourists. Then near dusk they went to the key spot.

They hid the coach and horse on a by-path, and set their trap. It was in a narrow nonChroma avenue between two small Black Chroma zones; no one would stray far from this path. Throe hid in black bushes with a rope, while the two women donned torn old clothing that hardly covered them. In fact they looked very poor and very buxom, with artfully wild hair. Aspect's brown skin tint was long gone; she was no longer a golem. Even if their prey had been the ones she had encountered in the game, they would have been unlikely to recognize her.

"Remember, we want them to be caught in the act," Aspect reminded the others. "If they don't do it, we have no right to take them."

"They'll do it," Ennui said. "I saw it in their minds. The men like to abuse women, and the woman likes to abuse women too. They make quite an ugly team."

"Still, we need to catch them. We can't punish folk for what they might do, only for what they do do."

"Agreement."

When their mind check signaled the approach of the trio, they commenced their act. "Oh, what is to become of us?" Aspect wailed forlornly.

"Hush, sister, we can surely find our way home," Ennui reassured her uncertainly.

"But home is far away, and we have no idea where we are, and no one at home knows either! Oh, those wicked men! To think that we trusted them."

"They were bad ones," Ennui agreed. "Brigands, really. Not all men are like that."

By this time the trio had caught up to them. "What seems to be the problem?" the young woman inquired, though they had surely heard the details during their approach.

Aspect turned as if startled, making a small gasp of surprise. "Oh! Who are you?"

"Just a maiden with her brothers," the woman said. That much was true. "Seeking no mischief." That was untrue; they were scouting the situation to see what offered.

"Thank the planet!" Aspect exclaimed, inhaling, while Ennui looked more wary. "My sister and I are lost and need direction. Where is Village Corncob from here?" That village was a fair distance, and one this trio had never been to. That meant that the two of them really were stranded far from home.

"Why, I'm not sure," the woman said. She turned to her brothers. "What do you think?" She wasn't asking about the village.

"It's a go," one man said, eying Aspect's shapely bottom that her inadequate skirt did not sufficiently conceal.

"I don't understand," Aspect said.

"We'll take care of you," the man said, grabbing her arm.

"Sister!" Ennui cried. "These are more brigands! Flee!"

Aspect screamed and tried to run, but the man hauled her in, holding her fast with an arm around her neck. Ennui also tried to escape, after wasting time dumbfounded, but the other woman tackled her.

Then it was exactly as in the game. The second man ripped off Aspect's shirt and yanked down her skirt. She struggled ineffectively, not using her real strength. In a moment he bared his erect member and wedged it into her crotch, finding the place. He shoved with force, entering her fully, completing the rape.

That's it, Aspect thought. *He's done it, and the others are accomplices.*

Complete stage two, Ennui thought.

Then it changed. Aspect clamped on the member inside her, holding it in a viselike grip. It could not be torn off in the manner of a golem member, but it did hold the man painfully in place. She reached up with her supposedly ineffective hands to catch the lapels of his shirt in a cross-armed grip, digging the edges of her crossed wrists into the sides of his throat. It was a blood strangle, squeezing the buried carotid arteries that supplied blood to the brain, and in seconds he was unconscious. He sagged against her as she released his captive penis; she had no further use for it.

"Hey!" the brother said, catching on that something was amiss. He had been holding her in place, but her action had been so fast and masked that he had missed most of it. Then he gagged as a lasso caught him from behind, dropping over his head and tightening around his neck. He let go of Aspect and tried to get hold of the rope, but it jerked him off his feet as it throttled him.

The sister started to protest, but found she had a problem of her own. Helpless Ennui had suddenly turned competent, and put her in a harsh submission hold. In a moment she too was unconscious. Throe had not been joking when he said that Ennui was now stronger than he was; it was true, and she was in no gentle mood.

Throe came forward. "Remind me never to antagonize either of you Amazons."

"We'll be enticingly weak women again soon, when we revert," Aspect said. "Now for stage three."

They carried the unconscious trio to the hidden coach and dumped them inside. Throe used cord to tie their hands and feet together, then joined the coachman in front, leaving the captives in the charge of the women.

As the coach started moving, following Throe's instructions, the captives recovered consciousness. "What?" the rapist demanded groggily.

"We are taking you for a ride," Aspect said. "You will not be returning."

"Huh?" He tried to struggle, but couldn't get anywhere. Throe knew his business; the bonds were secure.

"You are cheaters, rapists, and killers," Aspect said. "Mostly indulging your foul appetites in the guise of a game, but not averse to doing it for real when opportunity arises. You raped me, and so I am punishing you."

He was not quite ready to believe it. "You bitch—what did you do to me?"

"I strangled your penis and throat. You will feel the bruises if you concentrate."

He hardly needed to concentrate. He winced as he took stock of himself.

The other two were reviving. "You're not helpless women," the woman said. "You set us up. Why?"

"Remember a young woman you befriended at the golem game two days ago?" Ennui asked her. "You set her up for rape and murder."

"She was a fool," the woman said scornfully. "A plum for picking."

"Sometimes fools have friends."

"We didn't hurt her," the rape man said.

"Not physically," Ennui agreed. "Not directly. But it was still unfair, and it was an ugly shock for her."

"It's all in the game. Next time she'll know better."

"Next time perhaps you will know better too," Aspect said. "You had better, because I doubt your new community will tolerate much of your nature."

"What are you talking about? What new community?"

"Limbo," Aspect said succinctly.

"Huh?" He had never heard of it.

But the woman had. "You can't! That's for political crimes."

"It's for folk we can't afford to have in circulation. Technically you aren't bad enough to kill, so we are merely removing you from our society."

"We'll come back!" the rapist said threateningly.

But the woman was pale around the gills. "No one comes back from there."

"And perhaps those other game players who knew your ways will take warning from your mysterious disappearance," Aspect said.

"In fact, perhaps that type of game will be shut down," Ennui said. They shared a certain grim satisfaction.

In due course they arrived at the Limbo lake. Throe approached the boatman, who knew him. The three tied people were put on the boat.

"Please!" the woman cried, her toughness gone.

Aspect shrugged. "You never can tell the future. Should the king ever need you, he'll fetch you. Meanwhile, do your best to fit in. Your old life is finished."

The boat moved across the hot water, disappearing into the night. The deed was done.

The coach took them back to Triumph City by dawn. Throe gave the man a bonus gemstone. "Forget this day and night," he said.

"Forgotten." The coach moved off.

"Realization," Aspect said as they walked to the ferry. "We were several hours in the Brown Chroma zone. We could have divested ourselves of the ikons."

"Negation," Ennui said. "I tried it, without success. There must be stored magic that takes more than a day to dissipate."

Aspect sighed. "Then we'll have to arrange a longer stay in Chroma zones."

"We can travel," Ennui agreed. "And have one last great sexual fling before reverting to normal dull women."

"There will always be a place for dull women," Throe said.

"With dull men," Aspect said. "Lovable dull men."

They all laughed, understanding each other. But Aspect feared this was going to be more of a challenge than they had anticipated. How long would the ikons retain their power while in Chroma zones? This could be an extended excursion.

⁀≈

They waited silently at the Traveler's Exchange, preferring to answer some other traveler's specification than to make their own. That would help them remain anonymous, here in Triumph City where someone might recognize them.

In due course two men stood in the center. "We are returning to our home village Applesauce after delivering our season's produce," one said. "We have a covered wagon with bedding and enough food, but aren't good hands at women's work. We'd like a woman, no fault, for the trip. We can trade for transport across the Chroma zones, so she won't have to."

There were a number of woman in the Exchange, but none responded. It might be that none were going that way, or that none cared for the busy nights that no fault travel with two men promised.

Ennui exchanged a glance with Aspect. It didn't matter where they went, so long as they remained for a sufficient time within Chroma zones. Applesauce was a fair distance; this should do it. They could certainly handle two rustic men, but would pretend reluctance.

Aspect raised her hand. "My friend and I are going that way, lacking trading goods."

The man looked at them. "Done." He was evidently a fair judge of the physical forms of women.

They gathered privately and exchanged introductions. "I'm Andy," the one who had made the announcement said. "This is my friend Bummer."

"I am Speck," Aspect said. "My friend is On."

"We are going beyond Applesauce," Ennui said, "but your bedding and food will help us on our way."

"And your womanly expertise will help us on ours," Andy said.

"About no fault: we prefer to get our rest at night," Ennui said, playing it coy. "Shall we say once early, one on one, and we have our own bedding?" Part of her remained surprised by the coolness with which she negotiated; her old self would never have had either the nerve or the sexual power to compel strange men.

There was a pause. "You are handsome women," Andy said. "We would prefer you sharing our beds."

Ennui made a show of considering. "Do you wager?"

And licked his lips. "In a fair game, with fair stakes, yes."

"We wager. If we win, we get to sleep alone, after one event for each of you, each night. You win, you get us in your beds for an hour."

"Two hours."

Ennui exchanged a glance with Aspect. "Done. What wager?"

"Scissors/paper/rock?"

"We're not much on luck. We'd prefer some contest of skill."

Andy laughed. "About our only halfway skill is telling stories, and not the kind you ladies might care for."

Ennui had heard a fair number of stories over the years, being a good deal older than she looked. Since her purpose was to make a show of reluctance, and lose, this was fine. She and Aspect would get intense sex for two hours, while on record as not seeking it. "We can tell stories too."

The men considered that chance of winning two hours. "Who judges?"

"The villagers, first stage we get. You tell one, we tell one, they vote."

"Deal!"

They went to the men's covered wagon at the nearest Chroma zone staging area. It wasn't fancy, but it was well made, to handle the heavy load of canned applesauce it had delivered. The supplies weren't fancy but were adequate. There was room for four mattresses, but it would be more comfortable if they were put together, two by two. *We lose, we forget to leave after two hours,* Aspect thought. Ennui agreed. The men would not be sexually active all night; the male ambition was generally greater than male performance. But they could probably be tapped once or twice during the night, and in the morning. The novelty of clasping women this shapely would surely rev them up considerably.

The Blue Chroma proprietor came to check with them and collect the trade. "Got an animal resting now. Ready in an hour."

"Satisfactory," Andy said.

When they were on their own again, Andy turned to Ennui. "How soon is early?"

Ennui smiled. Oh, he was eager! "Now, if you want. But that's it for today, unless you win the wager."

"We'll take it."

Andy had the first turn. He took Ennui inside the wagon while Aspect and Bummer remained outside. Ennui sat and removed her shirt, then slid off her skirt. It was shadowed inside, but there was enough light for him to see her clearly enough.

He pursed his lips. "I knew you were a looker, but you're more than that."

"Much more," she said. "Are you staying dressed?"

"Negation." He had been distracted by the sight of her. He hastily got bare. His erection sprang up as his trousers came off. He was certainly ready.

She didn't make him wait. She pounced on him, bore him back, and lay on top of him. She found his member and fitted the connection, then slid down to make it deep and tight. She found his face and kissed him.

He erupted. He couldn't help it, as she had intended. "Deal," she whispered in his ear. "If you can come again without falling out, I'll count it as one."

He rose manfully to the challenge. Such was the excitement of the occasion, he managed to maintain penetration despite softening. She lifted her upper body so that her breasts hung down, just touching his chest, and let his hands fondle them. She was rather proud of those breasts, never having had a pair like them before the ikon. She loved proving their power over men, and they did not fail her this time. Before long he stiffened again, and she let him roll her over so he could finish it his way. He was phenomenally grateful—and she had had enough contact to climax twice herself.

As she did this, she pondered the extent of the change she had undergone in the past year and a half. She had been a frowzy aging woman who had never related well to men or sex or, indeed, life itself. She had gambled her life on finding a new lifestyle, and succeeded beyond her dream. Havoc, the barbarian, had transformed her life. But that was only stage one. She had remained herself, in a remarkable new role as the king's most trusted friend.

Then Havoc and Gale had turned Glamor, and given Ennui and Aspect their ikons to hold. And that seemingly innocuous act of trust had transformed the two women, at first subtly, then remarkably. Now they not only were capable of attracting men sexually, they craved the sex itself. Repeatedly. At first Ennui had thought it was the unfamiliar joy of being desired. Now she knew it was straight raw desire. Stage two. She was having sex with a man she'd never seen before an hour ago, because she needed frequent sexual fixes.

The original Ennui would have freaked out at the very notion. The stage one Ennui would have disdained it. But the stage two Ennui actively sought it.

And what would stage three bring?

She had to be rid of the ikon. She adored what it did for her, but her rational mind, also enhanced by the ikon, knew this had to end. It was like being high on a happiness spell rather than on reality. There was bound to be a consequence.

Andy subsided in bliss. "Gotta win that wager," he gasped.

She wanted him to win too. That was the ironic horror of it.

They dressed and got out of the wagon. "'Bout time," Bummer said. His trousers were bulging impatiently. He and Aspect scrambled into the wagon.

Ennui remembered about playing coy. "But if we win, we sleep alone," she reminded Andy.

"We'll keep our word. But you sure showed me—and I'll bet your friend is showing Bummer right now."

"So you both know we're worth the wager."

"We know!"

The men didn't really know anything, fortunately.

When the others emerged, Bummer looked dazed. Aspect had surely educated him about city-style sex.

"Now we need to plan," Ennui said. She had plenty of experience organizing things for the king; it came naturally to her. "If we play this right, we can gain lodging and maybe even a good evening meal at a village, so that your supplies will stretch farther."

"Doubt," Andy said. "But we're willing to be surprised again."

"We have a wager," she said. "We can use it to gain more than just our private settlements."

"Interest."

She explained. The men listened, and nodded. "If you can set it up, we'll go along," Andy said.

The animal came, a blue six legged rhino, huge and surly but obedient to its master. The entire wagon was strapped to its back, and it lumbered on at an amazing speed. The ride was rough; this was second class service, all the men could afford. But it was fast enough. By day's end they were at the far side of the Blue Chroma zone.

"Now let's see if we can sleep in style," Ennui said. "If we can proffer entertainment, villagers may be willing to trade."

"And we'll get our contest," Andy said, licking his lips. The sexual sample had whetted his appetite for much more. That was the beauty of playing coy.

Ennui approached the blue camp attendant. "Question: we'll be moving on tomorrow. We'd like to trade for lodging at a village tonight by telling stories. Is there a village near?"

The man eyed her. She knew she looked rag-tag, by no accident. "You don't look like a minstrel troupe."

"We aren't. We're amateurs. But we'd like to give it a try."

He shrugged and pointed. "Walk that way."

"Appreciation."

They walked along the blue path, through blue field and forest. Ennui had visited Chroma zones many times, but always briefly, and they remained intriguing. Probably to the zone natives, these shades of blue were as good as full color, and they didn't even notice the lack of variety.

As she walked, Ennui rearranged her clothing to flatter her outline and offer sufficient peeks of flesh. Aspect, picking up on her cue, did the same.

The village was blue too, and all the people in it. The four visitors were immediately the cynosure; they were the only non-blue folk there.

The village elder came out to intercept them. "Introduction: I am Elder Condor of Village Deuce."

"I am On, and my companions are Speck, Andy, and Bummer. We are travelers weary of the road who would like to trade for a comfortable night's lodging. We are amateur storytellers."

"Not minstrels?"

"Not minstrels," she agreed. "Yet we have an angle."

"Question?"

"We two women would prefer to sleep separately. The men want us in their beds. So we have a wager: whoever tells the best story wins the case. But we need judges to decide the issue. We propose to tell our stories to the villagers and let them decide."

The Elder considered as Ennui coincidentally turned, showing her profile to advantage. He surely recognized the interest the villagers would have in a case like this, regardless of the merit of the stories. Sex was always intriguing, especially when there was a conflict of interests. Particularly when there were shapely women involved. "You will announce this?"

"Agreement."

"Two votes: on the better story, and on whether to provide accommodations for the night."

"Agreement."

Soon they were in the center of the village circle. The villagers were assembling, the children sitting on the ground in front, the adults standing outside. There were a fair number, as Ennui had suspected there would be, because of her ploy. Sex was accepted as an instrument of trade, but the idea of it being partly involuntary was compelling.

"Confession," Andy murmured. "I'm nervous. I've never been a public speaker."

"This won't work unless one of you tells a story," Ennui said. "I can set it up, but we can't tell your story."

"I'll do it," Bummer said. It was the first time Ennui had heard him speak. Apparently he saved his words for important things.

When the villagers were ready, Ennui took the center and started talking. This was another thing the ikon facilitated; it gave her confidence and stage presence.

"We are four travelers," she said, turning slowly so as to address all the spectators. "Two innocent women and two lusty men, strangers to each other before this journey. We women want merely to get where we are going, several more Chroma zones distant, and have agreed to do housework as trade for a ride in the men's covered wagon. But for some reason the men want us in their beds at night. Something about no fault, whatever that is."

She paused to allow a murmur of amusement to pass through the audience, then elaborated. "Obviously a bed is just about big enough for a single person; two people just get in each other's way. It's uncomfortable. So we prefer to sleep alone. Yet they are insistent. We don't understand their demand. They are just so unreasonable." She opened her robe for a moment, flashing the audience with a brief full length view of her torso. She had to do it several times as she rotated so that those behind and to the sides could get their peeks. This time the murmur was one of appreciation for her outstanding body. Now everyone knew what the men wanted, and that her profession of maidenly innocence was merely a ploy.

"Finally we made a deal," she continued. "Or rather, a wager. We would have a contest telling stories, and the winners, the tellers of the best stories, would have their way. But we need judges, folk who will fairly judge the merit of our stories and decide which is superior. Thus we have come here; are you good folk of Village Deuce willing to help us?"

Elder Condor made a show of counting responses, though it was already clear that the villagers were solidly in favor of this role. If the intrigue of deciding the fate of would-be lovers was not sufficient, the flash of her bold breasts surely was. They wanted to see more of her. "The villagers agree," he announced. He was evidently pleased; this was turning out to be better entertainment than anticipated.

"Thank you. We do appreciate it." She paused. "Of course if we are good enough, we would appreciate a decent lodging for the night, for we are weary of wagon accommodations."

The Elder answered for the village: "If you are good enough."

Ennui nodded. "Traveler Bummer will speak first, then the Lady Speck." She walked to the edge of the arena and sat down beside Andy, while Bummer got up. He looked a bit nervous, but was game, perhaps inspired by the wager.

"My story is for men," he said. That gave them warning: it was apt to be raunchy. In most villages children were taught about sex early, but there were exceptions. No children moved, so that was all right. "Once on Planet Counter Charm there was a man who had a type of magic seldom seen: he could turn back time a few seconds. That meant that when he made a mistake, he could step back a bit and play it over. When he did that, he was the only one who knew it. Mostly he just used it to get rid of pain or embarrassment, like when he hit his thumb with a hammer he could step back and next time make sure to get his thumb out of the way. Or when he was out in the field, and thought he was alone, and pissed or bared his bottom to poop, and some old maid walked by just then and saw him, he could step back and wait for her to pass before he showed his stuff."

The children in the front tittered. They knew about getting hurt by accident, and about showing bottoms to piss or poop. They would like to have magic like that.

"Now this wasn't exact," Bummer continued. "When he stepped back, it was never quite the same again. Sometimes he missed his thumb and hit his finger instead, and would have to step back again. Or the old maid would be there a little earlier and see him anyway. But generally he could get around trouble, if he stepped back often enough.

"One day he traveled with this woman, no fault. She was really pretty, like those two." He glanced meaningfully at Ennui and Aspect. "But though she said she was willing, she said she had a problem, and it probably wouldn't work. He wasn't worried; he figured she hadn't done it before and was scared, so he'd be very gentle the first time. He discovered she had a special talent of her own: she could make something jet, just by touching it, if it had a jet in it. That was nice when they were thirsty in a desert; she touched a cracked rock and the crack spouted clear water for a moment, which they caught in a leather bucket and drank. But when they got together in bed, naked, and he clasped her, his member jetted the moment it touched her. He was spent, and he hadn't even gotten into her. Bummer!

"'That's my problem,' she said. 'I can't have sex with a man, because he can't get into me before he spouts. I'm doomed to be an old maid!' Well, now; he knew he had to do something about that. So he stepped back in time and got his manhood back inside him, raring to go. She didn't know he'd already tried it. This time he tried to get into her fast, but the jet was faster; the first touch set it off. Bummer again. So he stepped back in time again and asked her to try it with her mouth, but it didn't help; he just got stuff all over her face. Double bummer!"

This time the children burst out laughing. That was a fine joke!

"So he stepped back from that, and she never knew about that embarrassment. But he was really hot for her, and here she was ready to do it with him if he could just figure out a way. But how could he, when he couldn't even touch her? Then he thought, hey, it wasn't exact, and maybe this time he could use that to get around the problem. So he told her to have patience, and he touched her and jetted, but this time he went on into her while he was still hard. Then he held onto her tightly, and stepped back just a bit in time without letting go. Sure enough, he had his potency back, but he was already inside her. Now he pumped away in style, and had a fine jet into her center. It was great, because she was really nice inside. 'How'd you do that?' she asked, amazed. So he told her about his magic, and how he'd used it to reverse his jetting but not his penetration. 'No other man can do that,' she said. 'I can't let a prize like you go; I'll have to marry you.' 'Okay,' he said, knowing no other man would ever get into her. And that was how his magic brought him happiness."

Bummer's story was done. The audience applauded politely; they liked the story. It wasn't new; no story on the planet was completely new, but there were variations, and he had told it well enough.

Now it was Aspect's turn. "Once on Counter Charm there was a young woman. She was a village girl who would soon have to marry, but she wasn't lovely, and the man she longed for paid her no attention. He wasn't even interested in playing Tickle & Peek with her. She knew that soon he would marry a pretty girl, and her chance would be lost forever; she would have to marry the village lout. She knew she had qualities that would impress the man she loved, and that she could make him happy, if she could only get past the problem of appearance. But how could she do that?"

Ennui looked around, and saw the nodding heads of several older girls. They identified with this problem. Tickle & Peek was a standard device for girls to get the attention of favored boys; they could arrange to show a good deal of leg or breast in the process of supposedly helpless ticklishness, and boys were generally interested. When that didn't work, the girl was to be pitied.

Ennui got up quietly and went to the center of the stage, where she squatted.

"One day, struggling with her problem," Aspect continued, "she walked out into the countryside and came to a forest pool. She lay down beside it and wept. 'What's this?' a voice inquired. 'You look sad enough to croak.' She hastily looked up, as she had thought herself to be alone, but there was nothing there except a six legged frog. 'Yes, I am a frog,' it said. 'But I was once a princess. Kiss me and I will resume my natural form and marry you so you can live happily ever after.'" Aspect was doing all the talking, for this was her story, but Ennui faced her in the manner of a big frog. She was a prop.

"'But I'm a girl,' she protested. 'I can't marry a princess.' The frog considered. 'You do seem to have a point. Well then, kiss me, and I will grant you the gift of music, and go find me a prince to marry.' 'What good will music do me?' she demanded. 'I don't know, but it's all else I've got. It's a good gift, because it's magic music. You can do a lot with it.'

She thought about it, and concluded that it was better than nothing. So she kissed the frog, and the frog turned into a princess, complete with a royal gown, glass slippers, and a sparkling little crown." Ennui stood, trying to look regal. "She lifted her hands and gestured. 'And here is your reward, the gift of music,' the princess said, zapping her with magic. 'But remember, it takes time and practice and concentration to learn to use it well.' She departed." Ennui returned to the edge of the stage.

"The girl wasn't sure the princess had really given her anything, so she tested it. She had never had any flair for music and couldn't sing, so that would be a good test. She opened her mouth and sang a note." Then Aspect struck a pose and sang a note. It was strong, firm, even, and melodious. The audience was impressed. Ennui knew it was the ikon enhancing it, as it had when they performed before.

"Surprised, the girl sang several notes." Aspect did so, and they were excellent notes. "She realized that she really had been given the gift of music. But though that might enable her to participate effectively in a chorus, it wouldn't get the attention of the man she loved, who was tone deaf. So it really hadn't changed her situation. Disconsolate, she walked back toward the village.

"Suddenly a bear charged her." Ennui was now the bear, walking on hands and feet. "It had been stalking her, but she had been too distracted to notice. Now it intended to kill her and eat her before she got back to the safety of the village. She looked at it and screamed—and the bear fell over as if it had struck a wall, its six legs scrambling in air." Ennui did that, though she had only four "legs" to lift, in the process proffering a considerable Peek to one section of the audience. "She was amazed; what had happened?

"The bear rolled to its feet and came toward her, growling. All she could think of to do was flee, but she knew it would catch her. Then to her surprise she sang the four notes she had just practiced—and the bear rocked back as if struck on the nose. This was astonishing; could the mere sound of her voice hold the creature off? As it turned out, it could; she was able to sing the bear into complete retreat." Aspect sang a simple melody, and Ennui fled.

"The girl realized that there really was magic in her music; that was what had driven away the bear. Still, that would not get her the man she loved; he was not afraid of bears. She walked on toward the village. But when she came to the little bridge over the stream that supplied the village with water, she discovered that the supports had given way and the bridge had collapsed into the water. She was unable to cross, because there were crocs therein. But then she wondered: if her voice could stun a bear, what about a croc? She had to cross the stream, because it was getting late, and it was dangerous outside at night.

"So she sang, and walked down the bank to the river. The croc there did not move. She stepped into the water, still singing, for she knew the effect would end the moment the song did—and her foot did not splash. Instead it touched the surface of the water and stayed there."

Aspect paused, looking down at her feet, as if amazed. The children looked there too imagining the river.

"She took another step, singing, and her foot remained on the surface. She walked across the water! When she was across, quite dry, she stopped singing and turned to look back. Could she really have done that? Even the croc looked amazed, and disgusted. Well, now! This had real possibilities. What else could this magic music do?

"The next few days she experimented whenever she was by herself. The powers of the music seemed endless; in fact it was as if she lived in a Chroma zone. But she didn't; she was a nonChroma girl. No one in her village had magic. She knew she would be resented if she let her talent be known, so she resolved to conceal it. But then how could she use it to win the man she loved? Finally she tried a special kind of magic: to use illusion that only he could see to make her seem lovely.

"She waited until he was leaving the village." Ennui now assumed this role, clumsily striding as if in the manner of a man, garnering a few laughs. "Then she joined him, as if by coincidence. 'Greeting,' she sang brightly. 'Acknowledged,' he replied gruffly, for she was not the kind of company he craved. He liked pretty and sexy women, and she wasn't either. 'I wish to marry you,' she told him. He burst out laughing, thinking it a joke, glancing at her." Ennui pantomimed the laugh. "But his laugh gave out in the middle, for he saw a lovely face. 'Huh?' She smiled. 'I think I can be what you like.' 'You're wearing a mask,' he said. 'Negation. Feel my face.' He did so, and the illusion made it feel the same as it looked." Ennui felt Aspect's face. "Still he doubted. 'And I like—' 'Feel these,' she sang, opening her shirt to reveal burstingly full breasts. He did so, and was satisfied." So was the audience, for

Aspect had opened her own shirt to illustrate the story, showing breasts that were every bit as nice as those described, and Ennui gave them a good feel. That got a considerable laugh. "'How—?' 'I'll tell you after we are married.' At which point he got canny. 'I want to know it works, first.' 'Very well.' They went to a place beside the path, and she lay down and let him have at her body." They did not act out this part. "'Stop that fool singing!' he said."

Aspect stopped her own singing narration. "Oops." And the audience related. What was the girl to do now? If she couldn't sing, she couldn't keep up the illusion.

"Fortunately he was already plunging into her, and didn't notice that she had reverted to plain. While he worked, she thought desperately, and got an idea. She resumed singing, but this time modified the spell to make him like her voice as well as her body. So he no longer complained. Satisfied, he agreed to marry her, for she did seem to have all that mattered in a woman." Aspect smiled knowingly, and the women and some of the men smiled with her. "After they married, she told him about the frog and the magic. He, not being entirely stupid, realized that this could be quite useful. So he kept the secret, and they prospered. All because she had kissed a frog."

The audience applauded vigorously. The villagers had liked the story, perhaps as much for Aspect's appearance and the incidental acting as for the familiar content. In fact the applause was louder and more sustained than it had been for Bummer's tale. Ennui realized that could be a problem, because they wanted to lose, not win. But the contest was far from over.

⁓⁓

Now it was Andy's turn. He looked determined, surely because the sight of Aspect's breasts had reminded him what was at stake. He was nervous about public speaking, but knew he would lose his hot night in bed if he defaulted. So he visibly nerved himself and started in. "There was this guy, this ordinary man who had just got dumped by his fiancée. She told him he was of no account, had always been of no account, and always would be of no account. The worst of it was she was probably right. He was so beat by that that he decided to go to the Cave of Death and die. No one who entered it ever came out; it was sure suicide. Maybe that would make his ex-fiancée sorry."

Andy paused, uncertain how this was going. Aspect caught his eye and smiled: he was doing well. Encouraged, he resumed his narrative, not thinking to question why the opposition should be helping him. "So he came to the cave and peered in. It was totally dark in there, and he was scared. But he couldn't back off now; if he returned to the village everyone would laugh at him for lacking the courage of his convictions. Somehow that seemed worse than death did. So he gulped in some air, cranked up his posterior, and marched boldly into the gloom.

"For a moment there was nothing. Then he heard a voice. 'A man!' It sounded like a woman. This surprised him; what was a woman doing here? So he stopped walking and peered into the darkness, seeing nothing. 'Who?' he demanded. 'It's me, Autopsy,' she replied. 'I can't see you.' 'No one can see me; I'm a ghost.' 'A ghost!' he repeated, appalled. 'Well, this is the Cave of Death. What did you expect—warm luscious living flesh?' That made him realize that he was being foolish. Of course there were ghosts in here; where else would they be? 'Well, I guess I've come to join you. What's it like being a ghost?' 'Oh, it's awful! I hate it.' She burst into sobbing. That made him feel bad; he didn't like hearing a woman cry, especially a ghost woman. 'Aw, don't cry, Autopsy.' 'Oh? What are you going to do about it? Restore me to life?' 'I don't know; is it possible?' 'No.' This annoyed him. 'Then why did you suggest it?' 'I wasn't suggesting it.' 'Yes you were! You said—' 'I was being sarcastic.' 'I hate sarcasm.' The ghost paused, then softened. 'Why did you come here?' 'That's none of your concern.' 'Yes it is, if you're going to be a ghost I'll have to associate with you for all eternity. Are you of good character?' 'What is this—a test to see if I'm okay to die?' 'Yes.' That set him back. He didn't know how to refute it, so he answered. 'I'm not a good enough character to rate well with my fiancée, so she dumped me. Now I don't want to live.' 'Oh, that's so sad.' 'Are you being sarcastic again?' 'No.' 'So I guess if I'm not good enough for here, I'm not good enough for you, so maybe I'd better find another place to die.' 'Let's not be hasty. I was, and I regretted it. Are you sure you really want to die?' He considered. 'It's not that I really want to die, it's that I can't live without my fiancée.' There was another pause while the ghost considered. Then she said 'I am not alone here. I have two friends. Let's exchange introductions.' 'Okay, I guess I've got nothing much better to do. I am Buffoon.' 'I am Autopsy, as I said, and my friends are Necropsy and Thanatopsy. They are also ghosts.'

"Somehow that didn't surprise him. Those were weird names, but they all seemed female. Buffoon felt a stir of interest. 'Okay. Let me see you.' 'I can't to that.' 'Why not? If we're introduced, we ought to meet face to face.' 'It's because in death we each have only a fraction of our living abilities. I can be heard, but can't be seen or felt.' 'Oh. I guess that makes sense. How about the others?' 'Necropsy can be seen, but not heard or felt.' 'Well, then, let's see her.' 'She's sort of shy. She's afraid you won't like her.' 'What, she's ugly?' 'No, she's beautiful. But men don't like beauty without substance.' Buffoon had a similar sentiment, but didn't think this was the occasion to mention it. 'Let's see her anyway.' 'But she's naked, because that's how she was when she died.' Somehow this didn't bother Buffoon as much as it might have. 'I promise not to make any nasty cracks.' 'Very well then, she'll risk it. Remember, you promised.' 'I promised,' he agreed, intrigued.

"In a moment a pale glow appeared in the cave. It swirled and formed into a vaguely female shape. This clarified into a lovely nude woman. She had a cute face, pert breasts, a shape that fell short of an hourglass but was obviously trying to get there, and long firm legs. Her bright hair waved out of her head and framed her like a cloak. 'This is Necropsy,' Autopsy said. 'She's the loveliest creature I've ever seen!' Buffoon exclaimed. The divine figure smiled hesitantly. 'Do you mean that?' Autopsy asked. 'Sure I mean it! If I had a girl like her to clasp, I wouldn't be coming here to die.' 'Hearing that makes Necropsy practically expire with pleasure.' Now Buffoon was really curious about the third ghost. 'How about Than—Than—' 'Thanatopsy. She can't be seen or heard, but can be felt.' 'Well, I guess I'd better feel her, then.' 'She's naked too. We all are. We didn't want to spoil our nice clothes when we died.' 'Understanding.' He didn't understand, but it seemed the expedient thing to say. 'Here is Thanatopsy.'

"Then something touched him. It felt soft and smooth and thoroughly female. 'Hi, Thana,' he said. 'You feel good.' 'She appreciates your appreciation,' Autopsy said. This was really interesting. 'May I hold you?' 'She says affirmation.' So Buffoon put his arms around the figure he couldn't see, and it was really nice. There were breasts against his chest, and a face close enough to kiss, and a truly evocative torso, by the feel of it. Things proceeded naturally, and he kissed her, and felt her kissing him back. 'Nice, really nice,' he said after a moment. 'You must have been something really special when you were alive, because you're great dead.' For answer she kissed him again, and guided his hands to her shapely bare bottom. 'You know,' he said, 'if you three are as nice to me when I'm dead as you are right now, I won't mind dying.' 'But when you're dead, you'll be limited too,' Autopsy said. 'You will be a talker, a viewer, or a toucher. We prefer you alive.'

"That made him do some serious thinking as he reluctantly turned Thana loose. 'I wish you were alive, all three of you. But I like you pretty well as ghosts. Are you stuck here in the cave?' 'We could leave it, but what would there be for us outside?' Autopsy said. 'Here in the darkness Thanatopsy and I can pretend we might be seen, and Necropsy can pretend she might be felt. But out in human society we would be known for what we are: mere ghosts. We'd expire of humiliation, so to speak.' 'I see your point. I guess you're better off here.' 'Will you stay with us, alive?' 'Well, you know I like your company. You haven't told me once I'm no account. But there's nothing to eat here. I'd soon be dead of starvation.' 'True,' she said sadly. 'You're better off in human society.'

"But the dialogue had him thinking. He did like these ghosts, and not just because one was nice to talk to, another was nice to look at, and the third was nice to feel. They accepted him as he was, and wanted him to live. His lost fiancée seemed distant now, less worth missing. There was something here; could something more be made of it? Then he got a wild idea. 'You really want me to be with you?' he asked. 'Yes we do,' Autopsy said. 'You're the first live person who has been willing to associate with us, knowing what we are.' 'You three are the first women who seem to think I'm worth being with. But just what could we do together?' 'We can do everything, in thirds," she said. 'I can talk with you, Necropsy can be visible for you, and Thanatopsy can touch you.' 'But can I touch her? I mean—' 'We know what you mean. Yes, you can. But touch is all; no sight or sound.' Buffoon was afraid he'd turn them off, but now was the time to find out. 'I'm a man. What I want in a woman is sort of basic.' Necropsy gazed sadly at him. 'We know,' Autopsy said. 'The idea of being with a live man really turns us on. But we're still confined to thirds.' 'But you'd be willing, if you could do it.' 'Eager. But—' 'I may have a way.'

"There was a pause, but he knew they were interested, because Necropsy was looking at him with excitement and Thana kissed him on the ear. 'How?' Autopsy asked. 'Well, it involves some, uh, overlapping.' 'We're ghosts. We can occupy the same space, if that's what you mean.' 'Affirmation. Suppose you all three get together, so all of your bodies overlap.' 'Like this?' Autopsy asked, as Necropsy overlapped her so that it seemed to be the visible mouth speaking. 'Affirmation,' he repeated. 'If you can hold that pose, I can do all three things with you at once. You'll seem just like one living woman. I could take you out into human society, and no one would know. Are you interested?' 'Affirmation!' Autopsy said in glad wonder. Then she stepped into him, or rather, the three of them did, and kissed him. Things proceeded, and soon they were in an embrace that could not have been closer. They felt just like a woman, outside and inside. 'That's great!' Buffoon gasped. 'Now there's just one problem. Folk'll wonder if I'm seen with a constantly nude woman.' 'We don't need to be visible all the time,' the lovely affectionate figure said. 'We can be together for you alone, in the comfort of your house. We don't need to shop or wash or anything. When you have visitors, you can explain that your wife likes to be natural in her own house.'"

Andy looked around at the audience. "So Buffoon thought it was going to work out. What do you think?"

There was a great round of applause. The villagers agreed, and liked the story. It was evident that a good many of them had not heard it before; it wasn't in the repertoire of local minstrels.

Now it was Ennui's turn. "Once there was a brother and a sister in a nonChroma zone, named Tuck and Nip. They were equivalent in age, he being the third child in the family, and she the fourth." Ennui paused just long enough to let the implication register: they were siblings, but not full blood related. "Nip was a fine strapping girl, growing tall and strong, and she liked active play. Girl things like sewing and cooking turned her off. Tuck, in contrast, was frail for a boy, not at all muscular, though he had good coordination in his hands. So when they had chores, they arranged to exchange them, so that she hauled the heavy water buckets for him, and he sewed fancy doilies for her. Their parents didn't know." Ennui paused so that the children in the audience could finish their titter. There was a lot that parents didn't know about children, regardless of the Chroma. "Their elder siblings knew, and might have told or teased them, but the elder boy had a secret girlfriend he didn't want known, and the elder girl had a wart on her bottom she didn't want known, so they held their peace. That's the way it is, in families." There was a chuckle that spread beyond the children.

"Then their family moved to another village to take care of an ailing relative. The two elder siblings remained in the original village, for they were coming up on marriage age, but Nip and Tuck were ten, and had to remain with the family. They considered, and made a momentous decision: they would switch places. Nip donned trousers, and Tuck a dress. They were of equivalent height, but Nip was the solider figure. Their parents, distracted by the care of a difficult elderly person, either didn't notice or didn't care, as long as the chores were done. So the folk of the new village came to know Nip as a boy and Tuck as a girl. They pretended shyness, and never played Tickle & Peek." This time the whole audience laughed, well understanding why.

"But as they come up on the age when boys discover qualities in girls and girls consider prospects for future homesteads, there was a problem. Nip was developing breasts and Tuck wasn't. Their charade couldn't continue much longer. Nip was interested in boys, and Tuck in girls, but any romantic association was not feasible in their present modes. They pondered and fretted, and finally concluded that they would have to change back to their real genders. By this time they knew the young folk of the new village pretty well, including many of their embarrassing secrets, so they were able to escape ridicule when they made their secret known. Actually there was some respect for it; they had done a bold thing, switching genders. In fact, several girls who had shared sewing parties with Tuck were pleased to continue association, but now they batted their eyes at him instead of sharing girlish secrets. The boys were less accepting of Nip, because she could scythe better than most of them and was taller than some of them. But one big boy who had trouble attracting girls because he wasn't handsome was interested. As it happened, his younger sister was a fourth, and he got along well with her, so he didn't mind Nip's being a fourth. It was also the case that her scything had built up her chest muscles, causing her freshly unbound bosom to become prominent. He liked that. Meanwhile his little sister, who wasn't great with sewing or cooking took a shine to Tuck, and soon was trading Peeks for sewing. In the end, Nip and Tuck married the other brother and sister, and Nip did most of the man's work for her household, while Tuck did most of the woman's work in his household. Their spouses were glad to let it be, and when they had children, they pitched in and did their share, and their neighbors never knew."

Ennui was done with her story, and there was applause, but less than before. The villagers preferred the three ghosts to the exchanged roles. So it was even, and the issue had not been decided.

The elder made it official: "We see your wager undecided. We also are not sure your stories are worth a night's lodging. Tell one more, with all of you participating together, and if that moves us, we will grant your lodging."

Aspect knew they were being pushed, but there didn't seem to be a choice. "Let us consult."

They consulted. "How can we settle the wager by a joint story?" Andy asked.

"We can't," Aspect said. "We'll have to settle it by a game of chance. But first we must secure the lodging. What story can we tell that will move them to give us what we want?"

"I know one about ghosts and brothers and sisters," Bummer said. He described it briefly, and it seemed viable.

"You're the brothers, we're the sisters," Aspect said. "The non-actors narrate."

"Agreement." They hastily worked out spot details, and then addressed the audience.

"There were once two brothers," Andy said, standing in the center beside Bummer. "They were named Bum and And, for the elder and the younger, and they needed to marry, but they had been away from the village for some time on business, and now all the eligible maidens were taken. So they traveled to another village, but the folk there didn't know them, and no girls were interested, as they were just ordinary folk. They were decent, but not handsome, so did not make a winning first impression. So they went to another village, with no better luck. And another, and another, always courteously denied. They were worthy men, but were caught by circumstance."

"Then two sisters heard of the traveling men," Ennui said, moving to the center with Aspect as the men faded back. "They were named Speck and On, and they had to marry soon, but did not like the available prospects. They cared more about character than appearance, and were presentable but not beautiful. So when the two men came to their village, they welcomed them and agreed to marry them."

"Now you might think that such a hasty set of marriages would not work out well," Andy said. "But as it happened, compared to what the brothers had feared they would have to take, the women were pretty." He glanced across the stage at the two women, who opened their cloaks to show nice forms.

"And as it happened," Ennui said, "the men were competent workers with good situations. They took their new wives back to their village, and it was good. They fell in love, Speck with Bum and On with And, and in due course each couple had two children. They agreed privately to switch husbands for the fourths, when that time came, and their families would be complete." Ennui went to stand with Andy, embracing and kissing him; she was On, of course, and he was And. Aspect and Bummer, the other couple, also joined.

"Then tragedy struck," Andy said.

"Speck needed to go to trade in a neighboring village, and Bum was busy, so And went with her for protection, lest there be brigands." Aspect and Andy walked together to the other side of the stage. "On the way a magic storm crossed the trail. They tried to flee it, but it was too swift. They tried to find shelter, but there was none close by. They simply had to hunch down in their cloaks and hope it wouldn't be too bad." The two kneeled on the stage and lowered their heads, side by side.

"But it was a dagger storm, surely conjured by some evil magician," Aspect said. "Sharp knives rained down on them. And tried to shield Speck with his body, but the knives cut through him and got to her too." The two acted it out, shaking as phantom daggers struck them, then collapsing on the ground. She was pleased to hear a child in the audience crying; it was real for the youngest.

Bummer stepped to the center of the stage. "And so they died," he said. "The villagers found them a few hours later. It was a blow to everyone, but especially to their spouses, Bum and On, when they learned." He put his face in his hands as if grief-stricken, then turned to pantomime telling Ennui. She made a gesture as of tearing her hair, then collapsed, so And comforted her, somewhat awkwardly.

After a suitable pause, Ennui took over the narrative. "But they had children to care for, and were required to remarry. Rather than seek strangers—for the village still lacked suitable partners—the two survivors married each other. In that manner they formed a family with four children, and were not required to have more. Two children had their own mother, and two had their own father, and the parents had been close throughout, so it was not as bad for them as it might otherwise have been."

"But there was a problem," Bummer said. "Bum still loved Speck, and On still loved And, though they were dead. On and Bum could not stand to touch each other; it would have seemed like a betrayal of their loves. So they lived together like brother and sister."

"Yes this was not easy for them," Ennui said. "On longed to be clasped at night, and Bum longed to clasp. Each understood the other's grief and need perfectly, but neither could abate it. So frustration was added to the burden of their grief. Bum turned surly, and On dreamed of rejoining her beloved in death. The children noticed, but did not comprehend the cause. They were locked into a slow downward spiral that threatened to destroy the compromise family."

Now Aspect and Andy rose from the floor. "The ghosts of the dead partners saw this, and were restless," Aspect said. "They had children who needed a good home. They did not want to see those children orphaned again. But what could they do? They were ghosts; they had no substance, and would scare anyone they appeared before."

"But they knew they had to do something," Andy said. "They could not return to life, so needed a way to make the living folk be satisfied with their roles. What could that be?"

"Then they thought of something," Aspect said. "It was chancy, but it was all they had, so they agreed to try it."

"Speck went to see On, in the middle of the day when she was alone," Andy said. "Speck took faint illusion form, and spoke in a whisper, which was all she could manage. 'On,' she said. 'Hear me.'" Aspect stood before Ennui, gesturing. "On stared at her. 'What's this— a ghost? Am I dying at last?' 'No, beloved sister, you must live, for the sake of our children. You must find love again.' 'How can I do that? I can never love another man.' 'Then you must pretend, for his sake and for the children's sake.' 'Confusion!' 'You must emulate me, and go to my beloved, and give him solace. Then at least he will be comforted, for a while.' On laughed. 'I could not do that, and if I did, I would not fool him for an instant.' 'Still, you must try. Don one of my dresses, do your hair like mine, and copy my voice.' 'I would seem just like what I am: one woman pretending to be another, cruelly teasing a good man who does not deserve further grief.' But Speck insisted, and prevailed on On reluctantly to don the dress, change her hair, and copy Speck's voice. Since they were sisters, there was a fair resemblance to start with, and these efforts did make her resemble Speck." Andy shook his head. "But it wasn't enough. It was clear that though the emulation might fool a passing villager, it would never fool the man who loved Speck. 'There's no help for it,' Speck said. 'I must merge with you, beloved sister, to complete the effect.' 'How can you do that?' 'Like this.' And Speck stepped into On, her ghostly substance overlapping the flesh of her living sister." Aspect stepped into Ennui, and covered them both with her cloak. After a moment the cloaks separated, and Aspect's sank down to a huddle, as of a thing that had lost its animation.

"Then On left the house," Andy continued. "She went to the field, where Bum labored alone, for the other men did not want his surly company any more." The cloaked figure walked to the center of the stage, where Bummer was now moving his arms as if working at something. 'Beloved,' she said softly. Bum paused to stare at the concealed figure. 'You sound like—it can't be.' 'It can't be for long,' the figure said. 'But for an hour, I exist.' 'I don't believe it. You're dead.' 'Yes, but for an hour I live. I had to come to you, beloved.' 'This is a cruel hoax. Show your face, impostor.'"

The figure threw off the cloak, and there was Aspect. There was a general gasp in the audience, then a knowing murmur. The two women had exchanged places while covered by the cloaks. But it was understood: this was the living woman emulating the dead one, with the dead woman's magical help.

Bummer stared at Aspect. "It's true," he said. "You have returned."

"For an hour," Aspect agreed. "Come, beloved; let's make the most of it."

"Agreement!" He embraced her and kissed her, and she returned the affection passionately. Then Aspect stepped out of her dress while Bummer hastily stripped, and they covered themselves with the cloak as they lay on the ground. It looked a lot like masked sex.

"After they made love, they talked," Andy said. "It was so good to be together again. But then the time was up, and Speck had to depart before the spell wore off. They dressed, and kissed once more, and she was gone, leaving Bum happily bemused. At dusk he returned home. He thought about telling On about his experience, but concluded that she might misunderstand, so he was silent. But he was no longer surly."

Now Aspect took over the narrative. "The two ghosts were pleased at how well their effort had worked. But that was only the beginning. Now it was time for the other couple. Bum visited And, and broached him in similar manner." Andy stood before Bummer, gesticulating, while Bummer shook his head. But Andy kept after him, and finally Bummer agreed to change clothing, color his hair, and try to emulate his brother. They merged under the cover of the cloak, and separated, and Andy walked to where Ennui worked in the house. The audience understood that it was the living man imitating the dead one, with the help of the ghost.

Andy appeared before Ennui. "Beloved," he said.

She turned to face him, startled. "And! It can't be."

"It can be—for an hour." Then he enfolded her, and kissed her with such passion that some of the children in the audience squirmed, finding this part dull. They made love under the concealment of the cloak, and as the hour ended Andy departed, leaving Ennui visibly dazed.

"And so On, too, had her joy," Aspect continued. "But because of her prior experience, she knew that it had not been the physical And who had visited her, but Bum with And's ghost. And surely Bum knew it also—that his prior tryst had been with On and Speck's ghost. Did it matter? She was in doubt."

Then Bummer returned from his work in the field, shown by his march across the stage. "I have been thinking," he said.

"So have I," Ennui replied.

"The other day my beloved came to me in the field and gave me great joy."

"Today my beloved came to me in the house, and gave me similar."

"They were ghosts."

"Borrowing human bodies."

"Ours."

"Ours," she agreed.

"I will always love your sister Speck."

"And I your brother And."

"Yet there are ways in which you favor her."

"And you him."

"Do you think they are trying to tell us something?"

"Or perhaps show us?"

"That they would not consider it a betrayal if we loved elsewhere," he said.

"So that they can rest in peace," she agreed.

There was a silence. Then they came together and kissed, and clasped. "Perhaps I could love again," Bummer said. "You have many of the qualities of your sister."

"And you of your brother," Ennui agreed.

"And when it comes to sex—"

"Agreed."

Without further dialogue they lay down together, covering themselves with the cloak.

Andy and Aspect walked to the center of the stage. "Now at last we can depart," he said.

"Agreed. The living will be happy again, and take good care of the children."

"And what of the dead?"

"Perhaps the living have shown the way," Aspect said.

"We have worked well together."

"And we died together."

"We deserve some solace too," Andy said.

"Agreement."

They embraced, and kissed, and lay down together, covered by a cloak.

After a pause, all four players got up. "And so all was set to rights," Andy said. "And our story is done."

The applause was loud and long. The villagers had liked the story, having been surprised by its ending, which was new. "You'll have lodging," the elder agreed.

The lodging turned out to be a single small house with nice appointments, a supply of food, a washing area, and just one main chamber largely filled by a huge bed. Aspect looked around. "It seems we did not rate separate lodgings," Aspect said.

"We can throw fingers and take separate halves of the room, whichever way," Andy said. "Or the bed and the floor."

Aspect glanced at Ennui, who nodded. "We don't need to throw

fingers. The story turned us on. But I would like to be with the one I
died with, this time."

"And I the one I lived with," Ennui said.

"Done!" the men said almost together.

"Let's eat, then take turns on the bed," Aspect said, knowing the
men would have another idea.

"Let's start with the bed," Andy said.

"One couple starts with the bed," Ennui said. "We throw fingers
for that."

"Odd is us," Andy said.

Andy and Bummer threw fingers, and it came out odd. Ennui
and Bummer set about fixing a meal while Aspect and Andy stripped
and got on the bed. There was no foreplay; he was on her and in her
and climaxing almost instantly, and she with him. Aspect really had
gotten hot from the story; it had been a fine interaction.

"Our turn," Ennui said.

Andy and Aspect laughed and got off, not dressing. Bummer and
Ennui jumped on, and were at it with similar speed. Aspect watched
with interest, as she had not often gotten to watch such action when
not participating. It revved her up again.

When the two were done, and fell apart, Andy and Aspect got on
the bed with them. There really wasn't room for four abreast, so Aspect got on top of Bummer and Andy got on Ennui. This mixing was
another turn-on. The women had done it with three women and one
man before, but not with two and two. The men turned out to be more
than willing to experiment, and soon Bummer was into Aspect from
below, and Andy into Ennui from above, while Aspect and Andy turned
their upper bodies toward each other and kissed and fondled. It took
a while, since they had all had sex very recently, but in due course
Aspect felt Bummer's climax building. She clamped her cleft around
him and stuck her tongue into Andy's mouth as her own joy came.
That set him off, and his reaction set Ennui off, and they finished in a
chain reaction, long and slow, so that they did overlap.

"Let the ghosts beat that," Aspect gasped as she finally collapsed
on Bummer, milking the last of his essence from him. Andy's hand
remained on her breast, and hers on his buttock as they lay there in
their pile for a while.

After a while they got up and had their supper. They took further
turns on the bed, Aspect with Andy, Ennui with Bummer, seeing what
they could do. Eventually they slept, finding a way to fit all four of
them on the bed: The women had the center, the men the edges, with
their heads on the women's breasts as pillows. Whoever woke and
stirred was taken on by whomever of the opposite gender woke, and
then returned to sleep. It was a wearing but glorious night. The men
by this time had caught on that the women were as eager for sex as the
men were, but had the sense not to remark on it. They knew better

than to question a situation they liked extremely well: full access to two beautiful, experienced, and ardent women.

But they still hadn't found out how to rid themselves of the ikons that were responsible for such excessive passion. That was increasingly worrisome for Aspect.

⋙⋘

In the morning they slept late, recovering, then had breakfast. "You two are some special women," Andy said.

"Merely travelers," Ennui said. "No fault."

"You want to try the next Chroma zone the same way? It worked pretty good last night—better than I expected. We could tell the same stories in a new zone, like a troupe."

"We're game," Ennui said.

"Listen, we don't want to pry, but we're getting curious as hell. We're just regular men, but you two are not regular women. Is there anything you can tell us?"

Ennui glanced at Aspect. They had demonstrated sexual capacity unlike that of normal women, and the men were justified in remarking on it. What part of the truth could they share?

Aspect came through with a slice of it. "We have what you might be called a curse. It makes us want sex as much and as often as men do. It was fun at first, but now we want to be rid of it. We have men of our own, but we're wearing them out. So we're traveling, looking for a cure."

"Seeing if you can use it up!" Andy exclaimed. "That explains a lot."

Ennui had not thought of it that way, but it could be valid. If they not only starved the ikons of their magic source, but invoked them heavily, they might use up their power faster. "Something like that," she agreed. "We travel anonymously because we don't want to embarrass our men. After you two, we'll try others. If the curse has a limit, we'll find it."

"We're glad to help," Andy agreed. "Anytime."

They had been a good two hours without sex. "Appreciation for your understanding," Ennui said, moving into him.

"Okay!" He joined her on the bed, and they had another hot round of sex. Ennui had spoken truth: she did want to use it up, if she could. But it was no chore; she was eager for it, and now she had a rationale.

Aspect and Bummer followed, performing similarly. Then they packed and departed the house, checking out with the elder. "We threw fingers," Ennui told him. "We women lost."

"We men cheated," Andy confided. "Wouldn't you?"

The blue elder smiled, knowing they were joking. "If you pass this way on your return trip, we will be interested in more stories. What you lack in polish you make up in enthusiasm."

"We wanted good lodging," Ennui said. "We had to perform."

They went to the staging area, and soon were on their way across the next Chroma zone, a fiery Yellow. Modesty was no longer necessary, so they had several bouts of sex while floating.

As the day waned, they were in a White Chroma zone. They went to a White village and bargained with the White elder for lodging. Soon the villagers assembled, and they told their stories again, refining them as they went, and their performance was satisfactory. There was always an excellent market for tales, even poor ones, and theirs were perhaps middle range.

This time they had two beds in the white apartment, and could have slept apart. They didn't; they formed two couples. But by now the men were wearing thin, and a single bout of sex was enough. It was getting time to find new men.

The third day saw them past the men's destination, and they went on alone. "Well, it was fun," Ennui said.

"But we still can't divest ourselves of the ikons."

"Agreement. I've been trying."

"Similarity."

"Maybe if we stayed several days in a single Chroma zone, instead of passing through nonChroma zones, however briefly," Ennui said, musing. "We don't know what the recharge rate is."

"Worthwhile."

They bargained for transport, selling no fault sex to larger groups of men, and delivered more than enough to satisfy. They had become sexually indefatigable, able to climax repeatedly in rapid order. Not merely able, or willing, but desirous. They pretended to be good sports about the numbers of men, but actually it was an ongoing hunger. Faking climaxes was no good; only real ones eased their obsession for a time.

Then they came to a large Green Chroma zone with a nature trail. "Are you thinking what I am?" Ennui asked.

"We could take days to navigate that trail by foot."

They went to the trail entrance and bargained for admittance. The green men in charge considered, having eyed them appraisingly. "You plan to night at the trail stops?"

"Affirmation."

"A number of rangers stay at those stops, maintaining them and the surrounding forest, also acting as guides. Two nonChroma woman would be a novelty. No fault for those you encounter?"

"Agreement."

"Then here are your passes for indefinite stay thereon." He paused, his gaze on Ennui's displayed cleavage. "I wonder—"

Ennui stepped forward. "No fault."

They stepped into his private chamber. The green man turned out to be as virile as any other, and as appreciative of her charms. "I was not aware that nonChroma women could be so shapely and ardent," he said as they concluded.

"We are from the big city. We find Chroma men interesting."

"Gratification. Perhaps when you exit, your friend—?"

"She surely will," Ennui agreed, committing Aspect to a similar session. It was fun making men happy, considering how easy it was.

They set out walking the trail, in no hurry. Walking, too, might draw on the ikons' power, because their magic made the women virtually indefatigable. Walking, sex, and continuous immersion in a Chroma zone—if anything could do it, this should.

Greeting.

"Why hello, Swale," Ennui said aloud so that Aspect would know. They were avoiding telepathy, their general policy in Chroma zones. Translucent specialized in mind reading, and was good at it, but any Chroma could do it, and some Chroma folk surely did do it. So they kept their minds locked, and gave no evidence of their ability

"What are you doing here?" Aspect asked. "I thought you were in another region." Naturally they did not refer to the Glamors or their mission.

"I am," Swale said, borrowing Ennui's mouth with her consent. "But they need privacy at the moment, so I am catching up on the local news. Spanky says you are traveling, but she doesn't know why."

Ennui took back her mouth. "Read it in my thoughts."

The succubus did. "Oho! You have been naughty girls."

"It facilitates travel," Aspect said, smiling.

"And you didn't invite me along!"

"Welcome," Ennui said. "Though we are trying to use up our sexuality."

"Forlorn effort, as long as—oh, I see. Do your better halves know?" Swale meant the Glamors.

"You can inform them," Aspect said. "We do not wish to cause them concern."

"I will. But for now, I prefer to remain with you. I promise merely to observe, so as not to subvert your effort."

"Pleasure," Aspect said. "How goes it in the other region?"

"Mixed. Some phenomenal discoveries. Do you know what ifrits are?"

"Demonic spooks in stories," Ennui said.

"There are real ifrits there." And in the course of the next hour, speaking in careful generalities, Swale informed them of the discovery of astonishing cloud-like entities. Also of serious problems handling massive illusion. It was fascinating.

Then they told her of the game rape and murder of Nonce, and how they had gotten vengeance. "Ooo, glorious!" the succubus said. She liked anything sexual, especially if it was illicit or violent.

Only when their stories had caught up did they become properly aware of the wonders along the nature trail. They were not random; it was a veritable garden, with many varieties on exhibit. There were nut trees, fruit trees, and flowering trees of many types. Some were tentacled, the kind that carried carriages through the forest. "Oh, Havoc would love this," Ennui said.

"Gale too," Aspect said, looking down at the thick mosses lining the path.

"Augur too," Swale said. "He's Red Chroma, but he specializes in plants. He's quite a lover, too."

"That relates?" Aspect inquired.

"See that love orchid? One of those men could make it sing."

They looked at the orchid. It was a sturdy shrub with a single giant flower shaped like a supine human female torso. It had phenomenal green breasts, broad hips, solid thighs, and a gaping vulva.

"Just what a man desires," Ennui agreed, impressed. "No arms to get in the way, no head to talk back, no feet, just the essentials."

"I understand such flowers get heavy patronage," Swale said. "The men know they aren't real women, but they are so sexy and obliging that it doesn't matter."

"But what point?" Ennui asked, intrigued.

"They get some nourishment from the semen. But mainly they stick pollen to the bodies of the men, and this gets carried to the next flower they touch. So the plants really are breeding, just not in exactly the way their clients do."

Ennui got a wicked idea. "Are there male orchids?"

"I believe so. After all, women walk these trails too."

They walked on, alert for male orchids, and soon found one. It resembled a muscular man's torso, and unlike the female flower, had a head with a handsome face. Farther down was a tight belly with a small projecting erect member.

"I should think it would be larger," Aspect said, contemplating the member.

"Women don't go for size alone," Swale said. "It has other features."

"I'll try it," Ennui said. She had been several hours without sex, and missed it.

"Embrace it and set it," Swale advised. "When you're ready for the action, kiss it. That's the signal."

Bemused, Ennui removed her clothing and straddled the torso. She set the member at her cleft so that it was as far in as was feasible considering its size, then lay on the torso and put her face down to kiss the mouth.

The torso came alive. The mouth returned her kiss. It had a sexy sweet taste that turned her on. The torso sweated, coating her belly and breasts with moisture that caressed her skin and made her nipples swell. The member abruptly swelled to penetrate her completely, with a peristaltic rippling along its expanding girth and length. Part of it spread out along her cleft, wetting it with a slick ichor that generated a warm pleasure. It spread up to her clitoris, surrounding it, and suddenly the pleasure intensified.

"Oooh!" she moaned, in orgasm before she knew it.

The member pulsed, and she felt it jetting thick fluid. This, too, generated pleasure that radiated outward from her groin. Now the rapture was at her mouth, breasts, and cleft. She was transported by the triple climax, kissing the mouth, pressing her breasts into the torso, and clenching involuntarily on the stem, milking it of all it offered.

Slowly it faded. Embarrassed for her wanton display, she lifted herself off the plant. Sticky green moisture covered her front. She would have to wash it off.

"That wouldn't show on a green woman," Swale said. "She'd carry it to the next male flower and rub it well in."

"Now I appreciate what travelers see in such plants," Ennui said as she wiped herself off and dressed. "No man ever delivered a climax like that."

"Plants don't go for nuances of personality or commitment," Swale said. "Just for what works."

"It certainly works!"

"Next one's mine," Aspect said.

"But that won't propagate the plant," Ennui protested, only half joking.

"There will surely be other orchids."

They walked on, admiring the other plants. Ennui realized that it was fortunate that the Nature Trail was cultivated, because otherwise there would have been a mix of predator plants. Of course she and Aspect were more or less invulnerable to physical attack, but other travelers weren't.

There was another female orchid, then another male, and Aspect did strip and try it. She was almost comical to watch as she reacted, writhing and moaning in bliss; Ennui was glad Aspect hadn't laughed at her, and she kept a straight face now. She understood exactly what it felt like.

"Think what boy and girl orchids could do for each other," Swale said.

"They surely are immune, even if they could travel around to do it."

"A walking sex orchid!" Swale said, laughing. "What a market there would be for that."

They did pause at two other flowers farther along. This time the effect was not as potent. They were developing immunity, or perhaps the ikons were acting to counter what could become a dangerous habit.

Before evening they came to a closed campsite. They approached the green gatekeeper. "Passes, please," he said. Then, glancing at them, he eyed them with new appraisal. "No fault."

"Agreement," Ennui said.

The accommodations were good, as was the food. Ennui got to shower and change. Then she joined the gatekeeper for the night, and Aspect joined the other station worker. The green men were evidently intrigued by nonChroma flesh, and also by the alert minds of the two women, but the greatest appeal was of course the vibrantly shapely bodies.

Ennui thought about that as she settled to sleep after exhausting the green man's wildest dreams. When they gave up the ikons, this would cease. They would lose their invulnerability, their shapes, and their seeming youth. Also their extreme desire for sex. Could it be worth it? Yes, to hold their good men. But what about for itself?

Eternal sex is overrated, Swale thought. *I am in a position to know. I'd trade it all to have my ordinary living body back.*

"But what of this wonderful power over men, that makes traveling and trading so easy?" Ennui asked, subvocalizing so as not to disturb the man sleeping next to her.

You would not be traveling at all, if you didn't have that. You don't need it for your job at the palace.

And that was true. "Can you detect any diminution in the power of my ikon?"

None.

"But it should be fading, with all our walking and sexual activity in a Chroma zone."

Let me verify. She felt the succubus checking her body in the way that only a spirit could.

In a moment Swale had her report. *You won't like this. Your body is drawing magic power from your Glamor.*

Ennui was shocked. "But it's supposed to be the other way! We support our Glamors, so that they never run out of magic."

It seems they support you similarly. Fortunately they are staying mostly in nonChroma zones on Counter Charm.

This was appalling. They could be putting their Glamors in danger by depriving them of their magic. "We have to return to nonChroma!"

In the morning, lest you reveal something to your companions.

The succubus was correct. "You must advise the Glamors, and tell them to remain in nonChroma until we can get out of this Chroma zone."

Agreement. Parting. Swale was gone.

Ennui could do nothing at the moment, so willed herself to sleep, another ability she had discovered since taking the ikon. She remained horrified, but at least they had discovered the problem before doing irreparable harm.

In the morning she advised Aspect. "Swale has returned to tell the others, so they can protect themselves, but we need to get out of here promptly."

"Agreement!" Aspect was as disturbed as she was.

They did not complete the circuit, which would have taken several more days. They reversed course, stopped for nothing, and by midday were back at the entrance. They paused only long enough for Aspect to fulfill their commitment to the main gatekeeper. Then they were on their way to the nearest nonChroma zone.

"I think we do not want to trade for Chroma passages," Ennui said. "We must follow the nonChroma trails.

"Agreement. We can walk it all if we have to."

As it turned out, they didn't have to; they were able to bargain with traveling traders for wagon rides. They did not encounter Andy and Bummer, because those two traveled across Chroma zones; perhaps that was just as well, because they didn't want to discuss their supposed curse again.

They rode by day, taking men into the rolling wagons for agreed trysts. When the wagons camped by night, the two women set out alone to walk the next lap. They were indeed indefatigable, and did not feel the lack of sleep; it seemed they could take sleep or leave it. This was a real test of their ikon powers. By morning they had reached another staging area, and caught another trading caravan.

In two days they were back at Triumph City. Their men were glad to see them, but surprised by their manner of return. And appalled by the explanation.

"We can't give up our ikons, in more than one sense," Ennui told Throe. "But I beg you, as Aspect is begging Chief, not to give up on us yet. We'll do our best to find another way."

"We'll support you throughout," he agreed. "Meanwhile it is just as well you are back. The mocks have a problem."

"We'll handle it, whatever it is." Because Ennui and Aspect were the real powers behind the mock throne.

Ennui caught Throe up on their spot adventures during the excursion. She checked in on Nonce, who was recovering nicely from her distress, knowing that the perpetrators had been effectively dealt with.

"Spanky was a great help," Nonce said. "We've been friends throughout. She consoled me."

"That's right—when Havoc first came, Bijou was First Bath Girl—"

"First Mistress of the Bath," Nonce agreed.

"Spanky was second, and you were third. You moved up to First when the others went to other duties, and I think you won't be returning there. You have become my associate, and Aspect's."

"It is a royal privilege."

"I'm glad you had Spanky when you needed her."

"Agreement!"

Then Ennui and Aspect went to talk to the mocks.

Swale's brother Berm was an excellent imitation of King Havoc, wearing the royal robes with flair, and of course the crown was real. The ten magic Chroma gemstones conflicted with the real Havoc's Glamor magic, so he now used an imitation crown, as did Gale. That was just as well, because it lent substantial protection to the mocks, who needed it.

Spanky made just as good an emulation of Queen Gale, royally garbed, with her hair styled correctly and her expression carefully schooled. No one would guess that she was a former bath girl, except for her larger bottom, which she never showed when on duty. She gazed at the mock king with adoration she didn't need to feign, for she did love Berm. Swale had remarked on that; she was so pleased to see her brother with a really good girl. The bath girls *were* good; they were carefully selected to be pretty, smart, honest, and discreet, because they washed the body of the king and served any other need he might have. They normally moved on to other positions of privilege, and excellent marriages. Swale knew Spanky well, as she often inhabited her, though never when the two had sex. The succubus wanted no part of sibling incest. "But if she ever obliges some other man," Swale had remarked, "I mean to be there to help her swing that outstanding ass."

Things had worked out remarkably well. That seemed to be the way with Havoc; when he wasn't wreaking havoc, he was putting things together in rather neat fitting ways. He seemed to have a special talent for that, comprehending the nuances of human interactions and capacities in ways that should have been beyond a mere barbarian. Ennui herself was an example, as was Aspect, and of course Symbol. Old vessels turned to marvelous new purposes.

Ennui bowed her head as she came into the royal presence, maintaining the facade. "Sire."

"Good to see you, Ennui," Berm said with the correct degree of royal gruffness. Spanky came forward to embrace Ennui and Aspect in token queenly manner, smiling graciously. She did it exactly correctly, for Aspect herself had taught her how.

The king got down to business, having little time to waste on amenities. "In your absence we ran afoul of a clerical problem."

"Apology, Sire, for being absent when there was need."

"Negation," he said, waving a hand to dismiss it. "The office had a query and the clerk couldn't answer; if anyone can fathom it, you can."

"Best effort, Sire."

"It seems three siblings disappeared. A coach was seen in the area with the king's bodyguard aboard. A slender straw, but the fourth sibling came to petition for information, in case there was a royal connection."

Oops. Throe had been recognized. He had ridden up with the

coachman, to guide him to Limbo, and someone had seen him. So they had not gotten away with it cleanly.

"The king would have dismissed it out of hand," Spanky said mischievously. "But the fourth sibling is a pretty girl. She's still here."

"Jealous wench," Berm said, spanking her bottom. He liked to do that, and she liked to receive it. It was a barbarian mannerism they had invented.

Berm must have suspected their involvement, considering Nonce's case, so was giving them the chance to cover it properly.

And how would they do that? She needed time to think. "Sire, allow me to research in the records. We do keep track of coaches and bodyguards. May I report to you in an hour?"

"Granted, in the audience hall," he said carelessly, and turned away.

Spanky followed, leaving a significant glance behind. She was close to Nonce, of course, as they had been bath girls together, and surely approved the action. But the king's reputation must not be sullied. The mocks were fervent about that; they existed to protect Havoc's name.

They went to Ennui's office. She didn't need to research; she knew exactly what had happened, and knew Havoc and Gale would approve. In fact Swale should already have informed them of the escapade. Had Havoc handled it himself, the trio might not have made it to Limbo; they would have been dead. He liked Nonce.

"How do we wiggle out of this one?" Ennui asked Aspect. "That pretty girl is waiting for an answer. She surely knows the nature of her siblings, and suspects they overstepped."

"It's always the unthought of detail that catches you," Aspect said. "Anonymous coach, anonymous women, known bodyguard. We have to explain him."

"Why would the king's bodyguard have anything to do with three rogues?"

Aspect smiled. "Not with three rogues. With two women. Was he slumming, or fetching them for the king's amusement?"

"Explain the two women," Ennui agreed.

"Why not the truth: they were bait for a trap."

It was coming clear. "Because there was a rumor of brigands in the area, and the king hates brigands."

When she reported back to the king, Ennui had changed her clothing, hair style, and makeup to look closer to her real age, and dowdy. Sure enough, the fourth sibling had been summoned to the audience. The elder sister had been fit and comely; this younger one was more than comely, just rising onto marriage age. Havoc would indeed have noticed her, and tried to help her.

The king and queen were seated on their audience thrones. The girl stood with head bowed, awaiting notice.

"Proceed," the king said.

"Introduction," Ennui said. "I am the king's private secretary. I have researched this matter and learned that the king's bodyguard was indeed on a mission to that region. It seems that there was a suspicion of brigands in the area, but such outlaws can be hard to catch; they tend to fade away when authorities show up. The king became annoyed, and declared that firmer action must be taken. Therefore there was set what is called a honey trap: two innocent maidens were placed stranded on the trail where the brigands might pass. Guards under the authority of the king's bodyguard waited in ambush. Ordinary travelers would have helped the maidens, or at worst ignored them. But one small band showed by its actions that it was brigand, the two men attempting to molest one maiden, the female holding the other maiden for her turn. The trap sprang, the brigands were captured, and summarily exiled. They turned out to have no prior evidence of brigandage, or they would have been executed."

Ennui met the young woman's gaze. "Now it may be that your siblings ran afoul of those brigands and came to bad ends. In that case you can be satisfied that justice has been done. The brigands will not return. Are you satisfied?"

The girl looked as if she had narrowly dodged a thrown spear. "Satisfied," she agreed faintly.

"The audience is concluded," the king announced grandly. "Accept our hospitality this day and night, and we will see you to your home on the morrow."

"Appreciation, Sire," the girl said with evidently mixed emotions.

Ennui retired to her office. The girl *had* known the nature of her siblings' diversions, and realized that she might be implicated. Ennui had offered her an implied exoneration, and she would have a royal story to tell when she got home. Would Berm actually take her to bed for the night? Probably not; Spanky would resent it, and despite her prettiness, the girl might have some of her siblings' propensities. Best not to get too close to her.

So the spot problem had been dealt with. But not the larger one of the ikons. What were they to do about them?

Ennui sighed. They would have to ask Havoc. He would understand, and come up with something. But she wished they had been able to handle it on their own.

Chapter 9—Illusion

"Trouble with the ikons?" Havoc asked, dismayed.

"Swale was with Ennui," Gale said. "They wish to divest themselves of their ikons."

"Question!"

"The ikons are changing them, Havoc, you know that. They once were two rather staid middle aged women; now they are youthful sex bombs."

"Agreement. What is the problem?"

She laughed. "You know what. They're not themselves any more, Havoc. They're losing their identities. They would rather reverse the process."

He remembered how the Ladies Ennui and Aspect had approached him, intimating that they would like to have sex with him. That had set him back, because it did not match his notion of them. If they reverted, that would relieve that awkwardness. "Then let them revert, once we find another place for the ikons."

"They have a place: in the crowns."

"Objection: we can't carry our own ikons."

"The real crowns."

Then he saw it. "The ones we don't wear! Ideal."

"But they can't let go of the ikons. They seem to have become attached, and can no longer set them aside. So they traveled in Chroma zones, hoping to cut off the magic so that the ikons would not be able to hold on—and discovered that the ikons were drawing power from their primaries."

"Us," Havoc said, seeing it. "To protect themselves from separation, in case of a threat to their bearers. Makes sense."

"But since the ladies don't want to risk weakening us, they immediately returned to nonChroma and are on their way back to Triumph City. That leaves the problem unsettled."

"There must be a way. We can tackle it when we return to Charm. Can they wait that long?"

"They'll have no choice. Swale says they are indulging in an orgy of sex, trying to use it up before they revert. Meanwhile we'll have to ponder how to accomplish the separation. It may be best for Symbol, also."

"But she's a naturally sexy creature."

"True. Maybe for her the ikon will be no problem." Gale faced him. "Now we have three choices: sleep, discuss the illusion challenge, or sex. Do you have a preference?"

"It is a formidable challenge, even with the help of the ifrits."

She unveiled her right breast. "I inquired whether you have a preference."

"Maybe sleep will be the best preparation."

She exposed her left breast. "I inquired—"

"The left one," he said hastily, kissing it.

Then, laughing, they clasped each other for a fast hot connection.

"Remind me to tell you that I love you," she murmured as they finished.

"Negation. It's my turn."

"Aww."

"I love you."

"Since when?"

"Since that first Peek when we were children. You had the nicest little bottom."

She bopped him on the buttock. "I've still got it."

"And I still love you."

Weft appeared beside them. "*Please*. We're trying to sleep. Turn down the emotion."

"If you don't stop being the jealous female," Gale said severely, "I will fetch Warp and kiss him right on the face."

"Outrage," Weft said, disappearing.

"And you weren't even bluffing," Havoc said.

"And I have the kiss to prove it. You'll have to take it." She kissed him. "And now it's my turn: I love you."

"And I have your bottom," he said, taking hold of it.

They snuggled on into sleep. It was fun being lovers when they weren't busy being married.

In the morning they organized for the attack on the illusion. The Glamors had hashed it out, and were prepared for a slow but certain penetration. They had concluded that all they needed was a marked path through it; it was not necessary to nullify the whole thing, assuming it could be done. A single path should be comparatively simple.

"Want to go too," Weft said as Havoc kissed her parting.

"Negation," he said. "Not safe. We don't know what we'll find. You stay with Symbol and your Ifrit friends."

She looked rebellious, but did not argue further. The child was getting possessive of him; he assumed it was a phase. He set her down with the others, and she went to join Igor.

The illusion party lined up at a station they had set up at a convenient adjacent nonChroma zone. Havoc took Ini's hand. She had the altar, and would indicate the direction. Futility would remain just outside the illusion zone with the tapestry map. The Red Glamor and the Gray Glamor Avian would be liaison for this initial penetration. They knew that the outer illusions were fairly simple; it was the inner ones that were likely to be the challenge.

The first illusion was a courtyard amidst stone ruins of a castle. That was interesting; the day before if had been a grassy valley. It had changed. Which was of course why they needed direction, map, and marked trail; no single indication would be proof against shifting illusions.

He glanced at Ini without letting go of her hand. A strange woman stood beside him. That was Ini as changed by illusion. For one thing her face, arms, and legs showed clearly, while the real Ini was completely swathed. The illusion had given her a costume like that of the Red Glamor, and a face like—

He smiled. It was his own face on that body. The illusion was taking aspects of all of them and putting them together in different combinations.

He concentrated in the manner he had practiced, nullifying the visual illusion. Slowly it cleared, and he saw swathed Ini again. "Report," he said. "We stand amidst stone ruins. Ini has my face and Red's clothing."

Garbled words came back at him. He looked to their source and saw swathing. That would be Red, in Ini's garb. She was repeating what he had just said, but he couldn't understand her because he had not nullified the sonic illusion. She could understand him, however, because that was the nullification she was focusing on.

The illusion was doing exactly what the ifrits had indicated, drawing on the natures of the intruders to confuse them. It allowed just one aspect of illusion to be nullified by one person, with effort; that was evidently according to its rules. But was that all?

He did not bother to penetrate the illusion form of the Red Glamor, as that was not necessary to his progress. It was enough to know that she would relay his message to the others, who would note it, and Futility at the edge would mark his progress on the tapestry map. Once he had reached the object, that map would enable others to do so.

Meanwhile, he was impressed. It was one thing to be informed that the illusion was dynamically interactive; it was another to experience it. This scene seemed quite real in every respect. When he penetrated its visual aspect, seeing the barren plain it covered, the sounds and odors of the courtyard remained, and the feel of the stones at his feet. And the moment he stopped concentrating, the sight returned. He was standing near a wall; he put his hand out to touch it, and felt the mossy stone. A six legged lizard scooted away with a faint squeak of protest.

"Experiment," he announced. "I can see that there is no wall beside me; I shall try to walk through it." He let go of Ini's hand for the moment.

He focused, getting the true vision again, and stepped into it. And banged his chest and arm against the wall. It was a solid jolt, unbalancing him; he wind-milled his arms, but banged into the wall again. He sank clumsily to the ground/floor. "Oof!"

There was the sound of sobbing behind him. Ini was holding a dripping handkerchief to her face.

Newly cautious, he focused his vision again, and saw that she wasn't crying, she was laughing. She had seen enough of his motion to understand what had happened.

Negation. I got it from your mind.

Oh. That did not improve the situation. *Embarrassment,* he thought.

Now let's make love, while Gale can't see.

Havoc got back to his feet. Something was wrong; Ini was not one to sneak around. And why were her thoughts coming through ungarbled? "Ini," he said aloud. "Did you just—"

He cut himself short. Ini wasn't telepathic. She wasn't even able to nullify any of the sense illusions except sound; only the Glamors seemed to be able to accomplish even that much. So she hadn't seen him fall, unless the illusion had showed it. It couldn't have been her.

He had just learned something. The illusion didn't have to garble; it could make seeming mental sense if it chose, just as it made seeming visual, sonic, and tactile sense. They had agreed not to use telepathy because of the garbling; now he knew that was not the only reason.

"Report," he said. "I tried to walk through the wall, but it felt real and I crashed and stumbled. Then I heard Ini sobbing and thought she was laughing, and received a seeming mental seduction invitation from her. Most of this was illusion."

After a moment he looked at Ini again, nulling the illusion. Now that she had heard his report, she knew what had happened. She held a handwritten sign: I DID LAUGH.

Oh. He had reported his intent, then exclaimed "Oof!" and she must have pieced it together.

Then he looked at Red. Her sign said I PROPOSITIONED YOU.

So Red's teasing invitation had been transposed to seem to come from Ini, otherwise coming through intact. They couldn't even trust the illusion to be completely wrong. It relayed what it chose. That had nervous implications.

"Ini," he said. "What do you see here?"

After a moment she held up her plaque. STONE COURT.

He nodded. "Observation: we are experiencing the same illusion setting. Only our companions are garbled."

He gave them time to relay his observation, then took Ini's hand again. This time it felt like the claw of a bird, but his null vision verified that it was gloved human.

"Question: direction?"

Ini lifted the hand he held, pointing it ahead. That was the direction of the object they sought. They stepped across the court as he watched to be sure there were no real gaps in the real surface. Reality was the plain.

But as they stepped through the arched doorway, reality changed. The plain became a glade in a forest, the arch a set of trees with branches crossing overhead. That made him pause again. How could reality change? He was penetrating the illusion, so should have seen what was there throughout.

"Pause," he said to Ini, letting go of her hand again. He stepped back through the archway, nulling the visual illusion.

The plain returned. Experimentation showed that there was after all a limit to his ability; it could null only the immediate illusion, not the more distant one. So the near part of the plain he saw was real, the far part illusion. He had been fooled into thinking that all of it was real.

He made a report on that, then took Ini's hand again and stepped on out of the ruin, concentrating on near reality.

Ini stopped walking. He knew because he found himself stopping. He glanced at her, then ahead, forgetting for the moment to null. And stood amazed.

The illusion scene had changed far more than the reality, or perhaps it was merely the larger scene expanding from the partial one they had been in before. It was a glade formed by trees and towering ruins, trunks and columns mixed, as if the portals of a great ancient castle had been centuries overgrown. But that was only the background. The setting was filled with odd people, mostly clothed, of several different sizes, with wings. The wings were in addition to their human limbs, three of them encircling each waist. Most of the folk were standing, but some were flying, lying horizontally in the air as their birdlike wings spun rapidly, propelling them forward.

Havoc took time to assimilate the picture. It was another composite of features, this time human and avian. The Gray Glamor was a three winged bird, so that was the source of the wings. The people, male and female, were like Havoc, Ini, and Red, each a bit different but with a family resemblance. Most were going toward an elevated stone stage where several people stood. It was evidently some kind of gathering.

Ini tugged at his hand. He checked to see whether this was real or a touch illusion, then saw her sign: MOTION BUT SCENE UN-CHANGED.

Oh? He looked again. People were still streaming toward the stage by foot and by wing, but no more had arrived there than before, and there were just as many at the periphery. So they weren't actually getting anywhere. Smart Ini had caught on before he had noticed. So this was an animated yet unchanging illusion scene. That was another new effect.

"Report: we see an assemblage of winged people of different sizes." He described them, and the manner the larger scene did not progress.

Two women were walking along a path toward the stage clothed in pale robes and barefoot. One turned back to the other, glancing at her and lifting her hem, making a flirt of her head as if to say come on, we don't want to be late. But the other hung back, disdaining the event. Then the first spied Havoc and Ini, smiled, and signaled them.

And there was yet another novelty. The image figure was making eye contact, inviting him along. This was truly interactive. But what did it mean? That the illusion was trying to get the visitors to participate in the illusion ceremony?

He focused, nulling the scene, and saw the empty glade. There were trees but no towers; all was natural. No pitfalls, so it wasn't that sort of trap. The young woman was pretty and well formed; Red must be the body model. But she was all illusion, so if he went to her he would be relating to nothing.

After a moment the illusion woman shrugged and walked on toward the stage, her companion reluctantly following. Both had wings but weren't using them. Havoc felt half disappointed, half guilty. Meanwhile the other folk continued flocking stageward.

"Report: we were invited to participate in the gathering, by a comely young winged woman. Haven't accepted yet."

He looked again at Ini. "Direction?"

She held up her sign: INDETERMINATE.

"The setting is interfering!"

SEEMS SO.

So Iva was correct on this point too: they had to play the game by the illusion's rules. This setting was evidently on the way to the object, because the altar had pointed to it, but the altar could not point beyond it until they were through it.

Was the illusion woman trying to help them—or to lead them astray? He suspected the latter. But what else was there to do except enter the setting?

Havoc wasn't satisfied with that. The illusion was trying to prevent passage to the hidden object. Cooperating with it was bound to get him nowhere.

But he did have to play the game. What were its rules? Was he supposed to go along with the mock woman and learn something from her? To reject her? Ignore her?

The two women appeared again as the illusion recycled. This time Havoc went to her, holding Ini's hand so she would know where he was. With his other hand he took the illusion woman's hand, and it felt completely real. He kissed her, and her lips felt not only real but responsive.

But she still wasn't there.

"Welcome, Havoc," the woman said.

So now the illusion had picked up on his name, and was addressing him ungarbled. He already knew that after this mission was done, he wanted to learn mastery of this type of display, as it was superior to anything he had known on Charm. How could a setting that had remained for centuries and had no conscious input be so relevantly apt? This was intriguing and frightening.

He let the illusion govern, as he didn't need to constantly verify her nonexistence. The woman was a pleasure to view, with her loose robe not at all concealing the esthetic outlines within it. "Appreciation." He let go of Ini's hand.

"We must formally meet the queen. Then we shall be free for pleasure."

"Apology. I must pause to consult with my associates."

She frowned prettily. "Must you? Whatever for?"

"I must report that I am talking with a lovely woman, with whom I am about to meet the queen, and then share pleasure. I must learn whether they have any objection."

"Impatience." But she waited.

In a moment he nulled the vision and turned to Ini, who held up her plaque. WE HEAR THE WORDS YOU DO. BUT THEY HAVE NO ORIGIN.

He had thought as much. Ini could penetrate the illusion of sound so as to hear the reality, which was silence. At least it wasn't dangerous.

Then Ini seemed to speak. "Go with the maid, Havoc. I will find a handsome man."

That was more illusion, and Ini herself would be hearing it. She knew he would not be fooled. "Can you track me by sound?" he asked her. "As I track you by sight?"

AFFIRMATION, her plaque said.

"Then stay close."

He faced the woman, who had not moved. That was one thing about a programmed illusion: it reacted to direct input, and had no volition otherwise. His parameters were beyond its capacity, so it ignored them. "I will go with you."

"Appreciation." She took his arm and guided him toward the stage. Her female companion was no longer in evidence.

He was getting along well with this illusion. He had no doubt that he would be able to converse with the queen, receive her blessing, and then go to a private place with this nice nameless woman and have sex with her, all of it seeming quite real if he did not null the visual aspect.

But would this get him through the setting? He doubted it. After all, the purpose of the illusion was to lead him astray, to prevent him from reaching the object it guarded. Why should he allow it to do that?

But what was the alternative? He had to grasp and honor its rules, or there would be no way through. How could he go along with it and *not* be led astray?

Then he had an inspiration. "Apology," he said. "I just remembered something important I forgot, and must return for it."

"Confusion."

"Regret." He turned to face away from the stage. He saw the faces of numbers of folk of all sizes, all proceeding toward the stage. This setting was not even pretending to be realistic; the different sizes of animated people showed that it was crafted. Even if they had existed, they would not have had identical proportions; the larger ones would need larger legs and wings. So this was meant to be understood as a challenge, assuming that the designers of this illusion had any such intention.

The path he was on wound back into the forest, and others were walking along it. He would be going against the current, as it were.

He started walking. The oncoming folk moved around him without pausing, some afoot, some flying, none paying him any other attention. The flying ones generally had less clothing, and it was filmy to the point of translucency. Most were female, their breasts and thighs evident as they were carried by their central wings. The illusion had also caught on to the appeal of such anatomy to a visiting human male.

He encountered the two women walking their course. The young one caught his eye and smiled invitingly. He shook his head. "Regret," he repeated. It seemed the recycled figures had no memory of their prior interaction with him. Why should they, since they didn't exist?

He proceeded to the edge of the glade, to the forest. He stepped into the shadow of the forest—and was in the next illusion field. He had fathomed it.

This one was all stage, and he evidently had a front seat in the audience. A line of buxom women were dancing, kicking up their scantily skirted legs in unison to show their well fleshed thighs to the junctures. But Havoc, not one to miss incidental details, noticed that their heads were those of birds, and some of them had three or four breasts. Nothing like good composites to make it interesting.

He stepped back into the glade, making sure Ini remained with him. She was not in sight until he nulled the visual aspect; then he saw her, and beyond her Red and Gray.

"Report: the key to the flying people glade is to go opposite to the apparent folk." He glanced at Ini. "Direction?"

She came to the border and pointed at right angles to the path. Well, now. So the next obvious setting was a wrong one, no way through, or at least not on the way to the object. That meant that this was a puzzle not limited to the obvious. He liked that.

He took her hand and stepped off the path, into an apparent thicket of thorns. It opened into another stagelike setting, this one consisting of a checkered floor with a number of people standing to the sides. Those on the right were all male, ranging from king and bodyguard to a row of boys. Those on the left were all female, ranging from a queen and Amazon guard to girls.

"Observation: it's a chess game, men against women." He gave Ini time to relay the message as he considered it. The pieces were properly laid out for the opening, each confined to his or her square. Obviously this was a game to be played. It must have been drawn from the minds of the humans, for surely the ifrits had never played chess. It was a game of ancient Earth, thousands of years old, its pieces and rules long since fixed.

Surely the setting required that the game be played to a conclusion. But which side was supposed to be the victor?

"Question, Ini: do you play chess well?" For of course she knew the game; every person on Charm knew it, and all the other games. Humans were a gaming species.

AGREEMENT.

As he had expected. She was a very smart woman, surely a tough opponent. Havoc himself was one of the best players he knew, though he had not touched a piece since becoming king.

"Play the women, to win."

She went to the female side. He went to stand behind the male array. His pieces were White, which meant he had the first move. He focused, willing it.

The boy standing before the king stepped forward two squares. Pawn to E4.

Ini's pawn girl stepped forward to D5.

Havoc smiled. This was likely to be interesting as a game, apart from its significance as an illusion setting.

They played it through, taking time to do it right. Havoc noticed with a certain fond bemusement that his king rather resembled himself, and the opposing queen resembled Ini when her features were visible. The illusion was still drawing on what it had. The male secondary pieces, the rooks, bishops, and knights, were all strong men in body with appropriate clothing and emblems: castle turret, triangular hat, horse's head. The female pieces were more delicate and interesting, because they were bare breasted. When a male piece took a female piece, he squeezed her and she swooned. When a female piece took a male piece, she kissed him and he stumbled dizzily from the board.

It was a good game, and Ini turned out to be the better player. The king, defenseless, was at last trapped in a corner, unable to escape.

Seeing that, he lifted his sword and stabbed himself through the chest. He fell dead, untouched by any woman. Had it gone the other way, the queen surely would have taken poison rather than be raped by one of the males.

And the scene shifted. It was the new setting. It hadn't mattered who won, just that the game be fully played.

"Report: chess motif navigated. Next illusion field is a city, but not like any I have seen. Towering buildings, cloudy sky, vehicles flying magically above the streets. Throngs of people below." He glanced at Ini, nulling the vision. "Direction."

Ini approached. PAUSE. PROBLEM.

That was not good. "Problem?"

WEFT HAS ENTERED THE ILLUSION ZONE AND IS LOST THEREIN.

Havoc felt a wash of irritation, pride, and despair. That willful child had slipped her halter and followed him in. That showed initiative and commitment, but also reckless nerve. This was certainly mischief; how could he make his way through the visions, knowing that his daughter's life was threatened? For she could certainly blunder into real danger.

"I must fetch her," he said anxiously.

AGREEMENT. BUT YOU SHOULD NOT GO ALONE LEST YOU ALSO BE LOST.

She had more than a point. "You must mark the site, and Red and Gray must mark the route."

THEREFORE DEVA WILL GO WITH YOU.

Havoc felt a blast of ire from the direction of the Red Glamor that even the illusion couldn't entirely mask. Red had made no secret of her hope to get him alone and seduce him; it was a game with her. Now Deva, the Yellow Glamor of Demons, would have that chance instead. But that was only a peripheral concern for him; he wanted to find Weft in a hurry, and Deva would surely be as helpful as any. "Appreciation."

In a moment she appeared. She looked like a classic vampire with excellent fangs, but he recognized her even before nulling the vision because not all her fiery halo had faded. She carried no plaque, but could surely communicate well enough without it.

"Can you track me?" he asked her.

In a moment Ini held up her plaque. BY SOUND. WHISTLE AS YOU WALK.

He pursed his lips and whistled tunelessly. Deva nodded. Good enough.

Now he focused on Weft. He knew her well; she was his favored child, in the theoretically neutral ambiance of the family, and they had a mind connection. He oriented, and felt its faint trace. He nulled the vision halfway, paying attention to walls and trees because of his experience with the formidable illusion of touch.

Weft was not in the vision city. Her signal was from another direction. He found a street leading that way and followed it, knowing he would soon be out of that particular illusion field.

He was. The chessboard squares reappeared, but the people had been replaced by animals of a number of types seen on Counter Charm. They were moving in one direction, like the gathering of winged people, but instead of a stage there was only a continuation of the path. Weft was that way, so he followed, with Deva following him. The path narrowed and crossed the surface of a sea, the animals treading it without concern.

Then the waves of the sea turned red and surged higher, lifting and twisting the path. Some of the animals were thrown off, to land in the water—where large snouts appeared to take hold and drag them screaming beneath. If Weft were caught in that, she would be terrified; she was not yet two years old.

The path curved, but Weft's mind did not. Havoc strode off the path, into the sea. He could see by nulling the vision that there was no sea, just level ground, but he felt the water swirling around his legs, then on up to immerse all of him. He choked; he knew it wasn't real, but he felt the water engulfing his face, cutting off his air.

He spread his arms and swam upward, reaching the illusion surface so that his head cleared the water. His real vision showed him still on the ground, but now he could breathe.

The scene had changed. The water was calm, leading to a tree-lined shore, a phenomenally colored skyscape above. Weft was there, somewhere.

He reached the shore and waded out to the trees. Beyond them were ornate buildings, tier on tier, each rising from mist like an island. The path reappeared, this time a huge ribbon of material suspended from great cables. Havoc had not seen anything like it on Charm; what was the illusion's source of this vision?

Weft was in one of the buildings, which now loomed like a castle of many turrets. He ran to it, but its monstrous doors were closed, and his touch would not pass through them. There seemed to be no handle or latch; how was he to open it?

Deva caught up to him. She lifted a hand to warn him back. Then she took hold of a metal ring fastened in the door, lifted its base, and let it fall. It struck the wood and made a sharp sound: a knock.

After a moment the door swung inward, opening. Inside was a gloomy jungle. He tried to relate to the trees, but they were illusion, having no reality. Too bad; real trees might have helped him, as he was their Glamor.

He tramped through the jungle, following Weft's trace. It led to a large-boled tree with a small door in it. This one had a handle. He opened it and entered a room that was much larger than the size of the tree could have allowed. On the wall hung pictures of bears dressed like a man, a woman, and a child. "The tale of the three bears!" he exclaimed.

Deva nodded. The illusions were now drawing from stories. Weft had heard that tale, and evidently understood enough of it to form the scene. Was she playing in it? There was after all a little girl therein; she was that.

A winding stair led to another floor. He followed it, the illusion accommodating him as he stepped though reality remained bare ground. Upstairs was a chamber with a small bed. The cover and sheets were rumpled; someone had just been there. Weft, taking a nap in baby Bear's bed? But where had she gone?

Deva pointed to an open window. Beyond it was a massive twisting vine, so gnarled and rough that it could be climbed. "Jack's beanstalk," Havoc said, recognizing another children's story. Were they going to have to climb that to find Weft?

Deva stood before him, gesturing. What was on her mind? Did she have a better way to catch up to the child?

She took his hand and led him to another chamber. There was a larger bed, looking very soft. Mama Bear's. Deva lay down on it, beckoning him as she bared her breasts. The illusion made her look like an utter hag with rotting melons, but his null-vision showed her in her golden beauty.

She was taking this opportunity to seduce him! Instead of looking for the lost child. Angry, Havoc shook his head and turned away.

She bounced up and caught him. She drew his head in close to hers. "Trust me," she mouthed.

Reluctantly, he acceded. He joined her on the bed, kissing her and stroking her.

And there was Weft, blasting out ire. She was jealous!

There was the answer. Weft had been playing a game of tag with them, but couldn't let them turn aside for sex. Deva had indeed known what she was doing.

"You little mischief," he told the child with mock severity as he picked her up. She looked like a ferocious bear cub, and her body felt furry, but he saw through the illusion just long enough to be sure of her identity. "You weren't lost at all."

Not, she agreed complacently.

"I received your thought!" he said, surprised.

I null mind talk.

"You null telepathic illusion," he agreed, speaking aloud so that Deva could follow the dialogue and relay the news to Gale and the others. Weft would hear his voice garbled, but could receive his parallel thoughts directly. "So you know where the minds are. That's how you tracked us."

Agreement. She was pleased with herself.

"But I am nulling sight illusion, not mind illusion. So how did *I* track *you* as you teased me along?" He couldn't help it; he did like her cute independence and was impressed with her growing magic abilities. He couldn't be mad at her, as she knew.

I sent you my mind.

Havoc was amazed. "You null it both ways?" But obviously she was doing so.

Deva, now standing before them, made a gesture as of her jaw dropping. None of the Glamors had realized this was possible. But of course most senses were input rather than output; telepathy was both. Nonetheless, they hadn't thought to try. Weft had beaten them all in that respect.

Delight.

Havoc looked at Deva. "Can you null outgoing sound?"

She focused. "Do you receive this?"

"Agreement!" Their interpersonal contacts had just become much easier, thanks to this revelation.

He kissed Weft. "Appreciation. Now I must take you back to Symbol."

Negation. I'll fuss.

Havoc eyed her sternly. "We're used to that. It's not safe for you here."

Like this: Then she let loose a mind-wincing scream of anguish and desolation. It was a mere demonstration, but it made him shudder with remorse.

Deva smiled. "You can't do it, Havoc."

"We can't let children make the rules. It's a matter of discipline." He prepared to retrace his path through the illusion fields.

Weft broadcast another wave of utter horror and fear. He felt as if he were torturing her to death. But he nerved himself and tried to take a step. The amplitude increased, blasting away at the remnants of his determination.

"They can all feel that panic," Deva said. "They'll be wondering what you are doing to that poor innocent waif."

"Blackmail!" he snapped.

"Superior force," Deva said. "Yield to the inevitable."

Deva was right. He couldn't do it.

The awfulness faded, to be replaced by warm comfort. The little mischief knew she had won. Again.

"But we're hopelessly off the route," he said. "We'll have to return to the base and start over."

Mommy's doing it, Weft thought. *It's her turn.*

It surely was. "Meanwhile, we'll make our way back and see what we can do with two-way communication. You have helped us, Weft." He glowered at her. "But you'll still have to take your scheduled nap."

Awww. She nestled in his arm, well satisfied.

⋙ ⋘

Gale followed the markers through the ruined courtyard and the winged humans settings, declining the invitation of a handsome man to go meet the king. Havoc had reported encountering a comely woman here; evidently the illusion tuned in to the person, proffering appropriate distractions. She was impressed.

Next is the chess game, the Red Glamor's thought came. *You must play it to conclusion.*

Gale entered the setting. There were the male and female pieces set up for the opening. "Idea," she said. "Fool's mate is fast."

"Agreement," Ini said. She looked like a scantily clad strange young woman, but Gale knew she was fully gloved, veiled, and swathed. Havoc had discovered that they could null speaking illusion as well as hearing, just as they could the telepathy sending and receiving. That was a great help. Gale herself was nullifying touch illusion, so that she could walk through walls if she had to. She carried a staff to use to probe ahead, because she could still step into a real wall or off a real cliff if not careful. But so far the real terrain seemed to be reasonably flat, without such traps. With Ini's speech and Red's mind contact, she hoped to make it safely through. Weft had been naughty, but had significantly helped them.

Gale took the White men and played for the obvious trap. Ini obligingly walked into it, and soon was checkmated. And the fabulous alien city appeared. It had worked; the illusion didn't care or perhaps didn't know about collusion, so long as the rules were followed.

This was where Havoc had deviated to go after Weft. Now Gale would go after the object. "Direction."

Ini could not point, because Gale could not penetrate the visual illusions. So she did it by speech. "Not this field. Turn to your left and walk."

Gale did so, though she had to march through a building to do it. She nulled the feel of it and forged through the stone and cement, her staff before her, tapping the ground and feeling for any real obstacles. She was really moving blind, but it did not seem like it because the setting surrounded her. Only when she was inside the wall of the building did she have the feel of sightlessness, and that was just for a moment.

She emerged not to the interior of the building, but to a broad barren plain. There was nothing but dry grass covering it. That could be treacherous too, because it could be illusion masking a deadly dropoff. If she fell she could fly, preventing mischief, but that would violate the rules of the illusion and spoil her chance to reach the object they sought. So she continued questing and tapping with the staff. Better to be slow and sure.

"Request," Ini's voice came. "Pause while we make our way though the building. We can't go through the wall."

"Agreement," Gale said, glancing back. And blinked: there was no wall behind her, just a continuation of the plain, all the way to a far horizon.

Curious, she stepped back—and found herself within the stone again. It was there, in illusion; she just had to cross the boundary. The illusion fields were discontinuous, each seeming to occupy the whole area, but actually circumscribed. That made sense, as it meant there could be a great many in a small area.

She returned to the plain and gazed around. What was the purpose in a featureless plain?

Then she saw a cloud in the distant sky. It was tiny; her thumbnail held at arm's length could have covered it, had she been able to see any part of her own body. She couldn't; the illusion had rendered her as part of the plain, invisible.

"Present," Ini's voice came from close by.

"How did you track me? I'm invisible."

"Red now is nulling mind illusion, and directed me. I also hear you when you speak."

"We shall have to speak often, in this setting. Direction?"

"Toward that cloud."

Gale looked at the cloud. In that brief time it had grown substantially, and now her spread hand at arm's length would hardly cover it.

That must be the point of this setting, Red's thought came.

"To navigate the coming storm," Ini agreed. "It looks fierce. Can we handle it?"

Indeed it did look fierce. The clouds were boiling outward, darkening dangerously, lightning was spearing down repeatedly, and a funnel was descending from the base of the array. "Tornado," Gale said.

"That will blow us away," Ini said. "We aren't nulling touch. So far we've been all right, honoring the limits, but that will bring the touch to us."

Agreement.

Gale realized they had a problem.

"Wait," Ini said. "I'm being an idiot. There's no problem."

"Could have fooled me," Red said. "We Glamors are invulnerable, and you may be too, with that ikon, but if we get blown away we won't be able to help Gale much."

"We won't get blown away. We'll feel as if we are, but that's illusion; it can't actually move us if we don't move ourselves. All we have to do is hunker down and wait it out."

She was right, and just in time. The tornado was almost upon them. "Let's hunker," Gale said.

They clustered together, facing each other, kneeling and putting their heads together, pulling their shirts over their faces. The storm struck, the howling becoming piercing, the wind battering at their backs. The wind intensified, wedging between them, hauling at them. Sand blasted across, obscuring everything. Then it got under them, heaved, and suddenly they were sucked into the air, whirling. Equilibrium vanished; there was no balance to be had.

Gale opened her eyes, peering down below her shirt. They were flying inside the funnel, rising to a tremendous height above the plain, surrounded by a spinning wall of sand. Then she penetrated the illusion of touch, and felt the ground under her knees, and there was no pressure at her back. It was all sensory, none of it real.

Share with Ini she thought to Red, opening her mind.

"Weird," Ini gasped after a moment. "I see it, I hear it, I smell it, but now I know I don't need to feel it. That helps."

Just wait it out, Red thought.

They did, and soon it passed. They broke their formation and watched the tornado moving away. "So I was correct," Ini said. "It couldn't actually move us, though I felt as if I were being tossed far into the sky."

"You were, in the illusion," Gale said.

"Now we can move on, having handled this setting."

Not yet. Gaze there.

The lightning had started several grass fires. Now they merged and swept toward them, whipped by rising wind. The grass was only knee high, but it was thick enough to support a solid sheet of flame that rose in places to head-height and looked furiously hot.

"That makes me nervous," Ini confessed. "It may be illusion, but I'll feel the burn."

She had a point. Buffeting was one thing, but pain was another. Gale could lift Ini and carry her over the fire, escaping it, but that was Glamor power that would probably violate the illusion requirement. They needed a realistic way to escape or survive the fire.

"I'm an idiot again," Ini said. "The heat of a plains fire hardly penetrates the ground. Even a shallow covering of sand will shield against it." She got down and started scratching at the ground with her gloved hands.

The woman called herself idiot, but she wasn't much of one. Twice she had come to understandings the Glamors had missed. Gale and Red got down and helped her excavate dirt, Gale using her staff to pry out rocks.

They moved readily, and a hole formed. This was illusion responding to input; such motion caused the ground to give way. In moments they were down to sand, and it was mounding up to the sides. Then, as the fire caught up to them, they threw themselves into the hole and swept dirt and sand over themselves, including over their shirts, used to make air pockets over their faces.

The fire passed across. They felt its heat, but two things mitigated it: the layer of dirt, and the fact that there was no grass to burn immediately over them, so the fires passed around more than over. It was uncomfortable but bearable. There wasn't even any smoke; that was rising, not sinking.

They waited until the heat faded, then climbed out of their shallow grave. "Why do I think this is not the end?" Gale inquired.

Because it isn't, Red thought. *See that heavy rain.*

The fire had burned itself out, but another cloud was coming, and this one was raining rather than blowing or setting fires. They could see sheets of water descending, like rivers pouring over dams, and the plain was flooding. Soon it was washing around their feet, and rising.

Havoc found it hard to breathe under water, Red thought. *We will too.*

"We'll just have to swim," Gale said.

"Concern," Ini said. "Floating and swimming does not seem like a sufficient challenge."

Then Gale saw a fin projecting above the surface of the muddy water. "It's not," she agreed grimly. "Sharks."

Where could sharks come from, on a rainy plain?

"This is illusion," Ini said. "It has its own rules."

This time Gale came up with the answer. "It draws from our knowledge of creatures. That means they must follow the rules we remember. Sharks are not as aggressive as some think; they are cautious about unfamiliar things. They seldom encounter helpless humans in the water; most are fishermen with nets and fish spears, who will also spear a shark if they get the chance."

"Too bad we lack a spear," Ini said nervously. The water was surging around their waists, and the fins were circling closer.

"We have what will pass for one," Gale said, lifting the staff. "The end is blunt, but they don't know that. Also, you have material that may resemble netting. A smart shark won't risk it."

Ini nodded and stripped her swathing, becoming invisible. The wrappings formed into an extremely crude semblance of a net.

As the water rose higher, they gave up their footing and started swimming. Gale held her staff in one hand, like a spear, and Ini played out her netting.

A large shark decided to risk it. It swam in close, jaws gaping. Gale hefted her mock spear and made as if to hurl it. The shark sheered off. Then, reconsidering, it returned. This time Gale poked it in the snout. Surprised, it retreated.

One came at Ini. She spread her net toward it, and it too retreated. The sharks did not know what to make of this group, but evidently didn't care to chance getting within kill or capture range.

The waters sank. The illusion was not lasting long, and they had survived it within its rules. Soon they stood on the dry plain again—as they had been throughout, could they just have sensed it. Ini put her swathing back on, but Gale wouldn't have known it if she had not mentioned it as she did so; it had been visible when used as a net but faded out otherwise. Gale's staff had similarly shown up in the illusion when it emulated a spear. It seemed the illusion fields did play fair.

"Direction," Gale repeated.

"Toward that mountain."

Gale saw a mountain that she suspected had not been there before the flood. She headed for it, tapping the ground with her staff, and the others followed. Soon they reached it, and Gale ascertained that there was a real slope underlying the illusion slope. Was that meaningful?

The route was across the slope, which extended up on the right side and below on the left side. As they traversed it, snow began to fall. It increased rapidly, becoming a blizzard. Snow piled up on the ground, forcing them to tramp through it, because they could feel its cold resistance against their feet. Gale didn't bother to null it; she wanted to feel what the others felt.

"Odd that it's not colder," Ini remarked.

She was right; the snow was firm against their feet, but the air wasn't cold. Was there a glitch in the illusion? She didn't trust that. Why should snow not be cold?

She looked around. The downside continued to a drop-off that looked unsafe. The upside extended past a boulder and on to a distant mountain peak that was now clothed in snow. Above it the bright light of Vivid shone, reflecting off the white surface. The storm had faded.

"This makes me nervous," Gale said.

"Agreement," Ini said. "This setting has something in mind."

Yet the snowstorm had passed and the day had turned bright. What could it be?

There was a rumble. The three of them paused in place, trying to locate the source.

Red was first to catch on. *Avalanche!*

The rumble increased. Now Gale saw the snow starting to slide. It started far up the mountain, but was gathering force. They were in its path.

"It will sweep us down and over the drop-off," Ini said.

Gale looked desperately around. Could they run forward or back to escape it before the sliding snow swept across the path? No, the snow was moving all across the slope, and would catch them before they could stumble far enough to escape it. Already snow was nudging across the path, shaken by the reverberations of the avalanche; soon it would be caught up in the onrushing main mass of it.

Then she remembered something. "The boulder!" she cried. "Go!" She plunged uphill toward it, knee-deep in snow.

Toward the avalanche? But Red followed.

"She's right," Ini said, doing the same.

They struggled upward as the snow gathered momentum downward. They did not have enough time. As they neared the boulder, the vanguard of rushing snow crashed through.

But they were in the lee of the boulder. The snow divided to pass around it, leaving a temporary gap. They scrambled into that gap, escaping the rushing snow on either side. The clear section closed by the time the snow crossed the path; they would not have saved themselves had they not hurried closer to the boulder.

The rushing snow passed, coursing on into the void below. The slope was clear.

"Nice weather makes snow melt," Ini said. "When the slope is steep, it slides. I should have seen that coming."

Recrimination was pointless. They had survived by the rules of the setting. "Direction."

"Up the mountain."

They walked on past the boulder and up the increasing slope. There was no sudden shift to a new setting; the mountain was exactly as it appeared from the path. But Gale had a notion, and paused. "Bear with me." She returned to the boulder and carefully climbed up its rough surface. There was a real boulder here, so the climb was real. She reached the top, stood up, and looked around.

From this vantage she could see farther to the sides and down. There was something odd about the fantasy layout.

Then she had it. "This mountain has no base."

Both Red and Ini reacted. *Humor?* Red thought.

"The illusion mountain is floating. Observe for yourselves."

They joined her on the boulder, verifying that the path they had walked before crossed the base of a mountain that had no anchor. The drop-off they had seen before was not a mere steepening slope, it was the curvature to the base of the mountain, which hung over the waves of a broad sea.

"We are in a new setting," Ini said. "I feel dizzy."

Our sense of balance is being affected, Red thought. *I am no longer certain which way is up.*

Neither was Gale. She was starting to feel as if she were about to fall off the boulder. "I think we had better readjust."

They did so, climbing off the boulder and making their way down the slope to the path. As they did so, the scene seemed slowly to reorient, so that they were actually climbing. When they reached the path, it was near the top of the slope rather than the bottom. They went to what had been the drop-off, and it led to a rounded field sloping up toward a copse of trees. A rickety wooden rail fence crossed it. A rather normal pasture scene.

Except that the sea was now above them. It was the sky, a solid cloudbank level below, dark in the center, without upper limit. Other floating mountains hovered just below it, their broad bases facing up, their sharply pointed peaks angling downward. The view was dizzying.

"We seem to have turned over," Ini remarked.

Gale concentrated, nulling touch. It didn't help; the ground felt just as solid. It was balance or sight she needed to null, and she wasn't in a position to do that. "We are captive of the illusion," she said. "We shall have to play it through and see where it leads. Direction?"

"We are going the right way," Ini said, sounding surprised.

The illusion fields control direction, Red reminded them. *We don't know what way we are headed; our directional sense can't be trusted. Presumably the altar's orientation can be trusted.*

"Impressive illusion," Ini said. "I would not have believed it, without experiencing it."

"The ifrits wrought well," Gale agreed. "Now they can't enter these settings at all, and we find them challenging in the extreme."

They came to the fence. There was no gate. The path led to a crude wood stile so that they could climb over without disturbing anything. Beyond, the trees crowded in on one side, and the drop-off on the other side, making the way narrow but firm.

They followed the path as it twisted up a rocky slope to a higher level. Gale felt the heat of her exertion as she climbed. That was more illusion, since she was sure the underlying geography was closer to level, and in any event her Glamor power enabled her to exert herself without heating or tiring. Still, it was a nice country scene.

They crested the hill and followed the path as it wound down through yellow bushes to another fenced pasture. Another stile, then on to a river coursing through its deep channel. There was a wood bridge across it, with handrails.

"Negation," Ini said as Gale was about to step on the bridge. "Direction is down along the stream."

They followed the stream as it meandered though the small valley it had carved. It grew larger as it was joined by streamlets from either side.

Then it flowed over a ridge, forming a waterfall. And beyond the waterfall was—nothing.

They stood at the brink and stared. The water fell in a clear sheet past the edge of the mountain, and evaporated before it struck the boiling clouds below.

"Let's check the direction again," Gale said. "We might not actually get hurt if we jumped off, but I doubt the illusion considers attempted suicide a victory."

Ini tried again. "Ahead and down. In the river."

"So be it." Gale nerved herself and walked over the ridge, following the water. Her body tilted, and she found herself entering the water face first, but not falling. The liquid sheet parted around her and she entered a canyon girt about by stone structures and rushing waters. She was under the mountain, again, and yet upright.

In a moment the others joined her. "I think if I were not here on business, as it were, I should like to visit for pleasure," Ini said. "This impresses me, both as illusion and as scenery."

But where is it leading?

That was the question. They had encountered no further challenge or threat, unless rounding the mountain counted. Perhaps that was it; the average person might not be able to countenance the shifting orientations. So maybe they had navigated another setting after all.

Gale shared her notion with the others. "Agreement," Ini said. "We handled the attacking elements—wind, fire, water, snow—and then the vertigo orientations of the mountain. Different settings, different challenges. The next is bound to be dissimilar."

"Then let's get to it," Gale said, and marched on.

The canyon widened. The water moved to the left; their path to the right. Soon they were at the edge of a huge valley, with trees and houses below, clouds and houses above, their path cut into a slope so steep it was not far from vertical. A few cactuses and flowers clung to the grooves in the slope; otherwise it was barren.

The path led to a house or castle perched on the slope, and they entered a doorway. Steps led upward and downward.

"Direction?" Gale inquired.

"Up."

They stepped up. The stairway come to a landing, turned a right angle corner, and resumed ascending.

So it continued, for an interminable climb. They tramped up one floor, two, five, ten. "Surely there is a top to this tower, somewhere," Ini said.

"Somewhere," Gale agreed.

They continued, but so did the square stair. How high was it possible to go? This truly seemed endless.

Then Gale got a suspicion. The illusion wasn't interfering with their views of each other; Gale could see her own clothing and body, Red was garbed in red and was red herself; Ini was completely swathed. Why was it letting them be? Unless it wanted not to distract them from what they were doing. "Verify my reasoning," she said. "The purpose of the illusion fields is to prevent us from reaching its center where the object is. Therefore it distracts us in any way that avails. Could this be such a way—an endless loop?"

"Sense!" Ini agreed.

"In which case we are merely going around and around. It will never end, as this is accomplishing its purpose of diversion."

Obvious—in retrospect, Red agreed.

"So how do we make sure of it—just in case my notion is wrong?"

"Elementary," Ini said. "One of us goes the opposite way."

"Wouldn't that just separate us?"

"No if it's a loop. I'll do it." Ini turned and started down.

Gale wasn't sure of this. They did not want to get too far apart from each other. "If you don't find a way out in five floors, stop and return," she called.

"One floor should do it. You go on up."

Gale and Red resumed their climb. They turned a corner, then another—and encountered Ini, coming down.

"How did you get up there?" Gale demanded.

"Going the other way on the loop. This confirms it. We'll never get anywhere here."

Obviously so. Gale verified it by going down herself, and finding the others one floor below. They were repeating a single floor. "Curiosity: how is this possible, even in illusion?"

"Perspective," Ini said. "We aren't actually going up or down, just around, deluded by illusion."

Doubt Red thought. "We could be seeing mere images of each other, as we separate."

"We had better get this straight," Gale said. "If the illusion tricks us into separating, we won't be able to continue far."

"There is a central stairwell," Ini said. "We can see several floors up and down. Let's look."

Gale tried it. She went to the inner rail and peered down. One floor below, there was the back of the head of a woman who looked a lot like herself. Then she put a leg over the rail, caught her other leg against a rail post, and swung out so she could peer upward.

And found herself looking right up under her own flared skirt. She had nice legs.

Red came beside her and looked down. Gale saw Red's head appear above, beside the Gale figure. Their glances met. Gale stuck out her tongue. Red put her spread hands to her ears. They were definitely themselves.

"And how do we get off?" Gale asked.

"We use the landing exit," Ini said. "Having fathomed the trap."

Duh. Gale felt foolish.

Did the altar point us into this trap?

"I never thought to check, after the first indication for up," Ini said, chagrined. "The path led nowhere else. I just assumed—I'm an idiot again."

"Join the throng," Gale said, laughing. "You couldn't check while inside a setting anyway. Where does it point now?"

"Out."

They went to the nearest landing, which looked exactly like the one they had entered at, by no coincidence, and exited the tower.

The scene had changed. The steep valley slope was gone. Now it was a forest glade. Sweet music was playing, and four buxom nude young women were dancing in a circle.

"I think it's time to give Havoc his turn," Gale said, laughing.

Tomorrow, Red said. *We have had enough experience for the day. We need to digest it, so we won't make further mistakes.*

Gale and Ini were glad to agree.

"Announcement," Gale said. "We are leaving off now, for the day, at a setting of interest to Havoc."

They set about making their way carefully back.

෴

Havoc hugged Gale as she emerged from the illusion fields. "Appreciation for leaving those bare nymphs for me."

"You will have a better notion what to do with them than I would," she said, kissing him.

"I go too," Weft said.

"So you'll have a chaperone," Gale said.

"Awww." He picked up the child and they returned to the main camp. The fact was Weft would have her way; no one said no to a Glamor, not even a Glamor parent. She had taught him that. In due course he would impress upon the child the need for discipline, but not just yet. Gale was right about that: he was a soft touch for Weft, as she was for Warp, and Symbol for Flame. Parenting required certain weaknesses.

"I think we made progress," Havoc said as they settled for the night.

"We handled a number of settings," Gale agreed. "But we don't know how many more there are. There could be a perpetual loop of settings, just like those stairs."

"Negation. The ifrits made it, and they tell us there is a way through."

She nodded. "Agreement. Now seduce me."

"Whose turn is it?" he asked teasingly.

Weft appeared, scowling cutely. "Yours, Daddy. Get it over with."

Gale frowned. "I think I see a little bottom in need of spanking." But Weft had already disappeared.

"Lovemaking will never be the same," Havoc said.

"Do you regret adopting them?"

"Never."

"Agreement."

Warp appeared. "You better not regret it!" He vanished before Havoc could formulate a suitable threat.

"We should get Flame's permission too," Havoc murmured.

A ball of flame appeared. Havoc punched at it, but it flickered out before his fist touched it. The children's reactions were too fast for adults. Gale laughed.

They proceeded to their lovemaking, getting it over with. It was great despite the likely audience.

Next day Havoc lined up with Ini and Red, carrying Weft in a back-pack that enabled her to peek over his shoulder, and they moved through the several settings with dispatch, using Gale's notion of the Fool's Mate for the chess, and doing only one floor of the repeating tower before exiting. And there were the four dancing nymphs, on a grassy bank before a lake and distant mountains. Fortunately by this time Weft had gotten bored and fallen asleep.

Havoc looked around. Ini and Red had disappeared. He focused, and they were there, merely washed out by the illusion. "Observation: this setting is crafted to tempt a man, so must be mine to tackle. Remain close."

Agreement, Red's thought came.

He stepped out. "Greeting, maidens."

They ignored him. They continued dancing in their circle. Now he heard the music, a merry tune. A hoofed lad was sitting on the ground, his back against a tree, playing pan-pipes. Was he the one to be addressed?

"Greeting, Pan," Havoc said.

Pan ignored him also. The melody and dance continued unabated. That was unusual; it was as if Havoc had not entered the scene. Prior settings had reacted to the presence of intruders, seeking to divert them in some manner, or being diversionary in nature, like the endless stairs. So was this like the stairs? Holding him here until he figured it out?

Havoc didn't have the patience. "Nuisance!" he exclaimed, and marched toward the dancing nymphs. They were quite appealing as their flesh jiggled here and there, their hair swung around their heads, and their torsos flexed. Breasts and buttocks bounced with each footfall. They were linked by a chain of flowers they held and moved around to briefly obscure selected features of anatomy, calling them to attention.

He came up to the last one on the flower line, who was just passing him. She looked to be the youngest of the four. "Greeting, maiden," he repeated, and smacked her on the bare bottom.

The scene shifted. Now she was clothed in a simple white dress, standing by the edge of the lake, dipping her bare toe in the water. That was all; she dipped her toe, drew up her foot, dipped again, watching intently. She took no notice of Havoc.

"Enough," he said, and touched her dress.

The dress came away in his hand, leaving her naked. She stepped into the water, and waded ankle deep among lily pads. When she reached the edge of the shallow section she turned and waded back, showing her small breasts and moderate patch of pubic hair. It matched the color and texture of the black mass of hair on her head, an esthetic alignment. Her hips shifted intriguingly with each step, but there was nothing sexual about it; she was just a barely nubile girl wading alone.

Havoc knew he was misplaying it, but was annoyed by being ignored. How could he make an impression on this creature?

"Here is your dress," he said, proffering it. When she paid no attention, he touched her with it. It wrapped around her waist and hung low, the hem touching the water, leaving her nude above. Now her breasts seemed fuller than before, and her hair longer as it cascaded down her back. She stood there, seeing right through him.

"Come sit on the bank," he said, taking her hand.

The dress dropped into the water and dissolved. She turned and walked to the bank and sat there, one knee lifted. This provided an excellent view of her thigh, which was thicker than it had seemed to be before. Her breasts, also, were larger. This was a mature woman

"Every time I touch you, you get older," he said. "Where is this leading?" But she did not respond.

It was time for a more serious step. He bent down and kissed her sedate red mouth.

She held the kiss for a moment, then turned her face away. Now her breasts were solid to the verge of pendulousness, and her torso was thicker.

"I can keep this up if you can," he said. He touched her hand, and touched it again, and again, before she could withdraw it.

Her body became dark and wrinkled, her hair stringy. Her breasts sagged low. Her face was deeply etched with the lines of age, her eyes staring out like hooded lamps.

And Havoc realized that he was changing too. He couldn't see his body, but he felt it, getting younger. It was the illusion of youth, but uncomfortably persuasive.

How could he reverse this, before she died of old age and he became a baby? His touches made them both change. What was the opposite it touching? Nothing happened when he *didn't* touch her.

"Ini," he said. "How do I untouch her?"

Her voice seemed to come from the nymph. "Cause *her* to touch *you*."

Could that be it? He studied the nymph-crone, who was now shambling aimlessly through the water. He moved to stand before her, a bit to the side, so that as she walked her right hand brushed his projecting elbow.

She became a decade younger, and he a couple of years older. The change was proportional rather than fixed.

Satisfied, he got before her again, and got touched again, with another shift of ages. Several stages returned them to their original states.

But that merely undid his prior mistake; it didn't solve the riddle of this setting. How did he get beyond it?

He shrugged. Then he went to intercept her again, and her touch made him older and her younger. Several repetitions had him feeling like an aged man, while she was a breastless young girl. This wasn't getting anywhere either.

He touched her until they were where they belonged, then considered. "Any other ideas?" he asked Ini.

"We have established that her touch is the opposite of your touch," Ini replied, again seeming to speak from the mouth of the nymph. "We need to find what is the opposite of touching itself."

Ignoring Red's thought came.

"Ignoring," he agreed. "I will try."

He stood near the nymph as she waded. "I have been paying you much attention," he announced. "I shall now ignore you." He turned away from her, crossing his arms.

"You must not," she protested.

So now she talked! That was progress.

Continue ignoring her.

That was his thought. "Negation," he said, staring fixedly away from the nymph. "You are not worth my attention."

She came to stand before him, her breasts heaving, her face beseeching. "I will give you anything."

What now, Red? he thought.

Refuse her. That will indicate she can't distract you via sex.

That made sense to him. Besides, sex would be awkward with his little chaperone along; Weft would wake and protest the moment he got into anything like that. He also remained aware that the nymph did not exist; his vision nulling still showed emptiness there. He would feel rather foolish having sex on that basis, even if he could feel every nuance.

He turned away from the nymph again. "You ignored me when I was interested; now I am ignoring you."

"I misunderstood," she said, circling to stand before him again. "Please—I have so much to offer." She stroked her own slender body.

"You age when I touch you, and youthen when you touch me. I have no interest in relations with either an old crone or a young girl." He turned away again.

"We can take turns touching each other," she said, circling again. "I beg you! I can be so good for you."

The irony was that he was feeling tempted despite his knowledge. But he maintained his stance. "Forget it."

"Abject entreaty!" she pleaded, tears flowing from her lovely eyes. "I must serve you."

He hated tears. "Negation," he said with an effort.

Weft woke. "Go away, illusion!" she said. "You can't have Daddy."

And the scene reverted to that of the four dancing maidens. They had escaped the nymph.

But not the larger setting. The nymph had evidently been a mere diversion, not an exit. Which one of the others would open the way to the next setting?

"Don't be stupid, Daddy," Weft said. "It's none of them."

She had fathomed that? How did she know? "Question?"

"Used Voila's talent."

"You looked into the future?"

"Briefly," she agreed. "The nymphs' paths are all circles."

Amazement! Red thought. *We could have done that, if we had thought of it.*

"And we didn't," Havoc said, taken aback.

"Well, you're grownups," Weft said smugly.

"Guilty," Havoc agreed, reaching over his shoulder to pat her little hand. "So what other aspect is there to address?"

"Pan, dum-dum."

"Pan," he agreed.

"Question," Ini asked. "How does Weft use precog, receive thoughts, and speak ungarbled? She should be able to null only one, unless she can change modes much faster than we can."

"Don't," Weft said. "Red sends in clear, and you speak in clear and so do I. Precog—" She broke off, confused.

"Maybe that is garbled, and she didn't realize," Havoc said. "In which case one of the other nymphs may be the one." He eyed the most voluptuous of the maidens.

"Yuck!" Weft exclaimed.

Doubt, Red's thought came. *I tried it just now, and see the same circles she did. I think the illusion is not interfering with precog.*

"Conjecture," Ini said. "The ifrits did not know precog, so did not program it into the illusion fields. We may have a special advantage."

But best to verify. Try a circle, Havoc, and ascertain its authenticity.

"Agreement," he said.

"Disgust," Weft said.

If you interfere, Weft, I will emulate a nymph for Havoc to feel. My breasts and buttocks are real.

"Horror!" Weft sank down in her harness, tuning out. She knew when she was overmatched.

Havoc advanced on the sexy nymph, focusing on the near future. He saw the circle, with no path leading beyond. If that was accurate, he would find no way to get beyond the nymph.

The nymphs ignored him, as before, until he slapped the bottom of the shapeliest one. Then the others faded and she turned to him. "Why Havoc, I feared you'd never come to me," she said, delighted.

"I am trying to find a way past you to the next setting," he said.

"Will you show me the way?"

"Of course I will oblige you," she said, putting her arms around him. "You are such a great man."

"Observation," Ini said. "She did not address your question."

"Noted," he said.

"Yes, it does get boring perpetually dancing," the nymph said, answering his spoken word. "But now you are here, and we'll have such a great time together." She drew him into her and kissed him.

Havoc felt a wave of jealous revulsion. That was Weft, who it seemed was not completely tuned out. She tolerated his romantic interactions with Gale because she had to, but fiercely resented any other women. It was a phase she was supposed to grow out of in time; Havoc wasn't sure how long it would last.

So would making out with this nymph lead to the next setting? He stroked her back and bottom, squeezing the mounds of flesh. It was amazing how realistic the illusion of touch was. But how far did it go? He ran his fingers into the crevice of her bottom and found the lips of her vulva. She did not object. He ran a finger into her hot moist vagina. She made a low moan of pleasure, and squeezed on his digit as she clung to him. She was fully formed and eager for any part of him she could get.

But still she did not exist; when he nulled the vision she vanished, though her cleft still clasped his hand and her warm breath still tickled his ear. And the path of the near future continued its circle, not leading to any far future.

There was no future here, only the present. For surely if the illusion field handled precognition too, it would have shown him a path that led somewhere he wanted to go, or else garbled all the paths. It would not have let him see that this was a dead end, alive as it felt at the moment.

Satisfied, he decided to withdraw from the nymph and return to the main setting.

"First get your finger out of the pie," Weft said severely.

He laughed and obliged. She was an effective chaperone, all right.

"I am done with you," he said to the nymph. "I am ignoring you."

"But you can't!" she protested desperately. "Feel my flesh!" She took his hand and put it against a breast. "Everything is yours."

"Negation. I am gone." And soon he was, again feeling somewhat guilty for his treatment of the illusion.

The four nymphs were back, dancing to the music. It was as though his sessions with two of them had never happened; they were oblivious.

He turned to Pan, who was playing, never pausing even for a breath. That was a mistake. As with the automatic responses of the nymphs, a spot error of programming. It was almost impossible to think of everything, especially when you didn't know what kind of creature you would be diverting centuries in the future. Havoc remained highly impressed with the caliber of the illusion fields.

He approached Pan. "Greeting."

Pan ignored him. The music continued unabated. It seemed the scene was locked in until he touched one of its players. But why would he want to touch a goat-footed man? His actions needed to make sense in terms of the setting, or he would lose the progress he had made.

I thought the path would lead through him, Red thought. *But all I see is another circle beyond him.*

"Confirmation," Havoc murmured.

"Daddy, there's a path," Weft said. "From right here. But I don't see how to get to it."

"Idea:" Ini said. "Music."

And there it was. Havoc brought out his dragon scale. He strummed it, then played the same tune Pan was playing, accompanying him.

The illusion fuzzed but did not dissipate. He was on the right track, but not there yet.

He tried a different tune, clashing dissonantly with Pan. The setting wavered, the dancing nymphs losing coherence as they tried to match both melodies. They couldn't; they stumbled and halted. And the scene changed, along with the sound.

Pan remained, still playing his pipes, but now both he and they were different. His button nubs had grown into monster horns that curled around before his face. He applied his mouth to the hollow tip of one horn and blew, and the sound was a horrendous loud ooompah! that blew steam from his pointed ears. His eyes were giant flexing orbs that pulsed with changing colors and density. His belly was a gross face that stared intensely at Havoc, its eyes glinting. Below it divided into two legs that descended not into feet but merged into a nether creature, an imperfect mirror image, that in turn divided and merged, repeating until it faded from sight.

Look at the nymphs.

Havoc turned to look. They were as bad, with faces on their knees and bottoms for faces. They were dancing, or trying to; now their efforts looked more like struggles to escape some horrible fate. One of them turned her head around so that the other side of her posterior came into view; it was a visage consisting mostly of an orifice with great yellow teeth. The teeth clashed together, striking sparks, and the creature lunged toward him.

Havoc acted on spot inspiration. He focused not on nulling the illusion, but on enhancing it and joining it. His own face expanded, his mouth growing, his teeth lengthening into virtual tusks. He leaped to meet the clashing face, spreading his jaws so wide that he took in the whole opposing figure and bit its head off.

And he was in another setting. There were trees growing, but their trunks were not ordinary; they were closer to animal and human limbs, their ankles in the ground, their tops sprouting foliage. Some were animal and human faces, their necks in the ground, their hair sprouting leaves. Some were full human torsos, the males with broken off branches projecting like stiff phalluses, the females with knotholes for genitals and swelling wooden breasts. Every trunk was different; none were ordinary.

He wandered through the forest, nulling just enough to be sure it wasn't there and that Ini and Red were following. It seemed endless; this was an inactive setting he had to find his way out of. But he suspected that mere walking wouldn't do it.

"Precog, Daddy," Weft said.

He tried it. His near future paths diverged immediately, leading in every possible direction. He traced them farther, and saw that they became a tangle of crossings and mergings. No help there.

"Mask them, Daddy."

"Question?"

"Voila showed me. Filter out the bad ones so you can see the good ones. Good for middle future paths. Like this." But her mental demonstration was garbled.

"Show Red," he said.

In a moment the thought came from Red, showing the new technique. It was a deliberate fuzzing of precognition so that only unique paths were clear, the rest merging into background. He tried it, practicing, and soon there were just a few paths, and then one. It wound through the forest and disappeared.

"Appreciation." He followed that path.

It led to a very large, exceedingly gnarled trunk whose permutations seemed to include many figures. But there was something else about it. Obviously this was where he could step through to the next setting, but the difference was aside from that.

Then it fell into place. "You're real!" he said. "A real live tree." He focused and verified that it was the only real tree in this setting; all the others were illusion. He had caught on because this trunk was twisted but natural, while the others were unnatural. Also—because he was the Glamor of Trees, and related to them. He had sensed its nature by his Glamor affinity.

He contemplated it. The illusion had not changed it; it was completely natural. The challenge had evidently been to locate the real one amidst the false ones, and he would have done that in time without the precog path; the precognition had merely facilitated the process. But for the moment he had another concern. "You're not in perfect health, friend."

He put both hands on the trunk and extended his Glamor awareness. The tree had been growing in the illusion field all its life, and had never been near another tree of any kind. No insects visited it to aid in the pollination of its flowers, so it could not propagate. That made it lonely and facing extinction of its line. "You're not ill; you're depressed," he said. "With reason."

"What is the problem?" Ini asked.

"This tree is one of mine; I need to help it. But what it needs is not my constituency."

"Fetch Blue," Weft suggested.

The Glamor of Insects. They had five legs on Charm, and were different here, but insects were insects. "Agreement," he said.

Red sent a mental signal, and in a moment the Blue Glamor was in relayed mental touch.

"This tree needs insects," Havoc explained. "But they can't find it hidden deep in the illusion fields. Can you help?"

Affirmation. I will give the local bees the coordinates of the tree and an imperative to visit it. A mature flowering tree will be well worth their while.

"Can they find it through the illusion?"

The illusion does not affect coordinates, and bees lack imagination for illusion. They can find it.

"Send some now," Havoc said.

She did not argue; one Glamor knew the urgency of another when his clientele was in need. Soon a small swarm of the odd bees of this planet buzzed in. They circled the tree, orienting on the flowers, and went to them.

Havoc patted the gnarled trunk. "You are in business, friend."

"That's sweet," Weft said tearfully. "Happy endings always make me cry."

"Me too," Ini agreed.

"We are done here," Havoc said, touched by their reaction. "Appreciation, Blue."

Welcome, Havoc.

Havoc walked around the tree, and when he reached his starting point, the scene had shifted.

He stopped and stared, and so did Ini and Red behind him. They were floating in deep space, and something weird was in view. It was some sort of machine, like those of the White Chroma, but far larger and stranger. It was made entirely of metal, with projecting turrets from which scintillating beams issued. Smaller machines were circling it like wolves around a bear when hunting was lean. But machines were not alive and did not compete for food. "Confusion."

"It's a spaceship," Ini said. "Old Earth had them. That's how our ancestors were brought to Charm a thousand years ago."

"Amazement!" Havoc, as a villager, had not known much about such things.

"It seems to be a space battle," Ini said. "I read of those. The spaceships fired beams of light at each other that had the power to burn holes in their hulls. So it was like men shooting arrows at each other."

"How does the illusion know about this?" Havoc asked.

"Such ships must have visited Counter Charm too, and been noted. They could have delivered some of the creatures here, or perhaps merely scouted it before deciding on Charm."

Still, this is odd, Red thought. *I understood it was a colony ship that delivered our species. These are combat vessels.*

"Agreement," Ini said. "The history makes no reference to combat in space."

"Do the ifrits know?" Havoc asked.

I will relay the question.

Soon the answer returned. *There is a memory of something like this in the distant past. The ifrits knew more of the matter in prior centuries, but it was shut off at the time the illusion fields were made.*

That explained much. The ifrits had feared that the knowledge would help free the object the illusion imprisoned. So they suppressed the information, but left evidence of it in the illusion itself.

But this was distracting them from the business at hand. "We must find out how to get beyond this setting," Havoc said. "This is beyond my understanding."

Naturally. You're a barbarian.

"Agreement. Suggestions?"

"Ini knows," Weft said.

"I know that we are going in the right general direction," Ini said. "I am able to verify with the altar between settings, as we cross. But I know nothing about space battles. They are not part of my experience."

"Daddy, if you want to kiss Ini, I won't be jealous. She's nice."

"I have done more than that with Ini, in the past, and may again. Why do you think Ini knows the answer, when she doesn't think so?"

"Because she's so smart. She can figure it out. Also, her precog path is strongest."

We keep forgetting to use the precog, Red thought. *Weft has trumped us again, comparing our near future paths for comparative certainty.*

"Ele-mentary," Weft said, pleased.

Havoc turned to the region where the Air Chroma woman was, though overridden by the space illusion. "Discussion."

"I can't do precognition," Ini said. "So I must reason things out. I note that this is a repeating cycle, with a number of small ships attacking the big one, being opposed by a few smaller ships that match the color of the big one. The big one also fires beams of light from its surface turrets, that burn any small ships they touch, and the small ships fire light beams at each other. The mother ship's accuracy improves as the enemy ships fly closer, and soon most are gone and the rest are fleeing. Then the little ships return to it. Then the cycle repeats. It is a recorded battle that the large ship and its minions win."

"Now I *will* kiss you," Havoc said. "I pride myself on my observation, but I picked up on none of this." He nulled the vision enough to locate her specifically, embraced her, and kissed her. She responded hungrily; she did carry an ikon, and she did like him, though she knew he would never be hers.

"See—I'm not jealous," Weft said determinedly.

Well, I am, the Red Glamor thought. *He respects Ini's mind more than her body, and her body has improved.*

Quite true. Ini was a fine, smart woman, and Havoc did not regret any part of his association with her. "Analysis."

"The moment we act, the setting will react," Ini said. "If it takes us for an attacking ship, the mother ship will shoot us down, and we'll be out of the illusion. We don't want that. So we must try to emulate one of its own little ships, so that it will allow us to approach. Surely the way through this setting is inside that big ship."

"Agreement!" Havoc said. "I am minded to do more than kiss you, Invisible woman."

"Willing and eager."

"Not *that* far," Weft snapped.

They laughed. Neither Havoc nor Ini had been joking, and all knew it, but this was not the time. "Let me see what I can do." He concentrated, and formed the semblance of a friendly little ship around them. The illusion allowed this; it was part of playing by its rules.

Havoc did not know how such a ship was guided, but it didn't matter; he simply willed it to move into the scene toward the mother ship.

Immediately an enemy craft changed course and came toward them. "Avoid!" Ini cried. "Don't let it shoot us down."

Havoc willed their ship to dodge to the right. He was just in time; a beam of light coruscated just to their left. This was like an arrow; the next one was likely to score. So he turned around, oriented on the enemy, and loosed his own arrow. His aim was good, and it scored.

The enemy ship exploded with a brilliant fireball. But that attracted the notice of several other enemy craft. They converged.

"Trouble," Havoc muttered. He steered the ship into the remnant of the fireball, simultaneously turning it around so that it was ready to go back the way it had come. Then, concealed by the smoke and debris, he accelerated. They emerged from the smokeball and shot by two approaching enemy ships before they realized what was happening.

The enemy ships quickly reoriented, but now Havoc had a fair lead. He went toward the big mother ship. The pursuit closed, but now they were getting closer to the mother ship, and beams of light shot out and passed Havoc's ship, aiming for the enemy craft. The enemy ships veered away; this was too dangerous for them.

"Admiration. It's as though you have been a space fighter pilot all your life," Ini said.

"I have been a barbarian warrior all my life. Same principle."

They slowed as they approached the mother ship. "Look for an entry port," Ini said. "The small ships are taken inside the mother."

Havoc found one, and guided the craft into it. Some invisible hand caught hold and put the small ship into a rack. Then a port opened, and they had entry into the main ship.

But instead of a metallic interior, they were on the vertical slope of an infinitely tall mountain. Havoc stood on a tiny ledge perhaps halfway up. When he dislodged a bit of sand, it fell interminably until disappearing long before it struck the bottom. Eventually there came the faint sound of a splash: there was water down there in the darkness.

"Things are not what they appear," he said tightly. He nulled the vision, and saw that he was standing on a plain. But to navigate the illusion he had to focus on it, and that brought the horror of falling. He was terrified.

This one is different, Red thought. *The illusion of fear.*

Illusion? Of course! Havoc had not been much for hesitation or doubt as an ignorant villager, and less so now; this had to be artificial. But in what way was the illusion of fear different from the reality? He knew it was not genuine, but still felt it.

"Daddy, I don't like this," Weft said.

What could he say to reassure her? "Neither do I, honey. But we have to get through it."

"That way," she said, pointing over his shoulder.

There was a series of indentations in the cliff. Some were toe sized, some finger sized. They led to another ledge. Obviously that was the route.

Could he do it? He had made similar climbs before, but not at this apparent height, and not burdened with the off-balancing weight of a child. The niches looked slippery and treacherous; if anything gave way, he would plunge into the sea below. And what about Ini and Red?

Show the way. We'll follow.

He saw no other way. "Remember, Weft, what we see is not real. If we fall, we won't really fall, though it may feel exactly like it."

"I'll shut my eyes tight."

"And don't wiggle."

He nerved himself, unaccustomed to this emotion. He had always been one for action, and seldom felt fear, even before he was a Glamor or king. But he had always done what had to be done, and would do it this time.

But the fear was almost paralyzing. The height and depth of the cliff was awesome, and while he knew his fingers and toes were strong, he was in serious doubt about the solidity of the stone around the indents. Was it possible to climb to the next ledge?

What choice was there? He faced the wall and slid his left hand out across the surface, seeking a hold. His fingers slid around the place, then found purchase for two. But suppose there were creatures in those holes, stinging insects, worms with blood-sucking mouths? He would be helpless.

He poked his fingers in regardless, hung on, then slid his left foot out. It was bare, as it had to be; there was no aperture big enough for more than two toes. He found such a place, and wedged in his big toe and the next one.

Could his left hand and foot take his weight? They had to. He slid his right hand along the wall—and realized that there was no purchase for it. His left hand already possessed the holes. What was he to do?

No thought or voice came from the others; they knew he had to work it out on his own, without dangerous distraction. And he did: he put more weight on his left toes, stretched his right arm out to the right side as a counterbalance, and slowly pulled his left fingers out. He slid them farther across the wall, seeking holes beyond.

He found them, and worked his fingers in. Then he moved his right hand across before his face until it found the first finger-holds. They weren't angled quite right, but he wedged in his middle and fourth fingers before his precarious balance was lost. Now both hands were anchored.

It was time for the feet. He had to vacate his toeholds to make way for his right foot. That meant stretching out precariously, suspended almost entirely by his four fingers. Was it possible? He was tempted to go back to the ledge, where at least it was safe. He fought that urge down; the ledge was nowhere.

His left foot found a farther indent, and his toes gripped it as well as they were able, taking weight off his fingers. He brought his right foot across to the first spot. Now he was entirely on the wall, dependent on his straining digits.

"I'd rather float," Weft said.

"Agreement!" he gasped. He had become dependent on Glamor powers, and hated being without them.

The scene darkened, and he heard something. After a moment he recognized it with horror: wind. A storm was brewing, and he was stuck on the wall.

He gritted his teeth and quested farther. He had to do it quickly or not at all, because he would be lost if that storm caught him. That meant risk taking. He hated it, but had no choice.

He moved across, finger by finger and toe by toe, as the storm

approached. Just before it struck, he achieved the other ledge, and
sat on it, panting with nervous relief. The storm blasted at him, but
couldn't dislodge him from the ledge; it was too solid. Soon the wind
and rain passed, giving up its futile effort.

"Is this what it's like for normals?" Weft asked.

"For nonChroma normals, yes. But most of them have the sense
to stay off ledges."

Havoc looked for the crevices beyond the ledge, so he could continue his laborious journey. And found a new horror. There were none.
The wall was featureless. The only route was between the two ledges,
not beyond them.

"What now?" he asked, stymied.

I think this is a test of courage, Red thought. *What do you fear
most at the moment?*

"Falling."

Then you must fall.

He couldn't argue with the logic. There had to be a way through
this setting, and the only way left was down, into the water below. If he
had the courage to jump.

He considered, reminding himself that this wasn't real. He wasn't
really risking his life and that of his daughter if he jumped. But if he
failed to jump, he was risking the success of their mission.

Again he nerved himself, fighting off fear that threatened to paralyze him. "Hang on, Weft," he said. "Whatever happens. And hold your
nose."

"This stinks," she agreed.

Then he stood at the edge of the ledge, and jumped. He did not
dive, because that would not have protected the child; he jumped clear
of the cliff and dropped feet first. He felt the air rushing by during the
long fall, then the solid blow of the water as they struck.

And they were in a new setting. This one was strange; he seemed
to be on another cliff, but his sense of balance indicated it wasn't
vertical. It was angled at about forty five degrees. But when he shifted
position and sand dislodged, it fell at right angles to that wall. It was
as if he stood in a wind he couldn't feel, that was blowing things counter
to gravity.

But he was getting the hang of these illusions, with the help of
Weft, Ini, Red, and their limited precog ability. It was mainly a matter
of fathoming their natures and beating them at their games. So they
forged through one setting after another, finding their keys and leaving them behind, marking their route. There was a buxom female
mummy whose windings concealed the horror of millennia old flesh
and bone. There were distorted human figures and animals. There
were weird watercraft floating down turbulent waters. There were rivers that turned into roads, and on into rainbows. A woman whose
copious skirt became a separate scene in itself, that they entered for

the next setting. Disconnected eyeballs. A coach that propelled itself on giant insect legs. Animated human skeletons. The images were losing their power to surprise or defeat.

And suddenly they were out of it, and into a large chamber without illusion. The precog paths converged, leading toward its center. The object they sought.

≈≈

Gale was nursing Voila at the edge of the illusion fields when the news was relayed through: Havoc had made it to the center. She was glad, but didn't celebrate; she knew that whatever had required such extensive burial would not be easy to handle, even millennia later. They had merely gotten past the first hurdle.

She returned to the main base camp, where Symbol was entertaining Warp and Flame with an illusion story. The remaining two children had been persuaded to behave only by the promise that once the way was won through the illusion fields, they would be taken there. "Havoc made it," she said. "Weft helped. They haven't seen the object yet; they are waiting for the rest of us to join them. Which we shall do tomorrow."

Symbol had just one question: "Is it safe?"

"Surely not. But it's a risk we have to take."

She went on to a conference with Ivo and Iva Ifrit, whose invaluable assistance had enabled this to happen. The ifrits could not penetrate the illusion fields, because they spread across Chroma and nonChroma zones and distorted ifrit senses as much as human senses. But the Glamors were reporting everything to them.

"Now you have won through to the center, a thing we are unable to do," Iva said. She was in solid form for this dialogue, because Gale was reluctant to assume cloud form during the tension of their infiltration of the illusion fields. "How will you handle the thing the illusion sphere restrains?"

"First we must find out exactly what it is."

"It is a machine, a thing without life, but motivated and dangerous."

"We have no experience with such a thing."

"Therefore you must be prepared, for it is dangerous."

"We shall certainly investigate it."

"Doubt."

"Question?"

"The whole of your planet ejected it rather than try to tame it. The whole of our planet isolated it rather than destroy it. These things were all that could be done. You must not assume you are safe."

She was making sense. "What can we do, that we do not plan to do?"

"You have one key magic ability we lack. That may be useful."

"Precognition," Gale agreed. "But it's really very limited."

"Your child does it best."

"Negation! I'm not taking my baby there."

Voila, asleep in her crib, woke suddenly, fussing.

Gale stared. "Horror! It's a wrong decision."

"She knows," Iva agreed.

Voila did indeed know. Gale ascertained that the baby had no idea of the specifics, just that she needed to be there. That meant that it was an extremely broad path, that would narrow when she got closer to the place and time. The other Glamors, including Gale, had learned to see briefly into the future; the baby could see farther, for her range had been growing. On occasion it was eerie, as they verified something days later that confirmed an episode of Voila's anticipation. There was more to this magic than the adults or other children yet fathomed.

So it was that next morning Gale reluctantly put Voila in a backpack and went to consult with Havoc in the center of the illusion fields. She made her way through the chain of key transitions marked on the map and by Glamors at the sites, followed by Symbol with Flame and the Blue Glamor baby-sitting Warp, diverting him with weird ugly fascinating bugs. It seemed pointless for them all to go, for Havoc, Ini, and Red were already circling the illusion-free perimeter, verifying that their magic powers were restored. There was no reaction from the machine in the center; it was oblivious, uncaring, or defunct.

Gale navigated the route faster than they had done before, because they now knew what was essential, but she remained impressed by the variety of the settings. She played her hammer dulcimer to change the music of the dancing nymphs, and made her way to the single real tree, now comfortably serviced by bees. The space battle amazed her with its magnitude and scintillating drama, but Blue reported that Warp loved it. He would. The fear at the sea cliff was horrible, but now she knew that she didn't have to claw her way to the next ledge; she simply jumped from the first one. And so on through, until at last they emerged to the inner region.

Voila screamed in terror. And something stirred in the center of the circle. It was a huge metal thing with projecting spikes and spinning wheels. It came right at them.

Gale leaped back into the illusion, taking Voila with her. Blue and Symbol did the same, but in different directions, protecting their charges, and she knew Havoc would act appropriately. She plowed through a scene with cows grazing between the ruined buildings of an ancient city, turned, and waded into the wall of the solidest building she could find. Then she hunkered down, silent. Fortunately Voila had stopped screaming; her foresight surely warned her that that was not a good thing at this time.

She heard the whirr of the machine as it pursued. There was a dull thud and the anguished scream of a cow, followed by a crash as the alien thing collided with the wall. Then it ground on, departing. They had escaped it.

When it seemed it was safe, she emerged from the wall and wended her way back to find Havoc. She met him part way, as he came searching for her, carrying Weft, seeing her though the illusion, using his vision nulling capacity. He caught her and hugged her, and kissed Voila over her shoulder.

"Question?" Gale asked weakly as Blue and Symbol appeared with their charges. She was relieved to see that all were safe.

"You appeared, Voila screamed, and the machine launched toward you," Havoc said. "It had not moved before. Now we know it is functioning and alert. It surely saw me before, and Red; why did you set it off?"

"Agreement: that was my question."

"Now we have seen how the illusion field balks it. The machine sees, hears, and feels the settings, and can't forge through walls lest it damage itself. It is subject to the same limits we are, except that it may not be able to null any of the senses. It got turned around and ejected, probably thinking it was still pursuing you."

"Reassurance," she agreed dryly. "Second question: why did Voila scream? That's what triggered the pursuit."

The Red Glamor appeared, with swathed Ini; the illusion no longer covered any of them, so that they kept company with the cows. "She reacts to threat before it happens," Red reminded them. "She knew the monster was about to attack, giving you time to escape."

"But it didn't attack anyone before," Havoc said. "How is Gale a threat to it if we are not?"

"Not Gale," Ini said. "Voila."

And that had to be it. Voila—with precognition. The machine recognized her as a danger, and tried to destroy her. She had reacted in terror before it acted.

"Problem," Ini said. "Voila screamed because the machine was about to attack. It attacked because she screamed. Paradox."

"Point," Red agreed. "Had she not screamed, it would have waited longer, for her to get within range. Her scream showed she had caught on, so it had to act. So why did she scream?"

"This taxes my barbarian intellect," Havoc said, smiling. They all knew that his mind was on a par with Ini's. "She can see the paths, so knew what a scream would do."

"Don't be dumb, Daddy," Weft said. "She screamed because it frightened her. She knew it was alert and menacing. She says it's a Mino."

"Question?" Red asked.

"Bull-headed man," Weft explained patiently. "In a puzzle."

"The Minotaur," Gale agreed. "In a labyrinth." That was from Symbol's illusion shows, the story of a man who navigated a labyrinth to encounter a monster trapped in the center.

"Apt analogy," Ini said. "So she saw—Mino—and was terrified, and screamed without considering the paths. She is after all a baby. That showed the machine that she had caught on, and it charged, as a lurking panther does once a deer spots it. Ideally it would have waited for the herd to get closer, but then it has to act before they all spook. Paradox lost."

"So she foresaw the lurking danger, not the specific attack," Gale said.

"Problem," Havoc said. "We do have to get close, in order to capture it and take it back to Charm."

"Problem compounded," Red said. "A pebble we might carry. A monster machine we can't."

"It would have to be dismantled and transported piecemeal," Ini said.

"As if it will sit still for being taken apart."

"Challenge," Ini agreed, her veil smiling.

"Observation," Havoc said. "The illusion fields have stopped covering us, and perhaps won't balk our departure, now that we have made it to the center. But they exist to stop Mino from escaping, and surely won't let us move him out, in however many pieces."

Voila laughed.

"Interest," Red said. "She knows something we don't."

"That's why she's here," Gale said. "I didn't want to bring her into this danger, but the ifrits say we need her here, and she agrees. We had better find out what she has in mind."

"Complication," Red said. "She's under four months old. She lacks language."

"Negation," Weft said. "She just doesn't speak your words. She knows what's what, because of the precog."

"Agreement," Warp and Flame said, almost together.

"Truth," Ini said. "She relates to the children, as we saw when they negotiated for learning to become clouds. We have to appreciate that however young she is, Voila *is* a Glamor. There has never been so young a Glamor before, and never one who was Glamor before growing into the norms of human behavior, with such a supportive environment. The three children were close, but they were rejected by their families and put in foster care, which surely set them back. Voila is the first to have complete, supported openness to the Glamor state. The other child Glamors have been interacting with her, providing the benefit of their experience. She is showing us the true Glamor potential." And the three children nodded; they know they had been stultified, which was why at first each had shown only one magic ability.

"Which it seems is beyond our imagination," Havoc said.

"She'll be a terror when she grows up," Red muttered fondly. "The others are bad enough." She smiled at Weft, who smiled back. The two understood each other, to a degree, as did Warp and Blue, who had to an extent taken his interest now that Gale was occupied with Voila. Each child needed the special attention of at least one adult.

"And I understand Voila," Weft said smugly.

"Then Weft will translate," Gale said.

"Delight," Weft said. She liked being important. Warp and Flame frowned but did not protest.

They settled on scattered stones while the cows continued to graze. Probably they were sitting on the ground, but the illusion masked that. Gale lifted Voila from her backpack and held her in her lap. Weft settled on Havoc's lap, facing them.

"Review," Havoc said. "I said that the illusion fields would not let Mino out, even in pieces, and Voila laughed. Why? What are we missing?"

Weft leaned forward, reaching across to take Voila's tiny hand. "Question?"

They remained in silent communion for a moment. Then Weft's mouth fell open. "Amazement!"

The adults exchanged a glance. What had Weft learned?

The child recovered. "She says Idyll will let Mino go, when he is tame."

"Who is Idyll?" Havoc asked gently.

"Idyll Ifrit." Weft waved her arms. "Here. She's listening. She's real old."

Now more than one adult jaw dropped. "The illusion fields!" Ini exclaimed. "One huge ancient ifrit!"

"But the ifrits can't enter this region," Red protested.

"Because they don't want to overlap another ifrit," Havoc said. "The ancient ifrits didn't make impenetrable illusion, they formed a Glamor ifrit. Here, around the menace. Idyll."

"Which explains how the illusions can be interactive," Ini said. "They are consciously controlled. The setting would be permanent, but when any creature enters them, Idyll takes over and modifies them to address the intruder. It also explains how the illusions can be continuous, crossing different Chroma zones and even nonChroma zones. A Glamor—drawing magic power from some other region, a distant ikon."

"Many ikons," Weft said.

Gale was as amazed as any. "How can Voila know that?"

"Idyll's talking with her. Mind contact."

"But telepathy is scrambled here!"

"Not for Idyll."

And of course the ifrit who was scrambling the senses of others would not have to scramble her own. "Why does she talk to Voila rather than us?"

"Voila's mind's open," Weft explained. "Same's when she turned cloud first, and precogged first."

There it was, as Ini had conjectured. The adults in their certainty were far less open to new things than the children, and the children less than the baby.

"Can we talk directly with Idyll?" Havoc asked.

"Doubt. I'm barely feeling her mind, and I'm not nearly as stultified as you grownups." She was still increasing her vocabulary. "Voila's the only one who can, because—" Weft paused, surprised again. "Not just because her mind's open. Because she's the greatest of all the Glamors, or will be when she grows up, and Idyll's the greatest of all the ifrits right now. They relate. Idyll's what Voila will be."

"Idyll's the strongest ifrit?" Havoc asked. "And a Glamor?"

"Stronger than all the other ifrits put together," Weft said, translating. "And all the other Glamors."

"Than all of us?" Red asked.

"Affirmation. That's why she could limit you. She could have stopped you entirely if she wanted to."

They digested that. After their experience in the illusion fields, it was believable.

"Voila will do, for now," Gale said. "Tell Idyll we are glad to meet her, and hope to work with her to take Mino away from here."

Weft communed again with Voila. "She knows. She wants to get rid of Mino. That's why she let you in. Then she can fade out."

"She wants to die?" Red asked. "That is, cease to exist as an entity?"

"She's been here a long time. She's tired."

Surely so! Yet she surely had all the knowledge of the ancient ifrits, including feats of illusion like none seen since. What a waste it would be to lose that.

"She says it's a burden," Weft said.

"She's answering my thought?"

"Sure. It wasn't shielded."

"But ifrits don't know telepathy."

"She says it's not exactly that. We're all in her cloud, so she knows more about us. And she likes you, Mommy."

"Flattered." What a discovery this was! Gale had at first thought that their study of the ifrits was a diversion during the frustration of their effort to penetrate the illusion fields; now it was clear it wasn't. "And she's a Glamor. Why aren't the modern ifrits aware of Glamor status, then, apart from our examples?"

Weft concentrated, working on a difficult transfer of information. "I think—it's like us," she said at last. "Only so many Glamors, and Idyll is all of them. No room for others."

"Glamors have constituencies," Havoc said. "Why did she leave that poor tree isolated from insects?"

"Different. They don't relate to life forms. Just to—whatever."

Gale realized that they could study the different modes of Glamor another time. "Right now we need to deal with Mino," she said. "How do we tame him?"

"Idyll doesn't know. She keeps him cooped, but he mines magic and she can't touch him directly."

"But if she's that strong, why can't she handle a mere machine?" Havoc asked.

Voila laughed. "He's not mere," Weft said. "He's stronger than anything. The ifrits had to make Idyll just to handle him."

"She must know something about him, to coop him."

"Just that's he's a dangerous machine who can null magic."

"Why doesn't he null the illusions and escape?"

Weft communed, getting the answer via Voila. "Because there's nothing there. The illusions are mostly projections—no magic to take. You couldn't even null single senses if Idyll didn't let you to make it fair."

The adults shared another glance, chagrined.

"But there is something else," Weft continued. "Idyll says now you have a hard choice."

Gale was wary of this. "Question?"

"To go home now, or to tackle Mino."

Havoc laughed. "Decided."

But Gale's wariness remained. "Question," she repeated.

"If you tackle Mino and win, and maybe you can if you all work together, gratitude and cooperation. If you lose, all of us will be trapped here."

Now Havoc became cautious. "Clarification: how can Glamors be trapped? Mino has such power?"

"Maybe. Idyll doesn't know, because there weren't little Glamors like you when Mino came so he didn't fight any. He mines magic, and maybe can take Glamor magic too, because Glamors aren't illusion, they're real."

"If he sucks the magic from one Glamor, the others will retreat to consider alternatives," Havoc said. "We won't be trapped."

Weft struggled to get the complicated concept into words. "If he beats one Glamor, he'll know how to beat all Glamors. But even with just one, he would use it to get free, and that can't be allowed. So all of us would have to stay here in—in—"

"Indefinitely," Gale said.

"Negation," Havoc said, and the other Glamors agreed. "Mino might catch one of us, but not all."

"Idyll would keep us," Weft said. "Indefinitely, until something comes to tame or destroy Mino."

The Glamors exchanged grim glances. Such a threat had to be empty, but they didn't like it.

But Gale knew Weft, and Voila. There was more here. "How would

Idyll do this?"

"By intercepting our magic beams from our ikons. Voila's ikon is already here, with Symbol. Idyll's letting its magic through because she relates to Voila. The others are sending from outside, and she can stop them. That will make us all regular folk who can't get through the illusion fields when she doesn't want us to."

This was a chilling prospect. "Idyll can do that?"

"Affirmation. She doesn't want to, because she likes Glamors, especially Voila, but Mino is just too dangerous."

"Mino is just a machine! We should be able to handle him, once we learn more about him."

"Clarification: the regular ifrits have a distorted history. Here is the real story. Mino is a scout sent by a galactic machine culture to survey planets for mining magic. Many like him were sent out, and the machine masters come to suitable planets as convenient and needed. They may take mil—mil—"

"Millennia."

"Millennia to come, because there are a lot of planets in a lot of space, and they finish one before moving their heavy equipment to the next. When they are done mining, there is no magic left. So we don't want them here, but they will come sometime. Idyll thinks in about another century. Everything was planned for then, to be ready."

Gale kept her voice unnaturally calm. "Why does Idyll think they are coming then?"

"Because Mino came to Charm, surveyed it, and sent out his report. The signal goes at light speed, which is pretty slow. If Mino had completed his round, he would have gone back faster himself, but when he came to survey Counter Charm the ifrits trapped him and stopped him from going. They knew to do it because they saw what happened on Charm. So only that signal went out, and judging by his report, his culture is about fifteen hundred light years away. It went out fourteen hundred years ago. So if they need magic, they'll come soon's as they get it. Maybe later, if they're not in a hurry, but we need to be ready then, to be sure."

Havoc whistled. "Four centuries before humans colonized! This crisis has been long in the making."

"Conjecture," Ini said. "They could come sooner, if they missed their scout and tracked his course."

"Doubt," Weft said, concentrating. "They have so many, they send them out pretty randomly and don't follow them. They wait for them to return, or to send their signals. It's more ef—ef—"

"Efficient," Gale said. "But this suggests that they have overwhelming force, at such time as they apply it. How can one or two planets possibly oppose such a culture?"

"By taming Mino and making him tell, or taking him apart and studying his parts to figure out how he was made and how his magic shields work. Then we can make something to stop the machines, which would be like him only moreso."

"And the ifrits plan to be ready in another century to do that?" Havoc asked.

"Idyll doesn't know. She thinks something in Charm is getting ready. It's a cooperative effort: Counter Charm holds Mino captive while Charm develops the means to deal with him and his kind."

Ini nodded. "And meanwhile humans came along, and Charm Glamors evolved, and now we are tackling it. Suspicion: we are being used."

"Clarification," Havoc said tightly.

"The loom, the tapestry, the altar—all helping us to locate Mino. How do we know that Mino himself didn't arrange that, to get us to come here to free him? Or that something else doesn't want us to tame him and then use his power for some nefarious purpose? We may be best advised to take the first choice, and go home without tackling Mino."

"Mino did not," Weft said, receiving an answer. "He sent only one signal, then was stifled."

"But *something* is helping us," Havoc said. "We do need to know what and why."

"Agreement," Weft said. "But Idyll knows you mean well and can be trusted. If you beat Mino, she'll help you take him back to Charm."

"But if we don't, she'll hold us prisoner," Gale said.

"Regret," Weft said for the ifrit. "Mino must be stifled. You must prove you can do it. So it's safe to let him out."

"Understanding," Havoc said. "So now we have our hard choice: Tackle Mino?"

Gale was highly conscious of the presence of their four children: they were subject to the same risk as the adults, but she hated it more. Yet she knew Havoc would want to tackle the challenge. After all, they had traveled between planets just for this. So she temporized. "Need more information. Does Idyll have advice?"

"Negative and positive," Weft said. "Don't tackle head-on; he will suck out your magic and store it in a can. If you get more from your ikon, he'll take that too. You'll just be giving him more magic. But maybe you can tame him by punching in the access and control codes."

There was hope! "Definition."

"The machine masters use a series of symbols called codes to control their sub—sub—"

"Subordinate."

"Units. Only the right authority knows the right code, so no one else can use that unit. When the machine masters come, they will use the codes. But if we use them first, Mino will be tame and serve us."

That certainly seemed to be an easier way. "Does Idyll know the codes?"

"Negation."

"Can they be guessed?" Havoc asked.

"Doubt. They are complicated, and if a mistake is made, Mino will kill the one trying, because he's an impostor."

"Glamors are hard to kill," Havoc said.

"Not when their magic is sucked out."

The magnitude of the problem was becoming apparent. "We don't know the codes, and dare not guess," Gale said, summarizing it. "And we won't have magic when trying. This seems hopeless."

"Voila says there is a path."

Gale pounced on it. "Can she precog the codes?"

"Uncertain. But there is a path she can follow."

"This seems likely," Havoc said. "Follow Voila's precog one step at a time, and get the codes."

"But that means Voila will have to approach Mino," Gale said, shuddering. "After it already tried to kill her."

"Mixed," Ini said. "It went after her because she sounded the alarm. It probably doesn't recognize her as a person."

"Huge comfort," Gale said tightly.

"She wants to do it," Weft said. "But can't, yet."

"Question?"

"Mino won't let anyone approach without sucking out their magic."

"And Voila's precog is magic," Gale said.

"But there's a path."

"Conjecture," Ini said. "Mino may not know of precog. He surveyed all magic existing when he came, but has been isolated since. He may not recognize it."

"That seems likely," Weft said, translating again. "Idyll did not know of it, so did not block it. Mino probably doesn't know either. His harvesting of magic is selective, not general; each type is detected, shielded, and channeled to storage. But he still won't let a human with any other magic approach."

"Idea," Warp said. "Space ship."

"Irrelevant," Gale snapped.

But the Blue Glamor held up her hand in a caution signal. "Reasoning," she said to the child.

"Mino came from space. The machine masters will come from space. He'll be watching."

"But we don't want them to come yet," Blue reminded him gently.

"Illusion," he said. "Show him them coming, so he thinks its them. Like the spaceship scene in the fields. Then send in Voila."

"Genius," Blue said, kissing the top of his head. He squiggled with pleasure.

Gale was impressed. It was indeed a good idea. "Idyll?" she inquired.

"She'll do it," Weft said. "But if it doesn't work—"

"We will be hostage," Havoc said. "Vote?"

They voted, including the children. They decided to try it, as it could be a quick and easy way to fulfill their mission. None of them were ready to give it up.

They worked it out, and soon put it into practice. The upper dome of the sphere of illusion had been showing an accurate replica of day and night, which abruptly changed any time Mino tried to fly out, baffling him with shifting illusion. Now it showed a tiny speck growing rapidly until it shaped as a metallic spaceship much like the one in the regular illusion setting. They did not know what a machine masters ship would be like, but judged that after fourteen hundred years the design could have changed, so Mino would accept it as a legitimate variant. Mino seemed to; his disk sensors were orienting on the image.

The ship loomed close, then hovered in place, a feat Idyll had seen Mino perform. From it came a much smaller unit, close in size and design to Mino himself. This dropped down to land nearby with a shaking of the ground. All illusion, but so realistic that Gale was inclined to believe it despite knowing better.

Now it was her turn. She walked to the shuttle, masked by illusion. Then, carrying Voila in her backpack, she walked directly toward Mino. She felt her Glamor magic depart; Idyll had cut off her contact with her ikon back on Charm. Voila's ikon with Symbol was also intercepted. Both of them still had magic, because their bodies took it from the surrounding ambiance. But that would end as they came close to Mino, where all magic had been sucked dry.

Except, perhaps, for the one Mino shouldn't recognize, therefore wouldn't mine. Precognition.

Gale wore a metallic suit that made her look like a person made of metal. She hoped that Mino would take her for a machine, though her living nature was plain enough. Maybe a living subject of the machines, some kind of sapient creature or even an animal. For all they or Mino knew, the machine masters had some living creatures working for them, slaves from captured planets. Why use superior machines for menial tasks?

One of Mino's disks oriented on them. That was all. Gale kept walking, guided by the single type of magic that remained to her, the paths. Precognition, enhanced by Voila. The paths diverged and merged, crossed and overlaid, but the firmest one led straight toward the giant machine.

Gale controlled her apprehension, which bordered on fear. She knew that their lives were the least of what they were gambling; the fate of the other Glamors depended on them, and perhaps of two planets. She focused on the paths; that was all that really mattered at the moment.

The firmest path led to a panel set in the side of the machine.

Now Gale faced it and focused on her hand. She moved it parallel to the panel. Then, guided by a hot/cold aspect of the path, she closed her fist and used her knuckle to tap on the panel with a special cadence. It was, she hoped, the access code.

The panel moved. It slid aside, exposing a pattern of buttons. She moved her hand over them, and felt warm over one. She used one finger to push it in. It clicked and rebounded as she withdrew her finger. And Mino had not destroyed them. Yet.

Guided by her enhanced precognitive awareness, she slowly pushed other buttons. She did not count them; she merely focused on each in turn, following the path. She had no idea what they did or meant; it was merely what enabled the two visitors to survive.

Then she pressed the wrong button. Her finger simply missed; she saw it happening and couldn't prevent it. Doom!

But immediately Voila's correction came. Gale pressed that wrong button twice more, rapidly, negating the error, then went on to the correct one. It seemed that provision had been made for animal mistakes. Gale felt weak in the knees.

She completed the series by striking a broader bar at the base: the one that confirmed the series and said to activate it.

The panel slid shut. Another opened: an entry to the interior compartment of the machine. Gale saw wheels, rods, and screens therein. Their specifics were beyond her understanding, but their general nature she understood from the precog paths. This was Mino's center of control.

They had tamed the machine.

Chapter 10—Finale

Augur stared at Ini. "Astonishment!"

"Empathy," she said. "We were all surprised by how simply it came out. But Mino is now tame, and you seem best to pilot him to Charm."

"But I know nothing about machines. Surely a Glamor should be in charge of this important artifact."

"The Glamors wish to remain away from it for now, for reasons of their own. So we mortals will ride in it."

Augur exchanged a glance with Aura. They were alone with Ini, for now. "Confidentiality."

Ini smiled knowingly. "Conjecture: not for further sex with my invisible body."

"Confirmation," Aura said, forcing a mock frown.

"Concurrence."

They understood each other. That was not surprising, because they had not only adventured together, and had more than casual sex, they had developed a genuine friendship. They liked each other and would not play each other false. In fact, they had already agreed to try to retain association after this mission was done. Ini hoped to marry and settle as their neighbor when they married, and they would exchange fourths. It would probably have to be in a nonChroma zone, as they were of three different Chroma. Probably Triumph City, working for the king, as the Ladies Ennui and Aspect did. But that was in the nebulous future.

They retreated to Augur and Aura's chamber and took seats in a triangle, facing each other, leaning forward to put their heads close together so they could converse quietly: the red man, blue woman, and swathed invisible woman.

"Suspicion," Augur said. "There are deeper currents."

"Agreement! This capture of Mino, the alien machine, was entirely too easy. Gale took Voila and used precognition to fathom the access and control codes that tamed the thing. Now, it seems, the Glamors govern him, and he obeys their will implicitly. That is why he is available to transport us home. He is really a small spaceship, a technological marvel from a far distant mechanical culture, sent here to identify suitable magic for mining and exploiting. We shall need to study him and understand him well enough to be able to repel the more sophisticated machines of his culture at such time as they arrive to proceed to serious mining. We have preempted him, theoretically."

"Doubt," Augur said, and Aura nodded. "What confirmation that the codes really worked?"

"The fact that he now accepts Glamor directives, and obeys. He has laid himself entirely open to their will."

"Insufficient. He could be pretending."

Ini nodded, but her words were contrarian. "Why should he do such a thing? The Glamors will not forward his mission. They may even destroy him after his usefulness to them is done. Certainly they will glean information from him to oppose his culture, at such time as it comes here. Mino must know that, if he has the wit to fake conversion."

"Because this is an avenue for his escape from confinement," Augur said. "He was not able to free himself from the illusion fields for more than a thousand years, and could not now, without the aid of the Glamors."

"The Glamors could not give him such aid," Ini said, still arguing. "Idyll Ifrit—the illusion fields—warned that if the Glamors lost their contest with Mino, she would confine them too, and she has the ability to do it."

"Disbelief!" Aura said. "Nothing can confine Glamors."

"Except another Glamor on her home territory," Ini said. "Who can intercept ikon signals."

"Reassessment," Aura said. "There is more here than we appreciated."

"Conclusion," Augur said. "If Mino could not escape alone, and could not escape by capturing the Glamors, his remaining path is to cooperate with them, or seem to."

"Fear," Ini agreed.

"Question," Aura said. "The Glamors are not stupid. Surely they recognize the chance of such a ploy. Why are they risking it?"

"Hypothesis," Ini said, and this was clearly the essence of her concern. "The Glamors suspect, and are risking it, because they are in a similar situation."

"Confusion," Augur said, knowing she had thought this out and needed their judgment.

"They have a mission: to fathom the mystery of their own origin, which was evidently not chance. The changelings, the altars, ikons, the loom, the tapestry, all signal that the Glamors were evolved for a purpose, and they must understand that purpose before they can rest. They need Mino to forward that exploration; the signals brought them here to him, and he, confined as he has been, could not have arranged them. If they do not get Mino, they probably will not be able to complete that quest for knowledge. So they must capture him, or—" She paused.

"Or cooperate with him," Augur said.

"Awe," Aura said. "It is a game both sides must play, lest both sides lose."

"But the stakes," Augur said, appalled. "Two worlds!"

"Better to leave Mino alone, and remain ignorant," Aura said. "Rather than risk the worlds for the sake of curiosity."

"Negation," Ini said. "If Mino remains captive, that will not stop the machines from coming; his signal went out fourteen hundred years ago. They will come, and we will be unprepared."

"Unless they tame him and learn how to oppose his culture," Augur said. "So they can't leave him alone."

"Their curiosity about their origin is therefore merely the motivating pretext," Aura said. "To get them to tame Mino, a thing they would not otherwise know of, let alone attempt, however uncertain the outcome."

"Concurrence," Ini said. "Your thoughts echo mine."

"Except," Aura said.

"Precognition," Augur agreed. "With that, they should know the outcome."

"Agreement," Ini said. "The one form of magic Mino did not know about."

"*If* he did not know," Aura said.

"Assume he knows," Ini said. "That he can read the future paths too. And sees victory."

"But Glamors are not readily fooled," Augur said. "They can emulate the powers of the dragon seeds, which are precognitive or at least clairvoyant. And the youngest is best: Voila can see far. She would not be deceived."

"Agreement," Ini said. "But I see no compromise here; the two sides can not align for mutual advantage in the long term, however they may in the short term. Victory can't go to both, but neither should participate without that prospect. Someone must be mistaken."

"Surmise," Aura said. "Game, outcome unknowable."

"Some games are like that," Ini agreed. "Scissors/Paper/Stone can't be predicted, because the outcome depends on simultaneous variables. It must be played to determine a victor."

"Both sides lose if they don't play," Augur said. "Each side has the chance of victory if they do play. So they must play, though it is a gamble."

"But it's a game between a horrendous machine and a baby," Aura said. "With worlds at stake."

"That is my fear," Ini agreed.

They looked at each other, mutually appalled.

Havoc appeared, with little Weft. "Some ifrits will travel too: Ivor,

Iva, and their four. They will set up a base for an ifrit enclave on Charm. They will have to travel in solid form, and will be most comfortable in your company."

Augur was astonished anew. "Welcome," he said faintly.

"We thought it best that you become acquainted with Mino together, today. Tomorrow we make the trip."

None of the three protested. They did not want to voice their conjecture or their fear, which could be mistaken.

Other Glamors appeared. In a moment they transported Augur, Aura, Ini, and Futility to the center of the illusion fields, where the huge machine that was Mino squatted. The ifrit family was already there. "Greeting," Iva said to Augur. "Interest."

"Interest," Augur agreed. "Trepidation."

Weft appeared, having transported herself. "Excitement! Space travel."

Warp and Flame appeared, with Symbol. "We'll help," Warp said, floating toward the machine.

Augur glanced at Havoc. "Question?"

"Affirmation. The children will ride with you. Should there be a problem, they will notify us."

They were small children, but they were Glamors. Their presence was an indication of the confidence Havoc had in the machine. But Augur noticed that the youngest, Voila, was not in evidence. He suspected that the Glamors did not want their leading precog in the possible power of Mino. He agreed emphatically.

The interior of the machine was surprisingly capacious; there was room for the seven adults and seven children. A chamber was set up with a chamber pot, and another with a broad bed. The human children were already trying both out, urinating in one, bouncing on the other. Symbol, Aura, and Iva kept wary eyes on them. Futility settled in a corner, indifferent to both children and machinery.

Ini joined Augur and Ivo. "I have an inkling," she said. "This is similar to White Chroma science magic, except with nonChroma coloration."

"Weird."

"Agreement. It seems the machine culture operates mostly with Science. I would not have thought so much could be done with it, but I am becoming a believer. To learn the mechanisms, we have but to touch controls and gaze at the screen."

"Fun," Warp said, floating across to join them. "And we can precog too."

Augur marveled that the child referred to precognition, as that had supposedly been the secret magic that defeated Mino. But perhaps it didn't matter, now that they had done it. If they had done it.

"We mortals can't precog," Ini reminded the child. "You will have to do that."

"Enth—enth—"

"Enthusiasm," Ini said without smiling.

"Agreement." Warp floated past the array of buttons. "This." He indicated one. "I can't touch it. Mom said she'd drop a nightmare on me if I touch anything."

"We won't tell," Ini said.

"But Flame will. She's watching."

Flame happened to be in line beyond Ini, so Augur could see her without being obvious. She was indeed watching. "I will press it," Augur said, and did so. As he did, he saw a wisp of fire flare near Flame; she was annoyed that her brother had not transgressed. There was evident sibling rivalry, and the nightmare threat was surely severe. They were Glamors, but still very much children.

The blank panel above the bank of buttons glowed, then showed a picture of the terrain outside. "A window!" Augur said.

"An image," Ini said. "An illusion picture. I suspect it can show other scenes."

"Illusion," Ivo agreed, evidently intrigued.

Warp oriented on another button. "Don't touch this yet. It's the drive."

They reviewed the essential buttons, with Augur and Ini making careful mental notes. They should be able to guide the craft through space; most of it was automatic.

Assuming it would allow their control, once it escaped the illusion fields. Augur did not see what continuing reason it would have, but surely Voila's precognition did. The game would not be ending yet. Still, it made him nervous.

Aura and Symbol joined them at the control panel. "The children pronounce the facilities adequate," Symbol said. "We're ready to return to the camp and organize for departure. Who is to stay here overnight?"

"Augur and Ini," Aura said. "They're in charge of the ship."

That seemed to be the case. "Well, there's a good bed," Ini said.

"If we are not needed here," Iva said, "we prefer to go where we can revert to normal. It is more comfortable."

"Welcome," Augur said.

The other adults, children, and ifrits departed. Alone, Augur and Ini looked at each other. "It occurs to me that our association may soon be ending," Ini said. "Candor?"

"Desired."

"I do not wish to separate from you and Aura."

"Reciprocation. I speak for Aura too."

She hesitated. "I have a notion."

"Other than sexual?" he asked teasingly. He knew she would not speak of their suspicion of Mino; that was forbidden, here within the malign machine. They would speak only of other things, perhaps allaying any suspicion Mino might have.

She began removing her swathing. "Agreement. But sex would facilitate discussion."

This intrigued him. Of course they would have sex; it was expected in a no fault situation like this, apart from their friendship. What would she find difficult to broach? It could be anything, but there was one thing he hoped it was.

He stripped his own clothing, and they adjourned to the bed. She was now invisible, but close and warm. There was something special about stroking such a fine body while looking right through it. Maybe it was like being in the illusion fields, nulling the vision illusion while still experiencing all the others. "Question—"

"Yes, it could be likened to the multi-sense illusions," she said, fathoming his thought. "But I am real and feeling." She pressed closely against him and kissed him avidly.

There was indeed something about being with a woman he respected, who so clearly wanted his passion. She wasn't Aura, but she was still well worth his attention. And what would Mino think of the act of sex, something surely well beyond his experience?

They had loving sex, then lay beside each other looking at the ceiling. "Perplexity," he said. "What can be on your mind that you are cautious about speaking?"

"I don't want to return to Charm."

"Surprise!" But not entirely.

"I mean, permanently. I'll make this trip because the Glamors need me. But if I can, I want to settle on Counter Charm. Yet two things make me hesitate."

"Empathy."

"You have thought of it too?"

"Aura and I are of different Chroma, and unwelcome in our home zones. We have no ties to other regions. Except, in a manner, to this one. We like the planet, and the ifrits."

"Concurrence! But though the ifrits can emulate the human form, they are not human, and I would be lonely as the only human here. So I wondered—" She trailed off.

"So did we. We do not wish to be the only human beings on the planet. But there is much else that appeals."

"The continued study of its plants and animals," she agreed. "And the ifrits. The Chroma zones. A lifetime's research."

"We could raise children here. Exchange fourths."

"If I had a man of my own," she agreed. "But that, for me, is a lesser decision. If the two of you will stay, so will I."

"Deal, if we are allowed."

"Deal," she echoed.

Ennui and Aspect made it a point to take no official note of Havoc's absences, since theoretically he had never been away. The mocks covered it, doing an excellent job. But privately Ennui had to choreograph the exchanges of kings and queens, so that there never appeared to be duplicates.

She got private with Spanky, who was emulating the Lady Gale. "They are returning tonight, and will show the children."

"Appreciation," Spanky said. "The children are kept private, and Bijou shows on occasion as the Lady Symbol, but too long an absence could make for suspicion."

"Understanding. That's why I asked them to show the children and Symbol immediately. They'll be traveling again soon."

"Again?" Spanky could not conceal her disappointment.

"Sympathy. I know you want to get off-stage and relax. But there is one more aspect of the mission. Thereafter it should be done, and you and Berm should be free."

"We want to marry as ourselves."

"Soon you will," Ennui said. Then she kissed Spanky and returned to her office. The mocks had been doing wonderfully, but it was stressful being king and queen, and they were understandably eager to retire from these roles.

Havoc, Gale, Symbol, and the children would return on schedule, and immediately make a public appearance with the children. Berm and Spanky would revert to themselves and spend time as aide and bath girl, so as to be convenient the moment they needed to resume their roles as mocks. It was fairly routine, and finely tuned.

Havoc appeared before Ennui's desk, startling her. "Surprise!" she said. "Early."

"Deliberate. Others may be aware of our schedule, and we have to scout the terrain unobserved, if possible."

"Cooperation," she agreed, knowing he was here for a reason.

Gale appeared, holding the Voila. "Baby-sitting," she said, holding forth the baby. "For an hour."

"Delight," Ennui said. She had done similar many times before, and really liked the little girl.

"I will prepare," Gale said. "Parting." She vanished before Ennui could answer.

"Summon Aspect," Havoc said, remaining.

Ennui sent a mental signal, and the Lady Aspect arrived promptly. She admired Voila, and took her turn holding her. Everyone liked the baby; Ennui suspected it was a Glamor trait, radiating pleasantness.

Then Havoc got serious. "So you want to be rid of the ikons."

"Agreement," they said almost together. "They are transforming us and maybe be dangerous to you if we ever get caught in Chroma zones."

"At present I need you as you are. But when this mission is completed, which may be within a month, you will be welcome to part with them."

"Except," Aspect said.

He nodded. "Except you can't. I have not yet thought of a way, but will focus on it—after the mission."

"Appreciation," Ennui said.

"The mocks—we hardly see them, thanks to the efficiency of the exchanges you arrange. How fare they?"

"They are in love and will marry the moment they are free of this service. They have performed very well, and are deserving."

"Agreement. They will retire from the King's Service with the King's favor."

"And what did you discover on Counter Charm?" Ennui asked, letting her suppressed curiosity emerge now that the necessary routine matters had been concluded.

"Fortunate you asked," he said, smiling. "I want you to meet our friends Ivo and Iva and their children. Set aside a Chroma wilderness region for them; they will settle there."

"Question?" Ennui asked. She had never heard of this family, and she was in a position to know all of Havoc's acquaintances.

"Complicated," he said. "Remind me to explain." He vanished.

They were left with the baby and a mystery. But then Swale came. *I will explain. They are an ifrit family, coming to colonize Charm. Nice folk, but not human.*

Swale had described the ifrits before, but only as floating clouds. This was new.

Spanky entered the office, emulating Queen Gale, wearing the crown and gown. "We need to coordinate tonight's exchange," she said. Then paused, seeing the baby. "Surprise! They're back already?"

"Not officially," Ennui said. "Tonight's still the time. We're baby-sitting for the moment."

"Oh, let me hold her!" Spanky was especially interested in babies now, as she anticipated marriage and family, and for the moment her delighted fresh youth showed through the role.

Aspect extended Voila, who was sleeping, and Spanky took her. She smiled tenderly, and Ennui was struck by the perfection of the emulation, because she looked exactly like the real Gale. How fitting that she be holding Gale's baby.

Voila woke screaming. Dismayed, Spanky tried to rock her in the cradle of her embrace, but she waved her arms wildly about, screaming unremittingly.

Ennui leaped to take the baby, comforting her, but her crying continued.

"Dismay," Spanky said. "I don't know what I did."

"You're emulating Gale," Aspect said. "She must have been startled to realize you aren't her. Not your fault."

"I'm so sorry. I never would—"

"We understand," Ennui said. "These things happen."

Voila continued crying, gazing at Spanky, struggling, reaching out as if to catch hold of her. It was as if she wanted to do something, but was terrified.

"I am agitating her," Spanky said. "Apology. Retreat." She left the office.

But that allowed Voila to relax only gradually. Something had certainly set her off, but what?

She knows something, Swale thought.

"She knows Spanky," Aspect said. "Spanky has on occasion nursed her. She can't be frightened of her."

"Agreement," Ennui said. "It must have been something else."

Something awful. The succubus was alarmed; her thought was tense.

Finally Voila fussed herself into troubled sleep, still quivering. They took turns holding her, mystified. She had never been a fussy baby, and had always had an uncanny awareness of her surroundings, because of her precognition.

"Precog!" Ennui exclaimed. "Did she see something coming?"

"But Spanky would never hurt her."

"No threat to herself—to Spanky."

They stared at each other. "Horror," Aspect said.

Voila woke and resumed crying, despairingly.

"Must warn her," Ennui said.

They hurried to the Royal chambers and knocked on the door. There was no answer. They entered, having that privilege as a business and personal prerogative, and found Berm and Spanky, still emulating King and Queen, sitting in supportive chairs, slumped.

Swale screamed soundlessly. *My brother!*

They did not need to touch them; mind contact sufficed. Both were mind dead. They had been assassinated.

Voila continued whimpering. She had seen it coming.

Appalled, they sought immediate help. In moments Throe and Chief were there, summoned telepathically. "What could have done it?" Ennui asked numbly. "They were protected from hostile magic by their crowns."

Throe considered. "Were they," he said, and it was not a question. "Ugly conjecture: the crowns were booby-trapped, maybe long since. Someone doesn't want Havoc to complete his present mission, so he was assassinated. Only they didn't know that he wasn't wearing the real crown, but a perfect fake. So the mock king and queen got blasted instead."

It made horrible sense.

"Havoc isn't going to like this," Aspect said.

Ennui almost laughed, hysterically. That was surely the understatement of the year.

"But we have to tell him," Throe said.

Ennui nodded, dreading it. "I'll do it. I can reach him." Because she still carried his ikon.

She signaled Havoc. *Emergency. Horror. Outrage. Grief.*

Aspect made a small scream. "Voila!" Then she clarified, speaking as she answered Gale by thought, using the connection of Gale's ikon. "Voila safe. The mocks dead. Assassination."

Ennui realized that in her distraction she had been remiss; of course Gale had feared for her baby first. She should have identified the victims.

Havoc and Gale appeared. They didn't take the baby or even ask what had happened. They merely looked at the mocks, and then an illusion picture appeared. It showed the mocks, still looking exactly like Havoc and Gale, entering the chamber. The Gale figure was talking, evidently distressed. The Havoc put his arm around her shoulders, comforting her, and she turned into him. The love they shared showed, beyond mere emulation. Then they sat in the chairs while she explained exactly what was bothering her, he listening sympathetically.

The Glamors were using their magic to run the recent past again, in illusion. Somehow Ennui wasn't surprised that they could do this.

Suddenly Berm put his hands to his head, as if to lift away his crown, his face a mask of agony. Then he slumped in the chair. Spanky, horrified, started to rise, to go to him, but was overtaken by her own agony, and slumped back.

"The crowns," Chief agreed. "We'll have them analyzed, but we know what we'll find."

"Untraceable mischief," Throe agreed grimly.

But Ennui's gaze was on Havoc. As the scene with the mocks reverted to the present, his face become composed, expressionless. But the air around them seemed to heat, and the scene shimmered as if reality were illusion. There was the feeling of a huge hidden storm with ferocious cross currents, of pressure building toward a volcanic eruption.

Ennui was Havoc's closest friend, no longer because of the oath they shared. She knew him extremely well. She had never seen him this angry. She was afraid.

And Gale's expression and mood matched his exactly. No mitigating influence there. They both liked the mocks, and had promised them rewards that now would never be granted.

"Curse!" Havoc swore, and the outwash of feeling hurled Ennui into the wall, gasping. Then both Glamors vanished.

Voila whimpered. Ennui realized with numb surprise that she was still holding the baby, having somehow cushioned her against the violence of Havoc's reaction. Probably she didn't need cushioning, being a Glamor herself, but she did need comforting. Ennui patted her back. "Reassurance," she murmured. "They haven't forgotten you. They just don't want you with them when their moods are this ugly."

The baby looked at her, and relaxed. She knew it.

Aspect, Throe, and Chief were braced against other walls, where they too had been hurled. "There will be a reckoning," Throe said.

"A dreadful reckoning," Aspect agreed.

Ennui looked at Voila's little face. "You tried to warn us," she said. "And we were too dull to understand."

"All they had to do was remove their crowns," Aspect said. "Voila was reaching for Spanky's crown."

"Normally Voila's siblings are there to translate," Throe said. "Or Gale. This time they weren't. You couldn't know."

So close. If only she could have comprehended, in time.

"Get out of here," Chief said. "Put on your public faces. No one else must know of this. We'll handle it."

They surely would. And so would Havoc, in another venue. Ennui relaxed—and dissolved into tears. She hadn't done that in decades.

Voila's little hands caught at Ennui's shirt. Positive feeling radiated from her. The baby was comforting *her*. That was weird, but it helped.

⁊⁊

Havoc and Gale arrived in their house in the crater mountain. "Take turns letting go?" Gale asked.

"Daren't."

"Understanding. Summarize instead?"

He nodded. He was so tight he feared to release any part of the iron control he was maintaining on his emotions. "We fetched Mino. Looked at tapestry."

"Tapestry had changed," Gale said. "Showed a new multi-Chroma zone."

"Which seemed to be in a polar region: cold, cracked."

"But which planet? Checked altar."

"Altar pointed new direction," he said. "Toward Charm."

"Meaning our Counter Charm mission was done. Now we are ready to tackle the last of it."

This actually was helping; he could feel the tension abating slightly as they talked, putting it in context. "So we jumped ahead to check before the others arrived. Choice between two polar regions."

"Left Voila with Ennui for safekeeping for an hour."

"Jumped to north pole. Huge cracks in ice, wide, deep, long."

"Floated over them, invisibly," she said. "Peered down."

"Penetrated illusion. Saw signs of activity."

"Descended to investigate. Landed on ledge. Tripped magic detector."

She nodded. "Caught by surprise. More sophisticated magic than anticipated in supposedly barren region."

"Withdrew to consider," he said. "Dropped into our private residence, here."

"Wondered whether the proprietors of the detector had fathomed our identity. We were wearing our robes and crowns."

"Received emergency mind call from Ennui," he concluded. Black rage welled up again. "They tried to assassinate us."

"And got Berm and Spanky instead," she agreed. "Innocent victims."

"I am more angry about them than about us," he said grimly. "Kings are natural targets. But I promised Spanky a fourth."

"And Berm is Swale's brother. He was her mainstay."

Havoc paced the floor, trying to work out more rage. "We don't know who they are, but we do know where they are."

"They surely think we are dead in that valley," Gale said. "That our bodies may never be found. So no one will come after them."

"This quest was merely for information," he said. "Until now."

"Until now," she agreed. "So we have the element of surprise. But let's consider carefully, to be sure we encounter no other surprises ourselves."

"Agreement. We can bypass magic detectors. I doubt they know we are Glamors."

"But they might," she said. "Assume they do, for safety."

"Assume they know," he agreed. "Could beams from the crowns blast the minds of Glamors?"

"Negation. We are virtually invulnerable."

He shook his head. "Then why try it, knowing it could not succeed?"

Gale nodded. "Revision: they must not know. If they set up the crowns, they must also know that Glamors could not wear them, and if we did, they would not be harmed by the beams. So it would make no sense. All that does make sense is that they don't know we are Glamors, and believe we are wearing the real crowns, and can be wiped out by them."

But now he argued another case. "To assassinate a king is an act with consequences. We discover their activity, they try to destroy our minds—surely this would lead to quick and thorough investigation that would reveal their guilt and bring savage punishment. Why would they do it?"

"Doubt," she agreed. "Surely they would not. Not right then, at any rate."

"So we are nowhere. Maybe too angry to think sensibly. We need another mind. Maybe Ini."

Gale smiled briefly. "You like her."

"Agreement." He smiled too. "But don't get a notion about leaving me on the theory that she could substitute for you. No one can substitute for you."

"Awww."

They kissed. They were getting the rage under control, though it was far from passing.

Havoc pondered. "Let's fetch her."

"She's on Mino, in transit between planets."

"We could still fetch her."

"Negation," she said. "Everyone would know something was up. The children would blab. Where would our element of surprise be then?"

But he had hold of a notion, and did not want to relinquish it. "She can't substitute for you, but you could substitute for her. Take her place on the ship, so no one knows she's gone, while I talk with her."

"The children would know."

"You can handle them."

She nodded again. "Take Futility instead."

"Question?"

"She's not as smart, but she's coldly practical, and you don't like her."

He looked at her, surprised. "You are jealous of Ini?"

"I try to be."

He had to laugh. It felt good. "Futility, then. But I may have sex with her."

"Knowing she hates it."

"Unlike Ini. You have calculated precisely."

"I want your mind working, not your feeling."

He made a show of sighing. "Futility it is."

Gale's features changed, and she came to resemble the dancer. The emulation wasn't perfect, but she would fine tune it when she saw the woman directly, assuming her clothing and hair style. She would become Futility, for a while.

They jumped to the ship, invisible. Augur and Aura were playing cards with Ivo and Iva while the four little ifrits watched, better behaved than human children; Symbol was playing catch-the-fireball with Flame, not getting burned because the balls faded just before she touched them; Ini was watching the progress of the ship in the screen, explaining nuances to Warp; Weft was quietly watching Futility, who sat alone, tuned out. Weft was the dangerous one; she would immediately recognize the exchange.

Havoc touched the girl and sent a thought. *Mischief. Must take Futility for a while. Keep the secret.*

Weft loved secrets, especially with her father. *Warp will know.*

But meanwhile Gale was touching Warp, swearing him to secrecy too. Then Havoc jumped to Futility, touched her mind so as to put her into stasis, took hold of her and jumped back to the house at the rim. Gale would become visible as Futility vanished, taking her place.

He set Futility in a chair, freed her consciousness, and let her go. She jumped, startled, gazed wildly around, then caught on that she was no longer on the ship. "Sire!"

"I need you."

Her hand went to her blouse. "Of course. Gratitude remains, which means I am willing as well as obliging."

"For dialogue."

"Question? That is not my strong suit."

"For objective, cynical analysis."

She made half a smile. "Qualified." She focused on the room. "Unfamiliar."

"You may explore it as you wish, while we talk."

"Appreciation." She stood and began exploring the room.

"Gale and I explored likely terrain, and found something, but were observed. We returned home—here—and learned that the mocks, Berm and Spanky, had been mind-blasted by the crowns they wore. The crowns Gale and I do not use; ours are fakes, as we don't need protection."

She froze in place. "I was not close to them, but they were courteous to me, and I wished them no evil."

"We were the targets of attempted assassination; they were the victims. We are angry."

She nodded. "Now I understand the brooding power I feel in this room. I thought it was from something else, but it is you."

"Confirmation."

"There will be hell to pay. You did like them."

"Agreement. I fear I am not thinking straight. I want your take." He described their conjecture about the lack of knowledge of their Glamor status, and their doubt that the folk of the polar crevice would be responsible for the assassination attempt.

Futility considered, turning slowly in place with her dancer's grace. "I betrayed you once, and was banished to Limbo. Were I to try it again, I would be more circumspect. Since I would obviously be under suspicion, I would arrange to have some other party do it, with no apparent connection. Someone who did not know me, or even of me. Who thought it was his own idea. So that interrogation could never implicate me. Then my proximity to you would not matter."

"So it could be the crevice people?"

"It could be, if they have secrets that required desperate protection. The timing suggests it."

"But they would not do it directly."

"Certainty. Guilty or innocent, there will be no discernible connection. Have you investigated the crowns?"

"Pause." Havoc shot a thought to Ennui. *News on the Crowns?*

Detonated by remote. Throe traced it to a wandering laborer who found the device and triggered it without knowing its nature. Now tracing prior possessor.

Appreciation. He broke.

Futility smiled. "Confirmation?"

"Agreement."

"Consider: if the assassination is successful, the authorities may be too busy choosing a new king to make a proper investigation. Perhaps only the dead king knew exactly where he was going or what he was seeking. The new king may not know or care what the old one was up to; he has a learning curve of his own. The palace will be in disruption. Chances of escaping discovery may be better than even. Still, not worth the risk unless the risk of the old king's action was worse. What could be there, that warrants such a measure?"

"The secret of the changelings, who are slowly taking over the planet."

"But you are one of them! Why investigate that?"

"To become my own master."

"Understanding."

"You must complete the journey in the ship. Carry the tapestry a while longer. As the mission finishes, you will have your reward."

"Belief."

She came to him. He touched her, nulled her, and jumped back to the ship. They made the exchange, and returned to the crater.

"She called it," he said. "No traceable connection to the crevice folk. No exoneration."

"Then we must investigate further."

"Agreement."

"Unnecessary reminder: investigation, not action. Until we know enough."

Because she knew he was apt to indulge in a destructive orgy against those responsible for the assassination, perhaps before every person in the chain of culpability was identified. She was as hurt and angry as he, but less likely to explode. The enemy would not fare better with her justice; the denouement would merely be quieter, and there would be fewer loose ends. "Agreement."

"Strategy?"

"Act now, before they realize the king is not dead."

"Obvious. Act how?"

"Turn ifrit, infiltrate crevice, observe."

"Thought: bring Voila?"

For her superior precognition. It was best to keep the baby girl away from Mino, for a reason it was best not to think about too openly, but she could be of real help in this case, and safe in cloud form. "Agreement."

Gale disappeared, returning in a moment with Voila, who had

not been surprised. Precognition was a marvelous advantage, but the baby's ability remained eerie. Havoc had become accustomed to being better at most things than those he dealt with, other than other Glamors, but it remained unsettling to have his own baby plainly superior in this respect.

Voila chortled. She knew this, too.

They jumped to the neighborhood of the crevices, dissolved into clouds, floated to the nearest crevice offshoot, and infiltrated. The air was deathly cold, but the ifrit form had magic to conserve heat and could handle it for a short time. Because they were Glamors, they could handle it indefinitely.

Havoc went first, following the main crack as it fed into the network. Gale and Voila followed, giving him time to clear the entry point, remaining in tendril contact. The true ifrits did not have telepathy, but tendril communication was about as effective for this purpose. Gale was careful, while Voila was enjoying the experience, having both parents to herself on a mission.

Soon they found the activity. A line of men were carrying boxes to the surface, where there were dogsleds taking loads of boxes south. Havoc floated around the boxes and infiltrated them, analyzing their content. It turned out to be magic crystals, one Chroma to a box.

"Revelation," Havoc communicated via tendril. "This is where the magic gems come from. They are mined and crafted here, and shipped out for trading."

"We never thought to wonder about their origin," Gale responded. "They are everywhere, and precious. It must be a lucrative industry."

"One the king should control. But would they kill a king to protect their business?"

"If they use the crystals to maintain power beyond the reach of the king."

"If they make the crystals," he thought, "they surely have the power to corrupt those in the crowns."

"Therefore have the will and the means," she agreed.

There came a thought of negation.

"Voila sees a path," Gale said. "It suggests that the crystal miners are innocent of this crime."

"Surprise! Innocent?"

"A false lead. Someone framed them. That's why they're going about their business as usual. They may not have realized that it was us their magic detector tagged."

"Who would frame them in such a way?"

She sent cold laughter along the filament. "Who else? The one we seek. Hoping to distract us."

"By killing our friends? That does not abate my ire."

"Nor mine," she agreed.

There was a signal of confirmation from Voila, who had caught the reference to Spanky. And another: a picture of a path leading to the south pole. She was too young to understand planetary geography, but Havoc recognized the gist.

Gale recognized it too. They had learned a lot about geography since leaving their home Village Trifle. "Shall we withdraw and turn this present matter over to our minions?"

"Agreement." Havoc was annoyed at being led astray even briefly. But he would soon be back on the true trail, and those responsible for the murders would pay.

They propelled their vapors back out of the crevice. They had set off no magic detectors; the miners did not know they had been investigated. This had been the first test of the cloud formation on Charm, successful.

The real challenge was still ahead.

ॐ ॐ

Aura gave up on the cards, which were interesting but pointless for her, as she did not require entertainment or diversion. She went to join Ini at the viewing screen.

"Question," Ini murmured. "Did you note anything different about Warp and Weft?"

"Both unusually interested in Futility."

"Agreement. That seems odd, as they had no interest in her before."

"Feasible to ask?"

Ini shrugged. "Why not?" She glanced at Warp, who had now left Futility and was returning to watch the screen. "Question?"

"Mommy came," he said.

Astonished by this diversion, Ini tried to clarify it. "Gale is elsewhere, not on this ship. She sent a thought?"

"Negation," Weft said. "She emulated Futility. Dummy Warp was supposed to keep the secret."

Warp floated off the floor, angry. "You blabbed too!"

"We'll all keep the secret," Aura said quickly. "Just us four. Why did Gale do that?"

"Daddy wanted to talk with Futility," Weft said.

"To have sex, dummy," Warp corrected her witheringly.

"Doubt," Ini said. "Havoc has readier partners, me included. You know that."

"Ask her," the boy said rebelliously.

Aura exchanged a glance with Ini. "I will ask her," she said. "Keep the children here." She knew Warp and Weft would cooperate, because they wanted to know too.

The children became instantly interested in the screen, which was showing Charm looming large. Aura walked across to where Futility sat.

The woman ignored her, but Aura was undeterred. "Gale took your place for a time. Why?"

"Not your business."

"Warp believes it was to have sex with Havoc."

The woman was plainly annoyed. "Negation. He wanted my opinion. I gave it."

Aura was surprised again. "Opinion?"

That irritated Futility farther, causing her to say more than she must have intended. "The mocks have been assassinated. We considered motives. Now leave me alone."

Surprise became astonishment. This was ugly news. She left the woman and returned to Ini. "Mocks assassinated," she whispered in her ear.

Ini stared at her. "Havoc won't like that!"

"Tell! Tell!" Warp and Weft clamored, almost together.

"Part of the secret," Aura said quickly. "Berm and Spanky have been killed."

Both little faces froze. Then both children burst out crying. Aura picked up Weft, and Ini took Warp, hugging and comforting them. The others in the ship surely noticed, but pretended not to. They knew that something private was occurring.

Futility stood and came to join them. "You should have left it alone. But now that it's out, conjecture: this relates to the quest. The intended targets were the king and queen."

That added to the horror. Of course! The mocks emulated Havoc and Gale almost perfectly; the assassin would have thought they were real.

"Further," Futility said. "The tapestry has changed."

"This relates?" Aura asked, perplexed.

"Change in mission," Futility said. "Coincidence?"

Ini nodded. "Let's look at the tapestry."

Aura remained confused. "Question?"

"To see if it has reoriented. The work on Counter Charm is done. Now it is Charm's turn. If a new region has been targeted, there could be resistance from those associated with it. The tapestry may tell."

Futility brought out the tapestry and unrolled it. "Changed," Ini said immediately. "But I don't know what it shows."

"It's on the screen," Warp said.

They held the tapestry up beside the screen. Sure enough, certain broad features coincided. "Polar region," Ini said. "Not sure which one."

"Can we overlay the images?" Aura asked. "That should establish an alignment, if there is one."

Ini hesitated. "Perhaps."

Why had she hesitated? Then Aura realized: Mino was listening. How could he help it? They were inside him.

Then she realized two more things that complicated her concern. First, this business might not be relevant to Minos' interest, so its exposure didn't matter. Second, if they made a show of concealing it, that would make him suspicious. Better to proceed, and hope that it didn't matter.

"Let's see if it's feasible," Aura said. "Hold the tapestry up before the screen."

Futility did. The tapestry was opaque, blotting out the picture on the screen. That was no good.

"Projection!" Warp said. "Illusion."

"Do it, Mino," Weft said.

Abruptly a translucent image appeared just before the tapestry. Both pictures could be seen, one through the other. The children had directed the machine, and the machine had done it. That was a bit unnervingly interesting.

There was no match. But the children followed up. "North pole, Mino" Warp said.

The superimposed image rotated as if the planet were turning on a mounting, until the north polar region was centered. There were crevices there, and crevices on the tapestry, but it was plain that they did not match and could not be made to match.

"South pole, Mino," Weft said. The children were enjoying this.

The globe rotated again. "The folk there must be getting motion sick," Futility said, and both children burst out in giggles. That surprised Aura in another manner: she had thought the woman had no interest in children, these or any others. But of course one quip did not necessarily mean anything.

The south polar region centered. There was no match. Aura was almost relieved.

"Align," Ini murmured.

The image turned about its axis until it suddenly matched the image on the tapestry. The two sets of crevices aligned exactly.

The children clapped their little hands. "It works!" Warp exclaimed.

"Perfectly," Weft agreed.

It did indeed. They had located the new area marked by the tapestry. They knew where the next mission was.

They shut down the image and put away the tapestry. There was nothing else to do now except complete the journey between planets and see what the Glamors had in mind next. Mino had already been given the destination.

"Where are we going?" Futility asked.

"Death Valley," Ini said. "Where the Ladies Ennui, Aspect, and Nonce foraged for the threads to make the tapestry. It's very private."

Mino moved to enter the long shadow of Charm: the night side. He dropped toward the dark ground. There was no light; Mino did not need it to see his way.

They landed gently. "We have arrived," Ini said. "There should be a habitable cave nearby."

"Cave men!" Warp cried, delighted.

They disembarked, using handlights. "Beware mini-Chroma zones," Ini said.

But there was a clear path that wound between zones toward a low hill. Someone had made it, and Mino had landed beside it. The cave itself was lighted internally and was stocked with supplies: food, water, bedding, bathroom facilities. "They were evidently comfortable here," Aura remarked.

"But lonely," Symbol said.

"Because they didn't have children," Weft said wisely.

"Surely so," Symbol agreed, not quite smiling. "Now are you ready for an illusion show?"

They were always ready for that. So while Symbol distracted the seven children with the show, Aura and Ini went about making a meal. Ivo and Iva were uncertain what to do.

"Regret," Augur told them. "The Chroma zones here are generally small and shifting, as I understand it. Unsafe to assume your natural form; you could be caught by changing zones. Can you endure in condensed form this night?"

"Uncomfortable," Ivo said. "We have been condensed for some time already."

Weft appeared beside them. "I'll tell Ennui. She'll fix it." She vanished.

Aura laughed ruefully. "So much for the distraction of the illusion show! Glamors will not be contained."

Weft reappeared. "She's on it." She returned to the illusion show.

The Red Glamor appeared. "Apology for our neglect. We had a distraction. We'll take the ifrits to their new range now." The Yellow and Green Glamors appeared behind her.

The ifrits hardly had time to bid parting to their human friends before the Glamors clasped them, with the Yellow Glamor taking the four children in a group, and disappeared. Suddenly Aura, Augur, Ini, Symbol, and Futility were alone with the three children. The cave seemed oddly empty, despite their number.

They were there for the night and the next day, passing the time as convenient. Then at dusk the Glamors came again. "Mino will take you to the south pole," the Red Glamor said. "We have prepared a camp."

It seemed to Aura that they were trusting Mino a great deal. Even if they didn't trust him, taking him along on their final mission seemed entirely too risky. But she remembered that they did need him; they couldn't complete their mission without him. So it made sense. But who was using whom? She wished she could be sure.

They trooped out to the big machine, and Mino lifted and flew silently across the planet, not directly south. Aura wondered about that, then realized that if anyone was watching, spying the machine by its temporary blotting of the sight of stars or Counter Charm as it flew over them, this indirection would lead them astray. In any event, any southward angle would lead them soon enough to the pole.

It did. Mino landed in a nonChroma snowstorm. Since the poles were the only large regions of perpetual cold on the planet, this had to be in the vicinity. They had to don heavy clothing before going outside.

"How did you know where we're going?" Aura asked Ini, who was at the screen, directing the machine.

"Warp gave me coordinates he got from Havoc, and I gave them to Mino."

"Coordinates?"

"A kind of grid that parses the planet with imaginary lines. Regular folk don't use them, but Glamors and machines do, it seems, because they can't trust the shifting Chroma zones."

"Confusion."

Ini nodded. "How can imaginary lines be more accurate than real physical planetary features? It is a challenge of understanding. I can explain after we get inside, if you're interested."

"Appreciation."

The hatch had opened and the others were filing out. They were linking hands as they exited, because the flying snow was blinding. Aura and Ini were the last two.

The storm bashed at them, making them stagger as the hatch closed behind them. But there was a beaten path whose sides were walls of snow, making it impossible to wander astray. Aura clung to Augur's hand before, and Ini's hand after, and tramped along.

The path deepened, with the walls rising, until it was a small canyon. Then the packed snow arced over the top, and it became a tunnel. That cut off most of the wind and made progress easier. But they still held hands; it was reassuring.

The passage curved and recurved, then debouched into a chamber large enough for all eight of them to stand. When Ini was inside, Augur set a sheet of ice across the aperture, cutting off what remained of the draft. Then he pulled away a similar ice panel at the opposite side, and they entered the main chamber, which was much warmer. "Airlock," he explained. "Separates us from the outside. Concept from space."

"I saw no such device on Mino," Aura said.

"That is because Mino is used to transporting machines that don't breathe or require air pressure," Ini explained. "But because his kind sometimes has to transport living creatures, the concept and ability exists, and the Glamors invoked it. So no airlocks there, but the ship was airtight for that trip, with fresh air provided."

Now Symbol picked up on it. "Mino could have let the air out in space, suffocating us?"

"It wouldn't have paid him to do that," Ini said. "The Glamors would have been annoyed."

Futility was interested too, and not pleased. "But he could have?"

"He has that capacity, yes."

The dancer's mouth thinned. "They were gambling with our lives."

"Not really."

Now all of them were grimly interested. "Explanation," Aura said.

"Analogy: story of hippo and croc, perhaps dating from Ancestor Earth. Mother hippo, huge and fat, with baby hippo, vulnerable. Dozen predator crocs sharing water hole in drought. Mother tolerates them, but mouths the leader croc, lifting him up without biting. He knows better than to protest; she could crunch him in half, though she's a herbivore. Then when crocs get prey and are in a feeding frenzy, mother pushes baby into their midst, and takes a nap. What happens?"

They thought about that. "Nothing," Futility said. "They touch that baby, they die. They know it."

"She makes sure they know it," Aura agreed, impressed.

"The Glamors put their babies in Mino," Symbol said. "And went away."

Ini nodded. "Assume they might gamble with our lives. Would they also gamble with the children?"

Aura mulled that over. The three children were adopted, but she had seen them with their parents. They were Glamors, perhaps impossible to kill, but it would surely be death even to try. "Negation."

"I have seen Havoc angry," Futility said musingly. "He reminded me of Void."

"It was a demonstration!" Auger said, amazed. "Mother hippo to leader croc: try it if you dare. And he didn't dare."

"Surely for good reason," Ini agreed. "The Glamors could have taken us back to Charm the way they took us to the other planet. They didn't. They were making a point."

"Point made," Aura said. She was just as glad she had not seen it this way while in space; she would have been considerably more nervous.

"Now explain it to us," Weft said. "What about crocs?"

Symbol smiled. "Granted. This way." She took the children to an alcove, and soon was demonstrating with dolls and gestures.

The chamber was set into ground, rather than snow, and had a ceiling of wooden beams and boards. There was a stove in the center, radiating heat. There were several adjacent chambers, some with beds. There was a kitchen area, with food supplies. This was a residence, or perhaps an inn, hewn from the wilds. Evidently the Glamors had been busy while the mortals and children traveled.

Aura settled into a chamber with Augur. "I suspect the worst is to come," she said. "Let's do what we can while we can."

He agreed. They made love, and slept, finishing out the night.

In the morning Aura thought to see about breakfast, but Symbol was already on it, feeding the children and setting up for the adults. Futility, surprisingly, was helping. She saw Aura, and shrugged. "Envy."

"Question?"

"You with your man. Symbol with children."

Aura was surprised. "You desire this?"

"Now I do. Quality man, quality children. I lacked experience with either, in my prior life."

"Understanding. Can you find a quality man?"

"Readily, now that I know what to look for. After the mission."

"After the mission," Aura agreed. But that was a giant imponderable.

☙ ❧

The Lady Aspect was startled to see the Red Glamor appear. "Problem?" she asked. She realized belatedly that the Glamor was not alone; there was another woman with her. She had been told to prepare, but hadn't known exactly for what. They had been scrambling to prepare a suitable Chroma zone, no easy matter.

"Introduction," Red said. "This is Iva Ifrit."

Aspect reacted with automatic poise. "Greeting, Iva. I am the Lady Aspect, social assistant for King Havoc."

"Acknowledged."

"You reserved a region for the ifrits?" Red asked.

"Confirmation. Ennui set it up."

"Show me there." Red put her hand on Aspect's arm, and suddenly they were hovering in the dark air above the pyramid city of Triumph.

Nonplused, Aspect had to demur. "Ennui knows. I'm not good at outside locations."

They were back in the palace. Ennui was just entering Aspect's office, trailed by the Green Glamor and a handsome young man. "We have to deliver the ifrits to their zone," Ennui said. "Follow me." The Glamor touched her, and both vanished, leaving the man behind.

Red touched Aspect again, and now the two of them stood in a glade in a Red Chroma zone under the pale light of Counter Charm. Before either could speak, the Yellow Glamor appeared, with Nonce. Then the Glamors were gone. "Question?" Nonce inquired, evidently nonplused.

Then the Glamors were back, with Iva, the man, and four young children. "These will be your contacts," Red told the ifrits. "But right now they are needed elsewhere. Check this site for their eventual return."

"Appreciation," Iva said.

Then the visitors fuzzed and began to dissolve into vapor. "Astonishment!" Nonce said.

"Swale explained," Ennui said. "They are returning to their natural form. They are sentient clouds from Counter Charm."

"Now you will join us," Red said, putting her hand back on Aspect's arm.

"Wait!" Aspect cried. "If we are to leave Triumph, we have to install the mocks."

"Swiftly," Green said, evidently annoyed.

"This can't be done swiftly," Aspect protested. "We have to prepare them and the palace personnel. There has been a recent—change."

"I'll start it," Ennui said. "You stay here and get to know the ifrits. And explain."

Green took Ennui away. They had arranged for Bijou to emulate Gale, and had rousted out the minstrel who had first emulated Havoc for repeat duty. But they had not yet been notified it was official. They were definitely not yet ready.

Aspect knew that the Glamors were in touch with each other, so an explanation to one would be to all. So while the ifrits dissolved into clouds, she reviewed the necessary spot preparations, to ensure that no outsiders caught on to the fact that the real Havoc and Gale were absent. The murders of Berm and Spanky had brought not merely grief, but chaos to the mock system.

"A day," Red said grudgingly.

"We shall get it done in a night and day," Aspect agreed. She know the Glamors wouldn't tolerate any more lost time.

Meanwhile the ifrits were making an amazing transformation. Their entire bodies were evaporating, forming red clouds. The children completed the process first, and floated into the forest. The two adults had more mass to dissolve, and were forming larger clouds. In due course they too floated away.

"When you need to contact them," Red said, "come to this spot and wait. They will find you, and one will assume human form so that you can converse. They had been long in condensed state, so were desperate to return to their natural forms. Once they have acclimatized, they will be amenable to brief condensations."

Aspect thought about how it would feel to have to be in some unnatural body form, and hoped she understood.

When the ifrits were gone, the Glamors took Aspect and Nonce back to the Palace. "Be ready," Red said, disappearing.

They did their best. Bijou had emulated Gale before, including sessions with Havoc himself, so she was quick to orient. The minstrel had been out of it for over a year, and had entanglements elsewhere, but understood the need. Both were promised that this would be of brief duration, but no exact time frame was clear. They reviewed the royal social and business schedule, drilled in the necessary information, and talked seriously with the palace staff members who would be their closest support. Ready or not, they moved into the royal suite within a day.

The Glamors came for Ennui, Aspect, and Nonce, and took them to what turned out to be the south pole.

Ini was there, and Futility, and red Augur and blue Aura. Symbol was with the Glamor children. The succubus Swale touched Aspect's mind, checking in. Everyone except the Glamors. They had a rather nice underground station complete with bedrooms and cooking facilities.

After the initial round of greetings, Aspect took stock. "Does anyone have a clear idea what we are doing here?"

"Apart from helping the Glamors make their final assault on the mystery of their origin, no," Ini said. "However, there are things that should perhaps be clarified."

"Please."

"We have just had a considerable experience on Planet Counter Charm, and some of us hope to return there to stay once this mission is done. Similarly, some ifrits are starting a colony of their kind here on Charm."

"Awareness," Ennui said.

"We also have the object we traveled to fetch: the spacecraft machine we call Mino. He is theoretically tame, but some of us have doubts. However the Glamors evidently believe that he will not betray our effort. It seems his participation is essential to the mission; the altar I carry and the tapestry Futility carries suggest this." She paused a moment. "But we are not clear why the participation of the three of you is required."

Was it safe to tell?

Little Weft had been listening closely. Now she spoke up. "Voila knows. She says you should tell."

And the baby Glamor was precognitive, as were the children to a lesser extent. Voila seemed to be asleep, but there was no reason to doubt the information. Ennui caught her eye and nodded faintly.

Aspect smiled. "Conjecture: we are here less to help than to achieve separation from the ikons we carry. Ennui carries Havoc's ikon, and I carry Gale's, and this possession has changed both of us significantly, as others may have noticed. We have become different creatures, and wish to return to our natural states. But we are unable to separate from the ikons. This is thus part of the Glamor mystery, and its solution may also free us."

"I can separate from the altar," Ini said. "And Futility from the tapestry."

"And Nonce from the loom," Aspect agreed. "But those are not personal ikons, and seem to follow different rules. What of Symbol with Voila's ikon?"

"I think I could separate, if I wanted to," Symbol said. "But it is becoming more difficult."

"Attachment takes time," Ennui said. "You have had less time."

"Question," Symbol said. "Why do you want to revert? Your ikons have indeed changed you, but for the better, no offense. You are younger, prettier, stronger, smarter, and much sexier now."

"But we are not truly ourselves," Aspect said. "And our men prefer us as we were."

"Surprise. No offense, but men—" Symbol shrugged.

"Are unpredictable," Ennui said. "Apparently not all want shapely sexy eager creatures."

"Weird." Symbol picked up Flame. "Yet there are other things in life."

"Candy," Flame agreed. "Fireballs." One appeared in the air before her.

Several adults laughed. Then they compared notes on things, getting comfortable with the current situation. Aspect, Ennui, and Nonce settled into a room together; they had been associating for more than a year and were compatible.

They rested and slept, catching up on what they had lost during the night. Then they rejoined the others. Nothing seemed to have changed; the Glamors had not reappeared. Aspect found this curious, after their prior urgency to get all supplementary parties here.

She approached Ini. "Question?"

"The children say that the Glamors are still scouting the approach. It seems to be as challenging as the one on Counter Charm. They are using Voila to fathom the paths."

Aspect saw that the baby was gone. Gale must have taken her.

"They must have expected a faster resolution," Ennui said.

"Agreement," Ini said. "It may be that the interaction with Mino complicates it."

"Confusion."

Ini looked at little Weft. "Question."

"Tell," Weft agreed. Evidently she knew.

Ini nodded. "We suspect that the special code that tamed Mino did not really work, but that Mino pretended it did so that the Glamors would free him from captivity on Counter Charm. We believe that Mino and the Glamors need each other in order to proceed with this mission, but that their ultimate purposes are profoundly different. Mino is here to hold these two planets for his machine culture to exploit at its convenience. Neither the Glamors nor the ifrits want that, because that mining is likely to destroy the magic of both planets and make them uninhabitable for most of the entities that are here now. So we fear betrayal at a critical moment. The Glamors may have a similar suspicion."

"We do," Weft said.

"So the likely actions of Mino must be factored in. The Glamors and the machine may have a common interest at the moment, in fathoming the mystery of the planets, but their ultimate objectives are different. Each must consider carefully to gain advantage, without ruining the join effort. One thinks of the Prisoner's Dilemma."

Aspect drew a blank, and was sure others did too. "Question."

"It is a riddle dating from old Earth. Two criminals have been captured and jailed, but the warden is aware that the evidence against them is circumstantial. He needs more to get a conviction. So he confines the two separately, so they can not communicate with each other, then makes each man an offer: if he will confess and implicate his companion, he will be freed, suffering no penalty, while his companion will be sentenced to ten years in prison. If he does not confess, and his companion does, than *he* will be the one to get ten years. If both confess, each will get five years. If neither confesses, there is sufficient case against them only for one year of prison for each. They are then given time to consider their decisions, separately."

"I'm not easy with this," Aspect said. "It smacks of palace politics. Each prisoner will do the selfish thing."

"But the best chance for both is for neither to confess," Ennui said. "Then each gets only one year, instead of five years or even ten years."

Ini nodded. "This is where trust is required. The dynamic of the whole is not the same as the dynamic of the individual. You will probably be better off confessing."

"Confusion."

"Perhaps we can show it in action," Ini said. "Pretend I am the warden, while the Ladies Aspect and Ennui are the prisoners. I proffer each of you the deal, then confine you in separate cells. What do you choose?"

"No deal," Ennui said. "I would not take my freedom at my friend's expense, and know she would not betray me."

"Agreement," Aspect said. "We trust each other. So the warden's ploy wouldn't work."

Ini smiled. "Now let's try the Ladies Aspect and Futility. What are your choices?"

"Confession," Futility said promptly. "If she remains true to form, I go free. That's my best option."

Ini faced Aspect. "You suspect she'll do that. So what do you do?"

Suddenly it was harder. Aspect trusted Ennui, but was not close to Futility, and knew the woman would do the selfish thing. That would cost her ten years. "Confess," she said reluctantly. "That cuts my penalty in half."

"And punishes her for betraying you," Ennui said. "Now I see it. Our choices will vary, depending on our partners in crime."

"Suppose you don't know the identity of your partner?" Ini asked.

They considered, and concluded that confession was better, because it limited the penalty.

"So let's relate it to the current situation," Ini said. "We have what amounts to a contest between Voila and Mino. If Voila wins, our worlds are saved. If Mino wins, they will be destroyed by having all their magic mined out. If neither wins, there will be some intermediate muddle that penalizes both sides to greater or lesser degree. It is not a physical or mental battle, but one of choices. The one who selects the best path benefits most. We assume their precognitive powers are even, so their chances are even. What choice does each make?"

"But they are communicating," Aspect protested. "So they can make a deal that benefits both."

"Negation," Ini said. "Neither side can be certain the other has integrity; each could lie to gain the victory. So they are in effect isolated, like the prisoners."

Aspect nodded. "So victory goes to the one that manages to deceive the other, or to find the better path."

"That is the way I see it," Ini said. "Of course this is not a perfect analogy. There is no warden, and there may not be any mutually beneficial solution. But neither side can afford to lose. Refusing to play the game means loss; Mino would have been left helpless in the illusion fields of Counter Charm, failing to accomplish his purpose in existence, and the Glamors would never solve the riddle of their origin or learn how to stop the eventual onslaught of the machine culture. So both do play, seeking victory."

Ennui shook her head. "Question. Mino is our enemy, yet we are working with him. Couldn't he turn on us and kill us before the Glamors can intervene?"

Now Futility smiled. "Negation. He's a croc, and we're protected by mama hippo."

"Confusion."

"It is a story I told earlier," Ini said. "The mother hippo has the capacity to destroy the croc, but won't do it unless he harms her baby. The croc knows that, so leaves the baby alone, even when the mother is asleep. The Glamors evidently have the power to nullify Mino, I presume by surrounding him with impenetrable illusion, but allow him freedom as long as he serves their purpose. So he cooperates by making himself useful, and can be trusted as long as that truce remains in effect. Eventually there will be a showdown, and then we'll discover whose precognition is superior."

"Misgiving," Aspect said.

"We are in a serious conflict of interests," Ini said. "Worlds are at stake. So we compromise by working with the enemy, each hoping for eventual victory."

"Depending on the judgment of a baby who can't even walk or talk yet," Ennui said.

"Voila's a brat," Weft said. "But she knows what's what, and she's a Glamor. We've learned not to cross her, because she sees farther ahead than anyone. We think she can take the machine."

"I sincerely hope that is the case," Aspect said, feeling weak. She had become accustomed to oddities since interacting with Glamors and possessing the ikon, but she had never imagined a contest like this, with such stakes.

～～

Gale nodded. "Agreement. We can't locate it on our own, even with precognition." She glanced over her shoulder at Voila, who had fallen asleep in her pack. "We'll have to use the map and altar."

"Regret," Havoc said. "But that's why we brought the mortals: as a backup in case of need."

"And why we brought Mino," she said. "Whom we were pretty sure we would need."

"Agreement."

They jumped to the camp house. The mortals and children were well settled in, some playing group games, others in dialogue. There was immediate attention.

"We foolishly hoped we wouldn't need you," Gale said. "But we do. Here is the challenge: somewhere there should be an entry to the stronghold; Voila indicates there is. But there is strong aversive magic on many levels that prevents us from locating it. It interferes with precognition too. It seems to be independent of Chroma, so this is no ordinary waste. We believe the map and altar will show the way through it, but the route is unlikely to be pleasant."

"We are accustomed to unpleasant service for the king," Futility said, and everyone laughed, including Havoc: she was referring to sex. Gale knew the woman didn't find sex distasteful, merely superfluous unless required as a social tool. She was reportedly quite good at it when she chose to be.

"We believe we should form a line, a human chain, with the leader picking out the route," Gale said. "That way no one will blunder into anything lethal. We will need map and arrow up front."

"Disbelief," Futility said. "I will get to lead?"

"Through an unpleasant emotional landscape," Gale agreed. "Ini second, with the altar."

"Question?" Ini asked.

"Explanation," Gale said. "We have been exploring, and have encountered what in stories of old Earth is a minefield of emotions. Fear, revulsion, sickness, depression, rage. Also positive ones that lead to dead ends or hazardous terrain. We believe the map will identify the zones to be avoided, and the arrow will point to the objective, as it did on Counter Charm. But there do not seem to be illusions, merely feelings. It is apt to be an odd challenge."

Symbol looked wary. "Experience. Some things are best not shared with children."

"Objection," Warp said. "We're not just any children."

Gale picked him up and kissed him, causing Weft to turn away in disgust. "You're *our* children. There are certain things we try to protect you from."

"Like what?" he demanded.

"Like fear, grief, and sex."

He shrugged. "We'll risk it." Weft and Flame nodded.

Gale made a small roll of her eyes. "We saw that!" Flame said, spinning off a fireball.

"She can't help it," Weft said. "She's *adult*."

Gale got down and hugged them all. "Some day that will be your fate, if you're unlucky."

"Awww," they said together, then deteriorated into giggles.

They formed the line, all of them bundling up to withstand the deadly cold. Havoc lead the way to the edge of the aversion field, then vanished. He and the other Glamors would be watching, then following when the path was marked.

Futility led the way into the field, obviously pleased to be a leader in anything. Ini followed, murmuring directions. It was immediately apparent that this time the altar indication was not constant; it changed as they moved.

Futility stopped, then backed up a step. She swallowed before speaking. "Nausea," she explained. She held up the tapestry map, which showed a bilious patch ahead.

"Bear left," Ini said.

They bore left, skirting the nausea zone. But in a moment they ran into a fear zone. Futility stopped again. "Terror." She indicated a blue patch on the map.

"Bear right," Ini said.

Futility did so, looking less pleased than she had been. Gale was third in the line, and saw that there were generally thin regions of colorlessness between the patches. They were threading through these.

They got the hang of it, and made progress. Then they came to an impasse of sorts: the way was blocked by a patch of disgust that seemed to be too intense to tolerate. But the bypass was a physical challenge: a steep-sided ice pit. "I might get through that," Gale said. "Boosted by magic. But the rest of you would have trouble."

"Agreement," Ini said. "Surely better to expire of disgust than of hypothermia trapped in a pit."

"You lead then," Futility said. "I can't stand it."

"I'll lead," Gale said. "You follow." She mentally marked the spot the map showed, then plowed ahead.

The disgust hit her like a pail of wormy garbage in the face. But it was emotional rather than physical. She wanted to deal with it, scour it out, expunge it from the universe. Instead she forged on through it. After a few steps it abated; she was back between patches.

She turned to look back. Ini had followed; no one else. She was appalled. How could they get through if the line was not maintained?

"Stay here," she told Ini. "I'll do something."

"I was in your lee," Ini said. "It helped."

So her Glamor magic had made a wake. Another discovered nuance. Gale forged back through the disgust, and reached the head of the line. She took Futility's hand. "I can suppress it some. Stay close." Without waiting for a response she reversed course again, hauling the woman along.

They made it. Gale deposited Futility with Ini and went back again. This time she found Augur with Weft. She got an idea. "Lead him across," she told the child. "Hold his hand."

Weft smiled and did so. They went ahead while Gale went on to the next: Aura with Warp. She sent them ahead, then found Symbol with Flame. After that there were just Ennui and Aspect. She took Ennui's hand and led her through, then returned for Aspect.

They regrouped and resumed progress. The next patch was grief: not for any specific loss, just the feeling. Futility and Ini moved around it, and so did Gale.

There was a scream. Gale whirled; that was Flame!

Sure enough, there to the side the little girl was running, screaming. The emotion of fear had gotten to her and send her off the path. There was a crack in the ice ahead of her, a veritable crevasse whose depth was not obvious.

Gale started after her, but a hand caught her arm. It was Augur. "False!" he said.

"That's my child!"

"No, Flame's with me," Symbol called from farther back.

Gale looked. There was her daughter, still in line. She looked back at the running child—and there was nothing. It had been just a projected impression, all in her mind.

"It's not all aversion," Augur said. "It's diversion—one way or another."

"Agreement," she said. "Appreciation." She kissed him.

"I saw that," Aura said, trying to frown.

"Oh, all right," Gale said, and kissed Aura. Warp and Weft almost fell over laughing.

They moved on, handling the aversions with greater ease now that they understood them.

They came to a featureless windswept plain. There was nothing, not even aversion.

"Here," Ini said. "The arrow has stopped."

"And it's the center of the map," Futility said.

"But there's nothing here," Gale said. She tried to query Voila mentally, but evidently the baby was asleep. Then she caught on. "Down. This is the entry."

Havoc extended one arm. "I'll melt off the ice."

Nothing happened.

"Now that's curious," he said. "I seem to lack fire magic." He looked at Flame, who had arrived with Aspect.

The child concentrated, but no ball of fire appeared. "I can't do it," she said, alarmed.

Soon they verified it: this region nullified their magic, including telepathy. "It must cut off our access to our ikons," Gale said. "We know that's possible."

"We mortals don't depend on ikons for telepathy," Aspect said. "But we're blocked too. It must damp out magic itself."

"Yet it's not a region of no magic," Ini said. "It's an Air Chroma zone."

"Affirmation," Symbol said.

That hadn't occurred to Gale, but the women were in a position to know, being of that Chroma themselves. Gale had become accustomed to doing magic regardless where she was, so had largely tuned out of Chroma zones; and in any event, this snowy region had seemed like nonChroma. But who could say what color the Invisible Chroma was? Only its facility with illusion made it apparent at all.

Now she felt naked and insecure without her magic, no more potent than the normal folk. She did not like it.

"This is surely why we need Mino," Ini continued. "He doesn't use magic."

"He uses Science magic," Augur said.

"And maybe precog," Gale said.

"I stand corrected. I should have said he doesn't depend on magic in quite the way we do. He mines it. Thus he may be able to nullify the magic that restrains us here."

"I'll fetch him," Havoc said, and started back along their path in the snow. "Mark a place for him to land."

They set to work scraping snow by hand, forming mounds in a large circle. Then they stood around that circle, so that their bodies further defined it.

Mino came. The machine floated through the air high enough to avoid the null region, then dropped to the marked spot with a muted crash. The port opened and Havoc emerged. "It nulled his flying magic too, near the ground," he said. "But this is something he can handle. I have explained. He will harvest the magic where he is, leaving mere reality."

They watched as Mino mechanically extended metal plates. They touched the snow around him, and the snow disappeared. It seemed to be translucent ice. Then that too faded, to reveal a dark hole.

"This is reality?" Gale asked. "We were standing on nothing!"

"On a magic ice surface," Havoc said. "Covering the entrance."

Mino's metal feet rested on the snow and ice beyond the harvested circle. Now he extended it outward, and dropped down into the hole. The descent continued as he harvested the magic below, eroding his own supports.

"We can ride him down," Havoc said, and jumped to the top of the machine's metal dome. Soon the others joined him.

In due course they settled into a large cave. Gale tried again to reach Voila's mind, and this time found it. "Magic is working again," she said.

"So Mino forced an entry by nullifying the protective illusion," Ini said. "Now we are in the sanctum. It feels intense."

"It does," Gale agreed. "Flame, try a fireball."

The little girl did. A giant mass of fire exploded before her, half blinding them all before it dissipated.

"I meant a little one," Gale said reprovingly."

"That *was* a little one," Flame said, awed.

They experimented further, and found that all types of magic were much stronger here than usual. The ambiance enhanced performance.

"And we're merely at the entry," Ini said. "I suspect the effect increases farther in."

Gale received a signal from Voila. "It does," she said. "In fact, that's the least of it. There is power of other kinds here."

"We have already seen some of it," Havoc said. "If it can nullify Glamor magic, it can surely do more. Best to proceed with caution."

"This from the wild barbarian," Gale said, laughing. Of course she knew that Havoc was anything but wild in reality; he was an exceedingly smart and careful man, which was one reason others tended to underestimate him.

"Query Voila," he said. "I don't want to blunder into anything we can't handle."

Gale did. Voila extended her precognitive awareness, and a flood of information came in, confusing in its complexity. It wasn't the baby's thoughts, but the raw material, beyond Voila's ability to process.

"Help me," Gale said to the other children. "Limit, parse and translate."

"It's huge," Weft said. "We can only bite off little chunks."

"They'll do."

"Who made this?" Havoc asked.

"The sphinxes," Warp said. "When they had to set up for the changelings and altars and loom and stuff."

"Amazement," Ini breathed. "Just like that, the answer to your quest."

"What's the main power of this site?" Ini asked.

"It broadcasts mood," Weft said. "To the whole planet, from here, following the lines of Chroma dif—diff—"

"Differentiation," Gale said.

"And it's as fast as light," Weft concluded.

"What is the nature of ultimate reality?" Aspect asked, smiling.

Flame looked at her. "Simplify."

"What does the future hold? It's not a serious question; no one really knows that."

But Flame gave her a serious answer. "Voila knows short term. Mino knows long term."

This drew the interest of the other adults. "Two different types of precognition?" Gale asked.

"Sure. Hardly need the enhanced information flow to know that. Mino's a linear precog, Voila a parallel. Do you know the terms? I don't."

"Linear," Gale said. "In a line. Parallel, several lines next to each other."

"That's it. Mino can see way down a hundred years along one line. Voila can see a hundred lines for the next minute, maybe ten up to an hour, but then they mostly fuzz out except for the strongest ones. But a year's about her limit on the longest."

Gale controlled her excitement. "So which one can see who wins this contest?"

"Neither," Flame said, frowning as she read this bit of the data stream from Voila. "Voila can't see far enough to know for sure, and Mino can't untangle the near lines well enough to pick a winner."

"Then why is he here helping us?"

"Because all his long lines lose if he does nothing, and he can't do anything unless the Glamors let him loose."

That aligned with what they had suspected but had not told the children. "And why did Voila cooperate in this, if she doesn't know whether it helps?"

Flame hesitated. "I can't say."

"She doesn't know?"

"She knows, but I can't say. It's weird."

Gale let that pass, lest she disrupt the information she was getting. "How can anyone know who wins?"

The little girl concentrated. "They can maybe find out together, if they cooperate."

"Why would they do that?" Gale asked, surprised.

"They want to know."

Of course. Why battle for supremacy if you can discover the winner without fighting? "Is there any other way to find out?"

Again the concentration. "No."

Gale looked at Havoc. "Opinion?"

Havoc looked at the others. "Vote. Do we let them cooperate to find out the ultimate victor between us?"

"Us too!" Weft cried.

"Granted."

They voted: seven adults and three children. Only Havoc and Gale of the Glamors were present; all other Glamors were staying out of range of the machine, forging a sphere of illusion to confine him. Mino was not free, and surely knew it. This was perhaps all that guaranteed his continuing cooperation. The other Glamors, human and animal, were using the multiple-sense illusion technique they had learned from Idyll, and were able to contain the machine, though only by constant vigilance and effort. The battle between them was constant, as Mino probed for weaknesses and the Glamors shored them up. But this impasse couldn't last forever. They needed to know.

The decision was eight to two. Only Symbol and Futility, the two most cynical members of the party, voted no. "It's dangerous for the children," Symbol explained.

"Can't trust the machine," Futility said.

"Do it," Havoc said.

Nothing happened. "How is this set up?" Ini asked.

"They're doing it," Weft said. "Leave them alone."

So simply! Gale tried to tune in on Voila's mind, and discovered an amazing phenomenon. That little mind was a conduit for a huge focus of magic power. It felt like a monstrous cable extending to the stars.

Then the cable dissolved, and the baby slumped in her pack. It was done.

"Verdict?" Havoc asked tersely.

"Confirmation of what Mino thought," Flame said. "They have to be together, or both lose. Everybody loses."

"Together?" Gale asked, not liking this at all. "How?"

"On the same side."

"And if they are not, how does everybody lose?" Havoc asked.

"Another culture comes and takes over," Flame said. "Not human. Not machine. Different."

Now it was making sense. "They saw the future together," Gale said carefully. "Together, either our side or the machine side will win. Apart, both sides will lose. To nonhuman, nonmachine aliens."

"Agreement."

"And if we get together, how do we determine which of us wins?"

"They fight," Flame said. "Voila and Mino. Winner takes all."

Gale looked around the circle. She didn't need to read any minds to know the general feeling of horror.

❧

Augur shook his head. This had come to a dismaying pass. How could a four month old baby fight a big thousand-plus year old machine? Yet the Glamors were seriously considering it.

They settled in the cave, which was comfortable rather than freezing, and camped for the rest of the day and the night. The Glamors conjured food, bedding, and whatever else the group needed, including toys for the children. Augur, Aura, and Futility helped Symbol entertain the children while Havoc, Gale and Ini discussed the ramifications of the information available here and potential mechanisms for the contest. Augur knew he should participate in that discussion, but for the moment he didn't want to face the strange prospect that loomed. By common consent, none of the adults with the children mentioned it.

"Is any of this real to you?" he asked Aura in passing.

"Some," she said, smiling. "The children are cute, apart from their powers. Let's have nonGlamors ourselves."

"Agreement."

She glanced at Mino. Warp and Weft were floating around him, playing dodge and tag, trying to confuse his observation panels. "Do you think the machine likes to play with children?"

"Doubt. He's just making sure they don't push a wrong button."

"They have short-range precognition, shorter than Voila's. He doesn't, so he has to watch them, and even so they fool him sometimes. It seems to be about even, for their game. But he may be studying them to learn how they do their precog."

"He's a machine. Can he learn an ability he's not programmed to do?"

"I wish I knew." She moved off, distracted by Flame. Things tended to be hectic when the children were around, even when routine.

They slept the night, and had a conference in the morning. "We were guided by our own limited powers of clairvoyance and precognition," Havoc said. "That's why we required all of you to come here, inconvenient as it may be for some." He glanced rather fondly at the Ladies Ennui and Aspect. "We believe there is need for some of you, but we couldn't tell which, and didn't want to risk lacking the right one. Now the situation is coming clearer."

"Concern," Aura said. "Should this discussion be in the presence of our opponent?"

"Yes," Havoc said. "Because we have worked out the nature of the settlement we must make with Mino. Clarification: he sees long, we see short, but both are needed for the answer. A path that ends short does not connect to the long path, so we have no advantage staying short. A path that ends long but has no clear connection to a short path is of no use to either party. It's a path that has no access. We need to find the path that extends all the way from here to a clear answer, perhaps a century hence. Working together, Voila and Mino saw that no paths are continuous unless we work together, so it is to our mutual interest to locate those 'together' paths we favor. We shall now do that."

"Mystification," Aura said.

"Voila is people oriented," Havoc said. "She can better appreciate a person with a mission, than the mission itself. Surely when she grows older she will be more independent, but we can't wait for that. We mean to settle this matter today. If we win, Mino will join us, suffering himself to be reprogrammed to be our servant. If Mino wins, we will deliver Voila to him as hostage, with her mother to care for her. This does not mean that harm will come to her; indeed, Mino will want her in the best of health and sanity, because he needs her to keep the path straight. The rest of us will come and go, but Voila will remain in the machine. The other children may visit her freely, but only in the machine. She will grow up there, and may marry and have a family, but she will never leave. She will be the guarantee that none of the rest of us will make mischief for Mino, both by her nature and her person."

"Horror," Aspect said.

"Compromise," Havoc said. "The stakes are even. The contest is between Voila and Mino, and the loser will serve the winner, and the power of their unification will make all else irrelevant in terms of the ultimate fate of the planets. Voila may live in Mino anyway, if she wins, to facilitate that future vision, but will be free to come and go. So there may be little apparent distinction between victory and defeat."

"Except for the fate of two planets," Ennui said grimly.

"Affirmation. Questions?"

"Have we a choice?" Augur asked.

"No more than Mino. We don't want to be destroyed by any other alien culture. By joining forces we have the chance to prevent that."

"But it's only theoretical," Augur said. "We can't know what aliens may come in the far future."

"Negation," Havoc said. "Mino knows of the other galactic cultures the machines have encountered in the past. A number of them are expansive in nature, and in time will almost inevitably come this way. They all need resources, and these two planets represent an extremely rich potential harvest. Mino sent the signal out fourteen hundred years ago, so we are known. Secrets are hard to keep; if the machines don't come soon, someone else will race to grab the treasure first. Chances of escaping are minuscule. Even if we lose, we may be protected for a century, until the machines come. That's better than the alternative."

It seemed tight. "How is this contest to be handled?"

"First, each of us must decide on a firm course of action or inaction," Havoc said. "Or perhaps merely think pleasant thoughts. Each is different; whichever one directs the course will make a unique path to the future. One of those paths will be the one we want."

"One?" Ennui asked sharply.

"One. All others will be for Mino."

"Dismay! How can that be?"

"In the normal course Mino would have won, had the ifrits not

captured him. That did not change the outcome, it merely complicated it. Now, with the involvement of the Glamors and Voila's precognition, we have an even chance for victory. Because she can select that
single course, and Mino can't prevent her."

Symbol looked relieved. "So we win after all."

"Negation. She will choose the course, but she can't see it to the
end. Only Mino can do that. So she may choose wrong. All factors
considered, the odds are even; they agree on that. It is a fair match."

Augur still mistrusted this, and saw that the others did too. "How
does she choose?"

"Each of us will stand in a circle," Havoc said. "Voila will float
past and choose one of us. She will sense the ambiance, and select the
one whose course seems most promising. Once her choice is made,
Mino will announce the victor."

"Mino!" Aspect exclaimed. "Confusion."

Havoc smiled. "You wonder how we can trust Mino to announce
correctly. There are several answers. As a machine, he may be inca-
pable of lying; that is a sophisticated living sapient sort of thing. Regardless, the truth will not be changed by it, as Voila's choice will not
be changed. She will not see the far future, but she will know if Mino
lies. So he has nothing to gain that way; his best course is to honor
our agreement. He will tell the truth, either way."

"Doubt," Symbol said.

"You lack precognition." Havoc glanced at Ennui and Aspect. "You
have the dragon seeds, which signal untruths. Did I say anything false?"

"Negation," Ennui said, and Aspect nodded.

Augur did not find this entirely persuasive, because as he understood it, the dragon seeds were of limited scope, not in the league of
this contest; how could they know what no one else did? But evidently
the Glamors accepted it and were ready to gamble the fate of worlds
on it. What could the others do but go along?

They formed the circle. Gale let the baby go, and she floated into
the center. Augur kept forgetting that she was a Glamor, with Glamor
powers, regardless of her age. She couldn't walk, but she could use
magic to fly. She couldn't talk, but she could communicate by telepathy. She couldn't truly reason, but could perceive the near-term consequences of choices. And, it seemed, she could save two worlds—if
she chose the right person, with the most promising course.

Voila floated first toward her mother, who had just released her.
Gale extended her hand, and the baby touched it. Then she floated
on; this wasn't the one.

She approached her father. Havoc extended his hand, and it was
touched. And rejected.

Aura was next. Augur hoped it wasn't her, chiding himself for his
selfishness; he wanted to complete this mission successfully, then retire to Counter Charm with Aura, Ini, the ifrits, and whoever else was

interested. If she were chosen, what would be her role, her obligations? Would she have to take up residence in the machine?

But Voila touched Aura's hand and floated on. Augur himself was next. Somehow that prospect did not bother him as much as it had for Aura; he didn't want it, but would handle it if he had to. He had no idea how to guide the worlds to an effective defense against galactic invaders.

The baby touched his hand and floated on. Aura took his arm, her grip shaking with relief. She had been similarly concerned.

Voila went on to Ennui, who seemed no more eager for this dubious honor. Then to Aspect. And finally to Symbol.

"I can't do it," Symbol said. "I have children to take care off." But she held forth her hand. And was passed by, evincing similar relief.

All seven human adults had been checked. Were none of them right? How could this be?

Then Voila floated down to Warp. It was to be one of the children? This was a surprise.

It wasn't Warp. She went on to Weft, and passed her by too. At last she came to Flame. "Agog!" the child exclaimed expectantly.

And passed her by. A ball of flame appeared, intensified, and exploded into nothingness.

The adults shared glances of mixed relief and dismay. It wasn't a child, but neither was it an adult. How could this be?

"Does this mean that no one marks a path for our victory?" Augur asked grimly.

Havoc glanced at Weft. "Ask," he said.

"There's a person," Weft said. "But he isn't here."

"Where?"

Weft spread her hands. "Somewhere. And there's something odd. Don't know what."

"Can she locate him?" Gale asked.

Weft concentrated. "Yes. Hot cold."

"Then we'll look," Havoc said. He stepped into the center of the circle and took Voila from the air.

"Take my pack," Gale said.

They set the pack on Havoc's back and put the baby inside it. "Direction," Havoc said, slowly turning around.

In a moment he stopped. "On our way," he said, and disappeared.

Augur looked around. "It seems we must wait."

"So must Mino," Aura said. "Maybe he knew that none of us was right, and thought he had the victory."

"But she saw through it," Ini said. "She can't be fooled that way."

If Voila really did know, Augur thought. What did Weft mean by "something odd?" This had been presented as a straightforward choice of people and paths, but he suspected that it was more devious than that.

Havoc jumped to the ifrit reservation. Could it be an ifrit? Weft had said there was something odd. That could account for it. The ifrits did not want the two worlds ravaged any more than the humans did.

But there was no "hot" here. Voila's mind signaled north of here.

Havoc jumped again, to a region well north of Triumph City, half expecting the direction to reverse. It didn't; the way was still north

Then he caught on. "The miners!" he said. "The ones who were framed for the assassination of the mocks." He jumped to the crevice at the north pole they had explored before.

But here the search became difficult. Voila had a direction, but it was not possible to follow it literally, because the cracks did not go straight. It could take a long time, and he didn't care to take it.

The minions of the king had not yet cracked down on the miners. It would come, but it was no simple operation. Throe was organizing it now, getting his men into place for an orderly operation.

Havoc was more direct. He followed a crevice deep down, discovering that the north polar region, like the south one, was an Air Chroma zone, its color invisible. He nulled the intruder-alert magic and reached the warm residential section. He collared the first miner he encountered. "Take me to your leader."

"Irritation. Who are you?" the man demanded.

"I'm King Havoc. Don't you see my crown?"

"Annoyance. That's a fake crown. I'm a miner; do you think I can't tell real magic gems from fake ones? Now stop wasting my time, impostor, before I hit you with some real magic."

This set Havoc back. The man was right: he was a miner, he could tell the difference, and these were fake stones. Havoc didn't want to reveal his Glamor status.

Then he got a nudge from Voila, who did not understand the details of the situation but knew the most feasible path. "Then turn me in to your leader as a fake king."

"Satisfaction. You asked for it," the man said. He snapped his fingers, causing a flash of red light. It was a signal.

In a moment an older man appeared. "Problem?"

"Confirmation, section manager. This faker pretends he's the king." The miner walked away.

The manager turned to Havoc. "Observation: You look like the king, you're garbed like the king. But that fake crown is a giveaway. Question: what's your business here?"

Havoc's clairvoyance informed him that this man had no knowledge of the king's supposed assassination. That confirmed the conjecture that the miners were being framed for the assassinations. "I need to see the leader of your zone."

"Warning: you are about to see the interior of our brig for intruding on private premises. How did you get in here?"

"Your intruder alerts are inadequate. Now summon your leader."

"Surfeit," the manager said. He concentrated.

Magic coalesced around Havoc, and was repelled. Then Havoc focused his own magic, and lifted the manager, pinning him against the wall.

The manager stared at him. "Amazement! You are not what you seem."

"Your leader," Havoc reminded him as he let him slid back down to the floor.

The manager snapped his fingers, emitting a blue flash. Another man appeared. "Man of mysterious power here to see you, Duke," the manager said. "Air Chroma sorcerer or equivalent."

Duke eyed Havoc appraisingly. "Follow, stranger." He turned and walked away.

Soon they were in a comfortable subterranean office. "Introduction," Havoc said. "I am King Havoc."

"Question: can your baby float?" He evidently knew that the king had adopted magical children.

Havoc reached over his head, lifted Voila out, and let her go. She floated. Duke eyed her, and magic swirled, but did not affect her. The man had tried to nullify Air Chroma magic, and verified that there was none.

Duke bowed his head. "Sire."

"Explanation," Havoc said. "On occasion I have private missions. I use a mock king to emulate me, so that my absence will not be noted. He wears the real crown, as I have magic of my own. You and your minions were right to doubt me."

"Sire, how may we serve?" Duke, also, had no knowledge of the assassinations.

"I am in search of a person who may be somewhere in your zone. Deliver that one to me."

"Name?"

"Unknown."

"Description?"

"Unknown."

"Question?"

Havoc reached out and fetched Voila in. "Speak categories."

Duke nodded. He was quick to relate, as effective leaders generally were. "Male."

Havoc mentally relayed the concept of maleness to Voila, and received her confirmation. "Yes."

"Age below eighteen."

"No."

"Between eighteen and forty."

"Yes."

"Chroma: Air."

"Yes." That made sense, as this was an Air Chroma zone.

"Miner."

"No."

"Administrator."

"No."

"Service person."

"No."

Duke paused. "Sire, we are running low on categories."

"Try what remains."

"Visitor."

Now Havoc hesitated. "Perhaps."

"Sorcerer."

That was interesting. Ini's sister Ine was a sorceress, capable of magic well beyond that of ordinary zone dwellers. "Probably, but not entirely."

Duke smiled. "Trader."

"Yes. Amplify."

"We mine, but are isolated from other zones. We are Air, and trade with an Air trader sorcerer who travels to the more populous zones. Other mining zones trade with other traders for other Chroma. Our trader brings us necessary supplies, as our zone has no viable gardens or animals for food. We suspect he cheats us, but we would not get a better deal from another trader, and can not afford to antagonize him." He sent a mental impression of huge amounts of Air crystals required for food. Indeed, it was a ruinously unfair exchange rate. The trader was squeezing both ends, thus amassing much material wealth and power.

So these folk were in regular business, and were not outlaws. It was the middleman who was the unscrupulous operator. "You will soon have a better deal from the king," Havoc said. "The trader will have other concerns."

Duke smiled, appreciating an excellent opportunity to rid his zone of an oppressive yoke. Havoc's reputation as a barbarian who took his word seriously had reached him. His cooperation became complete. "His name is Hoard. We do not know his residence, but he has an Air mistress who remains here; she might know."

"Summon her."

Duke snapped his fingers, making a green spark. In a moment a very pretty and fetchingly garbed young woman appeared. "Present," she said, curtsying.

"Where does Trader Hoard reside?" Duke asked.

"Why, with me, when he visits."

"When at his home."

The girl hesitated. "I wouldn't know."

Duke scowled, knowing she was concealing something.

But Havoc read her mind, and got a shock. "I have it. Appreciation. My administrator will contact you to discuss terms of trade. I verify only this guarantee: they will be substantially better for you than the ones you have had hitherto, with prospects for further improvement. The king appreciates cooperation."

Duke bowed his head again. "Appreciation, Sire."

"Parting." Havoc jumped to that site, which was in a small Air Chroma zone not far from Triumph city. The mistress had known, but been barred from telling. There was fear in her mind; Hoard was a brutal man, and quick to punish transgressions. She wished to be free of him, but dared not say so.

Yet that was only part of it. The mistress had received news of the appearance of the king at the polar region, and relayed it to Hoard. So Hoard had known what Duke did not.

Hoard was probably the assassin. His bribery connections were surely sufficient.

And they would have to work with him, to save the planets? Havoc was extremely wary of that. He had a serious score to settle. He remembered his night with Spanky; she had been a fine girl, undeserving of her fate. And Berm, Swale's brother, a worthy young man. The one who had killed them deserved a brutal execution, not the support of Glamors.

Hoard's residence was a veritable castle that was real, not illusion. Havoc surveyed it clairvoyantly. It had no service personnel, but huge storage chambers filled with Air Chroma crystals. The man had been truly named; he hoarded the source of his power. Surely he didn't want the king catching on and demanding the king's tax, which would be formidable.

There was no doubt now: this was the person. But how could they ever cooperate with such a criminal?

Havoc reached back to touch Voila's little hand. *Clarification*, he thought.

And got it: the key here was not positive, it was negative. That was what was odd; Voila had not quite grasped it until she got this close. Instead of endorsing a good agenda, they needed to eliminate a bad one. They were not going to work *with* this man, but to prevent him from working with Mino. By killing him.

"Satisfaction," Havoc muttered grimly. He jumped to the south pole to return Voila to Gale.

"Progress?" Gale inquired.

"Vengeance," Havoc said. "Victory when it is done." He showed her a quick mental summary, and jumped back to the castle.

He considered the situation. He wanted to be sure of taking out Hoard, and to acquire or destroy his hoard of crystals. But because they were magic, matching the man's Chroma, they would give him great magic power. A Glamor's power was no greater than that of a trained Chroma person, in his Chroma zone; the strength of the Glamor was that he could take his power with him, anywhere, not limited by the zones. A man with unlimited Chroma crystals could do much the same. It depended on his ability and experience. And this man, as a sorcerer, would have considerable. He was dangerous.

What Havoc needed to do was separate Hoard from his Chroma and crystals. Then the man would have no magical power, and could readily be dispatched. But that would surely not be easy to do, if he chose to remain in his castle. That set up the first step: remove the trader from his castle.

But first he had to do the honorable thing: give the man a chance to surrender to justice. Havoc hated the necessity, but he had to follow proper form. Damn these civilized obligations!

He used his clairvoyance to locate the man in the castle, then jumped to that chamber. Air Chroma folk were naturally invisible, but usually formed illusion images about their natural contours, making themselves visible and handsome, and this one was no exception. Havoc could see him plainly, and in any event could track him by his sound and solidity, as well as his mind.

As it happened, Hoard was with another person, a young woman. A lovely Green Chroma girl, surely another mistress. He probably had them wherever he did business, and at home. He was in the process of licking her full right breast, while she stared over his shoulder, for the moment allowing a natural expression of resignation to form. She of course had no magic here; she was out of Chroma and largely help-less. Men often liked to possess women of other Chroma, if they had the chance. Especially if they got them out of their Chroma. This girl did not like to indulge sexually with men of other Chroma; that was why she had been selected, apart from her beauty. Her mind was quite open; she hated being handled like this, and not just because she had been forced to give up the Green boyfriend she loved and would have married, had his desperate family, and hers, not been bought off by the rich Air trader. She had to do it.

Hoard did not see Havoc, but the girl did. Her eyes widened and she inhaled to scream. That mashed her breast into the man's face and alerted him. He turned his face toward Havoc, baring his teeth in anger as the girl stifled her scream.

"Introduction," Havoc said. "I am King Havoc."

"False!" Hoard snarled. "He's dead."

That confirmed his guilt, since no one outside the palace was supposed to know. "Clarification," Havoc said. "His mock is dead—the man who emulated him when he was elsewhere. That man wore the real crown. I recommend that you confess complicity and submit yourself to justice for that assassination."

"Laughable." The man stood, assessing Havoc. He was stout, of middle height, but clearly sound of body.

"Let us agree, for the sake of dialogue, that someone is dead, by your design," Havoc said. "That is murder, regardless of the identity of the victim. Will you submit to justice?"

"Negation!" An almost invisible air crystal appeared in Hoard's hand. He could do magic regardless, here in the Air Chroma zone, but the power of the stone would enhance it.

Havoc's smile was genuine. This was the answer he had wanted. "Then send the girl away, for you and I about to settle accounts."

Instead of responding verbally, the man hurled a bolt of fire at Havoc. Now the girl did scream as fire engulfed him, but it had no effect.

"I take this to mean that you wish to compound your crime by trying to take out the real king," Havoc said as the flames flickered out. "For this the penalty is death, by order of the king."

"Fuck your penalty," Hoard snapped. He dropped the spent crystal and summoned another.

Havoc addressed the green girl. "Depart this chamber and this castle swiftly; it is not a safe place. I will give you one minute to get clear before I destroy it."

The girl did not even scramble for her clothing. She lurched to her feet and lunged for the door, her green breasts bouncing. Hoard did not even notice; he was focusing on his next attack.

A huge heavy stone came down on Havoc's head, the weight of it more than sufficient to crush his body to pulp. But it stopped just as it touched his hair, and hovered there. Then it fragmented into a mass of gravel and dropped to the floor around Havoc, who lifted one hand casually to cover an obvious yawn. He was counting off the minute.

Hoard dropped the second spent crystal and summoned another. Each crystal had enough magic to power illusion pictures for a year, or more substantial effects for lesser periods; this was wasteful extravagance. But of course the man had an almost unlimited supply.

A pit opened up under Havoc's feet. He floated in place. A giant croc leaped in to bite his legs, but its teeth shattered without scratching the material of the trousers.

"The minute is up," Havoc said. "Now let's do something about those crystals." He focused, and conjured a rack of them from the nearest storage chamber. Each crystal was carefully packed in a wooden frame that prevented it from touching any other crystal. There were about a hundred of them on the rack, spaced out on multiple shelves.

Hoard seemed to be almost frothing at the mouth as he cast about for something that would make a suitable impact. But now he stood and watched, amazed that Havoc had been able to conjure so many crystals so readily. It seemed he still doubted that Havoc was genuine, and in any event didn't know he was a Glamor.

Havoc took one from a shelf and extracted it from its housing. He set it back, and took another, denuding it similarly. He set it against the first and took a third.

"Idiot!" Hoard exclaimed. "You can't do that!"

"Question?" Havoc inquired innocently as he set the third against the first two.

"The magic—too many too close will detonate it!"

"Doubt," Havoc said, setting a fourth crystal. "Let's experiment."

"Disaster!" Hoard said, reaching for the rack. But his hand stopped short, halted by Havoc's magic. "You barbarian hick, you'll start a chain reaction!"

"True? That should be fun." Havoc took a fifth crystal.

Belatedly the man caught on. "You rectum! You know!"

"Perhaps." Havoc took a sixth crystal. He held it a moment. "Do you wish to reconsider about submitting to justice?"

The man lunged at him. Havoc held him off with magic deflection, and set the sixth crystal with the others.

The magic of the close crystals interacted. They quivered, glowed, heated, and exploded, dissipating their magic in energy. The effect spread to the others despite their isolation, and they went off like a series of bombs.

Havoc jumped outside the castle. The green girl was there, still bare, staring at the light spearing out from the castle. "It is just beginning," Havoc said, conjuring her a green cloak, which she donned almost unconsciously. "In a moment I will take you home." He conjured one of the crystals and handed it to her. "Take this; it will repair the fortunes of your family and restore your prospects for a good marriage."

The effects in the castle intensified as the chain reaction spread to the storage chambers. Light flared out from the windows and muffled explosions sounded. Then the castle flew apart, the stones landing in a pile of rubble. All the remaining crystals were gone.

"Where do you live?" Havoc inquired.

The green girl told him. He touched her arm and jumped there, delivering her home. He knew she would be all right; the single salvaged crystal was immensely valuable for trading.

He returned to the ruined castle. He had wreaked some satisfying havoc, but it wasn't enough. It was time to finish off Hoard, after letting him suffer briefly.

But the man was gone. Havoc was sure he had survived the destruction of the castle; he clearly knew enough magic to safeguard his body. So where was he? Havoc was not nearly done with him.

∽≈

Ennui stood gazing down at Voila. Such a little baby, yet so much magic power! She had enabled Havoc to locate the person they needed. Now all Havoc had to do was take out that man, avenging the assassination of the mocks, and winning the contest with Mino. They were close to the end.

A man appeared. He looked around, then took a step toward Voila and disappeared. He was of the Air Chroma, and going for a hostage.

The baby screamed and started to float away. But Ennui realized with a terrible certainty that she wouldn't get clear in time. This was a sneak attack that had caught the Glamors off-guard. Even Voila had been relaxing, not watching her paths.

Ennui leaped between the intruder and the baby, shielding Voila with her body. She collided with the invisible man and grabbed on to him, determined to prevent him from reaching the baby.

There was a wrenching sensation. Then she found herself unceremoniously dropped to the ground. "Bitch! Why did you have to get in the way?" the man demanded as he reappeared.

So she had succeeded in balking him. She looked around. They were in a well appointed chamber, surely one of his many houses. "To deny you your hostage," she said. "You're the assassin."

"Good guess," he said. She realized that he didn't know she was telepathic; few nonChroma folk were. "Who are you?"

There seemed to be no harm in telling him. "I am Ennui, the king's personal secretary." And he, she had from his mind, was Hoard, a cruel and selfish trader and sorcerer unlimited by ethical concerns.

He nodded. "Young and shapely, of course. The king has good taste in mistresses. I have heard of you."

But evidently he hadn't heard enough; he was assuming too much. He didn't know her true age, either. "Fortunately I am useless to you. Soon Havoc will come for you; I don't know how you got away from him even this long."

"He destroyed my castle and most of my crystals. Somehow he has very strong magic. I thought no nonChroma folk have magic."

Ennui shrugged. "Havoc is Havoc. He has what he has."

"Bitch! You are mocking me." He swung his fist at her.

Ennui didn't move. She knew the blow would never land. "Yes, you turd." It was fun using gutter language where it was warranted.

Surprised, Hoard looked at his hand. "You have magic too! And you know it."

Oops. She shouldn't have given that away. She had been too cocksure, and careless. She stifled any further retort.

"He has magic, when he shouldn't. Powerful magic. He's a Glamor!"

Damn. He was catching on.

"And you're his closest associate—his oath friend. I remember now. You're the one he trusts most. Glamors have ikons. You have his ikon!"

What use to deny it? "I do," she agreed.

"I know something about ikons. They gather magic and transmit it to their Glamors. You may be a better hostage than his brat baby."

"Doubt."

"Because if we keep you out of your Chroma zone, you can't transmit that power. Better, I'll take his ikon and destroy it. Give it to me."

That was another thing he didn't know. "Take it," she said, smiling. She held the little tree out to him.

He tried, but his hand sheered away. "Set it down."

"I can't."

He considered. "Probably true. But it doesn't matter." He approached her, moving slowly. "I'm not hitting you, I'm just taking hold of you." It worked; his hand closed on her wrist.

Then they were at another place. This was a small square building in a desert region. They entered. Inside it was an empty room. "This is an Air Chroma zone," Hoard said. "Your ikon is no good here. It won't be long before he runs out of magic. And I still have enough of mine."

Could he be right? Surely not, yet she was apprehensive.

"So all we have to do is wait," he said smugly.

Ennui reviewed their situation. Ordinarily, if Havoc got weak, one of the other Glamors would come to his rescue. But Gale was overseeing the mission at the south pole, and the other Glamors were maintaining the illusion shield so that Mino had no hope of escape before settling the contest. So there was no one watching out for Havoc; he was on his own.

Except for Ennui herself. She could help him by warning him away. *Havoc!* she thought. *Stay away from me! It's a trap.*

A crystal flickered. "You're doing magic!" Hoard said. "My magic tuner's flashing."

She stifled her thought, but it was too late. She had given away yet more information.

"But what magic?" he asked rhetorically. He peered at the crystal. "Telepathy! You're communicating with him."

What was the use? "I warned him away," she said.

Hoard formed an ugly smile. "Let's see if he can stay away, when you tell him what I'm doing to you." He caught her by the arm, and his hand did not veer away. "So you're running out of power yourself. You can't resist me any more. So tell Havoc I'm raping you, because it will be true. He interrupted my liaison with my green girl, so he owes me one. You'll certainly do." He ripped at her clothing.

She tried to fight him off, but he was right: her ikon was running out of power and was no longer shielding her. He stripped her and threw her on the floor. "What a figure! I haven't had a nonChroma shape like that in months. Now tell him."

She lay there, pinned, resisting him in the only way she could: by refusing to call Havoc.

"Tell him," Hoard repeated. "Or I'll make you hurt. I can do that now."

He thought that would make her capitulate? "Hurt me, you flatulent pig," she said. She had never been a bold or brave woman, until the ikon protected her; now she was determined to be so on her own.

He dropped his head to her shoulder and bit, hard. The pain was awful. She screamed, and involuntarily let out a mental signal.

Havoc appeared. "Now we finish," he said.

A crystal appeared in Hoard's hand. Fire danced around Havoc. It didn't affect him. Hoard stood, dropping an expended crystal and summoning another. More fire appeared. Havoc shrugged and stepped away from it. A third crystal appeared, and more fire. Havoc yawned.

Ennui caught on. "He's using up your reserve of magic!" she cried. "I can't send you more; I'm here too. Get out of here, Havoc!"

"And let me torture her to death," Hoard said. "Your oath friend. I'll make her scream as I rape her, and scream again as I cut her up, bit by bit. You can't stop me if you're not here."

"Go!" Ennui screamed.

Havoc scowled. He took a step toward them—and metal bars dropped from the ceiling. Havoc just managed to step back in time to avoid getting struck. Then he was bathed by fire again, and this time it was evident that he felt it; his magic was being depleted and was almost gone.

"Havoc, go while you can," Ennui said.

Hoard whirled and struck her. She managed to block it partly with one arm, but the force of the blow knocked her to the floor. She fell with a cry. She wasn't being much of a heroine.

Havoc grabbed the bars and strained, meaning to rip them apart. But they bent only slightly, and more fire drove him back. He had become vulnerable.

Hoard nodded. "You're prisoner. You don't have enough magic left to get out." He considered. "But you might be faking some, so I think I'll just leave you in there for a while, and you can watch me with this bitch. I want you to suffer before you die."

Ennui's horror was more for Havoc than for herself. She had led him into this trap, and now was unwillingly cooperating with the enemy to make it worse. She tried to fend Hoard off, but he was twice her mass and strength. He bore her down and bared his member, which was ready and eager. The man obviously liked forced sex.

She couldn't look, but felt Havoc's mind as he strained at the bars again, exhausting his last strength. His thoughts faded as he lost not only his magic but his physical resources. She realized that he had sent all he had left to her, to help her fight back. Now he was unconscious.

She was on her own—and she lacked the power to fight off Hoard's brutal brawn. She could not stop him.

She felt something odd as the man jammed her down against the cool stone of the floor. It was a faint tickle against her exposed back. Something was there, a bug, or—

No, it was the tendril of a plant, or a questing root. A bloodsucker, taking advantage of her helplessness? But Havoc was the Glamor of trees and plants, and she had his ikon. No plant had ever hurt her since she took the ikon. What did this mean?

It meant the plants were trying to help her, because it was Havoc's will. The vine was pressing against her back and bottom, spreading out, feeding her energy. It was an Air Chroma plant, but that didn't matter; it was Havoc's creature.

She was gaining energy, but not enough; Hoard still had her pinned, savoring the sight and feel of her body. "Come here, you luscious bitch," he said, deliberately loud enough for Havoc to hear. "Give me your soft bare breasts. Open wide your firm thighs. Show me your hot wet cleft. I'm going to give you a plumbing like none you've had before."

And she couldn't stop him, let alone throw him off her. She had renewed energy in her torso, thanks to the plant, but not in her arms or legs. All that meant was that she would represent a tighter connection as he forced his way into her.

Then she remembered something. Could she do it? She would have to. The fate of worlds might depend on it, for if Hoard defeated Havoc, Mino would win and everyone else would lose.

She struggled ineffectively as Hoard deliberately oriented his member, nudging her cleft and sliding slowly along it until finding the vulva. Ordinarily she loved such action, being hungry for sex, but not with him. "No, no," she protested faintly as he pushed in just enough to plug the aperture without going deep. He was savoring every nuance.

"Yes, yes," he rasped, and thrust forcefully. His member rammed all the way into her, a rough surprise after the prior toying.

And she clamped down on it, internally. Just as Aspect had in the game, and then in reality. Just as she herself had when teasing Throe. It was not the kind of hold a man expected.

"What?" Hoard didn't know what was happening. Good.

She wrapped her arms around his neck and hauled it down to her face, but it was no kiss she was trying for. She angled her head and bit him, aiming for the windpipe and jugular vein and clamping down. She got her teeth in his throat angled, off-center, over one buried carotid artery, but had a fair mouthful of his neck. She might be weak, but her vulva and jaws had leverage on extremely sensitive and vulnerable anatomy, and it was easier to hang on once she had the grips. Especially with the strength the plant was providing her.

"Oooo!" he moaned, struggling. But he couldn't free his hips because his member was firmly pinned, and he couldn't draw up his head because that would rip out his throat. Meanwhile his breath was restricted and the exit of blood from his head was being stifled, preventing new blood from entering. She was efficiently breath- and blood-strangling him. She had a literal death grip. She was not going to let it go for anything, no matter how hard he thrashed about. In fact, thrashing should make it worse for him. It shouldn't take too long, if she had the strength. And she did, because the plant remained against her back, sending what it could.

Hoard thrashed, moving her about. Her teeth dug in. Blood leaked from his throat and trickled into her mouth, and his member thrust with something other than sexual urgency. She was conquering him, and that gave her a possessive thrill. She climaxed, drawing her sexual joy from him with the knowledge that he was getting no such satisfaction. She had reversed the rape! Didn't that serve him right!

Belatedly he remembered to use his magic. Suddenly there was an explosion of light and heat around them. It burned the skin of her arms and made her hair frizzle, but she absolutely refused to let go of anything. She was so close to him that he probably couldn't do anything serious to her without hurting himself, and he probably wouldn't be able to make himself do that.

There was a hiss as something reptilian slithered toward her head. She wanted to flee it, but maintained iron control; it might bite her to death, but not before she bit Hoard to death.

Water surged up around her body and head, threatening to drown her. She reminded herself that it could be illusion, in which case it wouldn't really smother her. If it was real, it would get him too, because she was holding his face down as low as hers, beside her head. Regardless, she refused to let go. This was her last chance to be a heroine and she wasn't going to waste it. She hung on, determined to die in style. To take him with her.

Bright little stars and planets appeared, whirling around her head. The chamber seemed to spin like a whirlpool, curling down into some awful abyss. Void—they were spiraling into the stellar black hole! Utter doom. Still she clung.

She held him while his efforts waned. She was not going to make the mistake of underestimating him. His strength was ebbing but wasn't gone. She clung to her two desperate grips. She would hold him for eternity, if that's what it took. She was tasting blood, literally. Like a she-wolf she was slowly killing her prey. It was gloriously horrible. All around her was blackness, but she would not quit.

Ennui.

That was Havoc's thought. She couldn't answer physically, because that would let go of the man's throat, but she sent a thought. *Courage, Havoc! I'm not giving up.*

Ennui, he's dead. You can let go now.

She realized it was true. Hoard's weight was heavy on her, and he was no longer breathing. She relaxed at last in both places, and managed to roll the man off her. His eyes were bulging and bloodshot, his mouth open in agonized horror. She had, to use an expression she would never speak aloud, fucked him to death.

She stood unsteadily and walked to the bars. They remained tight; they were real, not magical. Havoc lay on the floor; he evidently lacked the strength to sit up, but at least he was conscious now. She reached through to touch him, and felt some of the plant's strength pass from her to him. "How can I help you get out?" she asked.

He smiled feebly. "Observation: you are free of the ikon."

She looked back. There on the floor where she had lain was the little tree. It had fallen away from her sometime during the struggle, when all its power was gone. She had killed Hoard by herself, with no magic except what the plant provided. Maybe he hadn't been prepared to counter that kind of attack.

"Agreement," she said faintly. Now they knew how to divest themselves of the ikons; it should work for Aspect too, surely in less difficult circumstances.

"Do not take it back. Fetch it with a net and take it to a nonChroma zone."

Of course! She made a sling of cloth from her torn skirt and used a shoe to push the ikon in without directly touching it. Then she donned her tattered clothing and made ready to depart. "I'll just keep walking until I come to the edge of the Chroma zone," she said. "There should be nonChroma there. I'll hide it there and return for you."

"Set it there and wait," he said. "I should have power quickly, once it's transmitting. I'll come for you, and will carry you and it back to Triumph City. Then we'll rejoin the others, without the ikon. They should be glad to see us."

"Agreement."

"I love you."

She laughed, knowing what he meant. "Just don't try to have sex with me."

He laughed too, somewhat weakly. "I was reluctant to oath you in friendship. Now I know it was my best move ever."

"Ditto."

She opened the door and stepped outside. The landscape was bare; this was an isolated cell in an isolated Air Chroma zone, surely a small one. All she had to do was walk. She was tired and battered, her clothing was in wet rags, her skin was blistering, her hair was a frizzed mess, she had been raped, she had just killed a man with crotch and teeth, she would soon enough lose her seeming youth and sex appeal, but she was buoyant. Maybe it was an exaggeration, but she felt as if she had just saved two worlds and redeemed her formerly meaningless life.

≈≈

Voila felt the relief as the path aligned. Now it was clear, and she had the victory.

Capitulation, Mino agreed. **The future is yours.**

She was glad, because she didn't want her family to be unhappy. It had been a struggle, because she had known she couldn't share her secret with anyone. She had had to do it herself, and she lacked the mind to be competent.

But now it was done, and she could share. But first she had to sleep. She was horribly tired.

She woke when she felt Havoc near. He hugged Gale, then the children, then queried Voila: *How?*

She answered, letting him read her mind. She shared their thoughts as he told Gale and the others.

"She couldn't see to the ends of the paths," Havoc said. "So it seemed she had to choose blind, and all but one led to victory for Mino. So he expected to win. But it wasn't sure until she chose, so he had to wait. She had a secret, and used it to find that one path."

"Which was Hoard," Ennui said. She was in newly conjured clothing and healing balm, and there was horror in her mind, but also the joy of redemption. "He had to be eliminated, so he couldn't team up with Mino and betray the planet."

"But we thought it was positive, one of our number," Gale said. "How did she know it wasn't?"

"She has a quality the machine lacks," Havoc said. "She's alive, conscious, and feeling, and therefore creative. Mino is programmed, without emotion; he must follow his set course. So she had options he didn't."

"But he could see the ultimate end to any path she chose. She couldn't. So she had no option but guessing—with the odds against getting it right."

"That's the logical analysis," he agreed. "But she found a way, by following the path that led to the way to choose the right path."

"Confusion."

It was shared by the others; Voila felt it in their minds. None of them had figured it out.

Now her siblings peeked. "I got it!" Warp exclaimed. "She did to him what she does to us!"

"The little sneak!" Flame said indignantly.

Weft nodded wisely. "Mino should have known better than to mess with her. She knows what's what."

"So what *is* what?" Gale asked patiently.

"She looked down each path just far enough," Havoc said.

"But she couldn't see the end of it," Gale said. "Only Mino could do that, and he wasn't telling until it was fixed."

"She didn't need to see the end," Havoc said. "It's like the old story about the two men chased by a bear: neither could outrun it, but one realized that he didn't need to; the only one he needed to outrun was his companion."

Gale's patience was fraying. "Relevance?"

"Revelation!" Ini said. "She didn't need to see the end of the path, she just needed to see Mino!"

Voila felt her understanding. Ini was smart. She was making sense of what Voila had done the only way she could: by searching until she found what worked.

"Confirmation," Havoc said. "She followed each path until it intersected Mino, and saw how Mino reacted. She couldn't see the end, but he could, and he knew whether it represented victory or defeat for him. He claimed victory or capitulated accordingly. She searched for the path where he knew he lost. That was the one."

Now Gale understood. "Mino defeated himself! In the near future—because she thought to look at *him* instead of the end of the path."

"She outran her companion," Ini agreed. "And the bear got him."

"Then all we had to do was secure that path," Havoc said. "Which Ennui did."

"I had to," Ennui said. "You were lying down on the job."

They all laughed, knowing from their minds what had happened. Havoc had been unconscious, his magic exhausted. It hadn't mattered who killed Hoard, just so long as it was done. Ennui had done it, at great peril to herself.

Voila napped again. When she woke, Mino had been reprogrammed, and was now really their friend. She linked minds with him, as she had before, and his analysis greatly facilitated her understanding. The adults were checking the remaining reaches of the caves, verifying the powers of magic they facilitated.

Recommendation, Mino thought, his machine mind very loud and clear. ***Explore the parameters.***

Voila extended her awareness through his to the ambiance of the cave, for now she trusted Mino and could share freely with him. He had an enormous store of information and processing ability. What he lacked was imagination and feeling. She possessed these things, far less than the adults or even the children did, but her small basis was enough to guide her in seeking more. She discovered that it wasn't enough. *Siblings* she thought. *Join us.*

What you fussing about now, brat? Warp demanded. Then he felt it. *Wow!*

You're linked to Mino again, Weft thought. *And this time you're letting us in.*

And what a merger it is, Flame thought. *Bigger than anything except Idyll.*

Their company helped considerably, as it always did, for they could organize their thoughts in words and remember them. *Help me explore the parameters,* she urged them. She had to borrow the word from an adult mind, as all she knew was the vague concept.

They did, joining their minds and feeling to hers, drawing on Mino's database. Five minds, questing through the ambiance that had been too large, complicated, and dynamic for any one mind.

Understanding came. The secret of the planet was here, its ultimate motivation. It had discovered awareness and desire with the arrival of the early colonists, starting with the demons and progressing with the mosses, fungi, and trees. Then the worms had come, evolving up through dragons, bringing conscious intellect. The planet slowly integrated each arrival, and benefited from it, adding its capacities to its whole. The last to come was the human species, with its ready intelligence, and it too was being integrated. It needed to be, because the threat from the machine culture was too great for the planet's other resources to handle. It had to have those minds to guide its process. Thus the effort of the sphinxes, who had not known the larger plan; they had simply implemented the urging that came from the planet.

It wants us to serve Charm instead of mankind, Warp thought. *To be part of it.*

Why should we do that? Flame demanded.

Weft had the answer: *to save us all from the machines, maybe a century hence. Voila beat Mino, but he's only one little piece of a huge galactic culture. We're going to need everything. All the business about the altars, loom, changelings, and Glamors—was to try to bring the humans in. So that all will not be lost to the machines.*

Correction, Mino thought. **The effort to integrate preceded my arrival. All species are ultimately one with the planet, on Charm and Counter Charm. But it had to be hurried, because of this threat.**

So is it really that bad? Warp inquired.

Confirmation.

And Mino was in a position to know. Sharing his far-reaching linear precognition, augmented by his existing information, satisfied them that he was correct.

Then we'll do it, Weft thought.

Do we tell the adults? Warp asked.

Not yet, Flame thought. They all giggled.

Voila napped again, but was aware of the several paths of the near future. She saw Augur and Aura settle on Counter Charm, and Ini too. Ini would keep the altar ikon and marry the Green Glamor and bear him three children, with a fourth via Augur, and they would be raised among the ifrits. Other humans would come, forming a small community, a village. Meanwhile Ivo, Iva, and their children would be joined by other ifrits to make an enclave on Charm, with Futility as liaison to the human community, basking in her importance. She would take an ifrit lover who honored her whims implicitly, demanding nothing, but also accommodate the Translucent Glamor when he wished;

that was another kind of importance. In time she would marry the Glamor and start her own family, though not required to, and demand her fourth from Havoc, annoying all the other women of the palace. The former bath girls, Bijou and Nonce, would remain associated, marrying well and also claiming their fourths from Havoc in due course. Nonce would return the loom ikon to its native village, fulfilling a promise. The loom's Glamor was the planet Charm itself. The ladies Ennui and Aspect, free of their ikons, would slowly revert to their middle aged natures, and be quite satisfied, as were their men, Throe and Chief.

Meanwhile the children would grow up to be suitable palace terrors. Symbol, enhanced by Viola's ikon, would somehow keep up with them. And Voila herself would in time become a young woman, the most potent of all the Glamors—just in time to tackle the next crisis. Not the machines, but a nearer one: Earth, coming at last to reclaim its colony and exploit the planets. That could not be allowed, but its denial was a tangle of paths that could not yet be unraveled.

Voila looked forward to it. Meanwhile she would spend much time with her friend Idyll Ifrit, learning all she could. It would be wonderful.

Author's Note

The three ChroMagic novels were written at two-year intervals, in 1998, 2000, and 2002. When it was apparent that Parnassus (the traditional publishing establishment) wasn't interested, I gave them to small publisher Mundania Press, which set up to publish them at six month intervals in 2003 and 2004. Now that's done, and I'll write the fourth and fifth novels, *Key to Liberty* and *Key to Survival*, if the first three do well enough to warrant it. That depends on factors other than merit.

Which naturally needs an explanation. At the time I proofread the galleys and wrote this Note, my personal life on our isolated tree farm was suitably dull, but my professional life was evincing potential. I spent roughly the decade of the 1980s on the bestseller lists with my fantasy, and the decade of the 1990s as a has-been. It wasn't that the quality of my writing declined, but that the quality of my publishing did. I saw that if I wanted to return to the bestseller lists, I could not depend on the publishing industry. So I oriented on the sister motion picture industry. It was a long wait as the movie outfits flirted with my various novels and series, but now things seem to have aligned and there are excellent movie prospects for three of my fantasy series. Should these materialize, the market for my fantasy will magnify, sales will increase, and a continuation of ChroMagic will become commercially feasible. So it has nothing to do with the quality of the novels or the dubious efforts of publishers, and everything to do with the movies. This is one of the magical realities of fantasy.

As I read the novel, I pondered its elements. It starts slow, with a good deal of reprise. This is necessary, as the vagaries of the marketplace mean that some readers will not see the prior novels and will start with this one. Some will have read one or both of the others, but some time ago, so that many of their details will have been forgotten. Those readers need to be brought up to date, lest they be confused. I have always tried to have each novel in a series be intelligible and enjoyable on its own. Some writers look askance at that; they feel that readers should be required to start at the beginning of a series, so no updates are necessary. There's no point in naming those writers; you would probably not recognize them, as they lose much of their readerships without understanding why. Other writers extend the principle to single novels: if a thing is mentioned once, that's it, and the reader had better remember it. I have on occasion been thrown by what seemed like a key element flying in late from left field. Once I asked the author about that, and he was disgusted with my obtuseness: he had distinctly mentioned that element fifty pages before. So he had. Yet for some obscure (to him) reason he never earned the living from his fiction that I do from mine. My rule here is THINK OF THE READER. So I try to see that all key elements are clear, and I remind the reader of them when they reappear after a fair amount of text. Do I do that too much in this novel? It is possible, because I noticed it. It's a judgment call, to make for the greatest clarity for the greatest number of readers without alienating those who are sharp enough to catch and hold everything the first time.

Does the novel work its slow way up to a worthwhile climax? It seems so to me: the fate of two planets, and the answers to enduring mysteries. There are a number of elements along the way, each with its nuances that integrate to form the whole. The ikons, children, ifrits, and Mino—I would hesitate to cover them more expeditiously. The ikons alone range from Glamor tokens to a fancy loom, tricky to understand. I also have certain conventions to follow, like the customs of the language and gender roles: Question, Curiosity, Outrage, Obscenity. With the exception of the Amazons, women don't take up swords and battle like men. They find feminine ways to handle their challenges. For example, the case of the lesbians in the Gray Chroma village in Chapter 4. Ennui and Aspect don't threaten the villagers, they find a way to encourage tolerance. When there is violence there, the Gray Glamor handles it, making the point with brutal efficiency as the birds destroy the malefactor. Women don't hesitate to use sex appeal to win rides across the Chroma zones, an advantage they have over men. One result is that there's more sex here than you can shake a penis at. The new Glamors are discovering their magical abilities, and of course the Glamor children too. There's a lot to cover.

Normally fantasy is low-research; I simply invent what I need. Even so, there was some work here. In Chapter 3 the challenge to move the altars about was adapted from a tile moving game on my computer. I made a diagram, figured out a solution, then put my characters through it. There was more to do there than showed in the text. In Chapter 9 the illusion challenge was another job of research. I wanted different scenes, so didn't depend on my own limited imagination. I dug out my collection of about twenty fantasy genre art books and went through them, noting remarkable images. Then I adapted some of them to the scenes. It was quite a challenge, but I trust varied and refreshing for the readers. Another bit of spot research came to naught: a reader mentioned that "nonce" is a prison term for sexual offenders, who have to be separated from regular prisoners lest they suffer harm. I didn't know that, so I looked it up in my collection of dictionaries, from the Oxford English down. Nonce means the present, for now, which is the way I see the girl Nonce; she's certainly no sexual offender. No indication of anything untoward; it evidently has not yet reached the dictionaries. So I'm letting her be.

Then there are the inset stories. I have an idea file where I have summaries of my ideas over the years, and when I need one I go there. Thus the little stories travelers tell. My hope is that readers will like this series not just for the main storyline, but also for its ambiance: that they'll like just being in this realm. The no fault traveling and inset stories are part of it. I like to think that the reader pictures him/her self in the scene, polishing his/her own little stories to win a night's lodging from villagers, before traveling on to experience new wonders. I want my readers to live in this realm for the duration of the series, preferring it to their own mundane existence. So they won't get impatient if there is not a cliffhanger every scene.

Reading the novel two years later, I hardly noticed the changes in viewpoint, but these were a struggle to work out. Each long chapter has two viewpoints, two sequences for each view, with three sets of major characters, until the last chapter, which has several, including the finale by four-month-old Voila. I was concerned with balance, giving each major character fair representation, and having chapters of similar length. It was quite a balancing act—unnoticed in the reading. Conclusion: maybe I should worry less about balancing and just focus on telling the story.

Something else occurred to me: I have charts detailing the arrivals of all the major species as the planet gets colonized by successive waves of things and creatures. But when did the funguses, bacteria, viruses, and amoeba colonize? They are obviously there, as they support their own Glamors, but they don't seem to be listed. The record must be incomplete. That needs to be addressed, some time.

As I read, I kept thinking of the next novel, when Earth comes to reclaim its colony. What a cast of characters I have ready for that! The Earth ship officers have the power to blast the planets from space, so can't be ignored or directly opposed, but how little they will know what they're up against. That sweet teen girl, Voila, daughter of the king—they might take her home as a hostage. Does her nonChroma magic work on planet Earth? There are amoeba on Earth; if they accept her, she'll have a global reach. Can she read the future there? If so, they'd be better off blowing themselves up to keep her away from Earth. That harmless dull boyfriend of hers, Iolo Ifrit—they may have something to learn about clouds back on Earth, too. And do they even see that robot ship following them home? Revelation: I may have to start writing the novel regardless of its commercial viability, being unable to wait to discover the answers.

—*Piers Anthony, March 17, 2004*

About The Author

Piers Anthony is one of the world's most prolific and popular authors. His fantasy Xanth novels have been read and loved by millions of readers around the world, and have appeared on the *New York Times* Best Seller list 21 times. Although Piers is mostly known for fantasy and science fiction, he has written several novels in other genres as well, including historical fiction, martial arts, and horror. Piers lives with his wife in Florida.

Want to learn more about Piers Anthony?

Piers Anthony's official website is HI PIERS at **www.hipiers.com**, where he publishes his bi-monthly online newsletter. HI PIERS also has a section reviewing many of the online publishers and self-publishing companies for your reference if you are looking for a non-traditional solution to publish your book.

Piers Anthony's largest fan-based website is The Compleat Piers Anthony at **www.piers-anthony.com**. The Compleat Piers Anthony contains extensive information about all the books and stories that Piers has written, as well as up-to-date information about forthcoming books.

Mundania Press LLC

www . mundania . com
books @ mundania . com

THE CHROMAGIC SERIES

1,000 years ago Earth colonized the planet Charm. But the population of Charm is now far removed from their ancient ancestors. Technology has been lost over the years but the people have something better--Magic!

Charm is a world covered by volcanoes, each erupting a different color of magic. Everything within a particular Chroma becomes that color. Plants, animals, insects, and even humans all become one color and can perform that color of magic. Traveling is dangerous because a person leaving their native Chroma home can no longer perform their color magic.

In **KEY TO HAVOC**, Havoc is a barbarian living in a non-Chroma village, where no one has magic. As a boy, he rescued a dragon that rewarded him with special magic; to sense pending danger. His gift becomes more valuable than he can imagine as he is suddenly drafted and forced to become the new king of the planet. He must perform his duties or be executed for treason. To make matters worse, the assassin who killed the former king is now after Havoc!

Hardcover 0-9723670-7-1
Trade Paperback 0-9723670-6-3
eBook 1-59426-000-1

In **KEY TO CHROMA**, With the help of the God-like Glamors, Havoc and his companions must set off in search of seven mysterious ikons to attempt to learn the secret of the Changelings ... a secret that could answer all of Havoc's questions, or lead him to his doom.

Hardcover 0-9723670-7-1
Trade Paperback 0-9723670-6-3
eBook 1-59426-000-1

Printed in the United Kingdom
by Lightning Source UK Ltd.
120567UK00002B/87